I0639863

BOYS OF BRIGHTON
VOLUME 1

M. TASIA

EVERYONE LOVES THE BOYS OF BRIGHTON

"I loved this book and I love this town. I hope there's going to be more."
—Melissa Lemons on *Gabe*

"An amazing read that was filled with lust, love, crazy hot sex, danger, action and so much more This is the first book I have read in this series but I will definitely be reading more in the future."
—Gay Book Reviews on *Sam's Soldiers*

"I was crazy impressed that the author made me teary over the ending of a relationship that I shouldn't have even been invested in. I didn't yet know these characters yet the author made me hurt for them. That takes some mad writing skills!"
—Love Bytes Reviews

"Jesse and Royce together have my heart. Jesse has it all by himself."
—The Book Junkie Reads on *Jesse*

"So much action, intrigue, drama and angst for the long awaited story of Grady and Ben. This was worth the wait. Sexy and sweet. I can't wait for the next."
—SamD on *Grady*

"I knew this one would be my favorite to date! There was something about Vincent that said awesome then came Tristan."
—Booky on *Vincent*

"This installment of the Boys of Brighton was so good! I loved Shadow and Randy 's story I was hooked from the first page to the last. This book was definitely worth the wait!"
—AG on *Shadow*

"I have loved this series from the very first story and this holiday novella is simply perfect. We get a glimpse of all our couples and what is happening in their lives while the holidays explode around them. I cannot wait for more!"
—bookobsessed on *The Holidays*

www.BOROUGHSPUBLISHINGGROUP.com

PUBLISHER'S NOTE: This is a work of fiction. Names, characters, places and incidents either are the product of the author's imagination or are used fictitiously. Any resemblance to actual events, locales, business establishments or persons, living or dead, is · coincidental. Boroughs Publishing Group does not have any control over and does not assume responsibility for author or third-party websites, blogs or critiques or their content.

BOYS OF BRIGHTON VOLUME 1
Gabe, Sam's Soldiers, Rick's Bear, Jesse, Coop
Copyright © 2023 M. Tasia

All rights reserved. Unless specifically noted, no part of this publication may be reproduced, scanned, stored in a retrieval system or transmitted in any form or by any means, electronic, mechanical, photocopying, recording, or otherwise, known or hereinafter invented, without the express written permission of Boroughs Publishing Group. The scanning, uploading and distribution of this book via the Internet or by any other means without the permission of Boroughs Publishing Group is illegal and punishable by law. Participation in the piracy of copyrighted materials violates the author's rights.

ISBN: 978-1-957295-43-5

To my family for their unwavering support.
I love all of you to the moon and back.

GABE

Chapter One

"So…uh…didn't think our morning included hanging off the side of a building…but at least we get out of the staff meeting." Okay, as far as jokes went, that one sucked, but Johnny was beyond freaked and slipping into hysterical very quickly.

Looking around the room at the black, soot-covered faces and only seeing sheer panic staring right back at him didn't help. Johnny knew he was pretty much on his own to come up with a plan. He was no hero by a long shot—truthfully, he was more of a behind-the-scenes kind of guy—but somehow he had to get these three women out of this burning building. They were running out of time; clouds of black smoke rolled upward into the room from the space under the closed door.

"Well, shit. Okay, you three need to find something to stuff under the door to stop that smoke from getting in here," Johnny directed before going over to the lone window and breaking the remaining glass in an attempt to get the attention of the fire department below, praying that none of the glass fell on anyone.

He took a moment to get his first really good look outside and so wished he hadn't. Three stories below was pure chaos. People were running and screaming, and there were police, fire trucks, and EMS vehicles everywhere; their flashing lights reflected off the grey walls. The windows five stories above his head and four over spewed smoke and flames into the cloudless sky.

So screwed, we are so screwed.

"Mr. Jeffrey, what do we do?" Josie clung to his arm and cried, turning her head from side to side, looking for an escape route. He had been mentoring her for weeks while she attended Brighton College. A brilliant, funny young woman intent on turning the world of graphic design "on its ass"—her words, not his. Johnny knew she would, too. He just had to get her out of this damn building first.

He glanced back out the window in time to watch as a beast of a fire truck with a long ladder attached to its back came right up to the front of the building. Firefighters began jumping off even before the truck came to a complete stop.

Please, please, please, God, let that ladder make it up here in time. Okay, brave face time. Brave face? Shit, do I even have a brave face?

"Josie, look at me." Johnny ordered and spoke loudly so the other two women huddled by the open window could hear him over the roar of the fire and sirens. "They just brought out the big guns. That ladder down there on that fire truck is our way out. Maybe we can find you a hot fireman while we're at it." He was trying his best to sound as if everything would be just fine when in truth, he was wondering if a person could survive a drop of three stories. He was not willing to test it out.

"Half of my family are first responders. I could hook you up," Josie responded, wiping away tears and laughing softly. "I haven't heard you talking about a man in your life either." She was desperately trying to act calm, but the panic in her eyes was unmistakable.

"Just waiting on the right one, Josie." *More like avoiding the wrong ones.*

Johnny continued the "brave face, sound calm" thing and failed miserably, but he had to keep these women focused on rescue and not the alternative. He knew damn well they couldn't go back the way they came. Even with the coats stuffed under the closed door, the smoke was starting to make its way into the room. Johnny noticed that the ladder was being maneuvered toward the building. In the background, he could make out someone on the ground yelling through a bullhorn for them to stay calm.

Oh yeah, yelling at me to stay calm is really going to make me calm! Seriously?

"It will never reach!" the short blonde from accounting cried. Johnny tried to remember her name, but with everything else going on around him, there wasn't much chance of that happening.

He was about to try and calm her down when they felt the building shudder. It may have only been a tremor, but it was enough to have all four people in the room screaming and clinging together in fear. His heart hopped around his chest like a ping-pong ball.

"I'll never see my baby again! Why did I ever come back from maternity leave early?" Janice sobbed on Josie's shoulder. She had been Johnny's assistant since arriving and was one of the best damn mothers he'd ever had the privilege of knowing. She'd spend every lunch hour at the daycare with Ben and prepared homemade, organic baby foods for him. Her office had a wall of fame showcasing her husband and son. Johnny had no idea why, but the thought of Janice's precious pictures burning to ash was making his stomach churn even harder.

"Yes, you will! You will be there when Ben takes his first steps and every single one after. You got that. We are not giving up!" Johnny had no idea where his courage was coming from, because it was definitely a new development. He had spent the last twenty-nine years of his life under his all-powerful father's thumb—well, at least up until six months ago he did. Johnny had made a clean break from his family once and for all, though "family" was a term he used loosely ever since his beloved mother died while he was still a child. While his father still dogged his every step, Johnny had learned to ignore and misdirect most of his attempts at contact and control. For years he was simply a casualty of his father's ambition. Now that he was free, Johnny prayed he still had a chance to find out who he really was, away from his family's influence.

His father, Dr. Thomas Jeffrey, and his staff were currently somewhere in Asia traveling with his third wife—no, fourth? The man was a slut, plain and simple, but Johnny was thankful his dad had at least waited until after his mom's death. Everything changed in his world when she was taken from them; the pain was suffocating at times. Johnny hadn't seen his older brother in over two years. He'd heard that Dr. Frank Jeffrey, the renowned plastic surgeon to the filthy rich, was currently in Costa Rica yet again, enjoying the hospitality of people with money and power. That had always been his brother's only motivator: power. He took right after the old man.

Johnny was the odd man out, you could say. He had no need for power and enjoyed a comfortable, middle-class life in graphic design, in which he owned Ikea furniture and volunteered at an animal shelter. His mere existence continued to be an embarrassment to his father. Well, that and the fact that Johnny was gay, which he just lumped in with all the other indignities his youngest son had made him endure over the years.

It began with the fact that Johnny didn't quite measure up—literally, he was 5'6" and a hundred and fifty pounds if lucky, compared to his brother's 6'1" and father's 6'3". Oh, he had the same curly blond hair and green eyes as his dear old dad, but where the other two were built like dump trucks, Johnny was all lean muscle from his love of swimming. The fact that he chose to forgo family tradition and not become a doctor was always a great topic of conversation around the holiday table.

"The ladder's getting closer. They're coming to get us." Johnny coughed loudly while trying to speak, holding a ripped piece of the drapes to his mouth. The smoke was really getting thick. He could barely see the far door through the black haze.

"Promise me you won't let me die here!" Janice begged him. "I have to see Ben again. This can't be it!"

The air outside was thick and black, the ground was covered in snaking fire hoses, and shouts rang through the gathered crowd; it felt surreal. The short, blonde-haired woman began to vomit on the floor from her violent coughing. Johnny remembered hearing somewhere that it was the smoke that might kill them first.

Great.

"Janice"—Johnny looked her straight in the eyes so she could see his sincerity—"I swear on my life, I will not leave without you." That was the best he could do, considering he wasn't even sure he was making it out of the building alive, but he would keep those thoughts to himself.

Janice gave him a hopeful smile and stuck her head back out the open window, attempting to get a tiny bit of fresh air. Johnny moved aside to let the three women huddle closer to the window even though they were all slumped on the floor trying to get away from the smoke. He kept hold of their arms as each woman leaned out to get fresh air; he didn't want them getting dizzy and falling out of the window, which of course, with his shitty luck, was exactly what happened.

Josie screamed. Her hands slipped off the ledge and half her body slid out the window. Johnny desperately grabbed at her waist, snagging her belt at the last second, leaving her dangling upside down. Johnny found himself halfway out of the window, desperately holding on to Josie while Janice and the other woman held onto his feet. A few remaining glass shards sliced into his hips. Screams from below echoed off the blackened walls. Johnny held on tight as Josie dangled in midair. Knowing that damn ladder had to be close, he just had to hang on until they reached Josie.

"We got her! Let her go," a deep voice yelled from just below him. Johnny turned his head to see the firefighters on the ladder gently holding Josie to them. *Thank God!*

He released his hold, allowing them to take Josie. The other two women pulled him back inside the window, blood staining the front of his shirt and pants from where the broken shards cut through his clothes and skin. That was when Johnny realized he was getting dizzy. He pushed another flimsy piece of fabric tight against his nose and mouth, but breathing was getting difficult.

"How many people do you have in there?" That same voice echoed into the room. Thank God the firefighters were back.

The women were coughing so badly they couldn't answer, so Johnny inched his way to the window ledge to yell out and noticed the ladder was now only roughly three feet away at most. Hope flared in him; they actually might make it out of this.

"Three now that you have Josie—two women and myself!" Johnny yelled just before another tremor moved through the building.

Screams from the remaining two women were cut short just before he was violently thrown to the ground by an explosion that came from somewhere below them. He turned his head to the right, trying to clear his blurry vision, and saw a leg sticking out from under a large filing cabinet.

Oh, come on!

Johnny crawled on his stomach to the overturned cabinet to find Janice trapped underneath. "Johnny! Johnny, I can't move it. It's too heavy. Please help me!"

"I told you I wouldn't leave without you…" Johnny pushed and pushed, but the damn cabinet moved only a few inches. He had to find something to pry the cabinet up so she could slide out.

As he crawled around the room, he noticed the flames were now licking around the edges of the door. *Time to go!* He turned to where the other woman should be by the open window, but she was gone. Sending up a quick prayer that the firefighter on the ladder had gotten her out, Johnny could do nothing other than continue to look for something to use to pry the cabinet. On the floor, a few feet away from the now flaming door, he saw a steel coat rack. Grabbing it, he raced back to Janice, only registering pain from the heated pole as an afterthought and pushing it aside. He had to get Janice out. He shoved the bar under the cabinet and started pushing. Thankfully the cabinet began to move…and then everything went to hell.

***

The building was coming down, Gabe knew it. After the last explosion, he and his partner, Lee, were able to grab one of the women huddled by the window and carry her down the ladder. There were two more people in that room, and he would be damned if he'd leave them behind. Seeing his cousin Josie hanging from the window had almost paralyzed him with fear, but thanks to his years of training Gabe didn't miss a beat. He grabbed her out of the air from one of her coworkers who held onto her, saving Josie from a three-story fall headfirst.

Another explosion rocked the back of the building and Gabe raced back up the ladder. He didn't stop at the top. He jumped through the window instead, desperate to find the trapped people. His turnout gear and oxygen tank protected him from the worst of the heat and the thick black smoke that filled the room, obstructing his vision as he scanned for anyone, hoping he wasn't too late.

He heard a loud scraping noise from the back corner. Easing his way closer, he was finally able to make out the same shorter man that saved Josie trying to leverage a filing cabinet off a trapped woman.

"Got the last two, Lee. One trapped," Gabe called into his radio.

"The building's coming down!" Lee answered. "I'm almost at the top of the ladder. Get them out here now!"

Gabe reached the man just as a loud whoosh sounded through the room and flames waved across the ceiling. Time to go. The man with the pole looked up at the flames…but instead of making a run for the window as Gabe had expected, he began to desperately push on the cabinet.

Maybe I'm jaded after all these years.

Gabe grabbed the man's shoulder. The guy cried out in pain before he turned to face him. The smoke was so thick that it was difficult to make out his features, but the burn marks on the guy's shoulder from the steel pole he was using were easy to see.

"You have to get out!" Gabe called. "The ladder is outside the window. GO!"

"No! I won't leave her! She's unconscious. I'll pull her out"—*cough, cough*—"if you can lift this damn thing."

Gabe could tell the man was serious about not leaving without the woman. He figured it must be his wife or someone he loved.

To have someone love you that much… You would never be left behind. He longed for just that.

He put both hands under the edge of the cabinet while the other man dropped the pole and grabbed onto the woman's arms. With one great heave, the cabinet was raised. The man screamed in pain but managed to pull the woman out before falling to the ground himself and coughing violently.

Gabe quickly lifted the woman into his arms and carried her to the window, handing her off to Lee before turning to pick up the last survivor who was still coughing on the floor. Gabe removed his oxygen mask and placed it over the man's face before stepping onto the ladder and heading down to the waiting EMTs. Now that they were away from the smoke, Gabe looked down at the man in his arms to find stunning moss-green eyes staring up at him. *Wow…just wow.*

Desperate for something to clear away the sucker punch that one look had delivered, Gabe could only come up with the other woman in the fire. "Your wife is going to be okay. We got her out thanks to your help."

Gabe gently placed the man down on the waiting gurney. Within moments, one of the EMTs removed the oxygen mask Gabe had given him and replaced it with one from a tank in their rig. Gabe noticed more burns on the man's hands and chest as well as bleeding across his abdomen.

The green-eyed man quickly pushed the mask away from his face. "Wife?"

"Building's clear, Gabe. Now we just need to keep it contained," Lee stated through Gabe's headset.

"Copy, on my way."

"Wife?" the man asked again, looking adorably confused, eyes squinting, leaving a cute little wrinkle between his eyebrows.

"Yes, the lady under the cabinet is already being transported to the hospital," Gabe replied, doing his best to not look into those beautiful eyes or at the tempting bottom lip that was currently between the other man's teeth. The man looked confused for a moment, and then his face lit up in happiness. It was like the clouds parted with just that one look.

Where the hell did that cliché come from?

"Janice! She's safe?"

"Yes, she's on her way to the hospital. You can meet her there when you're transported." Gabe began to back a few feet away; he had to get back to the fire and stop staring at the poor man.

Damn, I've been alone too long when I'm lusting after a married, heterosexual man.

Being a gay firefighter, it wasn't easy for Gabe to find the right partner. Sure, easy sex was always available, but he wanted a commitment. Men might think it was hot to date a fireman, but they soon found the hours he worked and the dangers he faced to be too much, and they would eventually leave.

"Wait, wife? Janice? No…I'm gay. She's my friend—" The man began coughing so violently he was gagging over the side of the gurney.

"We're outta here, Gabe," said Royce, his friend and one of the EMTs, before replacing the oxygen mask.

Gabe ran back over, catching the gurney before it went into the rear of the ambulance. "Wait, what's your name?"

"Johnny Jeffrey."

Gabe and Royce shared a look before Royce gave a slight nod and smiled. Then the doors closed and the ambulance sped away, leaving Gabe and the rest of the firefighters to battle the blaze into the late afternoon. Royce would keep an eye on the guy for Gabe as best he could. After all, the man had saved his young cousin's life, and he couldn't just ignore these intense feelings of attraction, could he?

Chapter Two

Gabe Mason walked out of the showers on his way to his locker on the second floor of the old, brick firehouse that had been a fixture on Main Street in Brighton, Texas since 1895. Gabe loved his job, being a fifth-generation firefighter, and all generations served right here in Brighton. The town was founded on a very simple principle that was as strong today as it was over a hundred years ago: family. Simple term, yes, but sometimes even the simplest terms could be warped by others whose views of what a family should look like differed from your own.

In Brighton, the townspeople embraced all lifestyles and family units. It was a pretty much a live-and-let-live kind of town. In the close-knit community of just over sixty-two hundred people, you knew your neighbors and nothing remained a secret for long— especially with the "White Hair Crew," as they were affectionately nicknamed. One of them was Gabe's very own Grandma Rose, with whom he had a dinner date this evening. After that, he planned on racing over to the hospital to visit Johnny.

Gabe stood staring at himself in the bathroom mirror while he dressed. At thirty-six, he wasn't over the hill by any stretch, but he had laid down some heavy rules for himself years ago. He was tired—tired of being alone and living alone with no one to come home to. His loneliness hung like a lead weight around his neck. But he swore off one-night stands and easy hookups; he'd lost interest in nameless sex long ago. There had been one man over two years ago that Gabe had thought he could spend his life with, but Chris had other plans, leaving one day without so much as a "screw you." Recently he'd been receiving e-mails from Chris every few days—e-mails he immediately deleted. Gabe had no desire to talk to the man after everything that had happened.

At 6'4" and two hundred and forty pounds of muscled fireman, Gabe's attributes always ensured a steady stream of willing partners, but he just wasn't keen on spending his life that way. He wanted a future, a family, a life where he was the focus of someone's love and need. He knew he was dominant; that would never change, and honestly, past lovers could never completely accept his need to be the alpha of the relationship. He had the desire to care for his partner and to be in control, both in and out of the bedroom, and he'd never found anyone to relinquish that control fully to him. Gabe wasn't all dom all the time, but he was the bear of the relationship. His need to hunt, gather, and protect was strong.

For what had to be the fiftieth time that day, the mystery man with those green eyes and curly blond hair drifted through Gabe's mind. Since the fire, he'd felt almost desperate to find Johnny Jeffrey. Gabe had called the hospital and spoke to his cousin, Sam, who worked as an ER nurse. He'd been receiving text updates ever since. Small towns, you had to love them.

So far, Sam reported that Johnny had suffered third-degree burns on his hands, shoulder, and chest and serious damage to his lungs and throat from smoke inhalation. Gabe wasn't sure what chemicals were being stored in the basement of that building, but the smoke was toxic.

"Gabe, Chief wants to see you," Lee yelled from the lunchroom.

"Thanks, Lee. Have a good night," Gabe yelled back before grabbing his bag and heading to the chief's office. Lee had been his teammate for over ten years. They watched each other's backs, and Gabe had even been Lee's best man at his wedding to his partner Frank. Lee and Frank were expecting their first child in the next few weeks. They had found a wonderful gestational surrogate to carry their baby. Gabe had always wanted children and hoped, if he found a partner, they would want children as well. A lot of the men he knew wanted nothing to do with diapers.

The chief was sitting behind a large wooden desk covered in paper, the same desk the chief's dad had used, and his dad before him. One day it would be Gabe's.

"Hey, Dad, what's up?"

"Is it too much to ask for you to call your old man Chief Mason when we're at work?" his dad questioned, not even looking up from his reports.

"Yes, Chief Mason, sir," Gabe responded with a quick salute for good measure.

The chief finally looked at Gabe, perhaps wondering where he went wrong, before he burst out laughing. "Sit down. I hear Josie's been released from the hospital already. Aunt Flo took her home. She's resting with mild smoke inhalation, but she'll be okay."

"Mom left a voice message for me to let me know. That could have gone to hell so easily. One second, I see her leaning out of the window, and the next, she's hanging from the damn thing. I just...I couldn't race up that ladder fast enough to grab her." Gabe shook his head, trying to remove the image of his cousin hanging in midair three stories above the ground. "She would have never survived the fall. Hell, she would have hit her head first." A cold shiver worked its way down Gabe's spine at the thought of Josie falling.

The sound of the rhythmic tick from the plastic clock above the door was the only sound, both men consumed by their own thoughts. The fear of what could have happened was etched in his father's eyes. The chief took a deep breath before he spoke again. "She'll be okay. We'll have to find out the name of that young man who saved her. He was taken to the hospital before I had a chance to ask."

Even though Gabe knew Johnny's name, and had called the hospital to check on him, there was no way in hell he was going to be telling his dad this unless he wanted his whole family swooping in and taking over. "I'll check." *There, that was impersonal enough, right?*

"You on your way to pick your grandmother up for dinner?" The chief gave him an odd look that had Gabe sitting a bit straighter in his seat.

"Yes, but why do I have the feeling you didn't call me in here to talk about Josie or to make sure I picked Grandma Rose up on time?" Gabe had the feeling his mother was involved somehow; his *mom radar* was going nuts.

"You know you're not that young anymore, son, and your mom, she—worries."

If his dad couldn't spit it out, then Gabe knew he was screwed.

"I know Mom wants me to settle down, but I haven't found the right guy yet." *Hope to rectify that very shortly with one green-eyed beauty.*

"How's all that 'not dating' going for you, son? For the last two years since Chris, you've hardly gone on a date or shown any interest in anyone, and your mom is getting desperate. She's calling in *the aunts*." The chief steepled his fingers and leaned forward in his chair.

"No, no way!" Gabe almost flew out of his chair and gave his dad his best you've-got-to-be-shitting-me look. The last time the aunts got involved with one of the nephews' love lives, the U.S. Marshals got involved. "Besides, I met someone." *I hope. Shit! Well, didn't take long to get that out of me, did it?*

Gabe's phone beeped with the text sound he had specifically set for Sam in case something urgent happened to Johnny. He knew he was acting completely out of character but couldn't seem to care. Sure enough, he reached for his phone, unconcerned if his father was offended or not; something could be wrong with Johnny.

Johnny's being admitted. Poor guy's burned pretty badly from that metal pole. They just finished removing the glass and suturing the wounds on his hips and stomach. Ended up with thirty-two stitches. Let you know when I have a room number, cousin.

Gabe simply replied, *Thanks*, and locked his phone. He looked up to find an assessing look on his dad's face.

"I'm sorry, Dad. It was important."

"Was that him, this man you met?" His dad actually looked hopeful. *Does everyone think I'm a lost cause?*

"No, it wasn't him, but it was about him," Gabe answered honestly, but knew his dad wasn't going to give up so easily.

"You know that's not going to work, son, so you might as well get right to the facts or we can beat around the bush and let your mom call in the aunts."

"That's low, old man." His dad simply laughed, leaned back in his chair, and waited. *Damn.* "His name is Johnny Jeffrey. I don't know a lot about him, but I plan on changing that the second he gets out of the hospital, probably sooner."

"The hospital? Is he okay?" His demeanour changed immediately. Everyone thought the fire chief was as tough as they came, but Gabe and his family knew the man was all heart.

"He's the one in that office building fire today, the one who saved Josie. Sam's been keeping me up to date on his condition," Gabe confessed.

"Why didn't you tell me you already found out who he is?" The chief commanded an answer, and Gabe knew he was sunk.

"Because it was more of a personal investigation, not one on behalf of Josie's family."

It took his dad all of two seconds to connect the dots, changing his expression from concern to shock.

"Well, what the hell are you doing here? I'll call your grandmother and let her know you'll reschedule dinner. You go on over there and check in. I'll deal with your mom and the aunts." With that, his dad picked up his cell phone and pointed at the door for Gabe to leave.

His dad was just like him, all alpha. If the man Gabe was interested in was at the hospital, then his dad would make sure no one got in Gabe's way when he wanted to be with that man. His mom was perfect for his dad; she allowed him the control he needed, while in truth, she kept the family and house running. Dad was just along for the ride. The man would move mountains for his wife— just the way it should be, in Gabe's opinion.

Gabe walked out one of the five bays that held the various fire trucks and EMS vehicles. They might be a small town, but they were responsible for four surrounding counties; therefore, they had a large police, fire, and paramedic presence. He threw his bag into the back of his Ford F-250 before climbing in, stopping to take a deep breath. He wondered what he would say to Johnny. Would Johnny want anything to do with him? Did he already have a boyfriend or partner? He hoped not, because Gabe wasn't sure he could back down. He had set his sights on this man and couldn't remember ever feeling this attracted and possessive so soon, not even with Chris. Gabe would just have to work around any obstacles that got in his way. Decision made, he took a second to text Sam to let him know he was on his way.

***

Johnny imagined this was what the poor people who had asthma felt like; every breath was a struggle and burned his throat and chest. The doctor wanted to keep him on oxygen and observation for the next forty-eight hours. Johnny wasn't entirely sure what he was going to do after that because both of his hands were currently bandaged like a mummy, covering his burns. Hell, even his right shoulder and part of his chest were bandaged, not to mention the multitude of stitches crisscrossing his stomach and hips. He was at a loss on how he would take care of himself. The concerned nurses had asked him for a number of a relative or friend they could call. Considering he was fairly new to this town and wanted nothing to do with his father or brother, he explained politely that there was no one.

His room was dark and he figured he must have fallen asleep. The pain medication they had him on was knocking him on his ass. He heard the rustle of paper and realized he wasn't alone. His heart raced, and Johnny's gut reaction was to panic, assuming his father had somehow found out about the fire and was here. Johnny quickly tried to push himself up into a seated position, but he didn't get far before he was crying out in pain from his burns and stitches.

"Easy, you're safe. Don't move. I'll get what you need, or you'll hurt yourself." Johnny was certain he was dreaming—either that or the drugs were really, really good. There was just no way that the mouth-watering fireman who helped him save Janice and carried him out of the burning building was standing over him, brushing back his hair and gently lowering him down onto the bed. Things like that just didn't happen to someone like him. It had to be the drugs.

"Johnny, you okay? Do you want me to get the nurse?"

Johnny reached out with one bandaged hand to check if he was indeed real, but the sexy fireman gently placed it safely back on the bed. "Careful with your hands. They're covered in burns and blisters. I can't imagine how painful they are."

"You're real? You're here in my room?" Johnny couldn't think of one good reason for Mr. Tall, Dark, and Handsome to be sitting in his room. But, God, he was nice to look at, even if he was a hallucination.

Who was he kidding? The guy was a god, from his confident attitude to his dark brown eyes and black hair cut military short. Hell, he was dressed in a shirt that was valiantly trying to win the battle to contain his muscles.... Johnny would have drooled if his mouth wasn't so damn dry. Unfortunately, his bed was in the way so that was where his perusal ended.

Shoot.

"Yeah, Johnny, I'm real. How are you feeling?"

Johnny was about to answer but realized he didn't even know Mr. Sexy's name.

"What's your name? Or I could just keep calling you Mr. Sexy in my head." If Johnny could have slapped his hand over his mouth, he would have. It had to be the drugs because he definitely said that last part out loud. He could feel his face and ears getting warmer and just knew he was blushing. Okay, smooth he was not.

The fireman smiled and Johnny was sure he saw a tinge of pink crawl up his neck to his ears. "You can call me sexy, but my name is Gabe Mason. Do you remember who I am?"

"You're the fireman who saved us from the building. Thank you for helping me with Janice."—cough— "She's been released, they tell me."

"Yes, she was by earlier while you were sleeping and left flowers. Strangely, being pinned to the floor saved your friend from serious smoke inhalation. Her husband will be bringing her and their son by tomorrow to visit with you."

"Ben. He's adorable, but I think it might be a while before I can hold him again." Johnny's throat felt like it had been rubbed raw and he began to cough harder. Between gasps for air, he managed to ask, "Was anyone hurt badly? Josie…someone caught her. Do you know if she's okay?"

Before answering, Gabe brought a straw to Johnny's lips so he could have a sip of water from the cup he held. "No one was fatally injured. Thankfully, we got everyone out in time, but there isn't much left of the building. Josie has been released and is resting at home. Thanks to you, she will be fine. We all owe you for what you did."

"If she and everyone else are fine, I'm good. Wait, what are you doing here?" Johnny could wish all he wanted that there were other reasons for Gabe to be in his room, but why bother dreaming? "Do you have questions about the fire?"

"Nope, I'm here for you, and from what I hear, you're going to need me." Gabe grinned, displaying a pair of dimples that could stop most women and men in their tracks.

"Why?" This was getting stranger by the minute. Johnny stole a quick glance at his IV bag, wondering what the hell he was on. Funny, this only made the handsome man laugh.

"No, you're not hallucinating, though you're on a pretty heavy painkiller. The problem is you have no one listed for your emergency contact or family. Who will be taking care of you when you're released?" The look of concern on Gabe's face was shocking to Johnny; he had no idea why this man would care.

Busted.

"I…ah…I'll be fine." He was not contacting his father. He would try and drag his ass back to the Jeffrey compound where Johnny could be "reconditioned" into a productive part of the family and, of course, less gay.

"No, you won't be. You have third-degree burns, thirty-two stitches and serious smoke inhalation. You won't be able to walk without losing your breath or falling over in pain, let alone care for yourself. You'll be coming home with me. I'll take care of you, and when I'm at the station, my family will help out."

Johnny wondered what alternate universe he had just woken up in where the handsome bear of a man wanted to take him home and care for him while he healed. *Oh, come on! That never happens in reality.* Johnny half expected a big-ass white rabbit with a pocket watch to come running through his room looking for his damn hole. "What…?"

The overhead lights to his room flicked on and the same friendly nurse he remembered from yesterday came walking in. "Good morning boys. Johnny, how are you feeling?"

"Good morning, Nurse Rouse. Johnny's having trouble speaking without straining his throat, so if you don't mind, I'll explain. He's having a lot of pain in his hands and occasional slow, labored breathing while he was sleeping and since waking. He attempted to sit up, but I don't believe he's pulled any stitches." Gabe answered before Johnny even managed to think to catalogue how he was feeling; strangely, Gabe was right. His hands were killing him, he was having a hard time catching his breath, and he prayed he hadn't pulled any stitches.

With that, Gabe Mason took over and Johnny couldn't find a good reason to complain. Gabe wasn't causing him any harm. In fact, if Johnny were honest with himself, he secretly wanted someone to just take control. He knew he was weak for wishing that. His father had physically beaten that into him—never show weakness, always be in control. Would he ever feel comfortable in his own skin? How could he expect to find someone to love him when he didn't love himself that much?

Gabe spoke to Nurse Rouse for several minutes. She looked maternally toward Johnny before leaving to get his medication and new dressings. Gabe turned to Johnny.

"I'll be back in just a few minutes. I have paperwork to fill out and I need to speak with your doctor to set up therapy after your release. Nurse Rouse will be back, but she'll wait until I come back to help with your bandages," Gabe explained before he leaned down and kissed Johnny softly on his forehead.

Johnny was so stunned he could only manage to nod his head in agreement before Gabe left the room. He hadn't a clue how long he sat there just staring off into space before Nurse Rouse came back in chuckling and shaking her head.

"What kind of drugs do you have me on because"—*cough*—"that just didn't happen?" Johnny gasped out, still not able to take complete breaths, but needing answers.

"Now, no more talking. You need to let your lungs and throat heal, doctor's orders. And honestly, I'm not one hundred percent sure what's going on either, but I can tell you I've known that boy and his family all my life. The Masons are good, honest people. His father's the fire chief and Josie's his cousin. But I've never seen Gabe riled up this way, and that's the God's honest truth. I think Dr. Green's head's still spinning." Nurse Rouse laughed before she attached another small bag to his pole and into his IV line. "Just lie back and relax. That pain medication will kick in soon enough and we'll be able to have a look at your burns and those stitches without causing you too much pain. Oh, and don't worry, Gabe's also a trained medic with the fire department, so he'll be able to help you with your medication, bandages, and therapy."

"Why?" Johnny knew he shouldn't speak, but he couldn't understand why this seemingly wonderful man would want to take care of essentially a stranger. His only guess was that maybe this had something to do with helping Josie, and since Gabe was her cousin, Johnny figured he couldn't be crazy, *right?*

"For two reasons—you saved my cousin's life and I'm interested in you."

Neither one of them had noticed that Gabe was back in the room. He went on, "I want to take care of you. If we had met on the street,

I would be pursuing you just the same as I am right now. That's just the way I am. Just because you're injured doesn't change that. It only changes how I go about it." Gabe held a folder and was standing next to a man who looked like an older version of Gabe.

Okay, maybe he's a touch crazy...but why the hell not?

"Okay, but if this is some drug-induced delusion, I'm going to be really pissed when I wake up."

Gabe laughed; it was a deep, full sound that made Johnny's stomach flip. The older man just smiled at Gabe. Johnny coughed again and Nurse Rouse placed a mask over his nose and mouth. The weird vapor made it a bit easier for him to breathe.

"Thank you."

"You're welcome, sweetie. Now, no more talking." Nurse Rouse smiled and began arranging long scissors, gauze, and various other medical supplies on a tray beside the bed. He had a very bad feeling he wasn't going to like this part.

Automatically, his eyes sought out Gabe, who was at his side instantly. "It'll be painful. I'm not going to lie. I will never lie to you. We need to change the bandages regularly to keep your wounds clean. Some of the blisters are breaking and weeping."

Johnny wasn't proud, but the sound he imagined a terrified puppy would make worked its way up his raw throat, and he slammed his eyes shut, not ready to see what his burns looked like just yet. He knew it was bad. The doctor had explained the seriousness of his injuries and likelihood of permanent scarring. Hell, he could feel the intense burning pain, and he really didn't need to see it.

"Easy, babe, I'm right here. I'm not leaving you. Just keep your eyes closed, okay? You don't need to look until you're ready. Listen to my voice and concentrate on that alone."

Without thought, Johnny did exactly what Gabe said to do. He kept his eyes closed tight and listened to this amazing man talk about his family, his crazy aunts and the U.S. Marshals Johnny supposedly saved him from, as well as his grandmother who belonged to a "white hair" group of some kind. He cried out in pain a couple times and Gabe was right there whispering nonsense into his ear, but it was the most meaningful nonsense Johnny had heard since his mother died.

Johnny was getting a little sleepy, he imagined from the pain medication, and began to drift off. He could hear Gabe talking to Nurse Rouse about his stitches, and then the older version of Gabe was giving some sort of directions for something, or perhaps it was a timetable or calendar because it sounded like plans. Johnny was too tired to care, and soon everything just faded away.

Chapter Three

Johnny blinked his sore, dry eyes a few extra times in an attempt to clear his blurry vision, because he sure as shit wasn't seeing what was surrounding him. The last thing he remembered was Gabe's voice calming him while Nurse Rouse changed his bandages, but now he seemed to have fallen down that rabbit hole and ended up in a flower shop. How long had he been asleep and whose flowers were these? He didn't have any close friends and his family would never have spent a dime on something so frivolous unless it happened to be for themselves.

But Johnny had to admit, it did look and smell like heaven in here, even if it all was sent to the wrong room. There were yellow and pink roses, calla lilies, daisies, carnations, and flower arrangements with so many different colorful blooms that he hadn't a clue what they were named. A beautiful sunflower sat proudly in a glass vase beside a row of balloons with various get-well slogans floating happily against the far wall. Another quick scan of the room assured him he was indeed alone and not in the same room from earlier. This one was much bigger and had a window with a view of a park across the street, so close he could make out children playing on a large jungle gym.

This was definitely not his room. His insurance would never even cover the window in this room—heck, his insurance company would have thrown him into the basement if they could get away with it. So how the hell did he end up here? Slowly, he became fully awake and noticed he was hooked up to oxygen and an IV still ran to multiple bags high above him. A clock on the wall flashed 3:19 p.m. He had slept most of the day away.

Then he saw the one thing that put the rest to shame in his eyes; on his side table in a tall, thin silver vase was a single blood-red orchid. Images of his mother slammed into him so quickly he felt light-headed—her beautiful golden hair and gentle blue eyes, sitting with her in her garden. He was tucked safely in her arms while her gorgeous orchids swayed in the wind around them. She would always bring him there when his dad was in one of his moods. Mom would sing loudly and tell him how much she loved him, all in an attempt to drown out the venomous words that spewed from his father's lips.

"You're my beautiful boy, Johnny. You know I love you to the moon." Her soft voice echoed through Johnny's head. *"I'll always love you."*

"Love you to the moon, Momma."

The world was safe for Johnny as long as he was in her arms; he knew this one simple fact from a very young age. Then she was taken away from him. The only love and light in his life was gone because some person decided to get high and drive. A young Johnny was left alone with the man who viewed him as a failure—he was too soft and too small to be a proper Jeffrey—and decided to set about correcting what nature had somehow screwed up—painfully.

The orchid was stunning and made Johnny feel that same love and safety from so many years ago. For one brief moment, he wished someone had actually sent it to him—because this was still not his room. Johnny had heard of mix-ups in overcrowded hospitals of course but never actually thought he would become one. Brighton didn't strike him as an "overcrowded" town, which was another reason Johnny had moved here. He needed peace. After all the years trapped trying to please his tyrant of a father, Johnny craved peace and acceptance.

Carefully, Johnny turned his head, trying not to pull on his burned shoulder too badly, but he was in desperate need of a drink to soothe his raw throat. Then, of course, reality came crashing in, reminding Johnny that he couldn't move his mummified hands, let alone pour himself a glass of water or even hold the damn thing.

Well, this should be interesting. Let it not be said that Johnny Jeffrey just gives up.

Johnny oh-so slowly pushed himself up into a sitting position using his elbows. His hands burned and his stitches pulled, but he proudly sat and reached over for the entire pitcher of water. He knew he couldn't wrap his hands around the smaller cup but the pitcher was at least three times the size, so he was able to lift it easily, even if painfully. Without a straw, Johnny had no other choice but to tip the jug back and drink from the spout, not exactly classy, but he was so thirsty he didn't care at this point.

The cool water felt painful against his dry, sore throat but all was going well—at least up until the door to his room opened and a small sprite of a woman with blonde hair and big blue eyes strode in. She carried multiple bags and another bouquet of flowers. Johnny was so caught off guard that the hold he had on the pitcher began to slip. Tsking, the woman dropped her load and rushed over. Smiling widely, she held the bottom of the pitcher in her hands so that Johnny could finish drinking.

"Dear, you should have called the nurse for help. I just stepped out for a moment to call home and pick up these bags from the car." The sweet, crazy lady rushed around Johnny, bringing the nurses' call button closer to his side and raising the bed so he could lean back. She even went as far as tucking him back in.

"Thank you…but I think you might be in the wrong room, or maybe I'm in the wrong room because I'm sure none of this is for me." Johnny gestured toward all the flowers, as if the mystery lady could somehow have missed the garden surrounding her.

"No, Johnny, this is your room, and I'm here to see you, sweetheart. Actually, you've had a few visitors, but you've been fast asleep since early this morning, according to Gabe. It's best you rest as much as you can anyway so that you can start to heal."

"I'm sorry…do you know Gabe?" Johnny gasped, his lungs burning with the effort it took him to talk.

"Gabe said you weren't supposed to be talking and exerting your lungs, so how about I explain everything, dear, and you just get comfortable."

Johnny figured he might as well hear her out because he was pretty much trapped in the bed at her mercy anyway. The little spitfire raced around the room adjusting the drapes and his bedding…again. She put a straw in the pitcher of water and pushed it close to the side of his bed, and then finally picked up her bags, depositing them on his dresser before gliding into the chair beside his bed. Johnny liked her immediately but was exhausted from just watching her. She looked to be in her late fifties, but she hustled around his room with the energy of a twenty-year-old.

"I'm Ellen Mason, Gabe's mom. You can call me Mom," she happily explained. "Gabe has been called in to cover a fire over at the Jaspers' farm. Seems one of their hay barns went up, and with all this dry weather we've been having, they're afraid it could catch to the nearby fields. Trust me when I tell you he didn't want to leave you, but this is the life of a firefighter, dear. That's when family comes in handy. I'm sure he'll be putting in for some time off now that he'll be helping you heal."

Mom? That was the only word he caught in that whole explanation. He hadn't used that particular word in a very long time, and strangely, he felt a warmth spread inside him.

"I don't understand." Johnny had to admit it was nice having someone care about him, but he still wasn't sure what to make of this whole situation.

"That's okay, Johnny. Just know that you have the Mason family to back you up, even though Gabe's banned everyone but me and his father from the hospital—something about not wanting to scare you off with all of us hovering at once. But we'll see how many we can sneak in before he catches on." Ellen gave Johnny a conspiratorial wink before digging into her bags. The more time he spent with Ellen, the more Johnny liked her. She seemed to be tough and gentle at the same time with a huge dose of mischief sprinkled in. He bet Ellen gave Gabe's dad a run for his money.

Johnny was curious now: Exactly how big was Gabe's family that he wanted them to steer clear of the hospital?

"How big is the family?"

"Oh, Johnny, honey, I'm going to have to draw you a chart on that because there's just no way you could remember them all. Let's see, to make it simple, I'll start with the immediate family in the area. Gabe's father, Roger, has three brothers and one sister, so Gabe has three uncles, four aunts, three younger sisters, two brothers-in-law, fourteen cousins, a niece, nephew, and Roger's mother, Grandma Rose." Ellen must have seen the panic in Johnny's eyes because she quickly added, "Don't worry, they won't visit all at once. I think."

That...that's roughly thirty! Oh shit! That's a lot of freaking people. And that was only the immediate family in the area? Leave it to me to find a cult, a very helpful cult, but still a damn cult.

"Johnny, you look a bit pale. Here, I brought you some of my famous chicken casserole, cut up in nice small pieces so not to hurt your throat. Hospital food will not be enough to get you healthy again." With that, Ellen pulled a plastic container from one of the bags. Honestly, Johnny was starving and the casserole looked amazing, but he just couldn't figure out how he would get the food into his mouth.

But instead of asking the obvious question, Johnny was still nervous about the room and the flowers. It would break him to pay for all this. "Ellen, how did I end up in a bigger room? My insurance isn't going to cover this, and the flowers"—*cough*—"who…?"

Ellen quickly moved his pitcher of water even closer so that Johnny could lean into the straw and take a much-needed drink before she began to explain. "You don't have to worry about the room, dear. Whatever your insurance doesn't cover will be seen to. As for the flowers, well, between family and friends, they've been arriving all day."

"But—," Johnny began but was quickly cut off by one look from Ellen.

"No buts, young man. You will not worry about the room and you will accept the gifts you've been given because you deserve them, and I will not hear another word on it." It quickly became apparent to Johnny that Mrs. Ellen Mason had dealt with men much larger than himself and had the steel backbone to prove it.

Therefore, Johnny gave the only acceptable answer. "Yes, ma'am."

Ellen laughed softly and smiled. "I knew you and I would get along. Took me years to get the men of this family in line, but you caught on right off."

Johnny also knew in that moment that they would get along just fine as well, and perhaps they weren't in a cult after all. But still, he needed to know who sent the red orchid closest to him. He decided against talking any longer and simply pointed toward the beautiful bloom.

Ellen caught on quickly to Johnny's attempt at charades. "Do you wish to know who brought that one?"

"Yes, please. It's important," Johnny replied, forgetting his decision not to speak, as he mentally rifled through everyone he might know who would remember his mother's garden. No one other than his father and brother came to mind. The flowerbeds had been bulldozed within a week of her death, replaced by a shiny new garage to store all of his father's vintage cars.

"This is from Gabe, dear. Actually, it's from the greenhouse he has in his backyard." Ellen answered with a great deal of pride. "Do you like orchids, Johnny?"

"My mother's favorite," Johnny gasped, deciding right there he really needed to get a handle on not talking for the time being. Picturing the hulking firefighter tending flowers in his greenhouse shouldn't have given Johnny this much joy, but it did. He wondered if Gabe would permit him to visit his greenhouse someday, maybe allow him to spend time sitting with the orchids for just a little while.

"Johnny, do you want me to call your mother to let her know what's happened?"

"Died...long ago."

"Oh, I'm so sorry, Johnny. And your father?"

Johnny simply shook his head, not wanting to open that painful door. Instead, he took renewed interest in his dinner, still trying to figure out how to get it from the container and into his mouth. Unlike the water, he couldn't simply pour it. Looking back toward Ellen, he noticed the sympathy flash in her eyes, but she quickly masked it with her normal enthusiasm.

"You've got to be hungry. Let's get you fed." Ellen retrieved silverware from her bags before turning toward Johnny. "Now, young man, you are about to have a real treat. This is my mom's recipe and, if I do say so myself, it's the best in the county, and don't you let Gabe's aunts tell you otherwise. They're just jealous." Johnny could tell each word she spoke about her family was laced with love, bringing home just how lonely Johnny really was.

He decided then and there he would accept the care of these fine people for the time he was allowed and soak up as much of these feelings as he could. That way, when he went back to his own solitary life, Johnny could pull on these memories to get him through.

Ironically, Ellen took over much like her son. It was quickly becoming a theme. Considering Johnny couldn't do anything for himself, he appreciated each and every gesture. She spoon-fed him the best damn chicken casserole he had ever tasted. When a young male nurse named Sam popped his head into Johnny's room, giving it a quick scan before strolling in, it seemed odd at the time. It wasn't until Johnny was informed that Sam was Gabe's cousin and he had chosen to ignore Gabe's decree to stay away from Johnny's room, considering he worked at the hospital, that Johnny understood the spy routine. Johnny was pretty sure that this would be a common occurrence amongst the Mason family members.

Sam, with the help of another young nurse named Amanda, checked all of Johnny's vitals and dressings, replaced a bag on his IV, and, much to his embarrassment, helped him into the bathroom and with his sponge bath. Through the entire humiliating ordeal, they repeatedly assured Johnny that this was nothing to be concerned about, that they were nurses and he was family after all.

Finally cleaned, fed, and medicated, Johnny was back in his bed and ready for a nap. Sam booked it out of the room once Ellen received a call from the chief to let her know that he and Gabe had made it back safely and should be at the hospital within the hour. Johnny knew the call was a warning from Ellen's husband to have everyone out of the room before Gabe arrived, but Ellen simply tutted into the phone before she hung up.

"Honestly, you would think my husband and son didn't know me at all. Of course there will be family sneaking in and out. What did they expect?" Ellen smiled before she placed her tiny hand on Johnny's uninjured shoulder and turned back to the television, which someone had rolled in while he was in the bathroom. Johnny snuggled further into the cocoon of pillows Ellen had amassed, while she got comfortable in a reclining chair beside the bed. They both went back to a movie starring Hugh Jackman and his muscles; thirty minutes later, Johnny and Ellen were both entranced.

"Do we even care what the plot line of this movie is?" Johnny finally asked after Hugh's fine ass flexed across the screen for a second time.

"Not a damn clue, but I can't look away," admitted Ellen without breaking eye contact with the screen.

"He has a phenomenal ass, I'll give him that," Johnny commented.

"Agreed," Ellen replied.

"Who has a phenomenal ass?" a deep voice asked, causing both Johnny and Ellen to squeal in fright. The water bottle Ellen was holding went flying across the room and into a bright green balloon, popping it.

Johnny looked up to see Gabe and the chief standing just inside the door, trying to contain their laughter, until the chief finally broke down and laughed outright.

"Roger Mason, how dare you sneak up on a person like that? You could have scared Johnny," Ellen admonished, but by the deep shade of red covering her face and ears, Johnny was pretty confident this had nothing to do with him.

"Don't drag me into this. I can't help it if your husband caught you ogling another man's ass." Johnny spoke softly through his own muted laughter at how flustered Ellen had become by this point.

"You were looking at that same ass, young man," Ellen shot while Gabe came around to the other side of the bed and brushed a stray blond curl away from Johnny's face.

"I can look all I want, *Mom*. Besides, you put the movie on." Johnny raised his bandaged hands and smirked like the little shit he was.

"Oh, now you call me Mom when we're busted." Ellen threw her hands in the air in mock surrender.

"I can see this may not have been such a good plan," the chief grumbled good-naturedly. "They seem like two of a kind, son. That can't be good for my blood pressure."

"I'm beginning to wonder that myself," Gabe laughed. "You look better, Johnny. How are you feeling, babe?"

"Better, thank you." He paused to cough. "Mom's taken very good care of me." Johnny was having a hard time dragging his eyes away from Gabe. He was like a damn magnet and Johnny was stuck. It could have been his chiseled features, his commanding presence, or the fact that he was drop-dead gorgeous, but in truth, it was Gabe's eyes. They were so dark and filled with concern, compassion, and something Johnny hadn't seen directed toward him in a long time—affection.

"Well, I can see you have everything under control here, son," Chief Mason commented as Ellen began to gather her bags getting ready to leave with her husband. The chief stepped forward with his hand out. "We weren't introduced before. I'm Chief Roger Mason, Gabe's father."

Johnny looked at the chief's outstretched hand for a moment before he lifted his bandaged hands into the air. Chief Mason's eyes went from welcoming to stricken in seconds.

"Ah, damn, I'm sorry, Johnny. I didn't even think."

"No worries." Johnny sighed before moving his hands aside. "It's nice to meet you, Chief Mason."

"Dad."

"Sorry…?"

"You can't play favorites, Johnny. If Ellen gets 'Mom,' I get 'Dad.'"

"Wha—?"

"Well, gotta go. I'll see you tomorrow, Johnny." Ellen rushed over and kissed both Johnny and Gabe on their respective cheeks. "I'll call you later, Gabe." In a flourish of bags, Ellen flew out of the door with a smiling chief in tow.

"Please believe me—my family is actually sane, although that may be hard to accept at the moment," Gabe confessed while they both sat staring at the closed door.

"Have you consulted a professional about that?" Johnny deadpanned.

"Uncle Henry's a psychiatrist…but he might be biased," Gabe answered, a huge smile showcasing those deep dimples set in the dark stubble covering his cheeks. Johnny knew he was lost if he spent any time with this man.

Does Gabe even know he's walking among us mere mortals? I don't stand a chance; this can never work out. I have to keep my distance. I can't let this destroy me when I inevitably fall for him.

Chapter Four

By the next morning, Johnny knew something was seriously wrong—well, more wrong than all his current injuries. At Johnny's urging, Gabe had finally left late last evening so he could get a decent night's sleep in his own bed after spending the day fighting a fire. Now Johnny wished he'd never said a word; then Gabe would be with him as everything turned into mayhem around him. Just after 4:00 a.m., Johnny woke gasping for breath. He felt like he was drowning. Every time he coughed, he brought up a disgusting, frothy, pink phlegm of some kind. All in all, he was beginning to panic.

After several X-rays, an ultrasound of his lungs, and blood and oxygen saturation tests, a respiratory specialist was called in to consult and Johnny was diagnosed with acute noncardiogenic pulmonary edema. It was caused not only by the damage from all the smoke he inhaled, but also by the chemicals in that smoke. He didn't care what the hell it was or why he had it. Johnny just wanted someone to fix it now. He heard someone say something about a membrane, air sacs, and capillaries, but what it all came down to was the fact that fluid was filling his right lung and his body was battling to get enough oxygen.

More bags of clear liquid were attached to his IV line as nurses rushed in and out of his room. Nurse Rouse was at his side checking machines, her hand flying across her clipboard. She tried to look calm, but the pinched lines around her eyes and lips gave her away. Something was seriously wrong.

"I've called Gabe, Johnny. He's on his way. Don't worry."

She tried reassuring him, but her continued monitoring of equipment and rigid stance confirmed she was worrying enough for both of them. *Great, just great. I'm finally building a life with a new job and home only to almost die in a fire, possibly lose the use of my hands and by extension my career, and now something else is going wrong. Perfect! And I didn't even get to play with the hot fireman.*

Okay, not the best time to whine about that one.

Every minute that passed, Johnny struggled a bit harder to breathe. His eyesight was beginning to get blurry. As teardrops of light filtered through, Nurse Rouse began yelling, but it seemed to be happening from so far away.

"Dr. Green! He's losing consciousness and his oxygen saturation levels are dropping!"

"Prepare to intubate. We have to secure his airway," Dr. Green ordered and people began to run. Or at least Johnny thought that's what they were doing, but really it was all just a blur.

Johnny felt detached from the entire scene, as if he were weightless, simply watching but not involved. He knew he should be terrified, perhaps he even looked it, but really all he wanted was a nap. He was so tired. Machines were wheeled in and Johnny's bed was lowered. By now, he was full-on hyperventilating, dragging each and every breath in through what felt like mud.

Nurse Rouse put a syringe to a port on his IV line before giving Johnny a troubled smile. "You sleep now, Johnny. You'll be just fine."

The last thing he remembered were machines ringing, shouts from a vaguely familiar voice, and Dr. Green's face above him before everything went black.

***

Johnny had been on the ventilator for almost two days, and Gabe had no intention of leaving him again, whether Johnny was conscious or not. At the moment he was being kept sedated to give his injured lungs a chance to heal as various medicines were administered through either his tracheal tube or IV. Also, waking up attached to a machine wasn't something anyone wanted Johnny to experience; he'd been through enough. Gabe had raced into Johnny's room as he was being sedated. The fear he saw on Johnny's face sent acid clawing up his throat. It was something he never wanted to experience again. Nurse Rouse assured him that Johnny wasn't fully conscious at that moment and would likely not remember what occurred; he hoped she was right.

The dark, empty halls were a reminder of just how late it was in the evening of the second day of his vigil. Gabe felt drained and exhausted, but he had to stay strong for Johnny; he would need him when he woke up. So there he sat reading an old horror novel out loud so Johnny would know he wasn't alone. Earlier in the day, they read the *Brighton Bugler* together. There were plenty of studies proving that unconscious people could sometimes hear what was happening around them, and if Johnny could, Gabe was determined to make sure he knew he was safe and that Gabe was there watching over him.

His mother and father had been by often, bringing food and clean clothes or just sitting and keeping him company. But honestly, all he needed was for Johnny to heal and open those clear green eyes of his. Gabe would wait right here until that happened. The remainder of the family were calling for updates but stayed away, not wishing to add the stress of a strange group of people to Johnny's recovery.

"Okay, we are never burying our pets in some messed-up cemetery. I think we'll stay with the mysteries from now on if you don't mind, or else I'll be having nightmares." Gabe laughed softly, and placed the now closed book on the small side table. He gently held on to Johnny's arm just above his bandaged hands. Fresh orchids from his garden sat closest to the bed. Gabe's mother had stopped by his greenhouse. The sweet scent of jasmine softly lingered in the air. "I pray you can hear me or even feel my touch and know you're not alone. I'll never be far away, baby. You only need to worry about getting better. Once you heal up I want to share so much with you."

Gabe knew his emotions were all over the place and took several deep breaths to calm the hell down. "You see, I'll tell you a secret. I'm not a safe bet for you, Johnny. Things have happened, things I can't change but have changed me. And the only reason I'm brave enough to tell you this now is because you're unconscious. I find it hard to trust people. I'm stubborn and bossy, and I need to be needed, if that even makes sense." Gabe rubbed the palm of his hand across the back of his neck before he continued. "There's just something about you. I've been drawn to you since the first time I saw you trying to lift that cabinet off your co-worker. My instincts tell me we could have something special, and if you let me, I promise to try my damnedest to give this my all."

Gabe sat for a few moments just running his hand up and down Johnny's pale arm, hoping that one day he would feel those same arms holding him tight. He just needed to concentrate on making that happen and not on any other possible outcomes.

"So this is where I find you." An all too familiar voice broke Gabe's peace. He clenched his teeth, enraged by the very thought of Chris anywhere near Johnny.

"How did you get in here? This is a critical-care floor. How did you even know where to find me?" Gabe tenderly tucked Johnny's arm back under his blanket before rounding the bed and closing in fast on his ex-fiancé.

The smug smile on Chris's face was quickly replaced by fear as his hands flew up in surrender. "When you didn't come home after a couple days I followed your mom here. I just wanted to talk, sweetheart."

"Talk... *What?* Who the hell do you think you are coming here after what you did to me?" Gabe grabbed Chris by his shirt and dragged him out of the room away from Johnny and to the nurses' station. He wanted a peaceful environment around Johnny so he could heal and feel safe. Chris was not going to ruin that.

Nurse Moore took one look at them and jumped into action. "Call security. This man isn't supposed to be on this ward." She, along with many in the community, knew Chris's history and the events of two years ago.

"Wait, wait! I just wanted to talk, Gabe. Can't you give me five minutes?" Chris snaked his hand up Gabe's chest and around his neck. "Come on, honey, you know you missed me."

Waving a red cape in front of a rampaging bull is insanity; those last words might as well have been flashing crimson for the effect it was having on Gabe. "Missed you?" Gabe grabbed Chris's hands and tore them from around his neck, repulsed by his touch.

"Yeah, we had some good times together, Gabe." Chris's voice carried across the room and held enough innuendo that no one was left wondering what exactly he was referring to.

"Miss what exactly? The lies, the theft, the embarrassment, the pain, the anger? What exactly was I supposed to have missed?" Gabe's voice came out calm though he was raging on the inside. All he knew was that this vile man needed to be away from Johnny now. "Leave now or be carried out."

Gabe pointed to the three security guards standing behind Chris; one was already holding his handcuffs at the ready. Chris took an appraising look around. Gabe imagined he was deciding whether or not he should leave without screaming the walls down. *How could I have ever found this man attractive? Sure, physically he's tall, blond, and handsome, but how did I miss the sickness inside him? Those same blue eyes that used to make me smile almost seem cruel.*

"Fine, I'll go, but we aren't finished, Gabe." Chris looked like a petulant child with his hands on his hips and nose in the air.

Yep, no idea what I saw in him.

Gabe simply shook his head as the three guards led Chris away. "I don't want him able to get back in here."

"Don't worry; now that we know, we can keep an eye out for him. I'll inform the staff that he's been warned. If he tries again, we'll call the police," Dr. Green stated as he joined their small group. Though the doctor had moved to Brighton just under one year ago, he had been a perfect fit in the small community. "Now that the excitement's over, let's go check in with Johnny and see how he's progressing."

"Yes, I didn't want to leave him alone, but I had to get Chris out of his room," Gabe agreed.

"Understandable." The doctor's pale eyes looked tired but determined. "Johnny's improving every day, Gabe. Soon we'll have him breathing again on his own."

"Thanks, Doc." Gabe resumed his position at Johnny's bedside. Johnny's body looked so small in the middle of the crisp, white bedding. The melody of beeps and bells became background noise once the doctor began examining Johnny.

Twenty tense minutes later, Dr. Green confirmed yet again that Johnny was definitely recovering. If all went to plan, he would be able to remove the breathing tube within the next twenty-four hours. Once that was done, he would reverse Johnny's sedation, allowing him to regain consciousness over the following days. Soon Gabe and Johnny were alone once again. Gabe managed to get a baseball game on the circa-1980s wood-grained, plastic-encased beast in the corner. He pulled his reclining chair over beside the bed, wrapped his arm around Johnny's, and began to explain how the Brighton Bulldogs made it all the way to the five counties finals last year and how Gabe would be sharing his season tickets with Johnny.

***

The deep timbre of a voice Johnny recognized flowed through him thick and heavy, pulling Johnny forward before the connection sliced clean away. If he tried to concentrate, the words would simply vanish even faster. The only time the familiar voice stayed long enough to make out what was being said was when he relaxed and let the sound cover him like a warm blanket. *Gabe.* The nothingness of the words meant everything to him. Gabe was here. He hadn't left; that was all that mattered to him.

Johnny swore there had to be sand embedded in his eyes and his throat was on fire, but he could breathe—not deeply but without too much pain. At least his mouth was empty now, no longer filled with what he remembered felt like hard plastic. Now he just needed to open his eyes to see Gabe, but they outright refused to move. The more he struggled, the more exhausted he became until sleep finally took him again. This routine replayed itself too many times to count, and Johnny had just about enough of this torment. He was determined to open his eyes this time.

Johnny reached out with his bandaged hands, searching for that sweet man who was humming softly in his ear, calming Johnny with his strength and reassurance. But Johnny didn't want calm right now. He wanted to be awake. He wanted Gabe. Thrashing harder against what had to be a chest, Johnny finally felt the dry scrape of his eyelids opening, and light poured in, blinding him.

"Li…t," he managed to push out as tears ran streaming down his face.

"Turn down the light. Hold on, baby. This will help." The wet cloth that covered his still tearing eyes felt like heaven. "Johnny, I'm going to bring a cup to your lips so you can have a small drink of water."

Oh God, yes, water please.

He felt the hard plastic being pressed to his dry lips, thankful for the fact that there wasn't a straw involved. At the moment, he wasn't sure he had enough strength to breathe properly let alone suck up water. The liquid cooled and wet his parched mouth, but the moment it reached his damaged throat, he began to gag. He was positive razor blades would have been easier to swallow. While a small amount stayed down, the rest was caught by another towel held to his chin by Ellen—*Mom*.

The wet cloth that had been protecting his sensitive eyes had been removed and, mercifully, the only light in the room came from the open window. The strong, handsome face of the man he'd been listening to in the darkness hovered over him smiling, showing off those sexy dimples of his.

"You're finally awake." Gabe's eyes filled with tears as he sucked in a deep breath. Even with his blurry vision, Johnny could see the tension melting away, leaving a happy, exhausted man in its place.

"Hi," Johnny managed in a rough, raspy voice that reminded him of a rusted hinge being torn open. It sounded painful, which was fitting considering it hurt like hell.

"Shhh, don't stress your throat, Johnny. Just rest." Gabe leaned down and kissed Johnny on his cheek. His eyes sparkled, even if they were surrounded by dark circles. "Is Dr. Green on his way, Mom?"

"Yes, dear," Ellen answered, still clutching the towel as her own eyes filled. "The nurse ran to get him. They shouldn't be long, son. Johnny, we're so happy to finally have you back, young man." She turned and sniffled all the way to the bathroom, where Johnny was confident she was taking a few minutes to pull herself together.

The only problem was, Johnny had no idea why everyone was acting this way.

Why is Ellen crying? Why does Gabe look exhausted? Why am I in a different room again? Shit, what's going on?

"What happened?"

Gabe cupped the side of Johnny's face with his large, calloused hand. Johnny leaned into the gentle touch, needing to feel him close. Something had changed.

"You've been unconscious and on a ventilator for three days, Johnny. God, I've never felt so helpless. They removed your breathing tube yesterday afternoon. Dr. Green and the nurses have been taking good care of you."

"I remember your voice... right? You d-didn't leave me." Johnny spoke softly, trying not to hurt his throat more than it already had been, but he needed to know if what he remembered was real or if he had imagined the whole thing. The warmth he felt when looking at Gabe only confirmed the man had managed to slip into Johnny's heart somehow, but that was impossible. They'd only met days ago and it sounded as if Johnny had been unconscious for most of it.

"No, I would never leave you, baby." Gabe brushed Johnny's hair away from his face and carefully tucked the covers around Johnny's body. The bedding looked dishevelled from his thrashing, but thankfully Gabe had been able to restrain him enough so that he didn't accidentally pull his IV line out of his arm or the oxygen tube from his nose. "I'll explain everything soon, but you need to promise me not to stress your lungs by talking. All you need to do is concentrate on healing. I never want to see you that sick ever again." Gabe's voice cracked slightly. This strong, brave man who spent his entire life saving others broke down at the thought of Johnny's suffering, and seeing that did something to Johnny. Johnny would have to examine that change later, when his head stopped spinning.

"Me either," Johnny agreed. Even though he still had no idea what had happened, the relief in Gabe's eyes was enough to confirm that his condition must have been grave.

Gabe slowly leaned down, bringing his face mere inches away from Johnny's. His eyes, the color of dark chocolate, seemed to glow from within. His soft lips lowered to caress Johnny's, tender and slow, with the light dance of his tongue against Johnny's lips. The moment was over way too quickly for Johnny's liking.

"I see our patient is awake," Dr. Green announced from the doorway and smiled wide before entering with a nurse. "How are you feeling, Johnny?"

"Sore... weak," Johnny answered, but ran out of breath again before he could continue.

"Okay, I'm going to ask you some questions and I want you to just nod your head yes or no," the doctor instructed while he placed his stethoscope in his ears. "Gabe, can you help Johnny sit up so I can listen to his lungs?"

Gabe slipped his arms behind Johnny's back and cradled him, slowly lifting Johnny until he was sitting upright in the bed. Dr. Green listened to Johnny's chest and back. Johnny wasn't sure what the doctor was listening for, but he was glad the man didn't ask him to breathe deeply or anything. He was pretty sure it would be a while before that happened, considering it felt like he had a truck parked on his chest. Mom came back out of the bathroom with her cell phone against her ear, smiling like a loon. Johnny was still struck by the fact that this family so easily accepted him into their fold.

The doctor continued with his questions and examination. Johnny concentrated on Gabe and not his discomfort as the gentle man kept hold of him. He could feel the flex and bunch of hard muscle under Gabe's shirt. After several minutes, Gabe was asked to lower him back onto the bed, but Johnny held onto Gabe's shirt for a few extra seconds, not ready to let him go just yet. Johnny didn't know why he was behaving this way, but no one seemed to mind as Gabe rubbed his cheek against Johnny's head and simply held him. Gabe let go after a few moments and moved only a couple feet back to allow the nurse to check his blood pressure and oxygen levels.

"Your lungs sound much better, Johnny," said Dr. Green. "They're healing nicely, but it will take a while before you're even cleared to leave the hospital."

"That bad?" Johnny asked.

"Yes, it was very serious. I don't think now's the time to discuss everything that's happened, considering you just regained consciousness and are still feeling the effects of being sedated. We'll give you some time to get your bearings back."

"Thank y-you," Johnny gasped, and agreed talking would have to wait until he could at least take a decent breath in.

"You're welcome." Dr. Green gathered a folder from the side table, bringing Johnny's attention to the bouquet of orchids in a clay vase beside his bed.

He looked up to see Gabe watching him closely. Johnny reached out to touch the beautiful pink petals but remembered his bandages at the last moment and pulled his hand back. Gabe immediately moved the vase to the edge of the small table so that it was closer to Johnny, making him smile.

"Gabe, can I talk to you for a moment?" Dr. Green asked before heading toward the door.

"Yes, I'll be right out," Gabe answered. "Just rest, honey. Mom's right here with you. When I get back, we'll get you cleaned up and comfortable."

Gabe followed the doctor out of the room and Ellen took his place at Johnny's side. "Here, Johnny, have another sip of water, dear. It'll be easier to keep down this time." He gave her an unconvinced look but obediently leaned forward toward the cup she held. The cool liquid did stay down this time and only burned his throat a little. "There you go. We'll keep up on the fluids until we can get some broth into you."

"Thank you, Mom." Johnny tried desperately to prevent his tears from falling, but there was nothing he could do to stop them. Quickly, he turned his face away from Ellen as the events of the last six months finally came to a head. Fighting to gain his freedom from his father, moving to a town where he knew no one, being caught in a fire, and now finding out he was kept breathing by a machine for the past three days. Christ, he couldn't even wipe his own eyes with his bandaged hands. It was all too much. Johnny figured he was entitled to a mini meltdown.

Ellen dabbed a soft cloth across Johnny's wet cheeks, and then her gentle hand brushed his curly blond hair back off his face. "It'll be okay, son, you'll see."

"How?" Johnny asked, while he fought to get himself under control. His hands trembled and nausea surged through his weakened body.

"Because you're a strong man and Gabe will accept nothing less than your recovery. He can be very stubborn when he wants something, and you've already fought your way off the ventilator. Johnny, you don't strike me as a man who gives up easily." Ellen continued to stroke his hair, as if calming a frightened child. Johnny realized, in essence, that's what he was to her at that moment. After all, she had already adopted him as her honorary son. "I know it's a lot to take in, but you have Gabe and all of us to rely on now."

He knew Ellen was right. He might have been through hell and still had months of rehab to get through, if not longer, but he now had the one thing he'd never dared dream of before: a family to support and care for him. In the last few years, his father seemed to lose interest in Johnny, and his older brother simply disappeared from his life. After his mother died, he was left with no one he could count on. Johnny sent up a silent plea, hoping and praying that he had finally turned a corner in his life where he was no longer alone.

Chapter Five

Gabe watched as Johnny slept peacefully in their comfortable new orthopedic king-sized bed that he had delivered late last night before Johnny was released from the hospital—and he did consider it *theirs*. After the last ten days spent with this amazing man, Gabe was positive Johnny was *his*. He could easily admit that Johnny was gorgeous. His curly blond hair and big green eyes were striking, and his taut body might not be as muscular as his own, but Johnny had well-defined muscles that Gabe couldn't wait to explore once Johnny was healed.

Johnny might be small in stature, but his spirit was strong and the stream of visitors he received after only living in town a few months was a testament to the man himself. Janice had cried on Johnny's uninjured shoulder, thanking him for saving her life and keeping his promise to not leave her behind. Her husband was so choked up that he barely spoke and only managed a broken "thank you" while rocking their son Ben in his arms.

Josie had visited each and every day once Johnny was out of danger. The first few times, she had been inconsolable after seeing the extent of Johnny's injuries, especially his abdominal wounds from the glass in the window. Over the following days, and with Johnny's unwavering support, Josie came to terms with the fact that it wasn't her fault that Johnny had been hurt and it was truly an accident. His recovery was finally progressing after the fluid was cleared from his lungs. Gabe didn't like to think about how close he'd come to losing Johnny, and he had to make a conscious effort to not dwell on it. Johnny was safe now in Gabe's home, where he would remain and heal.

Now that they were home, Gabe knew to expect his mother and grandmother at any moment. They probably had old Mrs. Walker reporting from across the street. Food should be arriving shortly thereafter with his three sisters. Then the aunts should be stopping by with their spouses and children. Dad had managed to keep most of the Mason women at bay and away from the hospital, but now all bets were off.

As far as Gabe was aware, only his mom, dad, Sam, and Josie had been to the hospital. After Johnny had taken a turn for the worse, Gabe had lived at the hospital with him, caring for the man he intended to spend a great deal of time with. Thankfully, many of his fellow firefighters were able to pick up Gabe's shifts, allowing him to remain at Johnny's bedside. Brighton was a close-knit community, and Gabe was certainly thankful for that.

"You know I can't sleep if you keep staring at me." Johnny's scratchy voice brought Gabe out of his thoughts.

"Sorry, babe, I'll go out to the kitchen. Do you need anything before I leave?"

"Can I come with you?" Johnny asked softly. Gabe knew his beauty didn't like being alone since the fire, and had awakened numerous times with nightmares.

"Sure, we'll go out to the living room. I'm positive the Mason women will be swooping in at any moment." As if to confirm Gabe's suspicions, the doorbell rang.

Johnny simply laughed at him and shook his head. "See, there's a benefit to my family not speaking to me. You'll never have to worry about the in-laws. Besides, I've met a few of the Masons already, and I haven't run away yet." He stopped to cough. "Not that I could run, but I can shuffle like a pro."

"Their loss is my family's gain. I want you just the way you are, and I'm not letting you go, Johnny. I hope you understand that I'm very serious about us." Gabe brushed a gentle kiss over Johnny's lips, wondering if he would scare Johnny off with that admission. He had been waiting patiently for Johnny to become comfortable enough to express how he felt about Gabe, but so far he had remained quiet.

Before Johnny could respond, the family grew restless and began knocking on the front door. Gabe lifted him, wheezing, into his arms and cradled him close to his chest. Gabe loved his family, but at that moment he honestly considered retracing his steps and hiding out in the bedroom with Johnny for the rest of the day.

***

Johnny was in way over his head. He'd allowed himself to begin falling in love with this sweet, sexy fireman. He'd never done anything impulsive in his life, but he'd so easily handed his heart and complete and utter trust over to the man carrying him in his arms, toward a family that might not approve of him. True, Johnny had already met Gabe's mom and dad, his cousin Sam, and had actually known Gabe's cousin Josie for months, but this was not a free pass into the graces of the remaining masses of Masons.

Fully expecting Gabe to place him on the couch, Johnny was a bit shocked when Gabe walked straight to the front door while still carrying him. Johnny had to confess he felt safe in Gabe's arms, but as soon as he could perform an activity without gasping for breath or buckling in pain, Johnny swore he'd be on his own two feet again. *The occasional cuddle and carry would surely be okay…* Oh, who the hell was he kidding? Johnny was right where he wanted to be—in Gabe's arms.

Gabe easily shifted Johnny's weight and opened the front door. "Hey, Mom, that was fast. Should we be expecting anyone else?"

"Oh, don't be that way. You knew darn well your father wouldn't be able to hold the rest of the family back once you got your fella home." The small sprite of a woman who had wormed her way into Johnny's heart in a matter of days breezed through the door and straight up to him. "Hello, Johnny, how are you feeling today?"

"Better, Mom," he managed in a scratchy voice.

"You poor dear. Your voice sounds so painful." Ellen placed her tiny hand on Johnny's arm.

"Johnny's not going to be talking very much. He has to let his lungs and throat heal. Doctor's orders, especially since his infection," Gabe commanded as he carefully brushed Johnny's wayward curls from his face yet again. "Also, tell your merry band of women that Johnny needs to rest, so keep the wild plans to a minimum for the time being."

"We promise to not drag him out anywhere until he's healed." Ellen dramatically crossed her heart, but the mischief in her eyes gave Johnny pause. *Wild plans?*

"I'll believe that when I see it." Chief Mason walked in with an elderly lady on his arm. This had to be the notorious Grandmother Rose. "How are you feeling, son?"

"Better, sir," Johnny answered again between gasps.

"Okay, that's it, no more talking. Everybody got that? If not, y'all can leave," Gabe ordered and turned toward the couches. "I'll not have Johnny overdoing it and ending up back in the hospital."

"Understood, son. We'll just have the women do all the talking; should be no problem at all," the chief commented. Grandma Rose promptly smacked him on his huge arm with her tiny manicured hand.

"Don't you be badmouthing the people that control your food, son, unless you're fond of tofu," Grandma Rose spoke while she walked right past Ellen and a contrite chief toward Gabe and Johnny. Gabe leaned forward so that she could kiss both men before sitting down on one of the two oversized couches.

Johnny was positive that, to any average person, these couches would be considered mammoth, similar to most of the furniture in Gabe's house. Johnny was pretty confident that he could get lost on them—seriously, fall asleep and never be found again. After taking a closer look around the room, Johnny realized Gabe's home truly reflected the man. It reminded him of a den designed for warmth and comfort. From the rustic stone fireplace and exposed wooden beams, to the open-concept design covered in natural fabrics and earthy tones, not a hint of color could be seen. Johnny could picture wonderful artwork on the walls and colorful throw pillows. He bet Gabe had no idea what to do with a throw pillow other than to, well, throw it. Yep, he could really add a punch of life to Gabe and their home—Johnny was shocked and quickly reined in his wayward thoughts before they went too far. *This isn't my home.*

Johnny finally noticed that Gabe had stopped walking and was now watching him closely as if trying to read his mind. It was a little unnerving how Gabe could do that.

"You can change anything you like, Johnny, but leave me my chair, okay?" Gabe pointed toward an enormous black leather reclining chair that looked so comfy.

Okay, that could stay.

Johnny simply smiled back at Gabe, both because he was unsure of what to say to such a generous offer and he wasn't supposed to talk. Gabe must have taken that as an agreement and kissed Johnny with as much passion as he dared in front of his family to seal the deal.

"Well, holy cow, Dad was right!" a voice yelled from behind Johnny.

Thankfully, Gabe hugged him a bit closer to his chest, preventing Johnny from jumping straight out of his arms. Instead, it triggered a coughing fit, which prompted women to scatter in search of water and the inhaler that the doctor had sent home with him from the hospital. Gabe sat on the couch with Johnny safely on his lap. His coughing caused tears to run down his face. Vaguely, he was aware of more women entering the house and a few other men. Knowing they must be Gabe's aunts and uncles, Johnny's humiliation was now complete.

"Johnny, look at me. That's it. I need you to take a big breath in."

Johnny nodded, and even though his sight was blurry, he kept his eyes locked on Gabe's, trying to calm himself and breathe in, trusting Gabe to get him through this. Johnny felt his inhaler being pushed to his lips, his bandaged hands stopping him from holding the tube himself. Within moments, he could feel a cooling sensation flowing down his throat and into his burning lungs. Gradually he began to breathe easier.

"There you go, babe. You'll be all right. Just need to keep the excitement down to a dull roar." Gabe brushed his chin over the top of Johnny's head before he kissed his forehead. This seemed to be a more intimate gesture to Johnny than simply kissing him on the lips.

"I'm so sorry, Johnny. I didn't mean to yell like that." Johnny turned to see a distraught young woman standing just a few feet away. He guessed her age to be around twenty. She had dark black hair like Gabe's but bright blue eyes like Ellen's. Easy guess, this had to be a younger sister. "I mean, I was shocked. I've never seen my brother look or act like that. I just...I'm sorry."

She seemed to deflate right in front of him, and Johnny couldn't have this bright young woman sad. "It's okay. I guess I'm still a bit jumpy," Johnny croaked out and gave her what he hoped was a reassuring smile. He truly didn't want her to feel bad.

"Okay, back to the no-talking rule." Johnny nodded his agreement before Gabe went on. "This is my youngest sister,

Francine, but we call her Frannie. She's attending Brighton College, the same as Josie, but Frannie's majoring in English." He could hear the pride in Gabe's voice as he spoke about his sister. No one in Johnny's family had ever spoken of him that way.

"I want to become a teacher someday." The young girl beamed, smiling from ear to ear, and put two bags on the large wooden coffee table in front of Johnny. "I brought lots of stuff for us to do while you're recovering. I know you can't use your hands properly yet, but we'll figure out a way around it."

Frannie's optimism was contagious and Johnny smiled before he snuggled deeper into Gabe's chest and watched Frannie unload board games, a tablet, a chess set, cards, and movies. Grandma Rose, as she asked to be called, sat right up close to Johnny and pulled out photo albums from her oversized bag.

"Now, Johnny," she said. "Before you get all mixed up trying to remember everyone, I'll start at the beginning with pictures."

"Dad, Grandma's brought her photo albums. Can't we just skip over the 'embarrass Gabe' part of the visit?" Gabe groaned into the back of Johnny's head. Johnny turned and gently nuzzled Gabe's cheek to reassure him that all would be fine and that Johnny was actually enjoying himself. He hadn't thought before he acted to soothe Gabe, but the look of complete adoration on Gabe's face was worth anything Johnny could give.

Before Johnny could begin his walk down memory lane with Grandma Rose, the aunts and uncles took the opportunity to introduce themselves one couple at a time. Johnny remembered Josie saying there were lots of first responders in her family, and Johnny quickly realized that was true. There were Cousin Sam's parents Aunt Jane and Uncle Jack, a paramedic; Aunt Dot and Uncle Henry, a psychiatrist; Aunt Casey and her life partner Aunt Marg, a pediatrician; and cousin Josie's parents Aunt Flo and Uncle Jim, a firefighter. Mom explained that the remaining fourteen combined cousins had decided to stay away so as not to completely overwhelm Johnny, but they were guaranteed to come by and introduce themselves throughout the upcoming weeks.

"Johnny, there isn't a way to adequately express how thankful we all are for what you did that day to save our daughter's life." Uncle Jim spoke softly before moving the board games aside and taking a seat on the coffee table in front of Johnny and Gabe, Aunt

Flo at his side. The large man was brought to tears when Josie walked through the front door and came to kneel beside her father. Johnny reached out and placed one bandaged hand on Uncle Jim's leg. He wasn't sure how to comfort the man, so he remained quiet. Gabe wrapped Johnny in the safety of his arms, providing the emotional support Johnny needed.

"When I saw Josie hanging from that window, my heart stopped. I was down on the rig manning the deck gun, knocking down the flames when I saw you throw yourself out of that window, grabbing for my daughter. You're family now, Johnny. Even if you weren't with Gabe, you would be family." Uncle Jim's hands began to shake slightly. "If you ever need anything, anything at all, you let me know. We can never repay you for what you've done, but we'll never forget it either."

The room fell silent and a troop of hummingbirds began maneuvers in Johnny's stomach. He considered how to respond to Uncle Jim's declaration; the man deserved honesty. "I—I was scared out of my mind. I'm not a hero, sir. If I could've found us any other way out of that building, I would've taken it." *Cough—cough—* "Hell, if I could've left the decisions up to someone else in the room"—*cough*—"I would have, but it just wasn't an option."

"And that's why you're a hero, young man. When it came down to the lives of three women, you stood up. You took control and you saved lives without concern for your own. Whether you want to believe us or not, it won't change how we feel," Uncle Jim explained before he leaned forward and gently hugged Johnny, followed by Aunt Flo and Josie; all were careful of his injuries.

"Whether you believe it or not, babe, you're a hero to this family." Gabe held Johnny snug to his chest "Now that's definitely enough talking for you. Let's have everyone else take over for now."

Gabe's other two younger sisters, Joanne and Kate, arrived not ten minutes later with their husbands and two children. The little four-year-old boy was Joanne's, and the baby girl was Kate's. Johnny was beginning to get the suspicion that this was a well-timed invasion. Food was cooked, and schedules worked out, so that when Gabe had to work, one of the many family members would be with Johnny.

"You don't have to change your schedules for me." Johnny didn't want everyone to have to put their lives on hold because of him. "I'll heal up and be out of your hair in no time."

A few of the women simply smiled and shook their heads, but Grandma Rose just came right out with what she was thinking. "My grandson won't be wanting to let you go if that constant smile on his face is any indication. So you might as well get used to the family, honey, because you're stuck with us."

Johnny glanced up to Gabe, who looked determined and simply nodded his head in agreement with Grandma Rose's statement. Some women went back to cooking, while others were invading cupboards and closets, calling out items that were needed as Frannie kept a running list. Grandma Rose continued with family photos and hilarious stories. Johnny knew he would love spending time with the women of this family.

He felt a twinge of pain and looked down at his bandaged hands. The doctors couldn't predict how much damage was done to the nerves in his hands or how much mobility he would lose until he was further along in his recovery. Johnny was scared. He had no idea what he would do if he couldn't use his hands. How would he survive or continue in graphic design? He had fought so hard for his career away from his father, and now it could be taken away from him.

"You okay, babe?" Gabe asked. "Are your hands sore?"

Johnny nodded, trying to keep to the no-talking rule as much as possible. He had learned early on that it was useless to play down his injuries and pain; Gabe seemed to know the truth whether Johnny wanted him to or not.

Gabe stood and placed him gently back on the couch. "We'll figure everything out together, Johnny. For now, I'll go get your medication. You just rest." Several Mason men and women watched their interaction with interest and simply smiled or nodded in some sort of silent agreement toward Gabe. At times, it seemed as though the members of the Mason family only had to look at one another to know what the other was thinking without speaking a single word.

"So is telepathy a Mason trait as well, and if so, when do I start my lessons?" Johnny asked the group of men and women gathered on and around the couches. Gabe's laugh was so deep and filled with joy that Johnny couldn't help but smile back at him. When Gabe was happy, he was contagious, and from glancing around the room, Johnny knew his family felt the same way.

"Don't worry, son. You'll catch on soon enough," the chief explained as Gabe carried on into the kitchen to retrieve Johnny's medication and water. He lowered his voice before he continued. "I haven't seen Gabe this happy in a very long time, Johnny. Just keep doing whatever it is you're doing."

Johnny had no idea what he was doing, but he was enjoying spending time with Gabe and his family. They were strong, loving, and hilarious. It hadn't escaped his notice that most of the men in this family were very dominant, take-charge individuals; even the men who married into the family were alpha individuals. But it was obvious the women of the family actually held everything together. The aunts owned a boutique on the main street called Hidden Treasures, selling artwork and crafts from local artists. Both Kate and Joanne were pediatric nurses, and their husbands, Dave and Rick respectively, were both police officers.

Just as Gabe brought back Johnny's medication and a glass of water, a few cell phones and beepers started to go off, including Gabe's.

"Here, sweetheart, take these." Gabe handed Johnny two pills and held the water for him to drink since Johnny couldn't hold a glass yet. Frustrating!

"We have to go, son. Everyone has been called in. We have a retirement home in Jenson on fire, and they're afraid it could spread to the nearby hospital," Chief Mason announced. Johnny noticed a number of the men stood, kissed their family good-bye, and went out the front door. That amazed Johnny, families who spent their whole lives protecting and helping others. Polar opposites of his own family. His father and brother might be doctors, but it wasn't to help others, that was for damn sure.

"Johnny, I've got to go. Mom and Grandma Rose will stay here with you until I come back," Gabe explained as he crouched in front of Johnny and cupped his cheeks with his huge hands.

"So will I," Frannie announced. "I'll help you, Johnny."

Gabe looked upon his youngest sister with such love. "Thank you, Frannie. I'm sure you'll help keep him out of trouble. Now, Johnny, I want you to eat and get some rest. I don't know how long I'll be, but we'll be back as soon as we can."

Johnny didn't like the thought of Gabe going out into danger, but he respected the man's choice to be a firefighter. "Please be safe."

"I will, don't you worry. I have someone important to come home to." Gabe gave him a quick kiss and followed his father out to his truck.

Johnny didn't know what to do. This was the first time since he and Gabe became a couple that Gabe would be going off to fight a fire, and he would have to wait at home and worry.

"He'll be safe, dear," Ellen said softly before adjusting the pillow behind Johnny's head. "I won't lie to you; it doesn't get better with time, and you still worry every time they leave. You have to be sure you love him completely to sign on for this kind of life."

Johnny had to agree. These women lived with men who ran into hell to save people while everyone else was running in the other direction. He respected their strength and courage. Johnny knew he was falling in love with Gabe; he felt it to his very soul. Johnny also knew he would never be able to walk away from the man, but old doubts still lingered. *Why would a man like Gabe want me?*

"I want Gabe in my life any way I can get him." Johnny went with the truth; these women deserved it from him. "I'm falling in love with him."

Ellen's smile lit up her entire face, while his sisters, aunts, and Grandma Rose gathered around to join in the conversation.

"Have you told him, dear?" Ellen asked before she brought the straw up for Johnny to take a much-needed drink of iced tea.

"No. Isn't it too soon? He'll think I'm out of my mind." Johnny thought for sure he was out of his own damn mind, so it wasn't a big jump to think Gabe would be as well. *There was no such thing as love at first sight or even second sight, right?*

"Honey, the way Gabe looks at you now, I'm pretty sure he's already in love with you as well," Aunt Flo announced while the other women simply nodded their agreement.

Johnny had a hard time believing that Gabe felt so strongly about him, but he kept those thoughts to himself. They finished dinner with very little dignity for Johnny as he was forced to allow Ellen to feed him yet again. His hands were so heavily bandaged there was no way he could hold a fork or spoon. The aunts, a few remaining uncles, and the two oldest sisters had left for the evening, and Johnny was just getting settled on the couch to watch a movie with

Frannie, Ellen, and Grandma Rose when the doorbell rang. Ellen went to answer it, and even without a clear view of the front door, no one could miss the tall blond man's entrance.

"Ellen, so good to see you again. Is *my* man home?" The blond literally walked right past a pissed-off-looking Ellen and invited himself straight into the living room.

Who is this guy and who the hell is his "man"?

Frannie stood and cut the man off before he could get any further. "You aren't welcome here, Chris. Gabe made that clear, so take your lying ass back out the way you came."

That was when the rude man finally noticed Johnny bundled on the couch. "Who have we here, the invalid from the hospital? This mouse can't be my replacement. Christ, did he have to stoop that low after I left?" Chris sneered at Johnny. From his designer jeans to his perfect teeth and hair, he was the exact opposite of Johnny.

Johnny had no idea who this person was, but he had some sort of relationship with Gabe and hated the fact that Johnny was in this house. That much was clear. He could feel his chest tighten, a sure sign of the onset of a coughing fit, and Johnny desperately didn't want whoever this Chris was to see him coughing his lungs out.

"You need to leave, now." Johnny croaked out, feeling the rattle starting deep in his chest. *Shoot, no talking, stop talking.* The women looked approvingly at him. Even though he was injured, he wasn't going to sit back and have someone push him around. Not anymore.

"What the hell is wrong with you? Tell me *my* Gabe didn't just pick up some stray he felt sorry for?" The disdain dripping from Chris's every word and his curled lip and cold eyes were truly amazing to Johnny. He thought his father was the only man who could pull off such contempt.

"That's it! Get out of this house right now or I'll drag your worthless ass out." Frannie was fuming, and Johnny noticed Mom was now on the phone. Grandma Rose stood right in front of him as if guarding Johnny. God, he loved these women.

Johnny could hear sirens in the distance and he figured Mom had called in the cavalry. He would have laughed, but he was beginning to gasp again. Johnny knew he soon would be coughing. He needed to calm down. Unfortunately, Chris didn't want calm; he wanted batshit crazy, and he actually lunged at Johnny. He would have knocked him and Grandma Rose off the couch if Frannie hadn't tackled the asshole to the ground. Apparently, Frannie knew self-defense. *Go girl!*

Uniformed officers came running into the house just as Frannie pinned Chris to the floor. The police officers handcuffed the now irate man and dragged him out of the house. "He's mine, you worthless little shit. He wants to marry me!"

That was news and the last straw for his attempted calm. Johnny couldn't catch his breath and began coughing violently. Through blurry eyes, he watched Mom run in with his inhaler.

"Johnny, honey, you look at me. I need you to calm and take a breath in." Grandma Rose looked him straight in the eyes. "You will not allow that awful man to hurt you and Gabe. You're stronger than that. Now breathe in."

Johnny obediently sucked in a bit of air and felt the mist working its way down his throat and into his burning, painful lungs. After a few minutes, it became a bit easier to breathe and Johnny was able to sit up slightly with Frannie's help. He looked around the living room to find an EMT and Joanne's husband, Rick, in his police uniform standing nearby. Groaning from embarrassment, Johnny lay back down on the couch, hoping the damn thing would actually swallow him up. No such luck. The EMT crouched beside the couch and gave him a friendly smile.

"Hi, Johnny, I'm Royce. You might not remember me, but I work with Gabe. I think it's best if we take you back to the hospital and have you checked out." Royce leaned over and wrapped a blood pressure cup around Johnny's upper arm.

"I'm fine, but thank"—*cough*—"you for your help." Johnny was not in any way wanting to go back to the hospital.

"Here, Johnny." Mom leaned over and placed her cell phone to Johnny's ear.

Confused, Johnny leaned into the phone and croaked, "Hello?"

"Johnny, don't speak." Gabe's voice was intermixed with sirens in the background. "You'll go to the hospital with Royce. It's not open for discussion. I'll be with you as soon as I can."

Now, what happened next Johnny would blame on the shock of the events over the last couple days, his questionable sanity, or a full moon, if there even was one. "Fine. Love you too," he croaked and carefully pushed the off button with his nose before Gabe could respond.

Shooting Mom a pleading look before lying back down on the couch, Johnny was dreading going to the hospital. "Don't give me that look, young man. I've dealt with men bigger than you my entire life. Besides, I didn't call him. His father received a report that police and EMS were called out here. Gabe was a little concerned, to put it mildly, and if my son got you to go to the hospital, then so be it. Now, let's move out!"

"Yes, ma'am," Johnny and Royce said in unison before Royce and his teammate lifted him onto the gurney and they were off back to the same place he had just left that morning. Johnny was devastated.

Chapter Six

Gabe was furious. How dare Chris come into his house and try to attack his Johnny. Shit, and on the first day he had Johnny home. *How was that even possible? Is Chris watching my house?*

Gabe had spent the next four hours fighting to keep the fire contained to the retirement residence and trying to calm his racing heart. Johnny had said he loved him; well, he actually said he loved him *too*, which meant Johnny knew how Gabe felt about him and he felt the same for Gabe. He just prayed that Chris hadn't screwed this up royally for him. Gabe finally found a man who filled the empty places in his heart, and he wasn't letting him go. For years he had been living half a life. Sure, he had his family, friends, and work that he loved, but he was alone and afraid to trust again. Now he knew with absolute certainty that Johnny was the perfect man for him, and it filled Gabe with a profound feeling of contentment and peace.

When he arrived back at the firehouse, Royce was waiting for him. "Gabe, you look about ready to kill someone. You need to calm down before you go to Johnny. The guy's been through enough."

Gabe stopped in his tracks and lowered his head in disgust. He knew Royce was right. He was ready to kill anyone who dared to hurt Johnny, and he needed to get a grip on his anger. "You're right. I just…Royce, I finally—"

"It's okay, buddy. Hell, if I had someone…" Royce looked off for a moment, and Gabe immediately felt his heart plummet. Royce's husband had died tragically in a car accident over three years earlier, and Royce had never been the same. His friends had hoped that with time Royce would heal, but the life and joy had been sucked right out of him, and it seemed as though he might never fully recover.

Gabe reached out to Royce and gave his friend a hug. Neither of them spoke for several moments, allowing Royce the time he needed to snap out of his thoughts. "You better get going. I know it has to be hell what you're going through with Chris showing up like that and Johnny back in the hospital. You need anything, you call me anytime."

"Thank you." There was nothing more to say. These men were part of his extended family and understood how important Johnny was to him and the hell he went through when Chris took off. Gabe had been there for Royce, just as every other person in this department had been, and they would all be there for Gabe—there was never a doubt.

He knew Johnny was safe at the hospital, but it still seemed to take forever to stow all the gear, shower, and have the chief drive him there since his truck was still at his house. Before his dad's truck was even in park, Gabe was out the passenger door and striding into the emergency department. There were familiar faces everywhere, but not the one he was desperate to find.

His cousin Sam stood behind the nurses' station and raised his hands in surrender when Gabe walked up. "He's okay, Gabe. Come on, I'll take you to his room."

Gabe was beginning to wonder exactly what he looked like to make Sam so compliant because even on a good day, his flamboyant cousin was about as compliant as a rattlesnake.

Raising one eyebrow in question, Sam smiled and answered, "You look about ready to blow, cuz."

"Sorry, Sam. It's been a long day." Gabe hung his head and apologized.

"Don't worry about it; you have a right. Who would have thought that asshole would just randomly show up and attack Johnny, especially after you had him kicked out of the hospital?" Sam sighed as he came around the huge glassed-in desk and led Gabe and the chief toward the elevators. "Johnny is nothing like Chris, thank God! I would have to slap you silly if you hooked up with anyone like that jerk ever again."

"Can't disagree with you on that one." Gabe laughed for the first time since leaving Johnny earlier.

"Hey, the guy saved you from the aunts." Sam shook his head before getting on the elevator and pushing the button for the third floor. "He's golden in my books."

"Well, I'm glad they finally dropped the charges against you, Sam." Gabe smiled innocently, desperate to keep a straight face. His dad, on the other hand wasn't as in control, which was apparent by the laughter coming from the corner.

"Laugh all you want, you two, but being arrested by Marshals while on a blind date your loving aunts set up *is not funny!*"

"Oh come on, how was Aunt Dot supposed to know there was a warrant out for the guy's arrest?" Now Gabe was laughing just as loudly as his dad.

"It wasn't a warrant; it was a man hunt!" Sam hollered just before he broke out laughing himself. Though it wasn't funny at the time, Sam had been cleared of any involvement in his date's thieving escapades. At the very least, it gave Sam an automatic lifetime ban on the aunts' matchmaking attempts.

Sam led them to a darkened room. It was almost 2:00 a.m. "They moved him up here about three hours ago. They want to keep him in for another few days, Gabe."

Gabe froze. "Why do they want to keep him? What's wrong with Johnny?" All kinds of scenarios were running through his head. What if Johnny had been hurt worse than he was told? What if the damage to his lungs was worse or if he had developed another infection?

"Doctor Green is trying him on a different medication to help heal his lungs with less pain to Johnny. But he has to be connected to oxygen and monitored during treatment, so it's best he stays here. The doctor asked to be paged when you arrived so that he could explain everything to you himself, but he was needed in surgery, so he'll be a couple hours at least," Sam explained as if it was completely normal. Gabe knew he was overreacting, but hell, this was *his* Johnny.

"Son, why don't you go on in and send your mother out. I'll bring your truck in the morning. I don't imagine you're leaving here tonight."

"As long as Johnny's here, I'll be here. Thanks for everything, Sam, Dad." Gabe hugged them both and turned toward Johnny's room.

"You have to tell him, son." His dad spoke softly but the words held enough pain to stop Gabe in his tracks.

"I didn't think we would have to cross this bridge so soon," Gabe admitted, feeling the sharp edge of a long-ago pain cutting through his well-healed wounds. All he wanted to do was start a life with Johnny, and now his past was bearing down on him.

"He's a good man. A good match for you, son, and he loves you. That's obvious, but don't let Chris destroy it before you even get a chance to start."

"Listen to your father," Ellen said as she softly closed the door to Johnny's room and joined the men in the hallway. "He needs to know. Chris said some pretty vulgar and condescending things, and Johnny needs an explanation."

Gabe clenched his jaw and actually felt himself getting hotter, causing his palms to sweat. The need to track down Chris and run him out of town was overpowering.

"Go in there. Johnny needs you, and you need him. Just be honest; he'll understand." Ellen kissed Gabe on the cheek, took his dad's hand, and walked back down the hall toward the elevators.

Gabe had to take a few moments to calm himself down and think before he went into Johnny's room. He had no idea how he was going to explain being with a man he believed loved him only to find out how big a sucker he really was. Years of plans—plans of marriage and plans for children—all gone because Gabe was just another easy mark. It didn't matter how many times his friends and family told Gabe it wasn't his fault. In the end, it was.

***

Johnny heard whispers of a conversation outside his room but couldn't quite make out what was being said. He had been asleep for almost two hours and only woke as Mom left his room. For what felt like the hundredth time, Johnny tugged on the mask covering his nose and mouth. He felt suffocated but he'd been warned numerous times not to remove it.

In truth, Johnny knew why he was so unsettled—Gabe wasn't here with him. Mom had told Johnny that the fire crews had put out the blaze and stopped the fire from spreading to the hospital and everyone was safe, but that had been hours ago and still no Gabe.

Johnny wondered if perhaps this Chris meant more to Gabe than even his family knew. Maybe he decided Johnny was too big a pain to be bothered? Truthfully, Chris was handsome, tall, strong, polished—in fact, he was everything Johnny wasn't. How could he even compete? Maybe he should just bow out gracefully before he embarrassed himself any further.

The creak of the door alerted Johnny that he wasn't alone. He turned to see the man that he loved and, he just realized, couldn't keep. *This sucked.*

"Hey, babe, you're awake. I thought you'd be sleeping." Gabe came to his bedside immediately and kissed Johnny's forehead, avoiding the dreaded mask still covering most of his face, or at least that was what Johnny hoped. "I don't want you to talk, Johnny. You need to rest your lungs."

Johnny was perfectly fine with not talking. He had absolutely no idea what to say anyway. *Sorry I ruined your reunion with your fiancé?* Not likely. Gabe looked upset; maybe he felt bad for having to send him on his way while injured. But Johnny had thought ahead and had the nurse bring in information on home care. That way, Gabe wouldn't have to feel bad about sending him home. He could hire a health care worker to come in daily. It would kill him, but he would do it for the man he loved. Gabe turned to place his bag on the floor by the bedside table and picked up the booklet on home care.

"What's this, Johnny?" Gabe's voice hardened as he asked, but before Johnny could even open his mouth to answer, Gabe stopped him. "Wait, you're not supposed to be talking, so I'll do the talking and you do the listening, okay?"

Johnny simply nodded, a bit confused by Gabe's angry reaction to the home care booklet. Honestly, he thought Gabe would be relieved. Gabe carried a chair closer to Johnny's bed and sat down heavily. It seemed as if Gabe didn't have the strength to stand any longer; he buried his head in his hands. Johnny couldn't help himself, and reached out to brush his bandaged hand over Gabe's short, dark hair—needing any sort of physical contact.

Gabe didn't even raise his head as he spoke. "You deserve to know who that person was that attacked you today."

Gabe finally looked up. The pain in his dark eyes hit Johnny hard and caused his heart to beat a tiny bit faster. "I'm so sorry that Chris tried to assault you. He should have never been anywhere near you, and if I have anything to say about it, he'll never be again." Gabe reached up and ran his hand down Johnny's arm; it felt like a caress. Totally confused at the direction this conversation was taking, Johnny remained silent for a moment because this was the strangest "it's not you, it's me" speech he'd ever received.

Gabe seemed to be caught in some internal struggle, and Johnny couldn't let this carry on. The poor guy had been nothing but wonderful to him. It wasn't Gabe's fault that Johnny had fallen in love with him. Gabe didn't deserve to have to feel sorry for loving someone else, even if it was that asshole Chris.

"It's okay, Gabe. I can make arrangements for home care. You don't have to worry about me. I won't press charges against your fiancé."

There, that sounded confident and not like my heart was breaking.

Gabe stood up so fast his chair crashed to the floor, and before Johnny could even register what was happening, Gabe had him cradled in his arms lying on the bed. Amazingly, his mask had stayed on.

"I know we've just started out, but I can't lose you." Gabe pressed his forehead to Johnny's. He could feel a tremble run through Gabe's body. "He isn't my fiancé. At one time, I thought we would be married and, hopefully, have children, but I was sucked right into his lies. We were together just over a year. He moved into my home, and we were making plans for the future. Chris played his part well. Friends and family began to make comments about Chris's odd behaviour and seeing him around town at strange times of day when he told me he was at work. But did I listen? Of course not, because the Chris that was home with me wasn't the same Chris he showed everyone else."

The self-loathing and pain in Gabe's voice broke something deep inside Johnny and he couldn't hold back the tears for this poor man. Gabe held him closer but averted his eyes before he continued. "People I've known my entire life, people that I trust with my life, and I didn't believe them. I gave Chris more trust than I did my own family."

Johnny had no idea when he had begun stroking Gabe's chest to comfort him, but he needed the contact even if it was through layers of gauze, and he thought Gabe might need it as well.

"I turned my back on my family and friends when I chose not to listen to them. This was all my fault. I believed his lies and when he took off one day without a word, I'm sure I was the only one surprised. He'd cleaned out the house of anything of value he could sell and emptied the joint bank account. Thank God I never gave him the combination to my safe or access to my personal accounts. Anything of real importance to me was in the safe and the bulk of my money he couldn't touch. Maybe deep down I knew not to give him access to those things."

Johnny tried to speak, to comfort him, but Gabe stopped him with just one devastated look. "Babe, please let me get the rest out. It gets worse."

Worse?

"At the end, before he took off, we had been organizing our wedding and even had lined up a gestational surrogate for our supposed children. I was a fucking idiot to trust him. The woman from the agency Chris had interviewed and 'thoroughly background checked' was actually his sister. She wasn't a real surrogate and had tried to get a portion of the fee up front before even going to the fertility clinic. I became suspicious and refused to even consider her before speaking to the agency. She disappeared about the same time as Chris. I haven't seen or heard from him in years, since the day he left right up until a few months ago. He sent me e-mails, which I deleted unopened, and then he showed up at the hospital when you were unconscious." Gabe gently cupped the side of his face, making sure he made eye contact with Johnny before continuing. "He never made it anywhere near you, baby. I had him out of your room and out of the hospital almost immediately."

Holy shit, that asshole! Taking advantage of Gabe's dream of having a family. Who does that?

"That was over two years ago, and you're the first man I've trusted since, outside my family and friends. The odd thing about that whole situation was that I had never given up that much control ever in my life, and, Johnny, I'm sorry but it'll be even harder for me to give up control now. That's something you need to know right from the start."

Johnny gave a soft laugh then gasped for air before saying, "I already know that. I trust you, Gabe. I know you were there keeping me safe. You'll always keep me safe." He knew down to his soul that Gabe would never do anything to harm him and would only look out for his best interests. He wasn't naïve enough to think there weren't going to be a few disagreements in their future, but they would work it out; they just needed to be willing to try.

Johnny had always considered himself to be a smart man, and he'd be damned if he was going to throw away the best thing to happen to him just because some jerk showed up. The only way he was leaving was if Gabe asked him to, and even then Johnny would be hard-pressed to listen.

Gabe's dark eyes cleared from his sad thoughts and past pain. He gently ran his thumb along Johnny's jaw and up into his hair, and damn if that didn't just make certain parts of Johnny perk right up. *I'm hurt, not dead.*

"You'll stay with me?" Gabe said softly. Johnny wasn't sure if that was a question or statement, but he nodded in agreement just in case. He wanted no misunderstandings. "I love you, Johnny."

"I love you too, Gabe." Gabe gently removed Johnny's oxygen mask before giving him a kiss filled with love and the promise of future passion. Johnny would have never thought that it was possible to feel clear emotions in a kiss, but Gabe made him a believer. He could feel Gabe's love for him loud and clear. He wouldn't doubt what Gabe felt for him again. He was a very lucky man and knew it.

Saying yes and staying with the man he loved was that simple and that complicated all at once. There was nothing more that needed to be said; they loved each other. Johnny knew the facts, made his choice, and his choice was Gabe.

Chapter Seven

Two weeks later

The interior of Hidden Treasures felt more like your favorite aunt's house than a store. Well, in Johnny's case, the store was owned by Gabe's four aunts and his mom, so it wasn't too far off base. The store smelled like fresh cinnamon rolls, which Aunt Flo baked religiously every morning while the others dusted and arranged beautiful displays of stained glass, jewelry, carvings, metal sculptures, colorful artwork, and much more from local artists. Several carved wood pieces of local wildlife and paintings of a nearby lake now graced Gabe's house.

Though several of Johnny's belongings had made their way over to Gabe's house, he still felt like a guest. No matter what Gabe said or the fact that they slept together in the master bedroom every night—though without sex until Johnny was physically cleared—it didn't help ease his worry that once he was better he would have to leave. He wasn't sure what it would take to make Gabe's house feel like home. In fact, if Johnny were honest with himself, he hadn't felt as if he had a real home since his mother had died. Perhaps he never would.

"Do you want to walk over to the diner with me and pick up lunch, Johnny?" Aunt Jane asked as she walked out of the back storage room carrying a stunning new watercolor painting delivered that morning.

Johnny's lungs had been healing very quickly after his second visit to the hospital, and all his stitches had been removed, but his hands were still mainly wrapped, making it difficult for him to handle daily tasks. Gabe was on shift at the fire station and refused to leave Johnny on his own just yet, so here he sat behind the counter as Aunt Jane and Aunt Flo helped customers and unloaded stock. Johnny desperately needed to feel useful again.

"How about I walk down to the diner and pick up our order and bring it back here for lunch?" Johnny suggested, liking the idea more and more. He could use the small walk across town to clear his mind. "It shouldn't take me too long."

"Are you sure, Johnny? How's your breathing today?" Aunt Jane asked, clearly not liking the idea of letting him go out on his own.

"Oh, let the poor boy go. He has to be suffocating under everyone's care. Johnny's well enough to walk down to the diner on his own." Aunt Flo winked at Johnny to let him know he had one sister on his side.

"But what about his hands? How can he carry the bag without hurting his hands?" Aunt Jane wasn't ready to give up just yet, but Johnny wasn't either.

"Just loan me one of your fabric reusable bags with the handles. Jesse can put our lunches in the bag and I can put it over my good arm." There, that sounded logical to Johnny, and before Aunt Jane could come up with anything else, he slipped the handle of the bag over his arm and headed for the front door. "I'll be back in less than ten minutes."

The tiny bell tinkling over the door as Johnny left the shop proclaimed his freedom. Okay, Johnny knew he was being a little dramatic and it wasn't all that bad, but he still took the time to enjoy the sun high in the sky on this cloudless summer day.

The air was thick with the smell of roses coming from the garden surrounding the library across the street. The sweet smell reminded him of the oasis Gabe had made for him inside his greenhouse. Once Mom mentioned the joy Johnny displayed in the hospital after being given the orchids both times, Gabe had immediately gone out and bought a large, comfortable reclining chair. He'd placed it in the greenhouse, filled it with pillows, and proclaimed it to be Johnny's spot. Now, in truth, that was where Johnny could be found most days, reading and relaxing, when home. He loved Gabe so completely. To anyone else the gift wouldn't have meant much, but to him it was the world.

Several people called out in greeting from across the street, waving as they walked by. In the past few weeks, Johnny had met more people than he could possibly keep straight, but it felt amazing to be part of a community. For the first time in his life, Johnny felt accepted just the way he was. No one wanted to change him or cared what his last name was. It was amazing and scary all at the same time because Johnny had learned painfully that peace never lasted long. He had felt it on one occasion while away at college, but it was fleeting once his father arrived. After that one unwelcomed visit, regular reports were sent to his father from each of Johnny's professors and his roommate suddenly found other accommodations, leaving Johnny alone once again.

Five minutes into his walk, the small hairs on the back of Johnny's neck stood on end. He looked around, but nothing seemed out of place. Johnny couldn't shake the feeling of being watched and quickened his pace toward the diner. The sunny streets suddenly felt like they were getting darker and closing in on him, but nothing stood out. He felt foolish by the time he walked through the diner doors. Johnny had been working hard to regain his self-confidence since leaving his father's estate, only to find himself almost running into the diner because he was spooked. *I guess twenty-nine years of fear and self-loathing will take more time to reprogram than I thought.* Several more people shouted out hellos as Johnny forced a smile and joined Jesse at the counter.

Jesse was new to town. According to the White Hair Crew, he had drifted into town looking for a new start. He looked to be only about twenty-five, but his weary brown eyes told Johnny he'd seen too much in that short time. Grandma Rose took a liking to him right off, which was a stamp of approval if there ever was one, and Jesse found himself with a job as a part-time cook and full-time waiter at the diner. He also was able to rent a room in the small apartment above it and began his new life all within the first week; the "Crew" worked fast.

"Hey, Johnny, it's good to see you out on your own," Jesse joked. He knew how much Johnny had been chomping at the bit to feel normal again. Although now, with his tiny hairs screaming out warnings, he wondered if it would be odd to ask Jesse to walk him back. "You here to pick up your aunts' order?"

"Yes, thanks, Jesse." He handed the bag over to Jesse who filled it with takeout containers. Johnny couldn't help looking over his shoulder and out the front window, but no one was there. He felt like he was losing his damn mind.

"Are you okay, Johnny?" Jesse asked, still holding the bag in his hand without handing it over to Johnny.

"Yeah, I think I just freaked myself out is all. It's nothing." Johnny felt stupid now that he thought about it.

"How about you let me decide if it's nothing." Jesse's voice was tinged with concern. He stood only a few feet away, still not releasing the bag to Johnny and not looking like he was going to without an explanation.

"Well, when I was walking over here, the hairs on the back of my neck stood up and it felt like I was being watched." Johnny rubbed his bandaged hand over his neck, trying to ease the feeling. "But no one's there. It's in my head; I'm just working myself up."

Jesse looked out the diner window and scanned the area before yelling into the back kitchen. "Clem, I'm walking Johnny over to his aunts' shop. I'll be back in a few minutes."

Clem, a giant of a man, came to the front, wiping his big hands on a dishcloth hanging from his apron. Johnny absently wondered if there was something in the water around here making most of the men the size of bears. "No problem, Jesse. Wanna stop and get the mail at the post office while you're out?"

"Sure, boss man." Jesse smiled at Clem. "There isn't another one of those packages in there for a special someone? Oh, I don't know, maybe a certain librarian…?"

"Go, you troublemaker, and leave my packages out of this," Clem grumbled happily.

"I'm just saying, if you gave Rick the chance, I'm sure he would be more than happy to check out your package." Jesse laughed, dodging the dishcloth thrown at his head. "We're going, boss man…so testy."

Jesse led Johnny out of the diner and scanned the area again.

"It's okay, Jesse. I just got myself all worked up over nothing."

"Well, it's better to be safe. If you felt it, I believe it. You can't go around ignoring things like that, Johnny. Trusting my gut has saved my ass a few times," Jesse assured him. Johnny had a feeling he spoke from experience and not just in an attempt to make Johnny feel less embarrassed.

Jesse kept a look out while telling Johnny all about Clem's crush on Rick, the librarian, and vice versa. They were exact opposites, and if Jesse could be believed both were trying desperately not to let the other know how they felt.

"It's a damn soap opera, Johnny. I swear I'm going to have to come up with a way to get them together before they miss out on something amazing. Chances like that don't come around every day." Jesse swore before getting a faraway look on his face.

"You're really a softy, aren't you, Jesse? You have all these tattoos and ride a badass motorcycle, but you have a heart the size of Texas. I can tell; no use in denying it. Besides, Grandma Rose already spoke highly of you, so you're as good as in around here." Johnny laughed at the stunned expression on Jesse's face, as if being accepted hadn't even crossed his mind as possible.

"Well, just don't go telling too many folks or my cover will be blown," Jesse teased before walking across the crosswalk a block down from Hidden Treasures. "I really like this town. It has a feel to it, you know?"

The sudden squeal of tires was the only thing that alerted them to a silver car speeding toward them out of a side street.

"Look out, Johnny!" Jesse yelled before he pushed Johnny out of the way, unavoidably placing himself in front of the vehicle. Jesse's right leg was struck by the car's passenger-side fender, and the blow threw him a few feet away from Johnny.

The car continued to race down the street and around the corner, vanishing and assuring Johnny that he could crawl to Jesse's side. People were screaming for help and running in his direction. The aunts came sprinting out of their shop.

"Jesse, can you hear me?" Johnny grabbed Jesse's limp hand, praying to God that the man who had just saved his life wouldn't lose his own. "Jesse, can you open your eyes? Please open your eyes!"

"Johnny, an ambulance is on the way. What happened?" Aunt Jane asked, while applying pressure to a wound on Jesse's leg that Johnny hadn't seen in his panic.

"A car came out of nowhere. Jesse pushed me out of the way— he saved my life, Aunt Jane. He can't die!" Johnny screamed, terrified Jesse would indeed die.

Jesse moaned before he opened his eyes. "I'm not going anywhere. At least, not yet."

"The ambulance is on its way, young man. You just lie back," Aunt Flo said softly. "Johnny's Uncle Jack is working today and on his way. They'll take good care of you, I promise."

"Th-thank you, ma'am," Jesse said between clenched teeth. The pain he was in was obvious. "Can someone call Clem and tell him I—I can't make it back today p-please?"

"I'm right here, son. Don't you be worrying about nothing right now." Clem leaned over and placed a few clean towels under Jesse's head. Police had arrived and were moving the crowd back. Kate's husband, Dave, was talking quietly to Aunt Flo.

"You just hold on, okay? My family will be here soon to help you." Johnny held Jesse's hand as best he could with his own still bandaged, but he'd be damned if he would let go of the man who saved his life, no matter how painful it was.

The sounds of sirens pierced through the crowd as an ambulance and fire truck pulled up. Chief Mason, Gabe, Uncle Jim, Lee, and Ben raced over with their bags and a backboard from the fire truck. EMTs Uncle Jack and Royce wheeled a stretcher from the back of their rig through the crowd and began to work on stabilizing Jesse. Royce carefully brushed his hand along Jesse's jaw and whispered something into his ear, causing Jesse to smile. Johnny was gently moved aside and found himself in Gabe's strong arms. *Safe.*

"Jesse pushed me out of the way. That car would have hit me, Gabe. It was coming straight at me." The severity of the situation was finally hitting home for Johnny. Someone had tried to run him down and poor Jesse was the one hurt. Johnny began to shake uncontrollably in Gabe's arms. He was quickly carried back into the shop and away from the crowds.

"Easy, baby, I've got you. You're safe now." Gabe murmured the reassuring words into Johnny's ear over and over again while rocking him from side to side.

Eventually Johnny was calm enough to breathe normally again. He hadn't even noticed he was hyperventilating or that Gabe had Johnny's inhaler in his hand. They watched as the ambulance sped away and the family walked back into the shop.

"We have to go to the hospital, Gabe. Jesse doesn't have anyone," Johnny pleaded, knowing how scary it could be finding yourself in the hospital all alone.

"We will, sweetheart, but I need you to tell us what happened first if you can." Gabe was assuring as he continued to hold Johnny safely in his arms, seemingly in no hurry to release him, for which Johnny was very grateful.

Dave took out his notepad along with another officer. Dad and the rest of the family who were on scene stood to the side. "Did you see who was driving the car, Johnny?"

"No. It was silver and came at us so fast. Jesse yelled at me to get out of the way, and then he pushed me just before the car hit him. The car would have hit me, Dave. I have no doubt about that, but I didn't look up to see who was driving. Maybe Jesse did. We have to go now, Gabe, please."

"Of course, Johnny. I'll take you there right now." Gabe set him on his feet and dug through his pockets. "Aunt Flo, can I take your truck? I'll leave the keys for mine. It's at the station."

"Of course, you go right ahead, Gabe. Jim will bring me your truck after his shift. Then we'll all meet you at the hospital." Aunt Flo and Gabe exchanged keys.

"But you're working, Gabe," Johnny began to argue. He'd caused Gabe to miss enough time from work already and wasn't going to add to it.

"I can't go back to work now, Johnny. Not with someone out there trying to run you down," Gabe stated as he gently held Johnny's face between his hands before kissing him fiercely, unconcerned of who stood around. Johnny felt Gabe's love along with his trembles of fear and understood that they both needed this connection to reassure themselves that they were both alive and safe.

"Gabe's right, Johnny. It's best if he stays with you now. I'll call a few more men in, just in case anything else comes up," Gabe's dad assured him, and placed his big hand on Johnny's shoulder. "Jesse has the Mason family to take care of him now."

"Thank you, Dad," Johnny answered softly, trying desperately to hold it together.

"Johnny, why was Jesse walking you back to the shop? Was there a problem at the diner?" Dave asked. The tight lines around his mouth and eyes, along with the barely suppressed growl in his voice were unmistakable, but thankfully that anger was directed at whoever was behind the wheel and not Johnny.

"When I was walking to the diner I got a strange feeling that someone was watching me, but I didn't see anyone or anything out of the ordinary. I told Jesse and he said to trust my feelings and that he would walk me back to the shop. If he hadn't, I would've..." Johnny's voice finally cracked and a sob broke free.

"Shhh, it's okay, sweetheart. You're safe." Gabe hugged Johnny close to his chest, seemingly unwilling to let him get even a foot away from him.

"But who would want to hurt me? I don't know a lot of people and everyone in town has been so kind to me. There was only one— *shit.*" Johnny managed to stop himself before he said Chris's name. No one had heard from Chris once he'd been released from jail. Gabe had him charged with trespassing and left it at that, hoping it was a strong enough message to never come back. "But it couldn't be, could it?"

Gabe looked like he was deep in thought before he wrapped his arm even tighter around Johnny and led him toward the door. "We can't count Chris out. No one has seen him, but that doesn't mean he isn't still around. I just can't figure out why he ever dared to come back here."

"We'll meet you at the hospital, Gabe. I need to speak to Jesse as soon as he's stable just in case he was able to see the driver," Dave said before leaving for his squad car.

The chief drove the fire truck back to the station with the rest of their crew, instructing Gabe to call him with any news. Mom met them in the hospital waiting room. Jesse was already in surgery to repair a fractured tibia and shattered kneecap. The surgery involved metal rods, wire, pins, and screws; Johnny began to gag and ran for the washroom after hearing what Jesse had to go through. *This is all my fault.*

Royce had been sitting with them since Mom, Gabe, and Johnny arrived and hadn't moved except to go get updates from the desk. Johnny knew Royce was a good friend of Gabe's and had lost his husband years earlier in a car accident, but he had no idea he was Jesse's friend as well. When he'd asked Royce how the two had met, the answer shocked Johnny but seemed to make complete sense to Gabe.

"Today—I met him for the first time today. At breakfast before my shift." Royce spoke as if stunned by what he himself was admitting. A warm smile replaced his worry for a brief moment. "I went into the diner and there he was, and now I just can't bring myself to leave him."

"That's the exact same feeling I had when I first met my Johnny. That's all it took," Gabe admitted and tightened his hold around Johnny. "I thank God every day that I found him." Johnny felt the love and warmth spread through his cold, tired body. He thanked God every day for Gabe as well.

Royce remained quiet after that; he seemed deep in thought. Johnny couldn't help but wonder if he was thinking of his deceased husband. They had been high school sweethearts, together over ten years. Gabe had explained to Johnny how devastated Royce had been and that he hadn't dated a soul in over three years. But here Royce was, waiting for word on a man he had only just met that morning but was unable to leave. Johnny hoped that both men would find the love he and Gabe were lucky enough to have found.

Over the next few hours, more and more family and friends began to stream into the waiting room. It had been over six hours since they'd begun Jesse's surgery and still no word. Dave came into the room with a file in his hands. He looked at Dad before coming to sit in front of Johnny, who had a feeling he wasn't going to like this.

"Johnny, Gabe, officers had a chance to speak with Jesse for a few moments before he was taken into surgery and, thankfully, he was able to identify the driver of the car. He gave us a description and we were able to show him ten different mug shots. Jesse immediately picked out this one." With that said, Dave opened the file and turned it so that Johnny could see the red, sweaty face staring back at him. Chris.

"Chris is trying to kill me?" Johnny couldn't even comprehend what Dave had just told them. He just stared blankly at the photo of a man he didn't even really know, who apparently tried to run him down. A cold chill ran down Johnny's spine and he began to shake. Gabe immediately gathered him into his arms, and Johnny buried his face into the side of Gabe's neck, trying to calm himself. Gabe stroked his back, speaking softly into Johnny's ear, telling him he would protect him and how much he loved him.

Of course the doctor would choose that exact moment to walk into the waiting room.

"Jesse Tribalt's family?"

Johnny stood along with Royce and every other Mason in the room. The doctor simply shook his head and spoke to everyone. "Jesse made it through surgery just fine. We were able to get the most serious of his injuries stabilized, but there'll be months of physical therapy ahead of him. We'll deal with that later. Right now we just need to make sure he heals properly without complications. Now only two of you at a time can see him until he's moved to his own room."

"Johnny, why don't you and Royce go and see Jesse. We'll wait for you here," Gabe suggested before kissing the top of Johnny's head. Johnny knew the family would want to huddle anyway with the news that Chris was out there somewhere, apparently planning Johnny's demise....

Okay, a bit too dramatic even for me.

Johnny just didn't want to deal with anything more from Chris tonight. He would deal with that asshole tomorrow. "Yes, I think that's best." Johnny didn't mean for his anger at the situation to come out now, but it was so close to the surface that the best course of action was to simply follow the doctor and Royce out of the room, and to face Jesse. The poor man had taken the pain aimed at him and saved his life. Johnny knew this was all his fault. How would Jesse ever forgive him?

***

Gabe knew this was all his fault. How the hell would Johnny, let alone Jesse, ever forgive him? He stared at the door long after Johnny had left, fighting his need to follow his lover.

"He will, Gabe. Johnny may be understandably upset right now, but he doesn't blame you for any of this." Grandma Rose took Gabe's arm and led him to a seat. Gabe hadn't spoken out loud; perhaps this "family telepathy" thing of Johnny's might have some merit. "And Jesse's never struck me as someone who laid blame at the wrong feet. What we need to be concentrating on now is finding Chris and taking care of and protecting both injured men."

Grandma Rose was never one to sit idly by when things needed to be done. Gabe straightened and squared his shoulders. He knew he couldn't let Chris destroy the future he had planned with the man he loved. "You're right. We have plans to make. We have to find

Chris before he has a chance to hurt anyone else. I just don't understand what he wants. He honestly believes I would take him back. That's insane."

Dave opened the file again and pulled out a few more pieces of paper. "After we arrested Chris and took him from your house, I had a feeling something wasn't quite right. Chris was acting violent one moment and calm the next. He was sweating even with the air conditioning on, and then he seemed almost confused at one point. I didn't find anything on him other than his wallet and keys, so I brought Doc Green over to have a look at him. Doc suspected some sort of drug use and decided to run some bloodwork on him, but we didn't get the results back until after Chris was released. I could only hold him for the twenty-four hours, and once he made bail, he vanished." Dave hung his head, seeming to take the events as a personal failure.

"Why didn't you tell us before? What did Doc find?" Gabe asked. Suddenly things were becoming a bit clearer.

"I honestly thought we'd heard the last of Chris once he knew he had no chance with you." Dave rifled through the pages before finding the one he wanted and handed it to Gabe. "Doc found methamphetamine in his bloodwork at levels that indicate long-term use. I've issued a warrant for his arrest and contacted his sister over in Houston, but she stated she hadn't seen him in over a year and that he owed her money." He shook his head and his lip flattened out; this was the same woman that attempted to steal money from Gabe. "I asked Houston PD to check his apartment. Sure enough, it's empty and the neighbors stated no one's been seen there in months. DMV records indicate that Chris does own a silver Honda Accord."

"Shit…he can't actually believe I would take him back?" Gabe's frustration was rising by the second. How could Chris just disappear without someone seeing him?

"My best guess is money." Dad's deep voice sounded just as angry as Gabe's.

"Money? Why the hell would I give that man anything after what he did to me?" Gabe could now understand Chris's odd behavior. Meth was a dangerous and deadly drug, but why he thought to come to Gabe for money of all things was truly ludicrous.

"Chris isn't thinking clearly if he's still using. All he knows is that he needs money to buy drugs and the one person who he could count on for money was unfortunately you, Gabe. In my opinion he sees Johnny as competition." Gabe couldn't fault Dave's logic; after all, he was police chief for a reason.

"Now that we know what we're up against, we can be better prepared until Chris is arrested," Gabe said. "We'll move Jesse into one of the spare bedrooms, and I'm pretty sure Royce won't be too far behind, but we'll need help when Royce and I are at work. Johnny won't be able to do much with his burns still healing." Gabe threw out the beginnings of a plan. Soon his family chimed in and a schedule was set.

Dad decided to call an old Marine buddy of his, who now owned his own security firm out in Colorado, for help securing the interior of Gabe's home. Gabe would do whatever it took to keep his love safe. Nothing was off limits, including hiring armed security specialists.

When Royce and Johnny came back from visiting Jesse, Royce quickly made plans to move a few bags over to Gabe's house so that he could stay in the spare room attached to the one Jesse would be recovering in. Johnny was strangely quiet, barely giving any suggestions. Eventually, he simply curled up beside Gabe and fell asleep. Once a plan was in place, Royce decided to stay at the hospital with Jesse, and Gabe carried a still sleeping Johnny back to his truck and drove them home.

Johnny woke halfway home but remained quiet and reserved even as Gabe began to undress him in their bedroom. Once he had Johnny's shirt off, his love placed soft kisses across Gabe's bare chest. His warm, wet lips left a trail of goose bumps on Gabe's overheated flesh. Instinctively, he flexed his hips, rubbing his straining erection over Johnny's stomach.

"Johnny, your doctor said we shouldn't raise your rate of breathing very high while your lungs are still healing, and you haven't even begun to recover from your burns." Gabe was desperately trying to be the voice of reason, but Johnny wasn't having it. He responded by rubbing his hard, jean-covered cock against Gabe's thigh, moaning softly at the friction.

"Need you, Gabe. Need to feel you against me. Please?" Johnny's green eyes shone bright. His pupils were dilated and his face and chest were flushed red with desire. He was simply gorgeous.

Gabe knew then in that moment that he would do whatever Johnny wanted, but at the same time, he would ensure that he was safe. He'd wanted Johnny since the first moment he saw him, and sleeping together every night with him in his arms only heightened that need. He would still make sure Johnny's lungs and burns weren't further damaged, but Gabe would give Johnny the physical connection and love he so desperately needed.

He easily lifted Johnny to the bed and quickly stripped them both of their remaining clothing before blanketing Johnny with his own body. Deep, guttural groans filled the room as their cocks rubbed together for the first time. Johnny's hips bucked, urgently rutting himself against Gabe's muscled abdomen. Wet trails of precum laced the thick, dark hair covering Gabe's stomach leading down to his hard, pulsing cock.

"Easy, baby, I'll take care of you, but you have to lie back and let me give you what you need. I won't have you injuring yourself." Gabe pressed his large body down further onto Johnny, essentially pinning him to the bed, trapping him and making Johnny groan even louder... *Interesting.*

"Put your hands above your head, Johnny, and don't move them," Gabe ordered firmly, his dominant nature charging to the forefront. Johnny's beautiful, slim, cut penis twitched and oozed more precum from its swollen pink head as he quickly obeyed and waited for Gabe's next order. Johnny was absolutely perfect.

"You won't move until I tell you to. Do you understand?" Gabe kept his voice firm while running his hands up and down the toned sides of his lover's body, caressing over muscle and soft skin. "If you move, I'll have to tie you to the bed."

Johnny's quick intake of breath and dilated pupils were all the answer Gabe needed; Johnny liked that idea...a lot. "You want that, Johnny, don't you? You want to be tied up so you're at my mercy." Gabe punctuated his statement by capturing Johnny's right nipple in between his teeth and sucking it into his mouth, making Johnny arch his back off the mattress and cry out in pleasure.

"Yes...yes, please, Gabe." Johnny's begging ramped up Gabe's arousal to the point that he had to squeeze the base of his cock to stop from coming on the spot. He lost his control so easily around this man.

Gabe released Johnny's swollen, red nipple and began nibbling and kissing his way down his body, stopping to press his face into his lover's pale blond pubic hair and breathing in his musky, male scent. Gabe wanted to make love to Johnny so badly he could barely think straight, but he knew they couldn't do that just yet, not with Johnny's many healing injuries. But he could give himself and Johnny the release they both so badly needed. In one fluid movement, Gabe raised his head and sucked Johnny's cock down to the root while keeping both of his hands firmly on Johnny's hips, stopping him from moving and possibly injuring himself.

"Gabe!"

After that, Johnny began babbling incoherently between moans of pleasure while Gabe sucked and licked at an almost frenzied pace. The taste and feel of the man underneath him was intoxicating. All too soon, Gabe found himself on the edge again, knowing Johnny was just as close. Gabe raised his massive body up and brought their straining erections together. Capturing them both in his large hand, Gabe pumped his hand and hips, moving his painfully hard penis against Johnny's, their combined precum lubing his hand as he jacked them both.

Johnny's hips jerked violently, losing his rhythm, evidence of how close he was to coming. His beautiful green eyes never left Gabe's as his breathing hitched and he moaned Gabe's name loudly before he came. The intensity of the love they shared and the raw desire he felt watching Johnny come sent Gabe into his own orgasm so fast that he had no warning. Gabe roared his pleasure. His balls pulled tight, his muscles seized, and the head of his cock felt like it was exploding with wave after wave of his release.

Gabe was, thankfully, able to keep his weight off Johnny while he struggled to come back from one of the strongest orgasms he'd felt in a very long time, if ever. He nuzzled the side of Johnny's face, placing soft kisses along his jawline before playfully nipping at his ear. Gabe always felt loved and contented having Johnny in his arms, and now was no different.

Johnny laughed happily and finally brought his arms back down to wrap them around Gabe's neck. "I love you, Gabe."

"I love you so much, Johnny. I'm sorry about everything. I never expected—"

"No, none of this is your fault. None of it." Johnny voice was filled with anger, and even if Gabe understood it wasn't directed at him he still didn't like having his love this angry.

"Hold on, baby, let me get us cleaned up and tucked in. I want you comfortable. It's been one hell of a day for you." Gabe carefully stood, walked to their attached bathroom, cleaned himself quickly, and then warmed a soft washcloth for Johnny.

The sight of his Johnny lying naked, eyes closed with a happy smile on his face, touched Gabe and brought him a sense of peace. He took a moment to appreciate Johnny's sweaty, sated body glistening in the soft light from the bedside lamp. His soft, curly blond hair scattered wildly across the pillow shone like a halo and was absolutely breathtaking. Johnny looked every bit the angel he was—*a debauched angel*, Gabe chuckled to himself—but still his angel. That one image of his lover would forever be etched into his memory. He gently cleaned Johnny's softened cock and lightly furred stomach before tossing the cloth into the dirty laundry. After tucking a tired Johnny under the covers and turning off the lights, Gabe joined him.

Johnny lay with his head tucked safely in the nook between Gabe's neck and shoulder, half of his body on top of him. They fit together perfectly in Gabe's opinion. His love had been quiet for such a long time that he thought Johnny had fallen asleep and was a bit shocked when he spoke softly.

"We won't let him destroy what we have, Gabe." Johnny held him tight. His voice might have been muted, but it was firm. "I won't lose you."

Gabe hugged Johnny closer until he was lying fully on top of him, safely wrapped in his arms. "I love you so damn much, Johnny. I could never go back to a life without you. I'll protect you and our life together, baby. I won't give you up."

"Promise me, Gabe."

"Promise, baby."

Chapter Eight

The next five days were chaotic for Johnny; between his own physiotherapy sessions for his hands, he was also preparing a room to become Jesse's home away from home. Gabe and Royce had taken care of all the medical supplies that needed to be stocked while Johnny and the Mason women concentrated on the comforting, homey aspect. Johnny had to admit that he was beginning to feel more and more at home here every day. He felt like a Mason, and the family made sure he knew they considered him one as well.

Stacks of homemade frozen dinners and casseroles were stocked in a new chest freezer in the basement and every cupboard was crammed full. If Johnny didn't know better, he would think the women believed the four men would never be able to find a grocery store again. He loved this family so much.

Jesse had been more than understanding once they told him who had tried to run them down, and no matter how many times he or Gabe tried to apologize, Jesse refused to allow them to take any of the blame. Jesse had stated repeatedly that Chris was responsible for his own actions and that Jesse was just glad he'd been there to push Johnny out of the way. Jesse also stressed to Johnny that he was to always listen to his instincts like they did that day; it saved his life. Johnny swore to Jesse he would never doubt himself again.

When Royce told Jesse he would be staying with Gabe and Johnny so that he and the Mason family could take care of him, Johnny expected all hell to break loose. Thunderclouds appeared in Jesse's eyes and he opened his mouth as if to argue the point, but Royce simply gave Jesse a look that Johnny had never seen before on the quiet man's face. It stated flat out, "I'm in charge, and I dare you to fight me on this." Jesse wisely and quickly agreed to temporarily move in. After the first few days of the four of them living together, Johnny began to see and understand the new dynamic between Royce and Jesse.

Jesse might be the muscled, tattoo-covered biker and he might have sixty pounds on Royce, who was himself a large man to begin with, but Royce was fully in charge and the much more dominant of the two. Jesse was in fact a gentle giant who seemed to flourish under Royce's strong, dominant nature.

Royce had shown he was no one to be messed with when Jesse's brother randomly showed up at the hospital one day and tried to have Jesse transferred out of state. Jesse's terrified look caused Royce to step in and have the brother removed from the hospital.

Apparently Jesse had been running from his family for much the same reason as Johnny. Though Jesse's family spouted religion and sin, and Johnny's father's interests centered on money and reputation, both families evidently believed pain was the best method to get their sons to comply.

Sadly, one afternoon while Johnny, Gabe, Royce, and Mom were helping Jesse get ready to leave the hospital, they saw the evidence of his family's attempts at "reconditioning" their gay son littering Jesse's brutalized back. Long, jagged scars covered almost every inch of skin. Royce quickly covered them before Jesse could realize anyone had seen his pain, and the family carried on as if they saw nothing. Johnny swore he would be there for his new friend if Jesse ever wanted to talk to him and would personally kick Jesse's brother's ass if he came near him again…okay, maybe Johnny would have Gabe kick the evil man's ass, but the intention was still the same.

Royce doted on Jesse, and Jesse soaked it up like a sponge. It was easy for anyone to see he had been starving for affection. Clem had assured Jesse that he would still have a job once he was healed enough to work again. Sadly, the doctors thought that would be months away at the very least.

All in all, everything was moving relatively smoothly right up until ten seconds before, when Johnny came out of the house to get the morning paper only to find the tires on his car had been slashed.

"Gabe!" Johnny screamed in fear as he began backing up toward the house while scanning the front yard, half-expecting Chris to jump out at any minute.

Gabe came barreling out of the house in only a pair of jeans. Royce was close behind carrying a baseball bat. Gabe snagged Johnny around the waist and led him back inside the house while Royce took a closer look at his car.

"What's wrong?" Jesse asked as he steered his wheelchair into the kitchen where Gabe sat Johnny on the counter and reached for his phone.

He handed the phone to Jesse before answering. "Call the police station, Jesse. Tell them Johnny's car has been vandalized and to send an officer out. I want both of you to stay here in the kitchen while Royce and I have a look around." Gabe kissed Johnny quickly and walked back out the door.

Jesse called the station and a deputy was on his way over. Johnny also saw Dante Snow's black SUV pull in. He was the scary-looking security professional that Dad's old military buddy had sent to help find Chris. So far, Chris was still out there somewhere, even after Dante and the police had found Chris's car and the room he'd been renting in the neighboring county. They all thought he would be caught soon. He had no vehicle or place to sleep, and every law enforcement officer in the surrounding counties was looking for him. Dante had installed security cameras around the house and an expensive security system to cover the interior. Johnny just hoped they had caught Chris on tape slashing his tires.

"It'll be okay, Johnny." Jesse gently took hold of Johnny's shaking, bandaged hands. Until then, he hadn't even noticed he was shaking.

"I guess knowing Chris was this close to the house has me a little rattled." Johnny tried to calm down, but with every passing second, it was getting harder and harder to breathe. *Shit.* Johnny knew the signs; he needed his inhaler, but for the life of him he couldn't remember where it was. Gabe would be pissed. Johnny had been caught a few times without it when he couldn't catch his breath, but dammit he was only going to the driveway for the stupid newspaper this time.

"Johnny! Johnny, what do you need?" Jesse asked and started yelling for Gabe and Royce.

"In-inhale—" Johnny tried to get the words out, but he didn't have enough air. His vision was dimming fast as tiny pinpricks of light sparkled in front of him.

Suddenly, Johnny was lifted from the counter and the plastic of his inhaler was pushed to his lips. "Breathe in, Johnny. Come on, baby, just take a breath in." Gabe's voice pleaded as Johnny struggled to get some air and his medication into his lungs.

Minutes passed by slowly, but, bit by bit, Johnny managed to get more and more medication into his lungs and his breathing became less labored. Gabe had him cuddled safely in his arms on one of the living room couches. Royce, Jesse, and Dante were still in the kitchen giving them some privacy.

"Easy, Johnny." Gabe spoke softly, letting Johnny burrow a bit deeper into his embrace. "I've got you, but from now on, you're going to carry your inhaler in every damn piece of clothing you have. There'll be one in every room and I'll tie one on a damn chain around your neck if I have to."

Johnny could only nod in agreement even though they both knew that plan wasn't practical. He'd been scared enough times when he'd been unable to catch his breath, and he could still feel Gabe's body tremor underneath him in fear.

"How many do you want?" Royce asked from the kitchen. Johnny and Gabe both looked up to see Royce with his cell phone in one hand while his other ran through Jesse's hair, soothing the man. "The pharmacy has to order more in if you want over ten."

"Five should be a good start. I want Johnny to have one near him at all times, and if that means everyone in the family carries one, then I'm good with that," Gabe answered and Royce went back to his call.

"I don't need family to carry my inhaler, Gabe. I'm completely capable of carrying my own damn inhaler. Just because I've misplaced it a few times doesn't mean you get to treat me like a child." Johnny cringed. He didn't know where all his anger was coming from, but it was coming on fast. "I'm an adult, fully capable of making my own decisions. I've been doing it for years before you came along. Just because I'm injured doesn't mean I've lost the ability to think rationally. I'm a capable person. This isn't permanent. I will get my life back!" *Oh shit!* Johnny was beginning to feel like a child, and he didn't like it very much.

"Johnny, I know you can take care of yourself, but please understand this is something I need to do, sweetheart. I don't think any less of you or that you aren't capable, but you knew my need to be in control and to have you safe right from the beginning. I can't change that, Johnny. I love you, and by letting me take care of you, you're helping to keep me sane."

"Keep you sane?" Johnny huffed. He knew Gabe was trying to make him feel better about his inability to keep track of his inhaler and the fact that he might never be able to use his hands the same way again, but keeping him sane was a bit of a stretch. The love he saw in those brown eyes was always his undoing, but today he was just too damn frustrated to care.

"Yes, Johnny. Hell, if anything happened to you, it would push me over the edge. That is the God's honest truth." Gabe's voice wavered, and Johnny began to understand that, by keeping himself safe, he was making Gabe content and calm. This was something his bear of a man needed to be happy, and Johnny would give him anything if he could.

"Fine, Gabe. I know you're only trying to keep me safe, but sometimes I feel like you don't even trust me to do that on my own. I feel like I'm being patronized. I'd have hoped that you realized by now that I'm a grown man." Johnny hoped to lighten the mood a bit, fearing he might have overreacted.

"Oh, I've noticed." Gabe's voice dipped low as he nuzzled the curly blond mess on top of Johnny's head, making Johnny realize he hadn't even had a shower yet. "And I'm sorry if I've ever made you feel that way, Johnny. It's just, with everything that's happened in the past few weeks, I need to know I've done everything I can to make sure the people that I love are safe. I trust you with everything I am; I never thought I would be able to do that ever again, Johnny. You've given me my peace of mind back, and I want to share everything with you." Gabe always sounded so excited when he spoke about their future, and Johnny desperately wanted to let his fears over Chris slip away, if only for a little while.

Over the past few weeks, they both had bared their souls and let the other in so completely that Johnny felt they'd known each other for years, not weeks. Though Johnny knew he loved Gabe without question and wanted to spend the rest of his life with the man, he feared all his happiness would be ripped away at any moment. He knew it was due to Chris and, once he was caught, Johnny would feel more secure, but as of this moment, Johnny felt anything but secure knowing Chris had been within feet of the house.

"Do you think it was Chris?" Johnny asked Dante as he, Jesse, and Royce joined them in the living room.

Dante placed his laptop on the coffee table and turned the monitor to face the group. "Yes, I'm afraid it was indeed Chris," Dante confirmed while the image on the screen displayed a thin, dishevelled-looking man viciously stabbing a long, serrated knife into Johnny's tires.

The room went silent as Chris went about, almost joyfully, from one tire to the next with a look of absolute bliss on his face. Johnny felt the cold chill of fear race through his body, causing him to shake slightly.

"That's enough. We've seen enough." Gabe gently tucked Johnny's head back into his nook and away from the laptop. Out of the corner of his eye, Johnny could see Royce comforting a pale Jesse much the same way. How could he have forgotten that Jesse was a victim of this lunatic as well?

"Are you okay, Jesse?" Johnny asked, his voice breaking slightly.

"Yes, I'll be fine. It was just a bit of a shock seeing him again after the last time. He…he had that same look on his face. It's like a fucked-up, gleeful rage. I…I just…" Jesse answered softly, leaning a bit further into Royce's chest.

"I've got you." Royce folded Jesse into his arms; Jesse was visibly shaking by now.

"I'm calling in Spider. He'll find that bastard." A clearly agitated Dante stormed out of the house, stabbing his big fingers onto his phone's screen as he left. "Spider, it's Snow. I've got a job for you."

***

Gabe helped Johnny from his truck and into a nondescript brick building that was causing Gabe an amazing amount of stress, but he was able to hold it securely under wraps for now. He was proud he was able to keep his hand from shaking and placed it possessively on Johnny's lower back before leading his love to the second floor. He had been planning this for weeks and hoped this would do the trick. Since Chris's little overnight visit six nights ago, Johnny had seemed much more subdued and quiet. Gabe didn't like it one bit. His Johnny was full of life. Even with his injuries, he would be humming around the house or out in the gardens. Chris wasn't going to take that from Johnny; Gabe wouldn't allow it.

"Are you going to tell me why we're here, Gabe?" Johnny asked softly. They made their way down the long, wood-paneled hallway, Johnny glued to Gabe's side.

"Not quite yet, baby. It'll just be a few more minutes." Gabe prayed he'd made the right decision and wasn't pushing Johnny too far too fast or this could bite him in the ass. "It wouldn't be much of a surprise if I told you, right?"

"I promise to act surprised." Johnny giggled and gave him the best damn puppy-dog eyes Gabe had seen since his baby niece. Gabe felt his heart lighten just a bit with the return of his playful Johnny; he wanted him to be happy. Johnny had given Gabe the most precious of gifts—peace. Since Chris, Gabe had been living day to day, tied up in knots without ever considering the future. His trust issues kept him firmly rooted in the past. Now his future lay before him, full of possibilities, full of love, full of the kind, gentle man beside him. Gabe considered himself a very lucky man.

"Not going to happen, baby. Besides, we're here." Gabe smiled and ushered Johnny into the office at the end of the hall.

Johnny walked hesitantly into the waiting area. Appearing unsure of what to do, he turned his questioning eyes up to Gabe. "Just take a seat, Johnny, and I'll let them know we've arrived."

Gabe quickly checked in with the receptionist before rejoining Johnny, who was sitting rigidly in the old, plastic waiting room chairs. "Johnny, I would never take you any place where you need to be frightened." He spoke calmly while rubbing soothing circles onto Johnny's back. Gabe had learned during their time together just how to calm his lover when he became tense or upset.

"Of course you wouldn't! I trust you completely, Gabe. I'm sorry if I made you feel that way. I know you would never put me in harm's way. I love you." Johnny spoke with such conviction in his voice that Gabe's heart beat just a bit faster with the love he felt for the man in his arms. "It's just that I keep expecting him to show up at any moment. I…"

Johnny immediately lowered his eyes and worried his bottom lip. Hearing him voice his concerns brought out Gabe's protective instincts and he gathered Johnny further into the shelter of his arms. Sometimes the depth of love he felt for Johnny would steal his breath and nearly knock him on his ass. This shy, brave man was Gabe's future. Everything that he had ever wanted and dreamed of was wrapped up in his arms at that moment.

"I'll do whatever it takes to protect you, Johnny. He'll have to go through me to get to you." Gabe tried to reassure Johnny, knowing every word he spoke was the absolute truth.

"That's what I'm afraid of. Look at what happened to Jesse; he was hurt trying to protect me. Who else is going to get hurt while Chris is trying to get to me? I can't handle the thought of that happening to anyone else." Johnny's confession hit Gabe hard. His Johnny wasn't concerned with the danger to himself. Gabe should have known this inherently good man wouldn't be selfish, even when faced with a psychotic man's rage. "If he showed up, you could be injured, Gabe, or the family. I couldn't live with it if anyone else got hurt."

"Oh, baby, don't worry about me. Chris won't get the chance. You've seen Spider; that man is truly scary." Johnny's eyes widened before he nodded his head in agreement.

To say the man Dante had called in to search for Chris was intense would be such a huge understatement. It would be as foolish as saying a world war was a slight disagreement. Thankfully, Dante had warned everyone before he'd arrived or Spider might have caused quite a few suspicious-persons calls into the police station. The huge man had eyes as dark as his black hair and he stood at least 6'5" tall with muscles hard-earned from years in the service and constant assignments around the world. After hearing a few stories passed through Dante, Gabe wasn't surprised to find out that Spider was a decorated war hero, having saved four other Marines from capture and leading them back to safety after their Cobra helicopter was shot down over Afghanistan.

In truth, even with his scary-ass exterior, Spider hadn't been anything other than respectful toward everyone. He was a former Marine turned security specialist/bodyguard working freelance with Dante for years, still protecting those who couldn't protect themselves. He and Dante had heightened security around the house, set up motion sensors, and secured the neighborhood, with all the neighbors' blessings of course. Again, thank God for small towns.

He helped elderly Mrs. Rose down the street carry her groceries into her home and then sat for tea. This last one seemed odd, but the man was a walking contradiction. Spider's presence caused people to pause; he exuded a lethal strength that made people not want to step a toe out of line. All Gabe cared about was that the man continued to use an almost gentle nature when dealing with Johnny, Jesse, or any of the Masons he'd met. Gabe knew Spider would turn into a lethal predator when he needed to protect the people Gabe loved, of that there was no doubt.

Grandma Rose seemed to just love the mountain of a man and had invited him out with the rest of the White Hair Crew. The sight of this huge, admittedly deadly man sitting at a table in Ms. Stephanie's bakery surrounded by elderly woman eating pastries and having tea would be forever etched in everyone's memory. You just don't see that shit every day.

"Mr. Jeffrey?" a young woman said softly and smiled toward them from the now opened doorway.

Johnny stood with Gabe and followed the woman into the back offices. Johnny's eyes were wide and hadn't stopped moving from one machine to another once they went through the doors. Gabe didn't even bother trying to figure out what half of the machines surrounding him did, but if they helped Johnny, he would gladly learn.

"Gabe?" Johnny's voice was just above a whisper when the woman stopped in front of a rather impressive-looking computer system with all kinds of bells and whistles. Again, Gabe had no idea what he was truly looking at beyond the keyboard and screen.

To give the young woman credit, she hadn't said a word. Gabe had told Mr. Parks, the owner of Parks Adaptive Devices, that this was a surprise for Johnny, and by the way that Johnny stood stone-still Gabe wondered if he had just made a huge mistake. He had wanted to give Johnny some of his freedom back and knew he had loved his job in graphic design before the fire had destroyed his hands. According to Josie and several others, Johnny was very accomplished and sought after by companies requiring his flair for design and original ideas.

"Johnny, I...," Gabe began to play with the hem of his white button-down shirt as the silence dragged on. Johnny turned around to face Gabe with tears streaming down his face. "I'm sorry. I thought—"

Whatever he was going to say was silenced when Johnny threw himself into Gabe's arms and began kissing him as if his very life depended on it. Only the soft giggles of the forgotten young woman stopped Johnny from full-out mauling Gabe. Johnny blushed beautifully when he pulled away to look at the table again.

"It's...it's amazing. I never dreamed, Gabe." Johnny began to touch each piece of machinery almost reverently with a look of awe on his face.

The patient young woman finally spoke. "I'm Becky. It's an honor to meet you, Johnny."

"I'm sorry, an honor?" Johnny asked, stopping his perusal for a moment.

The woman stepped a little closer to Johnny and Gabe almost felt silly when his protectiveness brought him to Johnny's side. As if the small woman was a threat, but Gabe couldn't turn it off if he wanted to, which he didn't.

The young woman simply smiled and, with great care, lightly touched Johnny's bandaged hands; there was sadness in her eyes. "I'm Janice's baby sister. You saved my sister's life in that fire."

A tear slid down Becky's cheek and Johnny immediately wrapped his arms around her, crooning softly as she cried on Johnny's uninjured shoulder. Gabe had no idea that Janice's sister worked here when he stopped by to inquire on the system, but the day was just full of surprises. After a few minutes, Becky got her emotions back under control and gave Johnny a watery smile while drying her eyes.

"Thank you, Johnny. I wish I could take away your pain, but at least I can help you with your surprise." Becky waved her arms over Johnny's new adaptive technology computer system. Gabe had been guaranteed it had all the necessary equipment to help Johnny return to his love of graphic design.

"You did this for me?" Johnny turned to Gabe, his eyes still red and puffy, and his voice wavered slightly.

Gabe pulled Johnny into his arms and nuzzled the side of his neck like he knew Johnny loved, and just as expected, he arched his neck to give Gabe more room. "I know how much you loved your job, baby, and since you don't currently have one to go back to, I thought if you had the right equipment, you might like taking on a few projects from home. Not that you need to work if you don't want to. I just want you to be happy."

Gabe didn't want Johnny to feel obligated to work. Gabe could easily take care of both of them, but he had the feeling his lover would never be comfortable with that.

"It's a breathtaking system, Gabe. Thank you. It's perfect, but…" Johnny's voice trailed off as he lifted his injured hands, the defeat as evident in his voice as on his face.

"That's why Gabe came to us," Becky stated cheerfully, while carrying another box full of parts that reminded him of game controllers of some sort toward them. "We get to customize this bad boy so that you can work with as few limitations as possible. Even if your hands don't regain their full mobility or strength, we can adapt the system to your needs."

Johnny chewed his bottom lip and looked at the system, as if afraid of it. Gabe didn't like that look at all. "Baby, what's wrong?" Gabe held Johnny a little tighter from behind, trying to lend his strength to his love.

"What if we try and it doesn't work? What if my hands are too messed up? What if I can never be normal again?" Johnny released a few of his fears in a flood of emotions that Gabe felt had been bottled up since the fire. Gabe thanked whoever was listening that he was here when Johnny finally was able to voice some of those fears.

"You've already gained back more feeling than you thought you would, and the doctors believe that, with continued therapy, you'll get up to 80 percent of your range of motion back. We'll do whatever it takes for you to feel as normal as you can. I know it won't be easy for you, and it'll take time, but I'll be there every step of the way. I promise you won't have to go through this alone, ever. I love you." Gabe held Johnny, waiting for him to make his choice about the computer system. They could leave now and Gabe would support his decision.

With one final nuzzle, Johnny bravely pulled away and joined Becky at the desk. He knew that in the past, Johnny viewed himself as weak at times. His history had forced him to believe this as truth. But anyone who met Johnny could see his strength and determination shine through, and over the past few weeks Gabe believed Johnny had begun to see it, too. Gabe moved back to lean against the wall and watched as she showed him something that reminded Gabe of a joystick he used to play video games with as a child. She began measuring Johnny's hands, then recorded his grip strength from another machine, while yet another checked his range of motion. Becky had him attempt to use the keyboard and a few other machines while she took notes on what Johnny could and couldn't manipulate with his hands.

Once done, she brought out a few adaptive devices and began to mount them temporarily on a few machines. She removed the keyboard altogether and replaced it with a touch pad covered in symbols and an attached thick-handled stylus, which Johnny used to touch those symbols. Also, she brought out a small microphone and attached it to the system. Then she asked Johnny to speak clearly into it as she programmed the necessary software.

Gabe stood in amazement as, in just over two hours, Becky managed to have Johnny working on a basic mock-up system with multiple temporary devices as his aids. Gabe knew it would take a few sessions for Johnny to feel confident using his new system, but from all indications, he was off to a good start. Johnny's smile stretched from ear to ear as the screen came to life and he navigated through the various programs. Every few minutes, Johnny would turn his head and search out Gabe to make sure he could see what Johnny had accomplished. Gabe simply smiled with pride at the resilience Johnny possessed; he never gave up. No matter how afraid he was to fail, Johnny pushed himself forward. Gabe wasn't sure if he deserved a man like Johnny, but he wasn't foolish enough to ever let him go.

"I believe that's about all I need to get started on this first round of changes, Johnny." Becky set her clipboard down and turned to Gabe. "I'll need you two to come back in about a week from now to try out all the modifications. I'll call you to confirm an appointment time."

"Thank you for doing all of this for me, Becky." Johnny stood and stretched the stiffness out of his back. His shirt rode up slightly, revealing the toned muscles of Johnny's abdomen, and Gabe's cock took notice and began to swell. Gabe quickly adjusted his stance so that his need for Johnny remained hidden in such a public place before he joined him by the door. Gabe desperately wanted to touch every inch of Johnny and make love to him for hours, but he held himself in check day after day until given the all clear by his doctors.

"It's my pleasure, Johnny. Don't worry, we'll get you all set up in no time at all," Becky assured and then led them back out to the front offices.

They said their good-byes and headed out into the Texas heat. Gabe kept Johnny tucked securely into his side, eyes scanning the area instinctively, looking for any and all threats. After lifting Johnny into his seat and buckling the seatbelt, Gabe kissed him deeply, exploring his mouth freely. After several enjoyable minutes later, Gabe finally broke away, allowing them both to breathe. The dazed expression in his lover's eyes stroked Gabe's ego just a bit, and he wanted to make it his mission to give Johnny that look every damn day.

"I'm so proud of you, Johnny. That took a lot of courage. How do you feel?" Gabe wanted to make sure Johnny was truly fine with today's events.

Johnny closed his eyes and took a few moments to gather his thoughts before he answered, and when he did, the love shining in his eyes just about floored Gabe. "You've given me back a part of myself that I thought would be lost. A part of myself that I had fought so hard to have away from my father. I—I can never truly explain to you what today has meant to me, Gabe. Everything I come up with doesn't seem strong enough a word for what I feel right now. 'Thank you' doesn't seem to be enough for everything you've done to help put my life back together. I love you, Gabe. I can't imagine ever being without you."

"And you'll never have to, baby." Gabe leaned in for another kiss, but the shrill blast of a horn cut through their peaceful bubble.

Gabe turned ready to tear a strip off whoever was behind them, until he looked up and saw a panicked Lee behind the wheel of his own truck. Gabe immediate went on alert, scanning the area again before he shut his truck door, instructing Johnny to remain inside, and quickly approached his friend and teammate.

Lee already had his window down and began talking even before Gabe made it to his door. "We have to get to the hospital. Frank's already there!"

"What? What's wrong? What happened to Frank?" Gabe's words came tumbling out of his mouth, fear that something had happened to his best friend's husband making the words blend together.

"No, he's okay. It's Lucy. She's in labor; the baby's coming. My son and your godson, let's move!" Gabe could tell Lee was almost in a panic. Lucy, Lee and Frank's amazing surrogate, was due over a week ago, but it finally looked like the little guy was ready to finally come out and meet his fathers.

"Okay, but park your truck over there beside mine, man. You can't drive like this. I'll take you to the hospital." Gabe pointed to the open parking spot and turned away from Lee, sure that his friend would follow his instructions.

Johnny's head was turned almost all the way around in his truck, trying to watch Gabe's approach, but he hadn't attempted to get out, which made Gabe eternally grateful. Until Chris was caught, Johnny's safety was first and foremost in his thoughts. He opened the driver's door just as Lee jumped into the backseat, eyes bright with nerves and excitement.

"Is everything okay?" Johnny asked, turning around to face Lee.

"I'm having a baby—no, Lucy's having the baby. She's in labor." Lee looked ready to throw up as Gabe pulled back onto the road, turning toward the hospital.

Johnny was just about vibrating out of his seat with excitement. "That's amazing, Lee. Congratulations."

Lee's returning smile was so big, Gabe had to wonder if it hurt his face. He was the picture of happiness. Gabe allowed himself a brief moment to imagine himself and Johnny in this situation. They had discussed having children. Gabe believed in absolute honesty going in and wanted to make sure the man he wanted in his life actually wanted children as much as he did. Thankfully, by the way Johnny's eyes lit up at the mere mention of having children, Gabe knew even before Johnny confirmed his suspicions that he did indeed wish to be a father.

A family—his family—and Johnny would be its center, just as he was now Gabe's home. Together they would build a future. Gabe reached over, taking Johnny's hand and kissing it gently. The happiness on Johnny's face added to Gabe's own joy.

My family.

Chapter Nine

Just over four hours later, Lucy delivered a healthy, seven-pound-six-ounce baby boy. Both mom and baby were doing great, and Johnny was beside himself with excitement as Sam led him and Gabe down to their room. It was early evening by now and the hospital was quieting down for the night—well, everyone else was quieting down for the evening except for the adorable, red-faced screaming bundle in Frank's arms. The look of complete adoration on Frank's face was serene compared to the panic-stricken Lee.

"Sweetheart, sit down before you fall down. Our son is fine; he's simply hungry," Frank whispered before placing a bottle to their son's searching mouth, and quiet descended.

Lee seemed to finally realize that Johnny, Gabe, and Sam were standing in the doorway. He quickly came over and hugged all three. "Come in and meet our son, Jacob Samuel Rogers."

Lee took position behind his husband who was now rocking the sleepy little bundle of blue. Lee's pride and love seemed to fill the room, causing Johnny to quickly blink back tears of joy for the two new fathers. Lucy lay comfortably surrounded by pillows and flowers, smiling happily from her hospital bed as she watched Frank and Lee bond with their new baby. After Johnny had met the woman for lunch weeks ago, he swore she was an angel sent to his new friends. She selflessly helped give the greatest gift possible—life, and thus created a new family.

Lucy had also made Johnny and Gabe an offer that left him speechless. When the time was right, she would gladly become their surrogate as well. Johnny had not known at the time, but Lee and Frank had set up the lunch date with that one specific purpose in mind. Lucy had heard about their story and wished to meet Johnny and Gabe to see if they fit and, according to her, they did. She had stated quite plainly that if she felt a couple could not or would not love their child with everything they had, then she would not give them that chance. Lucy was convinced, even with Johnny's injuries, that they would make a loving and happy family for any child lucky enough to have them. Johnny had never been more thankful for the generosity of others than he was at that very moment.

"He's so beautiful," Johnny sighed, his voice cracking slightly with emotion. "Welcome to the world, Jacob. Your daddies love you very much."

Gabe ran his huge, comforting hand up and down Johnny's back, speaking softly to Lee, but Johnny couldn't take his eyes off the tiny sleeping bundle. He was perfect.

"Do you want to hold him, Johnny?" Frank asked.

Johnny was excited for all of a few seconds before his smile fell and he remembered his damaged hands. "I don't think it's safe with my hands. I don't have much strength yet, and I don't want anything to happen." Johnny felt the disappointment like a physical blow. *What if I can't even hold my own children? What if I can't take care of them?*

Gabe must have felt his distress and was guiding Johnny toward a chair. "If you sit down, you'll be able to cradle him in your arms and I'll be right here."

Frank carefully laid Jacob into Johnny's waiting arms and Gabe crouched down in front of them both. Entranced, they sat, cooing and babbling nonsense to the now fully awake baby staring back at them.

The hours flew by and too soon it was time to leave Lucy and the new family for the night. Johnny was so overcome with emotions he actually shed tears before he gave the little bundle back to Lee, who smiled knowingly toward Gabe.

"I don't think it will be long before the two of you start having little ones of your own," Lee commented before laying Jacob in his bassinet beside Lucy.

Gabe looked at Johnny with such love that it made it hard to breathe, but this time he didn't need his inhaler; all he needed was Gabe. "Yes, I think once everything is settled, that will be something to consider."

Johnny was so thankful. All he had ever wanted was a family of his own to shower with all the love he had been saving up living with his taciturn father. He would give just about anything to have that, and he would fight tooth and nail to keep it.

Johnny took the opportunity to wiggle away, while Gabe and Lee made plans, and found the nearest washroom, with Sam in tow of course. Gabe would not allow him to be alone anywhere, not even a public washroom. Johnny didn't mind truly; he knew the dangers, had seen them firsthand and was in no hurry to experience them again.

"So, any news on the disappearing Chris?" Sam asked as he followed Johnny into the huge, eight-stall washroom. Large windows covered in an opaque film graced one wall, lighting up the entire room.

"Nothing since my tires were slashed. I'm getting really tired of that jerk."

"I don't blame you, Johnny. I don't imagine you'll ever feel safe until he's caught," Sam agreed with what Johnny himself had been feeling.

"I can't wait until he's in a nice, secure mental institution drooling all over himself." Johnny wasn't typically a spiteful person, but he was making an exception in this case.

Sam was laughing when Johnny came over to wash his hands, which wasn't easy with the few bandages that remained. "Well, there's the spitfire I know and love. Don't let that asshole have the satisfaction of causing you and Gabe any problems."

"Oh no, I won't. Gabe is mine, and I'll fight for him," Johnny assured Sam. He wasn't giving Gabe up no matter what happened.

"How 'bout we do that right now, you little homewrecker." The scratchy voice sounded almost painful, but when both Johnny and Sam turned to see Chris standing in the washroom doorway with a knife in his hand, Johnny's own voice failed and his vision dimmed for a moment.

Chris took a single step forward and Sam began backing up, putting himself in front of Johnny. No way would he allow that. Instead, Johnny grabbed a long-handled industrial broom left in the corner by the cleaning staff and stepped up beside Sam. It didn't matter that his hands were screaming in pain at even the loose grip he had on the steel handle; he wasn't going to let Chris hurt one more person. Johnny was done being prey to people who thought he was weak. Years of fear seemed to melt away, leaving a confident, stronger Johnny in its place.

At seeing Johnny's "weapon," Sam spun and grabbed the mop left in the same corner and crouched low, waiting for the first blow. The way Sam was positioning himself, Johnny knew he'd had some self-defense training, and Johnny decided then and there, once this was over, he was joining up for a class.

"Chris, you have to stop this. You're not thinking clearly," Sam tried to reason with the clearly agitated man. Chris's eyes were wild, the whites streaked red, giving him an almost possessed look. His clothes were streaked with what looked like mud and ripped in several places, causing Johnny to wonder if he'd been sleeping in the woods.

His hand shook as he lifted the lethal-looking blade directly toward Johnny. "That little bastard took my man, and he has to go. Then everything can go back to the way it was."

"You left Gabe, Chris. There's nothing for you to come back to." Sam was still attempting logic, but by the look in Chris's eyes, there wasn't a chance in hell logic was making it through Chris's delusion.

"He'll forgive me. Gabe loves me!" Chris hissed and took another step forward, confirming Johnny's original assumption.

"We're in a hospital, Chris. How do you even think you're going to get away with this?" Johnny had to try and keep him talking. Gabe would realize Johnny had been gone too long and come looking for him.

"It doesn't matter. Once you're gone, everything will be perfect again." Chris barked the words out, causing spittle to fly out of his mouth.

Obviously, what was left of his sanity was slipping away fast, and Chris lunged forward. Sam slammed the mop across Chris's head while Johnny brought the handle of his broom down on his arm, trying to dislodge the knife. Unfortunately, Chris only stumbled back but kept hold of the knife. The drugs in his system, obviously dulling the pain, allowed him to just keep on coming no matter how many times they hit him.

Shit, now what?

***

Gabe was beginning to wonder what was taking Johnny and Sam so long when Dante and Spider came barreling into the room. Lee and Frank stood protectively in front of Lucy and their baby, sensing something was wrong.

"Where's Johnny?" Dante asked, he scanned the room and Gabe went on alert.

"In the washroom with Sam. What's going on?" Gabe answered but was already heading for the door; he had to find Johnny now.

"We tracked Chris to the hospital. He's in the building," Spider announced as he moved alongside Gabe.

Shit! Gabe took off at a dead run with Dante and Spider right behind him. Gabe's fear and adrenaline caused him to almost tear the washroom door off its hinges, but what he found on the other side was truly terrifying. Sam lay on the floor, attempting to get back on his feet, while holding his hand across a gash in his left thigh. Johnny was standing over him protectively while using a broom handle to dodge the knife Chris was wielding. Johnny's grip on the handle was slipping due to his injured hands. There was blood streaked on the floor and walls and, other than Sam's obvious wound, Gabe wasn't entirely certain where it was all coming from.

The sound of the door crashing open alerted Chris to their arrival, and without a second thought, he rushed past Johnny and Sam, lifted a waist-high steel garbage can, and threw it through the window.

Before Chris jumped out, he turned to Gabe and screamed. "You're mine! I'll kill anyone who tries to take my place!"

Dante and Spider had pulled out their guns, but the area was too confined and the odds of hitting Johnny and Sam too great to take the chance of firing.

"You have no place with me, Chris. You come near Johnny or my family again, and I'll kill you myself!" Gabe swore as he ran to help Johnny and Sam. Chris quickly jumped through the now-empty pane of glass and onto an adjoining roof, followed closely by Dante and Spider.

"Gabe, we have to get Sam help," Johnny cried while putting more pressure on Sam's bleeding leg wound.

Gabe ran for the door, still surprised no one had come to check on the noise, and yelled for help. This time, when he returned to Johnny's side, he saw the open wound on the back of Johnny's right arm. Grabbing a stack of paper towels from the dispenser, he pushed them up against Johnny's injury to try and slow the flow of blood.

"Just hold on, Sam. Help is on the way," Gabe assured, while having Johnny lean his weight back against him because he was beginning to shake.

"No worries, cuz. We did more damage to that asshole than he did to us, eh, Johnny?" Sam spoke through gritted teeth, his pain evident to Gabe.

"Damn right! He won't make the mistake of thinking he can take us on again." Johnny's words came out strong and sure, even though he was shaking like a leaf.

Spider came back through the window he had previously jumped out of and knelt beside Sam. "Hey, how ya doing, Sam?"

"Oh, you know, just getting off shift, wondering whether to get Thai or Greek for dinner—you?" Sam chuckled softly before laying his head back down onto the floor. Gabe could hear footsteps running down the hall toward them. Spider stood, pulled out his Glock, and put his body between the door and the three on the ground. Gabe refused to let go of the towels he had pressed against Johnny's wound, and Johnny was not letting go of Sam's leg, so it was up to Spider to protect the three of them in case Chris doubled back.

Dr. Green, Nurse Rouse, and two other nurses ran into the room and stopped dead in their tracks when they got a look at Spider standing ready to take on all comers. It took everyone mere seconds to realize there was no threat here, and Spider turned back to Sam.

"Dammit, Spider, you scared the heck outta me!" Nurse Rouse yelled before pushing past the huge man.

"Help them please, Nurse Rouse. The police are on their way," he asked before he ran his hand gently down Sam's pale cheek. That was the one thing about Spider; he was always a contradiction. He looked scary as hell and was ready to kill to protect them, but then spoke gently and politely to Nurse Rouse. "I'll be back. The three of us will get Thai for tonight." Sam simply smiled as Spider stood to leave. Gabe had no idea the two men even knew each other past the fact that Sam was Gabe's cousin and he absently wondered who the third person might be.

"Did you catch him?" Gabe asked as he moved out of one of the nurse's way while she wrapped Johnny's arm so they could be moved to the ER.

"No, he jumped down onto an adjoining roof and into the parking garage where he carjacked a woman before we could get near him. Dante and the police are searching for the car."

"Is the woman okay?" Johnny asked as Gabe gathered him into his arms so Sam could be loaded onto a gurney.

"Yes. She was just shaken up. She was parking her car and Chris grabbed the keys and took off. I'll be back." With a final look at Sam, Spider left—out of the door this time.

"Okay, let's move." Dr. Green took off through the door with the gurney while Nurse Rouse held Johnny's injured arm. Gabe scooped Johnny up when his legs finally gave out as his adrenaline began to crash.

"Gabe, w-w-why am I shaking?" Johnny asked through his chattering teeth.

"It's okay, baby. It's the adrenaline and shock. We'll get you to the ER and they'll fix you right up." Gabe would accept nothing less.

"Don't leave me." Now that the danger was over, Johnny's voice seemed almost fragile to Gabe, and he wished he could go out and find Chris to rip the man apart himself.

"I'm not going anywhere." Gabe carried Johnny into an ER bay alongside Nurse Rouse who was still applying pressure to his bleeding wound.

Dr. Green stayed with Sam while Dr. MacGuire came in to assess Johnny. Twenty-six stitches later and Johnny lay sleeping on the hospital bed, the day's events having finally caught up with him. Gabe sat quietly in a chair just staring at his love, the terror of the day hitting home. He once again could have lost Johnny so easily tonight. They had been lucky, and he would never make this mistake again. Gabe would hire a personal bodyguard for Johnny until this was over. He wasn't going to risk the man who meant everything to him.

Family had been in and out between Johnny and Sam's rooms for hours, but it was well past 1:00 a.m., and now only Sam's parents, Uncle Jack, Aunt Jane, Gabe, Ellen, and the chief remained. Two deputies had been assigned to keep watch over the two injured men. Sam had to have surgery to repair an artery damaged by

Chris's blade and would recover, but the wound would leave a substantial scar. Sam quickly brushed the news away, stating that this would only add character among his many tattoos. Dave and the rest of his deputies were searching alongside Dante and Spider, but they had yet to call with any news.

Gabe couldn't help but worry how Johnny was going to take this latest attack. The guilt Gabe alone was feeling was excruciating. He just hoped Johnny wouldn't take the actions of an obviously insane man as his own responsibility. Hell, if anyone was responsible for this mess, Gabe knew it was he himself.

"Son." Roger stood in the open doorway, his face a blank mask. "Your mom brought coffee. Let's go for a walk."

"I can't leave him, Dad." Gabe was nowhere near ready enough to leave Johnny.

"I know, son." Ellen walked in carrying her bag-o-tricks, as the kids used to call it. Seriously, Mom had everything in that oversized purse. "I'll sit with Johnny while you go and get some air with your dad."

Gabe knew an order when he heard one and obediently stood, kissed Johnny on his forehead, and walked toward his father, who was holding two takeout coffees. Before he reached his dad, Ellen opened her arms wide, giving Gabe the type of hug a mom gives when they know their son is about to get some bad news. Gabe couldn't help but wonder what else could possibly be wrong compared to the rest of the day.

Pulling away from his mom, Gabe looked into her eyes, hoping for some kind of clue as to what was happening. "Love you, son. Now go with your father, Gabe." *Shit, it's bad.*

With one last look at Johnny, he took the much-appreciated caffeine and followed his dad out into the front courtyard of the hospital. It was late and the night was quiet. Gabe and the chief walked in silence for a few minutes, and Gabe had the feeling his dad was trying to figure out how to say something.

"Why don't we have a seat?" Roger pointed toward a concrete bench and waited until they were both seated to begin. "They caught up with Chris just outside Brighton. There was nothing that could have been done."

"What do you mean, Dad? Is anyone else hurt?" Gabe wasn't sure what he would do if he found out someone else had been hurt by this madman; he'd had enough.

"Chris wouldn't surrender and was firing on nearby officers," Dad explained, his lip curled back in disgust for what Chris had done.

"Oh, my God, did he shoot someone?" *Christ, how has everything gotten so out of control?*

"No, but Chris is dead, Gabe. Spider had no other choice; he had to protect the other officers."

Gabe sat motionless, breathing deeply to keep the coffee he just drank inside his rolling stomach. He'd wanted Chris stopped, but he certainly didn't want him to die, even after threatening it himself in the heat of anger. After everything Chris had put them through, Gabe still believed most of the violence was brought out due to his drug use; the man had needed help. Even after the years spent with Chris and the love he had thought they shared, Gabe couldn't honestly say he felt the grief he should feel for the loss of someone he once loved. Was that wrong? He did feel the grief for the loss of life, as Gabe spent his own life saving others, but beyond that was only relief, which brought on its own sort of guilt.

"Don't think for one minute that any of this is your fault, son, or any guilt for feeling some sort of relief that this is finally over and your family is now safe. You didn't cause this. Chris's own greed and addiction is at fault, and he is responsible for his own death, no one else."

As Johnny would say, family telepathy was apparently out in full force.

"I just never would have thought something like this could happen to us. Hell, my biggest concern months ago was whether I'd ever find someone I could trust again. Now Chris is dead and the man I want to spend the rest of my life with is lying in another hospital bed because of me." Before Gabe's dad could tell him yet again that it wasn't his fault, Gabe carried on. "I know, logically, you and everyone else are right. That I didn't cause any of this, but it will take time for my heart to feel free of all the pain this caused the people I love."

"I understand, son. The family is here for you and Johnny." Roger assured and placed his arm around Gabe to give him a reassuring hug.

"I'm lucky Johnny's still here after everything he's been through," Gabe admitted.

"That boy loves you. He's not going anywhere without you. That's the kind of love your mom and I have, and I treasure it for the gift it is every day. You remember that, son."

"I will, Dad."

"And make an honest man out of that boy sooner rather than later. Your mom wants a wedding to plan. That should keep the Mason women busy for a bit. See, win-win." The chief laughed deeply, but Gabe knew his dad loved his mom and all the Mason women, even if they drove the men nuts at times.

"My thoughts exactly." He would marry Johnny and start that family he had dreamt of for what seemed like forever.

Once everyone had left the hospital for the night, Gabe climbed onto Johnny's bed and gathered him into his arms. Johnny snuggled further into his spot with his face pressed into Gabe's neck before sighing contentedly and falling back to sleep. Gabe knew he was blessed; he'd been given this chance at happiness, and for that, he would be eternally grateful.

Chapter Ten

Two weeks later

Johnny wondered if a man could actually die from having blue balls, because if Gabe didn't give in soon, he just might find out. Hot make-out sessions, cold showers, and jacking off were just not cutting it anymore. His lungs had finally healed and Johnny could take a deep breath now without pain, but his burns were another story. Though half of his bandages were now gone, the scarring was extensive on his hands, shoulder, and chest. His skin in these areas now had an almost waxy, white color with a raised, leathery texture that seemed almost tight. Honestly, Johnny wasn't sure how he felt about his scars, but he would move past them somehow and he would start today.

The brilliant sun peeked in and out from behind the many clouds on this beautiful July day. Family and friends were over at Gabe and Johnny's house, and yes, Johnny finally accepted the fact that he was never leaving and was in the process of subletting his old apartment. He and Gabe had only been together a few months, but the love he felt for that man was immeasurable. They would spend days together when Gabe wasn't working, just talking while Gabe held him in his chair in their beautiful greenhouse. For the longest while, that was all Johnny physically could do anyway, so it gave the two of them the time they needed to really learn about each other—which was wonderful really, but Johnny wanted sex now! Having his very own hot, muscled firefighter around had switched his libido from a slow simmer to the "find any flat surface" category.

Johnny watched the wonderful Mason women fluttering around the backyard, fussing over the children and setting out numerous containers of food that they always insisted on bringing. They had taken Johnny under their collective wings and he finally uncovered the reason why Aunt Casey was never allowed in the state of Kentucky again. You had to love the aunts.

Royce and Jesse had moved in to Royce's house as soon as Jesse was able to get around with his walker. Johnny still went and checked in on him every day, and they had become close friends since the accident. Jesse stood under a tree holding onto his walker with Royce by his side while talking to Spider, Dante, and Sam. Sam had recovered but still walked with a cane. Spider and Dante had yet to make plans to leave Brighton and return to their homes, causing Johnny to wonder how much of that decision depended on Sam. Gabe was working through his own feelings of guilt in the aftermath of Chris's death. Therefore, along with Johnny, they were both seeing a therapist weekly. It would take time, but Johnny had no doubt they would both come out of this stronger, further cementing their bond.

Johnny slowly made his way toward Gabe, watching as he laughed and talked with the chief and his brothers-in-law. He had noticed the shadows slowly disappearing from Gabe's eyes over the weeks. Johnny imagined pain like that would take a long time to put behind you, but he would be there for his love, and Gabe knew it.

"Hey, babe, having fun?" Gabe opened his arms wide as he always did for him and Johnny walked right into his embrace. "How are your hands? You've been doing a lot of cooking today. Do you think it's time for you to take a break?"

Johnny knew Gabe was just looking out for him, but Johnny had to start moving people past the damage to his hands so that they wouldn't feel the need to worry about them—or worry about offending him by mentioning the scars, which nobody spoke about. Absolutely *nobody*.

Ah, Kate's husband, Dave, Brighton's very own police chief, would be the perfect accomplice in his master plan. "Dave, can I ask you a professional question?"

Dave looked shocked at Johnny's formal tone but answered anyway. "You can ask me anything, Johnny; we're family." Johnny noticed the rest of their family and friends were taking interest in the conversation and Gabe just look confused.

Perfect.

Johnny attempted to look as innocent as possible before asking with a straight face. "So, will I be able to get away with a crime now that I don't have fingerprints?"

Dave shifted his weight from foot to foot and continued to stare at him, clearly uneasy and unsure where to go with the touchy subject of Johnny's scars. *Well, the sooner everyone gets over this, the sooner I might get laid.*

So Johnny pushed on. "Oh, don't worry, Dave. I'm not talking about murder or anything. Maybe just a little B&E on the side, you know, to supplement my income since I'm still not working full time."

A few of the gathered men's mouths opened as if to say something and then closed again like fish out of water. It wasn't until Grandma Rose and Mom started laughing that Johnny finally lost it and broke into laughter of his own.

The men slowly began to clue in when all the women were almost rolling on the ground and gave in to their own laughter.

"Well, Johnny, I would advise you not to do anything in the county 'cause I know those hands and I'll bust you anyway." Dave chuckled before taking a swig of his beer.

"Damn, you mean I don't get a family pass? Well, that just sucks." Johnny pouted before he began laughing right along with everyone else.

Once his family and friends had finally settled down, Johnny looked around at the people who filled his new life with joy and love. He became serious, which was odd for him, but it needed to be done. The "let's not mention his scars" time was over.

"I love this family. I love Gabe and all of you, but these"—Johnny thrust his hands out palms up so everyone could get a perfect view of the bandages and gnarled, white leathery flesh that covered the palms of his hands—"are just scars, and worrying about offending me by talking about them or worrying that I'm traumatized by them isn't necessary. Yes, I'm getting used to them, and yes, I'm learning how to use my fine motor skills again with the nerve damage. But I'm okay with that and whatever else I have to do because Josie and Janice are alive and Ben has his mother. Anything after that is just gravy anyway."

Gabe wrapped his muscled arms around Johnny and lifted him until he was at least a foot off the ground and they were face to face.

"You're absolutely right, Johnny. You've shown repeatedly how brave and strong you are. We should have known this wouldn't get in your way. I love you so much, baby."

"I love you too, big guy. Now that we have that out of the way, are you absolutely positive, Dave? Not just one family pass?" The family continued to chuckle and Gabe lowered Johnny back to the ground.

Johnny turned to walk toward the picnic tables until he heard Frannie gasp and spun around to face Gabe who was now down on one knee with a black velvet box in his hand. Gabe opened the box with shaking hands, and Johnny was amazed he was still able to stand when he saw the beautiful bands inside. Two square, princess-cut diamonds sparkled in the sunlight and were surrounded by etched flames. They were simply stunning.

"Gabe—?"

"Johnny, there's no one else I would ever want to spend my life with." Gabe stood up and pulled Johnny into his arms. "I thought I knew what love felt like, but I had no idea, not until you came into my life. You've brought me so much joy and happiness; you own me. I can't live without you." Gabe's eyes became impossibly darker as he stared down at Johnny. "Will you spend the rest of your life with me—will you marry me and have a family with me?"

Johnny could feel his heart trying to beat its way out of his chest. Everything he had ever dreamed of was wrapped up in this amazing man, and that man wanted to marry him. How had he gotten this lucky?

"Yes." It was as simple as that, and the only word he could say before Gabe slammed his mouth over his in a devastating kiss that rocked him down to his toes. Johnny's life had been filled with feelings of inadequacy and loneliness until the day his life was saved, in more ways than one, by this courageous fireman. As Gabe carefully slid the symbol of their love on Johnny's finger and he did the same to Gabe, Johnny knew he was finally home.

Cheering and congratulations finally filtered through their bubble of happiness as the family swooped in. Plans were made, and the Mason women went into complete wedding mode. Mercifully, Gabe and Johnny would simply have to show up and nothing more according to the women. Johnny just knew he wasn't going to get off that easily. Still had to love those Mason women.

Hours later, with dishes washed and family and friends gone to their respective homes, Johnny found himself pressed against the living room wall, moaning loudly as Gabe mapped his mouth with his tongue. His hunger for Gabe drove his lust to unimaginable levels. Johnny needed the fabric between them gone, *now*. Gabe's thigh pushed between Johnny's legs, allowing him to grind his aching cock against it, desperate for relief.

Gabe pulled away and looked at Johnny through lust-hazed eyes. "Babe, I need you. I need to be deep inside you. I don't know how gentle I can be right now. That's why I've been trying to wait. I'm having a hard time controlling myself."

"Need...now." Johnny was so turned on that he was reduced to single words. His brain had shut down, caught in a haze of sensations and the driving need to feel the man in his arms fuck him into the mattress or the wall—or the couch; Johnny wasn't picky.

Apparently, that was all the permission Gabe needed. The sound of ripping material and buttons tinkling to the ground barely registered. His pants were next as Gabe's pace became frantic. Soon Johnny found himself and Gabe naked, wrapped around each other and pressed back against that same wall. Gabe's lips were rough, demanding, and driving Johnny closer to the edge by the second. He was all for making love right here, but it seemed his lover had other plans.

Gabe lifted him up higher while Johnny wrapped himself around Gabe and continued to explore his soon-to-be husband's mouth. It wasn't until his back landed on the soft blankets of their bed that Johnny broke the kiss. Gabe's eyes shone with all the love Johnny had wished for his entire life; this brave, compassionate man gave Johnny exactly what he needed. Gabe saw Johnny; he never looked through him, and he never thought less of him. He was Gabe's equal and he was loved.

"I love you, Johnny." Gabe's voice wavered slightly with emotion, but he pushed on. "You're everything to me."

Johnny's breath caught in his lungs. He had never been everything to anyone. He had spent his entire life as someone with little to no value to his father. Now he had everything. Gabe gave that to him.

"I love you more than I can explain, Gabe." It was true. Johnny knew Gabe would never fully grasp what he'd given to him, but

Johnny would make sure to show him every day for the rest of their lives.

Gabe growled, lowered his head, and took Johnny's cock all the way to the root inside his warm, wet mouth, tearing a cry of sheer ecstasy from Johnny. Gabe hollowed his cheeks, the suction sending tingles down his spine and causing Johnny to buck his hips further into Gabe's talented mouth. All coherent thought fled when he began to swirl his tongue around Johnny's sensitive glans; he was going to come soon if Gabe didn't stop.

"Going to...come..." Johnny panted desperately, pumping his hips upward.

Gabe immediately pulled off his cock with one last lick. "Not until I'm balls deep inside you, Johnny."

Gabe reached into the bedside table and pulled out a bottle of lube. Johnny was so desperate for Gabe's touch that he pulled his legs up to his chest to give Gabe better access.

"You're so beautiful," Gabe murmured before pushing one lubed finger into his waiting hole in a slow, maddening pace.

Johnny inhaled sharply and pushed back, that little bit of pain morphing into pleasure within moments, making him groan and pant. Gabe wasn't wasting any time. As soon as Johnny's body became accustomed to the invasion, he added another finger and then another. Johnny was delirious as wave after wave of pleasure raced through his body. He massaged Johnny's prostate with his talented fingers and Johnny swore, if it hadn't been for Gabe's hand on his hip, he would have shot straight off the bed. Johnny's cock was leaving trails of precum all over his stomach as he lay writhing under Gabe's capable hands.

"Gabe...please, I need you." Johnny wasn't above begging at this point.

Gabe pulled his fingers from Johnny, leaving him feeling empty for only a moment before he felt the blunt head of Gabe's cock at his entrance. Blood tests weeks ago confirmed no need for condoms. "Push out, Johnny."

Johnny knew it had been a long while since he had been with anyone, and other than Gabe's fingers, they hadn't made love yet, so the stretch and burn were no surprise. He pushed out and tried to relax as much as he could with what felt like a two-by-four trying to split him in half. Johnny didn't care; he simply needed Gabe inside him. Slowly, inch by glorious inch, Gabe slid into him until his balls rested against Johnny's ass.

Gabe hovered only mere inches from Johnny's face, holding most of his weight on his arms. The beads of sweat on his forehead were tribute to how much control Gabe was using in trying not to move and allowing Johnny time to adjust to his invasion.

Johnny had other ideas. Lifting his hips slightly, he began to impale himself on Gabe's rock-hard cock, desperate for relief. It seemed that was all the incentive Gabe needed. He pulled back so that only the head was still inside Johnny's ass before slamming back in. Johnny cried out in pleasure, meeting him thrust for thrust as Gabe set a desperate pace, his eyes never leaving Johnny's.

Johnny was panting and begging for more. Reaching between them, he grabbed his own leaking cock, needing more friction as he drove toward his own release. Johnny's actions seemed to spur Gabe on. The bed creaked and slammed against the bedroom wall, but Johnny didn't care in the least; all that mattered was him and Gabe. In that moment, the world drifted away and it was only the two of them. Their desire and love drove them higher and higher.

Gabe's movements became even more erratic as he pegged Johnny's hot spot over and over until the tingling in Johnny's spine spread, drawing his balls up tight. Johnny cried out as he shot cum over his and Gabe's stomachs. That was all it took to set Gabe off. His cock swelled, stretching Johnny even wider before he roared his release, filling Johnny with his hot cum. Moments later, Gabe collapsed on top of him, but Johnny figured that since he could still breathe that Gabe must still be aware enough to be holding most of his weight off of him. Without even pulling himself out, Gabe rolled the two of them over until Johnny was lying on top of him. The events of the day must have caught up with Johnny, because the next thing he felt was a warm cloth between his cheeks cleaning him. He hadn't even realized Gabe had lifted him off his chest or that he had gone to the washroom to get items to care for him.

"I can do that," Johnny mumbled into the pillow, not entirely sure if he liked being taken care of this way.

"I've got you, baby. Please let me take care of you." Gabe spoke softly, taking the fight right out of Johnny. He knew Gabe was a nurturer and the dominate one in this relationship, and Johnny was perfectly happy with that.

A few moments later, Gabe crawled back onto the bed beside Johnny and gathered him into his strong arms before pulling the blanket over the both of them and settling in for the night.

"Thank you." Gabe whispered so softly that Johnny barely heard him. He lifted his head to look at Gabe curiously.

"Thank you for what, big guy?"

Gabe smiled at him, and the love shining in his eyes made Johnny feel invincible. "I thought you were asleep, baby. That wasn't for you. I was thanking fate for bringing you to me." Gabe finished by kissing the ring on Johnny's finger.

A wave of love washed over Johnny. This amazing man was thankful to simply have Johnny just the way he was. There had to be someone looking out for Johnny the day of that office fire. In his heart, he wanted to believe it had been his dear mother, and he swore to her that he would never squander what he'd been given.

"Love you to the moon, Gabe."

"Yes, to the moon, Johnny."

SAM'S SOLDIERS

Chapter One

Sam scanned the ER. It was standing room only for the fifth day in a row. A new wave of party drugs hit town and it guaranteed a constant flow of disoriented, violent young patients and their terrified families and friends. Currently, three of them were being kept in their beds with the help of four-point restraints, and under guard to ensure they didn't try to hurt themselves or anyone else. Thank God for the security staff or it would be impossible for him to complete his work.

It seemed this latest batch of caustic chemicals provided the user with some damn serious hallucinations lasting over twenty-four hours. One young teen had been found weaving through rush hour traffic on foot. Naked. The nineteen-year-old boy explained he was trying to outrun the tiger that was stalking him—of course said tiger had pink stripes, spoke French, and was seven feet tall. Sam still sported the fat lip he received from another disoriented young woman who had been attempting to pull the IV line out of her arm. *Ah, the glamorous life of an ER nurse but I wouldn't work anywhere else.*

Sam laughed at his own thoughts while going through his final checks before handing his patients off to the evening shift. Once the handoff was given to the next shift and his reports were complete, he was running for the door as quickly as his legs would carry him. Considering he was still suffering from the effects of a knife wound to his left thigh, perhaps "limp" would be a more accurate description. Either way, he was outta there.

It had been a little over four weeks since Sam and his friend and soon-to-be cousin-in-law, Johnny, were attacked by his cousin Gabe's ex-boyfriend, Chris. The man was unstable and addicted to methamphetamines, a dangerous combination and almost lethal for

Johnny. But two unexpected things came out of that month from hell: Gabe fell in love and proposed to Johnny, and the two hot, tattooed ex-soldiers sent to protect Johnny were now waiting at home for Sam.

Yes, he knew he was a lucky man. At first when Dante and Jack—better known as Spider—had approached him with this arrangement, Sam had been a little shocked. Why would two men who were already lovers want to include him as their third? Well, their third lover for the time they remained in Brighton. That was the deal he'd made and now regretted. The three had been living together in Sam's house since his men checked out of their hotel after the first week they'd arrived.

In the past five weeks, he had lost part of himself to these men, given away the one thing he thought was safe, his heart. But Sam knew it was only a matter of time until they left on one assignment or another and back to their real lives together, without Sam.

"Hey. You tattooed freak, get over here," Mr. Renfrew ordered from his bed in the far corner of the ER. Mr. R. was a frequent flyer at Brighton General and one of the town's few bigots. Brighton welcomed all comers and family units, but there always seemed to be a few close-minded individuals kicking around. "Can you hear me or did all that ink fry your brain?"

"What's the problem, Mr. Renfrew?" Sam asked, knowing exactly what was coming next. The now smiling sixty-year-old slid his tray of food to the edge of the rollaway table and flicked it to the floor.

"Oh, look what happened. I guess you'll just have to clean that up."

"No, housekeeping will be called down to help you with that. Have a good night, Mr. Renfrew." Sam turned and walked toward the nursing station. In the background, he could hear good old Mr. R. cursing up a storm.

Sam wasn't sure which bothered the man more: the fact that Sam was gay or that he had two full sleeves of tattoos, and those were only the ones that could be seen when he was wearing his scrubs. Personally, Sam didn't care. The man had it out for him since he first saw him over five years ago.

"Mr. R. needs housekeeping. His tray fell off his table…again." Sam sighed in frustration.

"Oh, those damn tray poltergeists, can't they just stay in their own dimension?" Joanne laughed and bumped Sam in the arm, making him smile with her corny sense of humor. Joanne had the ability to brighten even the crappiest of situations. "I'll call them to come deal with him. You go home to those hot men of yours."

"Thanks, Joanne. I'm looking forward to having the next four days off." Sam rubbed the tight muscles on the back of his neck, trying to give himself a bit of relief.

"You boys have anything planned?" Joanne asked while filling out the seemingly never-ending pile of paperwork on the desk in front of her.

"Nope, just kicking back and relaxing. I need some down time in the worst way." Sam groaned as he stretched out his sore back.

Joanne grabbed the files out of his hands and began ushering Sam toward the locker room. "Okay then, off you go."

"But…"

With one final push from his friend, Sam was on his way home to the two men who filled him with a joy he could never fully embrace. The threat that they would soon leave always hung over his head. It was just a matter of time.

His house was lit up when Sam pulled the big-ass four-wheel drive SUV Dante and Spider insisted he drive into the garage. He looked fondly at his classic green 1965 VW Beetle convertible tucked safely into the corner. He missed the old girl, even if his men said it was a death trap. It was only slightly rusted, and he only had to fill the passenger tire with air once a day now. Other than that, she was almost perfect, as long as you never tried to move the driver's seat or adjust the mirrors.

"Soon, my beautiful car, we'll go out soon for a drive," Sam vowed.

"Not if I have anything to say about it," Spider stated from the door leading into the house from the garage. "That car will get you hurt or even killed, which is not acceptable."

Sam turned so quickly, he got his injured leg hung up on the tarp covering his car. His lunch bag went flying as he braced himself for the pain of hitting the concrete floor, but it never came. Sam had no idea how a man standing six foot five inches tall and weighing over two hundred and sixty pounds of muscle could move that fast, but the fact that he wasn't kissing cold stone at the moment confirmed he could.

"See, if it's not the car putting you in danger, it's the tarp covering the damn thing," Spider whispered into Sam's ear before straightening him up and placing him safely back on his feet. Enfolding Sam in his huge arms, Spider leaned forward, pressing his face in Sam's curly red hair, and inhaled deeply. He loved it when Spider wrapped himself around Sam's smaller body, as if he was protecting him from the world.

"It wasn't the tarp's fault or my baby. I'm just tired and clumsy," Sam explained, and Spider tucked him even closer into the curve of his muscled body.

"What's with the fat lip, sweetheart?" Spider asked as he gently turned Sam's face from side to side.

"Just another night in the ER. You know how it's been lately. We lost a fifteen-year-old girl today because of that poison they're peddling. There was nothing we could do." Sam felt that same sick churning in his stomach he always got after he lost a patient.

"Sam, I'm so sorry. Something needs to be done." Spider's voice held barely suppressed anger but Sam knew it wasn't directed at him. "I know the police chief is taking down as many of these new dealers as he can, but another crop of them just pops up after the first ones are arrested."

"Maybe you and Dante could have a look around? If anyone could figure this out, it's the two of you," Sam said without an ounce of doubt, his men could figure this out.

"Perhaps. Let's get you inside. Supper is almost ready. Dante's cooking chicken parmigiana with pasta, Caesar salad, and garlic bread." Spider tilted Sam's head upward and kissed him as if his life depended on it. The touch as explosive as ever.

"Wow, a greeting like that and all my favorite food for supper. What did I do to deserve this?" Sam teased as he straightened Spider's shirt.

Spider took his hand and led him into the house and to a kitchen that smelled of garlic, tomato sauce, and cheese, all the things Sam loved, along with the third man of their triad, whom he also loved. Dante was slightly taller than Spider but a bit less muscled, which wasn't saying a lot because there was still a whole lot of it filling the room. *Mine.*

Sam had to stop himself from immediately running into the man's arms. He'd greeted Spider, and now he felt an almost desperate need to have Dante pressed against him. Dante turned as they neared the counter and immediately opened those strong arms, to which Sam responded by taking a running jump into his embrace.

"How was your day, Trouble?" Dante asked before kissing him long and hard, not letting go until they both needed to breathe.

"Much better now," Sam gasped with a smile.

"He's tired. He almost tripped over the tarp. If I hadn't caught him, Sam would have been face down on the concrete. He could have hurt his leg, and he has a fat lip for his troubles today. Sam needs to rest tonight." Spider looked at Dante, and they did the one thing that drove Sam nuts.

"Okay, you two. What's up with the talking-no-talking going on? I thought we agreed you two wouldn't have your freaky mental discussions when I'm around. Everything gets said out in the open." Sam knew it wasn't a mental thing at all. Dante and Spider had survived through war and dangerous, life-threatening situations in the service and in the security field they worked in now. They had been lovers for the past eight years and simply knew each other well enough to understand what every slight variation in facial feature or movement of their eyes meant.

"Sorry, baby, we just want you to rest this evening. We'll take care of everything. You've had a long day," Spider explained.

"You go have a hot shower and supper should be ready by the time you're done," Dante said and placed Sam gently back on his feet. Sam knew something was up; heck, he was a Mason after all, and just like his other cousins he'd learned early on how to tell when something strange was in the air. Typically, it was *the aunts* and another one of their blind date schemes to marry somebody off. You had to be on your toes to have enough warning when it happened. Last time he hadn't been and had spent the night in lockup because of it.

"Okay, you two, I'll go have a shower, but don't think you're getting away with anything. We have four full days together," Sam said as he walked down the hall to their bedroom. He couldn't contain his smile; this had been the happiest he'd ever felt.

***

As soon as Spider heard the water running in the shower, he turned to Dante. "We shouldn't do this. We can't leave him."

Dante came forward and wrapped his arms around Spider. "It was part of the deal we made, Jack. We can't back out now."

"It just doesn't feel right to me, it's Sam." Spider knew it was part of their initial arrangement with Sam, but things had changed, hadn't they?

"We've got another mission. We have to head a security detail in two days. Besides, Sam hasn't asked us to stay. We can't make that decision for him." Dante backed away and returned to preparing their final meal together. Spider's heart raced, knowing this was the wrong decision.

"But I know he cares about us. I can feel it. He was meant to be a part of our team," Spider said, trying to explain what he felt to his core, he knew Sam loved them on some level. They'd spent the last five weeks living together, acting every bit like a family, and it had been plain to see how each of them felt, or maybe he was simply seeing what he wanted. The two went on to work silently on supper for several minutes until they both heard the water turn off in the shower.

"Sweetheart, look at me," Dante said, and Spider finally met Dante's eyes. Spider knew he was the one more likely to show emotions out of the two of them, but the pain he saw in Dante's eyes confirmed he felt the same way about Sam. "We have to carry on with our lives and let Sam carry on with his. It's selfish to force ourselves on him."

"But, Major, I don't believe we are. Do we really have to leave like this?" Spider still fell back on his military training when stressed.

"Leave?" Sam spoke softly from the doorway, a towel hanging low on his hips. His beautiful tattoos stood in vibrant contrast against his creamy white skin and lean muscle. His red hair was wet and standing up in odd angles and his beautiful brown eyes shone slightly.

"Leave?" Sam repeated, his face becoming a mask, showing nothing. "Is it time for the two of you to go back already?"

Dante released Spider, who stepped forward and held out his hand. Sam immediately took it, and Spider pulled him in close so both he and Dante could surround him. "Yes, Sam, we have another assignment." Spider thought the words seemed like a physical blow to Sam even as he tried to hide his response from them.

"When?" Sam asked in a strangled voice.

"Tomorrow morning."

"So this is my farewell supper?" Sam stepped back out of their reach and took a deep breath. "I should have guessed with all my favorites on the menu."

Sam was smiling now, but it didn't reach his eyes. Spider was desperate to touch him again, but didn't know if Sam would allow it. "We wanted to make the night special."

Sam looked around at the table set with wineglasses and his grandmother's good china. "It looks beautiful, thank you. I'll go finish getting dressed and we can start our last evening together." Sam stepped forward, gave both Spider and Dante a quick kiss on their cheeks, and went back to their master bedroom.

"Dante?"

Dante stood straighter and squared his shoulders, the same stance he always took when the hard decisions needed to be made. "We have to go, Jack. We both knew this couldn't last forever, and all three of us went into this knowing it would eventually have to end. Now is that time."

"Don't you feel it? The pull to him, the need to keep him with us?" Spider couldn't understand why Dante was fighting so hard to not allow himself to fall in love with Sam.

"Of course I do. But again, soldier, that's not our decision to make."

Chapter Two

Sam couldn't breathe, he was gasping for air by the time he reached the bathroom. His heart was trying to beat its way out of his chest and sweat poured down his face. *Yep, panic attack...great.* Sam hadn't had one in years, and he had to get himself together before he went back out. Now was not the time to lose it. Hell, he knew this was going to happen eventually; he had agreed to it from the beginning before he realized what he would be giving up when they left. It wasn't Spider or Dante's fault that he fell in love with them. Sam had to be responsible for his own actions and decisions, and not act like a frightened child hiding in the bathroom. Which was exactly what he was doing at the moment.

Sam breathed deeply, stood, washed his face, and then dressed quickly in a faded pair of jeans and his comfy purple sweatshirt. He needed comfort now more than ever to get through tonight and act as though his heart wasn't breaking. Sam had to let them go. It was part of their agreement, but mainly because it appeared they wanted to leave as quickly as possible. He had never really considered the fact that his men might be missing their lives, their team, and the action that came with their jobs. Sam couldn't be selfish, he had to let them go.

He opened the door and walked down the hall and into the kitchen to face the last supper they would have together as a triad. He could do this; he could make it through tonight. When he came through the doorway, Dante was busy plating the chicken parmigiana and Spider was filling their wineglasses with a rather expensive bottle of Merlot, the perfect pairing for the tomato sauce. They both looked up when Sam entered the room. He quickly pasted a smile on his face, even if it was killing him, and began what he hoped was the best performance of his life. Strangely, the aromas in the kitchen were no longer appetizing. In fact, his stomach was churning so badly he wondered how he was going to keep his supper down.

"Everything smells wonderful, guys. Thank you for all of this," Sam gushed, hoping he sounded close enough to his usual self to get by.

Spider pulled out Sam's chair and held it for him as he sat. "Thank you, Jack." Dante placed a dish worthy of any fine Italian restaurant's menu in front of him before they both took their own seats. He looked at the two men who had changed his world so completely and smiled as he thought of all the memories he would have. The three of them had had an amazing five weeks, and he wouldn't tarnish that memory by sobbing like a baby. Or worse, begging them to stay.

So, with that in mind, Sam dug into his supper with gusto but never really tasted a thing. They talked about the hospital, the recent drug problem, and Sam learned that Spider and Dante would be heading a security detail protecting an heiress of some sort; it sounded very important. Sam was again reminded that these men had important jobs. They protected and saved lives; he couldn't keep them from that.

"Sam…we—" Spider began, but Sam wouldn't let anything ruin their last night together, especially not an apology for doing what they had to do, or worse, a "thanks for a good time" speech.

"No, Jack, don't say anything. The three of us knew this day would come. I just want to spend this last night with the two of you. No more talking about what needs to be done tomorrow. It's going to come either way."

Both men seemed to consider this for a moment before Dante spoke. "Whatever you want, beautiful." He had called Sam beautiful from the first time they met in the ER when Gabe introduced Spider as the man protecting Johnny. Well, that and Trouble.

Spider stood, took two steps, leaned down, and lifted Sam from his chair, easily carrying him all the way to the master bedroom. Sam clung to him, kissing his neck and jaw, tasting his salty skin. If this was the last night they spent together, Sam wouldn't waste it with tears. They'd stopped moving and Sam felt a second pair of warm hands lifting his sweatshirt over his head.

Spider slowly set him down, but only broke the kiss to remove Sam's clothes. Soon Dante began undressing Spider as well. They were both down to their underwear, staring at a completely naked Dante, and what a breathtaking sight, tanned skin curving to the planes and valleys of muscle. Sam needed to touch, to taste, and was powerless to stop himself from going to his lover. Sam pushed aside the fact that, as of tomorrow, those words would no longer apply.

Slowly, almost reverently, Dante brought his large, calloused hand up to cup Sam's face. He sank into those chocolate-brown eyes of Dante's, the color such a contrast to his shocking white-blond hair, cut high and tight. His lips were soft and gentle when he kissed Sam. The sight of Dante's thick cock, hard and ready, made Sam ache to have that beauty filling him.

Spider's broad chest pressed firmly against Sam's back, and he couldn't help but notice Spider was now naked as well, leaving Sam the only one left standing in his boxers. Spider's hard cock rubbed against his lower back, and Sam's own penis was pushing out of the top of his tight underwear. Sam leaned forward for a taste of Dante's warm skin, and considering he only stood at chest level with him, Sam began with those tempting dark nipples. The soft groan was all the encouragement Sam needed as he licked and nibbled at the peaked nubs. He lavished attention on both until he became distracted by the eagle tattooed on Dante's pec and traced the black outline with his tongue. Sam had numerous tattoos covering his body, and each held a special meaning to him. Dante and Spider each had a version of that same eagle on their chests in honor of their many years of military service.

Spider's hands slid under the waistband of Sam's underwear, allowing the bothersome material to skim down his legs. Dante immediately squeezed Sam's naked ass cheeks, his large fingers kneading the soft skin and exposing him for Spider's attention. The first swipe of his hot tongue over Sam's hole forced a deep moan out of Sam's mouth; the pleasure was electrifying and all consuming, as it always was between them. Sam was drowning in the need he could see burning in Dante's eyes.

He heard Dante growl just before he reclaimed Sam's mouth in a passionate kiss. Spider had two fingers buried deep inside Sam, using only his saliva as lube, and he could do nothing other than allow his lovers to prepare him. Submitting to Dante and Spider's will in the bedroom allowed Sam to experience a whole new level of pleasure and freedom from the constant pressures of being an ER nurse.

Spider pulled away to give Dante enough room to sweep Sam into his arms and carry him over to their king-sized bed. By now, Sam was desperate for release but knew that would only come when his men were good and ready. Dante followed him down onto the bed and covered Sam with his own body, while Spider rifled through the bedside table for supplies. A well-used tube of lube landed at his hip along with one condom. A fist engulfed Sam's straining erection, jacking him at a maddeningly slow pace. Dante stopped his exploration of Sam's neck to groan loudly and began flexing his hips. It seemed Spider was stroking both of them.

Sam was so close. "Soon, can't hold back."

"On your hands and knees, beautiful," Dante ordered as he reached for the lube.

Sam rolled over as soon as Dante lifted up and Spider released his hard cock, which was now leaking precum onto the sheets. The bed jostled when Spider crawled to the top of the bed and settled with his legs spread and his gorgeous cock only inches from Sam's lips. The ten-inch shaft glistened in the soft light coming from the candles that glowed around the room. Sam had no idea when he had missed Spider lighting them, but he suspected that had something to do with the man currently thrusting three thick fingers in and out of his ass.

"Suck me, love," Spider moaned while stroking his cock; his pupils were dilated, and a fine sheen of sweat covered his chest. The endearment felt sadly hollow to Sam considering Spider was in the throes of passion and had never said the word "love" before when referring to him. The spongy head of Dante's condom-covered cock pressing against his lubed hole drove those thoughts from Sam's mind.

Slowly, Dante breached him, giving Sam time to adjust to his size and the stretch. By the time he was fully seated, Sam was panting and writhing in need, acutely aware that his own dick felt like it was about to shatter. The wide crown of Spider's shaft brushed back and forth across Sam's lips. The salty, musky taste exploded over his tongue and drove his desire even higher as he lapped at the wet slit for more.

Dante pulled back until only the head was left inside him, then slammed home over and over again. Sam arched his back, trying to get closer as Dante drove his cock deeper. Spider's straining erection stood tall, demanding the attention Sam gladly gave. He knew he'd never take the entire shaft down his throat, but he'd give it one hell of a try. Sam jacked Spider's erection, then sucked the almost purple mushroomed head into his mouth. The muscled legs on either side of his shoulders slowly fell open on a loud groan from Spider.

"Baby. Oh God!" Spider cried when Sam slapped his flat tongue against the head of his cock and fondled his heavy balls while stroking his finger over Spider's hole. He was close to the edge, and Sam would do anything to push him over.

Dante's steady growl increased with every powerful thrust, lost to his pleasure just as much as Sam. His ass cheeks were held open, giving his lover a perfect view of their joined bodies. Sam sucked harder, his tongue mapping the large vein on the underside of Spider's hard shaft. He bobbed his head up and down and pushed the tip of his finger into Spider's tight ass.

Spider shouted while cradling Sam's head between his spread legs. Sam wanted to please the men he loved, but more importantly, he wanted to taste and feel their pleasure. Spider's cock pulsed in his mouth as Sam swallowed, but it was impossible to take everything as it dribbled down his chin. The look of ecstasy on Spider's face made him feel at peace because he had given that to his lover.

Sam began to keen low in his throat as Dante moved faster, pegging his gland with every thrust.

"Yes, Trouble, come!" Dante roared loud enough to make the windows shake. Sam felt the tingle at the base of his spine shoot through his balls and out the end of his cock as he came all over the crumpled sheets underneath him. He could feel the heat filling Dante's condom, signaling his release.

Sam collapsed on top of Spider's hard body, dragging Dante with him. He was in the position that both soothed and enflamed him at the same time, between his men. After a few minutes, Dante lifted off them and went into the bathroom as Spider held Sam closer, making him feel treasured and wanted. Then reality seeped back into his lust-filled fog. They were leaving in a matter of hours. He wasn't treasured or wanted. Dante returned with a warm wet cloth and proceeded to clean Sam and Spider. The fact didn't shock Sam.

Dante was the leader, the one who took care of everyone else, including his lovers. *Lover…not lovers. After tonight, Dante and Spider will have each other and I'll be left alone, damn. You agreed to this… You agreed to this…*

"Let's get you settled, sweetheart," Spider said while positioning Sam in the middle of the bed, allowing both men to lie on either side of him. He loved the way they could move him like he weighed next to nothing. The three usually slept this way every night, another thing Sam would have to get used to, sleeping in this big bed alone.

Once all three were settled, Sam couldn't think of the right thing to say, so he did the only thing that made sense: he kissed his men. Bringing Spider close, Sam captured his lips, hard and demanding, tongues tangling. Slowly, the kiss changed from urgent to sweet, filled with emotions that none of them had ever spoken. When they parted, Sam could see a world of emotion in Spider's eyes, but again, neither spoke.

Before Sam had the chance to turn and face his other love, Dante cupped his cheek and lifted Sam's head from the bed, slamming their mouths together. The kiss was rough and desperate, confusing Sam with its intensity. After several minutes, the kiss began to gentle to the point that Dante was simply brushing the tip of his tongue over Sam's lips. The look in Dante's eyes was unreadable; the only sense Sam got from the expression was pain.

I need to tell them. They deserve to know.

But, all too soon, the long shifts he'd been working at the hospital caught up with Sam, and his thoughts and concerns clouded in the mist of exhaustion. Before he fell asleep, Sam came to a decision: he would tell his men exactly how he felt, how much he loved them, in the morning, and then let the chips fall where they may. Sam couldn't live with himself if he let the opportunity slip by without sharing his love with them.

Chapter Three

Sam stretched his sore muscles, enjoying the wonderful ache that came from their overnight activities. He smiled and spread out his arms, ready to cuddle up to one of his men, but the bed was empty, the sheets cold. It all came back in an instant like a slap across his face. They were leaving. Sam frantically scanned the room, finding nothing, and for the life of him, he couldn't figure out why the sun was coming through his bedroom windows because the sun wasn't on this side of the house until…afternoon. *No, no, no, no, no… They didn't…*

Sam sprang from the bed, threw on his sleeping pants, and ran out into the living room, again finding nothing. The kitchen, empty. The clock on the wall read after 3:00 p.m. They were to leave in the morning. He numbly walked to the front door and turned the lock. If Dante's Hummer was gone, then it was true, they'd left. Sam opened it slowly, wondering if the door had always squeaked this much or if it was protesting being opened as well. He lifted his eyes to find the driveway empty.

Gone. They'd left.

They didn't say good-bye.

Sam was now relieved he hadn't told them he loved them last night. He had managed to save that much of his dignity. He slowly closed and relocked the front door before falling to the floor and letting his pain flow freely through his shaking body until he was an exhausted mess. Slowly, he picked himself up and walked stiffly into the kitchen. He needed caffeine, maybe with a shot of whiskey. As if on autopilot, Sam stumbled to the coffeemaker, finding it ready to go, and pushed the button. He then looked around, finally noticing the kitchen and table had been cleaned from last night's supper. All that remained on the table was a sealed envelope and a set of keys.

Sam knew he must have been in a dead sleep to not hear any of the cleanup, which explained why he needed four days off after such a long stretch. But now, those days would be spent alone.

He walked over and lightly touched the edge of the benign-looking envelope. His name was penned on the front in Dante's perfect handwriting. Sam knew, unlike himself, Dante was perfect, always in control, sure of himself and his actions, the leader. Spider, although slightly bigger and more imposing, if that was even possible, was in fact the softer of the two. He had an ingrained sense of right and wrong and a heart bigger than most knew.

Sam took the keys, recognizing them as the ones he used for the SUV he was told to drive while the three of them were together. He walked to the door leading to the garage and opened it, knowing full well the vehicle would still be in the same place he'd parked it the night before, but he had to be sure. He grabbed the handle, opened the door, and flicked on the lights. And there it was, Spider's black beast sitting in its usual spot. *Yep, they've left it.*

Sam's stomach churned and bile worked its way up his throat. *Is this some sort of payment for the past five weeks?* He quickly turned off the lights, shut the door, and leaned his back against it, as if trying to keep the truth locked in the garage. He was nauseous and confused. They hadn't woken him to say good-bye, but instead left a "Dear John" letter and a new truck for his troubles... *I'm a rent boy! They paid for my time with an $80,000 vehicle. Idiot! I'm an idiot!*

Anger temporarily replaced his anguish, but Sam wasn't foolish enough to think he wouldn't be returning to the profound sadness many times over the next couple months, if not years. But for now he was pissed. *How dare they think I was nothing other than a warm body to fill their bed while in town! How dare they...they do exactly what they said they were going to do?* Sam's mental rant ended quickly. Dante and Spider did exactly what Sam had agreed to. There was no one to blame here but himself.

Sam straightened and returned to the kitchen, filled a cup with coffee, and pulled a bottle of Jim Beam from the cupboard above the refrigerator. There was a bit of dust on the top. He wasn't a big drinker, but now was the perfect time to give it a shot. Grabbing his coffee cup, the bottle of whiskey, and the envelope, Sam moved to his enclosed back porch, sat in his old recliner, and began to explore the benefits of alcohol with a vengeance.

Many hours later, the sun had set, and Sam sat alone in the dark with a now half-empty bottle and a still unopened letter sitting on the table beside him. He wasn't entirely sure if he wanted to open it. His home phone had rung a few times and his cell phone had finally died after chiming constantly for hours now. Sam didn't care. He had four days to himself, and that was all he wanted. He took a long pull from the bottle in his hand, having given up on using his coffee cup about an hour ago. The burn felt good; it felt right and fit well with his dark mood.

His sad laughter carried through the dark, empty house. Sam thought it would be hilarious if his friends and family could see the diva now. He was the outrageous redhead of the family, the one who made everyone laugh or yell, depending on which prank he'd recently pulled. They'd be shocked at the drunk-off-his-ass, sniveling lump of useless flesh they'd find. It was better to not answer the phone or turn on the lights. The world continued to spin outside his front door, but inside, Sam was safe, at least for now. He knew he would have to deal with this eventually, but later sounded perfect right about now. He took another swig from his bottle, sat back, and waited for sleep to take him.

Pounding came from his front door. Sam looked at the clock on the wall; it was well after 11:00 p.m. No one should be at his house at this time of night. So he sunk farther back into his big comfortable circa-1970s reclining chair, the same one he'd had since college, and cradled his bottle of whiskey to his chest in the dark. Whoever it was could just leave for all he cared. The banging finally stopped, and Sam was relieved for all of two seconds until he heard the lock turn and the front door opening. *Shit!*

Only certain family members, Dante, and Spider had keys, and he was fairly certain it wasn't his former lovers. His front door creaked its complaint, and Sam could hear several pairs of shoes walking into his front entryway. Sam knew the jig was up; he should have just answered the damn phone. Now he had brought them to his front door instead.

"Sam?" His cousin Josie's voice rang through the darkened house.

"You here, Sam?" Johnny, his soon-to-be cousin-in-law, asked. Sam knew that if Johnny was here, so was Gabe.

Footsteps began to fan out from the front of the house in all directions; it was just a matter of time until they found him. Sam knew it would be foolish to try to hide now but the thought had crossed his mind. His family loved him, and that was why they were here in the first place. *I just want to be left alone. Lick my wounds and never make this mistake ever again.*

Heavy footsteps headed his way from someone bigger than either Josie or Johnny. One of his many cousins, Ben Mason, stepped through the doorway and flipped on the light. He spotted Sam in the corner of the room almost immediately. "I found him!"

Sam raised his bottle and saluted Ben before taking another drink. His head was progressively becoming foggier. "C-congrats, cuz, you get the p-prizzze," he slurred before laying his head against the back of his chair and closing his puffy eyes.

The pounding of feet heralded the arrival of the search party. Sam opened his eyes to find Josie, Johnny, and Gabe, along with Ben standing around him and staring. Figuring they'd never seen him drunk before, he gave them a minute to get the full effect of the skinny, tattooed drunk man sitting in his sleeping pants, shirtless, hugging a bottle of booze to his chest. Sam figured it had to be a pretty impressive sight when no one spoke.

"Sooo, what brings yous all here"—Sam stopped to yawn—"to my place?"

Johnny was the first to step forward. He and Sam had bonded when they both were attacked by a knife-wielding madman attempting to kill Johnny. The madman was Gabe's drug-addicted ex who just wouldn't take no for an answer. He had stolen, lied, and cheated on Gabe years earlier and had returned to town in hopes of getting Gabe back. Unfortunately, Johnny became the target of the man's rage and drug-induced delusions. They had fought side by side, and both had been injured. That was the reason why sometimes Sam still walked with a limp.

"How come I didn't get an invitation to the party?" Johnny asked, his eyes holding a sheen of wetness that Sam saw him blink away.

"Sorry, this is def...def...nity a private party, just for me." Sam knew he was slurring but didn't care; this was his house after all. "Please leave."

"Not going to happen, Sam," Josie declared before rounding the short coffee table and squeezing onto the recliner beside Sam. It was a good thing they were both small, or she would have been sitting on Sam's lap. "Dante and Spider called earlier. They were concerned because you weren't answering your phone. When you wouldn't answer our calls, you left us with no other choice but to come over here and find you."

Sam loved Josie, he loved all his family, but now was not the time for a family get-together. "I'm fine...see?" He responded by lifting both arms wide, one hand still firmly gripping his whiskey bottle.

"You don't look fine, Sam," Gabe said before sitting on the couch that was along the opposite wall. "You're sitting in the dark all by yourself and drunk off your ass."

"I'm...I'm old enough to drink, mmmister. And it's my houssssssse." Sam took another long drink from the bottle before continuing. "I j-j-just need to be alone right now. So if you all could p-p-please...leave. "

"Ya, I agree with Josie, not going to happen, Sam," Ben said softly. "We know that they left."

Well, that was just great. Everyone knew of Sam's new status as a well-paid rent boy. His face heated with embarrassment. He'd hoped to get a few days' peace before having to hash this out with the family. "I guess that means the w-whole family knows. Well, shit, I couldna' get a few days. Dante an' Spider obviously had no problem telling everyone?"

"Dante and Spider were worried when you didn't answer. They had to leave. They have a new client," Johnny answered.

"Yep, thatsa 'bout right. S'all good." Sam's head was getting fuzzy, and it was becoming hard to concentrate.

"You don't look all good, Sam. We're here for you. We love you," Johnny said from his position beside Gabe.

"At least somebody does." Sam laughed at himself, all the while thinking how pathetic he truly was at that moment. "It doesn't mat-tter. It was p-p-part of the deal."

"We all know about the agreement. No one ever tried to hide that fact. They would have to eventually leave, but that doesn't make it hurt any less." Josie spoke softly. Her eyes were glassy, as if she were fighting to hold back her own tears.

Sam leaned in so their foreheads were together and hugged her close. "I fell in love with them, Jos. It's not their fault if they don't love me back."

"I know you love them, Sam. I'm so sorry you're in pain now." Josie hiccupped, tears now flowing freely.

"Hey, at least I…I gotta new truck out of it. Spider left his SUV, the ownership was just sitting on top of the letter, signed and dated." Sam laughed sadly. "I was a very expensive call girl…call boy… Hell, call someone. I'm sooo drunk."

"You are not a hooker!" Johnny yelled, scaring the shit out of Sam, making him jump a bit and drop the bottle of Jim Beam. Ben quickly grabbed it and set it on a table out of Sam's reach. "You had a relationship with those men. That was not a hookup, and that truck is not payment for services rendered. They care about you. Maybe they left the truck so that you'd be safe driving around town. Lord knows that Bug isn't safe."

"If they cared so much 'bout me, then why didn't they say anything? W-why didn't they stay? Why did they leave without waking me up to even say good-bye?" Sam was yelling by the end of his rant, and Josie was hugging him tightly. He didn't know when he'd begun to cry, but the tears were streaming down his cheeks and dripping off his chin.

Sam closed his eyes and surrendered to the sadness and pain. Everything after that became a blur. He felt Johnny cuddle up to his side, and he found himself sandwiched between two people who loved him, his family. He cried uncontrollably for what felt like hours, but was probably closer to ten minutes, and must have fallen asleep because the next thing he knew he was being carried to his bedroom by Ben. Josie tucked him in while Gabe placed a glass of water and pain relievers on his bedside table. *Yep, I'll need those in the morning.*

Even before his family had the chance to walk out the bedroom door, Sam had closed his eyes. Tomorrow would be soon enough to come up with a plan to set into motion the changes that needed to be made.

***

Dante got off the phone and pulled his anxious lover into a tight embrace. "They found Sam. He was at home, just not answering his phone."

"Is he okay?" Spider pulled back to look Dante in the eyes.

"From what Gabe said, Sam was a bit intoxicated when they found him." Dante tried to pull off nonchalance but knew he was failing miserably.

"Drunk? But Sam barely drinks. Even when we go out, he usually stops at one beer." Spider was now acting more anxious than before they knew Sam was safe, and Dante wasn't far behind, but they had to keep his fear under wraps and move forward.

"Well, apparently Sam and a bottle of whiskey got well acquainted. He'll have one hell of a hangover tomorrow, but he's fine." Dante released Spider and stood staring out of their hotel window at the skyline of Nashville, Tennessee, the location of their latest client.

Dante had missed Sam the minute he stepped out of the door early that morning. He had to push himself to continue walking away. His heart kept pulling him back to the man they'd left sleeping in bed, the man who had grown to mean more to Dante than he'd ever expected, but his head pushed him onward. Leaving was the right thing to do. Still, Dante had picked up his cell phone countless times, waiting for Sam to call; it was maddening.

"Did he read the note?" Spider asked from across the room where he was pacing a hole into the floor. "Did he see the keys? He can't be driving that death trap around."

"No, the note is still unopened, but Sam did mention the keys, something about services rendered and being a rent boy." Dante's voice was so low he was surprised Spider heard the horrible words.

"What! Sam thinks because I left my truck that we were paying him for the time we spent together?" Spider's voice held an anger that Dante seldom heard, but he knew that anger wasn't directed at Sam. It fell on Dante's shoulders alone.

"Yes," Dante spit out around the lump in his throat.

"I knew we should have waited for Sam to wake up before we left. We could have talked to him instead of running away." Spider's voice rose with every word he spoke until he was almost shouting. "We could have worked this out!"

"He didn't ask us to stay. He easily accepted everything when we told him we would have to leave. He even smiled!" Dante's childhood had been less than stellar. He'd been forced to live with one relative after another after his dad took off. His mom wasn't sober long enough to take care of him. He swore he would never be forced on anyone ever again.

"Shit, when did you become so shitty at reading people, Major? You're supposed to be one of the best. Government-paid, first-class education and all, but somehow you missed the pain in Sam's eyes when he realized we were leaving him. Christ, what the hell were you actually seeing?" Spider's pupils were dilated and his muscles were flexing, clear signs he was agitated. "I understand that you lived through your own personal hell when you were a kid, but you gotta see we weren't pushing ourselves on him. Sam's arms were wide open."

"No, Jack, I saw Sam smile and walk away like none of this had any effect on him. That's what I saw. He laughed and smiled throughout supper, like every other night. We made love, and he fell asleep. Not a thing to indicate he was suffering in the least." Dante knew what he saw, it had killed him at the time, but he also knew this decision had been the right one...*really?*

Spider looked at him as if he was about to sprout flowers out of his ears at any moment. "You honestly didn't see how he was fighting to hold it together all night, how he would look away and blink back his tears? I thought you would have seen it just as plainly as I did."

Dante was getting a sick feeling in the pit of his stomach. Could he have projected what he thought he would see on Sam, and not what was really happening in front of him? Memories of his family members' disgusted faces flashed through his mind. The loathing in their eyes as they watched his mother stumble into the house in the middle of the night stinking of cigarettes and booze. The smiles only came when they'd finally had enough and threw them out to be another family member's problem. "We left a note asking him to contact us to discuss things."

"Like cowards, and need I remind you he hasn't read it yet. How would he know anything since neither one of us were man enough to admit how we feel?" Spider's agitation was increasing, never a good sign.

"Shit." Dante dropped his head and rubbed his throbbing temples. Could he have been so wrong?

"I need to know why. Why were you so convinced that we had to leave before Sam woke up this morning, Dante?" Spider demanded, taking two steps toward him, and Dante heard the floor groan slightly.

He turned away from Spider to stare out the window. To be honest, he just couldn't face his partner at the moment. "Because I would have told him that I was in love with him. I knew we had to go before I lost the strength to walk away."

"You know I'm in love with Sam, and you've just admitted to being in love with him, now explain to me why we left! I wanted to tell him, but you convinced me that this was for the best. That Sam would have asked us to stay if he wanted us. We didn't even fight for him." Spider turned away from Dante. "In all the years we've been together, I've always trusted your judgment, always followed where you led, but I'm not so sure you got it right this time, Major."

"Neither am I, Captain," Dante admitted.

"I'm going back," Spider said. "When this assignment is over, I'm going back to Brighton."

"What?" Dante spun around to look at Spider. "You're leaving me?"

"No, I want you to come with me. I love you, and we love Sam. We should have never left him behind." Spider's eyes pleaded for Dante to understand, to agree. "Think about it, Dante," Spider said before walking over and, without missing a beat, claiming Dante's lips in a passionate kiss. Muscles flexed, solid bodies tangled together, and their tongues dueled for domination, ending with Spider submitting to Dante. "The three of us belong together. You can't fight this, sweetheart. We'll just have to wait until your brain catches up to your heart because you are one stubborn bastard when you want to be."

Dante wrapped his arms around Spider without responding to his comments. He knew his lover was right, but the eight-year-old boy left on another relative's doorstep couldn't accept that maybe this time he really could have his dream: a home and a family of his own that would never turn him away.

Soon Dante's body began to react to the hard, muscled man pressed against him. The two had been together for over eight years, and each and every day Dante was thankful for the blessing of Spider. Not only could Spider put up with Dante's issues, he understood, and the fact that the man he loved beyond reason could turn a simple hug into a night of passion was an added bonus. Their kisses turned harder, hungrier as Dante pushed deeper into Spider's mouth. Though they were roughly the same size, Dante was a bit taller, the perfect height to lean Spider's head back and take control of the kiss. Demanding his lover's pleasure.

When Spider moaned, the vibration went straight to Dante's balls, making them heavy. The need he felt for his partner never wavered from the first moment they met in the hot sands of a war zone a world away from home, and thankfully the feeling was mutual. Dante began to kiss his way down Spider's neck, the sweet taste of his skin driving him onward. Since Spider was fresh from his shower, he was only wearing a pair of black boxer briefs, making what Dante had in mind a whole lot easier. Moans filled the air as he made his way down Spider's gorgeous body, mapping it with his lips and tongue.

Spider's skin warm and soft over hard muscle, Dante nipped at one of Spider's tan nipples before carrying on to his target. By now Spider's hips were undulating forward, attempting to get friction on his hard cock. A wet spot had formed on his boxers, testament to how turned on Spider really was. *Time to move this to the bed. But first...* Dante went to his knees before the man he loved and began to mouth Spider's hard cock through the boxers' soft fabric.

"Baby, if you keep that up this is going to be over way too quickly," Spider gasped out between moans. "God, Dante, please make love to me."

Without warning Dante tore Spider's boxers open and sucked his beautiful cock down to the root in one motion. Spider screamed and his legs shook as he tried to stop himself from orgasming in Dante's mouth.

"Dante! I want to feel you inside me before I come," Spider demanded, but his hips kept pumping his leaking cock in and out of Dante's warm mouth. The taste of his salty precum and sweet skin drove Dante on, sucking harder while gently cupping Spider's heavy balls.

Dante was too far gone to make it to the bed; quickly he lowered the waist of his sleep pants and wrapped his hand around his own cock. He pulled away from Spider's shaft to concentrate on his furry balls, lapping and sucking until Spider began to pump his own cock. Spider's eyes were half closed, mouth open, panting between moans, skin flushed and a sheen of sweat glistened across his broad chest. *God, I'm a lucky bastard.*

Images of the third man in their triad flashed through his mind, his red hair and dark brown eyes looking up at him begging for release. Funny that Dante didn't feel like he was cheating on Spider by thinking of the man when he had Spider's cock back in his mouth, it felt right. His smaller body fit perfectly between them, his soft skin pressed close, the love they shared. *Love!*

If it was even possible, his cock got even harder and began to pulse. Knowing he had little time left before he came, Dante wanted to give his lover his release before his own. Burying his nose into Spider's pubic hair, Dante swallowed over and over again around his hard cock. He brought his wonderful, passionate partner to orgasm with a loud cry and drank him down. Seconds later Dante felt the telltale rush of heat down his spine, into his balls and out the end of his pulsing cock.

Dante licked Spider clean; the second he was finished Spider pushed him back onto the floor and licked Dante's softening cock, cleaning every last drop of cum he could find. Dante lay unmoving with his leg and arms spread, allowing Spider to do as he wished, before he curled up at Dante's side.

"I love you so much, Dante."

"I love you too, sweetheart. I can't imagine my life without you in it."

They sat silently basking in the afterglow of their lovemaking when Spider asked the one question Dante didn't see coming. "Were you thinking of Sam?"

Dante wasn't sure how to answer that question. Would his lover be angry that he'd had both men on his mind when he was loving on Spider? Would he understand? Hell, Dante didn't fully understand himself. But above everything else he needed to be honest with Spider. "Yes, he was there. Like he always is." Dante turned to face away from his lover, unsure how Spider would receive the news. Sam had been in Dante's thoughts since the first time he met the man in the ER of Brighton General.

Spider's large hand gently turned Dante's head so that they were looking eye to eye. He'd expected to find anger, sadness, even hate in those eyes, but what he saw wasn't even close to what he'd expected. Happiness.

"Dante, it's okay. Hell, it's more than okay. You love him just like I do," Spider reassured before cupping Dante's cheek and kissing him with such tenderness that no one would expect out of a man Spider's size.

"Do you think of him when we make love?" Dante asked.

"I think about both of the men I love whether I'm with them or not. I'm completely dedicated to both of you; I couldn't be with anyone other than my two men. We belong together." Spider's eyes begged for Dante to understand.

Dante pulled Spider to his feet and led him toward the bed; after long moments of touching and kissing both settled for the night. Long after Spider's breathing evened out, Dante was still awake trying to make sense of the last five weeks and how he'd fallen so completely in love with the adorable redhead. The big question was what to do next; for the first time in many years Dante felt unsure of his actions and he didn't like that one bit.

Chapter Four

Sam knew his brain had to be leaking out of his ears. His eyeballs felt like they had sand the size of small boulders floating around inside them. Everything around him sounded muffled and fuzzy, but that could have been because his head wouldn't stop pounding. Sam's throat felt dry and raw, and his body seemed too heavy to be bothered trying to move. He and Mr. Beam were no longer friends.

The heavenly smell of bacon filled his bedroom, but Sam's stomach wasn't ready to face the world just yet, so he burrowed farther under his blankets. Apparently, his late-night visitors had yet to leave. Sam honestly didn't mind as long as they stayed on the other side of that door; after all, he had everything he needed right here. A bed, bathroom, water, and most importantly, pain relievers for his tender head.

It was not to be as moments later, the door opened and his peace was broken. "Wake up, sleepyhead." Evidently his sister Jamie hadn't gotten the memo to leave him alone. "Come on, it's time to get up. Lunch is ready."

"Go away," Sam grumbled without even lifting his head to look at her.

"No can do, big brother." Within seconds, his fortress of blankets was unceremoniously destroyed, allowing sunlight to pour into his swollen eyes and causing him to hiss and groan in pain. "Oh come on. You're not a vampire, so stop hissing at me. Need I remind you that you did this to yourself, puzzle-boy," Jamie teased before opening yet another damn drape.

Sam couldn't help but smile at the nickname his sister had given to him almost ten years ago. Jamie was much younger than Sam, and he had turned nineteen and just begun to explore his fascination with tattoos. A young Jamie claimed that the tattoos on Sam's body were like puzzle pieces being put back together. Of course, Jamie was the only one allowed to call him by that name, and Sam actually had a stunning tattoo of his sister on his right shoulder blade made out of puzzle pieces in her honor.

"Let me die in peace, brat," Sam grumbled before slamming the pillow over his head and groaning again. *I'm going to die. At least she could leave me in peace while I do.*

"Nope." Jamie laughed, and Sam was powerless not to smile, at least until his pillow was torn away from his face. "Time to get up."

"Hey, give me that back!" Sam yelled, but immediately regretted it and grabbed for his aching head. "Oh, ouch...ouch."

"Serves you right for drinking half a bottle of whiskey instead of calling me when they left. What were you thinking?" All laughter fled from her voice. She sat down on the bed and wrapped her arms around a now silent Sam. "I'm so sorry, big brother. I wish I could take all this away."

Sam wanted to hide in his sister's embrace and pretend the last couple days never happened, but he couldn't. He had to face the world. "I'll be okay, Jamie. I knew what I was getting myself into. My eyes were wide open."

"I know, but I thought things had changed over the past couple weeks," Jamie said before squeezing him even harder. Sam had thought things had progressed past their agreement as well, but he had been so very wrong to have hoped.

"Things did change. I fell in love with them, which is just fabulous, considering they don't love me back." Sam slowly sat up and crawled to the edge of the bed, aiming his sore body toward the bathroom. "I would be grateful if you could relay that everything is fine to whoever else is in my house, and tell them to just let it go." He couldn't stand the thought of his family and friends looking at him with sympathy in their eyes, or worse, pity.

"But Sam—" Jamie pushed on.

"No, Jamie. Please, little sis." Sam smiled at his sister to take the sting out of his clipped words. "Please, tell them I don't want to talk about it. Not yet. I'm just not ready to rehash all the glorious details, okay?"

Jamie stood and walked over to Sam, pulling him into a tight embrace, as if trying to give Sam some of her strength. He loved his sister. After a few minutes of standing in the center of the room and holding on to each other for dear life, Jamie finally took a step back. With a slight nod, she gave her agreement and turned toward his bedroom door. "I'll see you in a few minutes." Sam wasn't so gone that he didn't realize it wasn't a question; it was a statement. She would come back in and drag him out naked if he didn't show his face in a reasonable amount of time.

"Yes, Jamie." Sam chuckled before taking the final few steps into the bathroom and closing the door, temporarily locking the world out once again.

Sam walked into his multihead, gray porcelain-tiled shower. He would sometimes dream about coming home after a long shift and just standing there, allowing the body sprayers to relax his tight muscles. The water brushing his body, the decadence making him feel special. This had been his one big splurge when remodeling his 1970s rancher, but now the shower felt cold and empty, even bigger than it used to seem.

Sam rubbed soap across his smooth chest, letting his mind wander for a moment. Almost immediately memories from the last time the three of them were in this very shower together a few days ago came flooding into his mind.

Rough hands and soft lips explored his overheated body, mapping their territory by feel, sharing long, slow kisses. Three bodies slid together, wet and soapy, in a dance of passion and need. Spider's big fingers were buried deep inside Sam, brushing against his prostate with each pass. Dante pumped his hard dick at a slow, almost torturous pace. They kept bringing him to the edge of release with their fingers, hands, and mouths but never giving him that last little push to fall over the edge.

You like that, sweetheart? You want me to fill you up, don't you? Sam moaned and reached for his hardening cock. *I think he does, Spider. Give our Sam what he needs while I suck this beautiful cock down.* Sam could almost feel Dante's warm mouth surrounding his shaft, and he began to pump himself faster. *Ready for me, baby?* The pressure and slight burn morphed into pleasure within seconds, leaving Sam panting with need. *That's it, feel me deep inside you, baby. All for you, Sam, always you.*

Spider began to buck his hips harder as Dante took Sam's cock back down his throat and swallowed repeatedly. Sam was so close. Wrapped in their cocoon of steam, Sam could feel the connection flowing between them, the love. It was in every touch, every word, and every look. Dante came with a muffled shout, shooting his seed onto the tiled shower floor. Spider roared just before filling his condom. Sam's balls drew up tight to his body as fire raced down his spine through his swollen balls and he came in Dante's waiting mouth. The beauty in that one moment almost brought Sam to his knees.

He sighed with contentment, but reality all too quickly began seeping into Sam's bliss. Slowly, he opened his eyes and found himself standing under the streams of hot water, holding his own spent dick in his hand, alone. No lovers, no forever, just alone. Anger raged through him. He released himself and balled his hand into a fist, then punched the glass soap dish as hard as he could before slumping down into the corner of the shower. He cried for the loss of the two men he loved, letting the water wash away his tears of loss and blood from his cut hand.

He didn't know how long he sat there, lost in his own thoughts, before a soft knock brought him back to reality. Thank God, he had a large hot water tank.

"Sam, are you okay, son?" Jack Mason, Sam's dad, asked before opening the door.

Sam stood and met his father at the tiled opening of the shower. Being careful to leave his left hand behind his back, he answered, "I'm fine, Dad. I'll be out in a few minutes."

His dad took one look at him and shook his head. "You're not fooling me. I'm your father, and I've been a paramedic a long time, so I can tell that you're in pain and I don't mean just the emotional kind either. Let me see it."

Gingerly, Sam brought his left hand around to the front of his body and displayed a bloody mess. His knuckles were cut open, and the back of his hand had a long, jagged cut running up toward his wrist. From what he could feel, Sam was pretty sure there would be glass found in there somewhere.

"Oh Sam. Get out of there right now. I need to wrap that to slow the bleeding before we can take a good look at it," his dad ordered while reaching into the attached linen closet for towels.

Sam turned and shut the water off before leaving the shower. He wasn't worried about his nudity in front of his father but was a bit concerned about the throbbing hand he had cradled to his chest. Sam was still unable to look his father in the eyes. Not only had he gotten himself drunk as a skunk, now he was headed to the hospital to have glass removed from his shredded hand. *God, I'm a mess.*

"Get this wrapped around you." His dad draped a soft bathrobe around Sam before gently covering his left hand with a smaller towel. Sam slid one hand after another through the sleeves of his robe, and his dad tied his belt. "Look at me, son."

It was an order, plain and simple.

Sam raised his head to look his dad in the eyes, expecting to see disappointment and anger, but instead finding compassion and sadness. "Now, enough of this. What's done is done, and no amount of hurting yourself is going to make that change. You understand, son?"

Sam nodded, unable to find his voice at that moment.

"You won't be doing anything like this in the future." Again, not a question but an order.

"Yes, Dad. I didn't mean to do it at all. I just got so angry." Sam attempted to explain what drove him to hitting the dish but thought better of it. Explaining what used to happen in this shower on a regular basis wasn't going to happen, ever.

"Okay, that's done then. Let's get you cleaned up for the ride to the hospital." His dad walked back out into the bedroom holding Sam's hand high into the air.

"You think I need to go to the hospital?" Sam asked while being ushered to sit on his bed. "We could probably take care of it here."

"You and I both know there's likely glass in there that needs to be removed. And we need to make sure you haven't done any major damage to the nerves in your hand," Jack answered before yelling for someone to bring him the first aid kit from the kitchen, which seemed to have the effect of bringing everyone in the house running. A herd of cattle would have made less noise.

"Here, what do you need?" Gabe ran in with a huge red first aid kit. *Where the hell did he get that?* Sam had the typical first aid kit in his house, not the industrial version.

"We need to stop the bleeding, get him dressed, and take him to the hospital." His dad was always a man who got straight to the point; why change now?

His mom, Jane, stood a few feet away with her back turned to them to give him privacy while Dad, Gabe, and Ben helped to bandage his hand and get him dressed. Jamie, Josie, and Johnny waited in the hall until he was completely dressed, and then they came in demanding answers.

"What happened to your hand? Oh God, how bad is it?" Jamie went into hysterics the minute she saw the amount of blood on various towels across his bed. "Sam, you said you were okay."

Before Sam could rush to explain, his dad took over. "It was an accident. Sam and I had ourselves a talk, and it's over." By the tone of his voice, everyone knew this wasn't up for discussion; it was over. Sam avoided eye contact with just about everybody, embarrassed by what he'd done.

"Okay, let's get you over to Brighton General to have that looked at," Ben said and helped Sam to his feet while his dad continued to keep his hand elevated.

"I'll bring the truck around," Josie said before rushing out of the door.

"How are you feeling, Sam?" Johnny asked.

"I'm okay, really. Hey, at least my headache's gone." Sam gave a halfhearted attempt to lighten the mood. He felt badly for making his entire family worry; it was just a broken heart, not a life-threatening illness.

His mom stepped into Sam's path and placed both of her small hands on either side of his face. She stood for a few moments simply looking into Sam's eyes, as if searching for something. Sam waited. It didn't take long before she smiled sadly and kissed him on his cheek. "You'll be just fine, even stronger because of it, my beautiful boy. Please believe me, in time this pain will lessen."

"I hope so, Mom," Sam admitted, because the pain he was feeling at that moment made it hard to breathe.

"It will. Just remember you have your family to lean on, whenever you need us." Jane Mason's face took on that same look of determination she got just after making a decision. "You can come home to stay for a while until you heal."

"I love you, Mom. Thank you for the offer, but I'm going to stay here. I'll be fine."

"I love you too, Sam. If you need anything, we're just a phone call away."

Six hours later, Sam found himself bundled up on his couch under the watchful eye of both Jamie and Johnny. The remaining family members who had invaded his house had gone to their own homes to sleep or they were on shift at the firehouse. Jamie was still on summer break, so she parked herself at Sam's side. Johnny could work from just about anywhere with his new personally designed laptop. He had suffered third-degree burns on his hands in an office building fire—the same fire in which Johnny had saved both Josie's life and that of another co-worker.

So now, Sam had babysitters and two weeks off to allow his hand to heal and have the sixteen stitches removed. Luckily, he hadn't cut anything major. The doctor did find pieces of glass in one of the larger wounds on the top of his hand and spent quite a while pulling them all out. Dr. Green confirmed that everything would heal just fine, but when he returned to work, Sam would have to be placed on light duty until he regained his strength in that hand. Sam felt like an ass. He'd learned his lesson and wouldn't be punching anything anytime soon.

"Do you need anything, Sam?" Johnny asked for what had to be the fifth time in the last hour.

"No thank you, Johnny. You know, you two can go home as well. I'm completely capable of taking care of myself." Sam felt bad enough for all the chaos he'd created in the last twenty-four hours; he didn't want to force them to stay.

"We're only hanging out for a few days," Jamie answered. "Besides, I have to return to fall classes in three days, and I want to spend them with you."

"And you know how I hate being home alone when Gabe's on shift at the fire station. At least here I've got you two," Johnny said, shrugging his shoulders.

Sam shook his head. He wanted to call bullshit on both of them but didn't have the heart. He knew full well they'd stuck around to help and support him, and he loved them for it. Now, if they were still here after two days, Sam knew he'd probably be reconsidering that statement.

"Thank you, guys."

"Anytime, bro."

"Definitely, anytime," Johnny agreed, still flipping through Sam's DVD collection.

Sam's cell phone began ringing with the tone he'd assigned for Spider. This was the third time it rang in the past two hours, and just like the last two times, he ignored it. Sam wasn't ready to talk to either of them, not yet. He couldn't begin to heal and move forward if he held on to a false hope that they would come back to him.

"Do you want me to answer that for you, Sam?" Jamie offered and leaned forward, as if to grab the phone off the coffee table.

"No, Jamie, please leave it be. I don't want to have to deal with that right now. Hell, I don't even know why they're calling me in the first place," Sam sighed. He was hurting and confused. *Why do they keep calling me? How can I move forward if they refuse to stay out of my life?*

"Maybe you should open their letter?" Johnny offered with a hopeful expression, pointing toward the sealed envelope beside his phone.

"Not quite ready to do that yet. I just want to let everything settle for a little while before I go digging into things. Please understand. This has to be the way I deal with it."

Johnny smiled in understanding as Sam's phone stopped ringing.

"I'm guessing Dante and Spider know about my little visit to the hospital?" Sam asked his two nursemaids. When neither would look him in the eye, he had his answer. "Why would you tell them?" Sam was embarrassed enough when he thought it was only his family who knew about his breakdown.

"They care about you, and they're worried," Jamie answered.

"Care about me? You've got to be kidding, sis. If they cared, they would have stayed, to hell with the agreement. But they didn't. There's nothing left to talk about. It's over. Hell, Jamie, they snuck out, for Christ's sake, so they wouldn't have to face me in the morning. It was nothing but a fling for them." Sam stopped to take a deep breath. None of this was Jamie's fault; she just refused to see the truth. "I'm sorry, Jamie. I don't mean to get upset with you. I have no right to be upset at all. They did nothing wrong. I knew what I was getting myself into from the start. They were always honest, and neither one of them ever treated me badly."

"It's all going to be okay, puzzle-boy. You have a lot of people who love you." Jamie cuddled closer to Sam and wrapped her thin arms around his shoulders. "You're stuck with all of us."

"I can live with that," Sam teased.

"So, which DVD marathon are we watching tonight? *Star Wars, Star Trek*, or *Dancing with the Stars*?"

"Oh honey, *Dancing with the Stars* of course," Sam said, grabbing a bag of pretzels off the coffee table covered in junk food and dragging his bottle of water closer to the edge.

The three cuddled, laughed, ate, and cried into the wee hours of the morning. Sam knew they were all waiting for his inevitable breakdown so they could help him put the pieces back together. He loved his family.

***

Spider stood with his back flush against the wall, but he still found himself surrounded by drunk college students. Another night, another party. Lights flashed in a rainbow of colors, while a dry ice machine created a mist to float around the partygoers. This assignment was wearing thin on Spider very quickly, and if Mandy Cartright's (heiress to the Cartright fortune) stalker didn't make a move soon, he was going to lose his shit. Dammit, if he was groped by another co-ed, he was going to pick Miss Cartright up and carry her surgically enhanced ass out of the club screaming like a two-year-old if he had to.

Spider turned slightly and made eye contact with Dante, who stood in a relaxed pose a few feet away from their dancing client. Actually, the girl's father was their client, but why argue over semantics? Spider wasn't fooled by Dante's casual stance. His eyes were dark, his jaw had a steady tic, and that one vein on the side of his neck was sending out a rhythm that would make any drum corps proud. Yep, his lover was pissed.

He scanned the crowd and found the four remaining members of their team scattered throughout the darkened club. Each of them wore earpieces so they could communicate no matter the distance or noise. Over the years, all six had worked together on hundreds of assignments across the globe, and they knew more about each other than most families. They were all military vets, across multiple divisions and disciplines of the armed forces, all under Dante's command. Even though they weren't in the service any longer, their new team and the lives they'd saved gave them purpose. Only one person was missing from their group in Spider's opinion, and he just prayed they could fix what they'd done to Sam before it was too late.

"So, did he pick up?" Shannon's voice came through his earpiece, breaking up the constant pounding of the bass. A Navy Engineer and one of the world's leading hackers, if Shannon decided to set her sights on you, there was nowhere you could hide.

"No," Dante answered flatly. The longer this assignment carried on, the less likely it would be for Sam to forgive them and give them a second chance.

"Well, you just gotta go back there and sweep the guy off his feet," Shannon stated, as if that wasn't obvious. They both knew they had a lot to make up for.

"Do I look like some sort of Romeo to you?" Dante grumbled as another heavily intoxicated blonde clung to his tattooed bicep.

The blonde's voice slurred across their earpieces. "Heyyy, baaaby, wanna dance?" Just to make sure Dante knew exactly what she meant by dance, the woman rubbed her chest along his arm and pressed it into her cleavage.

Dante carefully extracted her long black nails from his flesh, never taking his eyes off their client. "No, thank you, miss."

"Oh, come on, honey, we could have some fun." She wasn't giving up. Spider would have admired her tenacity, if he didn't want to walk over there and remove her bony fingers from his lover's arm.

Dante extricated himself from her hold yet again and then pointed his finger directly at Spider, who smiled knowingly in return. "That's the man I'm going home with. You don't stand a chance, miss. Run along and find someone else to play with." Spider couldn't help the rush of arousal that always came when Dante claimed him. The man had always been upfront and open when it came to Spider, never hiding their relationship or love. *I just hope he finds a way to show all of that love to Sam because I know it's there.*

Apparently, the girl didn't appreciate how polite Dante was being, or just didn't care, if her next statement was any indication. "You're a fag! Fuck, what a waste!" The bigoted disgust was nothing new to either of them.

"Hey, get away from my bodyguard, you slut!" Mandy Cartright flew across the floor and stood between the now irate blonde and Dante, as if to protect him. Spider thought it was sort of sweet.

"You have fags for bodyguards, Mandy?" As if the choice of who Dante slept with affected his ability to protect the young heiress. "It's disgusting."

Mandy laughed at the girl before answering. "What bugs you more, Faith, the fact that he's gay or the fact that he has better standards than to lower himself to fuck you?"

Shannon had slipped in behind the blonde undetected, preparing for the inevitable freak-out, and on cue the blonde went off, lunging for Mandy. Dante quickly placed Mandy behind his back, and Shannon easily contained the blonde with a few simple moves.

"Let me go, bitch!" screamed the irate woman.

"Oh, but, honey, you're my type. Don't you want to 'dance' with me?" Shannon purred into the blonde's ear, making the woman freeze to the spot. "Now, walk away and have fun, miss."

Shannon abruptly released the blonde, and the woman quickly melted into the crowd, never once looking back. With a nod, Mandy returned to the dance floor, as if all was right in the world again.

"So, boss man, we all know you're nowhere near being a Romeo. But you're going to have to learn if you even think you have a chance at winning Sam back. Remember, you two left the guy." Shannon carried on with their conversation as if the last few minutes with the blonde weren't worth discussing.

Spider remembered all too well how they had left Sam. This had been four of the most agonizing days he'd ever experienced, and he'd spent weeks in South American jungles in places where, if the heat didn't kill you, half the creatures within five hundred feet would happily do the job. After four days of unanswered calls, Spider knew they were running out of time to save their relationship. The longer they were away, the smaller the chance at a happy ending for everyone.

"I don't need to be reminded. Now get back to work and stay out of our personal lives," Dante ordered before shifting away from Shannon in an attempt to end the conversation.

"Little chance of that happening, Major. You've stuck your nose in our business for far too many years, sir." Jake's reply came through their earpieces, even if no one could spot him. Jake had belonged to a special ops unit of Marines before he retired. The man could hide in plain sight; he was absolutely amazing. His code name was Shadow.

"Yeah, Major, you and Spider have managed to ruin my sex life," Coop groused from his position beside the busy bar.

"Really? The last time we 'interfered,' we saved you from almost getting yourself killed by the same guy you were just getting 'friendly' with outside a bar in Sao Paulo. If we hadn't shown up, he would have had that syringe plunged in the side of your neck before you even had a chance to introduce him to 'little Coop,'" Spider reminded him as he continually scanned the room for threats.

"'Little Coop'? There ain't anything little about me. Besides, let's get back to your fuck-up, shall we?"

"Do you really want to have a life with Sam?" Shannon asked as she mingled into the crowd and disappeared. "That's the question, because you're not going to get it by sitting back and waiting."

"We have a job to do." Dante's voice was hard, and he refused to look Spider in the eye. Over the years, Spider had become proficient at reading the man he loved, and he knew Dante was struggling with his own guilt while trying to reconcile the ghosts of his past.

"So, on a scale of one to ten, how pissed would you be if say...I took a little look-see into your Sam?" Shannon asked in a voice that could melt ice in the dead of winter.

"What?" Spider yelled, causing several people to step a few feet away from him. "Why the hell would you do that?"

"Well, like you so eloquently pointed out to Coop, sometimes men think with their smaller heads. We have to watch out for one another. We're family," Shannon explained.

Dante was growling low and steady by now, his eyes scanning the crowd again. "You had no right, Shannon."

"You would have done the same thing if it were any of us." Vincent decided to join the conversation. He was typically the quiet one, ever watchful. Ex-Navy SEAL and specialist in hand-to-hand combat, Vincent could take down an armed man three times his size without a weapon in under three seconds. "So, whatcha find out?"

"Shannon," Dante growled a warning. "Leave it be."

"Calm down. I didn't find anything horrible. Only a few parking tickets. Oh, and he was locked up for a night by the Marshals a few years back."

"It was his blind date who was the criminal. Sam was cleared of any wrongdoing," Spider said, defending his love. No way would he allow anyone to say one bad word about Sam. The man truly didn't deserve it.

"Oh, I know that, Spider. Sam's aunts set him up on that date. Those women are scary crazy. I can't wait to meet them." Shannon looked up for a second and Spider could see the uncertainty in her eyes before she vanished back into the writhing mass of partygoers.

"Meet them?" Dante asked.

"Yeah, when we're done here," Jake answered on behalf of the four other members of their team. "What? You guys thought you could just leave us behind? Not a chance, boss man. We just have to set up a new base of operations out of Brighton."

"You guys want to come with us?" Spider asked in shock. He had never thought the rest of their team would want to follow them to the small town, but he was so happy they were.

Four resounding "Yes's" came across Spider's earpiece.

"Hey, did you know that Sam volunteers at the animal rescue in town as well as the free clinic on his days off?" Shannon asked.

"Yes." Spider and Dante both knew Sam had a deep sense of responsibility to his community. It was one of the things they'd admired about Sam right from the beginning.

"How about his decision to sell that VW Bug of his?" Shannon continued.

"He'd never sell that thing. He loves it. Christ, he talks to it." Spider could feel his heart beginning to speed up. He knew his Sam loved that old piece of rusted metal. Christ, Spider had left his own vehicle behind so Sam would be safe, but he'd never imagined he would sell his Bug.

"Well, I don't know about that, but the ad has been posted for over twenty-four hours." Shannon reappeared on the opposite side of the room.

Dante finally looked Spider in the eyes. They both knew how much Sam loved that death trap of a car. Something was seriously wrong with the man they loved.

Before Spider could think any further on why Sam would sell his car, he noticed an older male headed straight for Mandy. His graying hair stood in stark contrast to the purples, pinks, and blues around him. He didn't belong in here.

Spider began to move toward their client. "Male, gray hair, blue shirt, closing in fast." The man was within fifteen feet of the young heiress, who was dancing without a care in the world. *Shit!*

Spider and Dante were physically pushing people out of their way on the dance floor, the loud music easily drowning out any complaints. Ten feet away, an evil smile curved the man's lips as his eyes looked their fill of the young woman's body. *Sick bastard isn't getting anywhere near her.*

"Is everyone in place?" Dante asked.

Four affirmatives made Spider feel a whole lot better about Mandy's safety. Shannon came out of the throng of people and began to dance with their client. She leaned in, smiling and laughing, acting as if a possible stalker wasn't ten feet away. She had to make the scene believable. The two talked and danced while the man stood staring at the women. Shannon soon took Mandy's hand and led her from the dance floor.

"We're headed out the back entrance toward our vehicles, which should give this asshole plenty of time to catch up to us," Shannon confirmed.

"We'll meet you out there. Be careful," Dante confirmed. He and Spider broke off their pursuit and walked out of the club by the front doors.

"If you think an old man with some sick, delusional crush on a barely twenty-one-year-old girl could get the best of me, boss, then we need to talk." Spider could hear Mandy laughing in the background over his earpiece.

"In position, boss." Jake's voice cut into their conversation.

"In position," Coop whispered from behind a stack of steel crates.

"Same," Vincent confirmed as he climbed the side of a nearby building without a harness.

"Remember he could be armed," Dante said.

Spider slid his back against the red four-door he was using as cover. The sound of female voices was getting closer as Shannon and Mandy carried on a conversation sure to get her stalker's attention. They had practiced this takedown at least a half dozen times with the heiress. Spider only hoped that, when the time came, the young woman wouldn't freeze.

Dante was three cars over on the other side of the walkway the women were currently using. "How far back is he?"

"He's fallen back to about twenty feet. He's spooked," Vincent confirmed from his position. They needed the man to make the first move, to assure themselves he was indeed Mandy's stalker.

"Don't worry. We've got this, boys." Those words always caused Spider to cringe every time Shannon spoke them. "I'll have him right over here in just a minute."

Shannon took a big breath in, gave Mandy a devilish smirk, which the woman returned, and put on a performance bound to get any jealous stalker's attention. "Oh, Mandy, that hot young thing had his eyes all over you. I bet if we go back in there, we could find him, see if he wants to come party with us. My dad's gone away for the weekend, and the mansion has four stocked bars. By the looks of that huge bulge in the front of his pants, you're so going to get pounded tonight, girlfriend."

Mandy giggled like a schoolgirl. She was really getting into playing along with Shannon. "Really? You think he's interested in me? His father's the head of the board of directors on one of my dad's charities. Hell, his jeans were so tight, I bet they were cutting off circulation to his feet."

"Oh, honey, it's not his feet you need to have circulation." Shannon laughed, a huge smile covering her face. Spider knew Shannon was getting a kick out of "playtime."

"How dare you talk to Mandy like she's a common slut, you whore!" the man bellowed. Shannon and Mandy turned around and got their first look at Mandy Cartright's stalker. "Mandy's a good girl who needs someone to take care of her. To keep the vulgar and disgusting people in our society away from her. She's special! Step away from her!" The man pulled a six-inch hunting knife from the pocket of his jacket and pointed it at Shannon.

"Mr. Hughes?" That was all that was said by Mandy before the team converged on the man who had been terrorizing an innocent young woman. Dante took him to the ground, removing the hunting knife from his hand and throwing it out of reach. Spider pinned the man's arms behind his back and secured his wrists with handcuffs. The man struggled, but it was useless; they had him. Jake and Coop held their Glocks at the ready while both Shannon and Vincent stood protectively in front of Mandy, who by now was crying and slipping into shock.

"Call the police and Mr. Cartright," Dante ordered, and Coop put his gun back in its holster, grabbed his cell, and began dialing.

"Mr. Hughes, why?" Mandy yelled at the older man leaning against the tire of a car.

"You know him, Mandy?" Dante asked.

"Yes, he's one of the guidance counselors at my school. He was helping me bridge my credits over to the university." Mandy's eyes turned hard. "I even told the bastard how much my stalker was scaring me."

Spider would like to have a word with the person who ran the background checks on behalf of Mr. Cartright, because obviously they were incompetent or involved somehow.

Spider turned away from the sniveling, disheveled man with a disgusted grunt. This man had been in a position of power over Mandy, and he'd used it to take advantage of her. He was supposed to be helping her. "You won't have to worry about him anymore, Mandy."

"But I love you, Mandy. I did everything for you!" Mr. Hughes yelled out. Dante immediately ripped a piece of the hem of his own shirt and gagged the delusional man. No one wanted Mandy upset. They weren't going to give the asshole any more power over the frightened young woman.

Soon cars began arriving. Officers took custody of Mr. Hughes, placing the now mumbling man into the back of a cruiser, and the knife was taken into evidence. Mr. Cartright held Mandy tightly; it was easy to see how much he loved his daughter.

"We leave at 0600, Jack." Spider knew something was up because Dante had used his given name. "I've been a stubborn fool. I was so wrapped up in the past that I didn't realize I'd fallen completely in love with him." Dante stepped forward, pulled Spider into his arms, and kissed him thoroughly. "This doesn't mean I love you any less, you know that."

"Of course I know that. I love you and Sam. I love the three of us together," Spider said.

Dante's smile transformed his face, and Spider could do nothing but smile back. "Then we better tell the rest of the team, pack up, and head back to Brighton. There's this gorgeous, kind, redheaded nurse whom we need to beg until he takes us back."

"I can't wait," Spider agreed before dragging Dante in for a quick hug. He loved Dante and he loved Sam. No matter what happened, Spider wouldn't give up either of his men.

Chapter Five

Sam had finally been left in peace two days earlier, and he hated it with a passion, which surprised even him. Before he had Dante and Spider living with him, Sam didn't mind being alone—yet another thing that had changed in the last five weeks. The house felt hollow, quiet, and far too empty. That was just one of the many reasons he now found himself standing outside the Brighton Animal Shelter. Sam had been considering adopting a rescue dog over the past couple years but had never gotten around to taking the leap. Now was the perfect time. He had a huge, fenced-in backyard. He also had time and, most importantly, love to give.

Without a doubt, the last four days had taught Sam a valuable lesson: never, ever expect a happy ending. He missed all the little things the three of them used to do together. Mornings before work were reserved for snuggling under the covers and watching the morning news, unless the snuggling got carried away. Saturdays they went grocery shopping together, Fridays were date night, Sunday afternoons they watched sports and barbequed with friend and family. Now he was left to pick up the pieces and move on alone…well, he wasn't alone anymore.

He knew most people would advise him not to make any major decisions right then, but Sam was positive now was the perfect time. He could hear numerous dogs barking before he even opened the door. Brighton had a no-kill shelter that housed dogs that had been abandoned, abused, or simply surrendered because their owners would not or could not take care of them any longer. This would be the perfect place to find his new friend and give a dog a new start and loving home.

Sam would be lying to himself if he didn't admit hoping the pain would lighten a little with his new family member, but he knew in his soul, the healing would only come in time— a very long time, if ever. He still hadn't been brave enough to answer his former lovers' calls or to open the letter they'd left. He would eventually, just not today...or tomorrow.

"Good morning, Sam. You dropping off donations again?" Harry, the shelter manager, asked as he walked into the reception area. If two plastic patio chairs and an old Formica desk constituted a reception area, this was it. Sam filed that little tidbit of information away to be brought up during the next nurses' fund-raiser. Harry deserved better than this for all the good the man did; Sam would make sure that he got what he needed.

"No. No donations today, Harry. I think it's time I get myself a dog."

"Well, I wondered when you'd finally get around to that. You come in here every week to help out, and I've seen the way you are with the dogs. You're a natural. Come on back." Harry opened the door, allowing Sam into the private area of the shelter. Harry was in his late sixties and would require an assistant sooner rather than later, but there would be no talk about retiring for the man. This shelter was Harry's life's work. They would have to carry the man out when his day ever came.

Sam followed Harry into the kennels. The dogs lucky enough to be here received better treatment than they would have in a lot of places, which was an unfortunate fact, but in Brighton, donations and volunteers kept everything running smoothly. Each animal had their own good-sized pen with a bed, toys, water, and food. Hell, some of these poor animals had it better now than they did with their original owners.

Sam recognized most of the dogs in residence since he volunteered in the shelter, but he was looking for one particular golden retriever. Buddy had been surrendered to the shelter because his owner could no longer afford his medication and vet bills. Buddy was a middle-aged dog with Type 1 diabetes that required insulin injections daily and regular visits to a vet. You might as well have stamped "unadoptable" on the poor guy's pen, but it made no difference to Sam.

He and Buddy had a bond from the moment they caught sight of one another. A couple times a week, Sam would bring in another toy or treat, and Buddy would be waiting. The dog would follow him around the kennels and outside into the fenced yard as Sam cleaned the yards and pens or anything else needed. It was their thing.

Harry stopped directly in front of Buddy's pen. He knew who Sam had set his eyes on. Buddy looked about ready to explode with excitement when he saw Sam. "I believe this is the dog for you." Harry gave Sam a knowing look.

"Yes, he's perfect. Thank you, Harry. You have no idea what this means to me." Sam couldn't wait to bring this golden bundle home.

"I think I do, Sam." Harry placed a comforting arm around Sam's shoulders and looked pointedly at Sam's bandaged left hand.

Sam just looked at Harry, hoping like hell he wasn't talking about what Sam thought he was but doubted he was wrong. "You know, then? And I imagine half the town as well."

"Yes, it's a reasonably small town, Sam, and lots of people care greatly about you." He knew Harry was trying to be comforting, but the pit in Sam's stomach was growing by the second.

Sam shouldn't have been surprised to find out a good portion of the town already knew Dante and Spider had left, and Sam had injured his hand. The "white hair crew" knew all, and Sam's own grandmother belonged to it. But it still stung.

"Let's get Buddy outta there before he has a coronary from all that bouncing." Sam chose to ignore what Harry had said and concentrate on his new dog, who was currently darting around his pen like a puppy instead of the six-year-old he truly was.

Harry smiled, not missing the change in subject. Thankfully, he didn't call Sam on it but instead unlocked Buddy's pen. Sam was engulfed in a ball of furry happiness, tongue kisses, and excited barks, which filled the room. Exactly what Sam needed.

***

As Buddy settled on the backseat of Spider's SUV with his safety harness in place, Sam backed out of his parking spot. He still considered it Spider's truck even if his former lover had left it to him. Sam wasn't entirely certain why he was still driving the damn thing around or why he'd sold his Bug. It just felt like it was time to grow up. His family was still shocked by the news.

After all, Sam couldn't count how many times Dante or Spider had called his car a death trap and made him promise never to drive it again. But Sam had one last road trip in mind for the old girl before he handed his baby over to her new owner, and neither of his ex-lovers would ever know. *And why do I even care?*

Sam turned his vehicle around and was about to pull out onto the highway when he noticed the same man he'd run into at the grocery store that morning. He was now sitting in a car in the parking lot across the street from the animal shelter. That same anxious feeling twisted around Sam's spine and squeezed just as it had done when the same man physically ran into him outside of the grocery store.

It had occurred earlier in the day and the event had seemed so odd that Sam couldn't help but remember. His dark hair was gelled back, his black eyes seemed dead and if that didn't get his attention, the gun tattooed to his neck certainly did. Sam had quickly apologized for running into the man, even though he was pretty sure he'd done nothing wrong. The man's cold eyes regarded him and seemed to find him lacking somehow; he grunted before turning away.

I've never seen him around town before, and now twice in one day? Maybe he's lost. Maybe he's following me... "Yeah right! Buddy, let's go home, boy, because your new master is obviously losing his ever-loving mind." Sam laughed at his overactive imagination. "I can show you around your new home, and then we'll get ready for our little weekend getaway."

Sam was sure he was racking up a lot of check marks in the "things not to do as a new pet owner" column by taking his dog on a road trip, but in truth, the two had been around each other and working together every week for the better part of a year.

Buddy responded by shifting his tail into overdrive and setting a pretty impressive pace on the seat. The dark-haired man didn't even look up when Sam passed him on the road, which made Sam feel like an even bigger fool for thinking the guy was following him. After a quick stop at the pet supply store to pick up a doggie bed, toys, treats, and a bag of dog food half the size of Sam, they pulled into his driveway.

"This is your new home, Buddy. You have the run of the entire place." Sam parked the SUV in front of one of the two closed garage doors, released Buddy, and began unloading his doggie necessities.

He intended to leave the truck outside overnight, making it easier for him to get his car out at 5:00 a.m. for their little impromptu getaway, before he handed his car over to its new owner. He'd already given his travel plans to his family, letting them know he'd be camping, but he left out the detail of which vehicle he was driving. Oh, they all knew he had sold it, but they would throw a fit if they knew he was driving the Bug outside the town limits.

Sam carefully grabbed the cooler containing Buddy's insulin and syringes before locking the truck doors and following the golden ball of energy across the front yard to his front door. Sam loved his home and all the little touches that made it his. For example, the bright red front door or the rainbow flag hanging from a small pole beside the garage, and the front topiaries clipped into various animal shapes. Yes, Sam knew he was a bit different at times, but who doesn't love a baby hippo, elephant, or the family of bears all lit up at night with small twinkling lights? It was beautiful to Sam, and that was all that mattered. Even though Dante and Spider had teased him about creating his own zoo, they had helped prune his menagerie every Sunday.

Dammit, stop thinking about them. Maybe this is why they didn't want to keep me. I'm too...weird, out there, different. They carry guns. I carry a stethoscope. They're strong and capable. I'm a short, redheaded weakling about half their size, and useless in a fight. Their lives are filled with excitement and adventure. Mine's filled with long shifts and sick people. How could they want me?

Sam quickly unlocked the door and let Buddy in the house while juggling his new purchases and dodging his new dog. "Okay, in you get, Buddy. We need to get your insulin in the fridge." Canine insulin needed to be refrigerated and kept out of direct sunlight much like human insulin; essentially they didn't have many differences. Buddy would require two shots a day for the rest of his life, and canine insulin wasn't cheap. Sam could understand why his previous owner could not continue caring for Buddy and thankfully brought him to a no-kill shelter for adoption.

Buddy's insulin would be kept in a battery-operated cooler that charged from his car so that he would not be at risk. Sam placed his purchases on the kitchen table beside the bags he'd already had packed for tomorrow. Buddy had gone to investigate his domain; his clicking nails on the wood floor were a dead giveaway to his location, which was currently the back spare bedroom. Sam felt lighter today than he had in the past four. He was by no means back to normal, but he could breathe a bit easier. He missed his lovers. He missed the life they had begun to build together, from the simple things like folding laundry to the way Dante and Spider held him securely at night.

Stop it! Enough. I need to move forward, not dream about the past.

With that, Sam squared his shoulders and called for Buddy. "Come, Buddy, it's time to eat."

The golden retriever came into the kitchen and straight to his huge bag of dog food. Sam would be repackaging Buddy's food before packing it for their trip because that bag would never fit in his Bug. Sam placed Buddy's bowl beside the bag that looked like a hernia waiting to happen. He wrestled it into the pantry, cut open the top, and scooped the exact amount Buddy's diabetic diet called for. Sam was sweating by the time he set the bowl down in front of Buddy and decided to sit for a minute after retrieving the insulin from the refrigerator. As soon as Buddy was finished, Sam filled the syringe to the appropriate amount, held a thick layer of skin on the back of Buddy's neck, and gave him his shot. Buddy was so used to this that he didn't even move.

"Okay, let's go outside for a few minutes and then get the car packed. What do you think, boy?" Sam laughed loudly when Buddy jumped up and placed both his paws on Sam's shoulders. "You and me, Buddy. We'll take on the world together."

***

The next morning began dark and foggy. Sam would have to drive slowly until the sun rose and began burning the fog away. The two new best friends climbed into Sam's Bug, and he hit the button to open the garage door. Carefully, he pulled his vehicle out, not giving the truck a second thought. It would be safe to leave out in his neighborhood. Sam shut the garage and locked the place up tight. He was so excited about their little vacation he was almost dancing by the time he came back to the car. He turned, taking another look to make sure he hadn't forgotten anything, and dropped his cell phone into the puddle under his feet.

"Shit." Sam quickly picked up his phone but knew it was too late. The phone was completely waterlogged and useless. Sam quickly dismissed the thought of stopping to pick up a disposable one, knowing that would delay his much-needed trip. "Well, I guess we'll have to replace that when we get back into town, Buddy."

Within minutes, Sam and Buddy were driving down the on-ramp to the interstate and Inks Lake State Park. Clear lakes tucked away in the Texas hill country sounded just about perfect to Sam.

The sun was beginning to rise and the duo was just over fifty miles away, Sam singing to an old Bruce Springsteen song while Buddy barked along, when an explosion tore through a quiet neighborhood in Brighton. Spider's truck was blown wide open, leaving twisted pieces of metal strewn across the yard. An unsuspecting, now dead, car thief sat behind the wheel as the vehicle landed in the living room of Sam's house.

Chapter Six

A cell phone rang in the darkened motel room. Dante nudged Spider, who was still snoring and draped all over him. They had stopped at a motel a couple hours outside Brighton so Sam wouldn't be overwhelmed by six people showing up on his doorstep at two in the morning. Probably not the best way to beg for a second chance. The shrill sound coming from his phone stopped, only to begin again a few seconds later. Dante looked at the clock on the bedside table. It wasn't even 6:30 a.m., and he'd only been asleep a little over four hours. Someone was going to die.

Dante threw the blankets over Spider and grabbed for the offending piece of technology. "What!"

Dante knew immediately something was wrong when the only sounds coming across the phone were sniffling and crying and, in the background, sirens.

"Dante?" Johnny's voice cracked, and the man melted into a fit of tears.

"Johnny. Johnny…what's wrong?" Dante asked while pulling on his boxers.

By now Spider was fully alert, his own phone pressed against his ear, likely talking with the rest of their team in the surrounding rooms.

"What is it, Johnny? Is Gabe okay? Is he with you?" Gabe was Johnny's rock, and he would never allow anything to make his fiancé this upset.

"He's fighting the fire." Johnny's voice seemed so small.

"Did your house catch on fire, Johnny?"

"No. Is Sam with you?"

"Why would Sam be with me? He doesn't know we're coming home." Dante and Spider wanted to show up on Sam's doorstep and, no matter what, convince the man he was loved beyond description. They had informed Sam's parents they were coming, making his mom and dad very happy, but had told no one else. How Johnny knew was a mystery.

"His… His… I hoped that maybe you guys couldn't stay away and picked him up early." Okay, this was getting stranger by the moment, and the sirens in the background were becoming louder.

"Johnny, tell me what's happened." Dante placed his phone on speaker so that Spider could hear the conversation.

"Sam's house is on fire. They say Spider's truck blew up."

"Johnny, where's Sam?"

"We don't know for sure." Johnny began to wail, and Dante could hear muffled voices.

"Dante? Is this you?" asked Dave Graham, police chief and Sam's cousin.

"Yes, Chief Graham. What's going on with Sam's house? Where's Sam?" Dante was almost yelling by now, and Spider was already dressed and packing his and Dante's bags. A knock on the door alerted them to their team's arrival.

"We aren't sure where Sam is. One of the other firefighters stated he saw a body in the driver's seat of Spider's truck before we had to back off because of the flames. We just can't get close enough, at least not yet."

"Have you tried his cell phone?" Dante's brain began to process all the places he might be, because the body in Spider's truck was not Sam's. He'd been told by Sam's parents that Sam had planned to go camping, but he hoped to catch him before he left.

"Yes, it goes straight to voice mail."

"Is his Bug still in the garage? Did you call the campsite?"

"He sold the Bug, Dante. His reservation at Inks Lake State Park was cancelled, and we don't know why," Chief Graham answered, his voice laced with frustration and fear.

"Cancelled by who?" Dante demanded.

"The park office manager said it was done electronically through their website this morning," Chief Graham replied. "Dante, I just don't know what the hell is going on."

"That cannot be Sam inside that truck." Dante's voice became hard and edgy.

"It's not Sam." Spider's words came out strong, but his eyes gave away his panic. The other four members of their team stood around the room listening, waiting for orders. None of them spoke. "We would know if he died, Dante. We'd know."

"I don't know, guys, but I'm praying that this isn't what it looks like and that Sam is somewhere safe. A truck doesn't just blow up all on its own." Chief Graham spoke the words that were floating around in everyone's heads.

"We'll be there in two hours or less." Dante hung up the phone and faced Spider and their team. "We're outta here in ten minutes. I want to be in Brighton by 0800."

"Yes, sir!" rang out in the small space, and Dante knew all four would be ready in under five minutes. The team knew Dante and Spider didn't require words of sympathy; they required action. They would begin the search for Sam. If Dante and Spider said he was alive, then he was; that was all their team needed as proof.

"Dante?" Spider stood ramrod straight, his body rigid, his face a mask of complete agony. "That's not our Sam. He's not dead."

Dante walked over and wrapped his lover in his arms. The man was trembling with the amount of adrenaline running through his body. Spider was in complete mission mode. Dante knew he would hunt down all those responsible for this and find their Sam. "We'll find him."

"They were after us, Dante, but found Sam instead. We caused this. When we get Sam back, we're buying land and building our own place. It will be safer for everyone." Dante knew Spider was simply talking about their future so he wouldn't concentrate on the alternative.

Dante took Spider's soft lips in a powerful kiss meant to distract and reassure. Spider groaned before taking a few steps back. "I love you, Dante."

"Love you, Jack." Dante cupped Spider's cheek with his shaking hand. "We'll find him, baby, and he will yell at us and tell us what idiots we were for leaving him. Then we'll kiss him until he forgives us. There is no other option."

"It's going to take a whole lot more than kissing to get Sam to forgive us, but it's a place to start. Hell, right now, all I want is to hear him yelling at us."

"I know, love, I know. Let's get moving."

0758

The last eighty-seven minutes felt like being stuck in purgatory, unable to do anything more than run frightening scenarios through his head. Dante was driving like a man possessed, and both Coop and Vincent fought to keep up. Shannon was in the back of the second vehicle surrounded by laptops and weapons. She would find out which asshole was in the area looking for a little payback for prison time or forced poverty when the team and Feds took every drug-dealing penny away. Jake was on the phone in the third vehicle making contact with their friends at the Bureau and, more than likely, the friends the Bureau had no idea they had. All three vehicles were connected to one another through their secure communications system.

"Boss, I have an idea who might be in Brighton looking for a little revenge. He shouldn't even be free, and I'll need to confirm, but—"

"Who is it, Shannon?" Spider wasn't in the mood to play twenty questions. His Sam was out there somewhere.

"Miguel Martinez escaped a prison transport over three weeks ago in Colombia."

"Why the hell weren't we informed? We're only responsible for bringing that sadistic bastard to justice and destroying one of the largest cartels running drugs from Colombia to New York. Didn't they think he might hold a grudge?" Dante asked.

"Not sure, boss, but Banks is looking into it on his end," Shannon explained.

"We're just entering Brighton now, people; keep an eye open because I'm pretty sure the police should be on us before we even get near Sam's house," Dante instructed.

"Why's that, boss?" Coop asked.

"Sam's truck blew up this morning and burned down his house. Everyone in this town will be looking for strangers, and guess what, three strange SUVs just entered the town proper," Spider explained.

With that said, the sounds of sirens could be heard coming from up ahead. Dante and Spider lowered their windows so that they could be easily identified, as did each member of their team. They pulled their vehicles over as one cruiser stopped in front of their convoy and two more blocked off their retreat. Chief Graham stepped out of the lead vehicle. Spider knew the exact moment the police chief recognized them, his shoulders relaxing.

"Christ, you guys know how to make an entrance. I take it the other four people are with you?" the chief asked while waving his men to stand down.

Spider and Dante got out of their SUV, and the look of relief on a few bystanders' faces would have been comical if it weren't for the reason they were petrified in the first place.

"Yes, they're our team members," Dante answered.

"Have you found Sam?" Spider asked, cutting right to the chase.

"No, nothing yet. We just left his house. The coroner is on his way out to take the body to the morgue for identification."

"My team requests permission to assist you in this investigation. We can have clearance obtained within the hour." Dante's formal request seemed to surprise Chief Graham.

"We all know your team's probably already ahead of us, and you have more contacts than I could ever dream of. We'll sit down and make sure all of us are on the same page." Spider watched as Chief Graham let a bit of his professional mask fall, to show his pain. "We think it's Sam in the driver's seat, but we won't know for sure until the lab runs their tests. But honestly, who else could it be? It's your truck, Spider. You left it for Sam to use. He sold his Bug, and he's the only person living in that house."

"Sam's not dead!" Spider's yell caused more than one head to turn in his direction, but he didn't give a shit. The man he and Dante loved wasn't dead. They would know. *He* would know, because his own heart was still beating.

"Boss, we should move on to Sam's house. The coroner has arrived, and we need to gain access to the truck to find any evidence on what explosives were used. That could tell us a lot, if it's not already been washed away," Shannon reported to Dante before returning to her own truck, the same truck that was now missing Vincent.

"How does she know that?" Chief Graham asked.

"She's hacked into your systems, and Vincent already has eyes on the house. We should go," Dante answered unapologetically. He was a vision of complete control; no one other than Spider could tell how much it hurt him when anyone even implied Sam was dead.

They loaded up and followed the police chief back to Sam's house. "Where can he be, Dante?"

"I don't know, love, but we'll find him."

He reached over and grabbed Dante's hand, needing the contact. "The only other time I can remember ever feeling this scared was when you were shot back in Iraq." Spider admitted.

"I've been a stubborn ass when it came to Sam, but the thought of possibly losing him… It's killing me. It might be selfish and insane, but I need both of you. I love both of you," Dante confessed, keeping his eyes straight ahead but squeezing all feeling right out of Spider's hand.

They rounded the corner and drove onto Sam's street. Bile rose so quickly from Spider's stomach he thought he was going to be sick right in the front seat. The area around the burned-out shell that used to be Sam's home was covered in hoses from the various fire trucks parked on the street. Flashing lights bathed everyone and everything in an eerie flashing red glow.

The remains of Spider's truck could be seen sticking up out of what once had been the spacious, comfortable living room where the three of them had often made love. Spider's stomach turned once again, and he must have made a noise because Dante was murmuring words of reassurance and kissing Spider's knuckles in an attempt to calm him. Spider was panting, and he could feel sweat beading on his forehead. *He can't be dead, not our Sam.*

"Easy, love, I promise everything will be okay."

Black, charred timbers with small plumes of smoke covered the entire area, but the flames were out, and firefighters were quickly squashing what remained. The white coroner's van sat in contrast to the black soot and smoke, as if guarding the site until the victim could be taken away. It was a stark reminder that more than a house had been lost. Sam's family stood off to the far side of the neighbor's yard, watching and waiting at a safe distance—at least the part of the family that wasn't working the fire. Townspeople and friends stood on the other side of the road, no doubt waiting for word on Sam.

Dante stopped his vehicle halfway down the street and got out with the rest of their team. The Masons were already on the move and closing in fast. A weaker man might've been worried, but Spider was not a weak man. Even so, he had to admit, if only to himself, the

Masons were quite intimidating. A red, puffy-faced Jane Mason walked straight up to Spider, wrapped her arms around him as far as she could, and began crying softly. Spider noticed Jamie, Sam's sister, doing the same to Dante.

He gently held on to Sam's mother until her tears had stopped once again. A distraught Jack Mason, Sam's father, stepped forward and handed his wife and daughter tissues to dry their eyes.

"My son is not dead." Jane spoke with a determination that would make any son proud. "You boys will go out, find my son, and bring him home because whoever was in that truck, Lord have mercy on his soul, is not my Sam."

"Yes, ma'am, we intend to find him. We've brought along a few friends to help out," Dante answered and took a few steps back from Jamie so he could introduce their team. Once done, the four scattered to have a look around, because if someone did indeed plant a bomb on his truck, whether they intended to kill Sam, Spider, Dante, or all three, they might have left clues behind.

"The coroner's going in to remove the body now," Fire Chief Roger Mason informed them. The grim look on his face said it all. "Do you two want to come take a look before we move things, in case there's anything you can use to find this bastard? I know it's not fair of me to ask the two of you to do this, seeing as you three were dating not so long ago."

"Are dating, are lovers, and that's not our Sam in there." Spider walked past the chief. He knew it wasn't the man's fault, but his anger and fear drove him forward. *It's not Sam. It's not Sam. It's not Sam.*

The chief and Dante walked on either side of him as they approached what used to be Sam's bright red front door—now it was streaked black—and up to the burned-out shell of his truck. The coroner was already beside the charred body, instructing his assistants on how he wanted the remains removed. *This is not Sam!*

"Dr. Payne, we need a few minutes to document the scene," Chief Mason advised the coroner, who gave a respectful nod and began to back away.

"There's probably something you all should know before you go any further," Dr. Payne stated.

Dante stepped forward. Spider noticed he only glanced at the charred body. There were no distinguishable features left; actually, there was barely any flesh left due to the heat and flames from the fire. "What did you find, Doctor?"

"Well, with this being Sam's house and this the truck he always drove, I wouldn't be remiss in saying we all thought we'd find Sam's body behind the wheel. But we were wrong."

"Wrong? How can you tell? How can you be sure?" Spider asked, the weight of relief almost sending him to the ground.

"The pelvis of the person in the truck is visible because most of the flesh has been burned away. Whoever this is, she's female, not male. Her pelvic cavity is wider and deeper than a male's would be. This isn't Sam."

Chapter Seven

Sam sat with his back against a fallen log beside his small but toasty fire pit on his campsite inside Cedar Hill State Park. Buddy was sleeping at his side as he enjoyed the sunset on the second night of his camping adventure. He would have to leave tomorrow and return to the real world. The peace he'd enjoyed over the past two days helped put many things into perspective for Sam.

Yes, he loved Dante and Spider, and he would do just about anything to have the chance to tell them. So with that in mind, Sam decided he would drive to Nashville. After all, he still had another week off work. He knew his men and their team were on assignment there. He just had to find out which hotel was closest. Sam was determined to find them and come clean, tell them everything, starting with how much he loved them and didn't want to have to live his life without them in it.

If his cell phone were working, he would have answered their calls by now, but he'd have to wait until he was back in Brighton to get a replacement. Thank God, an elderly couple RVing across the country allowed him to use their laptop once he explained what happened to his phone. He easily cancelled his reservation at Inks Lake after seeing Cedar Hill and deciding it was safer not to drive any farther in his rusted-out Bug without a cell phone.

After the first day, he started to think more clearly, and Sam soon realized this whole situation wasn't all their fault. He was to blame just as much as they were. He hadn't asked them to stay, he hadn't confessed his love, and he hadn't given them any reason to believe he wanted them permanently. He knew there was still a chance that his lovers really didn't want a life with him and that he would be putting himself out there to be rejected, but he had to try.

The crack of a branch brought Sam out of his musings and put him on alert. *It's a campground. Of course other people are going to be around.*

Buddy woke and lifted his head, staring off into the forest as if seeing something Sam couldn't, which completely freaked Sam out. Another crack, closer. Weirdly, the noise seemed intentional, as if letting Sam know whoever it was out there was coming his way. He wished he had gotten a campsite near the main areas because at that moment, he was all on his own. Wait, he had a dog, which should scare away whoever might be wandering around. *But what if Buddy gets hurt?*

The footsteps had increased their pace and were now running in his direction. Sam stood and grabbed Buddy's collar seconds before the dog would have taken off into the woods after whoever the hell was out there. He couldn't let his dog get hurt. Buddy barked as the steps came closer. Sam could tell it was more than simply two people out for a sunset stroll. These strides had purpose, and there were many more than just two.

A sound came from his left, and he turned in time to see a huge man dressed in camouflage come walking out of the tree line. Another just seemed to materialize out of the trees themselves, and finally a woman sauntered into the clearing. *Oh shit!* Sam knew the basics of self-defense, but that was nowhere near what he'd need against these three.

"Well now, you wouldn't happen to be Sam Mason, would you?" Of all the things he thought she would say, that wasn't it, and he found himself nodding without thought. "You are a little cutie, aren't you?"

"What?"

She tapped something in her ear and spoke too softly for Sam to hear. The other two men looked relaxed, but by the way they kept scanning the area, Sam wasn't fooled. More crashing came through the trees, not even trying to be quiet, just before three men came running into the clearing. Sam couldn't breathe. He had to be dreaming. Maybe he was asleep, because his dream just came true. Dante and Spider stood only twenty feet away from him, and he couldn't move. He was frozen.

The other four people walked back into the forest without saying a word. Sam wondered if they were the team his lovers had always talked about. Buddy was now calmly sitting at Sam's feet watching the two men closely.

Spider took a tentative step forward. "Sam... I—" Before Spider could finish, Sam ran, as quickly as he could with a limp, across the distance that separated them and jumped into Spider's open arms.

"I've missed you two so much." Sam held on tightly to Spider, afraid he would disappear again. Warmth covered his back just before a hard chest pushed him more firmly into Spider's hold. He was sandwiched between the two men he loved. Sam had been afraid to dream this was possible, even after he made it to Nashville, but he couldn't have been happier.

"We've missed you too, Trouble." Dante nibbled and kissed the side of Sam's neck, sending little shots of electricity down his spine and into his balls. "We couldn't stay away."

"You couldn't?" Sam hoped that meant they would be staying this time.

"No, we couldn't, baby. I love you," Spider said, just before capturing Sam's lips with his own. The love, passion, need, and longing in that one kiss did more to convince him Spider was telling the truth than any words ever could. Jack loved him.

When their lips finally parted, Sam said the one thing he'd been desperate to say for so long. "I love you too, Jack."

Spider held him tighter and seemed to not be in any hurry to let him go. After several minutes, he released Sam into Dante's arms. Dante held him close without saying a word, and Sam was beginning to get a bit worried. *Maybe he doesn't feel the same as Spider.* But then he spoke. "Sam, please forgive me."

"Forgive you for what?" Sam couldn't imagine what Dante had to apologize for.

"I was an ass, a fool to have ever walked out your door. I just didn't want to force you to keep us. I couldn't live with that. I can take a lot of things, but being with someone who doesn't want me isn't one of them. I was a coward, plain and simple." Dante hung his head, seeming to be unable to look Sam in the eye.

Sam nudged Dante's jaw upward until he looked at him. "I love you, Dante. Do you love me?"

"Yes, God yes, I love you." The words flew out of Dante's mouth.

"Then we can work everything else out. Now kiss me. I've missed you." Sam would have laughed at how quickly Dante swept in for a kiss if he hadn't been drowning in the passionate and possessive way Dante's lips commanded his submission, which Sam freely gave. Spider was now at Sam's back, and Buddy was jumping excitedly around the three of them.

When the two finally came up for air, Spider asked, "So, is Buddy ours now?"

Sam should have known his men would remember Buddy. They'd come with him to the shelter to help out on numerous occasions. "Yes, Buddy is our newest family member. He's already checked out the house and backyard, and all meets with his approval."

The change was immediate. Gone were the happy, loving looks, replaced now with masks of anger. "What did I say? What's wrong?"

"Sam, I think it's best we sit down and talk." Spider retrieved Sam from Dante's arms and sat on the log by the fire, keeping Sam on his side. Dante joined them, taking both of Sam's hands in his own, and Buddy sat by Spider's feet.

"W-what's wrong, Dante? Is my family all right? You're scaring me." Sam was way past freaked out by now.

"Sam, I hate to have to tell you this, but your house burned down." Dante was watching Sam closely, as was Spider.

"It's gone? Is anything left?" Sam brain was stuck, not really comprehending. *My house...*

"No, honey. It's gutted," Dante answered softly.

"My trees?" Sam had worked on those for years; it was a passion of his.

"I'm sorry, Sam, with the fire, the firemen, and the hoses, there isn't much left," Spider answered, gently stroking Sam's back.

"How? When? How did it catch on fire? Was anyone hurt?" The questions were pouring out as fast as his mind could think them up. He wasn't stuck any longer. "Was it my fault? Did I leave something on?"

Dante stood and began to pace, while Spider continued to hold Sam close, still rubbing his back with those large, soothing hands. The anxiety and anger coming off Dante was beginning to scare

Sam. Not that he thought Dante would ever hurt him; no, something had happened that was bad enough to put Dante in this dark place.

"The SUV that we left for you blew up," Dante stated between growls.

"Blew up! How? Was there a gas leak? I didn't smell gas." Sam wouldn't have missed something like that.

"No, it wasn't a gas leak. Someone had rigged the truck to explode when the ignition was turned to the on position."

"A bomb, you mean a real *bomb* bomb?" Sam's mind was reeling from the news, and he knew he probably would have dropped to the ground if Spider weren't holding him safe.

"Yes, sweetheart, a bomb. We believe this has something to do with us, some sort of act of revenge," Spider explained.

"Revenge for what?" Sam asked.

"Taking down a drug lord named Miguel Martinez and stopping a billion-dollar drug smuggling ring from expanding into the U.S.," Dante explained as he continued to pace.

Sam sat back farther into Spider's embrace, trying to absorb all the information he'd just received. He was homeless. He and Buddy were homeless. Thank goodness, he had enough insulin for Buddy to get by for a few days. Then something important hit him. "Wait, you said the ignition had to be turned over for the bomb to explode. How…did…?"

"Someone attempted to turn the truck on to steal it. She was killed instantly," Spider answered.

"Who was she?" Sam asked, feeling even sicker knowing someone had died.

"Jo Trinity. She's known to your cousin and the rest of the Brighton police force. She was on parole for car theft when she went after your truck. They identified her through dental records," Dante explained.

"Oh my God, my family. They must have thought it was me in that truck." The realization that it could have been him finally hit home. "That was supposed to be me."

"But it wasn't you, and we're going to make sure it stays that way. We love you. I, Dante, and our team will protect you." The determination in Spider's eyes reassured Sam.

"Yeah, about that. I never thought I'd see the day when I was actually thankful you drove your Bug, but I thought you sold it?" Dante asked. "And what is wrong with your phone?"

"I did sell her, but I don't deliver her until I get back to Brighton. I wanted one last trip with my baby, and before I left, I dropped my phone in a puddle." Sam came to another realization. "She's all I have left, that, the clothes I brought, and Buddy, and I really don't own her anymore either." *Oh God.*

"You have us, sweetheart, and we're not going anywhere," Spider vowed.

"I've never been so happy that you didn't listen to us and drove that rustmobile out here, but she's really a danger," Dante said. "We can get you something safer, like maybe a tank, but I'll settle for a Humvee."

Sam laughed for the first time since their reunion was ruined with the news of the fire. "Does my family know I'm safe?"

"Yes, I'm sure Shannon has made that call by now." Sam knew Spider was right. From what he'd heard about the team, they were family to Dante and Spider.

"How did you find me?"

"Well, considering you weren't where you were supposed to be, the six of us have been canvassing all the campgrounds in the area." Dante's eyes became serious. "That is another matter we'll have to deal with. If you break your phone, you go and get another one. You don't go days without a way to communicate with anyone."

Sam felt bad for worrying them and his family, but how the hell was he supposed to know Dante and Spider were coming back or that someone wanted him dead? *Oh shit!* "Someone is really trying to kill me?"

"We're not sure if you were the target or us, but either way, we won't be taking any more chances until we get him back behind bars," Spider explained.

"Or an unmarked pine box," Dante growled, while continuing to pace.

Sam began to feel way too exposed out in the forest for this Miguel to find. "Should we go now? Is it safe?"

"You're safe, baby. Shannon, Coop, Vincent, and Shadow are keeping watch. We won't allow anything to happen to you. Now that we know about the threat, we can anticipate some of his actions and put him on the defensive." Spider spoke with a confidence Sam wished he himself had.

Now that Sam was coming to grips with everything he'd been told, he noticed how he was molded to Spider's side and his body reacted to his lover. He would deal with the house and would-be assassin tomorrow. Sam's hips rocked back and forth, giving his cock the friction it needed. Spider held him tighter, allowing Sam to spread his legs a bit wider and grind against Spider's firm abs.

"We could stay here for a while. My tent sleeps four, so we should be able to cram most of the two of you in there," Sam teased. Dante's and Spider's eyes were burning with desire when they both looked at him. Sam needed to feel close to them once again. His life had been lonely since they'd left, and a criminal blew up the vehicle he was supposed to be driving. "Wait, what are we going to do with Buddy?"

Dante gave a sharp whistle, and a few seconds later, one of their teammates came out of the woods, grabbed Buddy's leash from a nearby chair, and attached it to his collar. Buddy jumped with excitement; apparently he had decided these people were friends. "I'll take him for you. Has he had his evening insulin shot?"

"Yes. How did you know Buddy was diabetic?" Sam asked.

"We've been busy the past couple days. It's nice to meet you, Sam. I'm Vincent. I'll take care of Buddy tonight. Where are his supplies?"

Sam pointed to a duffel bag just inside the tent and a small cooler. "Those have everything Buddy needs, including his insulin. Are you sure you want to take care of him?"

"No problem, little boss," Vincent responded.

"What?" Sam asked.

"Little boss. You're the bosses' partner, and you're about half the size of them. Therefore..." Vincent smiled while making a circling motion with his hand, waiting for Sam to finish his sentence.

"Little boss," Sam answered.

"Exactly." Vincent turned and walked Buddy back into the woods.

"Where will your team be sleeping tonight?"

"Our team brought our trucks. Those not on watch will sleep in them," Dante explained.

"That can't be comfortable. Maybe we should go ho—right, I don't have one of those." Sam was having a hard time accepting that fact.

"Don't worry, sweetheart. Your parents helped us find a large house to rent just outside of town where we can all stay until we buy some land to build on."

"Land to build on? You're going to have a home in Brighton, not Florida?"

"Of course we are, all three of us, together. Well, and the team will need houses eventually."

Sam was so shocked he could barely form words. "You two want to build a home with me?"

"Of course." Dante came over and knelt before Sam, reaching for his hands. "Jack is the only other person I've ever told I loved them. For me, love is forever, and that requires us all to be in the same place." Dante looked vulnerable and unsure, both looks Sam had never seen on Dante before. "Do you want to live somewhere else, Sam?"

"No. No, I want to live with you two. I love you both, and I want forever with both of you," Sam quickly answered, unable to stand the concerned looks on Dante's and Spider's faces any longer. "I'm just shocked. You did just leave me less than a week ago."

Dante stood and took a few steps back, allowing Spider to lift Sam into his muscled arms and begin walking toward his tent. "We were sorry the minute we stepped through the front door."

"Then why didn't you just walk back in and come to bed?"

Spider looked at Dante but didn't say a word. Whatever it was, it seemed important to both of them. Finally, Spider spoke. "I've followed Dante's lead for more years and more missions than I really want to remember. We lived through hell, sometimes with only each other to count on. I'm ashamed to say I followed his lead this time as well when I should have just stayed in bed with you. I'm so sorry."

"I don't want to be responsible for the two of you fighting. I agree, at the time, you should have left with him. It was the right thing to do." Sam believed every word he said. Spider and Dante were made to be together. He would never make them choose. But then why did Dante leave? Was he just here to keep Spider happy, accepting Sam to keep Spider?

"Dante, if you really don't want to be he—"

Dante immediately lifted Sam out of Spider's arms and cradled him to his chest. "I want to be here with you, Sam. You two are my family. No, better than family; my family is disgraceful, nothing like the three of us."

"Then why leave?"

Dante seemed to think about it for a moment. "Can I explain everything in the morning? I'm not trying to avoid your question, beautiful. I just don't want it to ruin our reunion further."

"It's okay, Dante. I can wait until you're ready to tell me."

"Thank you." Dante looked at him with such love that Sam had no doubt the reason he left was important to him. "Now, Trouble, how about we see how the three of us fit in your tent?"

"Oh, I like that idea." Sam chuckled before taking Dante's lips in a hungry kiss.

***

Spider's heart was in his throat. Seeing his lovers kissing and rubbing against one another should have made any man jealous, but hell if it didn't turn him on more. Both men belonged to Spider, and tonight they would reclaim Sam, the final piece of their triad.

Dante carried Sam over to the tent opening, and Spider quickly pulled the flap aside. Dante put Sam down because there was just no way to get into the tent carrying someone. Spider followed Sam in and onto a pile of pillows and sleeping bags. He smiled knowing his baby liked to be comfy, even if he was camping. The tent was quite roomy, but add two large men to Sam and it got cozy real quick.

Sam took off his shirt, revealing his creamy soft skin and beautiful tattoos. Spider had many tattoos from his youth and his life in the army, but his didn't rival the colorful art gracing his lover's skin. He wanted to run his tongue over each line and taste every color, so he did.

Sam lay beneath him, arms above his head, as Spider explored to his liking, licking and sucking up lewd marks across Sam's collarbone. He could hear the hiss of water extinguishing the fire before the sound of the zipper sealing the entrance to the tent. Sam was writhing and moaning as Dante undid his jeans and pulled them free. Spider was lost in the feel and taste of his lover, and Dante took the opportunity to kiss and fondle Spider through his clothing. Spider was consumed by need. He wanted to feel Sam around his hard shaft while Dante's beautiful cock filled him.

"Dante, I need—" Spider groaned before returning to the luscious skin being revealed to him inch by glorious inch as he slid Sam's boxers down his legs.

Dante stopped and caressed the side of Spider's head. Spider looked up, and whatever he saw made Dante smile. Dante began to strip Spider of his clothing while he continued to explore the body of a very vocal Sam. Moans echoed through the silent woods, which could have been easily heard if there were any campsites close by. Thankfully that wasn't something they had to worry about. As for their team, well, they could just ignore whatever they heard, but were more likely to razz them about it instead.

"Please," Sam begged before Spider took his mouth in a bruising kiss. Dante pulled the last of Spider's clothing off, and his hard dick bounced freely against Sam's. He was desperate to get inside his fiery redheaded lover. Spider growled, beyond words to express what he needed. Dante handed him a small tube of lube that would have to do preparing both Sam and Spider.

Spider grabbed the lube and poured a liberal amount onto his fingers before breaching Sam's hole.

"Yes, Spider, oh God, yes. More." Spider added another finger, stretching his fingers wide so he wouldn't hurt Sam when he entered him. Dante took that moment to position his naked body behind Spider's and cover him completely. It was a position Spider loved. He wanted to be claimed by Dante as much as Spider needed to claim Sam. Slowly, one of Dante's large fingers circled his rosette until it loosened and allowed him in. Spider loved the burn and soon felt Dante adding another finger.

"I'm ready, Spider. Please fill me. Drive that gorgeous cock into my ass," Sam begged, slamming back onto Spider's fingers.

"I have to make sure you're ready, baby. I won't ever hurt you," Spider answered and added a third lubed finger. Dante did the same to Spider. It was as if Dante had waited, letting Spider set the pace. They were breached in unison, making Spider push back harder against the fingers giving him so much pleasure.

Every feeling heightened when Spider brushed Sam's prostate and sent the man flying, crying out his pleasure. Not to be outdone,

Dante pegged Spider's gland without mercy, causing Spider to yell and spread his legs wider. Spider heard tearing and felt a condom being rolled onto his sensitive cock. Moaning, he bucked into Dante's hand and turned his head, blindly searching for a kiss. He opened his lips and welcomed Dante in, his tongue controlling, searching, and causing goose bumps to rise all over Spider's body.

"Take him, baby. Make him ours again," Dante ordered in a rough voice.

Sam looked up at Spider, his eyes half-closed, his pupils blown wide, and his legs pulled tight to his chest, welcoming Spider in as he slid past Sam's outer ring of muscle. He waited until Sam's grip on his arms loosened and he nodded for Spider to move forward. Slowly, he pushed until he was flush with Sam's ass.

"So full. Spider, move... Please move."

Spider happily obliged and began a slow rhythm so that Dante could join them while he pleasured Sam. He felt the blunt head of Dante's cock brush against him, and Spider slid even deeper into Sam, waiting for Dante to claim him. Dante and Spider didn't use condoms; they had been tested long ago. With Sam, they used a condom because there was never a guarantee he would want to stay, but now that concern was over.

"We're going to all get tested again, and then we won't wear a condom with you, Sam. We're in a committed relationship now. We belong together," Spider explained to his lovers. They were together now, and he wanted nothing between them.

"Yes, we're family now," Sam agreed.

Spider looked at each of his lovers, content all three were thinking the same thing. Forever. Dante nodded and Spider stopped moving to allow Dante to enter him fully. The thrill and pleasure he felt was immeasurable. When each was buried deep, the lovers looked to Sam, who was squirming, trying to get more friction on his hard, weeping cock. *This is it.* They had talked about the right time, and this was perfect. They were all connected to one another.

"Sam, will you marry us?" Spider asked.

Dante added, "We want to be a complete family, partners and husbands. I know we'll have to figure it all out, and that will take time, but tell us you'll marry us someday. Well, legally one of us, but it will be the three of us, Sam."

Sam's eyes filled with tears as he stared at both men. "Yes" was all he said, but it was perfect.

Spider kissed Sam deeply while Dante kissed and sucked up marks on Spider's neck and then reached over and kissed Sam. He began to pump himself in and out of Sam's slick hole while Dante set a rhythm that soon had him pounding into their smaller lover. Sam didn't seem to mind. He was babbling incoherently and begging for more. Dante continued to suck up marks on Spider's neck, each suck sending lightning down his spine and into his cock, which was firmly buried inside Sam's body.

"Close, so close," Sam moaned. His legs were wrapped around Spider and part of Dante, the three bodies writhing together in a frenzied need that none of them could have stopped.

"Come, beautiful," Dante ordered.

That was all it took. Soon Sam was screaming his release as his warmth spread out against both Sam's and Spider's stomachs. His hole tightened around Spider's cock and began to squeeze with Sam's release, throwing Spider over the edge and into a world of pleasure. He could hear the roar behind him and feel the heat filling him, branding him with Dante's cum while the man gently kissed Spider's shoulder.

Spider looked down at a now unconscious but smiling Sam. "I think we broke him."

Dante chuckled and kissed Spider's ear. "He's not broke, love. He's perfect."

"Yes, he is," Spider agreed.

"Same as you, Jack. You're perfect. I'm lucky to have you in my life," Dante confessed before pulling himself slowly from Spider's body. That was the one thing he regretted most, being separate from his lover. Dante grabbed a towel and poured a small bottle of water over it before cleaning Spider and then himself. Then he wet another cloth while Spider disposed of his condom and began cleaning Sam. Spider arranged the sleeping bags and piled all their clothing near the entrance to the tent. He placed both his and Dante's Glocks on either side of the bed. Considering Sam would be in the middle, they would keep him safe.

Within minutes, they had Sam arranged even though he was still fast asleep, with a cute half-snore, pig snort thing going on. He and

Dante settled on either side of Sam and turned off the battery-operated lantern.

"I love you, Jack. I don't ever want you to doubt how much I love you now that we have Sam. I just—"

"Dante, I love you too, and I know that you love me. If anything, the love we share for Sam makes us stronger. There're three of us, a strong triad. We love together, and we fight together. Our private team."

"Yes, together." Dante paused, and Spider knew he was considering how to phrase what he wanted to say. "I'm afraid to be completely happy, Jack. Every time I think I'm happy, it all blows up. The only time I've allowed myself to be truly happy is with you. You have some sort of superpower when it comes to putting up with my bullshit, and now we have Sam. I love him, and I'm scared something is going to ruin this for us. If anything were to happen to either of you, I…"

"We won't let Miguel anywhere near him, and you know I can take care of myself. Now that we know he's in the area, we'll find him." Spider knew his lover wouldn't rest until Miguel was back behind bars, just the same as him. "I love you both, Dante. You two are my family. The rest of the team can play the parts of annoying brothers and sister."

Dante laughed just as Spider had hoped he would. "Good night, baby. I love you."

"Good night, Dante. I love you too."

Soon Spider could hear Dante's breathing even out until snores filled the tent. With the rest of their team on guard, they were given this one gift, time alone with Sam. Spider would thank any and all gods for the gift of Dante and Sam in his life. He would sacrifice his own to protect them.

Chapter Eight

Dante lay staring at the beautiful man in his arms—Sam, the man they loved and could've easily lost. He was still having a hard time being any distance away from his lover. When he'd seen that body in the burned-out truck, he had barely held it together. When the doctor had stated the body was that of a woman, Dante had barely kept himself from collapsing in relief. He knew he had remained firm with everyone else, telling them that Sam wasn't dead, but that bit of fear was much larger than Dante had realized.

He'd let his past almost ruin their future. He felt ashamed of his actions but knew he couldn't have stopped himself at the time. Sam deserved an explanation; he deserved the truth.

"Morning," Sam whispered from under a layer of sleeping bag as he stretched his gorgeous, lithe body and wrapped himself around Dante. "Where's Spider?"

Dante pulled Sam even closer, rubbing their naked bodies together. He'd missed how perfectly Sam seemed to fit between himself and Spider. He never intended to be without both lovers again. "He went to check in with the team. He should be back in about ten minutes."

Sam slid his body suggestively over top of Dante, bringing their hard cocks together. "Now what shall we do with the time?"

Dante laughed—it felt so good to laugh again—and kissed Sam until his eyes glazed over, his pupils dilated, and he was moaning and riding Dante's thigh for friction. He wanted to see to Sam's needs, but his conscience had him pulling back. Dante could see the confusion and hurt in Sam's eyes the moment he pulled away.

"No, beautiful, I'm not rejecting you."

"Then why?"

"I need to explain to you why I left."

"Is that why Spider's gone to check on everyone?"

"Yes, I wanted some time alone with you."

"You're not leaving again?" It crushed Dante to hear the fear in Sam's voice and to know he was the one who'd caused it.

"No, never again. We'll have to still go out on missions though. We can't give that up at this point, but we can pull back and allow the others to take the lead sometimes."

"Okay, tell me." Sam sounded like he was bracing himself for anything Dante might have to say.

Dante laid Sam down at his side and held him close, but Dante was still unable to look him in the eyes. He was positive if he did, he'd lose his nerve. Although he knew deep inside Sam would never turn his back on him, the fear he'd felt as a child still came rushing back.

"It's okay, baby. You don't have to tell me," Sam said. Dante hadn't even realized tears were running down his face—tears for his missed innocence, family and love, and all the things any child deserved but were withheld from him. "Sweetheart, I don't need to know. I love you. You love me, and Jack loves both of us. That's all that matters."

"No, I need to tell you. I need you to know why I sometimes react the way I do. Please, Sam, let me get this out."

Sam lay back down beside Dante. "I'm right here, and I'm not going anywhere."

Dante settled back and stared at the roof of the tent to center himself before he began confessing what had been his nightmare for thirteen years. "My mother was a drunk. The first twelve years of my life were spent taking care of her, up until the morning she didn't wake up."

"Oh Dante—"

"No, Sam, wait." Sam nodded and placed his head back on Dante's chest. "She wasn't a real mom. My dad took off, just up and left without looking back. For the longest time, I thought if I was the perfect kid, he would come back and Mom would stop drinking. No matter how much I did, it was never enough. One day when I was around seven, the landlord came with the sheriff and kicked us out because Mom had been drinking all the rent money away. For years, we bounced around between relatives' houses, some better than others, but it never lasted long. She would drink herself into a stupor and leave me to be cared for by whoever had taken our sorry asses in. I tried to make myself useful, but I couldn't keep up with my mother's fighting or when she'd destroy their belongings in one of her rages. Then we would be forced on the next in line.

"There was one uncle I stayed far away from. He liked using his belt more than Mom liked to drink. I was relieved when his wife made us leave, but it wasn't long before I was back. After my mom died, he was the only family member to claim me. That's when my new version of hell began. I was twelve, but he pulled me out of school to work in his construction business for free, and no one did anything to stop him. Not the school, not the rest of the family, no one. Within the first six months, I had three cracked ribs and a sprained wrist, and none of those injuries were from working on the jobsites." Dante felt Sam stiffen beside him.

"Yeah, my uncle had upgraded from the belt to a baseball bat. One day, I couldn't get my nose to stop bleeding, and I was getting scared. No one was home, and the only other people I knew lived two blocks over. I helped build their new garage, and they gave me food or money when they saw me. They were always nice to me. So I figured I would go ask Mr. and Mrs. Phillips how to stop the bleeding. Now, you need to understand that I had just turned thirteen but looked more like a ten-year-old because I was so malnourished, and I walked up to their front door covered in my own blood. The next thing I knew, the police were there with an ambulance. I was rushed away to the hospital with the Phillipses while the police went to arrest my uncle for child abuse."

Sam hugged him harder, as if trying to squeeze the horrible memories out of Dante. "I'm so sorry you had to go through that, Dante. What happened after the hospital?"

"The Phillipses petitioned the court to foster me. I went back to school, got my diploma, and joined the Army. The day I was shipping out, I overheard my par—the Phillipses talking to their friends about having no other choice."

"No other choice about what?"

"Me. Me of course. The one they were forced to take in, like my family had been, just this time around I didn't see it coming. They had been so kind to me. I had every opportunity, and they were so proud of me when I joined the Army, but in truth, they had no choice but to take me in."

"Did they say that? Did they actually say they had no other choice but to take you in?" Sam was leaning over him by now, looking him straight in the eyes.

"No, I left before they could say anything else. It was plain to see, and after that, everything changed. I stayed away on missions longer, sent cards home on holidays, only returning home once a year out of respect for everything they did for me."

"Did you ever ask them? Did you ask the Phillipses what they had no choice about?"

"No. Isn't it obvious? I was nineteen and leaving for basic training. Their good deed was finally over." No matter how much it hurt Dante to say those words, he knew they were true.

"Oh baby, I don't know about that. I mean, your life up until that point was hell, and I wish I could take it all away, but the Phillipses didn't have to do what they did. They wanted to, by the sound of it."

"Sam, you have one of the kindest hearts I've ever met, but sometimes things are just the way they appear. But I wanted to explain why I couldn't push you to accept us. I'm so sorry I put all those insecurities on you." Dante spoke while he nuzzled the side of Sam's neck. The purple love bites stood out from his tattoos and made Dante hard just thinking about how they got there.

"We're together now, and I understand why you would not want to put yourself in that type of situation again, but you have to know that I love you. I love you and Spider. You aren't forcing yourself on me. God, before you got here, I'd decided to go to Nashville and tell you both that I love you."

"Well, I'm certainly happy we found you first." Spider spoke from outside the tent, making Sam squeal.

"Spider!" Sam yelled. "You scared the hell outta me."

The zipper opened, and the handsome devil crawled onto their nest of pillows. "I'm sorry, baby, but I wanted to make sure you both were dressed before the team got here." Spider cradled the back of Sam's head and kissed him slow and gentle. Dante's cock was completely on board with watching his lovers make out. Once he released Sam, Spider leaned over Dante and kissed him with the same tenderness. The love shining in his eyes took Dante's breath away. "Good morning, my loves."

"Good morning, sweetheart," Dante answered while Sam crawled on top of Spider and began kissing the back of his neck.

"Good morning, big guy."

Dante could feel Spider's hard cock rubbing against his leg and responded in kind. Sam was busy licking and kissing any part of Dante's skin he could reach. A low moan escaped Spider's lips.

"Okay, guys, we gave you three all night to get this out of your systems," Dante heard Coop whine from just outside the tent.

Spider reached behind him and lowered Sam back down onto the sleeping bags. "Looks like it's time to go, you two. Here are your clothes. I'll go keep the wolves at bay. They're hungry."

With one last kiss to each of them, Spider left Dante admiring his firm, gorgeous ass as he crawled back out of the tent. He turned his eyes in time to see Sam slip into his jeans. Smiling, Dante stretched one last time. *I'm a very lucky man to have Spider and Sam want and love me. I'll do whatever it takes to keep this.*

***

Sam was nervous, even though he'd sort of met the four members of his partners' team last night, and they all seemed welcoming...but what if they really didn't want Sam around, or to move to Brighton to build a new home base? Everything could be different by the light of day.

"What's the matter, Trouble?" Dante asked while he finished tying his boots. Spider and the team were waiting outside the tent somewhere.

Sam kept his voice low. "What if they aren't happy about this? Having to move to Texas from Florida is a lot to ask."

Dante gathered Sam close to his body and held him. "I think you'll be surprised, considering the four of them moving here with the three of us was their idea."

"Really, they wanted to come with you and Spider?" Sam asked.

"Yes. They know there's no way we're giving you up. This is forever. So they made plans to move here right along with us," Dante explained while still holding Sam in his arms. "You mean the world to us, Sam."

"I can't imagine my life without the two of you in it," Sam admitted before Dante pulled him in for another kiss.

"Are you two dressed yet, because we're taking down that tent with or without you guys in it," a voice said from somewhere on the campsite.

"Sounds like we'd better go before we get packed away with the tent," Sam said.

"Don't worry. Spider would come find us." Dante laughed again and released Sam.

Over the next hour, formal introductions to the team were made: Shannon, hacker extraordinaire with the penchant for fast cars; Shadow, the giant who could hide in plain sight; Coop, king of the one-night stands and brute strength; Vincent, hand-to-hand combat specialist and animal lover, considering he and Buddy kept playing while the rest packed up Sam's campsite.

Sam watched as his men and their team worked together to break down and pack everything away in his Bug. When he went to get into his car, he was promptly removed from the driver's seat. "Hey! What—"

"I may have said that I was happy you took your car on this trip, but that does not mean you get to drive it back. Shannon will drive the Bug back because she, out of all of us, has the most driver training in all imaginable situations. That way if your baby decides to have a tantrum, she can handle it," Spider explained. "You will be riding back with me and Dante."

"My baby saved mine and Buddy's lives. Show some respect," Sam teased, but by the looks on both men's faces, it might still be too soon to joke about his death.

"Yes, and we will be eternally grateful, but we're not willing to push our luck," Dante said and walked over to his truck to finish loading their equipment.

Sam felt like an asshole. He hadn't meant to make Dante or Spider upset, but if he didn't laugh, Sam was sure he would have broken down a few times over the course of the last twelve hours.

Strong arms wrapped around his waist, and Sam was pulled back against Spider's hard chest. "It's okay, sweetheart. Dante still hasn't quite gotten over what happened. I think neither one of us will ever completely forget the hell of the past two days. Getting that phone call that your truck had blown up and set your house on fire was horrifying, but we knew it wasn't you in that burned-out truck."

"How did you guys know it wasn't me?"

"We were still able to breathe, and our hearts were still beating. It's hard to explain, but if something had happened to you, we would have known," Spider admitted. "Then finding out that someone had targeted you because of us and that you were out here somewhere not knowing you were in danger and unprotected, we were frantic to find you."

Sam turned in Spider's arms and laced his fingers behind his lover's neck. "I'm sorry, Jack. I would never knowingly cause either of you to worry."

"We know. I just think Dante is having a hard time accepting the fact he let his own insecurities take him away, leaving you alone and unprotected," Spider explained.

"But to me, none of this is either of your faults. The blame lies with Miguel Martinez alone." Sam stood on his tiptoes and tilted his head back, silently asking for a kiss that Spider eagerly gave. "I'm going to speak with Dante. He can't hold on to this guilt."

Sam found Dante at the back of his truck securing one of the three duffel bags containing their clothing and Buddy's supplies. Vincent had already given Buddy his insulin after breakfast that morning. Dante looked up when Sam rounded the side of the truck but remained quiet. Sam stopped a few steps away from him.

"Dante, I'm sorry I made light of what's happened. At the moment, it seemed like the only way I could deal with it all, without crying and curling up into a ball somewhere. I didn't take into account everything you and Spider have been through the past few days."

"Come here, Trouble." Dante motioned with his outstretched arms, and Sam took the final two steps forward to be enfolded in his lover's tattooed arms. "I understand that this is a hell of a lot to take in and that you're dealing with it all the best way you can, but when everyone kept saying you were dead, I just couldn't accept that. Then finding out we caused all of this… The man I love was in danger because something we did put him there. I didn't know whether you were safe, or if Miguel and his goons had you. I was terrified thinking you might be hurt. It's not your fault, beautiful. This is completely on my shoulders."

"No, Dante, like I told Spider, the only one to blame here is Miguel, no one else. Do you understand?" Sam placed a hand on either side of Dante's face and made him look him in the eye.

"But—"

"No! Do you understand this is not your fault?" Sam wasn't walking away from here without some sort of understanding.

"Sam, it's not that easy, love." Dante's eyes begged Sam to give him time.

"Will you at least try to see that what I'm saying might be right?" Sam asked.

"Yes, I'll try. But I'd feel a whole lot better with that asshole back in prison," Dante grumbled.

"So would I. Let's go home to Brighton. We have a man to catch, land to buy, and plans to make."

"I like the way you think, baby, but you'll be staying out of the catching part. Do *you* understand?" All the playfulness was gone from Dante's eyes, and he was suddenly serious. "We will not risk anything happening to you."

"Of course. I'm not trained to take on someone like that. You guys can catch him. I'll stitch him up afterward at the hospital, 'cause I'm sure he's not coming in without a few nicks and scrapes."

"You won't be going anywhere near him." Dante was firm about this, so Sam did the only thing that would appease his overprotective partner.

"Yes, sir."

"And don't you forget it." Dante smiled and swatted Sam's ass with his big hand, sending a jolt of electricity straight for his balls and causing Sam to softly moan. "God, you're beautiful, inside and out, baby. If you keep moaning like that, I'm going to have to take you out into those woods and give you a proper spanking."

Sam couldn't help but moan again. Neither of Sam's men had ever spanked him before, but maybe they should explore new areas in their relationship. Considering the speed at which his cock was filling, Sam was all for it. "Please."

Dante growled, dragged Sam closer, and claimed his lips in a bruising kiss, adding to Sam's need. "Sorry, baby, but we need to get back before your parents send the police chief and half the Brighton police force to retrieve you. We can revisit this tonight with both Spider and me giving you what you so obviously need, my love."

"You have yourself a date, soldier."

Chapter Nine

By the time they reached the rental house, Sam was positive he had seen every last resident of Brighton. When they'd finally pulled into his parents' house, the place looked like it was hosting a wedding with the number of cars out front and food in the back. Dante had asked if he wanted to go by his house, but it was already late afternoon, and Sam really didn't feel up to it. His men completely understood and decided to take him over in the morning.

Sam had been swarmed by Masons the moment he stepped out of the truck. He couldn't help but cry when his mom and dad hugged him tight. The one thing that really shocked Sam was his mother's behavior toward Dante and Spider. After they hugged him, his parents hugged his men like they were heroes and a special part of the family. Everyone thanked his men and their team for finding Sam and bringing him home safe. Sam agreed they did find him, but he was driving back home in the morning anyway. *Sheesh.*

It wasn't until Aunt Dot asked when the wedding was being held that Sam clued in; Shannon had spilled her guts. Sam's eyes found Shannon sneaking away from the table mouthing the word "sorry." Dante had quickly taken hold of the conversation, stating they had a lot to discuss and take care of first. That seemed to do the trick for the family and their wedding questions for now. Besides, Sam was not in any hurry to rush down the aisle. Johnny and Gabe were getting married in the next six months, so he could wait a few years, *right?* Just as long as he had his two men, he was happy.

Okay, right then he was exhausted but happy. Walking into the rental house, Sam expected to be confronted with a mess of bags and stuff to be cleaned up and put away but was pleasantly surprised. The three-story Victorian had been temporarily decorated, as much as the short time had allowed, by the amazing ladies of the family. A few pieces of furniture that Sam was told had been donated to the cause were scattered about. Sadly, none of his furniture was salvageable.

Now, Sam found himself tucked into a new king-sized bed in the master suite all by himself. When he'd said he was tired, this wasn't the response he'd expected. Of course his men explained that they had to secure the house and yard before going over information they had received about Miguel's whereabouts. It made complete sense, so why did he feel like he'd been abandoned? On top of it all, now he wasn't even tired anymore.

Maybe a little walk around would help. Maybe I can find one or both men and convince them to join me.

With that very happy thought in mind, Sam slid from the huge bed covered in the softest bed sheets he had ever felt. He knew the thread count had to be well over 800. He would know; he'd ogled a set at Saks when he was in New York, and this was definitely something he would never be able to afford on a nurse's salary. Sam had been so shocked by the size of the house that he hadn't paid complete attention to the rooms when he first walked in. This time, he stopped to admire what looked like new furniture and not donated hand-me-downs like he'd been told. Maybe his furniture wasn't completely ruined after all. Maybe it just didn't fit in with this pricey group. Sam found a few beautiful wood pieces that still had tags attached, and the prices almost floored him. He couldn't afford to put a scratch on the coffee table for that price.

The marble countertops in the kitchen shined along with all the stainless steel appliances. The hardwood throughout the house was original and breathtaking. The two-story ceiling in the living room easily accommodated the eighty-inch television attached to the wall and all the gaming systems underneath. This was not a simple rental house. Each room was partially decorated, and the more he looked, the more dollar bills began dive-bombing his head. *How can they afford all this?*

Sam was getting a sick feeling in the pit of his stomach. He went from room to room, finding big-ticket items mixed with a few things that looked a bit older but well loved. He found the library... *A friggin' library! Yep, definitely not in my tax bracket. I should have paid more attention when Spider drove us here. Hell, I don't even know what area of Brighton we live in.*

In the library, he found a small box of books half empty. Inside the box, he found Shakespeare, Arthur Conan Doyle, F. Scott Fitzgerald, and many more. Some of the books were even first editions. Sam might not have had the funds to buy something like this, but that didn't mean he was uneducated as to their value. Did these things belong to Dante and Spider—or were they the other team members' belongings?

They had discussed finances before when Sam became concerned they weren't taking jobs because of him. *Shit.* They had flat out told him that they had a small nest egg…*small nest egg my ass!* Sam hadn't even noticed that before now, and he had to wonder if he had even paid for anything other than the mortgage since they'd moved in with him. He hadn't. Sam couldn't help the anger that started to bubble up. He couldn't understand why they'd never told him. Considering all the things he'd already found, it was pretty obvious someone had a large bank account.

Sam didn't like where this was heading. Now that he didn't have a house anymore, did that really make him a kept man?

"Ah, here you are." Spider's loud voice in the quiet room made Sam squeal and jump back, dropping one of the books he'd been holding onto the floor.

Sam immediately picked it up and placed it back in the box. "Sorry, the book's not damaged. I won't touch them again."

"What? Of course you can touch them. They're mine. I like to read and collect old books." Spider gave Sam one of those looks that meant he knew something was up with Sam, and he would get it out of him.

"They're first editions. I have only a rough estimate of what they're worth, which is probably low, so no, I won't be touching them. Some are irreplaceable. Even if they were, I could never afford to replace them," Sam explained while backing away from the box like it was a viper ready to strike.

"Sam, what's wrong, honey?"

"You and Dante lied to me."

"Lied to you when?" Spider asked.

"Who lied?" Dante asked when he entered the room with the four members of his team and Buddy happily walking at his side. *Great, now I have an audience and a traitorous dog.*

"You told me the furniture and things were donated because my house burned down, but that's not true. Some of this furniture is brand new and expensive. The rest is well loved and expensive. Hell, it's all expensive. None of it I could afford on my salary. Why did you lie to me?"

"Wait, you don't know how rich these two bastards are?" Coop looked confused. "And you're with them anyway."

"Rich?" was all Sam could squeak, because now he was hyperventilating.

"He doesn't know?" Shannon asked.

"Quit talking about me like I'm not here. I don't know anything!"

"We didn't tell Sam."

That was enough of an admission for Sam, and he began to storm toward the library door. He would take his beat-up old car and his poor ass to his parents' house. One deal breaker for Sam was lies, and vague answers or omission were lying in Sam's books.

"Where are you going, Sam?"

"To pack my one crappy old bag and drive my crappy old car to my parents' house to sleep in my old bedroom." That seemed to shock them into action. *Maybe they're used to men falling at their feet because they're rich. Well, not this guy.* Sam didn't honestly believe that, but he was so angry he didn't care. They'd lied. He had never once hidden anything from them, but they sure as hell had.

"Wait, you would honestly leave them because they have money?" Shadow asked, his face looking as confused as Coop's.

"He's not going anywhere," Spider announced. "Sam?"

"No, Shadow. I wouldn't leave them because they're rich. I would if they lied to me. I didn't hide one thing from the two of you I opened my home and my life, but I didn't rate the same treatment. I don't care how many zeros are in your bank accounts. I just wanted your honesty."

Instead of answering Sam's rant, Spider held out his arms and Sam was powerless not to walk into them. "I think we need to have this discussion in private." Dante led the way to their room.

"What part of town is this rented house in? Is it even rented or did you guys buy it? And the land for building, is that here too?" Sam couldn't help it; the questions were flying into his head as quickly as he could get them out.

"We'll explain everything, sweetheart. It's not as bad as all that, is it?"

"I don't know, because you haven't been honest with me. Did you think I would be after your money? Because if you did, then you two don't know me at all." Sam raised his voice as he entered the bedroom.

"You think that?" Dante asked. He was now lying on their bed in his unbuttoned jeans and tight black T-shirt, and his feet were bare. Dante was simply gorgeous, and Sam just about forgot why he was angry. Just about.

"Yes, apparently neither of you thought to tell me the truth for fear of something. Small nest egg my ass! My guess is that you thought I'd only be interested in the money. Well, too bad. This middle-class nurse doesn't want any of it."

Dante sat up and gathered Sam into his arms as he joined him on the bed. It felt so good to be wrapped up in either of his men's arms. Spider sat on the other side of Sam, essentially cocooning him between them. Normally, this position would've made Sam feel secure and loved. Right now, he felt trapped and betrayed. Sam scooched farther back and out from between them.

"Sam?" Dante huffed.

"We need to talk," Sam explained.

"Yes we do, beautiful, but why can't we have our conversation while holding each other?"

"Because you two will distract me, and I need to keep my head on straight right now. I want the truth."

"Okay, Spider and I are worth roughly seventeen million dollars."

Oh God. I'm so screwed. They're millionaires and I'm an ER nurse.

"Sam... Sam, baby, breathe."

Sam dragged in big gulps of air. Dante and Spider had surrounded him again and were rubbing his back and arms gently; it soothed him, and this time Sam didn't pull away.

"Seventeen. Million. Dollars. Oh shit. Why didn't you tell me before now? Were you ever going to tell me?"

"Yes, of course we were going to tell you, but we waited until the three of us decided to be together permanently because we knew how you would react."

"React, of course I'm going to react to something like that."

"Yes, but what else did you initially conclude, once you began to notice the new furniture and electronics? How about my book collection I had shipped here overnight?" Spider asked, knowing full well Sam had said he would never touch the rare books again.

"I was angry. That's what I've been telling you."

"No, beautiful. What conclusion did you immediately jump to?" Dante asked.

Sam sat there thinking back to his tour through the house. First he noticed the furniture. "I thought my furniture would never fit in here with yours, that it was too shabby looking. And, hell, what thread count are these sheets, because I've never slept in something that felt so soft."

"It's Egyptian cotton," Dante answered.

"See, my sheets came from the local mall," Sam admitted softly.

"Now you know why we waited. We know you're not after our money. You didn't even know we had any. One other thing we knew for certain was that the minute you found out you would think you didn't fit here, and we can't have that. Besides, we liked your house and furniture. But it's truly all been destroyed," Spider explained as he pulled Sam farther back into his chest to comfort him.

Sam could understand that. Considering what happened, there really would have been no need to tell him if they were leaving anyway, but he still had his concerns. "I guess that's why it was so easy to give away your SUV."

"No. The reason we gave the truck to you was to keep you safe," Spider growled.

"I felt like a prostitute at first, as if you were paying for our time together."

"Never, never would we think that. You're worth so much more to us than any of this. You have to believe that." Dante's eyes seemed to beg Sam to understand.

"Can I ask how you became so rich? No, don't answer. That's none of my business."

"Everything about us is your business and only yours. My father passed away while Dante and I were in the service." Spider spoke calmly, though Sam could feel the tension in his body. "He left me a few investments and property worth a little over four and a half million. We invested well, and when we mustered out of the army and began our own business, we reinvested our fees for each assignment. Of course we kept a bit to live on, but most of it was invested or used to buy more property. Our missions pay very well, so it didn't take long for the money to start to multiply year after year."

"We trust you, Sam. We love you and want to share this with you."

"I won't be a kept man," Sam insisted. "I love my job, even if it pisses me off at times and doesn't pay a whole hell of a lot."

"Of course you'll keep your job if you want to. It's completely up to you. We just want the three of us to be together. Dante and I want to share everything with you."

"But I don't have anything to share with you, not anymore. I have a rusted-out car that really isn't mine, one bag of clothing, a dog, and a burned-out house." *I need to call my insurance company in the morning and get more insulin for Buddy.* Sam felt so overwhelmed; he now had a running list in his head of things he needed to get done.

"You have everything we need. You're perfect. You love us and accept both of us. This type of relationship isn't easy, but we want it with you."

"Is this our new house?" Sam asked.

"Yes, we bought it and the two hundred acres around it."

Sam took a deep breath. He knew they loved him, even if he didn't have anything other than himself to bring into the relationship, but he had to feel like he contributed somehow. "When my insurance pays off my house and after the remaining mortgage is paid out, I want to put the rest of the money into this house for any renovations or building we need to get done." If his men agreed to this one condition, Sam would feel confident they could work things out.

"If that's what you want, then that's great. The team have their own funds to build whatever they decide, but, Sam, I don't want to force them to move out of the main house. We've been a team a long time." Dante looked a bit unsure when he spoke.

Sam understood how much they all meant to each other. They risked their lives together on a regular basis. "I don't want to force them out either. They're your family."

"*Our* family. You're part of us now, and soon enough, those four will be driving you up the wall like they do us."

"I want to be a contributing member to the team. I have administration experience, and I could help in the office." The minute he said the words, Sam wished he could take them back. He didn't want to insinuate himself into their company.

"Thank God! If I have to try to figure out Coop's expense report one more time or explain why condoms and lube are not a company responsibility, I'm going to throw him out the nearest window," Dante said.

All three laughed, dispelling the last of the tense energy in the room.

"There are quite a few things that will need repairing or replacing in the outbuildings."

"Outbuildings? Do we have a barn?" Maybe they could get a horse. Sam had always wanted a horse.

"We'll get around to showing you in the morning. Right now, someone is deserving of his spanking, considering he didn't trust his lovers to know him well enough to predict what he would do the minute he learned about the money."

Sam's cock filled inside his sleeping pants in seconds, almost making him light-headed. He hadn't stopped thinking about Dante's promise back at the campsite. He'd only ever played in that world twice before, but nothing as all-consuming as this. Sam wanted everything with these two men, his lovers, his partners, and, in time, husbands. He wanted to experience it all with them.

***

Dante could feel his hand itching to redden Sam's luscious ass, but he knew Spider deserved the privilege of being first to move forward into possibly a new aspect of their relationship. He and Spider had always liked to play at the clubs in Florida on occasion, but this was different. They loved this man. Dante had almost caused them to lose this. Spider needed this; he could see it in the man's eyes.

Dante released Sam after a quick kiss and moved to sit on the bench at the foot of the bed. "Take off your sleeping pants and come to me, Sam." Dante made sure his voice was firm, brooking no argument from Sam.

Spider gave Sam a passionate kiss, tongues dueling, and Dante was hard just from the sight of his lovers. Spider brought Sam close and molded him to his body. Ending the kiss, Spider stood Sam on the floor beside the bed. Sam's eyes showed excitement and need. *Perfect.* Sam slid down his pants to reveal his beautiful cock, hard and pointing accusingly at Dante

"Come to me." Dante patted his thigh. "Put your body over my thighs—head down, ass up, Trouble." Sam took a deep breath and smiled at the endearment.

Dante barely held back a moan at the sight before him. Creamy white skin, broken up by the colorful strokes of each tattoo, lean muscle, and a round, firm ass high in the air.

"I'm going to let Spider deliver your spanking this time, love." Spider, who had been standing at Dante's side, looked like he might have almost swallowed his tongue. Dante caressed one perfect ass cheek while Spider took the time to calm himself before the first strike. He knew he had to always be in control to make this as pleasurable for Sam as possible and to give him an orgasm that would not be soon forgotten.

"Are you ready, Sam?" Spider asked, his voice gruff.

"Y-yes," Sam moaned, his hips flexing, trying to get friction from Dante's legs on his needy cock.

"Lie still or we might change our minds, baby." Dante was only teasing, but the speed at which Sam stopped moving confirmed how much he wanted this.

Dante removed his hand from Sam's ass and stroked his silky head of red curls soothingly before bracing Sam's body with his other arm. Spider stood in front of them and ran his hand over Sam's ass reverently before pulling back and landing the first strike, followed quickly by another. Sam grunted only once then relaxed further into Dante's body. Spider wasn't spanking Sam hard, but the burn was building with every swing.

The room filled with moans, slapping skin, and whimpers. Sam was responding wonderfully. His body was flushed, and a fine sheen of sweat made his skin glisten. His red lips were parted, and when he arched his back and looked at Dante, his eyes were glazed and unfocused. He was gorgeous. His pink ass was turning red and swayed erotically in front of him. Spider's face held the same desire as he imagined his own did.

Dante reached down between his thighs and wrapped his hand around Sam's weeping cock. It wouldn't be long before his lover came.

"Please, please..." Dante wasn't sure what Sam was begging for, but he would give the man anything he wanted. He pumped his fist in time with Spider's strikes, and Sam began to moan with abandon. "I'm going...to...."

Spider and Dante worked in sync. Spider stopped spanking and palmed both of Sam's red cheeks in his hands as Dante pumped his throbbing cock faster.

"Yes... Yes!" Sam screamed as Spider squeezed those burning cheeks gently. His body went rigid, back arched, and stream after stream of cum pulsed onto Dante's fist and leg. When he'd given everything he had, Sam collapsed against Dante.

Spider knelt at Sam's head, caressing his wet red curls and whispering words of praise and love. Dante caressed Sam's back and ass, comforting him while he came down from his release. Spider's eyes met his, and Dante wasn't surprised to see tears in Spider's eyes. This had been cathartic for them all, a new beginning for the three of them, no more doubts, no more secrets. A new life with the men he loved.

Chapter Ten

Over the next seven days, the team began to work out a routine of sorts, and Sam now considered himself part of the team after the third time he had to explain to Coop that charging a motel room he rented by the hour to the company was not an allowable expense. Or the time Shadow brought home a boa constrictor to be friends with Buddy. It took all of five seconds for Buddy to view the new addition as a threat and try to wrestle it from Shadow's arms. Needless to say, the snake went back to the pet store and Shadow was banned from choosing pets ever again.

Sam had worked up the courage to go over and finally see the damage done to his beautiful house. Dante and Spider hadn't lied. Everything from his grandmother's china to his rom-com movie collection had been destroyed. His bright red front door looked as if it had been hacked to pieces by axes, the edges charred black. Sam's animal topiaries were either burned or crushed by fire hoses and the firefighters who had worked the fire. In the middle of the burnt-out shell that used to be his home, Sam broke down in his men's arms while the team kept watch from a respectful distance. After all, a pissed-off drug lord was still in the area looking for a little payback. So Sam now had bodyguards and was on extended leave from the hospital. He only agreed to stay off work when Dante mentioned that Miguel Martinez wouldn't hesitate to kill anyone in his way. Sam could never risk anyone else being harmed, so he followed the rules, for now.

As the days carried on, Sam and his men's new bond grew, and now Sam was beginning to do the talk-no-talk thing with them. At first he didn't even know he was doing it. He would just look at one of his men, and they knew what he was thinking. Then the next thing he knew, Dante looked at him one day, and there it was, written all over his face and in his eyes. Sam was beginning to feel a part of their triad and couldn't be happier. His thoughtful men had arranged to have several shrubs delivered, and with the help of the whole team Sam planted them around the grounds. Next spring he would be trimming and shaping them into different animals; it would be the beginning of his topiary "zoo." His morning spankings had become a reassuring way to start the day, and hell if he didn't miss it the one morning when his men had to leave early. The three spent every night wrapped in each other's arms. There was no going back for Sam. He had never been happier in his entire life.

As it turned out, the outbuildings included a dilapidated barn that, once fixed up, would be perfect for a few horses. There was also a greenhouse, shed, and separate garage that required a bit of work to make them usable again. Apart from the barn, Sam would often be found in the greenhouse fixing the numerous tables that would serve to hold his seedlings, much the same as he was doing right at that moment. It had been a long day and the sun was beginning to set; Sam was almost done for the day when he noticed that today's bodyguard was missing. Coop had been just outside the greenhouse door earlier but was nowhere to be seen at the moment. Sam stepped out of the greenhouse and turned in a circle, looking for him, but he found nothing. A sliver of fear sliced through Sam's heart. Coop wouldn't leave willingly.

Dante and Spider had gone into town to discuss their next step to try to flush out Miguel with the police chief's help. Shannon, Shadow, and Vincent were in the house cleaning out the packed attic, a job Sam had narrowly avoided as he ran for his greenhouse. The night air was turning colder but the chill snaking down Sam's spine, as he scanned the area once again, had nothing to do with the weather. Coop might be a man slut, but he would never risk one of his team, those he swore to protect, his family.

Sam decided to start for the house as quickly as possible; the rest of the team would help find Coop. He made it two feet before a hand wrapped around his mouth and a gun was pushed to the side of his head. Terror raced through his body, making his legs weak. *Shit!*

"Well, look who we have here." A scratchy voice whispered into his ear. More men began to appear from out of the tree line, and Sam knew that either Miguel was in the group of men in front of him or he was the man with the gun to Sam's head. Either option was a death sentence. "Your men should have kept a better eye on their toy."

"Miguel, there's three more in the house, the fourth has been eliminated." One of the men spoke to the man behind Sam. *What did they do to Coop?*

Sam began to struggle to get his mouth free to warn the others in the house, but apparently Miguel wasn't someone to take any form of resistance lightly. The butt of the gun slammed down on the back of Sam's head, sending him to the ground. The stars floating in Sam's vision began to disappear into darkness. The last thing he remembered was looking up at the same man he had run into at the grocery store, Miguel Martinez.

***

Dante pulled into the long driveway leading up to the old estate. It had only been a week since he and Spider had brought Sam home, and he had been the happiest he could remember since before his foster parents' betrayal. It no longer mattered that he wasn't wanted by his parents or even his foster parents; he had Sam and Spider, two men who loved him and whom he loved completely.

"I don't like this. We haven't heard or seen anything from Miguel since the bombing. He's out there somewhere, and Sam's not safe until we find him," Spider groused in the passenger seat.

"We'll find the bastard and put him back in a cell." Dante was confident that Miguel wouldn't wait much longer to make his move.

"I can't shake this feeling that we're missing something." Spider wiped his hands down his face in frustration.

"What do you think it is?" Dante asked.

"I don't know, but my guts are twisted in knots right now. Something's not right." Spider turned his head and looked Dante straight in the eyes.

Dante pushed on the accelerator. Spider had had "feelings" before out in the field just before everything went to hell. Something was happening. They needed to find Sam now. Dante slammed on the brakes and skidded to a stop outside the front doors of the house. Spider flew out of his seat even before the truck had completely stopped, Dante right on his heels. They rushed through the door and into the foyer, and were met with silence. This house was never silent. Both pulled out their Glocks and hugged the walls, inching forward into the living room. The sight that met them sent ice shards of fear through Dante's veins.

Sam sat unconscious in a high-backed chair, his hands tied together in front of his slumped body, dried blood covering one side of his face. Shannon and Vincent, both handcuffed, knelt on the floor in front of Miguel Martinez and four of his men. He could hear Buddy whining and scratching behind the closet door. Shadow and Coop were missing. Dante could only hope they were still alive.

"Nice of you to join us, come in." Miguel's voice was broken and raspy. Dante noticed a large red scar running across Miguel's throat that hadn't been there when they took him in.

They both aimed their guns directly at Miguel. They would need to cut off the head of this snake to kill the body; in other words, kill Miguel to throw his hired guns into chaos.

Miguel turned his gun and aimed it at Sam's head. "Now, now… We wouldn't want to have to put a bullet in your lover's head. Put your guns down or I'll have my men start executing members of your team until I run out, and then your Sam dies."

Two of Miguel's men aimed their guns at Shannon and Vincent. Vincent looked angry enough to rip Miguel's arms off and beat him with them, while Shannon looked cold and calculating. Good, they would need that kind of rage to make it through this. Slowly, both Spider and Dante lowered their guns and placed them on the tables beside the couches.

"Good, now walk over here slowly and kneel before me," the deranged psychopath said in a calm voice as if this were a reasonable request.

"Not a chance, Martinez." Dante's anger and fear for Sam were getting the better of him.

Miguel slammed the butt of his gun against the side of Sam's face, knocking him from the chair and onto the floor. His unconscious body crumpled. Dante immediately moved forward along with Spider. They couldn't allow Sam to be hurt further, and if that meant kneeling in front of a drug lord, so be it.

Miguel had a crazy look in his eye when he had all four kneeling before him. *I have to think of something fast or we're all going to die.* Out of the corner of his eye, Dante saw a slight movement, and then it was gone. *Shadow.* If Shadow was here, maybe Coop was as well. Dante could only hope, because at the moment they were outnumbered and unarmed.

"That's where you belong, you filthy pigs. You think you can just take what's mine?" It was becoming clear that Miguel's sanity had slipped away behind bars. "You see what they did to me in there! They thought they could kill me. *Me!*" He tugged his collar farther away from his sweaty neck, exposing the long, puckered scar close to his jugular.

"You're a criminal. Everything you've earned was made through blood and death. If you wanted sympathy, you came to the wrong house," Spider bit out.

"Oh no, I don't want your pity. I want your pain." Miguel laughed, which came out more like a hiss with his destroyed voice. "I want you to watch me kill your team members one by one, then your lover, before I torture both of you and kill you. Or perhaps I'll keep the little man as my pet. I could use a bit of a distraction."

Spider went to stand up, but one of the goons pistol-whipped the back of his head, sending him to the ground.

"Enough! Time to die," Miguel ordered.

Before Miguel's men even had a chance to do as ordered, two of them lay dead on the ground, bullet holes in their heads, no doubt from either Shadow or Coop. Spider flipped backward, grabbed both Glocks, and threw one to Dante. Vincent and Shannon jumped up, their handcuffs easily falling from their wrists. Lock-picking was a skill all team members were trained in, and they always carried their tools in a compartment on their watches. Vincent took the third man's gun right out of his hands, dismantled it, and had the goon on the ground before he knew what was happening.

Spider ran over to cover Sam's prone body to protect him from the bullets flying between Miguel and Dante. Shannon was locked in a furious battle with the fourth man when he bent and pulled out a knife, aiming for her heart. Shadow appeared behind the man and, in one swift kick, knocked him unconscious. Dante looked back to see Miguel working his way toward Sam and Spider. He would not lose his lovers. Dante jumped from his shielded position, firing shot after shot at Miguel as he ran to protect his lovers. By the time he reached them and stood protectively over their bodies, all noise had ceased in the room. Miguel lay in a pool of his own blood with multiple gunshot wounds in his chest. Coop stood by the open backdoor, gun in hand, bullet wounds in his shoulder and chest.

Miguel and two of his men were dead. The other two were unconscious and currently being tied up by Shannon and Shadow.

God, Sam! "Sam, honey, open your eyes," Spider begged as he gently checked Sam's body for bullet wounds, thankfully finding none.

As Dante knelt beside his two men, he could hear Shannon on her cell phone calling for police and ambulance. "He's unconscious from the blows to his head, there are no bullet wounds. Help is on the way, Spider. He'll be okay. He has to be."

Coop slumped down next to Sam. "Is Sam going to be okay, boss?"

Vincent handed Dante a clean dishcloth to slow the bleeding from the multiple wounds on the back and side of Sam's head; his beautiful red curls were now stiff with dried blood. Shadow began to work on Coop's bullet wounds, and sirens could be heard in the distance. Sam hadn't moved. Dante and Spider cradled him between their bodies. Spider was whispering to Sam, telling him how much he loved him between sobs; Dante could feel his own tears running down his cheeks. He had just gotten his entire family back; he wasn't about to lose one of his beloved men.

***

The beeping from the various machines attached to Sam's silent form was slowly driving Spider further and further into a depression he was helpless to stop. It had been three days since the ambulance rushed one of the men he loved to the hospital with severe head trauma, and Sam still hadn't woken up. The doctors were treating him for a subdural hematoma, which had caused his brain to swell in his head, from the blows Miguel had delivered. If Miguel weren't already dead, Spider would have easily remedied that.

If the pressure became too high, it could prevent blood from flowing to his brain. They had him on a respirator providing oxygen therapy to make sure his blood had enough oxygen in it and to help reduce swelling. So far it was working. The swelling had gone down, but no one could tell them when Sam would wake up or if he'd suffered any permanent brain damage. The guilt and fear were crushing him, Dante, and his team. Coop had been the only other person to sustain serious injuries from two gunshots to his arm and shoulder; thankfully, neither wound was life threatening. Typically, the mouthiest member of their group, Coop sat stoically in the corner. Members of Sam's huge family had gone down to eat and to contact loved ones with an update. Sam was never left alone; Dante and Spider refused to leave. Their team brought them clothing and they showered in the doctors' lounge. The ER staff had been devastated when they brought Sam in to the hospital and had been checking in ever since. The room was full of flowers, get-well cards, stuffed animals, and balloons; the town had gone all out for Sam.

Sadly, Coop believed Sam's injuries were the result of his personal failure, that he should have kept Sam safe even if he had been outnumbered and ambushed. He'd tried to resign his position on the team, but Dante had thrown the paper back at him and called him an idiot instead. They were more than a team; they were family. Miguel Martinez was solely responsible for Sam's injuries and the team knew that.

Shannon, Vincent, Shadow, and Buddy were at home cleaning and fixing anything that might remind Sam of what happened. Even though he'd been unconscious for most of it, no one wanted him to have to relive it by walking into the house and seeing broken furniture, bullet holes, and blood because, dammit, they would be bringing Sam home soon. Dante stood staring out the hospital window, his eyes unfocused, as if he were lost in his own thoughts. He'd been quiet and withdrawn; Spider was becoming increasingly concerned about him.

"Mmmmyyy head hur…ts," Sam groaned from underneath his oxygen mask, Spider stood so quickly his chair fell backward and all three men rushed to Sam's side.

"Sam, baby, open your eyes for me." Spider kept his voice low, not wishing to add to his pain. "Coop, get the nurse."

Coop ran from the room as both Dante and Spider leaned over the bed, watching those beautiful milk chocolate eyes open. "What…hap—?"

"Easy, you're in the hospital, sweetheart. You're going to be okay," Spider whispered, praying like hell he wasn't lying.

"Miguel…?"

"Yes, Miguel came to the house, but he's dead. He'll never hurt you again." Spider took it as a good sign that Sam could remember Miguel was at the house. The doctor had told him that Sam might have memory loss or even trouble controlling his movements. At worst, he'd have to relearn certain things. It didn't matter to Spider and Dante. They would be there to support him and help in every way possible.

"Head hurts," Sam moaned as he attempted to raise his hands to touch his bandaged head.

"No, baby, you can't touch those. You're healing, and we don't want anything to stop that," Dante explained while gently lowering Sam's hands to the bed. Sam slowly took in his room, all the machines and flowers.

"Love you, guys," Sam mumbled before reaching for their hands.

"I love you, Trouble."

"I love you so much, baby." Spider's voice was cracking with emotion.

The door opened, and Dr. Green, followed by a nurse and Coop, came flying into the room. Before any of them could say a word, Spider raised his hands and whispered, "Softly, he's in pain."

"Good to see you awake, Sam, how are you feeling?" Dr. Green asked in a whisper.

"Head hurts."

"Yes, I imagine your head hurts quite badly. The nurse is giving you something for that." Dr. Green carefully lifted the edge of one of the bandages on Sam's head.

Sure enough, the nurse was holding a needle to Sam's IV line. Dr. Green began his examination, asking everyone other than the nurse to stand back a bit so he could work, but Sam had other plans.

"No...no...no," he cried when Spider and Dante were out of his sight. They quickly surrounded him with their arms, soothing his frantic cries.

"Okay, I'll work around the two of you." Dr. Green smiled and got to work. By the time he was done checking and rechecking just about everything Spider could think of, Sam was beginning to fall asleep.

"Well, I'm much happier with his progress today, he's awake and coherent. There will be physical therapy if his motor functions don't return fully, and the pain in his head will come and go, but we can control most of that with medication. We'll run more tests once we get Sam on the road to recovery."

"What are you saying?" Spider needed verbal confirmation.

"We're on the good side of this now. He's awake and knows who we are. That was the biggest concern. Now we can work with the rest. Unless something drastic occurs, Sam will recover, but we need to figure out if there are any permanent concerns. But from what I see now they should be few and far between," Dr. Green explained with a smile on his face.

Spider could feel tears gathering in his eyes and didn't care who saw them. He was a man who just found out his lover was going to survive. They would take Sam home and help him heal.

"Don't cry." Sam's groggy whisper melted Spider all over again. He was lying in a hospital bed worried that Spider was crying.

"I'm just happy, love," he explained. Dante came up behind Spider and wrapped his shaking arms around him. Spider turned, shocked to see his other lover in full-on tears. Dante didn't show emotions but Spider couldn't think of a better reason.

Dr. Green and the nurse had left them alone. Coop stood at the back wall far away from Sam. Spider could feel the man's tension from here. "Coop, come here."

"Coop's here? He's okay? I couldn't find him," Sam asked; he looked relieved.

"Yeah, I'm okay, little boss," Coop answered in a gruff, broken voice.

"Good, I was worried Miguel said you were taken out. Wait, why's your arm in a…?" Sam stopped midsentence as if searching for the right word.

"Sling, baby," Spider provided.

"Yeah, sling." Sam looked confused for a second as if the word didn't fit. The doctors had explained that Sam might be confused and need help for a while after he regained consciousness.

Coop stayed mute, so Dante decided to fill Sam in. "Coop was shot twice trying to protect you."

"But I didn't, Sam. I'm so sorry. I should have been able to protect you. Miguel should have never gotten near you." Coop spoke softly but it was impossible to miss the guilt in his voice.

"You did save me. I'm still alive." Sam smiled at the giant of a man, and for the first time in days, Coop smiled.

"We love you, Sam. Rest, beautiful," Dante commanded, and Sam drifted off into a restful sleep.

"He really is one of a kind," Coop stated in hushed tones.

"Yes he is."

Chapter Eleven

Sam knew what he was doing could either make their relationship stronger or destroy it all with this one decision. It had been ten weeks since he'd been released from the hospital, and thankfully, everyone had pretty much fully healed even though Buddy refused to leave Sam's side. He still had migraines on occasion, but Sam was able to make it through them now with minimal medication. He'd been placed on medical leave from the hospital because he still had small tremors in his hands every now and then.

The team would be arriving back from their first mission away since the attack. Sam had to threaten to cut both men off if they didn't go; neither were ready to leave him just yet but grudgingly followed through on the security detail. Sam sat in their living room with the two people who could heal the man he loved. Or annihilate him. *Now is not the time for second thoughts.*

"Mr. Phillips, would you like another cup of coffee?" Sam asked Dante's foster father.

"Yes, that would be nice, Sam, and please call me Frank. I must say, I'm still a bit surprised to be here after fifteen years of barely seeing or speaking to Dante after he joined the service," Frank said. He still looked a bit unsure.

"We're so proud of him and everything he's done." Mrs. Phillips seemed to gush with pride, which was not the response someone would expect from a woman who didn't want her foster son.

"Does it bother you that the three of us are in a committed relationship?" Sam had to ask. If they didn't agree with the three of them loving each other, then he would show them to the door before his men came home. *Maybe I should show them the door before Dante gets home. Christ, what was I thinking trying to fix this?*

"Heavens no. You young men have a right to live your lives the way you see fit. You're not hurting anyone. The love I see in your eyes when you speak of our son and Spider is all the confirmation we needed," Joanne Phillips confirmed. They had met Spider on one of the few times Dante went home. The knowledge that the Phillipses would fit in well in Brighton did nothing to quell his fears.

Sam could hear vehicles pulling up to the house. It was now or never; he had to come clean. "Frank, Joanne, I need to be honest with you. Dante doesn't really know you're here. I've invited you on my own."

"Why, dear?" Joanne asked, looking confused and a little bit more nervous than she had a few seconds ago.

"Because he's suffering without the two of you in his life, but he's too stubborn to fix it. You have to make him tell you why he became closed off toward you. It's the only way to fix this." *I hope.*

"Once Dante left for the army, we understood that he was out there protecting us, and we never wanted to upset him by forcing the issue," Frank stated. "But to be honest we always wondered why Dante was never the same after he left. We thought it had to do with his missions and the things he'd done and seen to protect all of us."

"You need to force that issue now. It's important. But I can't be the one to answer your questions. Please stay and wait for Dante to get home." Sam begged for his lover and his future; if they decided to leave, nothing would get worked out.

The Phillipses sat quietly for a moment, and Sam finally understood where Dante had gotten the talking-no-talking thingy from: his foster parents. Both were in their early sixties, but they both acted as if they were in their forties. They had been there most of the day, and when Sam took them out to meet Clyde, Sam's new Clydesdale/paint mix he'd received for his birthday, they seemed so excited. Sam learned that Mrs. Phillips had been quite the equestrian in her day. They helped with his feed, water, and seemed to love brushing his bay coat. Sam was amazed; nothing seemed to stop the two. What one couldn't do, the other could and vice versa. He only hoped that he had this much stamina when he hit his sixties.

"Okay, Sam, we'll stay," Frank answered, and Sam finally let out a breath he hadn't known he was holding.

"Good, 'cause they're home." All the nervousness and fear came flooding in when he heard the front door open and several pairs of boots headed in his direction.

"We're home, Trouble." Sam couldn't stand the thought that this might be the last time he'd ever hear that endearment if Dante decided Sam had gone too far.

"We're in the living room, guys." Sam's voice wavered slightly.

The footsteps grew closer, and his heart thundered so loudly he thought he might pass out. Spider came into the room first, his big smile faltering slightly when he saw who Sam was entertaining. Questioning eyes sought him out, but all Sam could do was concentrate on not throwing up or passing out; either was possible. Then Dante came in with the rest of the team. This was when Sam expected all hell to break loose, but instead, Dante smile dropped and he simply kept walking toward the kitchen. Sam jumped up from his seat and grabbed Dante's arm before he had a chance to leave.

"Please, Dante, just a few minutes, please. For me." Sam didn't know if he was begging for Dante's foster parents or himself.

Dante turned his head to look at him; a slap couldn't have done the job better than his expression. The rage and pain in those eyes was something Sam just couldn't unsee. He'd been wrong. Dante pulled his arm away and turned to greet their guests.

"Hello, Mr. and Mrs. Phillips, I hope you've had a nice visit. I have to get ready for another mission, so if you don't mind, I'll leave you to your coffee." Dante's tone was cordial but frosty.

"Son, please talk to us. Your mother and I came all this way to see you." Frank stood, his hand extended as if in a peace offering.

Sam backed away from Dante as the rest of the team left. Spider remained on the far side of the room, watching, waiting. He never once looked at Sam; instead, his entire focus was on Dante.

With one final look at the two men he loved, Sam turned away. He'd ruined everything. His stupid meddling had alienated one of his lovers, and surely the other wouldn't see his actions in any better light. With those heavy thoughts, Sam slowly walked to the one place he hoped would give him solitude: his greenhouse.

***

Dante stood frozen to the spot. He'd never frozen before. Not in any firefight, bombing, raid, hostage rescue… Nothing made him freeze, except the pain he just saw flash across Sam's eyes. Dante was furious to come home, excited to see his lover after being away for four days, only to be punched in the gut at the sight of his foster parents.

"Son, please tell us what we did to make you feel this way about us?" his foster mother asked.

"It's nothing. I'm not the person you remember, and you need to forget about me." He had to get out of here and find Sam. Dante didn't need to hear the excuses, the fumbled explanations as to why they didn't want him. *But they're here, why would they come all this way?*

"No! Young man, you will sit your ass down in that chair and talk to us." When Mom raised her voice, everybody listened. Dad immediately sat. Spider even came and sat down. Finally, Dante gave in and sat as well.

"Tell us, son, why you've shut us out for all these years?" Joanne asked in a much calmer voice.

"You would think you'd be happy to be rid of me." Dante had finally had enough. If they wanted to rehash this shit, he'd be more than willing to jump right in.

"What? We love you, Dante. Why would we want to be rid of you?" Frank asked.

"Well, I figured since your little talk with the McGiverns the day I shipped out, you would be happy to never see me again."

"McGiverns? You mean Toby's parents? What do they have to do with this?" Joanne asked, with a look of complete confusion on her face, and Dante felt the first inkling that more was going on here than he'd thought.

"I heard you. I heard you tell them that you had no other choice. No other choice but to take in the poor kid. The troubled boy with no father and a mother who drank herself to death. The worthless weight around your neck. Me."

There, it was all out in the open. *Let them explain that.*

"Oh, son. No, that's not what we were discussing—" Frank tried to explain, but was cut off before he could finish.

"Sure, what other reason could you have for saying those words?" Dante wasn't sure he could believe anything they said, but the little boy covered in blood standing on their doorstep all those years ago wanted to believe.

"It wasn't you we were referring to. We were discussing your uncle... We'd just had him sent back to jail," Mom replied in a hushed voice full of shame.

Now, that he didn't see coming. Dante sat there dumbfounded. He looked to Spider and saw the same reaction.

"He'd gotten out of jail a few months before your graduation, and he was supposed to stay away. We had a restraining order and everything, but he kept coming around. We tried to keep him away from you, but we knew he would have come that day to destroy all your accomplishments. So, that last time he tried to get to you, we called the police and had him arrested for breach of his parole because he broke the restraining order," Dad explained with the same shame as Mom. "We couldn't risk it. I'm sorry, son."

"We felt so much guilt, Dante. We didn't honestly know if he would show up. It was just the next logical step, and we had him jailed anyway." Mom began to cry, and Dante immediately went to her side, grabbing the box of tissues as he went.

"You did the right thing. He would have done anything he could to humiliate me if he had the chance." If Dante knew anything, that was it. His uncle was a vicious man who would have loved ruining Dante's big dream.

"You honestly thought we didn't want you?" his mom asked.

"Yes." That one word held so much pain that Dante had to lower his head. He had lost so many years with the parents he loved just because he wasn't man enough to face his own fear. It took a man half his size with enough bravery to fill this house to give this peace to him; he just needed to find him.

"You best go find that young man of yours, son," Mom advised. "He loves you two very much but I think you may have a few things to work out."

***

Sam gently ran his fingers through his growing seedlings. Flowers, vegetables, and herbs would soon be big enough for another replanting into bigger containers so their roots would have room to grow even larger. He absently wondered if one of the team members would do it once he was gone because he was sure, after that one look, his time here was at an end. Perhaps he should be packing. The Phillipses had probably been shown the door by now, and soon he would be shown it as well.

Tears streamed down his face, and Sam was powerless to stop them. He'd had everything he'd ever dreamed of, and single-handedly burned it to the ground. That thought just reminded Sam of his house and that he had nowhere to go. Sure, he could stay with his family, but he was a grown man. No matter how pathetic he was at the moment, he was still an adult, though he had nothing.

After a few more moments admiring the plants he painstakingly nurtured, Sam left the greenhouse and wandered into the woods surrounding the property. He loved to walk through the acacias and cypress trees; they always managed to ease his headaches so maybe they would work on his heartache, but he doubted it. Sam had been walking aimlessly for several minutes when Shannon walked out from behind one of the large cypress trees right in front of him. This time Sam didn't jump; he was getting used to the way the team could just pop up anywhere at any time. It had taken weeks and multiple screams to get to this point.

"You hiding out here, Sam?" she asked.

"Sort of. I wanted to take a walk through the woods one last time," Sam admitted.

"Last time? Why, you planning on not walking out here anymore?" Shadow spoke from a tree branch above Sam's head.

"Not by choice." Sam spoke softly, knowing they would hear him.

"You think boss man's going to flip on you for that little stunt you pulled in there?" Coop asked unapologetically as he walked up behind Sam.

"That was pretty ballsy, Sam," Vincent said, joining the other three.

"Stunt! I was trying to bring them all back together. I still believe that what Dante heard was misinterpreted. I could tell by talking to them that they love him." Sam just about shouted, his fear and sadness getting the better of him.

"Hey, we didn't say it wasn't the right move, little boss," Coop assured, holding his hands up in surrender as he backed a few feet away.

"Ya, boss man would never have done it on his own, and the four of us know just how much he misses his parents," Shannon agreed.

Sam was mentally and physically exhausted; he walked over to a tree and sat down beneath it. Sure, he may have done the right thing but he doubted Dante would see it that way. Slowly he lowered his head to his hands, feeling the first inkling of a headache coming on.

"Then why the hell haven't any of you brought his parents to him to have this out?" If they felt that way, Sam couldn't understand why they wouldn't do something about it.

"None of us are that brave," Shadow admitted as he jumped down from his perch. "He would have skinned us, but you're safe, he loves you."

"Safe? You didn't see the look in his eyes. He thinks I've betrayed him, there's no other conclusion." Sam could feel the tears sliding down his face again but just didn't care who saw them. "He'll never forgive me for this one."

Sam could feel the pain in his head getting progressively worse but his medication was in their bedroom. The back of his head began to pound exactly where Miguel had pistol-whipped him.

"Don't be so sure, little boss," Vincent stated as he picked up a limb, pulled out his hunting knife, and began whittling. *People actually whittle?*

"Dante loves you, Sam. I don't know that there is anything to forgive. You did this because you love him and want him to be happy. Your heart was in the right place." Shannon tried to calm him but Sam wasn't having it, his heart and head were hurting.

"Sam, are you okay?" Coop asked, coming closer to have a look at him. "Is your head hurting?"

"Yes, I'll need my medication soon," Sam admitted.

"Okay, let's get you back to the house," Shadow ordered.

"I'll be fine."

"No you won't. Don't be stubborn or you'll end up with another migraine," Shannon piped up from somewhere to his left; he didn't bother raising his sore head.

"This is where you're hiding." Dante's voice sounded playful, but Sam couldn't imagine why. Maybe he'd pushed him too far and he'd cracked? Sam didn't bother looking Dante in the eye; he continued to cradle his head in his hands.

"I'll have my things packed within the hour if you give me time. If not, I could probably do it in thirty minutes with garbage bags and the team's help."

"Oh, you're not going anywhere, Sam." Dante's voice took on a bit of an edge, as if the thought of Sam leaving was unacceptable.

Yep, he's cracked.

Sam wiped his face and finally turned to look Dante in the eyes. The hate and anger he expected was missing. *Why?*

"Boss, Sam's head's hurting. He needs his medication," Shadow explained.

"Oh, Trouble." Dante stepped through his team and gathered Sam into his arms, allowing a flood of tears to pour out of Sam. "Don't cry, my love." Dante kissed his cheeks and gently brushed away any remaining wetness.

"But... But I ruined everything."

"No, beautiful, you've given me the one thing I thought I would never have: my parents back." Dante's voice was soft and full of emotion.

"Really?" Sam asked, still unsure if he was actually hearing Dante correctly or dreaming the whole damn thing.

"Yes, they're inside right now making supper with Spider. Let's go and get your medication, baby."

"Supper?" Sam knew he was stuck in one-word questions but was powerless to stop himself. His brain was stuck. Of all the things he expected after what he saw in the living room, this wasn't even on the same planet. "But in the house you...?"

"I'm so sorry, Sam. I was just caught off guard and felt a little betrayed."

"I would never betray you or Spider. I just thought maybe if...if you talked...."

"I know that, Sam, but at the time, I was trying to process the fact that my parents were sitting in our house. I haven't seen them in years. I was a little shocked."

"You don't want me to leave?"

"No, never! We're a team, the three of us, for better or for worse. Plus these other four pains. I love you, Sam. I always will."

"I love you too."

"But somebody still deserves a spanking for going behind my back, though I admit, I would never have agreed to inviting them here," Dante confirmed.

"Did I hear the word spanking? Well, don't I have perfect timing?" Spider laughed as he walked up to the two. The rest of the team had vanished. He immediately lifted Sam away from Dante and held him close. "You did good, sweetheart. It's still not getting you out of your swats, but they'll wait until we get your headache under control and feel better."

Sam's emotions had swung from nervousness, fear, and doubt to relief, excitement, and love in the span of one hour, but standing here, wrapped in the arms of his men, he couldn't imagine ever being anywhere else. He was home.

"You've got yourselves a date, soldiers."

RICK'S BEAR

Chapter One

Rick sat safely behind his old wooden desk inside Brighton Central Library, cataloguing new arrivals on the library's database. The library was quiet today, lowering his anxiety greatly. The thundering of a Harley coming down Main Street immediately caught his attention. It was well past 8:00 p.m., and Rick was just about to lock the doors and finish his work alone. His eyes were drawn to the window. He finally gave in, stood up, and walked the five feet to the place he found himself standing regularly throughout the day, and he wasn't disappointed.

There on the street, parking his big black-and-chrome bike was Clem "Bear" Mitchell—a man whom Rick had to stay far, far away from if he wished to keep his dignity. Begging was never an endearing quality. But instead of Bear walking into the diner he owned across the street, he was headed Rick's way, and Rick found himself frozen to the spot.

Clem was a scruffy mountain of a man, a bear in every sense. Rick thought perhaps he was in his early forties. If his height sticker on the front door was correct, he stood six feet seven inches tall, and Rick had to wonder how much all those muscles weighed, but then again, it wasn't as if Rick could have Bear hop on a scale when he came to visit. In all honesty, Rick found himself staring far too often in the man's direction that he'd almost memorized every detail of the biker's body, so his best guess was over two hundred sixty pounds.

Well, considering the average height of a US male is five-nine, he is certainly above normal.

Rick groaned the moment he realized he was coming up with useless facts yet again. It was a habit he had whenever he was nervous or stressed, which was most of the time.

Bear was carrying a package in his right hand. Rick knew it must be another gift for him, and he was barely able to contain his excitement. Finally coming to his senses, Rick rushed over to his desk and tried to appear busy, without much luck. He heard the front door open and heavy boots thudding their way across the wood floors as they always did when this hulking man came to visit. The steps seemed to thunder through Rick's body. If he had just one wish, it would be for the ability to speak more than a few words to the man. Rick's social anxiety and shyness pretty much prevented that from happening.

God, what I'd give to be able to ask him out.

The footsteps stopped, and Rick knew Bear was standing right in front of his desk. Slowly, he raised his eyes and looked at the gorgeous man from under his lashes, the same man who occupied his dreams every night. Bear stood there in his worn jeans, black boots, tight T-shirt, and leather jacket, looking every bit the biker he was known to be. His dark blue eyes sparkled from underneath his shaggy chestnut brown hair, and his short beard was trimmed perfectly.

God, he's so handsome.

"Hello, Rick, how are you today?" Bear asked in a soft voice. It seemed to Rick that he was trying to make himself smaller, less threatening.

"H-hi, Bear," Rick stuttered. "I'm okay. How are you?"

"My day's getting better by the second." Rick knew Bear was teasing, but deep down, his inner romantic nerd wished that Bear were actually flirting with him.

"Can I help you with anything, Bear?" Rick asked.

"Well...ah..." Bear seemed nervous and unsure, not his usual demeanor.

"Is everything okay?" Rick asked as he stood and came around the desk. "Are you okay?" Rick might be too shy to do anything about his attraction to Bear, but he considered the man a friend, and if something were wrong, Rick would help.

"No, nothing's wrong. I just saw this and thought you'd like it." Bear held out his hand to give the small package to Rick.

Rick carefully took the gift, accidently brushing their fingers together and sending up a spark of the one thing Rick hadn't felt in a very long time—desire. "Bear, you know I told you the last time that you didn't need to buy me anything."

Bear's smile lit up his entire face. "Wait until you see it to decide."

With his interest piqued, Rick carefully unwrapped the brown shipping paper from the package and revealed a book, but not just any book, an original first edition, hardcover copy of *The Hunt for Red October* by Tom Clancy. "Oh, Bear, it's amazing, but I can't accept this. It has to be worth hundreds of dollars."

"I know how much you love Tom Clancy. It's yours."

"Bear... I—"

"Rick, is it too late to sign out a book?" asked Rachel, a young woman who'd just moved to Brighton from California a few months back. Rick hadn't realized they weren't alone and immediately took several steps away from Bear, who smiled knowingly.

"Yes, Rachel, go ahead. I'll lock up after you're done," Rick assured the young woman who'd become his friend.

Rick walked back around his desk, cradling his new book to his chest. He'd never received such a thoughtful gift before. Well, if you didn't count the two other books Bear had already given him. It seemed to make the big man happy, and Rick was having a hard time saying no to him.

"Thank you, Bear. It's perfect," Rick gushed just a little. He knew he wasn't macho in any way, shape, or form, but he did have some restraint.

Bear looked down and blushed, which shocked Rick. He'd never seen the big man blush, ever. They'd known each other for over a year now, ever since Bear took over the diner when the previous owner retired. He'd been visiting Rick for months. Every few days he'd come to the library to visit or, like today, drop off something he knew Rick would like.

"Rick, can you help me, please?" Rachel asked from one of the five computer reference systems located in the library. "I wanted to find something on Greek mythology."

"Yes, of course, Rachel," Rick replied. He would have liked to spend a little more time with Bear, and it must have shown in his face, based on what Bear said next.

"Why don't you come on over to the diner when you're all done and have a late dinner? Today's special is roast beef, mashed potatoes, and green beans. We even have apple pie for dessert." Bear gave him a sly smile, knowing full well Rick loved apple pie, which seemed to always be available when he ordered some.

Rick thought about it for a moment, calculating how many people would be in the diner at that time of night. It wasn't that he didn't like people; it was just that once those people became a group or crowd, Rick immediately went into an anxiety attack.

Typically, he would order pick-up and take it home, but he did want to spend more time around Bear. He might not be able to act on his attraction, but he could still be in his world.

Much like the moon orbits Earth at an average distance of 238,855 miles. Ugh. Useless damn information.

"Is it very busy after 8:00 p.m.?" Rick asked. He would have to mentally prepare himself if he decided to go.

"No, just a few regulars, sometimes people passing through," Bear assured him with a hopeful expression on his handsome face.

Who could say no to that? Not me, that's for sure.

"Okay, I'll come over after I lock up," Rick answered after a few more moments of uncertainty, and Bear's smile was so big that you would have thought he'd won some sort of prize.

"You've got a date, Rick. I'll see you soon."

With that said, the giant of a man turned and walked back out of the library, leaving behind a confused Rick. He just couldn't figure out why Bear kept coming around; it wasn't as if Rick was some sort of prize catch. It was a mystery.

***

As Bear jogged back across the street to his diner, the chain attached to his wallet jingled, and excitement coursed through his veins. Rick didn't know it, but Bear would be having dinner with him tonight. He would consider it a quasi-date of sorts but would take whatever the little man was comfortable giving.

Rick was such a gentle soul that Bear couldn't help but be drawn to him. Compared to his old life in Chicago, Brighton was his idea of heaven, and the brightest spot in it was the intelligent, handsome librarian.

The "White Hair Crew," Brighton's very own grandmothers and purveyors of all information to be had in Brighton, had taken Bear aside and explained that Rick was extremely shy and suffered from anxiety in large groups of people. So Bear would make sure they were seated at the back away from anyone else. Grandma Rose had noticed Bear's interest early on and had also explained that several years ago Rick had dated a man who had destroyed what little self-esteem he had gained. If he ever met the guy, Bear would clear any misconceptions about Rick's worth very quickly.

Bear walked into the diner, happy for the first time to see that only a few people were seated at tables. Jesse was working the grill, and Sarah, his waitress, was cleaning coffee cups off the corner booth.

"Evening, boss man," Jesse hollered from the kitchen, his apron covered in stains. His eyes were tired, but the smile on his face was genuine. Since Jesse's family started coming around, the man seemed never to have a moment of peace. His family and members of their fringe church had been banned from the diner property when they started in with their bigoted rants and how Jesse was a sinner and bound for the fires of hell.

He had protected Jesse at work and at his home, considering his apartment was above the diner. Bear had no idea why Jesse, who was madly in love with his boyfriend Royce, wasn't living at Royce's large house. But he stayed out of other people's business as much as he could. He would protect Jesse here, and Royce could protect him when he was out, but Bear still had a bad feeling about that whole situation.

"Hey, Jesse, how's it going?" Bear asked.

"Good, quietin' down a bit," Jesse answered in a husky voice.

"Are you coming down with something?" Bear asked.

"No, boss, I'm all good. Just not sleeping all that well," Jesse admitted easily.

"If you need time to rest, just let me know. I can fill in for ya."

"You're a good man, boss, but I'm okay for now," Jesse replied.

Bear doubted that but wouldn't fight with the man about it. Something would give soon, and Bear would be ready.

"Hey, Sarah, can you reserve a booth in the back for me, and seat any customers that come in near the front?" That request got both Jesse's and Sarah's attention.

"You got yourself a date, boss?" Sarah asked with a gleam in her eye. Both of his employees knew that he was head over heels for the little librarian and couldn't understand why Bear was moving so slowly. Simply, he desperately didn't want to scare Rick away. The man had suffered abuse in the past at the hands of someone who professed to love him; Bear would take his time.

"Yes, as a matter of fact. Rick is coming over for dinner once he locks up the library, and I don't want him anxious in the middle of the diner." Bear knew both were aware of Rick's anxiety; after all, Rick had lived in Brighton his entire life.

"Good for you, boss. Don't you be worrying about anyone buggin' ya. I'll make sure no one gets anywhere near the two of you," Sarah assured. "Not unless they want a tray upside their fool heads."

"What do you want me to make for your date, Bear?" Jesse asked, his smile so genuine, Bear couldn't understand why Jesse's family harassed the gentle man. "I have Rick's piece of apple pie already saved in the fridge. We only had one left."

"Thank you, Jesse. I think he'll want the roast beef special. Rick loves the roast beef," Bear answered.

"Yeah, and that's why you make it the special a few times a week because you know Rick will be coming over." Jesse laughed before going back to work on his roast.

"Man's gotta do what a man's gotta do," Bear mumbled as he walked into his tiny office and sat behind his old, laminated wood desk. The high-back office chair was what was important. With the amount of time he spent in the diner, he needed the extra comfort. Bear sat and his mind immediately wandered to the fascinating man across the street and the last time he had Rick in this very chair.

It wasn't the typical way one might think one man might invite another into their office—this involved Rick being carried over Bear's shoulder. A few weeks prior, Sam Mason's truck had exploded and his house burned down by a drug lord bent on revenge for his arrest. When word got out about what happened, the town went into lockdown, and Bear couldn't leave Rick unprotected at the library.

So once again, he did what he had to do. He had marched over to the library, helped Rick lock up, and carried him back over to the diner when Rick began to have second thoughts. Bear had walked right through the crowds that were looking for any sort of gossip or news and into his office to keep Rick away from so many people.

Bear couldn't allow this kind, beautiful man to be hurt, so he'd kept him safely in the office and kitchen for the remainder of the day. He'd bring him food and drinks as Rick read one of the gifts Bear had given him. As soon as Bear locked the diner doors, he gathered up a still-grousing Rick and drove them both over to Bear's house. After all, they hadn't found Sam or those responsible for the attack, so he wasn't taking any chances of Rick being caught in the crossfire.

He'd acted the complete gentleman all evening, giving Rick something to wear to bed, which ended up being one of Bear's T-shirts that reached Rick's knees, leaving Bear with a satisfied feeling. He gave Rick the guestroom, so no pressure. But when Rick unconsciously snuggled into him while they watched an old 80s horror movie, laughing at how easily victims seemed to forget how to run away from the slow-walking psycho, Bear was hooked on the man.

After that night spent with only a wall separating them, Bear had made up his mind. He would woo the smaller man and earn Rick's trust before trying for anything physical. Though he wanted those physical aspects like any red-blooded gay man, he would wait until Rick made the first move.

The next day, he'd driven Rick to work after a pit stop at Rick's house to clean up and to change his clothes before he opened the library. From that day forward, Bear redoubled his efforts to make Rick comfortable and feel safe with him and see if they were compatible on levels beyond physical attraction. Bear had learned patience over his hard-earned life; he'd wait until the gorgeous man was ready.

To look at the two of them, not one person would say they belonged together—they were pretty far apart on the spectrum of personality. Bear had grown up in the streets of Chicago, joined an MC before he could even legally drink, and spent well over a decade as an enforcer for the club. He was a rough-looking grizzly of a man, and he knew it; that was how he'd gotten his name. It made people think twice before messing with him.

Now though, he'd found peace in a small town hours away from any large cities. There were no more battles to survive—fighting to hold rank, respect, money, and, at the end, for the right to leave. Rick, on the other hand, was quiet, reserved, and avoided conflict at all costs. The beautiful man was shy and became anxious in certain situations, and this was at odds with Bear's loud, outgoing personality.

The tinkling of the bell on the front door brought Bear back to reality. His shoulders slumped when he saw three men walk into the diner, none of them Rick. Bear was about to return to his chair when he noticed that the three men had four pairs of feet. He took two steps to the left and found Rick waiting patiently, or hiding behind the men, almost invisible behind their bulk. Oh, his baby sometimes behaved meekly; they needed to work on that.

"Rick," Bear said. "Come on over here, honey."

The three unknown men looked at him strangely, then noticed Rick standing quietly behind them. They quickly moved out of his way.

Rick carefully stepped between the three other men and, with the shift of air, Bear got the distinct smell of liquor coming off the unknown three. *Great.* Bear just hoped none of them decided to pull anything, not tonight of all nights. But, by the way the men ogled Rick's ass, he could predict that wouldn't be happening. Bear pulled Rick close, making sure to establish eye contact with each of the three men. Two looked down, but the third stared right back. *Right, now I know which one to keep my eyes on.*

"Hi," Rick whispered into his chest, making Bear realize he was probably smothering the poor man. Bear pulled away slightly and began leading him away from the men and to the back. He should never have made Rick walk through those men and become the center of their attention, never. The guilt was choking.

"I'm so happy you came." Bear smiled; he just couldn't help himself. Rick was here, and nothing would ruin this night.

Chapter Two

Rick knew he was going to ruin this evening somehow. Heck, he'd already started by causing those three men to notice him. He'd planned to stand behind them, hopefully going unseen, until Bear had called his name and he had to walk through the group. Now his anxiety level was rising like a toxic tide.

"Easy. Look at me. Breathe..." When Rick looked up, everything looked fuzzy, and he noticed they were in Bear's office instead of at the table. "Breathe in and out. That's it."

After several minutes, Bear's handsome face came into focus, and Rick could finally speak. "S-s-sorry" was all he could manage to say.

"No, that was my fault. I should have never called their attention to you or made you walk through them with your anxiety. I'm the one who's sorry," Bear replied with a guilty look on his handsome face. "I won't ever do that again unless it's an emergency. I'll come to you instead, I swear."

Rick realized a while ago that Bear was aware of his "little quirks" but had never brought them up so openly before. He felt a bit embarrassed and found himself unable to meet Bear's eyes. "It's okay, and it's not your fault that I'm this way." That responsibility belonged to someone else entirely, a man so vicious it had taken four officers to take him down.

"This way?" Bear gently cupped both of Rick's cheeks so he couldn't look away again. "The way you are is perfect to me, never doubt that."

He looked so serious that Rick had no other choice but to nod his head in agreement.

"Okay, now are we ready to have dinner and apple pie?" Bear's smile brought out that one dimple he had on his left cheek.

"Oh yeah," Rick replied. "Did you know an average nine-inch pie holds roughly six medium apples?" He hung his head so quickly that Rick was surprised he hadn't given himself whiplash. *Damn nervous useless information, he'll think I'm a freak.*

"Yeah, we use around five or six depending on the size of the apple," Bear answered and carried on toward the front without one word of censure or even a strange look for his "info drop" as Rick liked to call his freaky behavior. It wasn't like he could namedrop, but boy he could spit out useless information like a pro. Maybe for a little while, Rick would be able to act as if his idiosyncrasies didn't matter and not have to worry about how he appeared to others.

Bear led Rick to their table by keeping a possessive hand on the small of Rick's back, and Rick had no idea why it felt so good there. *How can I be attracted to another giant of a man? Didn't I learn my lesson the last time?* Rick honestly didn't quite understand why Bear wanted to spend time with him, but Rick wasn't going to complain. He felt safe when he was with Bear, which was an odd feeling for him to begin with.

Over the next hour, Rick learned more about the man that occupied every dream he'd had over the past year. He knew Bear had been in a motorcycle club back in Chicago but had left it to "find a new life," as Bear put it, but he wouldn't elaborate further. What he did know still amazed Rick, who'd never left Brighton. All the places Bear had seen were a world away from Rick's reality.

"Here you go, sweetie, your apple pie." Rick looked up and smiled at Sarah. The older woman was an absolute angel to everyone.

"Thank you, Sarah. I absolutely love your apple pie," Rick stated as his mouth watered for a bite.

"We know, honey," Sarah responded.

"Hey! What the hell? You told me you didn't have any more apple pie, you old crone," yelled one of the three men who'd made Rick feel nervous when he'd come in. "What do I have to do, go in the back and give the boss a blowjob like little Mr. Bookworm here did?"

Rick immediately pulled his messenger bag off the table and placed it safely on the bench seat—Bear's gift was in that bag after all. He slid across the bench, putting some distance between himself and the irate man. The man's two friends were desperately clawing at the third man's jacket, trying to pull him back.

Rick's anxiety began to rise, and of course, he knew what was coming next. "In a recent survey, it was found that four out of ten people have dated someone from work. But in this case, you are completely mistaken. We're friends."

The drunk man stopped and just stared at Rick like he'd grown a second head. "What do I care? Are you some kind of idiot?"

Rick witnessed the change in Bear and sat fascinated as he went from attentive, charming dinner date to a hulking man who, with one look, could make most people shake. But the truly bizarre thing was that, instead of feeling fear, Rick felt excited.

What's wrong with me?

Bear gave Rick a strangely sad look before standing and placing himself protectively between the men and Rick. "I'd take your friend and leave. As you obviously know, I own this property and I'll ban the three of you from the diner if you don't go now." Rick could see Jesse coming out from the kitchen and Sarah on the phone. This wasn't going to end well.

Bear spoke calmly and logically. The men should have left, but of course that wasn't what happened. The angry, drunk man lunged at Bear, pushing him back onto their booth's table, effectively smashing his piece of pie all over Bear's back. Rick grabbed his bag and dived under the table, knowing full well his scrawny body was of no help.

He sneaked a peek over the edge of the table just in time to see Bear throw the man across two other tables and onto the floor. Rick was shocked by the show of strength. Bear turned to look at Rick, his face full of regret. He could hear sirens in the distance but retreated back under the table. Soon there would be more and more people coming in. Rick was cemented to the spot, all warm, fuzzy feelings gone as he listened to the smashing glass, breaking wood, and sirens blaring closer.

Rick pulled his knees up to his chest and his world narrowed down to the few square feet he was occupying on the floor. His anxiety was taking over and heading straight for panic attack territory. This was why he worked in a library. Other than his love affair with books, it was typically a quiet, peaceful place.

Rick's whole body began to shake, and he couldn't catch his breath. Everything around him seemed unreal, distant. Feet rushed by and men were pinned to the floor by police, but none of the chaos reached him. Painfully, Rick's mind traveled back in time. He remembered being curled in a ball, desperately trying to protect himself as steel-toed boots pummeled him over and over again. The memory was so real.

Only when he heard that soft, deep voice did he allow the world to creep back inside his bubble. A warm hand caressed his face. Rick knew those large hands—Bear. The world snapped back into place and sharply into focus. There in front of him was Bear. The man was only able to stuff half his body under the table, and he had blood dripping down his face from a cut above his left eye. He was safe, and Rick couldn't help but slide closer and curl into Bear's arms.

"Are you hurt, Rick?" Bear asked while running his hands all over Rick's body, as if looking for possible injuries.

"No, I'm fine, but you're bleeding, Bear." Rick was panicked and still could only hold on to Bear's shirt when he should have been helping him.

"It's nothing, baby. Let's just get you out from under here." Bear gently pulled Rick closer and out from under his makeshift Sentinel. Five police officers were in the process of dragging the three men out the front door. He'd met a few of the officers on a similar night many years ago.

Police Chief Graham was speaking to Sarah, and Jesse was cleaning up the remnants of one of the tables the drunk had landed on, while his boyfriend, Royce, hovered protectively and helped him clean. Bear never once let Rick go, for which he was eternally grateful. In fact, when someone came near them, Bear would press him closer to his body, never allowing anyone closer to Rick than two feet.

When Chief Graham came over, Rick naturally tensed. Dave Graham had been an officer on the Brighton Police Force all those years ago. Though Rick's memories flashed in and out, he did remember Chief Graham's kind words while he held a bloody cloth to Rick's forehead as he was loaded into the ambulance. The police chief smiled warmly as he approached, obviously not trying to scare the "spooked" man. Sometimes Rick wished he were stronger in other people's eyes.

Maybe I'm not as strong as I think I am...and I did just hide under a table...damn.

"Bear, we got them all rounded up. Are you hurt, Rick?" Chief Graham asked.

"N-no, just a bit shook up." Rick stood straight, but his voice wavered slightly.

"Good, we have EMS here to take a look at those three and Bear's head," he explained. "I'm glad you're not injured."

Rick felt about as tall as a snake. Here Bear was bleeding, and everybody was fussing about him, but he still couldn't move. Rick knew he was safe with Bear: that was the only guarantee at the moment and he would take it. Trust was the one thing Rick had a hard time freely handing out, especially after the last man who said he loved him was serving twenty-five to life for murder.

"Rick... Rick, honey, are you okay?" Bear's words brought him back to the present and the people surrounding him—Jesse, Sarah, Chief Graham, and the EMTs—and Rick knew he had to get out of there before he had a panic attack in front of everyone.

"I... I think I should go home," Rick stammered.

The dejection he saw cross Bear's face and his slumped shoulders confused Rick. He wasn't leaving their date because of what happened—well, maybe a little—but the main reason was the growing crowd in and outside the diner. Unfortunately, there wasn't the opportunity to explain as Sarah gathered Rick into her surprisingly strong arms and began leading him toward the back door.

"I'll walk with you, dear. My house is just one block over." Rick knew that was just an excuse but appreciated her attempt anyway. He turned before walking out the back door to see Bear having his head bandaged. His big blue eyes were filled with sorrow and locked on to Rick before he turned away to answer an EMT's question, and Rick was led through the door.

***

Bear watched those beautiful hazel eyes cloud with fear when that drunk bastard approached their table, appear panicked when under the table, and now they turned sad and confused before leaving the diner. *Great first date.*

"He looks a bit stunned, but he's not hurt, and Sarah will make sure he gets home," Chief Graham assured Bear when he wouldn't take his eyes off the back door.

"He may not be physically hurt, but you know just as well as I do that Rick's history doesn't bode well for a man of my size and strength. This little tussle sure as shit didn't help my case any." Bear tugged on his short beard; he'd considered shaving it in an attempt to look less intimidating to Rick, but that would leave his numerous scars out in the open, which could be worse.

"Yes, I can imagine this is going to be a bit of an uphill battle, Bear." Chief Graham rubbed the back of his own neck, deep in thought. "I know you're aware of what Rick's been through. I don't agree with the way the White Hair Crew informed you, but I do understand their intentions. They didn't want you to rush him or misunderstand his actions. But over the past few months Rick seems to have gained a strength I haven't seen in years, and the only thing that's changed in his life is you. You can't take what happened tonight to heart. I'm sure Rick doesn't blame you or view you any differently now."

"I wish I could feel as confident as you do, but you didn't see the fear in his eyes." Bear felt Rick's fear and rejection straight to his soul and would do just about anything to have a crack at a "do-over."

"Of course he was afraid, some asshole was attacking you, but he wasn't afraid of you. He was glued to your side," Graham assured.

"I don't know about that, Graham." Bear was sure he saw that fear directed straight at him.

The police chief shook his head at Bear before continuing. "We'll take those three to spend the night in the drunk tank. When they sober up and find out what they're charged with, they'll have more than just a hangover to deal with."

Bear couldn't care less what happened to those three. His dinner with Rick had gone down in flames. He was forced to show a man who had suffered severe abuse in the past just how dangerous he really was. He knew he had to protect Rick and Sarah, but Christ, why now?

He'll never look at me the same way again.

Chapter Three

Two weeks. It had been two long, agonizing weeks since their dinner disaster, and Rick still hadn't seen Bear anywhere near the library. Bear was avoiding him, plain and simple; there was no other logical explanation. Rick understood the reason all too well, but the heartache he felt because of it was new. Rick realized he was a freak, and dinner had just confirmed it for Bear. He'd been told many times in the past, from a man who'd claimed to love him, that no one would ever be able to put up with his "crazy shit."

After all, who would want a man who hides under a table when things get scary or who can't be in a crowd without fear of having a panic attack? Or the ever-endearing quality of believing that reading late into the night was a great way to spend an evening? What was he thinking? He could never have kept a man like Bear interested past a single date—well, a sort-of date.

Rick's mind had wandered back to that night so often, and now wasn't any different, but it wasn't fear that he'd felt that night. The sight of Bear's hulking body standing over him should have given Rick an immediate panic attack, but instead he'd felt protected, safe. Bear's muscles flexing with every move and the power exploding out of this kind, usually gentle man should have scared Rick half to death, but it hadn't.

To Rick it seemed Bear only used a small measure of his strength with the drunk man. He was never out of control. His eyes weren't ever wild and glazed over with anger, and hurting others didn't seem to be his idea of fun. At this point though, the fact that Rick found himself attracted to this big bear was simply sad because it was obviously one-sided. He huffed out a breath that he hadn't realized he'd been holding and lowered his aching head to his desk.

"Rick, are you all right?" Rachel's voice came from close by on the left and sent Rick flying out of his chair.

"Rachel, for the love of God, don't sneak up on me!" Rick gasped, trying to catch his breath. After a few moments, he continued, "Can I help you with something?"

"I was bringing back the book I borrowed a couple weeks ago on Greek mythology and hoped to have coffee with you," Rachel explained.

"Ah... Aphrodite, Aries, Hades, and Zeus. How did you like the book?" Rick asked as he gathered the papers on his desk into a pile, trying desperately to hide the fact that he'd been so distracted by thoughts of Bear that he hadn't noticed Rachel entering the library. Hell, a herd of cattle could have stampeded through and Rick wouldn't have noticed.

"What I'd give for a thunderbolt on occasion." Rachel laughed, placing Rick more at ease, but her next sentence changed that quickly enough. "Rick, I'd like to think we've become friends over the time I've lived here in Brighton. May I ask you a personal question?"

Rick's anxiety shot right back up; personal questions always did that. He didn't have anything against Rachel. He really liked her, in fact, but he barely handled getting personal with the people he'd known all his life, let alone a new friend, since the day his life had changed forever. "Rachel, I don't know—"

"Please, Rick, I wouldn't ask if it wasn't serious," Rachel almost begged. Hearing the waver in her voice, Rick wondered why she was becoming emotional.

He couldn't fight the pleading in Rachel's eyes and caved like a tower of sand. "Okay, go ahead."

"Why are you so sad and depressed lately? Is it because Bear hasn't been coming around the library anymore? Did you break it off with him, or did he?" Rachel quickly rambled off her questions, as if worried Rick would stop her at any moment.

Rick knew Rachel wasn't some sort of stalker. She was simply a caring friend, just the same as many of the people in Brighton, and she had obviously been added to the Brighton grapevine. Usually, he escaped most of the town's gossip; apparently, that time had ended.

"I'm sorry, Rachel, but I don't like to talk about my personal life." He didn't want to be rude, but Bear was the last person he wanted to talk about.

"I know, but it's just that you're even quieter now than you've been for months, and you're not smiling as much. I don't understand why Bear hasn't come over in weeks. Did you break up with him?" Rachel asked, the concern in her voice easy to hear.

"No, Rachel, I didn't dump him. Are you crazy? He's perfect. But you know I'm not everybody's idea of a dream man." Rick tried to laugh it off and made a mental note to adjust his behavior in the future. He didn't want to have to answer this question ever again. He couldn't sit here pining over someone so far out of his league.

Rachel took a long, hard look at Rick. As moments passed, he became a bit nervous. *Big shock, ugh.* Whatever she saw must have confirmed something, because she placed her borrowed book on the table along with two full paper coffee cups, nodded her head, and then turned around and left. Rick thought it a bit strange, but after all, who was he to talk about someone acting strangely? Strange might as well have been his middle name.

As a child, he had been quiet and withdrawn. As he grew, he became a bit of a loner. Oh, he was kind and helpful to everyone, but he had no one to call a close friend. Deep down, he knew that this was the reason he had been so easily sucked in by Bret's attention; he had no one else to turn to. *I should have known better.* Rick was just happy his ex was far, far away, even if it meant he would live his life alone. He'd accepted that long ago.

***

Bear was just finishing up the lunch rush when the kitchen door slammed open, crashing against the wall and revealing a pissed-off Rachel White. Bear had never seen the woman without a smile on her face, but she could pull off a look of disgust like a pro. Bear cleaned his hands on his apron and approached her slowly, as he would a spooked animal, still unsure how Rachel had gotten back here or why she was in the first place. Before he could ask, Sarah came running through the door.

"You're fast, missy, but I've got ya now." Sarah looked about ready to spit nails.

"I'm not leaving until I say what I have to say to him." Rachel's voice was calm, but her body screamed aggression and anger.

"Okay, Rachel, what's this all about?" Bear asked, more curious than upset.

"Rick, of course," she answered with a snarl.

That got Bear's attention like nothing else could, and Sarah backed down instantly. "What's wrong with Rick?" He began to untie his apron; he had to go find Rick.

"As if you have no idea. I thought you were different. I thought you really cared about him," Rachel roared. "He was my first friend in this town. When I was all alone, I could always go to the library and talk with Rick. Now he's sad and barely talks because of what you did."

"Sad...? Wait, Rick's suffering because of me?" Bear asked.

"What did you think would happen when you dumped him? You haven't gone anywhere near him in weeks, like he has some sort of contagious disease. Just because he's a little different doesn't give you the right to play with his feelings." Rachel's chest was heaving by the time she finished, but Bear's heart had stopped completely. The man he needed more than his Harley—and that was saying something considering that bike meant more to him than air— thought Bear had dumped him.

"I don't understand. Why would Rick think I was playing with his feelings?" Bear had always been confident of his actions, but lately he was beginning to wonder if he'd lost complete control over himself when it came to Rick.

"I think the two of you need to talk somewhere other than in the middle of this kitchen, Bear. Unless you want to share with the whole town." Jesse spoke softly and motioned with a tilt of his head toward the full counter and the other customers milling around in the diner.

"We'll finish this in my office." Bear led Rachel to the small room, his mind buzzing with questions. He'd decided to give Rick some time to hopefully soften his fear of Bear. He remembered that look on Rick's face all too well from the night of the fight. It had flashed through his mind repeatedly ever since.

Once the door was shut, Rachel went back on the offensive. "Rick's a wonderful man. He may have a few issues, but you'd be lucky to have him." By now her hands were slicing through the air in anger.

"Yes, I know I would," Bear agreed before hanging his head.

"What?" Rachel asked. Her mouth hung open and she gaped at him.

"Yes, I would be very lucky to have Rick, but you don't understand. He's afraid of me." Bear pulled on his beard—if he kept that up, he wouldn't have to worry about shaving it.

"Afraid of you? Where the heck did you get that silly idea?" Rachel seemed so shocked that she physically stepped backward.

"The night at the diner when we were attacked, I saw his fear while I was throwing that guy around. I bring up bad memories for him. I try my damnedest to prevent reminding him of Bret, but fate has other plans," Bear said, as he laid it out. The truth was the truth, no matter how painful it might be.

"Well, you've really assumed a lot, haven't you? But did you ever think to ask him before you had this great revelation all by yourself?" Bear didn't miss the sarcasm but decided not to call her on it, considering he deserved much worse.

"I didn't want to make it uncomfortable for him. I thought, if I gave him time, he'd give me another chance." Honestly, he never thought Rick would take his actions as a rejection, but now looking back, it definitely could have seemed that way. Bear had planned to slowly work his way back into Rick's life until the man felt comfortable again.

"Well, you know what they say about assuming things." Rachel cracked her first smile since entering the kitchen.

"You say I 'made an ass out of you and me,' you'll never eat in this diner again." Bear smiled to make sure Rachel understood he wasn't serious. "Now, if you'll excuse me, I need to go and clear a few things up with someone."

"You'd better. You don't want to see me get real mad," Rachel warned before she turned and left the office as suddenly as she'd entered the kitchen. She was right: he didn't want to see her real mad if this hadn't been it.

Bear sat in his chair, staring at his scarred hands. Could he have been so wrong? Had the fear he saw not been directed at him? The last two weeks had been its own special kind of hell, leaving Bear depressed, and so many times he'd had to stop himself from going over to the library. Another first-edition novel he'd ordered for Rick had come in, but Bear was unsure if he should give it to him or wait. Right now he needed answers. He had to lay it all on the line with Rick and hope his heart was still intact when this was all over—if he hadn't already blown his chance with the man.

Bear strode out of the diner and across the street; the walk had never seemed as significant as it did at this one moment. Either he would leave the library a happy man or be extremely disappointed, even heartbroken. All of these feelings were strange enough to Bear, but the driving need to be near Rick had never happened to him before. Sure, he'd had other relationships, but from the first moment he'd seen Rick and their eyes met, there was a connection he couldn't let go of.

He opened the heavy wooden door, taking a deep breath as he entered. His boots sounded like thunder echoing through the library, no matter how he walked. Had they always been that loud? Soon enough, none of that mattered because sitting behind the wooden circulation desk tapping away on his computer was the one man capable of causing him so much joy and pain. His blond hair stuck up in odd places from Rick running his hands through it, a nervous habit Bear had noticed early on. The man was simply gorgeous to Bear, in his rumpled, ink-stained clothing. Rick had no idea what he did to Bear. Rick's kind hazel eyes slowly rose and locked with his own; the only thing standing between them now was the desk.

"Hi." *Oh, that was smooth.*

"Hi," Rick tentatively replied.

"Can you take a break, please?" What he intended to say was not for public consumption or local gossip.

Rick looked a bit nervous but slowly nodded his agreement. "Janet, I'm stepping into the back for a moment."

Janet, Rick's assistant, came up to the desk and took Rick's seat. The walk to the back was made in silence, which usually never bothered Bear, but this time he could feel the unease coming off Rick in waves. Once alone in the storage room, Bear could no longer hold back. Quickly, but carefully, he gathered a shocked Rick into his arms and held him close, not saying a word. After only a few moments, he felt Rick relax into his arms and snake his hands up Bear's chest, almost making him purr in happiness.

"I'm confused, Bear. I don't understand why you're here after two weeks without a word," Rick said, pulling away from Bear's hold.

He immediately let Rick go, not wishing to restrain him in any way. "I'm sorry. I didn't mean to hurt you."

"Hurt me? What makes you think you've hurt me?" Rick asked, avoiding eye contact with Bear.

"I had a little visit from your friend Rachel. She's a hellion when she gets her back up," Bear explained.

Rick's face fell and he looked at the ground. "I'm okay, Bear. I might have misunderstood your intentions with regards to us. That's on me, not you. I'm sorry Rachel said anything."

"No, sweetheart, this is all on me." Bear wouldn't allow Rick to take any responsibility for this situation. "I'm the one who didn't handle this the right way."

"I still don't understand what you're saying, Bear." Rick was becoming anxious all over again. Bear could tell by the way he clutched his own fingers together.

"Rick, I'm interested in you. I want us to date exclusively. It kills me to think of anyone else taking you out on a date." Bear took one step closer to a now-silent Rick, which didn't bode well for him.

"Someone else taking me on a date?" Rick spoke with a squeak. "You think people want to date me? Are you insane?"

"Okay, not the part of the sentence you should be concentrating on right now, honey."

"Right… Right, um… You really want to date me, just me?" Rick's eyes were round, almost as if he were in shock.

"Yes, Rick." *So badly.*

"But what about my…quirks and anxiety?" he asked.

"We all have our own quirks and anxieties. It's just yours come out into the open more often. Other people's are buried deep. You're a kind, intelligent, and gorgeous man who I find absolutely fascinating, and I want to get to know you on a more personal level." There, he spelled it out as plain as he could without using drawings. Now came the part he dreaded, the possible rejection.

"Me?"

"You."

"You're sure?"

"Positive."

Rick became silent, seeming to take a moment to consider everything that Bear had said. He then flashed a mischievous grin, took three steps forward, and jumped into Bear's arms. "Good, 'cause I'd like that too." He smiled before slamming his lips over Bear's in a possessive kiss that rocked Bear straight to his toes. Bear easily took back control, gently pushing Rick into a nearby wall and commanding his submission, which came with a whimper of need.

Finally breaking the kiss, both men gasped for air—still wrapped around each other when they heard Janet calling Rick's name. His eyes were dilated and slightly glazed, his lips red and swollen. He was simply breathtaking to Bear, but he had to set him down before Janet walked in on them. Rick would be embarrassed, and Bear could never cause him to be. Gently, he lowered Rick to the floor and took a few steps back just as Janet came through the door.

"Mr. Johansson, story time is about to begin. The preschoolers are waiting for you," the young lady shouted. When she noticed Rick and Bear, she smiled wide and turned on her heel, and walked out just as quickly without another word.

"Um…I—" Rick stuttered and blushed deeply.

Bear wasn't going to allow Rick to somehow apologize for his actions and his open show of emotion, so he cut him off. "That was hot. Feel free to kiss me whenever the urge strikes you."

The glowing smile he received back from Rick made him feel ten feet tall.

"Did you know it takes 146 muscles to coordinate a single kiss?" Rick was getting a little fidgety again, so Bear reached for his hands. Rick's shoulders lowered almost instantly and he calmed. "I have to go, the children are waiting."

"Okay, you go do your thing, sweetheart. After you lock up, meet me for dinner tonight at my house," Bear stated. It wasn't a question. He wasn't going to let the man wonder about his intentions ever again. "We should talk about what happened at the diner."

"I'll be there by seven, okay?" Rick asked, looking a bit apprehensive but not fearful. That was all that mattered.

"Dinner will be ready," Bear promised as he turned to follow Rick from the room. "Do you want me to pick you up?"

"No, your house isn't very far, and I like to walk," Rick answered, still looking absolutely kissable.

Bear couldn't help but smile as he followed the flustered man back into the main part of the library. He'd said what he wanted to say, and Rick hadn't refused him. If it wouldn't have scared several small children, Bear would have scooped Rick up and headed for the door. But that wasn't going to happen, considering a dozen inquisitive eyes were watching their every step at the moment.

With one quick kiss to the side of Rick's head, Bear left. His mind was already riffling through his cupboards, trying to remember if he had all the ingredients he needed, and deciding a quick stop at the grocery store was in order on the way home. This meal would make up for the one that had been ruined; he'd make sure of it.

Chapter Four

Before he even knocked on the front door of Bear's 1990s-style bungalow, Rick could smell rosemary, garlic, paprika, and citrus; it was heavenly. He had never smelled anything so mouthwatering, and he didn't even know what was on the menu. He'd stopped at the liquor store and picked up a moderately priced Sauvignon Blanc, hoping he'd chosen properly. He was nervous of course, but he had to admit, if only to himself, he also felt a tiny bit more confident. He was dating Bear; he just couldn't believe his luck was this good. Who would have thought the giant man with the kind, gentle eyes was attracted to plain old Rick? But he wasn't going to second-guess it.

The front of the bungalow had a covered porch running its length. Rick could imagine a couple sitting out there after dinner, watching the traffic slowly drive by. *Ninety percent of new homes built in the southern states have porches, decks, or patios. No, no, no, Rick. No useless info dropping tonight.* After the impulsive kiss he'd given Bear in the library, Rick thought it best not to embarrass himself any further by spouting useless information, but then again, he doubted he'd be able to stop himself anyway.

"Rick?" Bear's soft voice brought him out of his internal struggle. "Do you want to come in?" Bear stood to the side, holding the front screen door open.

"In. Oh, yes, yes definitely I want to come in." Rick quickly gathered his messenger bag from the ground and headed toward the door. "I brought wine. I just hope it's the right one to go with dinner. I should have asked what we were having. I don't get invited to supper often... Do you even drink?"

"Easy, breathe, babe." Bear stood directly in front of him now, holding the wine. Funny, Rick hadn't even felt him take the bottle from his hand. "This wine will be perfect with seafood. We're having Moroccan prawns with couscous and a mixed salad."

"Really, wow, that sounds wonderful. You must be an excellent chef." Rick realized he shouldn't have been shocked. This man had been surprising him from the first time he set his eyes on Bear. "I didn't mean you're not an excellent chef at the diner…"

"I know what you meant, babe. I just like trying new things, and I love to cook." Bear blushed slightly before ushering Rick inside. "Come on in and we'll open this bottle up. Dinner will be another twenty minutes."

Bear's hand warmed Rick's lower back, and he was powerless to do anything other than walk into the house. He loved the feel of Bear's hand on him and was shocked that his first response was excitement and not fear. He could get used to this. It had been so many years since he'd been able to be this close to someone Bear's size without feeling crushing panic.

Rick was almost giddy by the time they reached the kitchen. Bear's house was much like the man—strong, clean lines. The furniture looked as comfy as he remembered from the day Sam's house had been blown up and Bear refused to allow Rick to be alone. Rick may have groused at Bear's overprotective nature, but secretly he'd soaked up the feelings of safety and care.

"Would you like a glass of wine, Rick?" Bear asked as he rounded the kitchen island and grabbed a corkscrew out of the top drawer.

"Yes, please. That would be wonderful," Rick answered. "Did you know that Sauvignon Blanc's green grapes got their origins as an indigenous grape from the Bordeaux region of France?" *Well, that didn't take long. "Info bombs" away.*

"Actually, I did." Bear gave Rick an appreciative look before continuing. "One of these days, I want to visit France and tour wineries just to witness the art of making truly delicious wines."

Rick would have never guessed that. It seemed this big, strong bear had more of an eclectic taste, which matched Rick completely. His own interests ranged from ancient Egyptian hieroglyphs to the prehistoric-looking frilled shark. Well, maybe his interests were a bit farther apart than a biker chef with an appreciation for fine wines. But it still counted to Rick, because until that point, he was wondering if a biker and a librarian could have anything in common.

"Here you go. Would you like to sit at the island while I finish our dinner?" Bear asked, holding a glass out to him.

"Can I help at all?"

"No need, everything is almost done. But I'd love your company."

He couldn't help but blush at Bear's words, and the way he was looking at Rick should have singed him. Bear had never looked at him quite this intensely before, and Rick liked the warm feeling spreading throughout his body. "I-I'd love to keep you company." Rick stuttered slightly, but he wasn't feeling any anxiety, only excitement.

Rick had noticed over the months that somewhere along the line he'd grown to trust and respect the big guy and no longer felt extreme anxiety in his presence. He couldn't remember feeling so at peace with anyone in such a long time. If he thought about the circumstances as to why that was too long, he might have actually cried. *Not so manly right now, are you?* Bret's voice echoed through his mind, his taunts, his hate and rage directed completely on Rick.

Rick pushed the troubling thoughts far away and concentrated on the present and the handsome man currently tossing a colorful salad and flashing a heart-stopping smile his way. He had to admit, Bear had a killer smile, both sexy and boyish at the same time. Rick had no idea how you could be both, but Bear pulled it off.

Rick thought it was past time for him to get some information of his own, because apparently Bear knew just about everything about him, which he honestly didn't mind in the least. It saved him a whole lot of explaining right off the bat. The "White Hair Crew's" hearts were in the right place. They would never have shared with a stranger, but they knew there was something between Rick and Bear.

The grandmas had helped Rick when he was at his lowest: just released from the hospital, all alone, having no family left, unable to care for himself with multiple broken bones. The grandmothers had moved in and didn't leave until Rick was back on his feet. They, along with other community members of Brighton, had saved him, and he knew it.

"Bear, do you mind if I ask you a few personal questions? We've never talked about your past, and mine's apparently an open book," Rick joked.

"Yes, about that, I never intended for the White Hair Crew to ah…tell me what they did, Rick. I would never invade your privacy like that. I even tried to stop Grandma Rose from sharing, but she swore it was important," Bear explained.

"I know you wouldn't, and those ladies can do anything they think is right. They kept me going when all I wanted to do was crawl into a corner and die," Rick admitted, shocking himself with how easily he'd just admitted that to Bear.

He didn't like to share that part of his life, but he felt safe to do it here. It might have been years ago, but to Rick, sometimes it still felt like yesterday. Bear stopped tossing the salad, wiped his hands on a dishtowel, and gathered Rick into his strong arms. He melted into the embrace.

"If you ever need to talk about anything, know I'm always here for you. You mean a great deal to me already, Rick," Bear explained, but there was something more in his eyes, something Rick was unsure he saw or not.

"Thank you. I care about you as well. I feel calm and safe with you. It's a strange feeling for me. I haven't felt safe in a long time." Rick couldn't seem to help sharing his feelings with Bear; he was easy to confide in, and they'd known each other for months now.

"You are safe with me, sweetheart," Bear assured.

"The amazing thing is that I believe you." If Rick knew just one thing, it was that.

Bear held him a bit longer until the timer went off on the stove. Then he kissed Rick's lips quickly and backed away to resume cooking. "Almost ready here. How about you take that pitcher of ice water to the table and I'll bring our plates out?"

Rick was still smiling and his lips tingled from the kiss, but he managed to answer. "Sure." It was the least he could do since Bear had everything well under control. He moved around his kitchen like a conductor, using a fork instead of a baton, and spices, meats, sauces, and vegetables were in his orchestra. The flavors and aromas he produced with food could outdo any music a philharmonic could perform.

Rick placed the pitcher in the center of the table and couldn't help but notice the candles and fresh flowers. Now Rick wasn't girly by any means, but who didn't love a little romance? Certainly not him. The table was set for two seated directly across from one another, within reaching distance but not too close to crowd him. Bear seemed to have thought of everything.

"Here we go, Moroccan prawns, couscous, and veggies. Nothing too spectacular, but the flavors will keep you coming back for more," Bear said and then winked at Rick.

"I'd come back even if you didn't feed me," Rick admitted before he could stop himself.

"I like the sound of that," Bear responded without missing a beat and placed both plates of food on the table. "Sit down and dig in."

The smells of paprika, rosemary, and garlic filled the room and Rick's senses. He picked up his utensils, cut the delicate prawn, scooped a bit of couscous, and slid it between his open lips. The flavors exploded over his palate, smoky and spicy with the couscous adding a third layer of taste. Rick closed his eyes and moaned deeply; this was heaven. He couldn't remember the last time he'd ever had something so flavorful. Now honestly, the diner served wonderful food as well, especially compared to Rick's own nonexistent cooking skills, but this was spectacular.

Rick opened his eyes to find Bear staring at him with a heated gaze that sent a warm rush through his body.

"Um… I guess you like it." Bear picked up his glass of water and downed the contents all at once. Bear's Adam's apple bobbed deeply behind his neatly trimmed beard as he gulped. *How can that be so sexy?* Rick could do nothing but stare at the sight. "You do like it?"

"Yes," Rick quickly answered. "You should put it on the menu at the diner, maybe as a special once in a while."

"I was hoping it wouldn't be too spicy for you, but it might be too different for the diner. People don't like change all that much," Bear explained.

"I love spicy food. There's roughly one hundred and forty varieties of chili peppers grown in Mexico alone." *Damn!*

"One hundred and forty, I didn't know it was that high," Bear responded, as if what Rick said was anything but weird.

Rick's fork stopped halfway to his mouth. "I'm sorry. I'm always spouting out useless information, mostly when I'm nervous, but it can happen anytime."

Bear reached across the table and took Rick's left hand. "There's nothing to be sorry about. I want the real you. I like the real you I've already gotten to know. I never want you to hide anything from me," Bear said earnestly.

"You do?" No one ever wanted him to just be himself. It was always, "couldn't you be more" or "maybe if you just," and one of the favorites, "just shut up."

"Yes, I do. Every day I want to see the real you, the one you hide away behind books." Bear so easily picked up on why being a librarian was his chosen profession. He loved books, and he had a place that was quiet, a place he could spout useless facts all day long.

"Okay." Rick would accept that. After all, Bear had never lied to him before, and he trusted him. "I'll try my best not to censor myself as much around you."

"That's all I can ask, sweetheart." Bear smiled, and Rick immediately felt at ease. He also noticed that Bear liked to call him by endearments, which Rick could get used to quite easily.

Both went back to their meals, but Bear refused to release Rick's hand, so they ate with only one. It got messy on occasion, but neither let go of the other. So instead, they laughed and talked their way through dinner and took turns cutting the other's prawns. Once they'd finished, they cleaned the kitchen together and were now sitting and drinking coffee on the living room sofa. They were still holding hands, and Rick couldn't have been happier.

"I still think you should offer a few new options on the menu, Bear. People will love it. You're an amazing chef," Rick assured him, knowing full well Brighton would love the amazing food his *boyfriend* cooked. Rick grinned at the thought of Bear being his *boyfriend*. He never dreamed he'd be able to say that word again without fear.

"Thank you, Rick," Bear said. "I wanted to make up for the dinner that was ruined."

Rick felt his cheeks getting hotter. He didn't want to be reminded about his embarrassing "frightened mouse" routine under the table. He'd been working diligently for years to become comfortable enough to be part of the community, but any acts of violence always seemed to drag him back to the night he'd almost died.

"You didn't ruin our evening. Those men did." Rick wouldn't allow Bear to take the blame for something that wasn't his fault.

Bear seemed to consider his next words carefully. "Rick, were you afraid of me during the fight?"

"I was afraid, but not of you." Rick set his coffee on the table and moved closer to Bear. "I don't think I could ever be afraid of you, Bear. I trust you, which is really important to me."

The smile that broke out on Bear's face was brilliant and genuinely happy. "I was so worried that I'd scared you that night. It killed me to think that I'd ruined the trust we'd built, and our friendship is so important to me. But don't get me wrong, I want more than simply friendship between us."

Rick inched forward, closer to Bear, unsure exactly what to do but desperately wanting to kiss him again. In the next moment, that decision was taken away from Rick when Bear grabbed him around the waist and crushed him against his own hard body. His soft lips covered Rick's in a possessive kiss that left them both panting. Rick ran his fingers through Bear's thick chest hair—well, at least the bit showing above the V of his shirt collar. Rick could feel Bear's hard shaft pressing against his stomach, matching Rick's own. It still shocked him that he had that kind of effect on such a strong, amazing man who could date anyone he wanted, but he wanted Rick.

"I've been wanting to do that since I first found you on my front porch," Bear admitted, still holding Rick close, as if in no hurry to release him, which fit in with Rick's own plans nicely.

"I feel so calm and safe when I'm near you," Rick admitted. "I worry that I'm mistaking those feelings for attraction, and I don't want to lead you on just in case." Rick had been concerned that he was mistaking gratitude for attraction. He never wanted to mislead Bear.

"I understand, but I believe your attraction to me is real. Mine is growing stronger every day. Were you attracted to me before you knew me, before you fully trusted me?" Bear asked as he settled Rick's body against his own, allowing Rick to lower his head to Bear's shoulder and relax.

"Yes," Rick finally answered. "I couldn't take my eyes off you whenever I saw you around town. I'd wished every day that I would be brave enough to introduce myself to you, but it never happened. I'd never been happier than the day you came up to me and introduced yourself. I could have danced on the spot, if it wouldn't have sent me into a panic attack."

"Then that's a good indicator that this is real, sweetheart. You were originally attracted to me physically, before you felt safe, before you had a chance to get to know me. Our attraction began as physical from a distance and progressed into a friendship where you began feeling safe with me, to trust me. Only then could we move forward with that initial physical attraction." Bear looked about ready to burst, his smile was so wide. "This is real, Rick."

Rick thought about it for a moment. Yes, he had been extremely attracted to the big, bearded bear of a biker from the moment he roared into town on his Harley to have a look at the diner he now owned. For weeks Rick had explained away his frequent visits to the diner for roast beef takeout because he loved roast beef. Yes, he had been in denial for months. Bear was like a magnet to Rick; he couldn't pull away.

They lay on the couch, gently exploring with their hands, Rick deep in thought.

"Are you close to your parents?" Rick asked, wanting to know more about the man who had become such an integral part of his world.

"They passed away in a car accident when Jenny and I were young," Bear answered, his voice just above a whisper.

"I'm so sorry." Rick knew that pain all too well. "Mine passed away when I was a teenager. Mom had cancer, and Dad gave up on life. My first year of college Mom died; the second year my father committed suicide."

"Rick, honey." Bear wrapped both of his arms around Rick, holding him close. It had been years since he'd felt the loss of his mother's death and the betrayal of his father's. He'd only thought of himself and not Rick when he took his own life, leaving Rick alone in the world to grieve and settle all his affairs. The tears that trailed down his cheeks and dripped onto Bear's dark blue, button-down shirt were sad evidence that he still hadn't healed from the loss.

"Easy, sweetheart. I've got ya," Bear spoke softly into Rick's ear, causing him to shiver with desire at the most inopportune time. "I'm so sorry you had to go through that, Rick."

"But you lost both your parents when you were young. You and Jenny, I assume she's your sister, you were left all alone." Rick couldn't even imagine the odds of two people in a relationship having both lost their parents.

"Yes, Jenny's my younger sister. She lives back in Chicago with my nephew, Joshua. Unlike you, Rick, we weren't left alone to face the world. My mother's sister took us in. Aunt Clair was never married and took good care of us as if we were her own. Jenny and I owe her our lives. If she hadn't taken us in, child protective services would have separated us. I might've never seen my sister again, let alone have a relationship with my nephew," Bear explained while holding Rick tight.

"How old is your nephew?"

"Eighteen months old. Jenny and Josh will be coming down for a visit in a couple months, and I'd like for them to meet you."

"Meet me? Why?" Rick could feel his heartbeat rising.

"Well, considering you're my boyfriend and I'm very proud of that fact, I want my only family members to know you."

"I've never been introduced to someone's family before, but I want to meet your sister and nephew." Rick put on his brave face; he could do this.

"But you were with Bret for years?" Bear slammed his mouth shut, as if just realizing what he'd said. "Sorry, I didn't mean to bring him up."

Rick pulled Bear closer, knowing full well that if Bear hadn't allowed himself to be moved he wouldn't have moved an inch. Rick curled into his arms and began to explain. "He was convinced I would embarrass him in front of his family and friends. We seldom went out in public together. He preferred me to stay at home."

"Embarrass him? How could you ever embarrass him? You're perfect." Rick heard no hint of sarcasm in Bear's voice but still couldn't fully believe what he'd said.

"Bear, no, I'm not. How can you even say that with a straight face? What about my anxiety and panic attacks or my spouting useless information every time I even get slightly anxious?"

"That isn't your fault, and you've been working hard to learn how to deal with them to eventually have some sort of control over the attacks." Bear seemed so sure of him; maybe he was getting better.

"Ms. Vine's been helping. She's an amazing therapist," Rick explained.

"Yes, she is, and you're an amazing person too, Rick. You told me how you could barely get out of your house and make it to the library every day to work, and that was only a couple years ago. Now you're in therapy to help with your anxiety, you go to work, you come over to the diner, and you said yes when I asked you to be in a committed relationship with me. You're such a strong man; you just don't see it. Someday I'll convince you." Bear eased both of them farther down until Bear was lying on the couch and Rick was lying on top of him.

"Bear, what are you doing?" Rick asked, almost breathless, loving the way their bodies slid together. The added friction of their clothing took the sensations to another level.

"Getting comfortable with my man," Bear stated, seemingly sincere, and Rick might have believed him if he hadn't flexed his hips, rubbing his hard shaft against Rick's own.

"Your man, eh?" Rick played along.

"Oh yeah, every last inch of you. Told you I would remind you every day just how perfect you are to me." Bear cradled Rick's head and covered his lips with his own. Gently, slowly, he coaxed Rick's lips open, allowing him entrance. Bear's soft lips were contrasted by the bristles of his beard. But instead of bothering Rick with their slight scratch, it actually had the exact opposite reaction and served to heighten his need.

Rick melted into the kiss, excitement coursing through him. Before Bear, Rick hadn't kissed another man since Bret, and that had been more years than Rick wanted to honestly admit to. He couldn't contain the moans that escaped, and he began to flex his hips, rubbing himself against Bear's hard, jean-covered cock over and over again. The fog of desire cleared a bit when Rick realized how huge Bear really was.

"That's it, babe, take what you need from me." Bear groaned, reached down, and grabbed on to Rick's ass cheeks, squeezing them before he spread his legs and ground himself against Rick. "Babe, what you do to me."

Rick had no idea what he was doing. Bret had never groaned like this, but he was making Bear moan with need. Such a simple thing, but the boost it gave to Rick's self-esteem was immeasurable. Bear moved Rick's shirt aside and began to suck up a mark on Rick's exposed shoulder, making him pant as desire rushed through him. Rick wondered if he was allowed to mark Bear. He'd never been allowed to leave any marks on Bret. The feel of Bear's mouth sucking and nibbling on his heated flesh was driving Rick closer and closer to falling over the edge. Again, it had been years since he had come with anyone else, and his nerves were starting to creep back in.

As if sensing Rick's slight change, Bear released the skin he was nibbling on and leaned his head back, exposing his neck to Rick. "Mark me, babe. I want everyone to know I'm yours."

Bear didn't say, "You belong to me." Rick had heard those words of ownership for years from Bret. Bear was saying, "*I* belong to *you*." That statement alone made all the difference in the world.

Without another thought, Rick latched himself to the side of Bear's neck and gently sucked on the salty skin. Bear responded immediately, rubbing his hard shaft at a faster pace against Rick's own while holding him securely in place by his ass cheeks.

"That's it, Rick. Yes, babe."

Rick released his suction on Bear's neck and rubbed himself against Bear in wild abandon until he realized just how close he was to coming. "Oh God, Bear. I'm going… I'm…" But it was too late. Fire raced down Rick's spine, through his swollen balls, up his shaft, and sprayed the inside of his jeans while he screamed his pleasure. The deep groan echoing through Bear's chest and tensing of his muscles confirmed Bear had found his own release.

Rick's world felt like it'd been turned on its axis the last few months. His view had changed, and he had Bear to thank for that. He'd given Rick a bit of his confidence back. He made Rick feel safe and gave him equal power in their relationship. Rick curled into Bear's arms, the happiest he'd felt in a very long time.

Chapter Five

Bear held the precious man to his chest as they both caught their breath and slowed their racing hearts. *God, don't let me have ruined this by pushing him too far if he wasn't ready. But he responded so beautifully to every touch.* Bear thought back on what they'd just shared and couldn't help but smile. He'd never dreamed that would have happened tonight. The passion and all-consuming need he'd felt not only from himself but the fiery responses from Rick were unmistakable; he wanted Bear just as badly.

After a few more minutes without a word from Rick, he began to get a sinking feeling. "Rick?"

"Hmmm," Rick answered sleepily.

"Are you okay?" Bear asked, his heart in his throat.

"Yes, perfect." Rick hummed and snuggled closer.

Bear let out a breath he hadn't realized he was holding. "Well, if that's all I have to do every day to make you believe you're perfect, it's no hardship for me," Bear teased and watched as those beautiful hazel eyes lit up.

"Yes, there are benefits to being my boyfriend," Rick joked and buried his face back into Bear's neck and bearded chin. The gesture felt so intimate. It was odd to feel that way after what they'd just shared, but the act of nuzzling Bear's neck for comfort felt personal on a different level.

"Oh, I already know there are," Bear agreed easily. With one last hug, he released Rick. "Come on, babe, we'll go get cleaned up before our jeans dry to us."

Rick stood on wobbly legs and waited for Bear to stand. Once he did, and after a quick kiss, Bear led them to the master bedroom's *en-suite* bath.

"Let's get you cleaned up." Since Rick had his back to him, he simply ran his fingers down Rick's back and went for the hem of his shirt to lift it off his slight body. Suddenly, Rick pulled away and backed into a nearby corner, holding his shirt tight to his body. Bear immediately raised his hands in a calming gesture and slowly stepped a few feet away. Since he'd set his eyes on Rick, Bear had researched panic attacks and read about flashbacks and fear-driven reactions, and as sure as he was standing here, Bear knew it was fear he saw in those troubled hazel eyes.

"Rick, babe, look at me." Rick's worried eyes turned to Bear, as if begging him to understand. "It's okay. You're safe. Just breathe in for a count of seven. That's it. Now hold it and then release slowly."

After a few more deep breaths, Rick began to visibly calm. "I'm sorry, Bear," he whispered and wouldn't meet his eyes. No way would Bear allow that.

"You have no reason to be sorry. I should have never come up behind you like that." Bear wouldn't let that happen again. He needed to be more conscious of his actions to keep Rick from reliving past events.

"It wasn't that, Bear," Rick admitted quickly, "And it wasn't you…exactly."

"You don't have to explain to me if you're not ready, babe." Bear would wait as long as it took for Rick to feel comfortable enough to tell him any of the details of his abuse.

"I want to tell you. I…I want to share my life with you. Past, present, and future." Bear's heart took off with those words…*future*.

"Okay, but can I hold you while you tell me, Rick?" Bear felt almost desperate to touch him.

"Yes, I wish you would." Rick let out a deep breath and took a step toward Bear, who met him halfway. Rick wrapped his arms around him, and he buried his face into Bear's chest. "I met Bret shortly after my dad killed himself. He was new in town and seemed nice enough. Bret knew I was vulnerable. I was the perfect mark. I had no one and then this guy comes riding into my life and wants me." Rick shivered a bit at the memory. "Well, I know all this now and how everything turned out for me." Bear was having a hard time keeping himself from growling at the mere mention of that abusive asshole.

"He took advantage of you, Rick. You're not responsible for a thing he did."

"I logically know this, but I fell for it all. Just like one in four other members of the LGBTQ community who suffers violence at the hand of their partners. At the time, I honestly believed it was my fault. If I could just be more or do more, he would love me," Rick admitted. "Sorry, another bit of useless information for you there."

Bear hugged him tighter to his body. "Nothing you tell me is useless, and I didn't realize the numbers were that high. But it's still not your fault, and you know that now."

"But I still have to live with the scars." Bear froze. He prayed Rick was talking about small scars, but by the reaction he'd received earlier, he had a feeling it was much worse than that. "He…ah… He would whip me with his belt when I did something wrong or if he was mad, which in the end was most of the time. I have a lot of scars…. I'm ugly."

Rick finally broke down, crying softly into Bear's chest, and all Bear wanted to do was figure out a way to break into the prison holding Bret, but that wasn't possible. He'd decided to show this kind man just how beautiful he truly was today and every day after that.

"Rick, do you trust me?" Bear asked.

"Yes." No hesitation, no question. Just a statement of fact, which lightened Bear's heart to hear.

Bear released Rick and walked over to his huge tub—he was a big man after all—and turned on the water before pouring Epsom salt in to ease Rick's tight muscles. "Come to me, babe."

Without any show of his previous fear, Rick stepped up to Bear. "I'm going to take off yours and my clothes. Then we'll get into the tub where we can get cleaned up, relax, and explore each other's bodies. If you don't want that to happen, I'll leave right now, but I'd rather just stay here with you. No pressure though. You can clean up on your own."

Bear gave him a few moments to raise any concerns he might have, but Rick remained quiet. Bear slowly raised his hand and stroked the side of Rick's soft, damp face, down his chest to his flat belly to the edge of his shirt once more. This time he moved slowly, not wanting to cause him any further fear. Gently, he ran his hands under Rick's shirt, slowly inching higher until he felt the jagged edges of healed wounds crisscrossing Rick's back. Bear's anger skyrocketed, but he kept his outward appearance calm. He didn't want to make Rick believe it was him that made Bear mad and not Bret.

"Ready, love?" Bear asked while pulling Rick's shirt up a few inches.

"Love?" Rick asked in a hushed voice.

Bear had known for a while now that somewhere along the line, over the many months he had been getting to know Rick, that he'd gone and fallen in love with the quirky, amazing man. "Yes, love," was all he could manage to say, but it was enough to bring a megawatt smile to Rick's face.

"I don't know when or even if I'll ever be able to say those words back to you, Bear." Rick hung his head. "That's not fair to you. I might be too damaged."

"It doesn't matter if you say it to me. I'll know, and you let me worry about what's fair to me." Bear cupped the side of Rick's head. "Now, let's get you out of these clothes and into that tub." He knew, with the amount of pain and betrayal Rick had suffered, it would take time for even the simplest of emotions to be shared.

"Bear, I'm...ugly. There's scars and burn marks on...on almost every part of my body."

"You could never be ugly," Bear stated, desperately trying to keep his voice even and calm. *Burn marks?*

Rick seemed to read Bear's thoughts. "Bret smoked. At least he didn't burn my face. He didn't want others to know."

Bear didn't say another word, because honestly, he wasn't sure what would have come out. He was so angry, but he wouldn't let that show in front of Rick. So he lifted Rick's shirt. The material slid over his creamy white skin until the tip of a red, slightly puckered scar began to be unveiled, then another and another. The sheer amount began to hit home for Bear. *The pain Rick must have suffered.*

He didn't slow down, not when he revealed three thin white lines across his chest or when he undid Rick's jeans and slid them down his legs, revealing one round cigarette burn after another. He finally stopped when Rick was left standing in only his briefs, and he began to remove his own clothing. Bear heard the gasp but didn't stop until he too stood straight in only his boxers, allowing Rick to look his fill and waited for the inevitable questions.

"Bear... How?"

"You know that I was in a motorcycle club for a lotta years, babe. I had to fight to get in, to rise in the ranks, to protect members of the club, to protect myself, to hold my rank, and to finally get out. Every scar, stitch, broken bone, and patch of road rash was earned over years of hell."

"Oh, Bear. You went through so much." Rick stepped closer and gently traced a large scar from a knife wound running across his rib cage, which he'd received as a parting gift from his MC along with his "shave." Even with the painful memories, Rick's warm fingers sent sparks of desire throughout Bear's overheated body.

"My beard covers a few scars from a straight razor 'shave' I was given the day I left. That's why I keep my beard full. So I hope you like facial hair." Bear was a bit self-conscious of the scars on his face.

"I like everything about you, Bear. Your scars are so much worse than mine. I shouldn't be complaining so much. I'm so sorry that was done to you." Rick looked almost ashamed for even mentioning his pain.

Bear quickly gathered Rick into his arms and held him tight. "Yours are not any less than mine. You suffered just as I did, babe. But at least I could defend myself. You couldn't against Bret. That in itself is a big difference."

Bear knelt and skimmed his hands underneath Rick's briefs, slowly lowering them to the floor and kissing a few scars on Rick's hips. His beautiful, slim penis was proportionate with his smaller, toned body, and he was already half hard, showing renewed interest. Bear kissed another long white scar on the front of Rick's thigh then stood tall, waiting for Rick to make his choice. Mercifully, it didn't take long. Rick ran his warm fingers around the edge of Bear's boxers, as if teasing him in his slowness. Bear squinted his eyes at his obviously playful boyfriend to see that beautiful smile playing across his face. *God, he's so gorgeous. I have to make him see that it's true.*

Rick must have decided he'd teased long enough and began to slide Bear's black boxers to the heated tile floor. His cock was already hardening, needing the kneeling, naked man in front of him even though he'd come less than thirty minutes ago. With a patience he was surprised he even possessed, Bear remained absolutely still and let Rick look and touch his fill.

Soft fingers traced the scar of an old bullet wound on his hip that Bear hadn't even remembered until that moment. He'd been in his early twenties when he and his friends were caught in a drive-by shooting back in his neighborhood in Chicago.

"Bear, is this what I think it is?" Rick's voice was hushed.

"A bullet wound," he answered.

"Oh my God, Bear. You could've died. I want you to promise me not to put yourself in danger again. Promise me." Rick was almost frantic by now.

Bear leaned forward and brushed his fingers through Rick's hair. "I can't promise that something won't ever happen, but I do promise to be careful; after all, I have you in my life now. That's one hell of an incentive to stay safe."

Rick nuzzled Bear's hand before leaning in and softly kissing the rounded scar. A rush of emotion and need slammed into Bear, and his cock filled fully. "Let's get you into the tub, babe, while the water is still warm." *Rick has no idea how sensual he really is.*

Bear bent and lifted Rick from his knees and carried him over to the now full tub. Without stopping to set Rick down, Bear simply stepped in and sat with Rick still in his arms. He turned off the water and lay back in the tub, letting Rick sprawl out on top of him. A comfortable silence fell as the two relaxed in each other's arms. There was no other place Bear would rather be.

***

Rick couldn't quite believe he was naked in a tub—well, not the naked in the tub part, but definitely the lying across his "boyfriend" was new. No more hiding his many scars and burns, he was naked without stress or fear. He hadn't been without clothing around another man, other than the hospital staff, since the day Bret was arrested.

Rick let his body relax, his head cradled by one large, hairy pec. Bear was a bear of a man—large, strong, and his chest was covered in a soft layer of hair. He didn't know how he'd gotten this lucky, but Rick would be eternally grateful for whatever he'd done to deserve this kind man.

He could feel Bear's hard length pushing up against his hip. "You know, a recent study found that the average length of a man's erect penis is five point two inches? You are definitely above average by at least two or three inches."

"Thank you, babe, I'm glad to know I'm above average," Bear responded, and even though there was no censure or anger in his voice, Rick immediately ducked his head. *Who talks about penis size with their significant other? No one. I'm such a dork.*

Rick kept his face turned away from Bear, but he should have known Bear would realize that something was off. "Hey there, what's wrong?"

"I... I can't believe I just info dropped the size of an average human penis while I'm lying in a tub with you," Rick mumbled.

"Well, I was flattered. I'm above average. Now, had you said I was below average, we'd have a whole different discussion," Bear teased with a lame joke and a huge smile on his handsome face. "And I want you to stop apologizing for the wonderful things that make you...you."

Rick stared into a pair of sparkling deep blue eyes. "I don't embarrass you, do I?"

"Not in the least, Rick. You could never embarrass me by being yourself, love." He tightened his arms around Rick and took his mouth in a slow, heated kiss. Bear slid his tongue lazily across Rick's swollen lips, making him moan for more. There was no mistaking who was in charge, but Bear never forcefully took control away from Rick. He felt safe with Bear and easily gave that control completely over to the man, knowing at any time it would immediately be given back to him.

"You're a gorgeous man, Rick. I must have done something right in this life."

Rick wanted to argue that he was the lucky one, but Bear's lips were beginning to wander to his neck. "So soft, so sweet," Bear mumbled between sucks and kisses as he worked his way down Rick's body. By now they both were sitting up with Rick on Bear's lap, his legs wrapped around Bear, Rick's head thrown back with Bear licking his way across his collarbone. He savored the warmth of the water and the feel of wet skin sliding against wet skin. The attention being lavished on him was something he'd never thought would be his again. Bear had given this to him.

"Feels so good. Please don't stop." Rick moaned. He wasn't above begging to have this continue.

Bear kissed Rick's chest, giving Rick access to his neck and shoulders. The hickey he'd given Bear earlier stood out purple on his tanned neck. An intense feeling of possession hit Rick. Now he wanted his turn to explore Bear's hard body, so he leaned on Bear's shoulder in an attempt to push him back into their prior lying position.

Bear stopped everything immediately and cupped Rick's face. "What's wrong, love? Am I moving too fast for you?"

"No, Bear. I just want my turn to explore your body." For the first time, Rick thought maybe he'd been too forward, but what Bear did next melted Rick's heart.

With a roguish grin, he put his hands behind his head and leaned back against the tub, showcasing the hills and valleys of his muscles. "I'm all yours."

Those three little words, "I'm all yours," made Rick almost giddy with joy. Bear was his. He'd shown his care and commitment to Rick. Now it was time to show him how much he belonged to Bear as well. With only the barest of touches, Rick began to trace the outline of each muscle and scar, kissing and licking as he went. The groans coming in a constant stream from Bear urged him on.

Rick straddled Bear's thighs, the hot water flowing and caressing his body as he explored. His hard cock throbbed at the realization that he had free rein over the sculpted body beneath him. This intelligent, kind man was so easily bringing Rick back into the land of the living after years of self-imposed isolation. Bear's big hands were no longer behind his head; instead they were massaging Rick's ass cheeks, causing him to undulate his hips and rub his hard cock against Bear's solid abs.

"Babe, you're so beautiful in your passion. I don't want to stop, but I'm going to come sooner rather than later if we keep this up," Bear panted out, not slowing down one bit.

"I don't think I can stop…" Rick's breath rushed out of his body as Bear sucked one of his tanned nipples into his mouth. "I want to come, Bear, please. Please, make me come again."

Rick couldn't resist Bear's wet, red lips any longer, and once Bear released his nipple, Rick dove in for a kiss that made his swollen balls ache. He could feel Bear's cock rubbing between his ass cheeks. Rick knew he wasn't ready for that step just yet; besides, there would be no unprotected sex until blood tests were done if they continued on this path. Thankfully, Bear seemed to sense this and lifted Rick to move him until their cocks were now touching. Bear wrapped one of his calloused hands around both and slowly pumped them together. It felt like heaven. Rick spread his legs farther apart, desperate to get closer to Bear.

"So beautiful," Bear whispered before sucking Rick's other nipple into his warm, wet mouth. His tongue laved the slight pain away as he nibbled.

The water in the tub sloshed over the edges and onto the tile flooring, but Rick couldn't stop now even if he tried. He was too far gone, his body responding with need he'd never felt before, not even with Bret. He couldn't get close enough to Bear, whose hand was moving at a feverish pace. Rick panted between moans as sizzling fire raced down his spine.

"Bear, I'm close…" Rick moaned, thrusting faster.

"That's it, babe, come for me." Bear growled as he took his hand from Rick's ass cheek and grabbed the back of Rick's hair, pulling lightly, making Rick arch his back and expose his neck and chest to Bear. Such a vulnerable position should have scared the hell out of him, but for once he felt no fear, only excitement. He felt free, free to experience such an intimate, vulnerable moment without fear.

That was all it took, as Rick found himself yelling out his release to the world. Within moments, a deep groan vibrated through Bear's chest. Before Rick had a chance to collapse back down on top of Bear, he was wrapped in his muscled arms and crushed against his chest instead.

They lay together in the water, neither saying anything. Words weren't needed in their warm, peaceful bubble. All too soon, Bear gathered Rick close and helped him stand, then pulled the plug in the tub before leading Rick over to a tile-enclosed shower.

Bear turned on the water and a stream of cold immediately shot out. Quickly, Bear switched places with Rick, protecting him from the cold with his body. Still neither spoke; it was as if the moment would be destroyed if they made a noise. Once hot water flowed,

Bear placed Rick back under the warm stream, reached for the body wash and began to clean Rick from top to bottom, with a gentle kiss every so often for good measure. No one had ever done this before. He couldn't help but feel cared for and would gladly take each and every gentle touch. Rick had been well used to the opposite for many years.

Once he'd finished, Rick took over, wanting to care for Bear in the same way. The lather he'd worked up skimmed down Bear's body, over the ridges, and mixing with his dark hair. He was an exquisite man. If Rick hadn't already come twice, he was sure his cock would be making a valiant effort to show interest; instead, he hugged the bigger man close.

Soon he was being led to bed. Rick hadn't even realized Bear had turned the water off until he was being dried by a fluffy white towel. He also hadn't realized how tired he'd become. At least tomorrow was Sunday and the library was closed. The master bedroom felt just like the man. Big, comfy furniture surrounded a bed Rick might have to make a running jump at to even get on. People said the kitchen was the heart of the home, but Rick knew this bedroom with its comfy chairs, large bookcase, and flat-screen TV was the heart of Bear's home, the place where he was most at ease.

Rick wasn't worried that Bear would try to take advantage of him while he slept; the man had his complete trust. There had been multiple opportunities for Bear to have done so already, and he hadn't. They both walked naked to the bed. It always amazed Rick that Bear was a foot taller than him and could probably bench-press him without much effort... *Hmmm. Great, now all I can imagine is Bear working out naked.*

They reached the bed and Rick was about to try to hop up when Bear grabbed him carefully around the waist and lifted him onto the king-sized mattress. Was it strange they still weren't speaking or making much noise? If it was, Rick didn't care. He hadn't been this relaxed and happy in years. Rick would do whatever it took to keep it that way for as long as he could, and it looked as though Bear was doing the same.

Bear pulled the blankets over top of the two of them, then gathered Rick to his side and gazed at him, his dark blue eyes full of emotion and easy to read. He kissed Rick until they both were breathing heavy. Without words, Bear had given him the sweetest of gifts, the gift he hoped to be able to share with Bear soon. Love.

Chapter Six

Two months later

If anyone had told Rick he'd be cleaning Bear's house mere months after they first started dating, he would have said they were insane. But he'd offered after all. Considering Bear was working at the diner all day and his sister, Jenny, and nephew, Joshua, were arriving tonight, the man needed help no matter how often he told Rick he didn't.

Jesse, Bear's friend and cook at the diner, had had another run-in with his bigoted family. He was okay, but his boyfriend Royce was too nervous there would be more reprisals coming and wanted Jesse to stay out of sight for a bit. The two had been through so much pain in their lives, Rick prayed that they'd just be left alone to their own happiness.

As soon as it happened, Bear had rushed in to help, of course. Even if he wasn't the boss, he would have done the same thing. Rick had learned a lot about his lover in the last two months. *Can I say lover if Bear still hasn't entered me?* It wasn't like they weren't doing a multitude of other things together, and Rick considered that sex.

Honestly, Rick really wanted that physical connection to Bear but would never base their relationship on that one aspect. What was between them was more than physical; Rick felt it on a soul-deep level. Though he still hadn't been able to speak any words of love to Bear, Rick knew with every fiber of his being that he was in love with the man. It felt like the words were blocked, unable to be freed. His therapist, Dr. Vine, had told him that this was completely natural after everything he'd been through. Rick still felt a measure of guilt for not being able to reciprocate the words to the man he was positive he'd fallen in love with.

They had spent a lot of time together over the past two months, and Rick couldn't have been happier. He especially enjoyed the Sundays they spent in Bear's bedroom reading or watching movies, just the two of them. Bear hadn't done anything to betray Rick's trust. He was truly an honorable man.

Rick's confidence had grown to the point that he could sit in the diner during the day and have lunch without making a run for the door. Bear had taken him to a small farmers' market and he'd managed to stay for almost an hour before his anxiety became too much. Bear had never once left his side, providing him with that bubble of safety the entire time.

Rick was beginning to feel comfortable in his own skin again. He'd never even realized just how much of himself he'd lost over the years. The pain of that realization had hit about three weeks previous. He would never be able to go back to the way he was before the abuse. Rick had always thought, if he worked hard enough, he could. Of course Bear was there to help him try to understand how much he'd changed and that he could never be that same man again but could grow into a new version of himself. The Rick he knew was dead, and the new Rick was discovering himself all over again after years spent in purgatory.

On the road to that end, Rick was meeting Bear's family, which was a normal enough occurrence, but to Rick this might as well be a firing squad. Bret had never wanted anyone in his family to meet him. Rick couldn't help but think he was the reason for that. Maybe Bear was just being nice when he invited Rick to meet his sister and nephew. *But what if I embarrass him? No, Bear has never lied to me. He loves me, and he's proud of me.* Rick kept that mantra going in his head as he continued to dust the living room.

Hours later, Rick was just putting the last juice box for Josh into the fridge when the front door opened. Bear wasn't due home for another hour, so Rick was a bit surprised but happy to have him back home.

"What are you doing home early, babe?" Rick asked as he rounded the corner to the front entrance, only to stop dead in his tracks.

"Well, honey, traffic was light and we just couldn't wait to get here," said a petite blond woman holding a small toddler with chestnut brown hair—Jenny and Josh. *Oh shit.* "You must be Rick."

"Um…um…yes." Yep, frozen to the spot. A thousand things ran through his head. He'd planned to be long gone before they arrived, because he wasn't supposed to meet them until tomorrow. He'd had it all worked out. He had a plan. He would be prepared to put his best foot forward, if he had one. But now that was all gone out the window, and here he stood in an apron, sweaty and dirty from cleaning all day.

"Rick... Rick, okay, look at me. Breathe. You're safe." Jenny spoke softly. She was the same height as him, so they stood eye to eye. She had the same dark blue eyes as her brother.

Rick slowly got himself under control. "I haven't had an anxiety attack in weeks. I'm so sorry, Jenny."

"No, I'm the one who's sorry. Bear told me you might be here, and I should have knocked instead of walking straight in."

"Unk Bear?" the adorable toddler asked, big blue eyes looking around the living room, searching for Bear.

"Bear's still at the diner. He should be home soon," Rick answered. "I'll go so you two can get settled in peace."

"Oh no, you don't. We should sit and talk, get to know each other." Jenny had a devilish look on her face and a sparkle in her eye just like Bear. Rick knew that look; things were about to get interesting.

With one final glance at the front door, Rick decided that making a break for it wouldn't leave the best first impression. So he smiled, wondering just how long it would take before Jenny realized he wasn't good enough for Bear and everything came crashing down.

***

Bear was late. The diner had been storming busy all day, and he couldn't shove people out the door fast enough. He missed his sister and nephew. He used to live for their visits; they had been the only bright spot in his life for so long. Now he had an amazing partner whom he loved and who helped fill the empty spaces in his life, along with his family. He was a lucky man.

Bear had tried twice to reach Rick on his cell phone, but there wasn't an answer either time. Rick had said he'd be going back to his apartment after leaving Bear's house, but he'd driven by and his place was dark. His sister should be at the house with Josh, but where was Rick?

His house was lit up when he pulled into the driveway. Since he and Rick had started dating and Bear had given Rick a key, he would often meet Bear at home. It always warmed Bear's heart to see his typically cold and dark house filled with light, love, and life. Bear knew Rick loved him; he could tell by every sweet gesture and touch Rick gave him. He could wait forever if he had to, just to hear it, and even if he didn't, Bear knew.

Jenny had said she might arrive early, but Bear was still worried about his love. It wasn't like Rick to not answer his phone, and he'd never just wander off without telling him. Once he checked in with his sister and nephew, he would go looking for his missing boyfriend to make sure he was okay. Considering Rick didn't drive, he couldn't have walked too far.

Bear parked his black and chrome bike in the garage and entered the house by the side door. What he found on the floor would be forever ingrained in his mind and heart. There in the middle of the living room was Rick surrounded by toys, holding an action figure and a very talkative toddler. Rick's clothes looked disheveled and wrinkled and his hair stood on end, but that big, beautiful smile on his face was magic, absolutely breathtaking.

Rick still hadn't seen him, so Bear leaned against the wall and enjoyed the sight before him for a few more minutes, going unnoticed. He was falling further in love with the amazing man who had been strong enough to give Bear a chance.

His sister came out of the kitchen and quietly joined him. "So, big brother, this is where you're hiding," she whispered.

"Just watching," Bear whispered back before hugging his little sister tightly. "Love you, sis."

"Love you too, big bro. Pretty nice sight, isn't it? Josh took one look at Rick and decided that they were best friends, and your wonderful boyfriend just rolled with it," Jenny explained with a huge smile on her face.

"He's amazing, isn't he." It wasn't a question; it was a statement that Bear believed wholeheartedly.

"Yes. You gonna keep him?" Jenny asked in an all-too-innocent voice to be his sister; she was digging for information.

"Yes," Bear answered without hesitation. He had every intention of keeping Rick as long as his love wanted him.

"Good, or I'd have to knock some sense into you. Considering I'm half your size, you'd have to bend over so I can do it," Jenny joked as she wound her arms around one of Bear's big biceps and held him tight. "I've missed you, Bear."

"I've missed you, too. When are you going to just give in and move down here?" Bear would ask the same question every time Jenny visited, and every time she would say she could never live in a town as small as Brighton. But Bear refused to give up, hoping someday she'd change her mind.

"Well, now that you've mentioned it, I've been considering making a few changes," Jenny mumbled. "Brighton's a nice town."

"What?" Bear said loud enough to alert Rick and Josh to his presence.

"Unk... Unk... Unk!" Josh yelled as he climbed off his Rick jungle gym and ran to Bear, arms waving wildly. Now if that didn't melt a man's heart, nothing could.

"Hello, little man, how's my favorite nephew?" Bear bent and hoisted the toddler high into the air, Josh laughing the entire time before grabbing Bear's beard and pulling.

"Unk... Unk!" Josh called out but was looking back at Rick, his hands doing the little "gimme" sign, and Bear's heart flipped. Josh was calling Rick uncle.

Rick stood and straightened his stained clothing. *Is that applesauce on his shirt?* "Hi, Bear, I'm sorry, I tried to teach him my name, but he thinks 'Unk' fits better."

"Well, I think 'Unk' sounds just about perfect." Bear bent and kissed Rick right there in front of his sister and nephew. Bear didn't plan on curbing his affection for his boyfriend while his family visited; of course he would never do anything too outlandish. "How was your day, babe?" Bear wanted to check in with Rick to make sure he wasn't overwhelmed or anxious.

"Great, actually. We've been playing and talking for the past couple hours. Josh loves the toys we got for him over in Houston when we went for the weekend." Bear had been proud to act like tour guide, considering Rick had never been out of Brighton before. Rick had had the strength to visit stores without having an anxiety attack and stayed right by Bear's side. Whenever Rick had needed to get away from the crowds, Bear had led him to a quiet space and talked him through any anxiety he might have. Dr. Vine had been impressed with Rick's progress. Bear was simply proud.

"You want to come get cleaned up with me?" Bear asked as he gently brushed a stray piece of hair off Rick's face.

"Bear, we have guests." Rick's blush went all the way down his slender neck.

Bear laughed. God, he loved this man. "Just to clean up. Besides, we're on a completely different floor."

Bear turned to his sister to hand her Josh, only to see her brushing away tears. *Why would she be crying?* "Sis, are you okay?"

"Yes, of course I am," she answered before turning away. "I'm just so happy you finally found someone. Now stop staring at me and go get cleaned up for dinner."

Bear wasn't fooled. Something was wrong. His sister did not cry, and if it took him all week to figure it out, he would. "Okay, Ms. Bossy. I'll just take a quick shower and be right back."

"You better believe I'm the boss, muscle head. Now start moving," Jenny joked before turning back into the kitchen. "Oh, and thanks for getting a booster seat for Josh. He doesn't like his high chair anymore because he's a 'big boy.'"

"Big boy, big boy," Josh repeated.

Bear grabbed Rick's smaller hand and rushed upstairs to *their* master bedroom. Though they didn't live together just yet, a lot of Rick's clothing had managed to make it over to Bear's house, and he spent almost every night, which was exactly the way Bear wanted it to continue, until every last bit of Rick's belongings were incorporated into his own. Once he had Rick safely behind closed doors, he couldn't resist his love any longer and bent for a kiss that left Rick pressing himself against him, rubbing his jean-covered cock against Bear's leg. *That's better.*

"How are you really feeling, babe?" Bear asked. "Any anxiety?"

"Excited now. Seriously, there's a toddler in the house." Rick laughed and snuggled into Bear's chest. "Actually, I feel fine. Not one bit of anxiety—well, maybe a bit at the beginning, but your sister has a way about her. She's like a whirlwind. I really like her and Josh."

"They like you as well. I'm glad you don't feel nervous around my family. I would like you to have a good relationship with them." Bear was absolutely serious about that. He loved Rick, his sister, and nephew, and he wanted the people who meant the most in his life to be happy. After all, the three of them were his only family in this world, and he intended to keep them all close.

Rick held him tightly, and Bear knew he shouldn't respond to Rick this way with Jenny and Josh in the house. But their bedroom suite was locked and they were an entire floor away from the kitchen on the other side of the house.

"I missed you today, babe," Bear whispered as he nibbled on Rick's neck, happy when Rick's breathing increased and a soft moan escaped.

"I missed you too, Bear, but we can't."

"Well, the way I see it, you're all dirty and I'm all dirty, so we both need a shower, and considering we have guests, we shouldn't leave them alone for very long. That would be rude." Bear smiled at the adorably confused look on Rick face. "So to save time, we need to shower together."

"Shower together, without fooling around?" Rick didn't looked convinced.

"Maybe a bit of fooling around, but I promise we'll be quiet."

"Bear…"

"Yes, babe," Bear answered, trying his best to sound innocent before walking into the bathroom, leaning into the glass-and-tile shower, and turning on the water. Without saying a word, he turned and began to undress Rick as though he'd agreed to the shower. But he wasn't saying no or pulling away either, so Bear didn't stop.

Surprisingly, Rick began to unbutton Bear's shirt, seeming to need to get closer to him. His warm, slightly shaking hands caressed his chest, running his fingers through Bear's chest hair, almost making him purr. Before long, both stood naked and the steam from the shower had filled the room, giving it an ethereal quality.

"Let's get you cleaned up, sweetheart." Bear took Rick's hand and led him into the shower, placing him under the warmth of the water. Bear wrapped his arms around Rick, hugging him close and pressing his hard cock into the small of Rick's back.

Bear hadn't attempted to enter Rick; he was giving Rick time to get used to him and to having another man touching him without feeling fear. He was prepared for the time to come, having stashed lube all over the house, including the shower. Bear would be exploring a bit further very soon. He just needed to make sure Rick was ready as well.

Rick turned in Bear's arms and began kissing his chest, starting with one nipple and working his way to the other then down his muscled abdomen until Rick was kneeling between Bear's legs, lapping at the head of Bear's hard cock. Rick left his hands on Bear's thick thighs and took his cock deeper down his throat, swallowing and nearly making Bear shoot.

"Rick, babe, I'm going to come." What was meant as a warning to slow down only spurred his lover on into doubling his efforts. "Oh, you little brat." Bear groaned as Rick smiled around his cock.

There was no stopping him now. The feel of his tongue lapping at his slit, the suction, and massage of his throat muscles drove Bear over the edge. He muffled his groan with his hand. As soon as Rick released him, Bear lifted Rick off his knees and pushed him chest-first against the shower wall then went to his own knees. Pulling Rick's butt cheeks apart, Bear buried his mouth onto Rick's tight little hole while Rick moaned into his arm, muffling the noise.

Bear loosened Rick's opening with water from the shower and his own saliva until he felt the outer muscles relax, allowing Bear to slip his finger inside his lover up to the first knuckle. Rick's body shook as he came all over the tile wall, screaming into his hand, trying desperately not to make a noise in his passion. Bear hadn't even touched Rick's cock before he came, definitely a boost to his ego.

Bear stood and cuddled Rick back against his chest under the warm spray. After a few minutes, Bear grabbed the body wash and went to work on his lover's body. The only reason Bear wasn't concerned about the silence was the huge smile on Rick's beautiful face that told him everything he needed to know. His love was happy.

They were almost done when Rick turned and cupped both of Bear's cheeks, making him stare deeply into those beautiful hazel eyes. Bear wasn't sure why they looked uncertain. Had he pushed too far? Wasn't Rick ready?

"Bear, I love you." Rick looked like he was ready to bolt. "I really love you. I know it deep down to my soul." He reached up, pulling Bear's face downward for one of the sweetest kisses he'd ever received from Rick. He brushed his lips across Bear's before gently separating his lips and allowing the smaller man entrance to his mouth. They kissed for several minutes before finally breaking apart.

"Rick, you've made me the happiest man, sweetheart. I love you so much." Bear reached out and wrapped Rick in his arms, holding him close.

"I know I've made you wait months before I could say it, but please believe I was feeling it for a long time now." Rick looked guilty and ashamed.

"I would have waited as long as it took, Rick. Lust fades, but love is seeing all of the other person's flaws, idiosyncrasies, mannerisms, and accepting them as part of the person you love. For that, I'd wait forever." Bear knew this as fact because he loved this little man from the top of his blond head to the bottom of his feet. His anxiety, panic attacks, and info drops were only parts of the complete package, and Bear couldn't live without the complete "Rick" package.

"I do love everything about you, Bear—even if it would be nice if you learned where the laundry basket lived," Rick teased and buried his face in Bear's chest.

Bear turned the water off and wrapped a large towel around Rick. "Hey, I've been getting better at that."

"Yes you are, honey. Now sometimes I only find a sock or underwear instead of the entire outfit you had on that day." Rick's smile was breathtaking, and it looked as if a great weight had been lifted from him. If it were possible, he looked even happier now. "Come on, we need to hurry. Your sister and nephew are waiting for us."

Rick reached out and took Bear's hand before leading them into the bedroom. After a few heated kisses and passionate touches, they finally made it down to dinner. Jenny's knowing look couldn't dim Bear's happiness. Nothing could ruin this week. He had his sister and nephew here with the man he loved, and Bear's world was finally settled.

Chapter Seven

Rick lay in the backyard covered in toys and assorted stains, yet again, with Josh currently crawling all over him. Rick had become his favorite jungle gym, and the little guy had become Rick's favorite toddler. They'd played and had adventures to the park and to the ice cream store. Rick was going to miss the little guy when he went home. To that end, Rick had appointed himself Josh's official playmate and spent as much time as he could with the little man.

He'd even taken his holidays early, leaving his assistant, Janet, at the helm, and whiled away his days with an adorable toddler. Bear had to take care of the diner, and Jenny seemed to have numerous appointments, but Rick didn't mind. He could truly be himself in front of Josh and never have to worry about being judged. That was the beauty of young children: They weren't jaded by others' views of what was considered normal.

Over the past couple days, Jenny and Rick had become close. They would spend hours talking while Josh slept and Bear was at the diner. He'd even info dropped strange facts on her without fear. Rick could honestly say the woman amazed him, raising Josh on her own while working full time—the exact opposite of Josh's father, who was a less-than-reputable man who'd walked out on them and signed away his parental rights within moments of Josh being born. But Jenny never felt sorry for herself. She, along with her brother's financial help, pushed forward and made the best life she could for Josh. To look at Josh, all you saw was a happy, healthy little boy. Jenny had done a wonderful job.

Bear and Jenny were out having a little brother-sister time while shopping for more groceries. Jenny had personally asked Rick if he could stay with Josh as she wanted to talk to her brother alone but didn't elaborate. They'd been gone for over two hours now, and Josh was just about ready for his afternoon nap when Rick heard the front door open. He picked up Josh and began to walk toward the sliding patio doors when Jenny came out, eyes and nose red as if she'd been crying.

Rick rushed to her. "Jenny, what's wrong? Are you okay? Where's Bear?"

Jenny smiled, though her lips trembled, and took Josh, hugging him closely. "He's in the house. Rick, I have no right to ask anything of you, but he'll need you now more than ever. Please go find him."

Without a second thought, Rick ran for the house. He had to find Bear; he had to find out what happened. *What if he's hurt? No...Jenny would have taken him to the hospital.* He rushed through the door and into the kitchen, but Bear was nowhere in sight and there were no groceries on the counter. What happened? Living room empty, bedroom nothing—Rick was getting anxious, and that was never good.

"Bear? Bear, where are you?" Rick yelled, giving up the pretense of calm.

"I'm in here," Bear's broken voice answered.

The office, of course. Rick ran from the bedroom, down the stairs, and across the house to find Bear sitting slumped over in his chair, his head in his hands, crying softly. Rick stood in the doorway, unsure what to do. Should he intrude or let Bear have a moment alone? He'd never seen the big man cry. The decision was taken out of his hands when Bear looked up. The pain in his eyes could have brought Rick to his knees, and he rushed forward into Bear's waiting arms.

"What's wrong? What's happened, Bear?" Rick asked, but the answer he received wasn't anywhere on his radar of possibilities.

"My sister's dying," Bear stated before burying his face in Rick's hair, seeking comfort he was more than willing to give.

"Dying? What do you mean?" Rick's brain wouldn't wrap around what Bear had said.

"She has pancreatic cancer." Bear's voice was laced with pain and disbelief.

"What about chemotherapy or radiation?" There had to be something the doctors could do.

"It's too far gone. It would decrease the quality of life she has left. Jenny has decided not to undergo treatment. It...it wouldn't change the outcome or the time she has." Bear spoke in a whisper, as if the words themselves were making the fact more real.

"I'm so sorry, Bear. What can I do?" Rick was desperately trying to recall everything he'd ever read about pancreatic cancer. *It spreads rapidly and is seldom discovered early. Life expectancy of four to six months when terminal. Leading cause of cancer death. Shit!*

"Just having you here with me will help, babe." Bear's voice broke as he spoke. He seemed to be curling into himself for protection. Rick began to shake. *No. I will not have a panic attack now! Bear needs me.* Rick breathed in and out, calming himself, and held Bear tight.

"I'm not leaving you. I'll do anything to help you and Jenny through this." Rick swore on his life he would stand beside Bear; the man had been a godsend to Rick. "Oh God, what will happen to Josh?"

Bear looked Rick straight in the eyes, the uncertainty palatable. "She asked me to raise him." Bear reached over to a stack of papers Rick hadn't noticed before. "She's given me her final papers, her will and life insurance. She's already taken all the steps necessary. Now all we need to do is agree."

"We?" Rick wasn't entirely sure why he was involved in the decision making.

"Yes, we." Bear gathered Rick into his arms. "Rick, I know this is one hell of a time, but I want you with me permanently. I want you by my side every day, and to go to sleep every night with you in my arms. I know things won't be easy, but I can promise to always love you and do everything in my power to make you and Josh happy."

"Bear, I don't want you to make decisions in such an emotional state. You might find it hard to have me around all the time, and I could really screw up a little kid with my issues." Rick was panicked. He didn't want to mess Josh up with his own issues.

"Rick, listen to me. Do you trust me?" Bear asked.

"Of course," Rick replied without hesitation.

"Then trust me to know what I want, and I want you here. I just need to know if you want that too." The uncertainty in Bear's voice caught Rick off guard. Bear was always so confident.

Rick buried his face in Bear's chest. Could he do this? Could he trust someone enough to let go of his safe place after everything he'd lived through? But how could he not? He loved Bear and had grown very fond of Jenny and Josh, and suspected it wouldn't take much time for them to squirrel their way into his heart as well. When he started adding everything together, there really wasn't any question. He respected and trusted this man.

"Yes, I'll move in with you." Rick hoped Bear could see the sincerity in his eyes and took a deep breath and plowed forward. "Bear, I love you. I want to spend my life with you."

Bear crushed Rick to chest, crying even harder, and for a brief moment, Rick thought he'd said the wrong thing—until he spoke. "If I needed to hear anything, it was that. I love you so much, Rick."

"We'll help Jenny through this, and make sure Josh is loved, safe, and happy." Rick had no idea how he would go about that, but heck if he wasn't going to give it his all. "I love you with everything that I am, and I promise to stand by you, Jenny, and Josh through all of this."

"What have I done to deserve you? Because I'll keep doing it." Bear looked caught between happy and devastated, and Rick imagined his own emotions would be messed up if he found out someone he loved was dying.

The two sat in silence for a long time, both caught in their thoughts. Bear held Rick close, refusing to let him even a foot away. Rick had so many questions and no idea where to start, but he knew Bear needed time to think, which he gave easily.

"It's just not fair after everything she's been through and raising Josh by herself." Bear shook his head as he spoke.

"They have you, and I know you've provided for them." Rick wouldn't let Bear minimize what he'd done.

"What?" *Or maybe I should have kept my mouth shut.*

"Um… Jenny told me she wouldn't have survived without your support. Your love, help, and money… She told me some of the things you've done for her and Josh. Bear, they've never been on their own. You've always been there. If I had to guess, this is why she knows you'll take care of Josh when she's…gone." Even saying the words made Rick sick to his stomach.

"When did the two of you have a chance to discuss me?" Bear asked. He didn't sound or look angry; he actually had a smile on his face.

"When you were at the diner yesterday. We spent the afternoon in the backyard playing with Josh and talking." The sick feeling in Rick's stomach was getting worse by the second. The thought of Bear's sister dying was paralyzing. Raising Josh, even scarier. *What if I mess this up?*

"We should go find Jenny and Josh," Bear said.

Bear snaked his hand to the back of Rick's neck and slowly lowered his mouth. He kissed Rick's with such tenderness and care that Rick felt like he was being cherished by the big man. Rick had never felt this depth of love ever in his not-so-illustrious life, and he would do whatever it took to keep hold of his new family.

***

In the end they had only two months with Jenny before she lost her battle with cancer, and she'd been buried in Brighton Cemetery three weeks ago.

Early on Rick had decided he would stay at home with Josh. The little guy had lost his mother! And as she'd become weaker, Josh became more attached to Rick. So, after a long talk with Bear, which turned into an hour of convincing Bear he wasn't giving up on his own dreams, they decided to let Janet take over as head librarian and for Rick to officially become a stay-at-home uncle.

In the beginning after Jenny passed away, both Bear and Josh were quiet and reserved. Neither seemed interested in anything, and Rick had to put his foot down fairly quickly, not giving them the chance to become depressed. Rick knew all too well the damage depression could do. He ordered Bear back to the diner and began taking Josh to the park every day to play with other children.

Rick knew it would take time to heal, and in the meantime, he would make sure he kept everything together so Bear could concentrate on the diner during the day and relax with Josh at night. The only problem with this plan was that Rick was completely exhausted; from groceries, playdates, and errands, to laundry, cleaning, and cooking, Rick was running on empty. But Bear was beginning to smile again and Josh was laughing more now than he had in months, so Rick would just have to suck it up. Even being intimate had taken a backseat since finding out Jenny was sick, and they'd never had the chance to explore further.

Josh had woken up the previous night screaming for his mommy, and Rick spent the rest of the night on the floor in Josh's room providing him with comfort. Bear had tried to take his place, but Rick outright refused, though now, walking home from the park pushing Josh in his stroller, he wished he'd taken Bear up on his offer. His head hurt, his body ached, and he had a strange chill running through him even though it was a warm, sunny day. He had to get Josh home for his nap and put in another load of laundry, so he increased his pace. He was walking quickly down the sidewalk, mentally going through his checklist of chores, and almost ran down Grandma Rose Mason as she came around the corner.

Rick immediately stopped, barely missing the older lady. "Grandma Rose, I'm so sorry. Are you okay?"

"I'm just fine, Rick, but you look a bit frazzled. Are you okay?" She watched him closely, making Rick a bit nervous. He remembered that look from when the White Hair Crew took over after he was released from the hospital, saving his life.

"I'm fine. I just have lots to do, and I think I might be coming down with something." *Or it might be that I saw that same beat-up gray car again. But it always leaves, so maybe I'm imagining things, or maybe it's someone that lives in the area, or it could be my anxiety causing me to be leery.* But every time he saw that car, he held Josh a bit closer and kept an eye on the other children in the park. He was going to report it today, but then he began to feel sick and wanted to get Josh home.

"Oh dear, you go on home and I'll bring over some soup later," Grandma Rose ordered.

"You don't have to bother, Grandma Rose. I'm sure it's nothing." Josh chose that moment to wake and stirred in the stroller. "I have to get Josh home for his nap, ma'am, but thank you for your concern."

Grandma Rose examined Rick a bit too closely for his liking; he didn't need her seeing how close he was to passing out in front of her.

"I'll talk to you soon, young man. You can't fool an old bird like me." With that, she turned and headed into the town proper. Rick imagined that the other ladies of the White Hair Crew were waiting at the diner for her. He just hoped he wasn't the topic of conversation for today, but knew he wasn't that lucky.

**

Bear sat behind his desk in his back office at the diner. It'd been three weeks since his sister had died, and the crushing weight of the loss was beginning to lessen just a bit, allowing him to breathe. Rick had been his rock; their positions had reversed in a way. Now instead of Bear helping Rick through his panic attacks and anxiety, Rick was helping Bear and Josh through their loss and grief.

Bear was so proud of his love. When he began to wallow in his own sadness, Rick had kicked him in the ass and forced him to work. Day after day, Bear would grumble all the way to the diner, and day after day, Rick would be waiting for him to get home, kissing him senseless when he entered the door.

Rick was holding Bear's world together, but it was way past time for Bear to retake his own responsibilities in their relationship. Jenny wouldn't want him to grieve too long; in fact, she would have slapped him upside the head weeks ago. The picture of his feisty sister lecturing him about living life and not wasting time made him smile.

"It's nice to see you smiling again, Bear," Rose Mason said from the open doorway. "May I come in?"

"Of course, Grandma Rose" Bear responded as he stood and patiently waited for the older woman to sit. "How can I help you, ma'am?"

"It's not me that needs your help. It's your Rick," she explained.

"Rick? What's happened? Where are he and Josh?" Bear stood and was about to round the desk, heading straight for the door, when Grandma Rose spoke.

"Sit down, young man, and I'll explain what I've seen over the past few weeks."

Bear sat immediately, gripping the edge of the table and squeezing it just to keep him in his seat. "Noticed over the past weeks?" *How could I have missed something for that long?*

"Haven't you noticed that he seems exhausted most of the time now? I've seen him all over town with Josh; I haven't seen that in years. Now don't get me wrong, I'm happy to see Rick out in the world again, but you've got to ask yourself, did Rick suddenly get over his anxiety, or is he pushing it down so that he can get through everything he now does during the day and making himself sick in the process?"

"But he hasn't said a word, and I-I..." Bear thought about the last few months and how little by little Rick had started taking on more responsibilities as Jenny became sicker. He'd even taken over care of Josh. "I should have seen what was happening in my own house."

"Don't be too hard on yourself. You haven't had it easy these past few months. This is not all your fault. Rick should have said something when he became overwhelmed. Now go home and talk to him before he runs himself into the ground."

Even though he wanted to run to his bike and get his ass home, his aunt didn't raise a rude man. He waited until Grandma Mason stood, and then he escorted her back to her table with the rest of her crew.

"We'll be over about six with dinner, and afterward, we're taking Josh home with us for a few days so the two of you can rest."

"But Josh is still just getting over losing his mom. He barely wants to be in a separate room from one of us. I don't think he'll want to leave," Bear tried to explain as gently as he could. He didn't want to offend these kind women.

"We're only three doors down. We could literally yell over the fences if we needed help, which we won't considering, between the four of us, we've raised twenty children, sixteen grandchildren, and four great-grandchildren. Now go."

The second she was in her chair, Bear turned and headed straight for the door. On his way out, he waved at Jesse, who was working on the grill, knowing the man would understand that he was headed home. Bear always wanted to go home when he was at the diner now that Jenny had died; he wanted his family, but he was well aware that he needed a thriving business to support that family, so he stayed. It was about time he took a few days off and got himself together, because it was obvious to him now that Rick was actually taking care of everyone including him.

Chapter Eight

The house was unusually quiet as he walked from the front foyer and into the living room, but Bear knew Rick and Josh were home; the stroller was by the entrance, and they never walked anywhere without it. Bear checked the kitchen and playroom; both were empty. He walked up the stairs to find his family sleeping in Josh's bedroom, Josh lying stretched out comfortably on the bed and Rick sitting twisted like a pretzel in a high-backed chair beside him.

Bear stood there for a moment and took a good look at his partner—and he did consider Rick his partner in everything, including the diner. He'd even had the papers drawn up showing their joint ownership for Rick to sign. Bear also wanted to discuss wills, but that could wait. The closer he looked, the more he noticed the dark circles under Rick's eyes and the deep stress lines between his eyebrows. *He's lost weight! How could I have missed that? This changes now.*

He bent and gently lifted Rick from the chair, not even waking him, and walked to their bedroom, undressed him and tucked him in without so much as a groan from Rick. Bear's guilt was growing by the second. How had he let it get this far? Before he left, he put a glass of water on the side table and quietly backed out of the room. After a quick check on Josh, Bear went downstairs to take stock of what needed to be done.

The living room was spotless, the laundry room only had one load to go in, and the kitchen had only a few dishes in the sink. Hell, even the grass had been mowed. Bear had a sinking feeling that Rick had been working his ass off to keep the house perfect for him and Josh. There was no excuse for allowing this to happen. He'd checked out after Jenny's death, and he'd been selfish and needed to repair the damage he'd done. Rick should have never been put into the position of caregiver for the entire house. Now that he'd seen what Grandma Rose was talking about, he was glad she and the other grandmas would be taking care of Josh for a couple days. He had a lot to make up for to earn Rick's forgiveness, so he headed straight for his office to make plans.

***

Rick felt warm and cozy. He couldn't remember the last time he'd just woken up in bed without having a toddler alarm clock going off. He looked out the window and noticed the sun was setting and the sky was alive with purples, oranges, and reds. *Beautiful*. Rick stretched his still-achy body, but his headache had eased a bit. Everything was still a bit fuzzy from just waking up, and Rick enjoyed the moment of silence.

Silence… sunset… Josh! Rick leapt out of the bed in only his boxers and ran for Josh's room, finding it empty. *Why am I in my boxers, and why was I in bed?* Doubling back for the stairs, he raced down and into the empty living room. He could hear noises coming from the kitchen and quickly ran through the door to find Bear working at the stove but no Josh in sight.

"Bear, where's Josh?" Rick knew he looked frantic, but this was his Josh who was missing. "I can't find him anywhere."

Bear turned and must have seen the panic in Rick's eyes. Quickly, he came forward and wrapped his arms around Rick. "He's safe, sweetheart, and he's with the grandmas three doors down." Yes, the four women had lived in a big, old Victorian together for the past five years. They cared for each other and kept one another company when they weren't out in the community volunteering.

"Oh my God, I didn't hear a thing. I'm so sorry, Bear. I should have heard something." Rick was rambling but couldn't stop himself. Josh could have been taken, and he wouldn't have been awake to protect him. "I'm screwing up already. The FBI's National Crime Information Center reported that 460,699 children were kidnapped in 2015, and I slept through everything." Rick's breathing became labored. He was gasping, and it felt as if his throat were closing up. He hadn't had a panic attack in over a month, but he knew all too well what this was.

"Rick, breathe with me. In… Hold it… Breathe out slowly and again." This went on for a few minutes until he could breathe almost normally. "There you go, sweetheart. Do you feel better?"

"Yes, thank you. I'm sorry I freaked out like that. It's been so long. Just further proof I'm unsuitable to care for Josh." The words hurt, but the truth was the truth.

"Honey, if it weren't for you, this house would have fallen apart weeks ago. You kept everything together before Jenny's death, Rick. You're not a screw-up. You're my rock, and after my sister died, you kept me going." Bear held him closer. "I need to ask for your forgiveness. I laid everything at your feet when Jenny got sicker, the days and nights I stayed at the hospital and left you to handle everything by yourself and take care of Josh."

"No. You did the best you could. Your sister was dying. She needed you there with her. Bear, never apologize for anything you did for your sister. Jenny and Josh are worth whatever we have to go through." The last thing Rick wanted Bear to do was apologize for spending every possible moment with Jenny.

"God, babe, you are one of the strongest people I know. How did I manage to get you to give me a second look?"

Strongest person? Rick doubted that, but he didn't want to argue the point.

"Well, you're handsome for one, intelligent for another, and—"

"Okay, okay. Dinner's almost ready. The grandmas brought a pot of chicken noodle soup, ginger ale, ginseng, and orange juice. Apparently you're sick, and I didn't even notice."

The guilt written all over his face was surprising to Rick. To him, Bear had done nothing wrong.

"You've done nothing to feel guilty for." Rick cuddled into Bear's chest. "I've missed you." Most nights Rick would be so exhausted by the end of dinner that he had to fight to stay awake until after Josh went to bed; that didn't leave much time for romance or to just talk.

"Well, isn't it good that we have a few days to ourselves then?" Bear smiled wide.

"What?" *Days, why days?*

"Josh is having a sleepover with the White Hair Crew for the next two days," Bear answered.

"Two days… Are you sure? He might be too much for them to handle for forty-eight hours." *And I'm not sure I can handle him being away that long.* Rick had grown to love the little guy; they'd bonded over cartoons and coloring.

"Don't let them hear you talking like that or you'll find out exactly how much is too much after they kick your ass. I love you, Rick, but I'm not fool enough to walk into the middle of that. You're on your own." Bear laughed as he walked Rick into the dining room. It felt like he'd stepped into the pages of some home and style magazine. The table was set beautifully with crystal, china, candles, and cloth napkins. Rick hadn't seen this since their second date almost six months ago.

Rick shook his head, thinking of everything that had happened since then, when his greatest fear was having a panic attack in front of Bear. Now he had to worry about boo-boos, the nutrition in their food, playdates, and soon potty training. On top of dealing with just about everything a two-year-old could possibly get into and making the house completely safe for Josh, time had flown by.

"I thought I'd make dinner special. We'll have soup and fresh baked bread. If in a couple hours you get hungry again, I'll make something more substantial. You're run down and we need to build you back up, sweetheart."

"The table looks beautiful, Bear, but I'm a little underdressed," Rick teased while looking down at his boxers and thanking fate that the drapes were drawn or the neighbors might be calling Police Chief Graham. "I assume you took off my clothes and put me to bed."

Bear began unbuttoning his shirt. "Yes, and we can't have you feeling underdressed." Inch by magnificent inch, tanned skin and dark chest hair were revealed to Rick's appreciative gaze. Soon Bear was working on his jeans, sliding them off his feet, followed by socks. Now he stood in all his almost-naked glory, and parts of Rick were starting to take notice.

"None of that." Bear reached down and cupped Rick's sensitive balls. "Not until you've eaten and are feeling better, babe."

"I'm better. Just needed a long nap and all's good." Rick didn't care if his body ached a little; he was getting himself some of the gorgeous bear in front of him.

"You're not foolin' me. Now sit that cute ass down, and I'll go get our food. Then after dinner, we can have a bath." Bear smiled knowingly.

Rick just hoped they were on the same page as to how he wanted to spend the next two days…in bed, but not to rest. The smell of chicken soup filled the room when Bear walked back in with two bowls and a loaf of fresh bread. He set the food down, then leaned over Rick's chair and slammed his mouth down on his, aggressively taking what he wanted—but Rick wasn't afraid. He was turned on. He knew he would always be safe with Bear.

After several long moments, Bear pulled away, leaving Rick's lips tingling and swollen from his kiss. Rick wanted more, but as soon as he reached for Bear, he backed away. "If you keep looking at me like you want to eat me, I'll take you right here on the dining room table. But you need to eat before we even consider anything else."

Rick sat back down, disappointed but hungry enough to let things be, and dug into a little bit of heaven in a bowl. The chicken was tender, and the thick egg noodles, carrots, and celery were perfectly cooked. *Yep, heaven.*

"Did you know noodle and broth soup originated as early as the 1200s in Asia, and in 1700s Italy people fed the sick noodle soup because it was easier to digest?" Rick didn't even give it a second thought that he'd info dropped yet again. Bear loved every part of him—if Rick was sure of anything, it was that.

"I knew it had been used as relief for the sick, but I didn't know when they started serving it. Do you like your soup, babe?" Bear asked.

"It's very good. The grandmas can cook. I've almost finished this bowl already. They had me back at a healthy weight within a few months of me being released from the hospital." Rick ducked his head. Leave it to him to bring up his past when he was with his amazing new partner.

"Rick, look at me." Bear reached over and took Rick's hand. "I want you to speak openly about that time in your life. I don't want you to edit your thoughts. I respect the strength it took for you to make it through the abuse, and it will be a part of you forever. I expect you to continue to share everything that beautiful mind thinks up."

Rick had no idea why he was getting so emotional, but tears sprang to his eyes, and he tried hard to blink them away to no avail. Bear leaned forward and wiped Rick's cheeks with his napkin. "Bear, I'd say I love you, but the words don't feel strong enough for us."

"You show me every day, Rick. I have been neglectful in telling you and showing you the same, but that changes now. No more of you handling Josh and the house alone. You're my partner, and to that end… I wanted to talk to you about something."

Rick went on alert. "Talk to you" had never been a good thing before, but this was Bear, his Bear. He had to trust in their bond, their love. Bear would never do anything to hurt him. "Okay, what is it?"

"Well, maybe you should finish eating before we talk about this?" Bear suggested.

"I won't be able to eat a thing now until you tell me," Rick answered honestly.

"Okay, well, I wanted to talk to you about the diner. You're my partner, Rick. We may not have a marriage certificate to prove it, but I'm in this for life. I want you to become my partner in the diner— you and me, partners at home and at work. I love you so much, babe. What do you think?"

The diner? Rick couldn't believe what Bear was saying. He didn't deserve half of something Bear worked himself to the bone over. "Bear, I love that you made the offer, but I can't. That diner belongs to you, and I'm not going to take half of that. It's not fair to you."

"You let me decide what's fair. I've willed the diner to you anyway, so you might as well get to know the business now in case something ever happens to me."

Rick sprung from his chair and straddled Bear's legs. "Nothing is ever going to happen to you, do you understand?"

"Easy, babe. I'm not going anywhere. I'm sorry, I should never have said it that way. I just want to share my life with you. I need us to be connected in all ways. I need to know you and Josh are taken care of. I've already changed my will to include you and Josh. I set up a trust fund for him to go to college, and the rest is left to you to take care of yourself and Josh."

"Of course I would take care of Josh, but, Bear, we've only been together six months. Don't you think it's a bit early to do this?" Rick certainly did.

"Not in the least."

"Are you insane?"

"Perhaps, but I'm not taking no for an answer. Rick, do this for me. After losing my sister, it reinforced that life is so short and we need to live it. I will always love and miss my Jenny, but I choose to live in the here and now, not wallow away in sadness. Do this for me."

Rick was speechless. Bear had just declared that he wanted Rick for life. He wanted to share everything in his world with Rick, and suddenly Rick wanted to do the same. "If you want to share your world with me, then you have to accept and share mine."

"Of course, honey, whatever you want."

Rick was getting nervous. *What if he's mad that I didn't share this information before now?* "Um… there's something I need to tell you, and I don't want to upset you."

"You can tell me anything. If we need to discuss it, we will, but there will not be any anger involved."

"If you want to share half of everything with me, then you have to accept half of my inheritance," Rick declared in a stronger voice than he'd intended, but this was important to him.

"Inheritance?"

"Yes, when my parents died, they left me a bit of land here in Brighton and roughly $414,000 in assets and investments. I never told Bret a thing about it. That's the only reason I still have it. Well, that and the fact that my parents' lawyer kept everything behind the scenes for me."

Bear was silent for a moment before he spoke. "I understand why you were cautious to tell me, Rick, but that's a lot of money and it's from your parents. I can't do that to you."

"Now you know how I feel." Rick smiled at the disgruntled look on Bear's face. "It's only fair. I'll sign whatever you want, only if you sign the same for me."

"Wow, you drive a hard bargain." Bear laughed. "We can talk to your lawyer about this. Then we'll decide the best way to proceed, okay?"

Bear leaned in and ran his warm lips across Rick's jaw, sending waves of heat straight to his groin. Rick arched his neck, desperate for Bear's touch, needing to feel Bear's lips on his body after what seemed like months with no chance for intimacy. Rick snaked his hand down Bear's rippled abdomen, into his boxers, and wrapped his hand around Bear's hard cock. God, he needed to feel Bear's body wrapped around his.

"Are you done eating, babe?" Bear asked as he continued to nibble his way down Rick's neck.

"Oh yeah, we can have something light later. All I want right now is you. Please, Bear, it's been so long, and I need to feel you inside me."

"You've got me, Rick. With everything I am, I'm yours." Bear latched on to Rick's shoulder and sucked up a lewd mark. "Let's get you into that bath. I'll clean this up later."

Rick was all for the new plan and leapt from Bear's lap, heading straight for the master bathroom, never once looking back, assured by the knowledge that Bear was hot on his heels and just as excited. As the tub filled, they divested each other of their boxers and wrapped around each other, writhing and kissing. Rick would never have enough of Bear.

When they finally came up for air, Bear spoke. "Tub's ready. I want you slippin' and slidin' all over my body."

"That can be arranged," Rick answered, then squealed like a little girl when Bear grabbed him around the waist and carried him to the tub, which was full of bubbles.

"Bubbles?" *When did he put bubbles in?*

"Serious slippin' and slidin'." Bear stepped into the oversized tub and placed Rick down before submerging himself in bubbles. *Oh, this is going to be fun.*

Rick slid himself right onto Bear's lap, combing his fingers through Bear's wet hair, and slipped Bear's hard cock between his ass cheeks, leaving no question what Rick wanted Bear to do to him.

Rick licked the tiny droplets of water running down the side of Bear's neck, causing goose bumps to rise all over his hard body. Rick moved on to Bear's chest while rocking his hips, sliding Bear's cock back and forth between his slippery ass cheeks.

"You ready for that, babe?" Bear asked, his voice scratchy, as if he were trying not to growl his excitement over what was coming.

"I've been ready for months. Make love to me, Bear."

Bear's eyes dilated until only a rim of blue was showing. His breathing increased, and Rick swore he felt Bear's cock twitch.

"Now, what about your bath?" Bear teased.

"We can soak in the tub later. Right now, I need you," Rick growled.

Without another word, Bear stood and stepped out of the tub, lifting Rick out after him. They quickly dried each other, taking special care not to rub their shafts too hard and risk coming right there and not getting to the main event. As soon as they were reasonably dry, they raced each other to the bed, laughing the entire time, and threw themselves onto the down comforter.

Bear pinned Rick to the bed, leaned forward, and sucked one light brown nipple into his warm mouth, causing Rick to cry out. The pleasure was so sudden, he arched his back to get closer to Bear, but it wasn't enough. He needed so much more.

"Please… More…"

"I've got you, babe," Bear assured him, his face hard lines, his piercing blue eyes partially hidden by his chestnut hair. He looked as though he was barely holding on to his control, which excited Rick more. He wanted Bear to lose control and take him now, and to that end, Rick reared up and took Bear's nipple in his mouth. The response was instantaneous. Bear's big hand came around and cupped the back of Rick's head, holding him in place, and deep moans filled the room.

Bear finally pulled Rick away and reached for the bedside table, pulling the drawer out a little too hard and scattering the contents all over the floor.

"Dammit," Bear cursed under his breath and jumped from the bed, no doubt in search of the lube. "Found it!" He popped his head up over the side of the bed and held the tube high, as if it were a trophy.

"Then get over here and use it," Rick answered in a huff. He needed Bear back in the bed *now*!

Bear crawled onto the bed like a predator stalking his prey, a primal look on his face. *God, he's gorgeous.* Slowly he came to hover over Rick. "Mine." The word should have scared the hell out of Rick, but coming from Bear he felt the exact opposite. He felt safe and cherished.

"Yours," Rick agreed wholeheartedly.

Slowly, Bear spread Rick's legs wide and put a liberal amount of lube on his fingers before leaning down and kissing Rick senseless. He could feel the probing fingers circling his hole and loosening the muscle to allow Bear entry. Rick knew Bear was being gentle. Rick hadn't been with another man since Bret, but he could barely handle the wait. Then mercifully, he felt one finger entering him, and his nerve endings sent waves of pleasure through his body. Then another finger joined until Rick was begging to be filled.

"Just one more, babe. I'm a big man, and I never want to hurt you." Bear's breathing was labored, his voice rough.

"I'm ready," Rick said impatiently.

"Not until I say you are." Bear gently slid in a fourth finger, making Rick writhe on the bed. Bear removed his fingers, pulled Rick's feet up to his shoulders, and slowly began to enter him. Rick thanked god they'd had blood tests done so that he could finally enjoy making love without any barriers.

The stretch and burn were intense, but he knew they soon would be replaced by pleasure, and he relaxed as much as possible. Inch by inch, Bear slowly pushed deeper until his hips rested against Rick's ass.

Bear was waiting for permission before he moved. The look of pained restraint etched on his face was evidence of how hard he was fighting. Within moments, Rick's muscles relaxed, and he gave Bear a nod that he was ready. The look of relief would have been comical if he weren't being speared by a two-by-four. After a few strokes, the pain morphed into exquisite pleasure as Bear pegged his gland over and over again. Sweat trickled down from Bear's body as they moved in sync against one another. Rick's legs bent almost to his chest as Bear's thrusts sped up.

"Yes, babe, you feel so damn good," Bear growled out.

Rick was too far gone to talk, only able to emit moans of pleasure. Bear was ruthless about hitting Rick's gland with every stroke until he was ready to come. "Bear, I'm going to come. Please don't stop."

"Didn't plan on it, love," Bear confirmed, his strokes faltering slightly as he got closer to his own release. "Come for me, Rick. Give me your pleasure."

Bear pinched one of Rick's hard nipples, and that tiny bite of pain was all it took for Rick to fall over the edge. Pure carnal bliss took over his entire body. Come splashed onto Rick's chest as a harsh shout from above him signaled Bear's release. There were no barriers between them, just as they both wanted.

Bear released Rick's legs and collapsed on top of him, but quickly rolled them both, so as to not hurt Rick, which was good because he didn't want to be crushed after the best orgasm of his life. They lay there panting for what seemed like hours.

"Looks like we need a shower this time," Bear joked.

Rick popped his head up at the mention of hot soapy time with Bear. *Wait, I just had explosive sex with him, and not ten minutes later I want to rub all over him in the shower. What's wrong with me?*

"Ah, you like the idea of a shower, don't you, you animal?"

"I don't know why I'm like this. I've never been so horny in my life," Rick admitted.

"You just needed the right person to bring it out in you, and trust me, I'm reaping the rewards of that." Bear crushed Rick to his chest and held him tight. "I love you, Rick."

"I love you too, Bear." Rick knew that to his soul. He would never be with anyone but Bear. His heart belonged to the man. "Now, how about that shower?"

Chapter Nine

"I don't think I'll be walking anywhere for a while, mister," Rick teased as he sprawled across the bed naked, the same bed that they'd spent the last two days in. There were takeout containers on the dresser and towels strewn around the room, but not a stitch of clothing anywhere to be seen.

"You deserve it for taking advantage of me last night and then this morning. You know I can't say no to you," Bear replied.

Rick laughed before letting reality seep back into their bubble. "We need to get cleaned up so we can go get Josh, and this time I'm taking a shower down the hall so you can't distract me." Rick missed Josh and wanted the little dude home.

"Okay, okay, but I'll take the shower down the hall and you stay here." Bear sat up, kissed Rick on his forehead, and got out of bed, heading for the dresser.

Rick felt the loss immediately but got up anyway and walked to the shower all by himself. How had he become so addicted to this man? Well, if there was a cure, Rick didn't want it. For the first time in his life, he was happy, really happy. He had a family now, people who loved him unconditionally and whom he loved back.

He showered quickly and dressed even faster. Josh would be waiting for them. The doorbell rang and Rick could hear Bear walking toward the front door, so he didn't hurry. He heard voices coming from the foyer and headed in that direction. At the last second, he glanced outside the kitchen window, seeing the same beat-up old gray car in the driveway with a large man sitting in the passenger seat. Panic struck him. He had to tell Bear; he might be in danger considering the same person had obviously been following him. Rick ran for the foyer. The voices were getting louder and Bear was almost growling at the tall, thin man standing in the hallway.

"You'll never have him, Heath."

"Yes, I will," the tall man yelled back.

"Bear, whoever he is, he's been following Josh and me when we go to the park. That's the same car I've been seeing for days."

"You've been stalking my family. Do you have a death wish, Heath?" Bear took a step forward, causing the intruder to step back quickly.

"Wait, you know him?" Rick asked, not sure if he'd heard correctly.

"Yes, unfortunately this sack of shit is the sperm donor to Josh. He sure as hell has never been a father." Rick had never seen Bear this angry.

"He's my son, and I want him back. He can't be raised by no fags." Heath sneered as he spoke.

Bear took another step forward and Heath took one back. "You gave up all parental rights a long time ago. You wanted nothing to do with him. We both know you don't want Josh. It's the money. You want any life insurance money held in trust, and as Josh's legal guardian you can dispense the money as you see fit. Well, sorry to break it to ya, but you aren't his legal guardian."

"N-no, that has nothing to do with it. I want to see my son."

Even Rick could read through that lie.

"You have no rights to anything, Heath, so climb into that piece-of-shit car and get out of Brighton before I let Police Chief Graham know why you're in town."

"Maybe we should involve the police," Heath said, but his eyes told a different story.

"Go ahead. I have all the court documents, and many contain quite a few references to your criminal record and time spent in prison. I'm sure the chief would love to sit down with you and have a little talk."

The venom in Heath's eyes would have cowed any other man, but Bear stood tall, his arms crossed, every bit the big, bad biker he was.

"This isn't over, Bear." Heath sneered and then turned his evil glare over Rick's body, making him feel dirty.

Bear moved to block Heath's view of Rick. "You better leave, and if you come back, I'll call the cops on you for trespassing—if you're lucky. If not, I'll take care of this myself. You have no legal rights here, so go find your cash cow someplace else."

"I'll be seeing you soon," Heath warned before storming back out the open doorway.

Bear slammed the door so hard that the coat rack shook and fell to the floor.

"What are we going to do?" Rick asked.

"We're going over to the grandmas' and picking up Josh. Then I'm making a call to Chief Graham. He needs to know there's going to be trouble in town." Bear looked grim, making Rick anxious.

"Trouble? You don't think he'll leave?" Rick asked.

"No."

***

Bear walked Rick over to the grandmas' house, his eyes scanning his surroundings the entire time. Two years, it had been two years since Heath had walked out on Jenny and Josh, leaving them both in the hospital after he'd signed the papers. Well, technically, Bear had seen Heath a few hours later out back of Rudy's Bar where he'd left him with a few extra bruises as a parting gift.

How dare he show up here and demand Josh! The fear he'd seen in Rick's eyes when he knew what Heath wanted was almost enough to set Bear off into a rage, and then Heath wouldn't have been safe anywhere. Bear typically wasn't a violent man. Men usually wanted to take a crack at him because of his size, see if they could take the big guy. They never could. But Bear himself never went out to find problems. This one had showed up on his doorstep and threatened his family.

Hours later, Josh was safely in bed and Rick was hovering as if Heath were going to jump out of the closet and grab Josh at any moment. So Bear was in his office, calling in a little help.

"Chief Graham please."

"May I tell him who's calling?" Ms. Judy, the dispatcher, asked.

"Bear Mitchell."

"One moment please."

"Graham here." The man sounded tired, and Bear felt guilty for bringing this to the place he now called home.

"Hey, Graham, we may have a problem." Bear spent the next hour filling the police chief in on Heath and going over his past illegal activity, sure that Heath was dirty again. He needed money; that was plain to see with his old car, ripped clothing, and dirty body. Also the second man, the one who'd waited in the car, was there for a reason. Bear needed to find out who the other guy was. After he hung up with Chief Graham, Bear made a check on every door and window and set the alarm.

When he reached the second story, he found Rick right where he thought he would, in Josh's room on guard duty. The stress radiated off him as he looked out the window through the blinds.

"He's not going to try anything. He's more of an annoyance than anything," Bear stated, but he didn't believe a word he was saying. He'd seen the desperation in Heath's eyes; he wasn't sure how far the man might go. But he wasn't going to announce that fact to his extremely freaked-out partner.

"You don't know that, they could try to come through the window. They aren't very bright if they think they can just walk in and legally get any of the money." Bear knew that Rick realized he was overreacting, but could do nothing to stop it.

"I'll be right back, sweetheart." Bear left Rick and went to the second spare bedroom, stripped the bed, and dragged the double mattress back to Josh's room. It wouldn't be perfect, but he'd do anything to calm Rick.

"What are you doing?" Rick asked when Bear came in.

"Well, I know neither of us is going to sleep unless we're in the same room as Josh. We might as well be a little comfortable," Bear explained, still astonished that the little guy was sleeping through all of this. Rick ran and got his sleeping pants on and grabbed extra bedding for their makeshift bed. After the bed was made, Bear went to change as well. It killed him that his family now had to live in fear on top of everything else.

Bear swore he wouldn't let anyone harm them. He let out a deep breath and sat on their bed. "Jenny… God, I miss you so much. We're trying to do the best for Josh. I think we're doing a good job, but this shit with Heath so soon after you left me… I don't know what I would do if Josh or Rick were ripped from me as well."

"We're not going anywhere, Bear," Rick said from the open doorway. His beautiful hazel eyes were glassy. He walked over and stood in front of Bear, and gently cupped his face. "We love you, Josh and me. We're going to have a long life together. We're going to raise Josh to be a good man, and we aren't going to allow that horrible person to take him anywhere." As Rick spoke, in between random words, he kissed Bear's lips so gently, almost reverently. "We trust you to keep us safe. None of this is your fault, and we will survive this too." Rick kissed each of Bear's closed eyelids before tenderly kissing his lips and walking out of the room.

Bear sat there for a while, thinking over everything that had happened. Two months felt like a years. The joy, pain, and sorrow he'd recently experienced could fill up a lifetime, for sure. Finally, Bear stood and changed his clothing before returning to Josh's room. Rick had the bed tucked right up close to Josh's "big boy" bed with its railings. As Bear looked closer, he realized Rick was sound asleep. Very carefully, he shifted the blankets and slid in beside his love. With one final look at the two people who meant the world to him, he swore to be the man they needed him to be.

***

It had been a week since he'd last seen Heath or his car, and Rick was beginning to breathe just a bit easier. The fact that he had his own personal bodyguard didn't hurt either. Dante, Spider, Sam, and their team of ex-military personnel named *Sentinel*, who lived and worked as a team taking on missions around the world, were now watching over them. Their home base was Brighton, and Police Chief Graham had called them in once Bear explained why Heath was in town.

Rick wasn't entirely certain of Heath's criminal past, but his bodyguards kept a close eye on him and Josh while Bear was at work. Even after Bear came home, Rick was sure he saw one of them wandering around the outside of the house.

There were six in their team: Shannon, Jake (Shadow), Coop, Vincent, and the bosses Dante, Sam and Spider. At the moment, they were at the playground with Josh and Shannon. Now, if anyone thought having a female bodyguard made you more at risk of attack, Shannon would be more than happy to correct their thinking. She was an adorable, blond-haired, blue-eyed Californian and perfect as his bodyguard. No one would think she was a threat to anyone. Little did they know that she was a renowned hacker, expert with knives, and had so many different martial arts under her belt that she would be able to defend them without breaking a sweat, which was good considering there were two men in Heath's car. They still didn't know who the second man was, but they would find out.

"So, Mr. Homemaker, what's it like staying at home with a two-year-old? I admit, he's a cute little guy, but 24/7... I just don't know," Shannon asked as she scanned the area for what felt like the hundredth time, but seemed so natural for her to do. Rick wondered what kind of life you would have to lead to work protecting others but doubted Shannon would elaborate for him.

"It's cliché, but honestly this is the hardest job I've ever had—and the most rewarding. I wouldn't change anything about my life. Bear and Josh mean everything to me."

"He is adorable." Rick gave Shannon a strange look. "I mean Josh, not Bear... Josh is adorable, and I can't figure out how this asshole is his donor."

Bear had informed everyone that Rick did not want Heath called father; he was simply a donor. There wasn't a fatherly bone in his body, and the thought of him wanting Josh for Jenny's life insurance money just proved it.

"I have no idea what Jenny ever saw in him, but I'm damn happy to have Josh. I just can't stand the thought of that man out there somewhere trying to figure out a way to get Josh away from us."

"You'll never have to worry about that happening. That's why we're here."

"We?" Rick asked.

"Yep, Shadow's wandering around here somewhere." The fact that Rick hadn't noticed Shadow wasn't that odd; the man's nickname was Shadow for a reason. He could disappear almost right in front of you.

"Are there always two of you? I noticed one of the team watching the outside of the house last night."

"Yep, safe as can be," Shannon confirmed with a devilish smile.

"Unk, Unk! Play," Josh called from the sandbox.

"You got it, little man," Rick answered. "Wanna come play in the sand, Shannon?"

"No thank you. I've seen enough sand in my lifetime." She laughed and got up to walk away. "I'm going to check the area. I'll be close by."

Rick felt a bit uneasy but nodded his agreement anyway; after all, he would have to get over the constant threat and carry on with life. *Maybe Heath has already gone back to Chicago.* Rick didn't think Heath would give up so easily, but he could always hope. Rick sat down in the middle of the sandbox beside Josh and prepared himself to be covered in the gritty stuff yet again. His generous little man handed him his toy truck filled with sand, which poured right down Rick's T-shirt. *It begins.*

"Thank you, Josh. Let's make a castle for all your cars to live in." They'd brought a bag full of his toy cars and trucks to play with in the sandbox and to share if any of his little friends showed up. At the moment they were alone in the park, which didn't help the whole eerie feeling, even with his bodyguards around there somewhere.

"Casl," Josh cheered.

"Yes, castle."

Buckets were filled with sand and a castle of sorts came to life, although one turret was listing left and the bridge was more of a lump of sand, but hey, it worked.

"Casl, casl, Unk." Josh's chubby hands clapped, spraying sand everywhere.

"Yes, Josh's castle."

"Luv you." Josh's language development was right on track. He tried to put small words together and liked to mimic what everyone said. Rick's heart turned over at the toddler's garbled words.

"Love you, Josh," Rick replied, hugging Josh close.

"Well, isn't that sweet, but he's my son," came an angry voice from behind Rick. "It's about time this brat made me some money."

Rick grabbed Josh and stood, turning to face the vile man. "He's not yours. He was never yours. You gave up that right a long time ago."

"Things change, and he's now useful to me. You can't keep him away from me," Heath hissed.

"Watch me." Rick wasn't entirely sure why he wasn't having a panic attack, because this deserved one.

Heath took one step toward Rick and Josh, and was suddenly on his knees with Shadow's hand around Heath's throat. Shannon was at Rick's side, cell phone in hand.

"The police are on their way," she growled and stood in between Rick and Heath. "What the hell? Josh isn't yours. You had your chance. Leave town or you'll wish you had."

Shadow was deadly quiet, his hand applying constant pressure to Heath's throat and making sure he didn't move.

"He said that Josh was going to make him money, which I don't understand. The life insurance isn't that much, and it's been invested for his college fund. We have no access to it."

Heath eyes glazed over with anger so vicious Rick took a step back and curled his body protectively around Josh. Shadow increased the pressure on his throat and Heath looked away.

"I need to get Josh away from him." Rick wanted to go home and lock all the doors. He felt too vulnerable out in the open. He had to protect Josh. "We need to go."

"Okay, easy, we'll get you guys back to the house as soon as the police arrive." Thank goodness there were sirens splitting the calm like knives.

Rick gathered Josh closer and began to back away from Heath, not wanting to take his eyes off the evil man. His black eyes were still watching them, like a crocodile on its prey. His matted hair was either dark blond or brown, Rick couldn't tell. It was obvious the man had fallen on hard times, but how did he expect Josh to make him money? Rick knew they had to find out and soon.

The police cars were stopping in the lot when Rick saw Bear's new SUV coming down the road. Bear had bought it the moment he knew they would be raising Josh. The relief he felt was instantaneous. Bear was here; he could take them home. Rick turned and rushed toward the parking lot with Josh safely in his arms. Police deputies were running in his direction, Chief Graham in the lead.

"Rick, are you or Josh hurt?" was the first thing he said.

"No, he didn't get a chance." Rick would be forever grateful that people with Sentinel's talents lived in Brighton. Bear was running full speed directly for them. In a matter of seconds, both he and Josh were wrapped in Bear's big arms.

"Unk…play," Josh exclaimed at seeing Bear. He was completely oblivious to the drama carrying on around him.

"Not this time, buddy." Bear looked strung tight as a bow.

"We're okay. He didn't get a chance to hurt us," Rick quickly explained, hoping to calm Bear's obvious fear.

"You shouldn't have to worry every time you leave the house. I'm going to walk the two of you to the SUV, and then I need to have a talk with Graham."

"We'll lock the doors," Rick responded immediately. Bear's face darkened even further, and Rick felt a need to explain. "The other guy's still out there somewhere."

"You shouldn't have to," Bear growled out.

"Grrrrrrr," Josh growled back at Bear and then started giggling like only a two-year-old could.

Bear looked stunned for a few seconds before he broke down and started laughing, breaking the tension just that quickly.

"Are you a bear like Uncle Bear?" Rick teased.

"Bear, bear, bear," Josh chanted.

"Okay, okay, let's get you guys in the truck." Bear led them back to their vehicle, never once letting go of either of them, as if they might vanish in front of him.

Rick cuddled a now-sleepy Josh before placing him into the safety of his car seat with his blue blankie. Rick got into the passenger seat and was about to shut the door when Bear grabbed it and held it open. With an almost panicked look in his eyes, Bear leaned in and kissed Rick deeply.

"I can't lose you guys. You two are everything to me." Bear kissed him one more time before pulling away and shutting the door. Rick sat there for a second, and Bear tapped on the window and pointed at the lock. Even though there were police officers milling around, he locked the door. After a few words with a couple officers, Bear walked over to where Chief Graham had Heath in the back of a police car. The officers he'd just spoken to waved at Rick and took up positions around the SUV. *Oh come on! Who would be dumb enough to even try to get near us?* But he loved Bear all the more for his concern.

Chapter Ten

Bear had never been so scared in his life. When he'd received the call at the diner from the police station, he nearly went out of his mind with fear. It wasn't until he held both of them safe in his arms that he finally allowed himself to calm a bit. Heath should have never gotten that close to his family.

He headed straight for the police vehicle holding the man who had brought all of this to his doorstep.

"Easy, Bear." Chief Graham stopped him just as he reached the vehicle. "You can't go and do anything I might have to put you in jail for."

"Don't care. I want answers." Bear stepped around Graham.

"Wait, if you get locked up, who will take care of Josh and Rick?" That stopped Bear in his tracks better than anything else could.

"That's low, Graham," Bear grumbled.

"But true. We'll take him down to the station and get it out of him. Rick told us that Heath said Josh could make him money. I'm not sure what he meant, but we'll find out," Chief Graham assured.

"There's another guy out there. He came to town with Heath," Bear said.

"We'll find him, Bear. I'll run Heath for warrants, but we can only hold him for twenty-four hours if nothing comes up," Graham stated, looking just about as angry as Bear felt.

"What! He's terrorizing my family and making threats to take Josh. How the hell is that not illegal?"

"That's for the judge to decide," Chief Graham stated. "Look, Bear, I know this bastard deserves a cell. I just need enough evidence to put him there for longer than twenty-four hours."

"Sorry, Chief, I know you're doing the best you can, but it's my family. Just give me a few minutes alone with him." Bear tried once again to step around the police chief.

"You wouldn't respect me if I let you near him." He gave Bear a pointed stare. "You know I'm right."

"Yeah, I know. Call me and let me know what you find out. I'm going to take my family home." Bear deflated slightly; he wanted answers.

"Of course. Go home and spend time with them. I'm sure it will make you feel a bit better." Chief Graham smiled for the first time.

"Thank you, Dave, I'll talk to you soon." Bear used the chief's first name because this was personal, and he knew that Dave would do everything he could to help them.

Bear walked back to the SUV, Rick's big hazel eyes watching his every step. After everything Rick had been through, Bear didn't want this ugliness to touch his family, but it was too late. Heath had made the first move. It was time Bear made a few moves of his own.

When they reached home, the White Hair Crew were waiting along with Royce, Jesse's boyfriend. Josh was fast asleep in his car seat, not a care in the world, and that was the way Bear wanted to keep it. As soon as they parked, the grandmas moved in like a SWAT team. Royce stayed in the background, scanning the area.

"Oh, my dears, are you okay?" Grandma Graham asked as she reached in to lift Josh out of his car seat. "Sweet baby had a big day," she said as Josh yawned and cuddled into the older woman.

"We'll go get him ready for bed. Rose and Betty will get dinner started." Again, the grandmas took over in their own caring way.

Bear held Rick close and walked up to Royce. "Good to see you, Royce."

"Hey, Bear, Rick. Jesse told me what happened when I got to the diner. I'm here to help. I'm on a four-on, three-off rotation, so I'll be spending the night watching the outside of your house," Royce stated and continued to scan the area.

Bear was shocked. Royce was a good man, but other than through Jesse, neither had spent too much time together. Now the man was here willing to spend his days off watching over his family. Brighton was certainly a special town.

"Are you sure, Royce?" Bear knew how hard the EMT worked and didn't want to take his days off away from him.

"Absolutely. That other bastard is still out there somewhere, and we need to make sure he doesn't get anywhere near Josh," Royce stated.

Bear was humbled by Royce's offer to help protect his family. "Thank you, man. I appreciate any help you can give."

Royce gave Bear a smile. "This is Brighton, Bear. You'll get used to the way things are done around here. More than likely, there'll be more people turning up to help in some way." Though he'd lived here for a year, he still wasn't used to people caring so much.

"Thank you, Royce. It means a lot to us." Rick spoke softly and his eyes were droopy. Josh wasn't the only one in need of a nap. He had been up with Josh last night. They were now taking turns each evening as Josh called for his mommy in the night.

"Babe, we got everything covered. Why don't you go have a nap for a couple hours before dinner?" Bear suggested.

"No, I'm okay. I'll go check in with the Crew."

Bear turned Rick so that he could look him in the eyes. "You're no good if you run yourself down and end up sick again. Go lie down. I'm here, and by the sounds of it, half the town is on its way as we speak. Nothing will happen to Josh while you rest."

"What about you? What if something happens to you? Josh isn't the only one I'm worried about," Rick admitted as tears filled his eyes. "I don't know how far these guys are willing to go to get to Josh."

"Oh, babe, I'm a pretty tough old bear. You have nothing to worry about." Bear knew what he was and had no issue with it. He was big, and between his beard and thick chest hair, he was a hairy man. He felt no need to be anything he wasn't. "Okay, now go rest, or do I have to carry you there?" Bear teased, eliciting a smile from Rick, exactly what he'd intended.

"Okay, Bear, I'm going to rest for a little while, but wake me if there's any news."

"I will, sweetheart," Bear agreed before lifting Rick up and kissing him with all the pent-up adrenaline that was still running through his body. He aggressively took Rick's soft lips in a brutal kiss, laying claim to the man he loved.

"Um…maybe both of you should go for a *nap.* " Royce's voice broke into the fog that was taking over Bear's mind. He quickly broke the kiss and stepped back. Rick seemed dazed and a bit wobbly but smiled wide and walked into the house.

"Wow, I might have to call Jesse to join me," Royce said.

"No you don't. He's watching over the diner. Wait 'til it closes and he's all yours."

"Oh, he's all mine all of the time." Royce had a predatory look in his eyes. Bear imagined he looked the same when he spoke of Rick. Royce was far more dominant than Jesse, who was twice Royce's size. If there was a gentle giant in Brighton, Jesse would be it.

"Let's get inside and try to figure out their next step." Bear knew this was far from over.

***

Rick woke to the sound of people talking in hushed tones, the soft voices echoing off the walls around him. *How long have I been asleep?* The sun had set and the light from downstairs filtered into the room, leaving eerie shadows across the ceiling.

He rubbed his eyes and rolled to the side of the bed but was blocked by another body. *Bear.*

"Hey, babe, you awake?" Bear asked in a soft voice.

"Yes, where's Josh?" Rick felt a bit guilty for his mind immediately going to Josh and not the wonderful man beside him.

"Asleep, stop worrying for a few minutes." Bear reached over and cupped the side of Rick's face.

"Sorry. How long have I been asleep?" Rick asked.

"You've been out for about four hours. I just came up fifteen minutes ago to wake you and thought I'd hide here for a while." Bear had a devilish look on his face.

"Hide?" Rick asked.

"Yeah, the community of Brighton is currently in our living room and kitchen." He laughed.

"What!" Rick asked, a bit louder than he'd intended.

"Well, not all of Brighton. I'm sure some of them stayed home."

"Why?" Rick was stuck on one-word questions, but he couldn't stop himself.

"To support us…somehow…"

"I can't do crowds, not right now, Bear. Not with everything going on. Maybe a small group but not a full house." Rick was panicking already.

"Give me a few minutes to clear them out, but first I need a little of this…" Bear kissed him lightly, barely touching lips. "And this…" He kissed a bit deeper this time. "And definitely this." Bear dove in, and Rick could only hang on for the ride. He devoured Rick with his lips and tongue until he was left panting with need. "There you go, now concentrate on that until later. We need to talk, okay?"

Rick didn't like the sound of that but nodded anyway. Bear got up and left Rick to his own thoughts. He wondered if his life would ever be just quiet and simple, a life where he and Bear could raise Josh in peace. He'd spent years trapped in an abusive relationship and living in fear. Now that he was free of that, this happened. Rick was wondering when he'd pissed off fate.

Soon he heard the front door opening and the voices quieting down. Rick rolled out of bed, changed out of the wrinkled shirt and pants he'd fallen asleep in, and headed straight for Josh's room. He found Grandma Graham reading a book while rocking in a chair at the end of Josh's bed.

"How is he?" Rick asked.

"Sleeping the sleep only a child could pull off," she replied with a warm smile.

"Ah, out like a light."

Rick bent down and placed a soft kiss on Josh's head, tucked the blankets around the toddler, and stood. "He's so innocent. I don't want any of this to touch him."

"You're a good man, Rick, but you'll never be able to keep the real world away forever."

"Can he at least be three before that happens?" Rick huffed and immediately felt like an ass. This wonderful woman was here to help. "I'm sorry, Mrs. Graham, I shouldn't take my frustration out on you."

"Oh, honey, that's nothing. Mr. Graham could get in a snit with the best of them. You aren't anything near that, and you have a good reason to be stressed," she assured.

"I'm still sorry. Are you okay up here?" Rick asked.

"Of course; if I had to count the times I've sat at the foot of a child's bed, we would both run out of fingers and toes," Grandma Graham teased before returning to her book.

Rick laughed softly, kissed Grandma Graham's cheek, and walk out of the room to face whatever awaited him downstairs.

One step after another, Rick felt like he was walking to his execution. He always felt this way in crowds and hoped most of the people were gone by now. He came to the bottom of the steps and took stock of who was in the room. Police Chief Graham stood against the wall, and the remaining three grandmas could be seen through the passageway into the kitchen, ladles in hand. By the smells drifting through the house, chili was on the menu.

Royce and Jesse sat on the couch, Royce's arm holding Jesse tight to his side. Dante and Sam were sitting on the loveseat; they were two of the three bosses of the Sentinel Team that had protected him earlier today. There was no doubt in Rick's mind that one or maybe two team members were outside watching the house at that very moment, making him feel a bit better about Josh's protection.

"Hey, babe, you ready to eat?" Bear asked.

"Maybe after I find out what we need to talk about." Rick was nervous. Whatever it was, he doubted it would be good.

"Okay, but you're going to eat right after," Bear stated. He reached for Rick's hand and led him to Bear's oversized chair. He sat and pulled Rick down onto his lap. *The news has to be bad.*

"Please just tell me what you've found out." *Before I freak out.*

Chief Graham pushed off the wall and took a few steps forward. "I want to assure you we're doing everything in our power to find the second man, but so far he seems to have vanished."

"Why do I get the feeling it's the second man and not Heath we need to worry about?" Rick asked.

"Because you're a smart man, babe," Bear answered.

"We were able to identify the second man in the car, with the team's help. It turns out his name is Luther. He's an underling for the Denefusi family out of Chicago," Chief Graham answered.

"Mafia, you're telling me that someone in the mafia wants Josh?" Shock wasn't a strong enough word for what Rick was feeling.

"Well, not exactly. Heath apparently owes the Denefusi family a large amount of money from a gambling debt. We believe he was trying to get the money to pay them through Jenny's life insurance. Of course, he wants nothing to do with Josh, just the money," Bear explained.

"That was pretty obvious from the beginning, but how does this Luther fit into this?" Rick asked.

"He was sent as a babysitter for Heath to make sure he didn't take off," Dante answered. "My contacts tell me this is some sort of a test for him. He gets the money, he moves up the food chain. He doesn't, then there's nothing for him to return to."

"Well, he's not getting anything. The insurance money is in a trust for Josh. There isn't anything for him to take back to his employers." Rick hoped that was the end of it but knew he just wasn't that lucky.

"He won't give up until he has something to take back with him. This is personal now," Dante explained, his voice hard as stone.

Rick was getting a sick feeling in the pit of his stomach. "Josh?"

Dante held Sam a bit closer before he spoke. "The Denefusi family are well known in various illegal activities. One is human trafficking."

"No!" Rick yelled and jumped off the chair. "You can't honestly believe that they'd..." *According to the Department of State's Statistics from 2000, there are approximately 244,000 American children and youth that are at risk for human trafficking.* More stats ran through Rick's head, each one worse than the next. *How can people do that?*

"Easy, babe, breathe for me. Come on, babe, breathe in, hold, let it out slowly. There you go, and again." Bear held Rick close, rubbing his back in comfort and helping him calm further.

"Sorry, I just..."

"No, you won't be apologizing for anything. This would throw anyone for a loop." Sam Mason stood, his movement a bit jerky. Rick knew Sam had had a major head trauma not long ago and he was still suffering the effects. "He won't get his hands on either of you."

"Either of us? You mean...?"

No one spoke. Even the grandmas had stopped working in the kitchen and each one was now looking straight at him. "M-me."

"If he can't get Josh, I have no doubt he'll go for the next best thing. They could get a lot for a handsome young man in countries far away from here, where the law can be bought." Dante's spoke softly, as if speaking the words any louder was offensive to him.

"But... I'm nobody. I lead a quiet life... Why?"

"When I said it was personal now, I meant they want their payback out of Heath's family one way or another. He isn't going after Bear. He'd be too hard to control," Dante explained.

"No one's getting near you. You'll have bodyguards," Bear assured.

"I can't live—we can't live like this, always being afraid." Rick's heart was racing. How had everything come to this?

"It's just until we find Luther." Bear stared straight into Rick's eyes, as if begging him to understand.

Rick decided to leave the whole bodyguard thing alone for now. He needed more answers. "What about Heath?"

"As it turns out, he had a warrant for his arrest out of New York for fraud. They're on their way to take custody of him," Chief Graham answered.

"Thank God. At least that's one out of the way. Wait, how are you sure of any of this?" Rick was pretty sure Heath wouldn't have told them anything.

"The contact I have in Chicago reported back. Luther has called in for options now that Heath is no longer in the game. The underboss gave him the green light to do whatever was needed to get his money back, including taking you and Josh," Dante explained, and Rick wondered just how deep Dante's contacts went.

"How much does Heath owe?" Rick asked.

"Roughly $126,500, as far as I could figure," Shannon, hacker extraordinaire, replied as she walked in from the back door along with Coop, who he'd heard was ex-military like the rest of the team. All Rick knew was the guy was the size of a house, bigger even than Bear. "Seems Heath liked the horses a little too much."

Rick was speechless. Because some lowlife had a gambling problem, he and Josh were now in danger. *How can this be happening to us? I finally have everything I've always dreamed of. The love of a good man and a family, and that could be all taken away from me at any moment.*

Rick squared his shoulders and stood tall. "I won't allow him to destroy my family."

"No we won't, babe, no matter what it takes." Bear wrapped his strong arms around Rick, and he melted into the man he loved. Rick would do whatever it took to save his family, whatever it took.

Chapter Eleven

After hours of making plans, Bear was happy the house finally cleared out. He checked and rechecked every window and door. Two team members, Coop and Vincent, were patrolling around the exterior of the house. The grandmas had gone home with promises of coming back in the morning. There was no use trying to persuade them not to; they'd show up anyway. If he was absolutely honest, Bear wished he had a grandma like one of those four, but he had no blood relatives left. Instead, he was creating his own family surrounded by people he cared about and loved.

Rick had gone up to bed half an hour ago, and he was anxious to join his lover. Bear's emotions had run the gambit today—fear, anger, disbelief, determination, and then back to fear. He couldn't help but wonder if he'd made Rick's life better or put him in more danger than his ex ever had. The guilt he felt weighed heavy on him, and his pride stung, having to rely on others to help protect his family, but he wasn't so proud as to not accept the help. His family needed protection.

Bear climbed the stairs and, after a quick check on a still-sleeping Josh, entered the master bedroom and closed the doors. Tonight he needed to feel his lover around him, feel the love and strength of their bond, and hold Rick safe in his arms. Rick raised his head off the pillow when Bear entered, his beautiful hazel eyes watching Bear's every move. It seemed like he wasn't the only one in need of comfort and reassurance.

"How are you, babe?" Bear asked as he began taking off his clothes. He heard Rick's breathing increase, and his cheeks were slightly flushed. *Oh, we are definitely on the same page.*

"I'm still a bit shocked by everything I heard tonight, but I don't want to think about that right now." Rick began to lower the sheet covering him to reveal his beautiful body inch by inch to Bear's appreciative gaze. This was what he needed after everything that had happened; he needed his lover more than air.

"Need you," Bear admitted softly, and Rick's smile lit up the room.

Rick watched as Bear stripped down, his eyes dilating farther with each piece that was removed. As soon as the last piece of clothing hit the floor, Bear crawled up from the end of the bed and over Rick's body, stopping to run his tongue up Rick's soft inner thigh, causing Rick's legs to shake. He gently spread Rick's legs wider, appreciating the way his large, tanned hands looked against Rick's soft, pale skin. He kissed up both thighs until he reached his destination, nudging his nose against Rick's soft balls, licking and sucking each before moving on.

"Oh fuck… Bear." He knew Rick was lost in his pleasure when he swore. "Please, oh God, yes."

"Lie back, babe, and let me take care of you," Bear instructed before taking another ball into his mouth as Rick's cock filled and hardened. If anyone deserved to be taken care of, it was his lover.

Rick's hands gripped the sheets harder, and he moaned softly, neither of them wanting to make any loud noises in case they woke Josh. Bear licked Rick's hard cock from base to tip over and over again until Rick was babbling and thrusting his hips upward, desperate for more of Bear's attention, an attention he was more than willing to give. He took Rick's beautiful cock into his mouth and sucked it all the way down his throat. Rick's hips raised right off the bed, his cries muffled by his own hand. Bear doubled his efforts, running his tongue over the sensitive head before dipping into the tip into Rick's slit, making him shake even harder. *That's it, get lost in your passion.* Bear desperately wanted to give Rick a few moments without worry.

Bear felt something hit his arm. He looked up to see Rick's smiling face and a bottle of lube. *Yes!* Bear took the tube, applied a liberal amount to his fingers, and went to work on Rick's sweet little hole. Once he had Rick ready, he lined up his cock and slowly pushed in. *Oh fuck yes. Oh yes, I'm home.*

Rick's eyes were wide open, staring straight at Bear, love shining in their depths. How had he gotten so blessed after everything he'd seen and done in his life? He swore to give thanks every day for the miracle that was Rick. He lowered his head and claimed Rick's lips in a desperate kiss. Bear shifted his hips in search of that little gland that would bring his lover so much pleasure. After a few tries, Rick lit up like a firework, and Bear knew he'd found it. Ruthlessly, he pegged Rick's gland over and over until Rick had to muffle his cries with a pillow and he wrapped his legs around Bear as he writhed on the bed.

"Bear... I'm going to..." That was all Rick managed to get out before he sprayed onto his stomach, his cock untouched by Bear's hand. His ass squeezed Bear tight, and two strokes later, he came deep inside the man he loved.

Bear lowered himself to his elbows and kissed Rick gently, reverently, as he slowly pulled free of Rick's body and lay down beside him. As soon as his back hit the mattress, he gathered Rick close and wrapped him in the safety of his arms. *If I could only keep the people I love safe in the real world so easily.*

"We'll be okay, Bear," Rick whispered, as if the words were precious. "We'll have a long life together, the three of us."

"Well, honestly, I'd hoped to make it more than three eventually," Bear admitted.

Rick's head snapped up and he looked at Bear like he'd grown another head. "In case you haven't noticed, I'm not a woman."

"Oh, I've noticed, but you do know there are such things as foster children, surrogates, and adoption, right?" Bear teased.

"You want to have more children in our family?" Rick asked.

For the first time in their relationship, Bear felt uneasy. "Yes." He had to be completely honest; he'd always wanted children even though he knew he was gay.

Rick immediately wrapped himself around Bear. "Yes, I want more children. I've always wanted a large family."

Bear's heart was near ready to explode. He'd finally found what he'd dreamt of his entire life. He would protect them with his dying breath.

***

It had been over three grueling weeks since Heath was taken to New York to face his charges. Apparently, he might be spending the next ten years as a guest of the state. They hadn't heard a peep out of

Luther, and Rick was beginning to wonder if he'd left for Chicago. But then again, if they'd been right, there was nothing left there for him.

It was a sunny afternoon, the heat of the day lessening as cooler weather moved in, but it was still seventy degrees outside. Josh was playing in the backyard while Rick visited with Grandma Graham over iced tea. Royce was somewhere around the house keeping watch and guarding the three of them. Rick had been told Luther would more than likely make a move under the cover of night, so the daytime was reasonably safe.

"How are you holding up, Rick?" Mrs. Graham asked as she poured the iced tea.

"Exhausted from always being on alert and ticked off, afraid, on edge, just to start," Rick answered honestly; he knew he could do so with the grandmas.

"It has to be stressful always waiting for something to happen," she replied.

"Yes, it feels like our lives are on hold. I just want to start living without fear. I've lived in fear far too long," Rick admitted.

"Dear, you will. If anyone deserves to find peace, it's you," Grandma Graham assured. Unfortunately, Rick didn't feel so sure.

"Now this was easier than I thought it would be," a deep voice spoke from behind the three of them. "You would think they'd have more than one lone guy guarding you and the brat." *Luther.*

Rick picked Josh up off the ground and held him close. He wouldn't allow anything to happen to him.

"What have you done with Royce?" Rick demanded.

"He won't be a problem anymore." Luther opened his jacket to reveal a gun. Rick's heart fell. Royce... He'd shot Royce. Rick felt the panic rising in him. He couldn't have a panic attack now. *Not now, please, God.* He had to fight and breathe deeply to clear his head.

"You won't get away with this. People know about you and what you're doing." Rick had to buy time. There had to be someone out there who would notice and call for help.

"I don't give a shit what anyone knows. Now let's go." Luther pulled out his gun. It had a long, round metal piece on the end. It was a silencer like Rick had seen on television, which had to be the reason they hadn't heard the gunshot. God, what would Jesse do without Royce? Rick's mind was racing. How was he going to protect Josh and Grandma Graham?

"You don't need all three of us. Let me leave Josh with Mrs. Graham. You don't want a crying baby to take care of. I'll go with you, and I won't make a fuss as long as you leave them alone."

Luther had already shot one person. It wasn't hard to figure out that he'd kill anyone in his way. Rick would sacrifice himself in a second to save their lives.

"No, now move before I put a hole in the old hag." Luther pointed the gun directly at Grandma Graham's head.

Rick had to think and fast. He couldn't let Josh be taken. "I have money. I can give it to you. You only need me."

Luther's eyes gleamed at the word—he had him, or at least he hoped he did. "I have roughly $400,000. You don't need the baby or Mrs. Graham. Just leave them here unharmed, and I'll give it all to you."

"Where is it?"

"I have to contact my lawyer to arrange the withdrawal."

"Call him. I want proof." Luther began to waver.

"You can keep the money and leave, and no one will stop you." Rick was grasping at straws now. How the hell would he make sure no one stopped him anyway?

"Call," Luther ordered.

Rick juggled Josh and reached for his cell phone. He pushed his lawyer's number, and after a few seconds, the phone rang on the other end.

"Mr. Jacobs's office. How may I help you?"

"This is Rick Johansson. It's urgent that I speak to Mr. Jacobs immediately."

"I'm sorry, he's in a meeting, Mr. Johansson. Can I take a message?"

"No, this is very important, you could say life or death."

"Please hold."

Luther didn't look pleased, but Rick held on to Josh and his phone, hoping like hell his lawyer would take his call or someone would show up to save them.

A few seconds later, he had his answer. "Rick, what can I do for you?"

Rick put the call on speaker. "I need you to tell me what my total worth is with investments."

"Rick, is everything okay?"

"Yes, please just tell me."

"Well, the last quarter your investment did rally and your net worth is roughly $486,000, give or take. Rick, are you sure you're okay?"

Before Rick had a chance to answer, Luther grabbed the phone out of his hand and disconnected the call before pocketing it.

Luther thought about it for a second before saying, "Give the kid to the old woman and get your ass over here. If this is a trick, I'll leave you in a bloody pool for the police to find along with the kid and the old bat."

"N-no trick. We just need to contact my lawyer after we leave and arrange a transfer of funds," Rick stuttered. He hugged Josh one last time and kissed him on the forehead.

"Unk… play me?" Josh asked, oblivious to the danger he was in. He was grateful Josh was too young to understand.

"Yes, you can play, but you have to go to Grandma Graham first, okay?" Rick explained.

"Get on with it before I change my mind." Luther was getting antsy, and his eyes scanned the backyard.

Rick handed Josh to Grandma Graham. The fear in her eyes matched his own, but he had to do this. Rick's eyes misted. "Tell Bear I'll love him forever." *Because I doubt I'll ever see him again* went unsaid.

"Dear…" Tears streamed down her face.

"Enough!" Luther reached out and grabbed Rick around the throat, no doubt leaving bruises, and pushed the gun to his stomach. "Time to go."

"I don't think so." Vincent and Coop came out of the bushes, guns drawn. *Where the hell have they been all this time?*

Luther wrapped his hand tighter around Rick's throat and pushed the muzzle of the gun to the side of his head. "Make a move and he dies right here."

Shit, don't panic!

Vincent and Coop lowered their weapons, and Mrs. Graham slowly backed herself and Josh to the safety of the house. Rick would be forever grateful to the amazing woman for protecting Josh.

"Now, we're going to leave, and if you try to stop us, like I said, his pretty face is going to have a big hole in it." Luther began to drag Rick backward toward the street.

Rick was being choked by the hand around his throat but didn't dare say a word. He couldn't figure out why he wasn't having a panic attack but had no time to dwell on the fact when his back hit the fender of a car.

"Get in!" Luther growled, shoving Rick toward the car door.

Rick reached for the car handle and glanced back at Vincent and Coop, guns in hand, knowing there was nothing they could do with Luther's gun still pressed to the side of his head. Would this be the last time he saw his home? Would this morning be the last time he saw his Bear? Thinking of the man he loved seemed to make him appear in a haze of smoke and squealing tires along with two police cars. *Damn, that was fast.* His face looked tortured as he ran toward them.

"Don't come any closer!" Luther yelled. "Open the damn door!"

"I will, just move that thing away from my head." Rick had no idea where his courage was coming from, but it was coming on fast. "You shoot me and you die, do you understand?"

"Shut up!" Luther's hand tightened around Rick's throat in warning, and he was positive his face was turning red.

Rick pulled the handle and the car door opened like a mouth about to swallow him whole, or that could have been his imagination.

"Luther, put the gun down and let him go," Chief Graham ordered, his gun pointing straight at Luther's head, but Rick knew no one dared to fire and accidentally hit him. Faces he'd seen all those years ago when they'd saved him from Bret now were in the same position. Rick was tired of being saved; he wanted to save himself for once.

Bear seemed to be stuck to the spot as police officers fanned out, but it was too late. Rick was being pushed into the car and over to the driver's side. "Drive!"

With one final look, Rick noticed Bear's angry face was in sharp contrast with the pain in his eyes. He started the car, put it in drive, and began to slowly drive away. Police officers allowed the car to pass once Chief Graham told them to stand down. There was still a gun pressed to the side of his head and no one had a clear shot at

Luther. Rick could see Bear and the officers in his rearview mirror getting into police vehicles and following.

"Drive faster! Lose the cops or you're dead," Luther warned.

"You'd be dead too considering I'm driving." Rick was getting angry. He'd had a gun pointed at him, Josh, and Grandma Graham. This man was responsible for God only knew what, but considering he would be willing to kidnap him in broad daylight, Rick was positive he'd done worse in his time.

Luther jammed the gun harder against Rick's head, surely leaving bruises. He could hear the sirens and see the flashing lights following them out of town.

"Where are we going?" Rick asked. Luther was sweating and his hand shook a bit with either adrenaline or fear.

"Chicago." *Shit!*

"I thought I was giving you the money to take back." Rick knew the answer even before Luther answered.

"Not anymore. Now shut up and drive faster!" It was obvious Luther wasn't thinking clearly anymore. "You're my bargaining chip now."

Where the hell did he think they were going to go, considering the entire Brighton police force was right behind them? They were reaching the outskirts of town when Rick made his choice. He wasn't leaving Brighton. Rick reached for his seatbelt and pulled it across his body.

"What are you doing?" Luther growled.

"Putting on my seatbelt," Rick answered.

"A seatbelt isn't going to save your ass, fag."

And that was the final nail in the coffin of Rick's decision. He wasn't going much farther or he'd be a dead man. Luther was watching out the back window when he should have really been worried about the man beside him. Once he was safely into the outskirts of town, without any innocent bystanders on the road, Rick sped up even faster than he felt safe driving, but this was his only chance.

"What are you doing?" Luther screamed.

Rick didn't answer. He was too busy looking for the right spot to ditch the car… Luther wasn't wearing his seatbelt. Rick had to hope between the airbag and seatbelt he'd survive, but if Luther had his way, Rick wasn't going to live much longer anyway. His thoughts were filled with Bear and Josh, the family he prayed he'd see again.

With one final look at the parade of police cars behind them, Rick turned the wheel and headed straight for the ditch. Luther was yelling, but Rick didn't stop. The gravel gave way to grass and the car lost its traction for a split second, but it was long enough for the car to veer toward the woods. There was nothing he could do to stop from hitting the trees head on. Shattering glass and the crunch of metal were the last things he heard before the airbag deployed and everything went dark.

Chapter Twelve

Bear sat in the family room of Brighton General Hospital waiting for word on Rick's condition. They'd taken Rick into surgery over three hours ago to remove a piece of metal that had impaled him on the left side of his abdomen during the car crash. Sam had been giving him regular updates ever since. The room was filled with people, from Chief Graham and Dante's team to three of the grandmas and various residents of Brighton. This town was truly one of a kind, and he was proud to be part of this community. Josh was at home with Grandma Rose and a few officers because Bear still didn't want to leave them alone.

Arriving at his house to see Rick being held by his throat with a gun to his head had almost sent Bear over the edge. He'd remained in control by the skin of his teeth, even though his fear and anger were driving him to rip Luther to pieces. He'd hopped into Chief Graham's police car and followed Rick and Luther out of town, never losing sight of Rick, desperate to come up with a way to get his partner back unharmed.

Bear got up and began to pace. *Where is Sam? What if something went wrong? What if...?*

"Stop that right now," Chief Graham said as he came to stand beside Bear and placed a comforting hand on his shoulder. "He's stronger than any of us ever gave him credit for, which I'm ashamed of. He saved my grandmother and Josh with his quick thinking, and he knew exactly what he was doing behind that wheel. He'll pull through."

"He has to," was all Bear said before he went back to pacing. He appreciated every one's efforts to support him, but the only person who could calm him now was Rick. They were just beginning their life together and it could all be over. The man he loved could be torn from his life at any moment. He couldn't even remember the last words he'd said to Rick that morning. How could he not remember? Bear's heart began to race faster when he saw Sam coming down the hall toward them. Bear didn't have the patience to wait and met him halfway.

"How is he?" he asked.

"Rick's out of surgery and in recovery. The doctor wants to talk to you, and Rick's asking for you." Sam's smile was wide and his relief was obvious.

Bear went to his knees, his legs unable to hold him up any longer. His relief left him lightheaded. He took his first full breath in hours. His hands were shaking. He opened his eyes to see he was surrounded by his friends, providing him with the privacy to pull himself together.

Bear stood and looked around the group. "Thank you. All of you."

"I'll take you to him." Sam had tears in his eyes when he turned to lead the way. Bear had to stop himself from running. He'd been given a second chance and intended to make the most of every minute.

***

Rick heard the soft creak as the door to his room opened. He desperately wanted to see if it was Bear, but his eyelids just wouldn't open; he was so tired. A warm hand caressed his cheek, and he knew his lover was with him. Rick sank into the feel of the touch, knowing he was safe.

Still unable to open his eyes, Rick managed a few important words. "Love you."

"Love you so much, babe. Rest now. You're safe. I'll be here when you wake up." Bear's deep voice was enough to send Rick back to sleep, at peace and loved.

Rick wasn't entirely certain what time it was, but when he opened his eyes, his room was dark. The only light came from the small window in his door and the machines blinking and beeping around him. He turned his head to find Bear sound asleep in a chair beside his bed. *That has to be painful.* Careful of his IV line, Rick reached out and touched one of Bear's big, tanned hands, needing to touch him more than the pain it caused him to move. Bear's eyes flew open as he scanned the room. They came to rest on Rick, his dark blue gaze sparkling with sudden tears.

"Hey, babe, how are you feeling?" Bear asked.

"Tired and sore but alive. What happened to Luther?" Rick asked, his voice was scratchy and his throat was sore.

"He's dead, babe. You never have to worry about him again."

Rick didn't know how to take the news. He'd essentially killed a man, but Luther was going to kill him. Could that be considered self-defense?

"No, don't you dare feel guilty for doing what you were forced to do. Luther had a past filled with pain and death of his own creation. He would have killed you and come back for Josh."

"Wait, Royce... What happened to Royce? Is he...?" Flashbacks of the gun pressed to his head and the horrible squeal of twisting metal slammed into him, and Rick suddenly couldn't breathe. For the life of him, he couldn't figure out why he'd be having a panic attack now when he'd just survived a kidnapping without one.

"Easy, easy, Rick. Royce is alive. He was shot, but it was a through and through, and the bullet didn't hit anything life threatening. Thanks to his quick thinking, he was able to alert the team and police to Luther's attack before he passed out," Bear explained quickly.

"Thank God no one was seriously hurt. Well, other than Luther." Rick still wasn't one hundred percent okay with the fact that he'd killed him by ditching the car.

"Honey, you were seriously hurt. You were impaled by a piece of metal from the engine when you hit the tree."

"It was the only way to stop Luther," Rick replied. He was just happy to be alive.

"I don't ever want you to put yourself in harm's way again, do you understand? I... I don't think my heart can take it." Something about seeing his big, proud biker coming apart in front of him made Rick's heart break. He'd done that to him.

"I'm sorry, I promise to try to keep myself safe," Rick agreed quickly.

"That was my job and I failed you." Bear hung his head. "I'll never be able to forgive myself for this. I should have been able to protect you."

"No, Bear, this wasn't your fault. There wasn't anything you could do. We had professional bodyguards, and Luther still got to us." Rick figured one way or another Luther would have gotten to them.

Bear still looked so upset, and Rick didn't know how to fix this. He only hoped in time Bear could come to terms with it. "I love you, Bear."

"I love you so much. We're a family, and I can't do this without you."

"I'm not going anywhere."

"Damn right you're not. We're a team, the three of us."

"Absolutely, I wouldn't want to be anywhere else than with my Bear."

Epilogue

Anthony Denefusi sat behind his large mahogany desk in the top floor of a building named after him in downtown Chicago. Being head of the family was a position he'd held for over forty years. The whole situation in Brighton didn't sit well with him. He couldn't allow himself to look weak in front of the enemies. He'd have to send another man to retrieve what was his. He really didn't care if it was the child or the money. One way or another, he would have what he wanted. No hick town in Texas was going to stop him.

He drew back on his cigar, letting the smoke drift up and over his head in a cloud of gray as he overlooked the city below, his kingdom. An uneasy feeling crept up Anthony's spine, and he looked around his darkened office, the only light coming from the Tiffany lamp on his desk. He quickly strode to his office door, finding his men missing and the hallway empty. Anthony ran back into his office to grab his gun out of his desk.

"Hello, Tony," a voice spoke from the darkness before he could reach his weapon.

Slowly, one by one, five men and one woman emerged from the darkness. One was even directly behind him—all armed and, obviously by their skill, lethal.

"How did you get past my men?" Anthony asked. He couldn't show fear or he was a dead man.

"You really should invest in better staff." A large, blond-haired man smiled. "Don't worry, they'll live."

"But the jury's still undecided about you," the woman said. Her smile was anything but friendly.

Anthony thought about the Ruger again in his top drawer.

"Try it, please try it," a huge man with black eyes and hair whispered, as if praying he would reach for the gun.

Anthony knew he was dealing with professionals and immediately took a step away from the desk. Without his men, he was vulnerable. "What do you want?"

"To have a little talk. Your response determines if you walk out of here in one piece or in a body bag," the meanest-looking of them all said. He had white-blond hair cut short and death in his eyes.

"Talk about what?" Anthony asked belligerently. He would never cow down to another man.

"Who," a smaller man with long black hair and ice-blue eyes growled so quietly that Anthony almost missed it.

"Talk about who?" he corrected.

"Bear Mitchell and his family."

"That family owes me a lot of money."

"No, Heath owed you the money, not his two-year-old son. We could take you to Heath's cell if you'd like to collect," the woman said.

"A debt is a debt." Whether father or son paid, Anthony would get his money.

A bundle of cash was slammed down on the table. "This should cover it."

Anthony didn't bother reaching for it. He wasn't about to make any sudden movement, unsure how trigger-happy these people were. By the looks in their eyes, they'd sooner shoot him than pay him.

"Who are you?" Anthony asked.

"Friends of the family who wouldn't hesitate to take out any threat that comes near them. This concludes our business. You've got your money. This is over. If we see any of your men or even hear that you're considering sending anyone to Brighton, we'll be back, and it won't end this well for you."

Anthony watched as one by one the group leisurely sauntered out of his office like they had every right to do so. He took the stack of bills and quickly counted it; the bundle contained the original debt plus ten percent.

If they thought that was enough after this insult, they were sorely mistaken.

JESSE

Chapter One

The headlights were blinding, but Jesse didn't dare pull over and stop on the side of the road. He pushed down harder on the gas pedal and picked up speed. He had to make it home before they caught up to him. *They ran me out of my home over ten years ago, why can't they just leave me alone?* Fear snaked up his spine as he watched mailboxes fly by his window.

Jesse had just closed up the diner where he worked as a cook and driven Sarah home. The waitress had been on her feet all night, and considering she was over sixty and still working five days a week, no way would he allow her to walk home no matter how nearby.

Jesse had been staying at his boyfriend Royce's house for the last few weeks, helping him recover from a gunshot wound he'd received in his shoulder while protecting their friends Bear and Rick as well as their nephew Josh from Josh's biological father. Before then, Jesse had been living in an apartment above Bear's diner since he'd arrived in Brighton, Texas.

He thought he'd be safe here, that they'd never find him, but he'd been very wrong. The lights were catching up, and he didn't dare go any faster on the rain-slicked roads. Jesse was beginning to panic, and he knew that was what they wanted, him to panic and make a mistake. Then they'd have him. *How do they manage to always find me when I'm alone? Someone has to be watching me.*

The car jarred violently over a pothole, causing the undercarriage to squeal out in warning. Ghostly trees lit by his headlights flew by as the houses grew fewer and farther between. Royce's house sat at the edge of town, only minutes away, but it might as well have been a hundred miles with the other car now kissing his rear bumper, pushing him to lose control. Jesse was honestly surprised he hadn't already lost traction. Why were they doing this to him all over again? He'd left town, lost everything he'd worked for, and lost his family and friends. Wasn't that enough penance for the sin of being gay?

Another jarring hit vibrated through the entire car, but he held on tight and kept his vehicle on the road. Jesse could see the pole light outside the main barn on Royce's property; he was almost there. There was a long driveway leading up to the little farm Royce had created, and Jesse was thankful for its length. He'd need a lot of room to slow down with how fast he was driving. The driveway had a soft curve leading off the road, so at least he wouldn't flip, he hoped.

Seconds later, he took his foot off the gas and veered onto the dirt driveway, fishtailing before he regained control over the vehicle. The lights in his rearview mirror disappeared, confirming that they had stayed on the main road, not daring to come near the house where there were witnesses. Jesse slowed the car, his hands shaking as he parked in his spot. His breathing was still coming out in gasps, and he couldn't stop the tears that escaped his eyes no matter how hard he tried.

He was just considering getting out of the car when his driver's door opened, and Jesse instinctively curled into himself and protected his head with his large arms. Even though he was 6'2" and weighed 245 pounds, Jesse wasn't a fighter normally. The only time he allowed himself to use force was when protecting someone else.

"Jesse, honey, it's me. What's wrong? What's happened?" Royce's calming voice bled through Jesse's fog of fear. "Was it your family again?"

Jesse uncurled his body and looked up at the man he loved so completely and nodded his head. "I don't know why my cousin and his buddies won't just leave me alone. It's been so long, almost a year since the last time, why now?"

Royce leaned into the car and held Jesse close, helping him to settle even further. Even though Royce was three inches shorter and sixty-five pounds lighter than Jesse, Royce was the emotionally stronger and more dominant of the two, and Jesse was completely on board with that. Due to his size, many men assumed Jesse to be the dominant one in their relationship. But Royce knew what Jesse needed, which made Jesse feel free to be himself for the first time in his life.

"I don't know why they're coming after you, Jesse, but we need to step up our security until we find out or have enough proof to have them jailed," Royce answered. But Jesse knew how they worked; they never attacked him when someone else was around to witness the abuse or threats. That was how they'd stayed below the radar back home, and what led to Jesse escaping one lonely night ten years earlier.

"They never try anything when someone else is with me. They have to have someone watching me, because they waited until I dropped Sarah off before they attacked," Jesse explained.

"I'm going to call Chief Graham once we get you inside, and tomorrow I'll drive you to work."

"What about your shoulder?" Jesse asked.

"It's healing up well enough, and I'm more than capable of driving safely. Even if I'm a shot-up paramedic on medical leave, I can still protect my boyfriend," Royce explained gruffly.

Jesse smiled. He couldn't help himself. He'd never had anyone protect him before. He'd caused indifference, disgust, hate, and even pity from the people in his old life, but never had he felt protected. Royce and Brighton had given him his freedom and peace; now he just had to figure out how to keep it.

"Thank you, Royce. I would feel better if you drove me." Jesse truly would. He hadn't ridden his Harley since members of his parents' fringe church showed up and demanded Jesse return with them to begin his rehabilitation for the sin of being gay. If he'd ridden his bike tonight, he could have been knocked off, which only brought out more questions. If they wanted to take him back, why would they try to physically harm him or worse? After the initial contact, he'd only seen his cousin and five members of the congregation from a distance. Why were they here now? *Something is not adding up.*

"Okay, that's settled. Now let's get you inside the house." Royce scanned the area. His left arm was still in a sling while his wound healed.

It warmed Jesse's heart to know he wasn't alone anymore. Ten long years of living a transient lifestyle, never staying in one place too long, had taken its toll on Jesse. When he'd arrived in Brighton, he thought maybe he'd found his new home. After he met Royce Evans, he knew he'd been right.

***

Royce got off the phone with the police chief, not feeling any calmer than he had before he'd called. They'd come and look at the dented bumper first thing in the morning and keep an eye out for the suspect's car, but there was nothing more they could do. Without a witness or more evidence, it was a 'he said, he said' situation. Jesse was relaxing on the couch watching some sort of reality show while Royce made his calls. Royce knew all too well that the other car involved would be gone in the next few hours, never to be seen again without having some bodywork done.

The chief had other crimes and issues to deal with, and stalking might not be top on the list of his concerns. Royce knew by the way the Redemption Squad—as he liked to call Jesse's family and followers—had upgraded to straight-out violence, something had changed. Proving that hurting Jesse or worse was now an option.

Royce couldn't stop his thoughts from drifting to over three and a half years earlier when his world stopped turning—the day his husband died. They'd been high school sweethearts and married once they both finished college. That day Royce's heart had been ripped out and his soul left ravaged and unrepairable—at least that's what he thought, until he laid his eyes on Jesse working in the diner one morning before his shift.

They'd gotten to know each other while Jesse was healing from a knee injury he sustained pushing their friend Johnny out of the way of a speeding car. Since that incident, Royce and Jesse had been together every day, only apart when Royce was on shift as an EMT for Brighton's Emergency Services or Jesse was at the diner. They'd either sleep at Royce's house or Jesse's apartment, but in truth Royce wanted Jesse in his home full-time. They'd been dating for over four months now, and Royce hadn't felt this alive and in love in a long time.

But the question still remained, how would he be able to protect the only other man he'd allowed himself to love? He had to figure it out because he wasn't allowing anything to happen to his Jesse.

The throbbing in his injured shoulder only brought back the fact that life was short and he needed to live it. He rubbed his arm, trying to lessen the pain without the use of painkillers.

"Your shoulder hurting, babe?" Jesse asked from the open doorway. Royce hadn't heard him approach. "Don't answer, because you'll just deny it. I'll go get the cream for your shoulder and meet you in bed." Jesse raised and lowered his eyebrows a few times and gave him a goofy grin. God he loved that man.

Before Royce could answer, Jesse was gone, undoubtedly in search of the muscle-relaxing cream he'd been prescribed. Royce's muscles would seize up around the wound, causing more pain than the actual gunshot did. Physiotherapy had helped, but the doctors kept saying it would take time to heal. The one thing he didn't have was time. The Redemption Squad had upped the pressure on Jesse, and he wouldn't stand for that.

Royce got up, double-checked all the locks, and set their new security system, which monitored any motion outside or attempted entry into their house. He knew his gorgeous boyfriend would be lying in their bed waiting for him, and if he were lucky, Jesse would be in only his boxers.

Sure enough, that muscled, tattooed body lay sprawled across the bed in only black boxers and a smile. Jesse's sandy blond hair spread out across his broad chest and down his abdomen. His deep brown eyes were filled with need and lust. He was such a contrast to Royce's own red hair and green eyes. Without a word, Royce began to remove his sling from his arm and immediately hissed from the pain. Jesse was off the bed in seconds, gently holding Royce's arm stable.

"I'll help you, Royce. Hold your arm while I unbutton your shirt and remove your pants."

"I can do it." The last thing Royce wanted was to look weak in front of the man who meant everything to him and whom he needed to protect.

"Please, Royce. Let me help you." With only a handful of words, Jesse managed to melt any resistance Royce might have had; Jesse excelled at that.

"Thank you, babe."

With gentle hands, Jesse unbuttoned Royce's shirt and slid it down his arms before placing it across the chair. His pants soon followed. Now they both stood only in their boxers and both equally hard.

"Lie down on the bed, Royce, so I can rub your shoulder."

"Can we skip the painful part and get to the fun stuff instead?" Royce was not looking forward to this particular massage. Though he still lay down and carefully arranged his arm on a pillow.

"No, but if you're good, I'll make sure you have all the 'fun stuff' you can handle," Jesse negotiated as he came to sit beside him with the medicated muscle-relaxing cream in his hand.

Royce smiled at his gentle partner, then lifted his uninjured arm over his head and said, "I'm all yours, baby."

"You're definitely all mine, and I'm all yours," Jesse replied while squeezing a small amount of lotion on his hand, and Royce prepared himself for the pain.

No matter how gently Jesse rubbed, the pain was instantaneous, and no matter how hard Royce tried, he couldn't keep the pain-filled groans from escaping his lips. Even though Jesse never rubbed near his wound, simply rubbing his cramping muscles felt like his skin was tearing apart.

"Easy, I've got you," Jesse whispered as he lightly moved his hands over Royce's skin and worked each muscle in his shoulder and arm.

After a few moments, Royce's sore muscles began to relax and his tension faded away. Jesse continued to rub until Royce melted into the bed, and he might have fallen asleep if it weren't for the warm, wet mouth that was suddenly sucking his cock in long, lazy pulls. He had no idea when Jesse had removed his boxers or stopped rubbing his arm, but Jesse was now doing something infinitely more satisfying.

"Yes, babe, turn around. I want to taste you," Royce suggested.

"Not this time, love. This is all about you." His deep brown eyes seemed to sparkle before Jesse sucked down Royce's hard cock to the back of his throat and swallowed.

Royce cried out in pleasure and spread his legs farther apart, giving Jesse complete access. He kept his left arm cradled on the pillow, not wanting to reinjure anything, but he couldn't stop from flexing his hips and fucking Jesse's mouth. Jesse began humming, and the vibration nearly made Royce shoot. His tongue laved the underside of Royce's cock from his balls to tip before sucking him down once again.

By now Royce had forgotten his pain, knowing that was what Jesse had intended all along. He was close to coming and warned his lover, "Soon, babe."

Instead of slowing, Jesse sped up and sucked harder. His tongue slapped the sensitive head of Royce's cock and dipped into the slit; that was all it took. Fire raced down his spine, his balls throbbed, and pulled up tight just before he screamed and came down Jesse's throat.

He tensed his shoulder for a moment and then every muscle in Royce's body relaxed. Royce could have fallen asleep right there but he would never simply leave his partner needing. "Let me take care of you, sweetheart."

Jesse raised his head and smiled at him. "No worries, I've already come, baby, just from listening to your moans and feeling your body react to me. I couldn't help myself."

"You always know what I need," Royce said. "Every muscle in my body is relaxed now."

"That was the plan. I'll go get cleaned up, and then we need some sleep. It's almost one o'clock in the morning."

Royce got comfortable and rearranged the pillow cradling his wounded arm, just as Jesse walked back into their room in all his naked glory. His tanned, muscled body was simply beautiful, scars and all. At first Jesse had been embarrassed when Royce saw the injuries he'd received at the hands of his family. Those brown eyes showed every emotion Jesse had, making it easier for Royce to determine when there was another run-in with the Redemption Squad or if he'd had a rough day.

His thick, uncut cock swayed as he walked over to the bed, crawled up beside Royce, and turned off the bedside lamp. "I love you, Royce."

"I love you too, Jesse. I never thought I'd be lucky enough to have this with you. Never thought I'd be able," Royce admitted.

"I'm the one who's lucky. I can finally trust someone again. I've lived for so long without a single person to trust, to believe in me like you do. You accept me just the way I am. I don't have to pretend to be the tough guy with you. I can be myself." Jesse's voice cracked as he spoke. "I'm sorry I brought those people into your life."

"Even if I knew you had a screwed-up family hunting you down, I wouldn't change a thing about our relationship. I still would have pursued you just as hard as I did. I wouldn't leave you after the first sign of trouble. I love you, all of you, no matter what's thrown our way," Royce assured him, and Jesse's eyes misted over with tears. "You and me, through thick and thin. I'm just glad you finally gave me a chance."

Jesse pulled the covers up over both of them and cuddled into Royce, his head on Royce's chest on the opposite side of his injury. They'd had to change the sides of the bed they slept on because Jesse now needed to lie on Royce's right side, so Jesse could still cover Royce's body with his own, without accidentally hitting his wound.

"You wore me down," Jesse teased.

"Well, thank God for that," Royce huffed. "Because I know it wasn't my suave, debonair pick-up lines."

"You're suave to me and very confident and charming." Jesse looked up, his eyes soft and expressive.

"Thank you, babe, that's all that matters," Royce said. "Now let's get some sleep. Chief Graham will be by in the morning."

Jesse laid his head back down on Royce's chest, his big leg slung over both of Royce's. It was their usual position and it didn't take long for Jesse's breathing to even out as he fell asleep. Royce stayed awake for a long time, working out how to better protect Jesse. He thought about asking the Sentinel Team for help, but knew Jesse would never accept that because someone other than himself might get hurt. The Sentinels were a group of former military personnel who called Brighton home, when not out on missions recovering or protecting others.

But what if Jesse didn't know and he asked only one of the team members to keep an eye on Jesse to keep him safe? That might work. He didn't like keeping things from Jesse but his safety came first. Royce felt a little bit better and decided to call the team first thing in the morning.

Chapter Two

Jesse stood in the back of the kitchen kneading the dough for the diner's signature fresh biscuits. The diner wouldn't open for another hour, giving him the chance to stock the kitchen. Sarah would be arriving thirty minutes before opening to make sure everything was set to go when people started arriving. It had been three days since his cousin and his people had tried to run him off the road, which only meant something was going to happen soon.

His muscles bulged as he pushed down on the dough before throwing a light dusting of flour across the counter and grabbing the rolling pin. Since he was opening today, the owner, Bear Mitchell, would be closing. At the moment, he and Bear were the only two cooks, but they'd scheduled interviews over the next couple days in hopes of finding a third cook to take the pressure off them.

He finished with the biscuits, placed the trays in the oven, and checked on today's special, roast beef, which was still cooking away in the second oven. Rick, the boss's boyfriend, loved roast beef, and it always made it onto the weekly menu. Rick was also the man Royce had been protecting when he was shot.

Jesse grabbed onto the counter—his legs always weakened when he thought back to the day he'd almost lost his partner forever. He knew it was only a small percentage of the pain Royce must have felt when his husband died. At least Jesse still had Royce.

While sitting beside Royce's hospital bed, Jesse swore he'd open himself completely to this wonderful man. Up until that point, Jesse had still held back, never fully trusting that his happiness would last. When the Redemption Squad showed up, he thought it would be enough for Royce to run in the other direction, but he'd stayed right by Jesse's side.

The shooting just proved how quickly everything could be ripped away from him and that he should make the most of each and every day no matter his past. With that decided, Jesse went about sharing everything with Royce, who seemed to be behaving the same way. Perhaps he wasn't the only one who'd had an epiphany that day. But Jesse knew that no matter how open he was, there would always be a part of him waiting for the end of his happiness.

After spending so much time together Jesse had decided he wanted to move in with Royce on a permanent basis but didn't know how to go about it, or if Royce was even interested in living with him just yet. True, they were doing that at the moment, but it had been to help Royce recover. So he kept quiet. He'd never lived with someone before, other than his parents, and that hadn't turned out so well. But he was willing to try. He loved Royce more than he'd ever loved anyone before. To be absolutely honest, living on the run didn't bode well for his love life, but he knew what he had with Royce was special.

The back door opened with a sharp squeal. When Sarah didn't automatically yell "good morning," Jesse went on alert. "Sarah? Are you okay?"

Nothing, not a sound. *Shit.* Jesse slowly walked to the kitchen door leading to the hallway, Bear's office, and the washrooms—still nothing. He leaned his head out of the doorway, finding the hall empty. Gradually, he stepped out of the kitchen, across the hall to the washrooms—still nothing. He walked out of the washrooms and made his way to the office. His hands shook as he opened the door and took a quick scan of the empty room.

There was only one other place left for someone to hide: the front of the diner. But he couldn't figure out how someone could have gotten past him. Jesse's nerves were frayed as he walked out into the front and along the counter, his eyes scanning every possible hiding spot, finding nothing. Was he losing his mind? No, someone opened the back door; this was all real. With a slam, he heard the door close and Jesse began to panic. Somehow they'd made it through the locked door.

"Jesse! Why would you leave the diner door open?" Sarah's voice carried from the back and into the front seating area, leaving him a little lightheaded in relief. "Jesse, what's going on, son?"

Jesse's eyes focused on the plump figure of a sixty-year-old woman in her waitressing uniform, apron and all. "I didn't leave the door open. I didn't even open it."

Sarah's demeanor changed in an instant. She scanned the area around her and pulled out her cell phone. Jesse finally snapped out of his fear-induced paralysis and went around turning on every light in the place. A loud knock was coming from the front door. Jesse froze. *Wait, my cousin and his men wouldn't knock.* Sure enough, it was Jake—or rather, Shadow from Sentinel. Jesse walked to the door, unlocked it, and let Shadow in.

"I'm sorry, Jake, we're not open yet, but I could throw on some coffee."

"Thank you, Jesse, but I'm not here for breakfast," Shadow said, before walking past Jesse and heading for the back entrance. *What's going on?*

The bell tinkled over the front door and Bear walked in, followed by Royce and Chief Graham. *Okay, something's up, Sarah's called in everyone.* Could whoever opened the back door still be here somewhere? Bear headed straight for the back without saying a word. Jesse figured he must be tired of having all this shit happening in his diner.

"Are you okay?" Royce asked as he wrapped his arms around Jesse. Even with their height difference, Jesse always felt completely surrounded and safe.

Shouts echoed from the office as Bear and Shadow dragged a man, who was cursing and still struggling to break free, up to furious Chief Graham to be handcuffed. "Quit with the whining. You broke the law so you must know what comes next. You get to spend some time with me and my officers. Won't that be fun?" The man struggled even harder but the chief had control of him.

When Chief Graham finally turned the man to face Jesse, he realized he knew that cruel, vicious look. Jesse stood there staring at his cousin, Jerry. He hadn't been this close to the evil man in a lot of years. Up until now, Jerry had always sent his cronies to do his work. Some of Jesse's worst punishments had been at this man's hands.

"He was under the desk in the office," Shadow said, the one place Jesse hadn't looked. "He couldn't get back out the door because Coop's now stationed out there."

Why are two members of Sentinel hanging around the diner when it's not open?

"You're all just disgusting fags, and God will punish you if you don't repent and change your ways. You destroyed your parents, Jesse, when you chose being gay over them." Jerry began to spout his hate-filled words in front of everybody. Jesse wanted to just go back to the safety of his kitchen. His embarrassment was complete when Jerry spat on the diner floor.

"Well, my God loves everybody no matter their race, religion, gender, sexual identity, or who they share their lives with, asshole. Being gay isn't a choice. We are born this way. When will you guys realize that?" Bear said as he gave the irate man a little shake.

"Let's get him over to the police station," Chief Graham ordered. "I have a nice cell all reserved for him."

"I have to go check my biscuits," was all Jesse said before he basically ran back into the kitchen.

Thank goodness they weren't burnt, because he didn't have time to make another batch; the front door would be opening in thirty minutes. He felt a presence at his back and knew it was Royce, but he didn't have the courage to turn around and face him. By the time his cousin and the men following him were done, they wouldn't have to drag Jesse out of Brighton; the townspeople would kick him out first. Though they were all nice to him, how long could that last with the Redemption Squad riding around spewing their hate?

"Babe, please turn around," Royce asked.

Jesse could never deny Royce anything, and this time was no different. He put the tray of biscuits down on the counter and turned to look at his partner's calm face, which in turn made him calm a bit as well. There was no anger or disgust on his face and his eyes held only concern.

"I'm sorry," was the only thing Jesse could think of to say.

"Sorry? For what, Jesse?" Royce asked as he took Jesse's hand.

"Everything. For the damage they'll do and the hate they'll spew. Like mud on a white sheet, they'll stain this community. This is all my fault. I brought them here."

"None of this is your fault. They followed you, and you didn't invite them. You're a victim in all of this, love," Royce argued.

"But the town?" Jesse couldn't believe that everyone wouldn't hold him accountable. He certainly held himself responsible.

"The members of this town understand what's going on and no one blames you," Royce said, wrapping his arms around Jesse. "You can't control the actions of others. They're responsible for themselves."

Jesse stood there in silence, hoping what Royce had said was true. He liked Brighton and wanted to stay. A few moments later, the sound of heavy boots coming down the hallway put him back on alert. He knew those big boots belonged to Bear, and he also knew his reckoning had arrived. Would he be fired outright or given time to find another job?

He let go of Royce and stood tall, looking Bear straight in the eyes when he walked in.

"Hey, Jesse, you okay?" Bear asked.

"Yes, boss. He just scared the hell out of me."

"I can understand that, and I think that's what he wanted to do. Well, now he has his own jail cell to skulk around in. Breaking and entering and trespassing are the start of his charges. Unless he has someone to bail him out, he'll be in there until his court date," Bear explained. "While I have you here, I wanted to talk to you."

Jesse deflated right on the spot. He was being fired. "It's okay, boss man. I understand. If you give me a couple days, I can have my belongings out of the apartment and it'll give me time to organize all my recipes for you." Royce squeezed his hand in support and stood silently by his side.

"What? Why would you do that?" Bear asked, looking honestly confused.

"That way you don't have to fire me outright. I can just leave. No guilt or upset feelings, I understand. I brought all this to your doorstep, and for that I'm truly sorry." Jesse lowered his head and waited.

"I wasn't going to fire you. I was promoting you. I'll need a manager to keep an eye on the new cook and teach him. With Rick and my nephew taking up most of my time, I need you to help keep the place running," Bear explained. "I was going to tell you later today but since I was here I thought I'd do it now."

"Manager? Me? But—"

"But nothing. You're a good man and I trust you."

"But my cousin and his friends aren't going to give up," Jesse stated.

"Yeah, I don't think so either, but we'll be ready for them." Royce's voice was hard and his jaw set.

"Yes, you have friends and bodyguards," Bear assured.

"Bodyguards?" Jesse asked Royce, who wouldn't look him in the eye.

"Back to the manager thing, babe. We'll talk after," Royce answered once again without eye contact.

"You bet we will," Jesse replied before turning back to Bear. "You really want me to be the manager of the diner? What about Sarah?"

"She's going to retire soon, and I need someone who can run the front and the back of the diner. I want you for the position. So what do you say? I could really use the help once we hire more people."

Jesse had never been allowed to manage anything, not even the everyday running of his family farm. Could he do it? Could he manage staff and the diner when Bear wasn't around? The excitement building inside him had already made the choice for him. This was his chance to show what he could do.

"Yes, I'll help manage the diner with you, boss man," Jesse said with his head held high.

"Thank God, oh, and it comes with a raise in pay, and you start immediately. We have two interviews this morning and two this afternoon. I want one new cook to start and then we'll add on more staff as needed."

"Thank you, Bear, for giving me a chance." Jesse was honestly thankful that after the events of this morning he still had a job, let alone a raise.

"Thank you for not running. You have a life here in Brighton, and we're not going to let them push you out of town." With that said, Bear turned and left the kitchen.

Before Royce could make a sound, Jesse turned and said one word: "Bodyguards?"

***

"Ummm…yeah, bodyguards," was all Royce could manage to get out. He wasn't one hundred percent sure what Jesse's reaction was going to be. It could go one of two ways.

"You hired a Sentinel to watch over me without telling me?" Jesse asked.

"Yes."

"Why didn't you tell me?"

"Because I was afraid you would say no, that it wasn't necessary. I need to protect you even when I'm not with you. I'm not saying you can't protect yourself, but I know you don't like to use violence and I worry."

Royce waited for the recriminations to begin, and he knew he deserved it for keeping secrets from Jesse. He waited another moment but nothing came out of Jesse's mouth. He just had a smile on his face.

"Jesse?"

That seemed to snap Jesse back to reality. He wrapped his arms around Royce, lifted him off the ground, and kissed him deeply before he said, "I love you."

Shocked, Royce replied, "I love you too, and I'm sorry I wasn't honest with you."

"You were trying to protect me, and I love you for it. No one has ever protected me. Only you," Jesse confessed.

Royce could feel his heart breaking for the boy who had to grow up without unconditional love and protection. It still amazed Royce that Jesse had grown into the amazing man he was. With his parents as his guide, Jesse should have been as evil as his cousin.

"I will always protect you. You mean so much to me. Jesse, you've brought me back to life. I was only existing after my husband died. I don't know how much longer I could have lived like that... I—"

"You're a strong man who lived through a horrible tragedy. You survived and are now helping to save me from my own family. Don't ever think you're anything but the amazing man that I love." Jesse continued to hold Royce. He seemed desperate to get closer after all the events of the day, and the diner hadn't even opened yet.

"I should let you get ready to open, sweetheart. I'll stay for breakfast before physiotherapy. Shadow will be around today to watch out for the other four men in Jerry's group. I don't want you to worry," Royce explained.

"How can I when you worry enough for both of us? Now go. I'm safe. You don't want me to get fired after I just got a promotion, do you?" Jesse joked.

"Okay, smart-ass, I'll leave you be," Royce stated before smacking Jesse's firm ass as he turned to leave.

"Leave my ass out of this." Jesse laughed.

"Never," Royce replied as he walked out of the kitchen doorway. *God, I love that man.*

Chapter Three

Royce grunted as the inevitable pain and burn ran through his arm and shoulder. He was convinced physiotherapy was just another name for torture, and the perky Miss Girard was obviously a master at doling it out. If he had to pull on one more massive rubber band, his mind was going to snap. Royce knew he was a bit testy; he could never stand being injured. Especially now that he was unable to do what needed to be done to the assholes who were stalking Jesse. Instead, he had to take a backseat and allow Sentinels and police officers to take the lead, leaving Royce frustrated and essentially useless.

Those two emotions he knew all too well over the last three and half years since Daniel, his husband, had died in a car accident caused by an impaired driver. The world he knew had ended that day, the love and life in his world was gone. For quite a long time he'd believed there was no reason for him to exist. He'd survived the loss only by the strength of his family and friends.

"Mr. Evans, you're not paying attention. I need two more reps before you're done for the day." Royce could hear the snap of her imaginary whip slicing through the air.

"Yes, ma'am." Royce had a very strict upbringing and no matter the pain his therapist inflicted, Royce always treated her with respect.

Royce pulled the band, stretching it between his good arm and his injured one. Each move was excruciating and Royce wondered if he'd ever be able to use his arm properly again. Would he still be able to be a paramedic? He'd never once regretted taking a bullet in an effort to save Rick and his two-year-old nephew, Josh. He'd been able to call in reinforcements before passing out from the combination of blood loss and shock. The front of the bullet wound took only a few stitches to close up but the exit wound had mutilated the back of his shoulder. The doctors had spent hours trying to put everything back together. Muscle and skin had been torn apart when the bullet exited his body, but at least he was still alive.

"There you go, all done. You did great, Mr. Evans. We'll get you back to your usual active self in no time," she said, but Royce still had his doubts.

"Thank you, Miss Girard, but I honestly don't see any improvement," Royce admitted.

"But you have improved. When you first came in here, you could barely move your arm. Now you can stretch it out from your body by at least eleven inches and you've got the glare down perfectly," Miss Girard continued to assure him.

"The glare?" Royce had a bad feeling that he hadn't been able to hide his dislike of physiotherapy all that well.

"Yeah, the 'I want to rip your throat out glare.'" She laughed as if it were nothing.

Royce knew he was turning red. This young lady was trying to help him and he repaid her with death glares. *Great.* "I'm sorry, Miss Girard, I—"

"Oh, don't you dare apologize. At least you never swore at me, I get that a lot," she explained as she stored all the various equipment back on the shelves.

Royce's anger at having to do therapy turned into a whole lot of respect for the plucky little woman who always had a smile on her face. "It still doesn't make it right. I'm sorry I took my anger out on you, even if it was through a look."

"Well, I accept your apology and believe me when I say you are making progress with your arm." Miss Girard smiled. "You'll be back to work before you know it."

"Thank you. I do appreciate your help, just not all the pain that comes with it," Royce joked.

"Nobody does. I promise it will get easier. Now I have to go. More patients are waiting on me. Have a good day, Royce, say hello to Jesse for me." Miss Girard smiled before leaving Royce to his own thoughts.

His need to get back to Jesse was irrepressible. One quick shower later and Royce would have been on his way to the diner if it weren't for the flat tire on his car. Without having the ability to change it himself with his arm in a sling, he called his best friend Gabe to help him. Gabe and his fiancé Johnny showed up minutes later and were in the process of changing the flat for him.

"How are the plans for the wedding going, Johnny?" Royce asked. It always warmed his heart to see the couple finally getting their happy ending. Their lives had not been easy but they'd pushed through and found each other in the end.

Johnny brushed his curly blond hair out of his face before replying. "It's going to be beautiful. We're having a huge buffet reception at the community center and we left the invitation open to the whole town of Brighton. That way anyone can stop by and celebrate with us."

"That sounds great, Johnny. It's going to be quite the party." Royce wasn't surprised by their generosity and was thankful Brighton was only a small town or his friends would go broke doing that.

Gabe stood up and joined the conversation, looking a bit unsure. "You know you're my best friend, Royce. Been for a hell of a lotta years. We've been through thick and thin both at work and in our personal lives. I was hoping you'd be my best man."

Royce was shocked. Gabe's family was so large he assumed that he'd pick a member of the Mason clan. Would he and Jesse ever get to the point of marriage? He hoped so. As for Gabe, he'd been his greatest strength after Daniel's death. He'd kicked Royce's butt more than once and brought him back from the edge more times than he could remember. "Yes. I would be honored, Gabe."

Gabe slapped him on the back out of habit and Royce groaned in pain. Gabe grimaced and pulled his hand away. "Oh shit. I'm so sorry, Royce, I completely forgot about your arm."

"It's okay, but you know what they say about payback," Royce joked between deep breaths. Gabe didn't think he'd reinjured him but the jarring movement had been painful.

Johnny joined them but was looking a bit worried. "Um…Royce, I was going to ask Jesse to stand up with me. He saved my life by pushing me out of the way of that car. We've become friends since then. Do you think he'll say yes?"

"I don't see why not. You guys are close. Jesse considers you to be his good friend," Royce said. The poor guy still had his moments of uncertainty, and Royce wanted to reassure him.

"Thank you, Royce." Johnny looked relieved before he turned his attention back to Gabe, and Royce's flat tire. *I must have picked up a nail somewhere that deflated my tire while I was in having physio, I'll get it fixed this afternoon.*

"Royce, come look at this," Gabe said, as he stood and stepped away from Royce's car. "Your tire's been slashed."

Sure enough, the sidewall of the tire had a roughly two-inch-long gash. It had to have been on the bottom half of the tire when it deflated for the cut to have been hidden from him. No wonder Royce hadn't seen it originally. He pulled out his cell phone and called Shadow. He didn't want to worry Jesse at work.

"Hello."

"Shadow, it's Royce. My tire's been slashed," Royce said. "Is Jesse okay?"

"Yep, I can see him in the kitchen right now cooking up a storm. The diner's really busy today," Shadow confirmed, allowing Royce to breathe again.

"Keep a close eye on him. I don't know if this is simply retaliation for having Jerry arrested or a way to keep me from Jesse." Royce didn't know which, but he would always make sure Jesse was safe.

"You got it," Shadow said before hanging up.

"Something's up. They're becoming more open with their attacks," Royce said to Gabe. "I just don't know what they're planning."

"You need anything you just call, we'll be there," Gabe assured Royce. He knew in his gut this thing was coming to a head. He just hoped and prayed he was there to stop it from hurting Jesse.

***

Jesse had been running around like a madman all day, trying to keep up with all the orders. The diner was becoming the new hotspot in town along with Lucky's, the only bar in Brighton. Jesse might never admit it but he desperately wanted to dance with Royce at the bar. He still had a hard time being openly gay in public after having been punished into hiding it for so long. But bit by bit Royce was bringing Jesse's true self to the surface every day. He could now kiss

Royce out in public and hold hands without always looking over his shoulder for his family. He'd never been this happy in his entire life.

"Two more specials, Jesse," Sarah ordered from the counter in front of the pass-through, then attached the order tickets to a metal railing above her head.

"Two specials, on it," Jesse answered.

The interviews for another cook couldn't have come fast enough. He'd already sat in on two interviews after the morning rush and had two more scheduled for after the lunch rush. So far, neither of the first two had the experience needed to jump in to a busy diner, and one even seemed a bit homophobic. Jesse hoped the afternoon interviews went better or he'd be working seven days a week indefinitely.

"Specials up, Sarah," Jesse called out.

"Thank you, sweetie," Sarah replied. "Oh and there's a young man out here who says he has an interview with you."

The guy was early, a good sign. "Thanks, Sarah, can you tell him I'll just be a few minutes?" Jesse scanned the dining room. Shadow was still sitting in the back watching everyone and everything. A couple sat by the windows, and a few others were spread throughout the diner. No one new, except for the lone man in a side booth, which gave Jesse the time to step out of the kitchen. He took off his apron, washed his hands, and went in search of what he hoped was their new cook.

Jesse walked out into the front of the diner and waited until he saw Sarah walking toward him. It gave him time to observe the young man. He had hair as black as ink and tattoos covering his slim arms. From the information Bear provided, he knew the guy was twenty-six, and by the looks of him he'd missed quite a few meals. His clothes hung from his body, but his eyes were full of hope as he looked around the diner.

"So what do you think, Sarah?" he asked when she walked behind the counter.

"I think he needs to eat. Poor boy looks half starved," Sarah said gruffly, a sure sign she was affected by the state of the young man.

"I agree. Hold on a moment." Jesse walked back into the kitchen, grabbed the bread and roast beef, threw on a basket of fries and went to work. A few minutes later he had a hot roast beef sandwich covered in gravy with a mountain of fries on the side. "Sarah, order up."

Sarah came to the window and gave him a knowing look. "And who might this be for?"

"You know darn well. I'll pay for it after he leaves. Tell him that I've been tied up and that I won't be able to see him for another fifteen minutes. That should give him enough time to get most of this into him. Tell him the meal's on the house, my way of apologizing for my being late."

Sarah's look softened. "You're a good man, Jesse Tribalt. Don't let anyone tell you any different."

Jesse could feel his face heating up. "Just go and stop sweet-talking me."

He watched as Sarah delivered the food to the obviously malnourished man. His eyes watered at the sight of the plate. Sarah said a few words and walked away with a smile on her face. Travis—this was the man's name, which Jesse also had learned from the boss man—looked toward the back and smiled at Jesse in what he assumed was thanks. He then dug in like a man who hadn't eaten in days, which by the looks of him was probably true.

"Good thing you did there. He looks like he's starving." Shadow spoke from across the room, causing Jesse to jump. At times, you never saw the man unless he wanted you to. It was amazing and annoying all at the same time.

"Will you stop sneaking up on me?" Jesse huffed and went on to clean the grill.

"Can't, it sorta goes with the gig…'Shadow,' remember?" he said with a grin that probably had melted many a man's heart, but Jesse was unaffected. He had his own man that made his heart beat.

"Then go and be a shadow in the front of the diner, not in the kitchen."

"Touchy, touchy Mr. 'I can't take a compliment.'" Shadow laughed as he walked out the door. Shadow was right of course; he had no idea how to take a compliment from someone. He'd never had them lavished on him in his past life.

Jesse went back to stocking up for the supper rush while keeping an eye on Travis's progress. He was about halfway through his meal when he suddenly stopped. He still looked longingly at the roast beef but didn't touch it. Sarah walked to his table and they spoke quietly before she headed back toward the kitchen.

Sarah walked straight up to Jesse, her eyes looking troubled. "He asked for a takeout container. I know darn well he could finish that plate but I think he's saving the other half as food for later or even tomorrow. Where does this poor boy come from? I've never seen him around town before."

"Somewhere in Arkansas, and don't you worry, I'll bring him a big piece of pie when I interview him. Which should be about now before the next guy shows up." Jesse had pretty much decided on helping Travis out. He just hoped the guy had some sort of cooking experience.

"Oh, the final interview called to cancel, so our boy Travis is it," Sarah said, with a sweet smile. "You want me to start showing him around?" She knew what Jesse was about to do, but really, how could he not?

"At least let me go make like we really had an interview, okay?" Jesse laughed softly.

"Okay, I'll wrap up his food." Sarah grabbed a takeout box and left the kitchen in a much better mood then when she'd entered.

What have I gotten myself into?

With one quick pit stop to pick up two pieces of apple pie, he was off to either get himself a new cook or make one of the biggest mistakes of his short-lived management career.

Jesse approached the table and the moment Travis saw him, he stood. Travis was much shorter than Jesse, with shoulder-length black hair and light blue eyes. He'd definitely been missing his share of meals. They'd have to fix that.

"Hello, Mr. Boone, sorry to keep you waiting," Jesse said.

"Call me Travis, Mr. Tribalt. It's good to meet you," Travis replied.

"Jesse, you can call me Jesse." Jesse reached out and took Travis's offered hand. His handshake was stronger than he had expected, his back was straight, and he looked Jesse right in the eyes. Whatever had happened to Travis hadn't broken the man. Jesse liked him right from the start. "So how about we eat these pieces of pie and talk? I hope you don't mind. I hate eating alone so I brought one for you."

"Thank you, that's very kind of you." Travis sat but wouldn't meet Jesse's eyes. "I see what you're doing."

"Feeding you? Well hell, someone has to." Jesse decided to be blunt and used the deep, "in command" voice he'd honed over the last ten years. "Now eat, and we'll talk." Travis immediately picked up his fork and dug in. Jesse didn't like trying to be dominant because he was never comfortable in that position, but in this situation it was necessary.

"So, let's discuss your experience. Where have you cooked before?" Jesse asked, hoping against all hope he'd hear at least one diner on the list, if there was even a list.

Travis wiped his mouth with his napkin and began naming diner after diner and a few full-blown high-end restaurants. "My last position was with Ray's Roadhouse just outside Dallas," Travis concluded.

Now Jesse's curiosity was piqued. He wondered why Travis would leave so many of his previous positions. "I know Ray's, their barbeque ribs are amazing. Can you tell me why you left your previous employers?" Jesse asked.

Travis looked away again before answering, "I didn't fit in well."

"Do you honestly think I'm going to leave it at that?" Jesse stated in the same no-nonsense voice. "Why didn't you fit in?"

Travis looked ready to bolt but he sat with his back straight, the complete picture of strength even though his eyes were panicked. He took a deep breath and looked Jesse straight in the eyes. "I'm gay. The bible belt wasn't too accepting of that or my tattoos."

It was so anticlimactic that Jesse almost laughed. If it weren't for the defiance in Travis's eyes, he might have. Did he not know where he was? Had he thought he'd be turned away because he was gay? Yes, in reality the world could be a hard place.

"I—," Jesse began, but was cut off.

"No, it's okay, Mr. Tribalt. I understand." Travis began to gather his takeout container and thin jacket.

"Perhaps you should wait for me to reject you before you assume I have." Jesse used his normal voice, no longer needing to be stern now that he knew why Travis was on a run of bad luck and straight-out homophobia.

"I'm sorry, what did you wish to say?" Travis asked.

Just than the bell over the front door tinkled, announcing the entrance of a customer. Jesse turned his head and saw Royce, Gabe, and Johnny headed for a booth. Royce smiled at him the entire way and caused Jesse's heart to speed up.

"You see those three men that just came walking in? The two holding hands are my good friends who are getting married in a few months, and the sexy redhead is mine." At Travis's stunned expression, Jesse continued, "Welcome to Brighton, Travis."

Chapter Four

Two days later, Jesse found himself in his favorite position, lying on the couch in his lover's arms—well, *arm*, because the other one was still in a sling—enjoying a quiet evening at home. Jesse was starting to think of Royce's house as their home—a dangerous feeling, considering they'd never discussed their living arrangement. Jesse wanted to talk about just that and was almost ready to back out, not wanting to risk pushing too far, but he needed something solid to hold on to. Now that Jerry was in town and everything he loved could be ripped away from him at any moment, he needed the reassurance.

He was lying with his back against Royce's chest, watching an old '80s action movie, and he didn't dare turn around for this discussion. "Royce, I wanted to talk to you about something."

Royce tensed, his arm tightening around Jesse, holding him closer. "Okay, baby, what did you need to talk about?"

"It's about our current living arrangement," Jesse explained.

"Yes, I've been thinking about that as well," Royce agreed.

Jesse was unsure if that was a good thing or not. Maybe he wanted Jesse to leave. He was getting nervous and suddenly wished he'd never brought it up. He could live without knowing, right?

"I...I..." Jesse stumbled over his own words, unable to ask for what he so desperately wanted.

Royce jumped in to save him. "Shhhh, sweetheart, it's okay. No matter what you have to say, I love you. Come to think of it, maybe I should start with what I want to see happen."

Jesse nodded his agreement. *Why can't I get the words out? 'I want to live together permanently,' see? Easy.*

Royce took a deep breath and said, "I want you here with me. Not just while I'm recovering but forever. I want you to live here with me. I know this may be moving too quickly for you but I can see us together long term. I promise to do everything possible to make you feel at home here."

Jesse's heart stopped. He wasn't sure he'd heard Royce correctly or simply dreamed that answer. "Can you repeat that?"

"I want you to move in with me permanently," Royce said.

Jesse shifted, careful not to jostle Royce's injured arm, but he had to look him in the eyes. "Again?"

Royce's expression softened. "Sweetheart, will you move in with me?"

"Yes. Yes, I'll move in with you. I love you," Jesse answered without a hint of hesitation. "This is what I wanted."

The smile he got in return from Royce was breathtaking, pure joy. Careful of Royce's arm, Jesse turned Royce's body until he was lying beneath him. Lightly he began to kiss his lover, feathering his lips over Royce's, teasing them both.

Soon the kiss deepened as Royce took control, leaving Jesse wanting so much more. He rubbed his jean-covered cock against Royce's thigh, desperate for friction. The couch was suddenly too confining; he needed more room to touch and explore. In a bold move Jesse ended the kiss, stood, and lifted Royce into his arms. Royce was a big man himself but Jesse was still quite a bit bigger and easily held him. Royce didn't say a word; he just wrapped his legs around Jesse's waist and went on to suck up lewd marks along Jesse's neck, driving his desire even higher.

By the time they reached their bedroom Jesse's shirt had a tear in it and Royce's sling was almost completely undone. Jesse made sure to handle Royce's arm gently. Even in his lust-fogged mind he would never hurt his lover. Every ridge of hard muscle brushed over Jesse's cock as Royce slid down his body. As soon as he was standing, Royce began stripping off his clothes as fast as he could with one arm. Piece by piece, Royce's beautiful, toned body was revealed and Jesse stood in place simply staring until his lover was completely naked. His pale skin was such a contrast to the red hair covering his broad chest and leading down to his large, erect penis.

"Baby, you have too many clothes on," Royce teased.

"Just can't get over how lucky I am. You're perfect, you're gorgeous, kind, smart, and sexy. I just don't know what you see in me sometimes," Jesse explained; he honestly believed every word he said.

Royce ran his hand across Jesse's chest and pinched his nipple, sending jolts of electricity down to his balls. Royce squeezed a bit harder, gaining Jesse's instant attention. "Now, I'm just going to have to prove how irresistible you truly are to me, baby, so you don't doubt that I'm the lucky one in this relationship."

"But—" Jesse tried to argue the point.

"No, Jesse, I don't want to hear you saying anything derogatory about yourself. You're breathtaking. I can't help but want to touch you whenever you're near me. You have the biggest heart and you make me so very happy. What you did for Travis, the kindness you showed him, meant so much to the man. And then managing the diner for Bear, you're trusted and intelligent. But most of all, you love me so completely I could never ask for more. Now get naked and kiss me."

In five seconds flat Jesse was naked, and kissing Royce like the man might disappear at any moment. He knew his fear was irrational, but he couldn't help but pull Royce closer. This was what love felt like. He never thought he'd be fortunate enough to have this opportunity, and needed to be closer to the man who taught him what love truly was.

Royce broke the kiss. "Up on the bed, baby. I need you."

Jesse eagerly did what he was told, crawling up on his hands and knees on top of the sheets, waiting for Royce to join him. He loved this position; having Royce's body blanket his own made him feel protected and cherished. A few seconds later, instead of feeling lube on his hole like he'd expected, he felt a warm, wet tongue, the sensation sending Jesse's head back as he moaned out his pleasure to the ceiling.

"Yes, yes please, Royce. Just like that." Jesse wasn't above begging his lover for what he needed.

"You like that, baby?" Royce asked with a devilish smile. "You like it when I rim you."

"God, yes." Jesse was losing control as Royce pulled his ass cheeks wider apart and dove in. Jesse began to shake. Royce reached around and fisted Jesse's hard cock, pulling the foreskin back and working his sensitive head. Royce pointed his tongue and entered

Jesse's hole, making him scream, unable to hold his desire in any longer.

Jesse widened his legs and rested his head on his pillow, his arms shaking so badly he could no longer hold himself up. Royce kept lavishing him with intimate attention that made Jesse babble incoherently into the mattress. His heart was pounding and all he could think about was how much he loved this wonderful, giving man. Jesse didn't know what life had in store for him, but he'd do anything necessary to stay with Royce.

Royce pulled away and knelt behind him, rubbing his hard cock between Jesse's ass cheeks. Jesse pushed himself up on his hands and began rocking back against Royce, desperate to feel him push inside, for them to be joined.

"Please, Royce, take me," Jesse cried out.

Royce growled and began pushing forward; inch by inch the pressure grew as Royce filled him. Thanks to blood tests done months earlier, there was no need for condoms, allowing for them to safely have no barriers between them. Soon all he could feel was pleasure building while Royce buried himself deep inside Jesse. Royce waited patiently until Jesse gave him a nod before he moved; he knew Royce would never intentionally hurt him. Royce sped up, and Jesse pushed back against every powerful stroke. He looked over his shoulder to see Royce holding his injured arm to his chest. *Shit, his injury, how could I have completely forgotten about his arm?*

"Baby...lie down so I can ride you." Jesse groaned as Royce found his prostrate and pegged it mercilessly, almost distracting Jesse from what he'd asked. "Royce, let me ride you, please."

With one final stroke, Royce pulled out and lay down on the bed beside Jesse. "Up you get, love."

Jesse couldn't help but moan as he straddled Royce's body and hovered above him. Royce's hard cock brushed against Jesse's ass, enticing him to lower himself down to take Royce inside his body. Royce was by far the more dominant one in this relationship; to prove that point, when Jesse leaned down for a kiss Royce held his head in place and took control almost immediately. *Oh yes, yes...yes...yes.* Jesse melted into his touch, happily submitting to the kiss as Royce pushed in deep.

In a matter of seconds Royce was thrusting upward, pegging Jesse's gland over and over again. His beautiful green eyes softened with love. There was no mistaking the look and Jesse couldn't help but respond. His entire being—mind, body, and soul—reached out to Royce in that moment, feeling a connection that went so deep, it was breathtaking.

"Take what you need from me, baby," Royce whispered, as if not wanting to disturb the shroud of love that surrounded them.

His body stilled, allowing their movements to be controlled by Jesse. Flexing his hips, he slammed down on Royce's hard cock over and over again until they both were beyond thought and moving on instinct. Royce reached for Jesse's cock and began to pump.

Jesse couldn't hold back. Without warning he came across Royce's stomach and chest, yelling his release to the heavens. Two strokes later Royce's warmth filled Jesse before he collapsed on top of Royce. His body trembled from the strength of his orgasm and Royce held him close, safe in his arms.

"I've got you, love...easy, Jesse." Royce spoke softly.

Slowly Jesse came down from his euphoric high and melted into Royce's touch.

"See? Irresistible," Royce said.

***

Three days later, Jesse had decided to go to work early. That morning he would begin packing all of his belongings from the apartment above the diner. He was excited to move his things into Royce's house—well, Royce and Jesse's house, as Royce wanted it called. Life had never been so "normal."

Everything I've ever wanted.

Royce drove him in, of course, concerned Jesse's family would try to attack him again. As they pulled into the back parking lot, Jesse noticed Travis's old, rust-covered car parked in the farthest spot away from the building. Since Travis hadn't been given a key just yet, he couldn't be inside the diner. He had to be in the car, but why show up for work hours early?

"Travis is awfully early," Royce said. His voice echoed Jesse's own concern.

"Let's go see what's going on," Jesse suggested. He'd been working with Travis for the past three days, and honestly the man knew his way around a kitchen. He was a godsend to the diner. Now Jesse just hoped his faith in Travis hadn't been misplaced.

Royce pulled up beside Travis. His car had seen better days and Jesse doubted it had more than a few miles left in it. They both got out and Royce immediately put himself between Travis's car and Jesse.

"I'll go see what he's doing here," Royce said. He turned on his flashlight, because they were still hours away from dawn, and walked toward the car. Jesse was now used to Royce's need to protect him, so he leaned against the back fender and waited for the all-clear.

As Royce approached the car and peeked inside, his stance went from cautious to relaxed in an instant, and he waved Jesse over. What he found in the backseat of the car was heartbreaking. There wrapped in a threadbare blanket was Travis, sound asleep. The man was living in his car.

As if sensing their presence, Travis slowly opened his eyes and shouted in fear. Once he realized it was them, he buried his head in his shaking hands. Travis scrambled to sit up when Royce tapped on the slightly open back window. "I'm so sorry, I'll leave. You don't need to worry about firing me." The grief in those pale blue eyes could bring a man to his knees. Jesse knew that look well; he'd worn it often during his time on the streets.

"You aren't going anywhere. You get straightened up and meet us in the diner and don't even think about driving off. In fact, give me your keys." Royce's voice had taken on a deep, authoritative tone that never ceased to thrill Jesse.

Travis didn't hesitate in handing over his keys. He recognized an order when he heard one.

"Ten minutes or I'll come out and find you, understand?" Royce asked.

"Yes, Mr. Evans." Travis spoke just above a whisper.

Jesse grabbed on to Royce's hand and pulled him away from the car and toward the diner. "Let's go pack up my stuff because Travis needs that apartment immediately. He can't stay in his car."

"I'll call Bear and check if it's okay with him that Travis moves in. I'm sure it'll be fine, but we shouldn't make any promises without his okay," Royce explained. So often Jesse found that he and Royce were on the same page; it gave him a warm feeling inside whenever it happened.

"Thank you, Royce. I think he might have tried to take off if you hadn't asked for his keys." Jesse knew they had to help Travis, with or without his cooperation—though it would be much easier if they could convince him to accept their assistance.

Jesse remembered his time on the streets, living in parks, washing in public bathrooms, never knowing where his next meal was coming from, and always on the move. There was no peace to be found, only survival. He went to bed hungry and woke the same way with no guarantee he'd make it through another day and sometimes even wishing for the suffering to end. It had taken months for Jesse to trust Royce enough to open up about what life was like living on the streets. To finally have the ability to share his suffering and fears with the man who loved him had been cathartic and felt like closing a door on a painful chapter in his life.

"He wouldn't make it another day living in his car. No food or water, and the thing's about to fall apart around him. When is his first pay?" Royce asked.

"End of the week, so another two days," Jesse explained, as he catalogued his belongings to see if there was anything he could leave behind for Travis. He decided quickly to donate his microwave, toaster, and a new bedsheet set that had never been used. That way, Travis wouldn't have to go out and buy things right away. Jesse also had canned goods, pots and pans, utensils, and secondhand furniture that Bear had gotten for him.

"He'll need money in the meantime; I've got forty dollars on me. That should hold him over, right?" Royce asked.

Before answering Jesse opened the back door, pulled Royce inside, and began thoroughly kissing him. His lover's soft lips became insistent, demanding entry to Jesse's mouth as tongues dueled and teeth nipped gently. Reluctantly they parted, gasping for breath.

"Baby, not that I'm complaining, but what was that for?" Royce asked, his eyes dilated and his pants bulging.

"Just for being you. You're such a good man, Royce, and I love you," Jesse explained while caressing his lover's cheek.

"Don't let that get out or my image will be ruined," Royce said.

"Hate to burst your bubble but everyone already knows you're a big softy." Jesse laughed. "I'll go pack, you call Bear."

He gave Royce a quick kiss and ran upstairs, taking two steps at a time. The heartbreak in Travis's eyes and the conditions in which he'd been living made this decision easy. Travis would move into Jesse's old apartment so he would be safe and could get back on his feet. Jesse had been in Travis's shoes when he came to Brighton and if it hadn't been for the "White Hair Crew"— Brighton's very own gang of grandmas—and Bear, Jesse had no idea where he'd be or even if he'd still be alive.

Jesse looked around his tiny apartment with new eyes. It may have been small but it had essentially saved Jesse from his old life. Now he hoped it would do the same for Travis.

Several minutes later Royce called up the stairs, "Babe, Travis is waiting."

"On my way," Jesse replied as he set a half-full box onto the bed with the others and then headed down into the diner. Jesse found Travis sitting in a booth while Royce was busy making coffee at the front counter. The smell of the brewing liquid floated throughout the diner and was like a siren's call.

Jesse sat in the booth on the opposite side of Travis. It seemed as though the man was trying to make himself as small as possible, and he wouldn't meet Jesse's eyes. "Travis, please calm down. You're not in trouble."

"You just found me sleeping in the parking lot, how can I not be in trouble?" Travis asked.

"Because I've been there, but I didn't have a car to sleep in, only a motorcycle," Jesse explained.

"You've been homeless?" Travis asked, looking shocked.

"Yes, for a lot of years I had all my worldly belongings in a saddlebag," Jesse confirmed. His memories flooded back of the one night he had to fight to keep his saddlebags from two other homeless men. It had been a bloody fight but Jesse had kept his belongings and left the area. "How long have you been homeless?"

"Almost eighteen months. I couldn't afford rent and food because I never knew when I'd have to leave again." Travis hung his head as he spoke. "I could hide my tattoos under a long-sleeved shirt but for some reason they always seemed to guess my sexual orientation even though I hid it. Someone would complain and the next thing I knew, I was out on my ass again. Either that or they'd make the working environment so toxic I had to leave."

Royce brought over three mugs of coffee and slid in beside Jesse. "We want to help you."

"Why?" Apparently Travis wasn't used to any acts of kindness. Jesse knew they could fix that. When he'd come to town all those months ago, he'd trusted no one and every day he'd waited for the other foot to fall, but it never did.

"Because you need it and we have it to give...but I know you have your pride so this isn't a handout. You're going to have to pay Bear for the apartment," Royce explained.

"Apartment?" Travis asked.

"Yes, my old apartment upstairs. I'm moving in with Royce. So it's available to you. It isn't big but it's better than your car and I'm leaving a few things behind you'll need." Jesse still couldn't believe he and Royce were living together; he'd never be alone again. *Thank God.*

"But I don't have any money." Travis looked panicked and his thin leg began bouncing even faster.

"Well, you have a job, you'll make money. Bear said that considering there's only ten days left in the month, he wouldn't charge you rent until the following month and he'd cut it in half until you get on your feet," Royce explained.

A knock came from the front door and Royce left to find out who it was. Jesse wasn't too concerned that it might be the Redemption Squad. They wouldn't have knocked.

"Say yes, Travis. A while ago I was given the same chance. Take it," Jesse coaxed. He wanted the poor guy to have the same opportunity he'd had and build a new life here in Brighton.

Travis's emotions got the best of him and his eyes filled with tears that spilled over and down his red cheeks. "Thank you for this. I don't know what to say. But I want the chance to live a normal life, a real life."

"Travis, why are you crying?" Officer Bo Mason stormed past Royce and crouched down in front of the smaller man, who was desperately trying to wipe his tears away. Even crouched Bo was still taller—the man was even bigger than Jesse. "Are you hurt? Did something happen?"

"I have a place to live, a real apartment here above the diner," Travis explained. "I finally have a job and a home."

Bo seemed to take a moment to digest what Travis had said. "That's wonderful, Travis. But if you don't mind me asking, where were you staying before?" Bo asked as he rubbed the remaining tears from his face. Travis looked mortified that he'd said what he did; he'd obviously let his happiness cloud his thinking and revealed more than he wanted to Bo.

Jesse and Royce looked at each other, both wondering what the hell was going on. They had seen the two talking and having lunch together on occasion but maybe there was more than simply friendship between them.

Before Bo could get an answer to his question, Travis jumped to his feet and backed away like he'd been burned. "I was in a motel until I could find a place."

Bo didn't look like he believed a word Travis was saying. He was a police officer after all; Jesse assumed he could pick out lies easily. "Then why were you crying?" Bo stood and took a step toward Travis.

"Because I was happy. They were happy tears." Travis looked ready to bolt. "I'll go grab my belongings out of my car." He seemed to realize what he'd just said and began backing away.

"Why is all your stuff in the car and not the motel room? Which motel were you staying at?" Bo asked as he continued to move closer to Travis. For every step Bo took, Travis took one backward.

"Why are you interrogating me? I haven't done anything wrong, officer." Travis was panicking and Jesse knew Travis didn't want to admit to Bo that he'd been living in his car.

"Bo—you know you can call me Bo and you're not in trouble at all," Bo answered. "I'll help you carry your belongings in."

"No! I mean no, there isn't much, I can handle it." Travis looked even more panicked then before, as if the thought of Bo seeing his car was tantamount to standing naked in the middle of the street. Then again, Jesse would have done anything to make sure Royce never saw some of the places he'd been forced to sleep at night.

Jesse could feel the chill in the air. Now that Travis was pulling himself together, he was also pulling away. Travis had not given anyone the cold shoulder in all the days they'd been working together. Something serious was going on between the two of them and Jesse would find out what that was.

Though he'd heard only good things about Bo Mason, he would still protect Travis if he had to; the man was vulnerable until he got his feet back under him. Jesse remembered all too well the vultures that used to prey on the weak when he was on the road, though he really doubted that was Bo's intention.

"I'll be leaving then. I just wanted to check in when I saw the lights on so early and make sure everything was okay." Bo seemed to have forgotten Royce and Jesse were even there; all his attention was on Travis.

Jesse had to do something to get Travis out from under the spotlight. "Travis, would you go pour Bo a take-out coffee, please?"

"Yes, Jesse," Travis answered, letting out a deep breath he must have been holding.

As Travis walked off, Jesse was counting down the seconds until the first question was lobbed his way.

"What happened to him? Where was he staying?" Bo asked.

"I'm sorry, Bo, but that's something Travis will have to tell you himself," Royce answered for the both of them, knowing Jesse wouldn't want to be spreading Travis's private information around.

"Is he safe?" Bo asked, turning his head to watch Travis working behind the counter. His eyes softened and his expression changed from concern to something a little more personal.

"Yes, he is now," Jesse replied.

"Thank you for giving him a place to settle into," Bo said. Jesse could tell that it meant a lot to Bo to have Travis safe, but why?

"You're welcome, but why are you so interested in Travis's well-being?" Royce asked, obviously not as patient as Jesse. He'd planned on leading up to that question.

"I'm a cop. I'm always concerned about the members of this community," Bo answered before looking away.

Jesse would have called "bullshit" on him if it weren't for Travis heading their way. Travis's cheeks were red and he was looking at everything and anyone other than Bo.

"Here's your coffee, Officer Mason," Travis said as he held out the large Styrofoam cup to Bo. Jesse just realized that Travis hadn't even asked how Bo wanted his coffee, he already knew. *Interesting.*

"Bo—and thank you, Travis." Bo smiled at Travis, causing the shy man's cheeks to become even redder. "You have a good day."

"Be careful on your shift," Travis said as he retreated into the kitchen.

Bo's smile was huge as he turned and headed out the front door. He seemed to have completely forgotten Jesse and Royce were even in the room.

"What was that all about?" Royce asked.

"I have no idea but I intend to find out." Jesse gave Royce an innocent look before he went to join Travis in the kitchen.

Chapter Five

Jesse had attempted to get answers every day they worked together, but Travis had yet to come clean about Bo Mason. Every time Jesse would bring him up, Travis would simply turn red and change the subject. Jesse wasn't willing to push too hard, but he had a sneaky suspicion the two were more than a little attracted to each other, much more than mere friendship. But Travis now seemed afraid to be in the same room as the man even though Bo would visit the diner every day. After hiring him, Jesse had quickly realized Travis was a shy person, but this was taken to extremes when Bo showed up.

It had been a busy night and they were finally getting around to locking the doors. Sarah was cleaning the dining area, and while Shannon, another Sentinel, stood guard, he and Travis began restocking and cleaning the kitchen. Jesse grabbed the two bags of garbage and headed for the dumpster out back. The night was warm, a slight breeze was coming out of the north helping cool the evening down.

The town was quiet. He liked the peace, considering he'd spent most of the past ten years hiding in big cities so that his family couldn't find him. The pace in Brighton appealed to every part of Jesse: it was slower, you knew your neighbors, and people helped each other. This was where he wanted to spend the rest of his life alongside Royce.

Jesse lifted the lid to the dumpster and threw the garbage in before locking the lid back down to keep the raccoons out. Jesse's skin began to crawl up his back and neck, a sure sign that he wasn't alone. He turned to find his cousin and two more men taking up positions around him.

"Hello, Jesse, I believe it's time this came to an end, don't you think? I have bigger plans that need to be attended to, and you need to disappear. Get him in the car!" Jerry ordered as his goons slowly moved in.

"Why can't you just leave me alone, Jerry? I left, wasn't that enough?" Jesse growled, squared his shoulders, and sized up the two men that flanked him. He was larger than each of them, but again it was three against one if his cousin decided to get his hands dirty.

Jerry's smirk and vicious glare were enough of an answer, but the asshole decided one last jab was in order. "You don't deserve to live and you certainly don't deserve a windfall. I do, not you!"

Windfall?

Jesse had no time to figure out what he meant as the two other men closed in; one pulled out a knife, and the other brandished brass knuckles. The first blow landed with a thud to his lower back, pain and nausea sending Jesse to the ground. They rained punches down on him; it brought back memories of the pain and suffering of his childhood. He was curled in a ball in the corner of his bedroom while others attacked him over and over again like rabid dogs.

I'm not that defenseless child anymore!

Something inside Jesse's mind snapped into place. He was a man and he would no longer allow anyone to abuse him. As he pushed himself to his feet, a metallic taste filled his mouth and he spat the blood out onto the ground. The men recoiled in astonishment but soon regrouped. Jesse caught the next fist before it had a chance to connect and twisted it, hearing a satisfying scream and snap of bone. Jesse was shocked at himself; in that moment he'd gained the physical and emotional strength to finally fight back. *One down, two to go.*

Just then, Travis appeared at the back door. His fists were clenched when he saw what was happening, he cursed and yelled into the diner for help and ran to Jesse's aid. *No, no, no,* Travis was still gaining weight and strength; he couldn't take on these men.

"No, Travis, get back inside!"

The one with the knife charged forward, blade aimed at Jesse's stomach. He easily dodged the knife and took the man to the ground. A loud groan came from behind him and Jesse turned in time to see Jerry kicking Travis repeatedly as his friend lay curled up on the ground. Jesse clawed his second attacker off him and dived toward Jerry when Shannon came out of nowhere, an avenging angel. With a few quick kicks of her own followed by jabs to Jerry's throat and chest, she had him on the ground moaning in pain.

Shannon turned to check on Travis and Jerry took the opportunity to crawl away into the dark. Jerry knew he'd lost, but no way was Jesse letting him go free after everything he'd done. Unfortunately, before Jesse had a chance to go after Jerry, the bastard with the knife decided to attack again. The ruthless man jumped in front of Jesse and began slicing the blade through the air; his eyes were bulging and he licked his lips as if he couldn't wait to taste Jesse's blood. Jesse dodged each blow up until he heard a loud moan from Travis and he lost his concentration, ending with him being cut along his right forearm, leaving a three-inch gash. Jesse yelled in pain and lost his last shreds of control. His friend had been hurt and these idiots were trying to kill him, not simply take him back.

The man lunged at him again. Jesse easily dodged the knife and brought his fist down on his attacker's jaw. He went down like a rock. The second man was still rolling around on the ground holding his broken arm to his chest, cursing and crying. Red and blue lights filled the parking lot as police cars raced in along with Royce's car and another truck he didn't recognize. Sarah must have called in the cavalry.

Within moments, officers were handcuffing the two remaining assailants, even the one with a broken arm. They were asking for names and information as to where they would find the rest of their group. Jesse wildly scanned the area; he swore and clenched his fists when he realized Jerry was gone. He'd gotten away. *Dammit.*

"Jesse, are you okay?" Royce's voice was a mixture of panic and anger.

"Oh God, your arm's been cut. An ambulance is on the way. We're going to get you looked at." "Is Travis okay?" Jesse looked frantically for his friend, forgetting his own pain. "Jerry had him on the ground and was kicking him pretty hard. Travis should never have jumped in to take on Jerry like that. Shit, how bad is he hurt?" Questions poured out in a jumble. Jesse was still running on adrenaline and wasn't feeling the full extent of the pain in his arm just yet. "He needs help."

"He's being taken care of." Royce took one of the clean cloths Sarah was handing out because the ambulance hadn't arrived yet and began to clean the blood from Jesse's arm, examining his injury. "Travis ran in because that's what friends do. He looks to be unconscious, but they'll get him to the hospital. He'll have the best care possible."

Jesse looked over to see Officer Bo Mason, out of uniform and off duty, cradling Travis's head while another officer was checking the downed man over for injuries. They moved closer and Royce grabbed another clean cloth and began wrapping Jesse's arm to slow the bleeding. While Royce did that, Shannon came over and looked at Jesse's injuries as well, cleaning blood off his face and checking the damage underneath. Jesse felt like he'd been through a meat grinder but he was more worried about Travis, who still hadn't moved or regained consciousness.

Royce lifted Jesse's shirt and gasped. "Oh sweetheart, you're covered in red marks and bruises."

"How badly are you hurt, Jesse?" Chief Graham asked as they joined the group that was still hovering around Travis's still form.

"I'll be fine, it's Travis you need to worry about," Jesse explained, unable to take his eyes off the unconscious man.

"The ambulance is on its way and you're going to be looked at as well," Chief Graham ordered.

"I'll be fine," Jesse repeated. There was absolutely no way he would take any medical attention away from Travis.

"You're going to the hospital. At the very minimum you require stitches and we need to make sure you weren't hurt worse than you think," Royce stated with authority, and Jesse could do nothing but agree it was for the best.

"Yes, I'll go to the hospital. Now someone explain to me why my cousin isn't still in a jail cell?" Jesse asked, his frustration at the situation and his fear for Travis turning his voice into a growl.

"He was bailed out within twenty-four hours. We took him and his friends to the town limits and told them if they came back to Brighton they would be arrested on sight. They agreed that only Jerry would come back for his court date and they all left without incident. We haven't seen them since. We'd thought they were gone, but obviously they're laying low somewhere. We'll hunt them all down," Chief Graham assured. Jesse could almost see the fire burning in Chief Graham's eyes. "This should have never happened."

"I just can't figure out why he won't simply leave," Royce stated, sounding just as frustrated as Jesse.

Jesse suddenly remembered what his cousin had said before they attacked. "Jerry said he needed me to disappear, he had other things that needed his attention and that I didn't deserve a windfall. Whatever that means."

An ambulance pulled into the parking lot and two of Royce's colleagues jumped out. "Who's in the most serious condition?" Danny, an EMT, asked before he noticed Travis lying on the ground surrounded by people.

"Travis. He was kicked in his abdomen multiple times and he's been unconscious roughly four minutes," Chief Graham said.

Jesse watched as the EMTs immediately went to work. Bo refused to leave Travis's side until one of the paramedics needed the space. What worried Jesse was the death glare that Bo was giving Jerry's men. He didn't want Bo to get into trouble now that he knew Bo was such a good man, and head over heels for Travis as far as Jesse could tell. Though neither man had said a word, their emotions were easy for Jesse to see.

Jesse pressed his body closer to Royce's, seeking the comfort only the man he loved could give. The adrenaline was beginning to wear off and the pain was beginning to flare throughout his body. Jesse knew he'd be covered in bruises from the punches and kicks that he'd suffered. It wouldn't have been the first time, but they'd heal. He prayed Travis did the same.

"Is the pain more severe in one place over the others?" Royce asked.

Jesse did a mental check of his body. His ribs throbbed, his jaw ached, but it was the cut on his arm that held his attention. Jesse lifted his arm. "I think this is the worst of my injuries."

"Okay, then we'll drive you to the hospital while the ambulance takes Travis," Royce said, leading Jesse to their car. Jesse looked back to see Travis being loaded into the ambulance and Bo running to his truck.

"Here we go, Jesse; we'll be at the hospital in minutes," Royce said as he helped Jesse into the passenger seat. The groan he let out when he bent over seemed to make Royce move faster.

"I'm sorry, Royce. This happened because of me," Jesse mumbled as he kept his face turned toward the window. He'd brought this to Brighton. He'd brought the men who'd hurt Travis. This was his fault.

"None of this was caused by you, baby. Jerry and his people are responsible for their own actions." Royce spoke firmly and logically. Jesse knew he was right, but his heart just wouldn't accept that. To Jesse, pain and suffering seemed to follow him around since he was a child. Even at a very young age his parents never "spared the rod."

His beloved grandpa was the only person who showed him any care and love. After he'd passed away and the rest of his family swarmed in, life became even more unbearable. As Jesse grew older, the slightest suspicion that he was gay meant the gloves came off. They no longer cared if they left bruises and welts, and there was no one left to protect him. Even after fleeing his home he was always on the move, never staying in one place long enough to be found. He'd let down his guard in Brighton and now the members of the town were paying the price.

"Jesse, Jesse honey, we're here," Royce said. He was watching him closely. "Are you sure you're not dizzy? Did you get hit in the head at any time?"

Jesse had been so lost in his thoughts that he hadn't noticed the car had even stopped outside the ER. The ambulance had already arrived and was offloading Travis's gurney. Thank God Travis's eyes were now open and he was talking to the paramedics and Bo, who was again by his side. Jesse thanked whoever was watching out for the little guy that he was awake and swore to have a talk with him about fighting someone twice his size once he had the all-clear.

"I'm okay, no dizziness," answered Jesse as he rubbed his sore jaw, reflecting on what had just happened. Jerry and his men attacked him where they could have been seen by anybody. They weren't hiding anymore and were prepared to attack him whenever the chance arose. His guilt was at an all-time high and he knew things were going to get worse.

"Let's get you looked at, love. Everything will be fine, I promise." Royce seemed so sure.

Jesse wanted to believe him, but he knew better. Jerry would never give up now, considering he'd just been humiliated. Jesse didn't want to have to run again; he wanted to make a stand here but was that fair to Royce and the people of Brighton?

***

Royce knew something wasn't right but Jesse refused to share what was on his mind. Jesse's silence was frustrating. Royce could handle yelling or crying, but silence drove him nuts. He knew Jesse was feeling guilty for Travis being hurt, no matter how many times he was told he wasn't responsible. Luckily, Travis didn't have any major injuries, but he did have a minor concussion.

They spent that night wrapped in each other's arms, both reeling from such an open and vicious attack. Royce was gently stroking Jesse's hair as Jesse ran his fingers through Royce's chest hair. The lovers were both quiet as they comforted one another, cocooned in the safety of their bed. Tomorrow would come but for this one moment they found peace together in the silence.

Still, days later, a fear like he'd never felt before after pulling into the parking lot to see Jesse fighting a man with a knife, still remained fresh in his memory. Royce had always been considered the calm one in chaotic situations, which had always helped, considering he was a paramedic. But when he saw Jesse covered in blood, he froze. The fear of having to bury the second man he'd ever loved felt like someone had reached around his throat and squeezed.

His husband, Daniel, and he had been high school sweethearts and after he'd died, Royce simply shut down for years. He never dreamed he'd have a chance to feel that type of all-encompassing love again until the day he'd met Jesse. Now he had the opportunity for a life filled with love and happiness that he refused to give up at any cost.

"So are you going to sit there and stare out the diner window like a lost puppy the entire time they're gone?" Gabe asked before taking another gulp of his coffee. "They're safe. Coop's with them while they shop. You know I would never put Johnny or Jesse in danger."

"I know, Gabe, but he's been distant from me since the fight. Jesse blames himself for everything that's happened no matter what I say. He thinks he brought all of this to Brighton and anything that happens is completely his fault alone," Royce explained.

"None of this is his fault. Jerry and the men who are following him are solely accountable for all their own actions." Gabe looked shocked to even hear Jesse was taking complete responsibility for everything that happened. "You mentioned the Sentinels are checking into Jesse's family to try to uncover what's going on."

"Yeah, they're trying to get as much information on his parents as they can to see if they can approach them for answers. I don't hold out much hope that they will be any help. For all we know they're the ones who sent Jerry here in the first place, but why?" Royce asked, still not taking his eyes off the street even though Jesse and Johnny had already gone inside the store.

"Royce…Royce, look at me," Gabe ordered, his tone sharp. Royce grudgingly complied and Gabe continued. "Tell me what's really going on."

Royce buried his face in his hands before answering, "I can't lose him. I can't lose another man I love, Gabe. I believe Jesse's thinking about leaving Brighton to take the danger away from the town."

"What? He wouldn't leave you." Gabe's voice had taken on a hard edge.

"He would if he thought I was in danger. I need him to stay here with me and make a stand, but I honestly don't know if he will," Royce explained.

"Have you talked to him about your fears?" Gabe asked.

"Every time I try to bring it up he changes the subject and the last time he left the room. What am I supposed to think?" Royce asked.

"You need to sit him down and talk. You're assuming a lot here. You don't know what he's thinking for sure," Gabe advised.

"He won't talk to me. It's as if by staying silent he's still trying to protect me."

"You never struck me as a man who gave up so easily or allowed anything to get in his way. I guess things have changed," Gabe suggested.

"Nothing has changed. I don't give up. Especially when it comes to Jesse. I'll pin him down tonight and get some straight answers." Royce knew that would be easier said than done but he had to try.

"Now that's the man I know." Gabe flashed him his usually carefree grin and went back to devouring his chicken potpie.

Royce would have to push Jesse into having this discussion. He was avoiding any mention of his cousin or the fight the other night and his family's involvement. It was as if it never happened. It was a strange way to look at it but still true. He had to get Jesse to let him in one way or another.

Chapter Six

Jesse sat in one of the oversized chairs in the center of the only men's store in Brighton as Johnny spoke with the owner. He'd asked Jesse to come with him today to look at suits for his upcoming wedding to Gabe. It had been almost a week since the attack in the parking lot and both he and Travis were back to work at the diner. Though Jesse had been avoiding any talk of the fight, he had apologized to Travis, who like everyone else, refused to blame him.

Jesse knew he'd been acting distant from everyone since the incident but he couldn't let go of the guilt he was carrying. It felt as though he couldn't stand up straight with the weight of it all sometimes.

"Jesse."

He looked up to find Johnny standing a few feet away. He looked nervous, which immediately put Jesse on alert. "Johnny, what's wrong?" Jesse asked as he scanned the area. Nothing seemed out of place but that didn't mean a thing.

"Nothing's wrong. I just need to talk to you about something," Johnny replied softly.

"But you're okay, right?" Jesse asked. He would do anything to make sure the gentle man was not hurt by any of this. Johnny was kind to everyone and deserved the good stuff out of life, not the shit following Jesse around.

"Yes," Johnny confirmed with a smile. "I just wanted to ask you something. It's important to me and I'm a little nervous."

"You can ask me anything. We're friends after all. If you need something I'm here to help." Jesse didn't know why Johnny was nervous, but he'd do anything to help his friend.

"I wanted to ask you to be my best man, and if you agree I brought you here today to get your measurements for your suit."

Johnny sat down beside Jesse, his eyes fixed on a mannequin a few feet away.

"So you brought me to get a suit before you even asked?" Jesse couldn't help but tease a little; in all good conscience he wouldn't make Johnny wait long for an answer. Or it might have been the fact that he couldn't hide the smile on his face. "Yes, I would be honored to be your best man."

Johnny turned, eyes bright with tears. "You will?" he asked.

"Of course. We're good friends, Johnny," Jesse assured.

"Before I came to Brighton I was never given a chance to build any real friendships. Only families my father deemed to have the right kind of children to associate with. The best money could buy," Johnny stated sarcastically. "Not one of them knew the real me or even cared."

"I care about you and I see the real you; you're a kind and generous man who I'm honored to call a true friend," Jesse said softly, not wanting others in the store to hear their private conversation. "Now how about we pick out a suit for me because we both know it's going to take a while for them to tailor it to my body." To stress his point, Jesse flexed his muscles, making Johnny laugh just as Jesse had planned.

Hours later, Jesse had been measured from top to bottom and way too closely to some personal places in between. They decided on a dark gray single-breasted, three-piece wool suit. Half the time it felt like Johnny and the tailor were speaking in their own special language about cuts, how it hung, vents…Jesse was lost but Johnny was happy, and that was all that mattered.

"You're going to look great," Johnny gushed. "Has Royce ever seen you in a suit?"

"Well, considering this is my first one…no," Jesse teased, and smiled at a happy Johnny. The man could light up a room when he smiled.

"He's going to be blown away. You'll rock that suit, I promise," Johnny said, and Jesse found he had a little less weighing him down compared to earlier. He had friends, he was a best man, and he had his first suit. All things he never thought would happen. Then add the man who meant everything to him, and his world was just about perfect. If only Jerry and his men would leave town, then it would be.

"How could I not look amazing with you overseeing everything? Now we need to get back to the diner before the guys send out a search party for us." Jesse laughed.

"Okay," Johnny said and the two headed for the door.

As they walked they discussed all the things a best man was responsible for, considering Jesse had no idea what it entailed. Thankfully, both he and Royce were in this together because Jesse had never been close enough to anyone to be considered their best man. Johnny was still talking about flowers and colors when Jesse noticed an older-model van with darkly tinted windows drive by for the second time. Johnny was oblivious to the possible danger. Either that, or Jesse was overly sensitive to changes around him. Jesse scanned the area in search of any one of the Sentinels who should be watching over him, and found Coop on the opposite side of the street, talking on his phone and watching the van like a hawk.

As they approached the diner, Jesse noticed two black SUVs were parked along the side of the road and one police vehicle was in the process of pulling over the van.

"Wow. I wonder what that guy did wrong to get Officer Bo's attention and why are there Sentinels here?" Johnny asked, watching Jesse closely. "Wait, is something wrong, Jesse? Are those the men who keep following you, your family?"

"I'm not sure. The van's driven down the street three times since we left the men's store. They're just being careful." Jesse was pretty sure it was Jerry or the last two of his men, but he didn't want to worry Johnny and ruin their day.

"Let's get into the diner. I'm so sorry you have to go through all of this," Johnny said as he sped up into an almost jog.

Jesse went with him and made sure to keep his body in a position to block any view of Johnny from the van. The last thing Jesse wanted was to have another person hurt because of his past.

When they opened the door, Royce and Gabe were already coming their way.

"We just saw the police and were coming to get you two. What's happened?" Royce asked while scanning the street. "Who's in the van?"

"Not sure but they've driven around the block three times so far. I guess it raised Coop's suspicions and he called in the troops," Jesse explained.

The four watched along with everyone else in the diner as two of Jerry's men were pulled from the van. Jesse hung his head in shame. *They'll never give up, it was only a dream that I could live in peace.* Solid arms wrapped around him, giving Jesse the strength to open his eyes and look down into a pair troubled green ones. Royce didn't say a word, for which Jesse was grateful; he just held him, lending Jesse his strength.

"You don't be worrying about those evil men, Jesse." A soft voice came from behind him. Royce released him, allowing Jesse to turn around to be met by two older men. Both had to be in their eighties, one with a cane and the other with a walker. Jesse had seen the pair in the diner every afternoon since he'd started working here. "My husband and I are too old to give those men a run for their money, but we have strappin' children that want to pitch in." Children. Jesse had often dreamed of adoption when he was a child, hoping his parents would send him away to be raised by anyone else.

Jesse stood in shock. These men wanted to help protect him, even though they really didn't know him. It was humbling.

Three middle-aged men stepped forward and shook Jesse's hand. "We haven't had the opportunity to introduce ourselves but Royce knows us well." The tallest of the three spoke: "I'm Bill and these are my brothers James and Chad. We'd be happy to volunteer to help in any way possible. We have a few hands on the ranch as well, who would like to help search for any of those bastards left. Nobody messes with the people in our town."

"Language, young man," one of the older men scolded. Jesse laughed, seeing how contrite Bill was.

"Sorry, Pa."

Before Jesse had a chance to say anything Royce stepped in. "Thank you, guys. We appreciate any help you can offer."

"Yes, thank you. I'm honored you want to help us," Jesse said. "Please stay safe though—they have no issue with using weapons and I don't think they're worried about anyone getting in their way any longer," he explained.

"Don't worry. We live in Texas. I'd say about eighty percent of the people standing in this here diner are armed," Bill said. To prove the point several people in the diner produced various handguns; even old Ms. Chan, who ran the local knitting club, pulled out a bedazzled .380 caliber gun from her flowered handbag. "And all of ours are legal. I doubt they can say the same."

"Let's get going, babe, that's enough for one day," Royce suggested, but Jesse could tell there was something bothering his partner. *Maybe he's finally getting sick of all this bullshit going on around him.* Jesse's heart plummeted like lead, and a sick feeling filled his stomach as he searched Royce's eyes for answers. Royce simply looked as concerned as Jesse imagined he himself was appearing right about now.

First he had to do something he dreaded doing. "I'm sorry, Gabe and Johnny, but I don't think I can be one of your best men. I don't want anything to happen at your wedding." Jesse couldn't risk anyone getting hurt at his friend's wedding.

Suddenly his arms were full of a distraught Johnny. "No, you're my best man, period. The wedding is months off and everything will be cleared up by then."

"I don't want to risk you." Jesse tried again but Johnny wouldn't hear it. He simply gave him a watery smile and followed Gabe to the door without replying.

"Let's go home, honey," Royce said. "The car's out back."

"Okay." Jesse agreed. By now the police were gone, taking Jerry's men with them. He knew he'd have to go to the police station eventually but would put it off until morning. Royce led him out the back door and into the passenger seat of their car. He felt numb. *Have I finally snapped?* After all the years of being hunted, the only safe place he'd ever had was no longer safe and the man he loved might be having second thoughts. Numb was the best way to describe it.

"Jesse…Jesse, honey, we're home." He looked out the window and was shocked to see they were inside their garage. He'd missed the entire drive from the diner. He got out of the car but stood rooted to the spot.

There, stored in the second half of the garage, sat his Harley. He hadn't ridden her in weeks. Jesse thought he should take her out for a ride. Her chrome gleamed in the sunlight coming in through the open garage door and her black paint shined. She was a beauty and Jesse had worked for years to buy her. Typically, before that, he went from town to town by bus. She gave him freedom, and right now if he were a decent person he would be hopping on her and taking the danger away from Brighton.

"Jesse?" Royce was at his side while he stood there and stared at his bike. "Tell me what you're thinking baby, please?"

Jesse thought for a long moment… *Hell no, I can't tell him that.* It didn't seem right to lay that worry on Royce on top of everything else, and still healing from being shot. "I'm okay." He hated lying to Royce but he had to protect him even if it was only from Jesse's own thoughts and fears.

"Bullshit," Royce growled. "If you don't want to talk about it, say that, but don't lie to me, never lie to me. Are you leaving me?"

"I should. It's for the best," Jesse answered, never once looking Royce in the eyes.

"But I love you. I'll protect you," Royce swore.

"You won't be enough. They'll hurt people to get to me." Jesse realized too late what he'd said, but before he could explain Royce took over.

"My love and protection isn't enough. If you're going to run every time life gets tough, then go, I won't stop you." Royce stormed into the house, leaving Jesse alone with his thoughts. He took a single step to follow Royce and explain, but stopped himself and with a deep sigh, turned around and walked toward his bike.

***

Royce heard the deep rumbling and knew his hopes that they could work this out had disappeared. The roar of Jesse's bike as it pulled out of the driveway and away from their house felt like a stab to his chest. Was it still "their" house? Was he coming back? Was he safe? Royce didn't have the answers and a sick feeling began to spread through his body. Jesse had left him. *Maybe I shouldn't have been so hard on him.* But Jesse was keeping things from him and Royce was frustrated. He'd spent the last few weeks afraid Jesse would be hurt or leave. *Well, he left.*

The pain was starting to set in. *Jesse left.* The realization hit home like a sledgehammer. *He left me.* Royce couldn't understand why Jesse hadn't taken his things with him. *Maybe he's coming back?* Royce didn't know what to think. He never thought Jesse would just take off like this because they'd always found it easy to talk things out up until now.

Royce wandered through his empty house room by room...rooms he'd hoped and prayed would be filled with children someday. He'd always dreamt of giving children with special needs a good home and viewed adoption as the option for him. But when Daniel had died, so had that dream, until Jesse came along. Now his pain was becoming intense, and Royce knew unless you'd suffered through the loss of the person you love, there was no way of properly describing it. But the closest he could imagine was paralyzing, painful emptiness creeping into his heart and soul.

Should he go look for him or wait here? What would he do if Jesse didn't come back? That one thought alone kept him pacing the floors. He stopped by the kitchen and grabbed himself a beer before continuing on with his silent vigil. The more he thought about everything that had happened, the more worked up he got. Hell, he'd already lost one man he'd loved. Royce couldn't help but wonder how he'd pissed off fate so badly that this was happening to him again.

Hours crawled by and Royce sat waiting. At two in the morning he surrendered to the fact that Jesse wasn't likely to be coming back. He'd been gone over twelve hours. Royce had already called Dante, one of the leaders of the Sentinels, to let him know Jesse had left. That had been hours ago, and he wondered if they were still out looking for him. Royce would still pay to have Jesse safe whether it was with or without Royce at his side.

He walked slowly to their bedroom, taking his shirt off and dropping it on the floor in the hallway, not caring where it landed. He continued on, leaving his pants at the bedroom door, boxers at the foot of the bed. By the time he crawled up onto the mattress, he couldn't hold back his sorrow and loss any longer. The last time he'd cried was at Daniel's graveside. Royce had thought he'd be impervious to that kind of pain again, but he'd been sorely mistaken.

Royce laid his sore head down, praying sleep would take him away into blissful nothingness. He hoped against all odds that this had all just been some sort of cruel nightmare and he would wake up at any moment with Jesse in his arms. But all the while knowing full well his reality had changed yet again and his future was uncertain.

Royce awoke hours later. He hadn't even realized he'd fallen asleep and had no idea what woke him, but something was different. He slowly opened his eyes; the room was dark but he could make out the outline of a large figure standing in the doorway. There was just enough light coming down the hallway to confirm that it was indeed Jesse. Royce sat up in bed, conflicting emotions running rampant through his mind and heart. He was overjoyed that Jesse came back but he felt betrayed at being left in the first place. Those two emotions alone kept him on the bed, silent. If he came back for his things, Royce wasn't about to beg. No matter how much he wanted Jesse to stay, the man had to want to stay first.

Jesse took a few tentative steps into the room. "Hi."

"Hello, Jesse." Royce's voice came out harsher then he'd intended, but he was tired of being left behind. First Daniel, though not of his own accord, then Jesse, who'd left willingly.

"May I come in?" Jesse asked.

Royce ached to cross the room and wrap his arms around Jesse but he stood his ground. If Jesse ran every time things got tough, this wasn't going to work. He loved Jesse completely, but that was the one thing Royce wouldn't be able to live with.

"Maybe we should talk out in the living room," Royce suggested as he reached for his sleeping pants because he didn't want to have to face this conversation naked.

"O-okay," Jesse stuttered and for the first time Royce noticed just how nervous Jesse really was.

Royce slipped on his pants and followed Jesse to the living room. He prepared himself as best he could for whichever way this turned out, but knew full well he'd be devastated if Jesse left again. Jesse turned on the lamps before Royce had the chance, so Royce went ahead and sat in one of the single chairs. He purposely stayed away from the couch because he wasn't confident what he'd do if Jesse sat beside him. The overpowering need to take the man into his arms was getting progressively harder to fight.

Jesse sat on the couch wringing his hands and refusing to look Royce in the eyes. "Royce, I-I'm sorry."

Royce wasn't actually sure which aspect Jesse was apologizing for, so he decided to ask. "You're sorry for what exactly: keeping things from me, not trusting me, leaving me? Or perhaps you intend to leave again, because I can't live with that. Always wondering if you'll take off when things get tough, leaving me alone again."

Jesse looked down at his hands; they were shaking. "I don't want anything to happen to you or anyone else. But I'm too damn selfish. I can't leave you, I love you. I should go and take all this trouble with me, but I can't."

Royce wanted to run over to the couch and hold Jesse, but they had too much to talk about before that happened. "Do you plan on leav...leaving me again?" Even saying the word caused Royce's heart to skip a beat.

"No...no, I'm not going anywhere unless you are and then I'm going with you," Jesse assured him.

"I need to be able to trust you. When you left you have no idea what that did to me." Though Jesse was back and said he wanted to stay with him, Royce's fear of being abandoned was high on his list of concerns

"I know I've damaged the trust we've built but I want a chance to repair it. Please give me that chance. I was so afraid of you being hurt by my family, I couldn't think of any other way of protecting you and Brighton from them. I was wrong. I couldn't even make it past the town line."

"Where have you been all this time?" Royce asked

"Willow Park. That's as far as I could go without you," Jesse answered. His eyes were red, with dark circles underneath, and his shoulders were slumped forward.

"Was a Sentinel with you? Were you safe?" Royce asked.

"Of course I was safe. You called them in when I left, didn't you?" Jesse asked but Royce remained silent. "After I'd hurt you so badly you still were concerned for my safety."

"Were you really going to leave me?" Royce had to know if there had been a chance.

"No, I just needed time to think clearly," Jesse admitted.

"And what have you decided to do about your family?" Royce asked, equally hopeful and afraid of the answer.

"That I make my stand here with you and the town of Brighton. I'm done running. I want to spend my life with you. I just need you to give me that chance. I'm sorry I left. I was sorry the moment I pulled out of the driveway. I know I hurt you and it's killing me to be this far away from you right now." Jesse's voice wavered. Royce could see the tears in Jesse's eyes and he couldn't stay back any longer.

Royce got up from his chair, went to Jesse, and held him in his arms "We'll work this all out, baby. I love you. It just kills me to think of you ever leaving again."

"No…I'm not going anywhere, I promise." Jesse's eyes were big, begging Royce to believe him.

"I believe you, love."

"You do?"

"Yes, Jesse, I do." Royce honestly did believe Jesse. If he were going to leave, he would have kept going tonight and never returned.

"God, I love you. I was so afraid you wouldn't want me back after I'd left," Jesse spoke softly before burying his face in Royce's chest.

"Just don't make a habit of it," Royce teased, wanting to lighten the mood. "Now I think it's past time for you to tell me everything that's been going through that beautiful mind of yours."

The two sat, holding one another tightly on the couch and talking until dawn broke through the living room windows and bathed them in light. They'd worked through their fears and hopes for the future, allowing Royce to finally be able to breathe again. Hours later they fell asleep bundled up together and still on the couch, neither willing to separate long enough to walk to their bed.

Chapter Seven

The pain was finally letting up as Royce pulled that damn giant rubber band for what felt like the thousandth time in the past few weeks, only now there were small weights on either end. He had to admit physiotherapy was finally paying off and Royce was regaining his strength. His movements were still jerky and he could only bring his arm out fifty degrees from his body, but it was an improvement. It had been five days since the incident that led to Jesse leaving. The two had talked more in those few days than they had ever before. It seemed to Royce that Jesse had released his demons that night and finally lowered his guard and let Royce in completely.

"Royce, can I talk to you for a minute please?" Miss Girard asked.

"Sure, what's up?" Royce responded as he set his equipment down.

"I know you and Jesse have been having a bit of trouble with his family and…" Miss Girard took a deep breath before continuing. "The other day a man came in here asking about you. Of course I told him that I didn't know if you were a patient and that I couldn't discuss anyone due to our confidentiality policy. But I could tell he didn't believe me. He handed me his card, asking me to give it to you." She handed over a matte black card with silver writing: Matthew Whitton, a phone number, and nothing else.

"Did he say what he wanted?" Royce asked, his mind racing.

"No, he just handed me the card and left," she responded, with worry laced through her voice. "I thought he might be one of Jesse's cousin's men but he didn't give me the heebie-jeebies."

"What did he look like?" Royce asked, hoping to at least have a chance of spotting him before the guy randomly popped up in front of him.

"He was short and slim with dark brown hair. Oh and he had the most interesting eyes, one was green and the other one hazel," Miss Girard replied.

Royce quickly rifled through what he knew about Jerry and his men, but none of them filled that description, and he doubted they would have left a card. Maybe it was unrelated, but Royce doubted he was that lucky.

"Thank you, Miss Girard. I'll find out what he wants. I'm sorry he came here and bothered you."

"It's not your fault, Royce." Miss Girard looked concerned but didn't argue further and went back to help another patient. Royce walked back to the locker room and grabbed his cell phone but instead of calling Mr. Whitton he called Shannon.

His call was answered on the first ring. "What's wrong?" She sounded ready to bolt over and Royce liked her even more for it.

"Everything's okay, but we have a new player on the field. He came into physio looking for me, and he left his card. I'm not sure if it's related to Jesse, but what are the odds some random stranger shows up when Jerry's terrorizing us?"

"I agree. The odds are slim it's not somehow related. What's the name on the card? I'll run a few checks," Shannon asked.

"That's what I was hoping you'd say. His name is Matthew Whitton," Royce replied and provided Shannon with the phone number on the card.

"On it. I'll call when I have any information." With that she hung up. Direct and to the point, that was Shannon.

Next he called Vincent, a former Navy Seal now working as a Sentinel, to check on Jesse.

Again his call was answered on the first ring. "Vincent here."

"Hey, Vincent. How's Jesse?" Royce asked.

"Good, he makes a mean fried chicken. The man's a wizard."

"I'm glad you're enjoying your time at the diner." Royce laughed. "We may have another problem." Royce went ahead and told him about the new arrival in town and his description, just in case he showed up at the diner.

After he hung up Royce went to have a hot shower to soothe his aching muscles. *Another month and hopefully I'll be able to put this all behind me and get back to work.* But on the flip side, Royce knew if he'd been working now he'd not be available for Jesse during this difficult time. So in the end it turned out to be in Royce's favor. He and Jesse knew it was only a matter of time before Jerry and any remaining men would try again. He just hoped they were ready.

One question that kept running through Royce's mind was, why would Matthew Whitton come here looking for him? Obviously, if he knew where Royce had physio then it stood to reason he knew where Jesse and he lived. Why not go there?

***

Jesse had settled even further into his new life now that his decision had been made. When he thought back to the hours he spent sitting in Willow Park and how close he'd come to losing everything because of his own fear, he was even more thankful Royce had understood and forgiven him. He no longer had that familiar anxious feeling running through his body. Oh, he was still concerned about what his cousin would do next, but that jittery feeling that seemed to always be just under the surface was gone. He'd settled, made his choice, and now waited for Jerry's next move.

Jesse still couldn't understand why Jerry was even bothering with him. His cousin literally hated everything about Jesse, so he figured it wouldn't be worth Jerry's effort to come after him. But here he was, in Brighton, still behaving like an asshole, the same way he had when Jesse was home. The man would never leave him in peace. The one thing he didn't have was an answer for why. His recent actions seemed a bit extreme, even for Jerry.

Jesse flipped the steaks on the grill and took a swig of his beer. The sunset was a mosaic of oranges and reds, and it filled Jesse with hope for a future where he'd spend as many evenings as possible just like this. It was all so very normal and exactly what Jesse had always wanted.

"Hey, babe, how are the steaks coming?" Royce asked as he brought out the salad and placed it on the table. The back deck on their house was big enough to hold a barbecue, table and chairs, and a few loungers. This was just one of the many things he'd never had a chance to enjoy before in his life, lounging and enjoying barbecue steaks at his home. He now had a home with the man he loved, a job, and a future. Jesse would fight until his last breath to protect this.

"They're almost ready, babe. How's everything else? Do you need any help?" Jesse asked.

"No, everything's ready to go when you are." Royce spoke as he came over and wrapped his arms around Jesse from behind. "Love you."

"Love you too, Royce," Jesse replied, and he felt every word down to his soul. He would be forever grateful to whatever hand had led him to Brighton. There had to be some divine intervention involved.

As he stood there safe in Royce's arms, he remembered his grandpa telling him that one day he'd get all the wonderful things in life he deserved. Now he knew his beloved grandpa was right because he had everything he'd ever wanted right here in Royce's arms.

"Sweetheart, there something we need to discuss," Royce said.

In an instant his calm vanished, replaced by worry yet again.

"Easy, Jesse. It's not that bad. I just need to know if you recognize the name Matthew Whitton."

Jesse froze. He hadn't heard that name in over fifteen years. "How do you know him?"

"He came looking for me, left his card. I take it you know him." Royce's voice was now laced with worry. "Did he hurt you?"

"No…no, he was my only friend back before grandpa died. I've told you my grandpa was the one who protected me as best he could, but after he died it all changed. Matthew's grandpa was good friends with mine, so Matthew and I would play together. He was the only kid allowed to have anything to do with me. Shortly after my grandpa's funeral Matthew's entire family moved away and I never saw him again. Why would he be here and looking for you?" Jesse asked while he flipped the steak, his mind racing to come up with any reason Matthew would be here and wanting to speak with Royce. *How did Matthew find me?*

"I'm not sure, love. Could it be someone with the same name?" He knew Royce was grasping at straws but it was in Royce's nature to try to find the bright side of any situation.

"Maybe…wait. Matthew had very distinctive eyes. One was green and the other hazel." Jesse thought that would be the best way to identify him. In all his years on the road Jesse had never seen anyone else with two different colored eyes.

"That's him. Miss Girard mentioned his eyes. I've called Shannon already to have a look into his background and any possible reason for him to be here, before I call him myself."

"But why would he come to you and not me?" Jesse asked.

"That's just one of the questions I have for him, babe. Along with why he's here now, of all times, and what the hell does he want?"

"Do you think he has anything to do with Jerry?" Jesse asked, almost afraid of the answer.

"We'll find out, Jesse. Try not to worry too much about it," Royce replied.

"He couldn't be with Jerry because he hated my cousin. Well, he and his grandpa hated my parents as well. I realized when I was older that they knew, they knew what my parents were doing to me. But the one and only time CPS came out, the other adult friends of my parents had painted me as such a problem child that I was never even interviewed. Matthew was the first person I told that I liked boys and not girls. I was young and had no idea what that meant. I thought it was normal until my parents figured it out and I was labeled a deviant, a freak."

"You are neither of those two things. You know that, right, love?" Royce asked as he squeezed Jesse tighter.

"I do now, but I still have my moments when I forget that I'm free of the world I grew up in." Jesse still feared he'd wake up some morning and find himself on another park bench.

"And speaking of that freedom, how about we go celebrate this weekend with dinner and dancing?" Royce asked.

"Celebrate what?" Jesse asked, but it was the second part of Royce's sentence that excited and worried him.

"Your decision to make a stand here with me. I'll contact a few of our friends to come and join us at Lucky's. We'll eat and dance with the people who are closest to us and we'll bring the Sentinels along as well. They deserve a thank you for everything they've done for us so far," Royce explained as Jesse plated the steak. "I love you so much, Jesse, and I can't wait until we start to grow our family. There's a lot of special kids out there who need good homes."

Jesse's heart would always skip a beat whenever he heard Royce speak of their future family. They both agreed that adoption was the way they'd make that happen. There were so many kids stuck in the system because they weren't babies anymore or they had a physical disability that adoptive parents didn't feel they could deal with.

Jesse and Royce didn't care about age or ability. They simply wanted to give children a home. A safe home, like the ones Jesse had dreamt of every night when he was a child living in his own hell. Knowing that Royce wanted the exact same thing with Jesse made that one last piece of his broken heart fall back into place. He finally felt whole again.

"We have so much room in our house we could take in at least five children." Jesse knew he was amped up by the prospect of being a daddy.

"Hold on, Mr. Excited. One child at a time and we'll decide as we go how many we'll bring into our family," Royce stated with a warm smile.

"Yes, sir," Jesse teased, but the heat burning in Royce's eyes only intrigued him more. "Do you like it when I call you sir, Royce?" Jesse asked as he placed the plate of steak on the table.

"God yes, but I don't need it. We do everything at your pace. It's about what you find comfortable."

Honestly, that was one request he'd be all too happy to fulfill. Royce's dominant nature was one of the many things that attracted Jesse. He could always let his guard down, showing his true self in front of Royce, and he knew he was completely safe. Jesse didn't foresee a problem. Every time he'd said the word up until now it had sent a thrill through his body. What impressed Jesse the most was that Royce was suppressing his own dominant nature, giving Jesse the time he needed to handle his family when he knew Royce wanted to take over and make the danger go away. *I love that man.*

"How do you always know when I need your reassurance?" Jesse asked.

"Well. I wouldn't be much of a boyfriend if I didn't know what my lover needed. I would do anything for you, love. You mean everything to me."

Jesse wrapped his arms around Royce, the only person in the world who truly knew Jesse and loved him even more because of it. "We should eat before it gets cold."

"With the heat we've been having I'm positive the steaks are safe. It's the salad we should be worrying about," Royce said, but let

Jesse go and pulled out a chair for Jesse to sit down before seating himself.

"So, how about the dinner and dancing? You interested, Jesse?" Royce asked before cutting his steak and taking a bite, moaning as he chewed. "So good."

"I'd love to, I really would, but I don't know how to dance. I never had the chance to learn." Jesse ducked his head and took a big bite of salad. He knew Royce was waiting for him to look up.

"Look at me, Jesse." He immediately looked up into those beautiful green eyes. "Don't be embarrassed. There are lots of people who don't know how to dance and many more who shouldn't. I'll teach you how, and we'll put it off a couple weeks until you feel more comfortable. You'll be fine, I promise."

"I don't want to embarrass you in front of your friends," Jesse admitted.

"You could never embarrass me, Jesse, ever, and they're *our* friends. Now let's finish dinner because your lessons start tonight," Royce said and then dug into his steak.

Jesse was so excited he doubted he could wipe the smile off his face. He was going dancing with his lover.

***

A few hours later and Royce figured it was a fifty/fifty chance his baby toe was broken, but he refused to limp in front of Jesse. This was only his first dance lesson after all, and of course he wasn't going to be perfect. His toe had a differing opinion. They would turn and attempt a few steps, all the while desperately trying to keep Jesse off his toes without much luck. They had been laughing so hard they'd ended up on the floor in tears. Royce's injured arm still tucked safely against his chest, even though his sling had been removed on his last doctor's visit, he was still careful. He laughed long and hard; he hadn't felt this happy or at peace in a long time. Jesse had given him back so many things he'd thought he'd lost forever.

Royce knew he would love Daniel the rest of his life, but he also knew he had plenty of love left to give. Daniel wouldn't have wanted him to stop living. In fact, he would have approved of Jesse.

Royce began to laugh harder and Jesse noticed the change. "Now that laughing can't all be from my two enormous left feet. Wanna share?"

He didn't want to keep anything from Jesse, but wondered if it would make him sad knowing he'd been thinking about Daniel. He took a deep breath and pushed forward. "Daniel."

"Daniel couldn't dance either?" Jesse asked. There was no change in his happy tone and the smile never wavered from his face.

"No, he could dance, but that's not what was on my mind. I think that Daniel would have approved of you."

The emotions that played across Jesse's face were easy to follow: shock, confusion, acceptance, happiness, and then tears. "Daniel would have approved of me?"

"Yes, I believe he would have. He was an amazing man and so are you. I'm very blessed." The moment he said the words he knew for the first time in over three years it was true. He'd been blessed to have the love of his husband before he died, and now he had Jesse and a second chance at a future.

"Can you tell me more about him, or is that not okay?" Jesse asked.

"Of course we can and I don't mind talking about Daniel. Actually I was kind of concerned you might never want to discuss him," Royce said.

"He's part of you and you love him. Of course I want to know more about Daniel. I know you love me. You are the one person that I'm completely safe with, and I have no fear you'll ever hurt me physically or emotionally," Jesse explained.

"I could never intentionally hurt you, babe," Royce stated as he pulled Jesse closer to him, both still lying on the hardwood in the living room. Jesse laid his head on Royce's chest to listen as he told the story of how two young boys fell in love and married in Brighton all those years ago. They relived the time they first met in high school, Daniel with his thick eyeglasses and Royce with braces, they were instant friends. They discovered girls together and neither of them could figure out what all the fuss was about. It wasn't until eleventh grade that they each realized they preferred boys to girls, but most importantly they were attracted to each other. When the story reached its inevitable tragic end, Jesse gathered Royce into his arms and held him close.

"He loved you so much, Royce. I'm so sorry that happened to the two of you," Jesse said.

"Thank you, baby. I know it was years ago but sometimes it still feels like yesterday. I don't ever want you to think that I compare the two of you, or that I somehow love you less because I don't. You mean the world to me. You're my everything," Royce explained.

Tears filled Jesse's eyes. "I know because you're the same for me. I've been given so much since coming to Brighton. I've been blessed as well."

Royce raised his good hand and, reaching behind Jesse's neck, carded his fingers through his thick hair, and pulled his soft lips closer to his own. The first brush sent Royce flying; it never ceased to amaze Royce the effect Jesse had on him. The need and excitement rushed through his body and straight to his groin. Their kiss turned insistent, demanding, as Royce took control and rolled Jesse onto his back.

"Clothes off, love," Royce said and began to unbutton Jesse's shirt.

"May I take your clothes off first?" Jesse asked in a soft voice that sent a thrill through Royce's body.

"Yes, Jesse, you may." Royce stood and helped Jesse to his feet.

Jesse gently unbuttoned and removed his shirt. He lowered his head and gently kissed the healed bullet wound on Royce's shoulder. "Please don't ever scare me like that ever again, Royce. I couldn't…sur…"

"Oh baby, I'm okay. I'm healing, and I'll do my best to stay safe."

"Promise."

"Promise, love," Royce agreed. He would take better care of himself. The last few years he'd never bothered worrying about the future or his health. He just didn't care. Now he had a whole new outlook, and he intended to stick around to enjoy his new life and love.

Chapter Eight

Matthew Whitton sat in a nearby tree watching as the lights went out in Jesse's house. He had to find a way to get close enough to have a conversation without being shot for his troubles. He wasn't an idiot. He'd seen the bodyguards and knew Jerry was in town with his crew. Hell, that's why he was here after all, to get near Jesse, but for entirely different reasons.

He had to protect his old friend and stop Jerry before he had a chance to follow through on his threats. Matthew knew the reason Jerry and the rest of Jesse's "family" wanted him to disappear. Matthew would never allow that to happen. He had the proof; all he needed was Jesse and then they could go to the authorities.

By the time Matthew knew he wasn't alone it was already too late. A large arm wrapped around his throat and a gun pressed to the side of his head. God, he was bad at this stealthy shit. Give him a computer and internet access and he'd show you just how competent he was; but physically, not so much. He worked out but his two left feet and lack of coordination sometimes made him look like a bumbling idiot instead of the respected computer genius he was.

"Where are your weapons?" a deep voice whispered into his ear. Matthew knew he should be scared out of his mind, and on some level he was, but that deep, gruff voice and the hard-muscled body at his back was a bit distracting. *I've lost my mind.* "Weapons?" the man asked again, adding more pressure around his neck. Matthew knew he was going to be bruised, but he figured that was the least of his concerns. This could be one of Jerry's men or one of the Sentinels; either choice would likely get him hurt. His own fear ramped up by the second as the arm kept tightening.

"No weapons," Matthew gasped. He knew if he ever carried a weapon odds were good he'd hurt himself first, before anyone else had a chance.

The big man didn't seem to believe him as he holstered his own weapon and began searching Matthew, never once removing his arm from around his neck. Matthew was holding on to the branch for dear life, knowing all too well how easily he could fall. He'd never been a good climber, but he had to keep tabs on Jesse somehow without getting close.

When the man seemed satisfied Matthew was unarmed, he loosened his grip on Matthew's throat, but only slightly. "Why are you here?"

"To visit an old friend."

"By hiding in a tree?"

"Better than being shot for my troubles by either side of this messed-up situation. I may be clumsy but I'm not stupid," Matthew admitted easily. He figured he was already screwed; he just needed to know which group had him. He prayed it wasn't Jerry's, as he still hadn't seen who the person was behind him. "Um…which side are you on?"

"You're part of Jerry's crew, so don't try to act all innocent now that you're caught." Jerry's crew, the thought of having anything to do with Jerry disgusted him.

"I have nothing to do with that scumbag! He can rot in hell for all I care." *Shit!* He'd let his mouth run away from him again, this could still be one of Jerry's men trying to trick him.

"What do you want with Jesse and Royce?" Instead of answering Matthew's original question, the heavily muscled man demanded answers of his own.

Even though he was scared out of his mind by now, Matthew couldn't divulge the truth to anyone but Jesse. "I need to speak with Jesse."

"Why?"

"That's between me and Jesse."

The arm around his throat tightened yet again. "Not anymore. I'm here to make sure you won't be getting anywhere near them. My friends are on their way, and I can assure you we'll get it out of you."

"Torture, great. Here I thought you were the good guys." Matthew was desperately trying to think of a way out of this.

The man seemed to loosen his hold around Matthew's throat. "Good guys?"

"Yeah, Sentinels. The ones protecting Jesse. Obviously you're one of Jerry's men. I've been watching you guys long enough to know you'd stoop to anything to get what you want."

"I'm not one of those assholes. How do you know the Sentinels?"

"My mind isn't as clumsy as my body, I can assure you." And, as if to prove his point, Matthew lost his hold on the branch and slipped through his captor's arms and off the limb. At the last second he managed to grab another smaller branch and was barely hanging on. His attacker was now trying to hold on to him, saving Matthew from falling roughly twenty feet to the ground.

"Hold on. I've got you." The man scrambled to reach Matthew's hand, but he was already slipping. *This is going to hurt.* He looked up just before he lost his grip. His eyes locked with the deep blue ones above him as his nails scraped through the bark. The last thing he saw before everything went dark were those blue eyes filled with terror.

***

"You don't have to go in, I can bring you a picture," Royce suggested. "You can identify him by a picture. It's safer."

"If it's Matthew, he's my friend and for god sakes he's unconscious. What can he do to me?" Jesse still couldn't believe one of the Sentinels had hurt his friend, or that Matthew was watching his house in the first place.

Royce grumbled as he took Jesse's hand and walked into the hospital room. Coop and Spider stood guard, still not trusting the new arrival. On the bed lay a man who was the grown-up version of his old friend: freckles still covered his face, his brown hair was still shaggy. All he needed was for Matthew to open his uniquely colored eyes and the picture would be complete. A large bandage was wrapped around his head; he had bruises around his neck, and a cast on his foot and ankle as machines beeped around him.

"He's Matthew Whitton, my best friend when we were children," Jesse confirmed. "How is he?"

"He has a slight concussion from hitting the ground and a broken ankle," Spider explained. "They're keeping a close eye on him but he should recover."

Jesse looked straight at Coop because he knew the man was the one who "captured" his best friend. "How did Matthew get all the bruises around his neck and how did he fall?" He couldn't help but feel protective of the guy. When they were little Matthew had always protected him. Jesse realized this was a strange reaction to a man he hadn't seen in years, but Matthew had been his only friend for so long. "He's half the size of you, Coop."

"The bruises are from my restraining him and he fell because he lost his grip on the branch and I wasn't fast enough to grab him," Coop admitted. But for the first time there was no sign of his patented melt-your-pants-off grin that he flashed at everyone. Though it never worked on Jesse, he knew there had to be several broken hearts scattered across the world because of that man.

"I'm sorry, Coop. He used to protect me when we were little, so I feel as though I need to protect him now. Matthew has always been a bit clumsy. He could trip over air." Jesse felt bad for assuming they were from a fight. Hell, Matthew didn't look big enough to fight off anyone.

"He mentioned that, and I should have been more careful but I honestly thought he was one of Jerry's men. Then he mentioned you and needing to talk to you, but not wanting to get hurt by Jerry's men or us." Coop rubbed his large hand across his forehead. "I'm just sorry he was hurt."

"So that's why he approached me first," Royce said. "He was trying to avoid all the people watching over Jesse."

"Matthew has always been smart. I remember how he rewired my dad's truck so that every time he pushed on the brake the horn honked." Jesse smiled as he remembered one of the few good memories he had from his childhood. There weren't many. "Has he woken up yet?"

"The nurse has been coming in and waking him every two hours because of his concussion, but he hasn't stayed awake long enough to answer questions," Spider explained. "Coop will be staying with Matthew until we're sure he's no threat to you."

"He's my friend. I know he's not here to hurt me," Jesse assured the group.

"It's been a lot of years, baby. You don't know him anymore," Royce said.

"I know it's been years, but I just can't see him changing into what Jerry and his friends are. People would make fun of him every time he dropped something, or tease him about his different colored eyes, and he never defended himself. But if one person said anything derogatory to me, Matthew was all over them demanding an apology," Jesse said. "Matthew was never able to physically take on anyone, but he was smart and he always found a way to exact his revenge. He saved me by his reputation alone multiple times. Especially after he accessed one student's private information, and threatened to reveal what he'd found if the guy or his friends ever touched me again. He did that when he was nine. I can't imagine what he's capable of now. We were best friends up until Matthew's family moved out of state. I've always missed him. He'd been my only friend for a long time."

"If I was your best friend, then why didn't you ever write me back or return my calls?" Matthew asked from the bed, his voice groggy and pain filled.

Jesse went to Matthew's bedside. "You're going to be okay, Matthew, I promise." Jesse's eyes filled with tears as he looked into the eyes-- one hazel and one green eyes-- of the man who used to be just like a brother to him. "I never received any calls or letters."

"I wondered if your parents were keeping them from you, and then when I got old enough to come back on my own, you were already gone. I've been looking for you for a very long time, knucklehead." Matthew laughed softly, and Jesse smiled at the old nickname they had called each other. "Your nasty-ass parents were no help, but I'm nobody's fool. I watched them, and every time Jerry packed to leave I followed him. Sometimes, when I found you first, Jerry would show up within the same day. I never had a chance to get to you before you were gone again."

Jesse should have known his best friend would look for him. A small cough reminded Jesse he wasn't alone and he immediately turned to Royce. "I'm sorry, sweetheart. I'd like to introduce my friend Matthew Whitton. Matthew, I'd like you to meet my partner, Royce."

"Nice to meet you in person, Matthew," Royce said and took Matthew's outstretched hand.

"Sorry about the stalking, but you were my only safe way in. It's good to meet you, Royce," Matthew said.

"Why are you here, Matthew?" Jesse asked.

Matthew's eyes were drooping but the smile on his face was genuine. "I often thought I wouldn't catch up to you. I have so much to tell you." His eyes closed even farther and Jesse knew he'd have to wait until Matthew was completely conscious before he got all his answers.

"He needs to rest. He can continue this conversation later," Coop stated, and Matthew simply rolled his tired eyes.

"Still bossy I see. Don't try to give me that smile of yours again. It's wasted on me. Go find some other guy to melt to his knees. I may be gay, but you're not my type," Matthew announced, and Coop looked stunned. Jesse guessed Coop had never met anyone immune to his "charms" before.

Spider began laughing but covered it with a cough. Soon enough Matthew's eyes drifted closed and Jesse took a chair to sit beside his bed. Royce did the same. Jesse knew it would be a bit before Royce trusted Matthew but that was okay; he had his friend back.

"You believe he isn't a threat?" Royce asked. "He has nothing to do with Jerry?"

"Yes, he's not here to hurt me," Jesse replied.

"How can you be so sure?" Spider asked.

"I've been on the run for so long, trusting no one. I was forced to determine if someone was a threat within the first few minutes of meeting them. Matthew isn't a threat to me," Jesse assured everyone.

"We'll see," Royce said, and Jesse smiled at his overprotective partner. Jesse loved every bit of him and wouldn't change a thing about the man he was planning on spending the rest of his life with.

***

Royce wasn't about to leave Jesse alone with Matthew until he was sure the man was on the up and up. So when Shannon from the team showed up with new information, Royce had Jesse leave the room with everyone else to get the rundown. Royce knew he was being illogical because Matthew wasn't even conscious but he couldn't help it.

"Well, professionally Mr. Matthew Whitton is quite the accomplished computer specialist, created and sold his first start-up before turning eighteen. Occasionally works with our government, large corporations, and other countries such as England. Nothing dirty that I could find. His entire family was killed in a vehicle accident outside San Diego when Matthew was twenty. He was the only one to survive, though barely, and spent months in hospital recovering. He works freelance now and is financially solid. The worst I could find was a speeding ticket from four years ago," Shannon reported.

"So he's clean so far, but I want Coop to stay with him until we're one hundred percent sure he's not a ploy to get close to Jesse," Spider said.

"I agree," Royce stated, pulling Jesse closer to him. Royce knew he was being over protective but he couldn't help himself; this was his Jesse.

"Matthew isn't a threat to me but if it makes you feel better, Royce, I accept the need for Coop to stay with Matthew. Did anyone think to ask Coop what he wants?" Jesse asked.

"Do you mind, Coop?" Royce asked.

"Matthew doesn't seem to want me anywhere near him," Coop replied.

"Well, that's a first for most men you meet. Typically you'd be making plans to hook up by now. It'll do you some good to be around someone who isn't falling at your feet," Spider said. "But I won't force you to watch him, Coop, I can put Shannon on him until Dante and Vincent get back into town. Jake is still going to be shadowing Jesse."

"I'll stay with him. Lord knows he needs a keeper," Coop said, and Spider smiled.

"Thought so," Spider replied. Coop shook his head and walked back into Matthew's hospital room.

Shannon left with promises of keeping in touch and Spider followed Coop back into the room. Royce was definitely sticking around to get to the bottom of why Matthew was in Brighton. This may have started as a search for an old friend, but there was definitely more to this reunion now. If Royce was sure of anything, it was that.

Hours passed as they waited for Matthew to wake again. The door squeaked open and Ms. Lucas, a veteran nurse Royce had worked with in the ER, came in. She woke Matthew, checked his vitals, and administered more medication through his IV line. "How are you feeling, Mr. Whitton?"

Matthew watched her every move. "My head's a little fuzzy and my ankle is really sore. What did you put in my IV?"

"I've given you a painkiller that the doctor had ordered you receive every four hours, which should help soon. If you need anything, push the button on the call bell. I'll be back in a few hours to check on you."

"Thank you, ma'am."

"You're welcome, now get some rest," she ordered.

Nurse Lucas left the room with a friendly nod to Royce.

"So did my report come back clean?" Matthew asked, as Coop raised the head of the bed so that he could sit up. "Before my head gets any fuzzier let's get the basics out of the way. You checked me out, yes?"

"We had to know, Matthew." Jesse sounded unsure as he explained and Royce sensed he felt guilty that they did a background check. He wouldn't stand for that.

"You're essentially a stranger to us. We had to check your background. Jesse had nothing to do with it. It was all me," Royce said, taking all the responsibility for digging into Matthew's past.

"Good. At least we're even now. I had you and Sentinel checked out long ago." Matthew smiled wide and carefully adjusted his pillow. "Nice work in Columbia last November, by the way."

Spider's demeanor changed almost instantly. "What do you know of that mission?"

"Well firstly, I'm surprised you don't recognize my voice." Matthew smirked at Spider.

Spider's face cleared. "Mouthy? Shit, you were the hacker we worked with on that one. I should have known that voice. You got us in and out of the hellhole and directly to the hostages. Why didn't Shannon uncover that fact?"

"She undoubtedly found information about me working with the government, correct?"

"Yes."

"I've buried the specifics so far down it would take a hacker ten times more capable than myself to access it. Since one hasn't been born yet, I'm safe. Shannon is great, don't get me wrong. She's kick-ass amazing, but she wouldn't have even known where to begin looking. If certain people found out all the things I've done, my days would be numbered, and obviously I can't even defend myself. So it's best for me to hide certain aspects of my life."

"What was our call sign?" Spider asked, obviously wanting further confirmation.

"Drift," Matthew replied.

"Why?"

"Because there was so much cocaine involved," Matthew told him, "it could have been drifts of snow."

"Shit, it is you!" Coop yelled, causing Matthew to grab his head and everyone else to jump. "You saved mine and Dante's life on the way out of that hellhole."

"Yeah, yeah, the two of you didn't blow up, but my head still might, not to mention my ankle. Keep it down, okay?" Matthew groaned in pain.

"Not that I want to interrupt your reunion," Royce said, clearly frustrated, "but we need to know why he came to Brighton and why he's been following Jesse." It was important they get to the bottom of everything involving Jerry. "Does this have anything to do with Jerry and his family?"

"Unfortunately, it does," Matthew said, "and Jesse's life may be at stake."

Chapter Nine

Royce pulled Jesse closer and asked, "What do you mean his life is at stake? Why?"

"Because Jesse has the power to take them down."

"Me?" Jesse asked. "I've got nothing."

"Can we have more specifics and perhaps a little bit less cryptically?" Royce asked. His patience was wearing thin. He needed to know how to protect his lover and why this was happening in the first place.

"When my parents and grandpa were killed in the car accident, I had to go through all their private papers and wills," Matthew explained as he tried to move his foot and cried out in pain. Coop grabbed a pillow from a nearby chair and gently placed it under Matthew's broken ankle.

"We should leave you to rest, you're in pain," Jesse said. "I'm so sorry about your family, Matthew. They were always so kind to me." He reached out and took Matthew's hand.

"No. I've waited so long to find you I need to tell you. It's been years since the accident, and I still miss them every day," Matthew said. "Do you know they offered to adopt you from your parents, but they wouldn't let you go?" Matthew looked wistful when he explained how his parents loved Jesse and wanted to give him a good home.

"No, I never knew," Jesse answered. "I would have jumped at the chance."

"We would have loved to add you to our family. At least now I know why they said no. I was going through Grandpa's papers and found a copy of a will that wasn't his. It was your grandpa's, Jesse."

"Why would he have Grandpa's will?" Jesse asked.

"I believe it was to keep a copy of it safe from other members of your family. I'm sorry, Jesse, but I read the will, hoping it would give me some insight into what was going on," Matthew explained. He blushed, as if revealing this information risked their friendship.

"It's okay. I'm sure it has nothing to do with me. My parents, aunt, and uncle would have taken everything," Jesse said. He leaned a bit farther into Royce, as if needing comfort from the memories.

"Well, you're right and wrong. They did take over the homestead farm and land, but they're running it as trustees until the real beneficiary takes possession of it."

"Real beneficiary?" Jesse asked. "Who else would Grandpa have named?"

"You, Jesse. You're the only beneficiary of your grandpa's will," Matthew said. "He left everything to you."

Jesse tensed in Royce's arms, "Me? He left the homestead to me?" Jesse said, incredulous. "Why?"

"Sweetheart, from what you've told me about your grandpa, he loved you," Royce said. "He wanted to provide for you. That's why he would have left it to you." He rubbed Jesse's back, comforting him. All the while, his own anxiety was choking him.

"My parents must have been furious," Jesse said, before wrapping his arms around Royce. That Jesse sought comfort from him made Royce feel ten feet tall and trusted.

"This is where everything gets a little illegal," Matthew explained. "You see, your parents, aunt, and uncle have been running the farm and pocketing the proceeds, since your grandpa died when we were children. They knew once you turned twenty-five everything would revert to you. They'd be accountable for all the money they took, over and above the generous trustee income they were paid to maintain the property for you."

"But they never told me," Jesse said. He looked to be in shock.

"Of course not, they never intended for you to find out. They ran you off before you ever had a chance of knowing, but now that a new lawyer has taken over the trustee income, they have a problem. Apparently, Mr. Foster wants to meet with you since he's found a few discrepancies in the old lawyer's paperwork. I can't prove it yet, but I think the old lawyer was in on it with your family. I have all the paperwork with me to prove everything I've said."

"How do you know all of this?" Spider asked.

"Hello, hacker extraordinaire…plus old Mrs. Gideon worked as the secretary in that law office for over thirty-five years. She knew your grandpa and suspected something was going on when I approached her. This is why I've been trying to find you. As well as you being my friend, I had to protect you before they got to you. Jesse, you can't allow them to get away with this."

"But what can I do?" Jesse asked.

"You go see that new lawyer and take control of your inheritance," Spider said.

"But I don't want the land; it only holds bitter memories for me."

"There are several good farmers back there who'd be more than happy to buy it off you," Matthew stated firmly. "Apparently your parents have been illegally upping the rent on the land every year. It's a good chunk of land and your family doesn't deserve any of it. They're horrible people." Royce noticed Matthew was getting winded and knew it was time to let him rest.

"Oh my God. That's what Jerry was talking about when he said I didn't deserve the 'windfall' and I had to disappear permanently." Jesse curled into Royce.

"Don't worry, baby, they won't get a chance. We'll contact that lawyer and get this all figured out. We also need to call Chief Graham so he's on the same page," Royce said.

"I'll call Graham and I'll let the team know we'll be heading out of town soon. Jesse, where is the homestead?" Spider asked.

"Idaho, just outside of Boise. But what makes you think I'll be going anywhere near there? I've never wanted to return to the place where my hell started. I'm sorry, but I can't." Jesse let go of Royce, stood, and walked out the door.

"I'm taking him home; it's been a long, stressful day. We'll talk about this again once Jesse has had a chance to calm down and Matthew has a chance to recover," Royce stated before following Jesse out of Matthew's room. He would talk this over with Jesse and figure out the best way of dealing with this inheritance. If his love didn't want to return to Idaho, then no way were they going. But that still wouldn't stop Jerry or the rest of Jesse's family; they had to be held accountable for their actions before they had a chance to get near Jesse again.

***

Jesse sat in the hot water of the tub, still feeling numb as the steam rose in swirls around him. Royce was sitting in front of him, offering his strength as he washed Jesse's body. Jesse had no idea what he'd do without the man.

"It just…it just never ends. I'll never have any peace," Jesse stated in defeat.

"Yes you will. Remember, this is where we make our stand. I'll do whatever you decide but there'll be no more running, baby. You're safest here and I'm sure we can convince the new lawyer to come down here to discuss what you want to do."

"What do I do?" Jesse asked.

"Oh honey, that's your decision. You need to do what's right for you and I'll back up any decision you make," Royce promised before he lay back in the water and motioned for Jesse to join him. Jesse slid across the large tub and cuddled up to his beautiful partner, placing his head on Royce's uninjured shoulder, their bodies entwined together in comfort.

"I know I shouldn't be shocked by anything they've done, but to keep my inheritance from me? Christ, I'm twenty-nine now and Grandpa died when I was fourteen; that's fifteen years they've been stealing from me." Jesse sat up quickly. "The abuse picked up after Grandpa died; do you think that was payback for essentially being written out of the will?"

"I think they were always abusive assholes. Perhaps it gave them some sort of sick validation for their actions in their own minds, but if it hadn't been that, I'm sure they would have found another reason." Jesse had mentioned his parents had never spared the rod with him even before his grandpa's death. "I'm also sure that that cult they belong to is benefitting from this arrangement as well."

"Fringe church," Jesse huffed. He didn't believe any real church would behave the way they had.

"You say tomato…" Royce teased, and Jesse knew he was trying to lighten the mood a little for him.

"I still can't believe any of this is true, but why would Matthew lie? It would explain why they wouldn't let me go in peace. They can't afford for me to randomly show up, but if I'm found dead then they would be my only living relatives and able to claim the land."

"What's on the homestead?" Royce asked.

"Farmland mainly. I don't know how much land there is, but we were considered one of the largest cash crop farms in the area. They kept me out of the way of most things; they just didn't want me around. How could parents not want their child?" Jesse asked. The pain in his own voice was almost too much.

"I don't know, sweetheart, but I'll always want and need you. I could never go back to my life before you came into it, so you're stuck with me." Royce's voice was firm so as not to leave any doubt of how serious he truly was.

"I don't think 'stuck' is the right word, baby, but I'm keeping you anyway." Jesse laid his head back down and soaked in the love coming from Royce.

It was hard looking back at everything that had been done to him and knowing it was all because of money, plain and simple. Jesse had spent his life trying to figure out why his parents hated him and now that he had a possible explanation, he felt hollow. Money was the one and only reason for making his life hell.

"I never wanted to go back to Idaho, Royce. I don't think anything could make me, not even this," Jesse confessed.

"Then we'll stay here and have the lawyer come to Brighton," Royce suggested.

"I don't want the property," Jesse admitted.

"Then you can sell it like Matthew mentioned."

"But it's my grandpa's." How could he sell his grandpa's land?

"Honey, it's been yours for the past fifteen years, you just didn't know it," Royce explained. "Sit in front of me so I can wash your back."

Jesse moved smoothly through the water and sat between Royce's open legs. Royce's hard cock slid between Jesse's ass cheeks, the silky skin rubbing seductively as he leaned back against Royce. All the time his own cock throbbed with need at being so close to his naked lover. Royce slid his hand across Jesse's shoulders and began to rub with those magic fingers of his, massaging as he washed. Slowly, Jesse's stress began to fade away as he groaned with each squeeze. Though Royce was forced to use mainly his right hand due to his shoulder injury, the man could still melt Jesse like butter

"That's it, baby, just relax. We'll figure everything out," Royce whispered as Jesse leaned farther back. Every move was carefully choreographed so as not to hurt Royce.

"They would have adopted me. So many years wasted that I could have been happy just because of a will. I love my grandpa but I wish he had just left everything to my parents, aunt, and uncle. That's all the four of them ever wanted. No wonder Jerry wants me gone: he and his parents would lose control over the land."

"I think Matthew was right when he suggested selling the land. You could do whatever you want with the money," Royce advised.

"What if I want to give it all away to charity, LGBTQ charities directed at helping youths?" Jesse asked. He truly didn't want any of the money and could remember wishing there had been a safe place for him to go all those years ago.

"That would be a beautiful way to honor your grandpa."

"You think so?" Jesse asked.

"Yes I do. I'm so proud of you, sweetheart. But we'll give it some time after the sale of the land before you make any decisions, which will give us time to research various LGBTQ centers and charities," Royce suggested.

"You're going to help me?" Jesse asked as he turned in Royce's arms.

"I'm at your side every step of the way, baby. As long as you want me to be."

"Forever. I want forever." Jesse wanted to spend this life and any others that they might be fortunate enough to have with Royce. He believed there was a higher power in this world and an afterlife. The way Jesse saw it, everyone was entitled to their own beliefs, and unlike his parents he would never force his views on anyone.

"So do I," Royce whispered, before covering Jesse's lips with his own. Jesse was always amazed by how soft Royce's lips were as they began to nibble across Jesse's jaw and down his neck. They were now facing each other, Royce's legs over top Jesse's, their chests touching, muscles straining to get closer as the kiss turned from gentle to demanding.

"I want you to make love to me," Royce said, stunning Jesse into silence. Royce had always been the top when they made love. Jesse had never thought to even ask because he typically preferred to be on the bottom, but on odd occasions he needed to feel as though he had the control. When everything was going to hell around them, Royce was still thinking of him above everything else. Royce wasn't a selfish lover. His love knew that Jesse needed to regain a bit of control after the day's events.

"Are you sure?" Jesse asked.

"Yes, baby. I want to feel you inside me this time," Royce murmured before he fisted both his and Jesse's cocks and began to pump. The feeling was exquisite, pleasure holding him on the edge with every stroke. "Are you okay with us changing it up, Jesse?"

"Yes. I need that tonight; how do you always know what I need?" Jesse asked.

"I've told you before, you mean everything to me." Royce began sucking up a dark mark on the side of Jesse's neck. *Oh, yes, mark me.*

Jesse had to stay in control; he wanted to make this amazing for his lover. "We need lube, sweetheart. I don't want to hurt you."

Royce leaned back, grabbed the bottle off the soap rack, and placed it in Jesse's shaky hands. This would be the first time he topped Royce; he realized it wouldn't happen often because they both preferred to make love the other way around, but he needed to feel that control tonight. Jesse's life had been filled with power struggles that always found him on the losing end. He'd never felt his own life was under his control, until he shared it with Royce. This was solid and secure, and Royce was his compass: no matter the storm, Jesse knew where home was.

Jesse raised Royce higher on top of his spread thighs, and Royce wound his legs around Jesse's body. They would make love face-to-face. He put a liberal amount of waterproof lube on his fingers and began loosening the muscles around Royce's hole. His love moaned out his approval. With utmost care he slid one finger up to the first knuckle, causing Royce to bear down, taking it in even farther. He was so tight.

"Yes, Jesse, more." Royce groaned his need and it was music to Jesse's ears. "Feels so good, baby."

A few minutes later he was able to insert a second finger. Jesse knew he was being cautious but he had to prepare Royce properly because he wasn't a small man. Small waves floated across the water in the tub in time with Royce's flexing hips. Soon a third joined in and Royce cried out in pleasure as Jesse rubbed his prostate mercilessly; he wanted Royce senseless with need when he entered him.

As soon as Jesse felt Royce was ready, Jesse pulled his fingers free; his own need was bearing down on him and he could no longer wait. He lifted Royce higher in the water, his hole directly above Jesse's hard cock. Slowly he lowered his lover, the combination of water and lube easing the way. The silky tight heat welcomed him in and he slowly bottomed out inside Royce. His face was a mixture of surprise and pleasure, as if he'd never felt anything like it before. *Wait, has Royce ever bottomed before?*

"So full," Royce moaned out.

"Royce, have you ever done this before?" Jesse asked.

Royce brought their faces together, beads of sweat sliding down the sides of their faces. "Only you, Jesse, only you. Now move, I need you to move." Royce moaned as he flexed his hips.

"I'll give you what you need." Jesse leaned forward and capturing Royce's kiss-swollen lips. Need like nothing Jesse had ever felt before washed through him. He lifted Royce until only the head of his cock stayed inside, and then lowered him back down over and over again. Cries and moans filled the room; water sloshed over the sides of the tub as their pace increased.

Steam filled the room, giving it an ethereal quality. The mirrors were fogged, and sweat dripped from Jesse's face as he drove deep. He was lost in a world of need and sensation, warm, wet bodies writhing in the hot water.

It didn't take long before Royce said, "Baby, I'm going to come."

Jesse wrapped his hand around Royce's throbbing penis and began to pump. "Come for me, Royce."

Seconds later Royce yelled and his body squeezed tightly around Jesse, signaling he'd found his release. Jesse managed two more strokes before his balls pulled up tight to his body and fire raced down his spine and out his throbbing cock, deep inside Royce's tight heat. His body shuddered and shivered even though the water was still hot. Moments passed as Jesse held on to a silent Royce, whose body was draped over his own.

"Baby…? Royce, are you okay?" Was he too rough? Did he hurt his lover? It would kill him if he had.

Royce lifted his head. His eyes were still dilated and his face was flushed, but the one thing that stood out was the huge smile on his face. "I'm perfect."

Jesse gently brushed a stray strand of red hair off Royce's face. "Yes you are. You're everything I could have ever wanted."

Chapter Ten

Jesse ran through the house to answer the front door; they were expecting company. He opened it to find Matthew being carried in Coop's arms followed by Police Chief Graham, Dante, and Spider.

"Put me down! I have crutches you know!" Matthew yelled.

"Yeah and you'll fall on your ass again! I'm not going to wait around until you break something else trying to walk with crutches," Coop yelled back. "You're a disaster."

Behind them, Jesse could see both Dante and Spider smiling at each other as if they alone had a secret they weren't sharing. Jesse moved out of the way and let their guests into the house. Royce came through the kitchen archway with a few trays of huge sandwiches and set them on the dining room table. Today would be the day he made his decision on how to deal with his inheritance. Bear and Travis were working at the diner, giving Jesse time to deal with everything that had been thrown at him the last few days.

"Jesse, tell him to put me down," Matthew begged.

"I'm kind of with Coop on this one, you with crutches is just an accident waiting to happen." Jesse almost laughed at the disgruntled look on Matthew's face.

"I know I'm clumsy but I think I can manage crutches."

"You couldn't this morning. What makes you think you can handle them now?" Coop replied calmly, like none of this was of any importance to him. "I was assigned to look after you and that's what I'll do until you're healed and leave."

The hurt that flashed across Matthew's face shocked Jesse but it was gone in an instant, replaced with a determination that made him wonder what the hell was going on between those two.

"Just park me in a chair please, I'll be fine," Matthew said in a monotone voice lacking any emotion.

Coop looked at Matthew for a moment before carrying him over to one of the big comfy reclining chairs, then immediately brought a dining room chair over to sit beside him. Matthew simply shook his head and pulled out a file folder from the bag around his shoulder as everyone else got settled.

"This is all the information I managed to collect since trying to find you all those years ago," Matthew explained.

He handed the thick file to Jesse, who held it at arm's length as if it would explode at any moment. To Jesse it might as well have been an explosive considering what it was about to do to his life. Things were going to change. He looked over at Royce, who was in the chair beside him.

"Forever, right?" he asked. He could handle anything but losing Royce.

"Forever, love," Royce answered easily before kissing him with his soft lips. "Always by your side."

With that bolstering his courage, Jesse brought the file closer and opened the cover. The first thing he saw was his grandpa's will sitting on top of a pile of paper with dates on them. He would read the will later when it was just Royce and him at home. Jesse picked up the will and placed the rest of the file on the table; he carefully folded it and placed it in his shirt pocket.

"You need to decide what you want to do with the property before Jerry gets around to trying again," Dante said. "The entire team is back from their missions and we're not taking on any more until this is resolved."

"You don't have to do that," Jesse replied. The last thing he wanted to do was take Sentinels away from all the other people they helped on a daily basis.

"Yes we do, you two are our friends, and Mouthy here is your friend. We've worked together before. I'm sure we can do so again to keep you protected," Spider stated bluntly.

Royce wrapped his arm around Jesse and spoke on behalf of the both of them. "Thank you."

"So let's get this started. If Jerry thought he was in for an easy fight, he was mistaken," Matthew said. "The bastard deserves some payback."

"Do you know what you want to do with the property, Jesse?" Spider asked.

Jesse looked at Royce again, took a deep breath and said, "I want to contact the lawyer and sell the land. I intend to donate it to finance centers for LGBTQ youths and teens, to make safe places for them to go."

"I'm proud of you, baby," Royce said while hugging Jesse closer.

"You haven't changed one bit, have you? I'd be honored to help you do just that," Matthew stated with a smile on his face. "Now let's make that phone call and set up a plan because once the family finds out you're intending to claim your inheritance they're going to explode. Jerry would have nothing to lose and considering he's only one bottle short of a case full of crazy, he'll come after Jesse."

Royce handed Jesse his cell phone. *This is it, no going back.* Jesse punched in the number for the lawyer's office and waited. The call was answered on the second ring. "King, Foster, and MacFarlane, how may I help you?"

"Mr. Foster please."

"May I tell him whose calling?"

"Jesse Tribalt."

The line went quiet as he was placed on hold. It didn't take long before the line was picked up again. "Mr. Jesse Tribalt! I've been looking for you…"

Jesse spent the next hour on the phone giving the lawyer a quick rundown of everything that had happened since the day his grandpa had died. Mr. Foster agreed it would be best if he were to come to Brighton to discuss the will and to begin proceedings on Jesse's behalf. After the call all Jesse wanted to do was decompress but they still needed to make plans for security.

"Baby, why don't you and Matthew go onto the back deck; you haven't had a chance to catch up," Royce suggested, making Jesse's heart turn over in love for his man. Even though he wasn't one hundred percent sure of Matthew, Royce was giving Jesse an opportunity to have a break and get reacquainted with his old best friend.

"Yes, I'd like that. Thank you, Royce."

"Love you, baby, and take sandwiches. You need to eat; you didn't have breakfast." Royce was right. He'd been too nervous to eat.

Jesse stood and Matthew attempted to do the same but literally tripped over his own cast. Coop easily caught him before he hit the floor and threw Matthew over his shoulder, grabbed a plate of sandwiches, and headed toward the back garden doors. Jesse took three bottles of water and followed.

By the time Jesse reached the patio, Matthew was already bundled in a chair with his casted foot and ankle resting on a pillow. Jesse was confused; one minute Coop was coddling Matthew, the next he was irritated by having to take care of him. Jesse set the drinks down as Coop turned to leave.

"I'll keep watch from the other side of the deck to give you two some privacy," Coop said before grabbing a spare chair, a sandwich, water, and then walking to the far side of the deck. Shadow was supposed to be watching the house but Lord knew where he was because he could blend in anywhere.

"Okay, you need to tell me what's going on between you two," Jesse whispered as he sat down beside Matthew.

Instead of answering, Matthew reached over and hugged Jesse tight. "I've missed you, knucklehead."

"I've missed you too, Matthew. You were my only friend for so long."

"You did well. I'm glad you finally found a safe place and people who love you. A special man to love you. I'm so happy. You deserve happiness after everything you've been through."

"Thank you, Matthew. What about you? Anybody special back home? Wait a minute, where is home? My parents never told me where your family moved to."

"San Diego, and no, I don't have anyone waiting for me. Who wants to be around a klutz? Hey, don't get me wrong, it may be cute for a little while but believe me, it wears thin fast enough." Matthew stared out at the back lawn as he spoke, seeming a million miles away.

"Oh Matthew, I'm sure there's someone—"

"I've tried. Romance was not meant for me, my friend. Now tell me everything that's happened since the day we left and don't leave out a thing."

For the remainder of the afternoon Jesse and Matthew sat reliving their childhood and the fifteen years they'd been apart. Some of the things Matthew had done seemed unbelievable, but the

Sentinels had confirmed he'd even worked with them, so he didn't doubt it. Jesse was impressed by how well Matthew had done for himself, and he didn't miss the fact that most everything he worked on was behind the scenes and involved computers. When they were younger, Matthew would never put himself out front, not unless someone tried anything with Jesse, and then he was like a wolverine.

"Do you remember what we promised the day you left?" Jesse asked.

"Yep, we swore never to forget each other and to always be friends, and I swore I'd come back," Matthew answered.

"And you did. I had been run off by then but you kept your promise. You came back for me," Jesse spoke softly. "I knew you would and I'm glad you're back in my life even if you live in San Diego."

"We'll see. I do work freelance, on my own terms, anywhere I want to. Besides, I won't be driving for a while with a broken right ankle." Matthew cringed when he tried to move his leg.

"True, so we have time to get to know each other all over again. I'd really like you and Royce to spend time together as well."

"You really love him, don't you?" Matthew sighed wistfully.

It wasn't a question, more like a statement, but Jesse answered anyway. "He means everything to me. I love him and want to spend the rest of my life with him."

The huge smile Matthew gave him was a little sad. "I'm happy you found someone. You deserve to be happy."

"What's wrong, Matthew?"

"Before I came here, I received my third 'Dear Matthew, it's not you, it's me…' letter. I think I've finally realized just how freakish I truly am."

"Freakish? You're not a freak. You're handsome, smart, and successful."

"I'm a mess who can't go a day without accidentally hurting himself. It's just not meant for me; I've come to realize that now. I have my work, I have my best friend back, and we're going to make your parents pay for all they've done. That's enough."

"Matthew—"

The patio door opened and Royce came out onto the deck. "Jesse, the White Hair Crew showed up with casseroles. How they knew we were all here is beyond me, but I think Chief Graham's grandma had something to do with it." Royce came up behind him and wrapped his arms around Jesse's shoulders. The White Hair Crew were a notorious group of the town grandmothers who believed it was their duty to take care of just about everyone. "How's your visit, sweetheart?"

"Really good," Jesse answered as he heard a chair scrape across the deck. He looked over toward Matthew to find Coop lifting him from his chair.

"Guess we're going to eat now," Matthew grumbled. "Next time ask me before you move me."

"You need to eat dinner, dinner is here," was all Coop said before he turned around and carried Matthew back into the house.

"What's up with those two?" Royce asked.

"Something, but I doubt Coop aka Manslut or Matthew aka Mr. Self-Deprecating are even seeing it," Jesse answered with a chuckle.

"Well, isn't that interesting, or at least it will be, once they figure it out." Royce laughed and hugged Jesse closer. "It'll be like seeing a bomb go off."

***

Royce lay awake with Jesse asleep in his arms. His injured shoulder had almost healed enough for him to return to work, at least on light duty inside the EMS/Firehouse. He prayed everything was resolved with Jesse's family before then or he'd go nuts at work worrying about Jesse even with the Sentinels guarding him.

He thought about everything they'd been through since they'd met. It had been crazy, between getting to know Jesse and convincing him to give Royce and Brighton a chance and being on guard for Jesse's family. The time had flown by. Royce knew the next few months were going to be tough on Jesse but he would be there to help every step of the way.

The words that Jesse had read to him from his grandpa's will were still floating around in his head. *"My Dear Grandson, You have been and will always be the light in this world to me. I'm amazed by your strength and kindness and know you will grow into a fine man. This is why I've left the homestead and all related lands to you as my sole beneficiary. You have my blessing to do whatever you feel is right with the land. I know you'll make me proud. I also want you to know that it's not wrong, loving whoever you want. Don't allow your father to influence any of your future decisions. Believe me when I say you will find a love that will fill all the empty places in your heart just like your grandma did for me. Be a smart man, and hold on to it as hard as you can because if anyone deserves to be happy, it's you. I love you, Jesse."*

Royce was pulled out of his thoughts when he heard the slight squeak of one of the garden doors opening and tensed, which immediately woke Jesse. Before he had a chance to speak, Royce placed a finger over Jesse's lips to stay quiet. Jesse nodded his head in understanding and Royce pressed his lips to his ear and whispered, "Someone's in the house, I need you to go to the bathroom and lock the door."

"I'm not going to hide while you're in danger. I'll come with you," Jesse stated firmly.

Royce didn't have time to argue. "You stay behind me." *Why didn't the damn alarm go off?*

Jesse nodded his agreement and they both slid out of the bed. The floor creaked under the weight of someone walking through their living room. *Thank God for old houses.*

Whoever it was, they were heading straight for the bedrooms. One door after another was opened on their way down the hallway. If he was trying to sneak up on them, the unknown person was failing miserably. Royce grabbed the baseball bat from behind the door. He'd kept it there for just this reason, but his injured arm would never have enough strength to do any serious damage on the intruder. He'd have to give it to Jesse. Before he had a chance to turn around a man cried out and crashed into the drywall in the hallway.

Royce reached for the light switch. To hell with hiding, he had to at least get some idea of what the hell was going on. What the light revealed would have been funny if it weren't for the fact that his love was the one in danger. There was little blonde-haired, blue-eyed Shannon handcuffing a man three times her size who was lying unconscious on the floor.

"You guys okay?"

"Yes, thanks to you. Is that one of Jerry's men?" Royce asked.

Shannon reached down and turned the man's face toward them, and Jesse gasped. "That's my uncle. What's he doing here?"

"We'll find out. The police are on their way as well as Dante," Shadow announced as he joined their group.

"Where were you?" Shannon asked.

"Dealing with another idiot outside, thank you very much," Shadow replied.

"Another one? There were two of them?" Royce asked.

"Yeah, you think you can identify him? He's handcuffed in the living room having a little nap of his own."

"Do you guys always knock people out?" Jesse asked.

"They're easier to deal with that way," Shadow answered before he bent down and picked up Jesse's uncle. Royce couldn't fault the logic.

"We'll meet you in the living room once we get a few more clothes on," Royce said while looking down at his sleeping pants; he'd be forever grateful that he wasn't naked. Royce and Jesse backed into their room and closed the door.

"Okay...everything will be okay, right?" Jesse asked in a small voice.

Royce immediately turned and gathered Jesse into his arms. "Of course, sweetheart. We'll figure this out together. Now let's get dressed; we're about to have a whole lot more company."

"I'm sorry, Royce; I never meant for any of this to happen."

"Of course not. You are not responsible for anything and I'll keep telling you that until you believe me. You're not responsible for your parents or the rest of that messed-up family. You're not responsible for your grandpa leaving you the land, and you're definitely not responsible for those two assholes in our living room." Royce punctuated each statement with a kiss; he would not allow Jesse to take any more responsibility for others' actions.

"Thank you, Royce, for always having my back and loving me through all this craziness," Jesse said as he held Royce tightly.

"Forever, baby. I meant it," Royce said. "Now get dressed."

Minutes later, hand in hand they walked down the hallway and into chaos. Chief Graham and a few deputies as well as Dante had arrived, and Jesse's uncle was screaming up a storm.

"Let me go, you freaks, or you'll be sorry!" his uncle yelled.

"The only thing I'm sorry about is not gagging you," Shadow growled. "But I'm willing to rectify the oversight now." He grabbed a dishcloth from the kitchen counter and shoved it in the irate man's mouth.

Royce was surprised the second man remained quiet, staring straight at the floor. Jesse was standing at Royce's side, silent and still.

"Royce, Jesse, guess you've had a party and forgot to invite me," Chief Graham said. "Jesse, do you know the second man?"

"Yes," Jesse's voice cracked when he spoke and the unidentified man was now staring directly at him. "He was the last man to whip me before I ran away. He's the one who made my life a living hell. He's my father."

Chapter Eleven

Jesse felt the blood drain from his face as he stared at the one man who had made his childhood a war zone. The man who would beat him until he prayed for it all to end was now kneeling on the floor in front of him. He was no longer the intimidating, menacing man Jesse used to fear. Now Frank Tribalt was a balding and overweight old man. The years had not been kind to him. It was obvious to Jesse that his father had been living a life of excess. If his bulbous red nose and swollen belly weren't evidence enough, the stench of liquor certainly made it clear.

"Do you want to leave the room, sweetheart?" Royce asked. "You don't have to be near him."

"Dirty fags," Frank grumbled in a scratchy voice that sounded like he'd smoked a pack of cigarettes all at once.

"Shut up or I'll gag you just as fast," Shadow threatened.

Frank pulled away from Shadow, knowing it wasn't an idle threat, and remained quiet, for now.

"No, it's okay, Shadow, let him speak. I'm never running again. You have no power here, Father, and let's just get past this homophobia you seem to love to fall back on. The truth is, it has nothing to do with my being gay. It really has to do with the homestead, doesn't it, Father? Or more specifically that it belongs to me, and not you."

"You don't deserve it." Frank's eyes bulged and his face turned red.

"Maybe I don't, but you certainly have no right to it and I bet I'll make better use of it." Jesse spoke firmly but never raised his voice.

"It's all mine!" Frank screamed, or he would have, if he didn't start wheezing. He was nothing like the man Jesse remembered.

"Wrong, Father. It belonged to me the moment Grandpa died. It was never yours. You were paid to look after my property until I came of age, nothing more. You've been collecting and keeping rent on lands that you didn't even own."

"You won't get away with this," Frank threatened.

"Watch me. Legally you're screwed, and when I sell the land, the money's going to LGBTQ charities. I'm not afraid of you anymore, Father." Jesse stared at the man who had filled his nightmares. Never again would he bow down to that fear.

Jesse turned and walked out of the living room and into the kitchen, away from the agony of his past, and closed the door firmly. By the time he reached the counter, Jesse was shaking but he'd done it. He'd stood up for himself to the man who had haunted him every day of his life.

"I don't think I could be more proud of you if I tried," Royce said as he stood just inside the kitchen door. "You're amazing, Jesse." He crossed the kitchen to gather Jesse in his arms, and kissed him deeply.

"I'm not amazing. I'm in here shaking." Jesse doubted brave people shook like a leaf. They stood tall and strong, didn't they?

"You are amazing. Lots of people shake after doing something stressful. Shaking isn't a sign of weakness. You were brave, baby; you stood up to him." Royce smiled wide, looking at Jesse like he'd lit the sun.

"I did, didn't I? I didn't run from him, I looked him straight in the eye and said my piece." Jesse had shocked himself by his own actions.

"You did great, sweetheart, and they're gone. Chief Graham took them to the station," Royce assured him. "The man looked absolutely gleeful at hauling them to jail."

"What will they be charged with?" Jesse asked.

"Breaking and entering to start with and whatever else we can pin on them with the help of your new lawyer. Fraud and embezzlement come to mind. Unfortunately, they'll probably get bail for now on the breaking and entering but once we have all the evidence your lawyer is collecting, they won't be getting out for a long time after that," Royce explained.

"I can't afford a lawyer for anything over and above my inheritance, Royce. I haven't got enough in savings," Jesse said.

"Yes we do," Royce replied.

"No, that's your money," Jesse argued.

"Do you want to share your life with me?" Royce asked flat out.

"Of course I do."

"Then this is the sharing part. We're in this together. No matter what happens, we deal with things together," Royce explained.

"Are you sure?"

Royce gently took Jesse's face in his hands and looked deep into his eyes. "I'm sure that I want to share every aspect of my life with you and you alone, sweetheart."

"Forever."

"Forever, love."

***

It had been two weeks since Mr. Foster, Jesse's lawyer, had set into motion the return of Jesse's inheritance. Royce had no idea what that involved, but he knew a lot of criminal charges were pending. Mr. Foster also gave Jesse access to a bank account that had been set up for him by his grandpa. No one had seen Jerry or his men again, and once they bailed out, Jesse's father and uncle left town. All in all things had quieted down and Royce had returned to work on light duty around the station house.

"It's good to have you back, buddy; I've missed you being around," Gabe said as he walked into the lunchroom. Considering EMS shared a building with the fire department, he saw a lot of his best friend.

"It's good to feel strong enough to work, but it's killing me to be away from Jesse," Royce replied. He'd spent every day with his phone tucked safely in his pocket on vibrate in case Jesse needed him.

"There hasn't been any sign of trouble for a while now, right?" Gabe asked, concern lacing every word.

"Yeah, it's been a couple weeks now but I doubt we've seen the last of this. They haven't tracked Jesse for this many years to just walk away now."

"Royce!" Fire Chief Mason hollered from his office. "Phone call."

"I'll talk to you later, Royce," Gabe said as he grabbed an apple from the bowl on the kitchen counter and walked back toward the truck bays. "Be careful, buddy."

Royce picked up one of the phone extensions and pushed line four. "Royce here."

"Royce, it's Chief Graham. I'm sorry to bother you at work but it couldn't be helped. Arrest warrants have been issued for Jesse's parents, his aunt and uncle, cousin, and several members of their group, along with the previous lawyer."

"Thank God for that," Royce replied, relief rushing through his body. *Jesse is finally safe.*

"Well, we may have a problem." *Shit, spoke too soon!* "They were able to track down Jesse's mom and uncle. His dad, aunt, and cousin are in the wind."

"Local authorities have no idea where they are?" Royce asked.

"They're on the run at the moment. They're facing some serious charges," Chief Graham answered.

"Did you contact the Sentinels? His father will go after Jesse." Fear replaced relief and Royce was just about ready to take off for the diner.

"Yes, I just got off the phone with Spider; they have three people watching the diner. They won't get anywhere near him."

"Okay, call me if you hear anything," Royce said, feeling a bit better knowing Jesse was being guarded.

The alarm bells started to ring just as Royce hung up the phone, bringing men and women running from all directions and straight for the trucks. Within moments two trucks were loaded up and pulling out of the firehouse. One ambulance followed and Royce found himself alone in the building. He couldn't wait to go back on active duty as a paramedic but now, with the hunt for Jesse's missing family members, perhaps he could wait.

Royce went ahead and restocked various equipment and then began cutting the onions and peppers for the spaghetti sauce he was making the crew for supper. The silence was broken when he heard a loud crash coming from one of the fire truck bays. Jesse grabbed a dishcloth and dried his hands as he walked through the building. The sound of metal scraping on metal sent chills down his spine and made him pick up speed. *What the hell!*

He ran into the bay to find a pile of spare axes lying on the ground in the middle of one of the bays. Royce stopped and scanned the area. He knew he wasn't alone, but was it a friend pulling a prank or something else? *Now would not be the best time for a laugh.*

"There you are, fag." Okay, so it was definitely not a friend. Jerry walked out from behind the second ambulance, gun in hand, evil smirk in place. Royce wanted to punch it off his face.

"What are you doing here? You'll never get anywhere near Jesse," Royce growled.

"Who said it's Jesse we came for?" Jerry laughed. "Now how would we get him to bring us the money if we kidnap him?"

"Are you crazy? They're looking for you." To say Royce was shocked would have been an understatement; he'd honestly not seen this move coming.

"I am and you'll do good to remember that." Jerry's eyes glazed over for a moment before he raised the gun once more. "Now move!"

"I'm not going anywhere with you," Royce yelled and took a step backward. The blast of the bullet hitting the wall to Royce's left proved just how serious Jerry was.

In the distance Royce could hear the fire trucks returning. He had to get Mr. Crazy out of the firehouse before the men arrived back. He knew Jerry wasn't above shooting an innocent person. "Okay, I'll go with you, but we have to hurry, the fire trucks are on their way back. They'll be here any minute."

"Put these on." Jerry threw a pair of handcuffs toward Royce, who discovered with a little maneuvering you can put handcuffs on all by yourself. At least his hands were out in front of him. "Let's go!"

Jerry rammed the gun into Royce's side and pushed him out the bay doorway and up to a waiting car being driven by Frank Tribalt with a bleached blonde, older woman in the passenger seat. Royce quickly realized that the woman had to be the missing aunt, and Jerry's mother. The trucks were getting closer; Jerry opened the back door and shoved Royce in. As he slammed the door closed behind him the fire trucks pulled in. The crew was jumping off as Frank pulled away from the curb. The last thing he saw was Gabe's concerned eyes before a bag was put over his head and his world went black.

***

Jesse knew something was wrong even before Police Chief Graham had said a word. He was sitting in Bear's office stunned into silence, unable to wrap his mind around what he'd just heard. Kidnapped, Royce had been kidnapped. Even though Gabe had called the police immediately after he saw Royce being shoved into a car and recognizing Jerry, they had still managed to get away.

All Jesse could do was wait for a phone call and their demands, if they had any. He would sacrifice himself for Royce without question. If they wanted the land back, they could have it, he just didn't care, nothing would be right again until he had Royce back.

Just as Jesse was about to lose it, Dante walked into the office, a storm brewing on his face. "I'm sorry, Jesse; I should have seen this as a possibility. We need to go."

"Go? Go where?" Jesse asked.

"We need to get you somewhere safe so we'll take you to our team's house, then we start tracking for Royce," Dante explained.

Jesse immediately jumped up from his chair and started for the door. Victor and Shadow were waiting in the hall. Chief Graham followed with three of his own officers. By the time they reach the massive compound that the Sentinels called home on the outskirts of town, Jesse was almost shaking. The grounds were beautiful and a big old Victorian sat proudly on top of the hill. The wrought-iron gates closed with a thud behind the caravan of cars, causing Jesse's heart to speed up. He could never stand being trapped. It brought up too many bad memories, but he knew these were his friends. He was safe, but what about his love?

"I will give them whatever they ask for to get Royce back, even myself if necessary. I don't want anyone to stop me if it comes to that," Jesse declared in a shaky but sure voice.

"It won't come to that. We'll have him back before daybreak," Shadow announced.

"How?" Jesse asked.

"Matthew and Shannon are searching for his cell phone signal as we speak; I guessed he would have it on him. Thanks to his kidnappers being either clumsy or inexperienced, they didn't take it away so we can track him anywhere with it. Come on inside where I know you're safe, Royce will kill me if you're hurt in any way," Dante explained as he led the way to the front door.

Jesse followed the group and was stunned by how differently the inside of the house was decorated compared to the austere exterior. Large comfy furnishings filled the living room, various gaming systems crowded around the massive television, and leather couches and chairs were arranged neatly throughout with thick wooden coffee tables and side tables.

"I know that look, not exactly what you expected from the outside. But when you have this many men living in the same house with a woman who managed to break the last coffee table practicing Krav Maga with Coop, you need durable, not fancy," Sam said as he joined the group. "Come in and sit down. Jesse, you have to be going crazy with stress and fear. I've brought you an herbal tea; it will help calm you."

Jesse didn't think anything could calm him other than having Royce in his arms again, but he sat and drank. Victor stayed in the room with him and Sam standing guard; the Sentinels weren't risking anything or anyone. The rest of the team and the police were just down the hall in a meeting room and Jesse was getting a bit frustrated at being left out of something that meant everything to him.

"You want to go in?" Sam asked.

"Yes, I need to be involved in the search somehow," Jesse answered honestly.

"Okay, you've calmed down enough that I don't think shock's a possibility any longer. You honestly were white as a ghost when you first got here and I was worried. I didn't intend to keep you away from the search," Sam admitted.

"Thank you for thinking about me. Honestly, I barely remember the drive here. I guess I needed the time to calm down." Jesse hadn't realized how close he was to going into shock but Sam was a nurse and knew the signs.

"Let's go see what they've found."

Jesse and Sam walked down the hall and into a large meeting room. Laptops were flashing maps up on a screen as Matthew and

Shannon did their magic. Officers and Sentinels were gearing up, and Jesse felt hope for the first time in hours.

"Matthew, did you find him?" Jesse asked as he approached the table.

"You bet we did, he's a couple miles outside town," Matthew answered. "The team will get him back for you, Jesse, they're the best. Trust me when I say that."

Coop was blushing nicely by now. Jesse hadn't ever seen him blush, but a single compliment from Matthew caused such a reaction. Jesse would have thought it was cute on any other day but not today; he needed his Royce back safe and unhurt.

"Victor and Shannon will stay here and watch over the three of you; we'll call in the moment we have him safe," Dante explained as the team checked and rechecked their gear and weapons.

Jesse walked up to the group. "Please be safe and bring Royce home to me."

Spider placed his huge hand on Jesse's shoulder. "We will, Jesse, I promise."

"You stay in the house until this is over," Coop ordered Matthew as he walked by.

"Yes, sir!" Matthew huffed.

"You just remember that, sweetheart." Coop smiled and walked out of the room.

"God help me." Matthew groaned before lowering his head to the tabletop and banging it a few times for good measure. "He's driving me insane."

"Yeah, well get used to it," Coop yelled from the hallway, and Matthew groaned even louder.

Chapter Twelve

The smell of musty, damp carpet filled Royce's senses and made him nauseous. His hands were numb and his head was throbbing as he looked up. The large, rusted hook his handcuffed wrists were hanging from was surely reinjuring his throbbing shoulder as he hung a foot off the floor. He slowly turned his aching head to look around the room for anyone else but he was alone. He had no idea how long he'd been unconscious, but the room was dark. He could hear people talking in another part of the dilapidated house, but he couldn't understand what was being said. There were old boards across the windows and stained, splintered furniture shoved against the mold-covered walls. Royce shook his head to clear his mind, but it wouldn't clear; everything seemed fuzzy and far away at the same time. *What did they do to me?*

The door squealed in complaint as it was opened, and three figures entered the room. It was too dark to see their faces until one of them decided to turn on a large flashlight. The trio who'd entered didn't shock Royce; unfortunately, he already knew who'd kidnapped him. But one damn thing did surprise him: Frank and the woman who he assumed was Jesse's aunt were holding hands as they came closer to him. He knew Jesse's mother was already in custody so this was a new development.

"I see you're coming around, we'll have to double the dose next time," Frank said with a cruel sneer.

"What the hell did you give me?" Royce growled.

"Oh, just a little something to keep you docile until we get our money." Frank confirmed what Royce had already suspected—he'd been drugged.

"Bastards, you'll never make it out of Brighton."

"Already have, sweetie," the bleached-blonde woman hissed as she approached. "We're miles away from that disgusting hick town."

Shit, if they made it out of Brighton how would anyone find him?

"Let me guess, you must be Jesse's aunt, Jerry's mother, and Frank's piece on the side." The flash of anger in her eyes disappeared as quickly as it had arrived.

"Good guess, young man, too bad the information will do you no good." Jesse's aunt leaned forward and kissed Jesse's father like her life depended on it. *What the hell! Disgusting.* "But I'm not the mistress. I may have married Frank's brother, but all I've ever wanted was Frank." Royce couldn't imagine why. "Once we have the money we'll start over someplace far away from here, our own little family."

Royce looked over at Jerry to see how he was taking the news that his mom and uncle were lovers, but the man seemed unfazed by it. *How can you watch your mother kissing your uncle without showing some sort of emotion?* Then Jerry laughed, shocking Royce further.

"You thought I would be offended or upset, why would I?" Jerry asked. "After all he's my dad."

Oh shit! That means Jerry is Jesse's biological half-brother.

"Enough! Jesse will pay anything we ask to get his 'boyfriend' back." Frank sneered; it seemed to be his natural expression. "You're the one who made Jesse believe he's more than the sniveling little shit he always was. I think it's time you learned your lesson, the same way Jesse did." Frank lifted his filthy right hand to reveal a thick black belt.

Royce knew what was coming; he'd seen Jesse's scarred back. Royce had no way of escaping or fighting back; this must have been how Jesse felt. He was hanging from the ceiling with his shoulder screaming in pain and on some sort of drug, so Royce doubted he could even walk if he managed to get free. Jerry came toward him brandishing a knife, and he proceeded to cut Royce's shirt off him and leave random shallow cuts across his skin.

"Now we'll see how long it'll take you to scream." Frank's eyes gleamed as he let the belt fly, landing a violent blow to Royce's right shoulder blade. His hanging body swayed forward from the blow. Royce held back his pain-filled cry; he would give them nothing.

Another blow landed dead center across his spine, slicing Royce's skin like butter. He could feel something wet sliding down his back and knew it had to be blood. One more blow and Royce had to grind his teeth together to stop from screaming.

"Silence? Trust me, you'll be a whimpering mess when I get done with you," Frank growled.

The door crashed open and glass shattered, interrupting the next strike, as the room seemed to explode into chaos. People were yelling, Jesse's aunt was screaming, and Frank was being slammed onto the floor. Royce's head was spinning, he assumed from the drugs and the pain, but he knew he saw Coop in the fray, confirming he was being rescued.

"Royce, Royce, look at me. Open your eyes." *When did I close them?*

He was having a hard time prying them open. He felt himself being lifted off the hook; he groaned in pain as his arms were lowered and then he was carried outside.

"You'll be okay, Royce. We'll get you to the hospital." He had no idea who was talking, his eyes wouldn't open and his senses were dimming.

"Drugs...put drugs in me," Royce slurred. He was so tired.

"Come on, Royce, open your eyes, Jesse's waiting for you." A deep voice said the magic word, "Jesse," and Royce forced his eyes open. "Good, keep them open, we'll get you to Jesse."

He was lying on his side in an SUV, a large first aid kit at his side. Someone pushed on his back, making Royce groan in pain, but he wouldn't scream. He refused.

"What drug did they use?"

"Don't... know," Royce barely got out before the world around him began to spin. He immediately closed his eyes. More pressure on his back made his head swim even further until blessed unconsciousness took him.

***

Jesse sat in the hospital waiting for word on Royce; they'd brought him in over two hours ago. The doctor said his kidnappers had given him a heavy sedative and that they'd have to stitch a few of the wounds on his back because they were fairly deep. They also had to go back in and repair the damage done to his reinjured shoulder. The pain at learning that Royce had been whipped the same as he'd been all those years ago sent Jesse into a rage to hunt his dad down and make him pay for all the pain he'd caused. Jesse knew that was impossible because his father was in a jail cell but the urge was still strong.

His love had suffered a pain Jesse knew so well, and the guilt was suffocating. Royce had been so concerned with protecting him that he'd left himself open to Jesse's family. Matthew had come to the hospital with him along with Sam, Coop, Dante, Spider, the White Hair Crew, Bo, and Travis. Dante had apologized again for not being able to predict Frank's move. No matter how many times Jesse said it wasn't his fault, Dante didn't seem to accept it.

They sat in silence until the doctor came walking down the hall and then the questions began to fly.

"How is he?" Dante asked.

"Is he awake?" Sam asked.

"Can I see him?" Jesse asked, desperate to get to Royce.

"Okay, okay… He's conscious, we've repaired his shoulder, but he'll have to go through rehab again, and his back lacerations took just over forty stitches to close. Yes, you may see him now, he's been asking for you, Jesse," Doctor Green answered. "We want to keep him for a few days until we're sure the drug is completely out of his system and to fight any possible infection."

"Will there be any lasting effects on Royce?" Jesse asked, fearful that Royce would be left with even more permanent injuries above and beyond his scars.

"None. The sedative will work its way out of his system quickly," Doctor Green answered.

Thank god, though Royce would still have to live with the scars, at least there wouldn't be any damage done by the drugs. The team and his friends grudgingly left with a promise to return in the morning. Royce's parents had moved to Arizona after they retired and would be arriving by morning as well. Jesse followed Doctor Green to Royce's room, his heart heavy. The lights were dimmed and Royce was sleeping, his handsome face peaceful. Jesse quietly sat down in the chair beside the bed. His troubling thoughts kept him company, and after a few hours the beeping of machines began to lull him to sleep. He laid his head down on the side of the bed; soon the world slipped away and Jesse fell into a restless sleep.

**

Royce woke to the soft snores of his love, his hand in Jesse's. Royce was lying on his uninjured side. The burning pain in his back and injured shoulder were intense but all he could think about was Jesse.

Jesse's head lay on the bed and Royce lifted his hand to run his fingers through Jesse's hair. He noticed the bruises around his wrist from the handcuffs; his other arm was back in a sling. Jesse's eyes flew open at the slight touch and his head popped up off the bed.

"Hi," was all Jesse managed to get out as his eyes filled with tears. Royce could see the guilt in those watery brown beauties. There was no damn way he was letting Jesse take any responsibility for what had happened.

"Baby, come on up here." Royce patted the spot beside him. The bed he was in was actually quite large.

"I'll hurt you." Jesse looked almost panicked.

"It will hurt me if you don't, besides there's lots of room." Even if there wasn't, Royce would do anything to be close to the man he loved, the man he was afraid he'd never see again.

Slowly, Jesse slid onto the bed, staying close to the edge, as if afraid to touch or get close to Royce. That wouldn't do. No matter how much pain he was in, his need to seek comfort and to comfort Jesse was all that was important. "None of this is your fault; remember what I've told you."

"But if it weren't for me, my family wouldn't have come after you. Wouldn't have hurt you." Jesse's tears began to fall as he spoke.

"If I had to choose between going through today one hundred times over or to have you, I'd gladly take the pain every time. You mean everything to me, Jesse. Do you understand that?" Royce swore every word he said was the absolute truth, hoping Jesse would believe him.

"I love you so much and it's killing me that you're hurt. You shouldn't have to go through any pain." Jesse still held on to his guilt like a vise.

"If anything I have a whole new respect for what you went through, and you were only a child. I always knew you were strong, but now that I had a little taste of what you suffered, and you being so young, I'm amazed by you." Every word was the truth. How a child had survived, let alone to come out as wonderful as Jesse, truly was a miracle.

Jesse inched a bit closer, carefully navigating all the wires and Royce's injuries, but the movement of the bed still made Royce groan in pain.

"I'm hurting you; I'll sit in the chair," Jesse said as he tried to scoot away.

"No! I need you beside me, baby. Please don't leave."

"I would never leave you," Jesse said before kissing Royce gently.

"Damn right, never," Royce agreed before falling into a restful sleep in Jesse's arms. Safe and loved.

Chapter Thirteen

The night was warm and the patio was packed, which was unusual for a Thursday night at Lucky's. Their large group took up half the outside space: Royce, Jesse, the Sentinel team, Matthew, Bear, Rick, Gabe, Johnny, Chief Graham, and his wife. They'd enjoyed a wonderful steak dinner and were now waiting for the band to start playing. They'd closed the diner early so that everyone all together could have an evening out. They were celebrating Jesse's recent purchase of a plot of land inside Brighton. It was the first step of his plans; he intended to build a group home for homeless LGBTQ teenagers from across the state.

His dream was beginning to take shape, and life had finally calmed enough for him to breathe easy again. Jesse took another gulp of his beer; he would try to dance with Royce tonight. Jesse hoped he didn't make a fool of himself or, more importantly, Royce. Again, no matter how scared he was, Jesse had dreamed of dancing at Lucky's with his love for a long time and he wasn't about to back out now.

It had been just over a month since his family had been arrested. They were being held in custody without bail in a Federal prison in Idaho. In that time, Mr. Foster had been working hard setting things to rights, organizing and retrieving all of Jesse's inheritance. It would take several more months to sell the rest of the land, but according to his lawyer, the farmers in the area had already inquired as to purchasing several hundred acres. Jesse had made sure to set the prices at fair market value. He wasn't about to gouge the hard-working people of his old town; he was sure his father had already overcharged them in rent for years.

Royce's injuries were healing well, even though his arm was back in a sling. He'd spent three days in the hospital; an infection caused by Frank's dirty belt had delayed his release. The stitches had been removed but the scars would be a permanent reminder of the cruelty of Jesse's father. A few days after Royce had been released he'd told Jesse what had been said in that old, rundown house. He had a brother. Jerry was his brother, not his cousin as he'd been led to believe his entire life.

Jesse was unsure how he felt about that discovery. With everything Jerry had done to him, it was hard to comprehend that through every beating Jerry had handed out he knew that Jesse was his brother. Jerry had taken great joy in hurting others, especially Jesse, and brother or not, some things couldn't be forgotten or forgiven.

Royce did the right thing by telling him the truth, although Jesse hadn't been all that surprised by the affair between his father and aunt. They'd always been extremely "close." Once when he was young, Jesse had caught them kissing. He'd been severely whipped for witnessing it.

"So when are you breaking ground on the new center?" Sam asked before taking a drink of his Coke; Sam was a designated driver tonight along with Royce, Chief Graham, and Gabe.

"Should be in the next couple weeks, once we finalize the rest of the estate. Over half has already been dealt with so Mr. Foster doesn't believe it will take too much longer," Jesse answered, his excitement evident in every word.

"It's going to be amazing," Matthew agreed. "It's a brilliant idea."

"I'm glad you think so because I have something important to ask you, Sam and Johnny," Jesse said. He leaned his elbows on the table and Royce laid one hand on Jesse's arm in support. The man was everything he'd ever wanted. "This may not be the best time to ask, but you know I need people I can trust to help me run the center, and I was hoping the three of you would…would want to take up positions within the center to help make it a safe and comforting place."

"Jesse, I'd love to help. What were you thinking the three of us could do?" Johnny asked.

"I was thinking you could help make the place feel comfortable. You're an amazing designer and I know you could make the rooms feel homey." Though Johnny was a graphic designer, he also had an interest in interior design. "Matthew, I was hoping you could help with setting up security for the house; a lot of the teenagers might be running from something or someone. And Sam, I was thinking of setting up a medical center inside the building just in case anyone requires medical attention," Jesse explained, all the while praying they would agree to help. He knew he was asking a lot of them, but he also knew these men were his friends and always open to helping others.

"Of course, Jesse, I'll help out," Sam said. "We'll get a small medical bay set up and I'll even come in to help out."

"No one will get on the grounds without us knowing, they'll be safe," Matthew swore.

Johnny's eyes sparkled and Jesse could see he was already designing the rooms in his mind. Jesse was blessed to have such great friends. "I'm in. It'll be comfy and welcoming. Most of those kids will have been on the streets for a while and will need all the comfort we can give them."

Royce wrapped his arms around Jesse. "I'm so proud of you, baby." Sam and Johnny were getting the same accolades from their men.

Matthew sat stoically until Coop put one arm around him and gave him a side hug. "It's a good thing you're doing." To anyone on the outside it was just a friendly hug but the smile on Matthew's face could warm even the most hardened of heart.

Jesse curled into Royce, enjoying the freedom to show his affection so openly. Since meeting Royce, and for the first time in his life, Jesse was looking forward to his future. Hell, he finally had a future to look forward to. He and Bear had discussed bringing on another cook to help Travis in the diner so that they could decrease the workload on all of them. Interviews began next week. They'd already brought on two high school students to waitress part time and help out Sarah.

Just then Travis walked in the door with Bo Mason on his heels, snapping Jesse out of his thoughts. They'd invited them both, but Travis was still walking on eggshells around Bo. Even after all the time Bo had spent at the hospital with Travis when he'd been hurt. No one knew for sure if they'd come alone or together. It seemed to Jesse that Bo wasn't giving up as he held the chair out for Travis to sit down before seating himself.

"Hey, Travis, Bo, we're happy you two could come tonight. Did you have a chance to eat?" Jesse asked. They could order more food, he was just glad that they could make it. Jesse really liked the both of them and Travis had become his friend.

"Yes, we ate at my house before we came," Bo answered, shocking everyone at the table and causing Travis to blush.

"Jesse, I've been thinking about the menu for the youth center. I've set up a list of healthy meals that would still be tasty to the teenagers. I worked for a health foods catering business for a while. I was hoping you'd have a look at it," Travis said, effectively changing the subject and steering it away from their dinner to a safer area of conversation.

"I'd love help with the menu and stocking the center, Travis, thank you." Jesse was overwhelmed with the support he'd received since revealing his plans to the people of Brighton.

They'd held a town hall meeting with the residents of Brighton where they had proposed the youth center project. With the help of Royce, Jesse had laid out their plans and answered everyone's questions. Several individuals had stepped forward to volunteer to help with construction. Jesse had hired one of the local family-owned construction companies, on the recommendation of numerous townspeople, to oversee the construction. The White Hair Crew were already on board, having decided they would cook for the center and help teach the kids how to cook for themselves along with other necessary life skills such as laundry. Teachers of various grades offered their time to help out as well.

There had been such a positive response that Jesse and Royce had filled quite a few of the volunteer positions that same evening. By the end of it Jesse had been so emotionally overwhelmed by their generosity that he'd shed tears in front of everyone at the meeting and for the first time he wasn't embarrassed. He felt their love and acceptance in return.

Conversations carried on around them inside the bar, but Jesse was now completely entranced by the handsome man at his side. Royce had kept his word and stood by Jesse through everything. They made decisions together and dealt with all the new legal issues as a team. Jesse would have to testify at his family's hearings, which he feared, but he knew it had to be done. He had to face each and every one of them. Without a doubt, Royce would be by his side providing him with comfort and strength. With each day that passed, Jesse's own strength grew, and for the first time he felt like his life was under his control.

"Love you, baby," Royce whispered in Jesse's ear before kissing him softly. Jesse no longer felt unsure; he was more confident and free with shows of affection toward Royce.

"Love you too," Jesse replied.

The band was tuning up on stage and Jesse's leg bounced even harder with nerves. He'd dreamt about this moment, the first time he'd ever danced with anyone, especially the man he intended to spend the rest of his life with. The band looked ready to start when a member who had to be the lead singer came up to the mic.

"This first song is dedicated to all those lovers out there." The first few notes of "Amazed" by Lonestar began to play and Royce stood, holding out his hand for Jesse. He immediately took the offered hand and stood, excitement coursing through his veins. Considering Royce's left arm was still in a sling, they had modified their positions so that they could still dance closely together.

Jesse took a quick glance around and saw Gabe and Johnny, Dante, Spider, and Sam, and even Bo and Travis as well as Coop holding Matthew in his arms, and all were on the dance floor. More couples joined their group and suddenly the dance floor was full, calming Jesse further; he wouldn't be the center of attention.

Royce's handsome smile seemed to glow in the stage lights; Jesse carefully wrapped his arm around Royce's shoulder and placed his left hand in Royce's right. Royce couldn't place his left arm around Jesse's waist due to his injury, but they managed. They found their rhythm as their bodies moved in sync and the world around Jesse slipped away. *I'm dancing...I'm dancing with Royce!* The words of the song ringing true in his heart, he was amazed by Royce. Jesse's new life was full and finally complete.

"And just what are you thinking about with that big smile on your face?" Royce asked as he brought Jesse's hand to his mouth and lovingly kissed Jesse's palm.

"About our life together," Jesse answered.

"And what about it?" Royce asked.

"One lifetime may not be long enough."

"Sweetheart, an eternity wouldn't be long enough, but as long as I get to spend every day with you I'm happy," Royce explained.

"Forever?" Jesse asked.
"Always and forever, love."

COOP

Chapter One

"Put me down," Matthew yelled for what had to be the tenth time in the last two hours. "Right now."

"You said you wanted to watch television, so here you go," Coop stated as he dropped Matthew onto the soft cushions of the couch.

"I could have walked with my crutches, ya know," Matthew groused as he straightened his shirt.

"It's cute that you think so." Coop smirked and walked toward the spacious kitchen. The entire first floor was open concept, making it feel spacious.

Matthew looked down at his casted right foot with disdain; it was the reason he was at Coop's mercy. It wasn't his clumsiness—it didn't matter that he'd fallen over his crutches a couple times since he'd gotten out of the hospital—Coop was just being bossy. Matthew wasn't just trapped in Brighton until he could drive home; he was trapped with a babysitter. Buddy, Sam's golden retriever, came over and sat beside Matthew, and he swore he saw sympathy in the dog's eyes.

Matthew had come to Brighton, Texas, to help his friend Jesse and protect him from Jesse's own family. It had taken years, but his friend's relatives were finally where they belonged: prison. Jesse was now using his inheritance to build youth centers for both LGBTQ+ and heterosexual homeless youths. Matthew was helping him with the security system because some of these kids would be running from one thing or another and might need protection. Jesse had been running from his own family for ten years.

"How's your ankle feeling, Matthew?" Sam asked as he sat down beside him holding a big bowl of buttered popcorn, which he held out to share with Matthew.

"Healing way too slowly in my opinion. I'll have killed Coop long before I'm cleared to drive," Matthew said with a huff.

"You could always fly home," Sam offered as a solution. "I mean, it's your choice. We like having you here, and I know Shannon is beyond ecstatic to have another computer geek in the house."

"I know I can stay, and if I go home, then I'll be stuck without anyone to help," Matthew admitted.

"Ah, so you concede you need Coop's help." Sam smiled wide.

"I need someone's help, not Mr. Bossy's," Matthew said in a huff.

"Deal with it, shorty. I'm all you got," Coop stated as he sat on the other side of Matthew, commandeered the bowl of popcorn, and handed him a bottle of water.

"You did this to me. Besides, aren't I cutting into your search time for your next one-night stand?" Coop had a reputation in the security field for his brute strength and his habit of sleeping with a new man every mission. Matthew couldn't afford to let his guard down and like the handsome man. He knew how that would end.

"You're not interrupting anything. The Internet is a wonderful thing. You'd be shocked what you can get on there," Coop said with that devilish grin Matthew knew melted men's hearts all over the world, but he had to remain unfazed. He couldn't give in.

But the small spark of pain that sliced through Matthew's chest was surprising, and he unconsciously rubbed at it. Of course Coop wasn't with him twenty-four hours a day; he could leave for a hookup any evening he liked. Why did that thought make him sick?

Instead of concentrating too hard on that fact, Matthew simply stared at the television, though he had no idea what they were watching. Coop sat there as if waiting for the next barb, but Matthew wasn't in the mood anymore, so he remained quiet and concentrated even harder on the giant seventy-five-inch flat-screen television. Sam moved over to another couch as Dante and Spider joined them. The three were the leaders of the Sentinels as well as lovers. Matthew fought to stay awake, but it was useless. He was just too damn tired and soon everything simply slipped away.

***

Coop felt Matthew's body go limp beside him, his head resting on Coop's shoulder. No man deserved to be as beautiful as Matthew was, and Coop knew better than to look too long. Matthew wasn't a one-nighter. He was the type of man who did relationships, and Coop didn't, period. Every man he'd been with knew the score before anything ever happened; Coop made sure of it. He didn't want to break any hearts, but he knew over the years that he had, even if it was unintentional. No one seemed to understand that he just couldn't have a romantic relationship; it wasn't possible, not anymore. When his need became too much, he headed to bars outside of Brighton to scratch that itch, or on missions if it was convenient, but lately he hadn't wanted to leave the compound.

He knew what he'd said to Matthew about hookups on the computer was a lie, and honestly, he had no idea why he wanted Matthew to be jealous, but he did. The lack of a response was enough for Coop to know he'd hit a nerve. *Why am I even concerned about Matthew? He's simply an assignment.* He'd been ordered to watch over the man until he was healed, and that was all. When Mouthy was healthy, he'd leave and everything could return to normal. Somehow that knowledge only made his tension worse.

Matthew's body lay relaxed against him, and a small snore broke the silence. *Why is it so quiet?* Coop looked up to see Sam, Dante, and Spider, who were cuddling on the other couch, all staring at them. The three were the bosses of the Sentinels, and his fellow members, Shadow, Shannon, and Vincent, were all on missions at the moment. The Sentinels worked as a group of heavily trained bodyguards and retrieval specialists; all were former members of the military.

"What?" Coop whispered at the three, who were all smiling, which was beginning to freak him out a bit.

"He doesn't see it," Sam whispered to Spider.

"Not a clue," Spider replied softly.

"Neither of them do," Dante said.

Coop was beginning to think he was being laughed at, and he didn't like it all that much. "What the hell are you three talking about?" Matthew squirmed a bit until Coop pulled him into his chest and spoke softly into his ear, and he fell back to sleep.

"It's nothing bad, Coop. You care for Matthew. It's just odd to see you reacting this way," Sam explained.

"I'm not acting any way different than I normally do. You put me in charge of him, and I'm doing just that," Coop explained as he pulled a cover over Matthew.

"Okay, Coop. Whatever you say. It's just nice to see," Dante said.

"You're imagining things, that's all," Coop grumbled, then slid his arm under Matthew's body and cradled him to his chest before he stood. He wasn't sticking around to be made fun of, and he wouldn't allow anyone to do so to Matthew either. "It's late. I'll take Matthew up to his room."

"Sure, Coop, whatever you say." Spider's voice followed Coop up the stairs to Matthew's room, which was directly across the hall from his own. He had to have him close by in case Matthew needed him.

He carefully maneuvered a still-sleeping Matthew through the door and to his bed. Coop had him almost on the mattress when Matthew's injured foot slid from the blanket wrapped around him. It slammed straight into the footboard of the bed, causing Matthew to wake instantly and let out a small cry of pain.

But instead of pulling away from Coop, Matthew held on tighter and buried his face in Coop's chest.

"Easy, beautiful, I've got you. I'm so sorry. Your leg slipped out of my hold," Coop explained.

Coop looked down into Matthew's eyes, one green and the other hazel, staring up at him in pain. Coop sat down on the bed with Matthew still in his arms as he arranged Matthew's legs to hopefully ease the pain. He turned back to Matthew to find him still staring at him. A tear slid down Matthew's cheek, and Coop gently wiped it away with his finger. His skin was so soft and his lips were full, and in that moment, all Coop wanted was to kiss Matthew.

As he leaned in close, Coop could smell Matthew's cologne and his intoxicating male scent. God, he needed this; he had to feel those lips on his own. Coop caressed the side of Matthew's face as he moved closer, waiting for Matthew to turn away or stop him. He did neither. Matthew's eyes had softened, and there was no longer any sign of pain. As he leaned down the last few inches, Matthew met him halfway.

His lips were even softer than Coop had imagined. The kiss was gentle as they explored each other for the first time. The excitement and need were like nothing he'd ever felt with any other man. He was already hardening in his pants. Their tongues dueled as the kiss deepened, and Matthew whimpered.

The sound of footsteps coming down the hall was as good as a cold shower any day, and Coop pulled away from a confused-looking Matthew. Coop quickly lowered Matthew onto his mattress and took two steps back just before Sam knocked on the open door and peeked inside.

"Hi, guys, just wanted to remind Matthew to take his medication before he fell back to sleep," Sam said as he stepped into the room, a bottle in his hand. "What's wrong?"

Sam looked between what Coop assumed were two red faces until he finally spoke. "Matthew hit his ankle on the bed."

Sam's look immediately changed from curiosity to concern. "Oh, Matthew, what can I do? Is there anything I can do to help you? Does it hurt more than before—wait, stupid question. I've got your pain medicine with me." With Sam being an ER nurse, he made sure Matthew didn't forget any of his medications.

Matthew's face was even redder than before, and his piercing eyes should have burned holes through Coop's head.

"I'll take it, but I don't like them. Coop, why don't you go? I'm sure you have plenty of other things you'd rather be doing," Matthew said, and Coop knew a dismissal when he heard one.

Without saying another word, Coop walked away and closed Matthew's door before locking himself in his own room. He didn't want any visitors right now. He'd kissed Matthew, and damned if he didn't want to do it again. But he didn't think Matthew felt the same way, if that death glare counted for anything. Coop wasn't sure if it was the kiss that was the problem, because Matthew had been kissing him back, or if it was something else. All he knew now was that the kiss had been amazing, he wanted more, and that Matthew was furious with him again. Not exactly a good combination.

***

Sam had left long ago, but Matthew still sat awake, staring out his window from the comfy window seat. The grounds were so beautiful; topiaries of different animals and twinkling lights surrounded the pool in the backyard. A large greenhouse sat a couple hundred feet from the house. A little farther away were the stables and a large building where the Sentinels stored their gear.

The property was stunning, and his small studio apartment back home in San Diego couldn't compare. He'd never really wanted more, though financially he could afford much larger. But, as long as he had his computers and gear, he was happy. Matthew touched his lips once again. Kissing Coop had been electrifying, and every time he thought about it, his cock began to fill. Then Coop had dropped him on the bed like he was a hot potato before anyone could see them kissing. *It's like...like he was, oh God, he was embarrassed about kissing me.*

Of course that's why Coop backed away from him so quickly. He wouldn't want Sam to see them together. Matthew's stomach churned even harder the longer he thought about the kiss. He'd been so distracted that he'd forgotten who he was dealing with. Coop had his share of men, powerful men who worked in the same field as Coop did. Some guy with freakish eyes and a notoriously clumsy history, standing only five feet six inches tall with plain brown, shaggy hair and freckles need not apply.

What was he thinking? He didn't want to apply. Coop was bossy and annoying, but most of all, he was the king of one-night stands. Matthew knew that's all he'd be in the end, and it was the last thing he would ever allow himself to be.

But the kiss, God, the kiss was exhilarating and gentle, leaving him wanting more but knowing that wasn't a very good idea. How was he going to face Coop in the morning after what they'd done? Matthew wished Coop wasn't Coop or, more specifically, the part of having multiple lovers across the globe. The rest of the man was perfect to Matthew.

He knew he'd just be another notch in a very long belt, and there was nothing he could do about it. Hell, Coop was probably going online right now as Matthew sat here pining over a kiss. *No way am I going to fall for that. The kiss meant nothing to Coop, so it will mean nothing to me.* That's the way it had to be, for his own sanity. Whatever happened, he'd keep his distance emotionally, but he wasn't so sure if he could manage to keep a physical distance. He was in so much trouble.

The next day, Matthew didn't have to worry about what Coop thought because he was back to his same bossy, overbearing self, as if nothing happened. Matthew couldn't blame him—it was the exact same thing he'd planned on doing—but it still hurt. Coop had shown up to his room right at 7:00 a.m., as he always did, and carried him down to breakfast. He parked him in a chair, filled two plates, and joined him as the rest of the team began to file in. Matthew had been told they'd hired Mrs. Walker the moment they settled into their new house. Not one Sentinel could cook, and they required someone full-time due to the sheer amount of food that needed to be cooked daily to feed this group.

Typically, the first two meals were informal. In the morning was a breakfast buffet, and lunch was the same, but supper was a sit-down affair. Whoever was home didn't dare come to the supper table in dirty clothes, or Mrs. Walker would take their plate away until they'd cleaned up. Matthew immediately liked the woman. She wasn't the least bit intimidated by the large men who lived in the big old house. Mrs. Walker was a member of the White Hair Crew, the grandmothers of Brighton. She took control of the kitchen, and Matthew had never eaten so well since his family had been killed all those years ago. *I wonder if Coop's parents are still alive. Stop that!*

Matthew had been imagining all kinds of strange things since that damn kiss, and wanted it to stop. Clearly the kiss had more of an effect on him compared to Coop, who was busy scarfing down two slices of bacon at once.

Spider, Dante, and Sam walked hand in hand into the kitchen and joined the table after they filled their plates. It would only be the five of them this morning. Buddy, their golden retriever, followed them in and came to sit at Matthew's feet. He couldn't help but pet the adorable dog.

After a round of good-mornings, everyone settled into their food and the dining room was quiet for several minutes. He dug into a mouthwatering ham quiche with flaky pastry, ham, eggs, and cheese—Mrs. Walker could cook. After they'd all finished their first plates, everyone except Matthew and Sam went back for seconds.

"So, how's your foot and ankle this morning?" Sam asked as he picked up his coffee.

"Better, thank you. I don't think I reinjured anything last night. I'm just a bit of a wimp, I guess," Matthew replied.

"No you're not. You have a metal plate and three screws holding your ankle together. You're no wimp," Coop said as he reentered the dining room. His face gave away nothing, but the words still shocked Matthew.

"I'm a wimpy computer geek, Coop, and a klutz. There's no changing that. If I could have, I would have long ago," Matthew answered, knowing full well that was the truth.

"You're an intelligent, beautiful person," Coop growled. "And I don't want to hear you bashing yourself again."

Matthew wasn't the only one shocked by that outburst, but everyone remained quiet as Coop sat down and dug back into his breakfast. Matthew sipped his coffee, his mind reeling from Coop's reaction. Jesse and his grandfather were the only ones who'd ever stuck up for him, even when he was the one bashing himself. Once the other three men were done with their second helpings, they slowed down enough to have a conversation.

"So what's on the schedule for you guys today?" Matthew asked.

"Well, we're preparing for a mission that will take us out of country for a couple days," Dante said. Sam didn't look happy about that, and Matthew understood it would be hard to send your partner—or, in this case, partners—into a dangerous situation. "And Coop will be coming with us this time."

Coop's head snapped up so fast the egg on his fork flew across the table. "What? I thought my assignment was Matthew until he healed. Who's going to be here to watch over him and Sam?"

"Shannon will be staying behind. We need her to hack into their systems for us and man a drone. And with that said, we need to have a discussion after breakfast, Matthew," Dante said, and this time it was Matthew's turn to be shocked.

"Oh…okay. Where do you want to talk?" *Don't say the office.* Matthew had learned that all major meetings and decisions took place in that room. If they went there, something was seriously up.

"Well, if you're done with breakfast, we'll take you to the office," Spider said.

Shit! "You'll take me? Is Coop not coming?" Matthew asked.

"No, this is a private meeting that doesn't involve Coop. Spider can carry you," Sam explained, and Coop growled softly before coughing to cover it up.

Why would he care if someone else carries me? You'd think he'd be happy to be rid of me for a while.

"Okay," Matthew finally managed to get out, and Spider walked around the table, easily scooping Matthew into his arms and walking away. Coop was suddenly on his feet, and Matthew had no idea what was going on.

"Stand down, Coop," Dante ordered as he turned to face Coop head-on.

What is wrong with Coop? Matthew's stomach began to churn with unease; he needed to defuse this situation. "Coop, I'm all right. I'll be back soon. Just sit down and finish eating. Maybe we could go to town later? I need to get out and get a few more clothes."

Coop's eyes softened and he sat back down. "We'll go shopping and have lunch at the diner in town." Buddy came over and sat at Coop's feet, as if sensing his anxiety.

"That sounds perfect," Matthew said, and Coop's cheeks reddened.

They continued down the hall, and now that Coop was out of his sight, that strange sick feeling churned in his stomach again. Maybe they would ask him to leave. The office was at the end of the hall away from the busy areas of the house. Spider sat him in a chair in front of a large, carved wooden desk. Sam sat beside him, Spider on the couch, and Dante in the huge office chair behind the desk. Matthew had never realized how scary this room truly was until now.

"Thank you for carrying me, Spider. I can't wait until you guys are gone for a few days so I can practice on my crutches without Coop throwing a fit."

"Make sure not to practice anywhere near sharp objects," Spider advised with a smile.

"You know, I have survived all this time all by myself," Matthew countered.

"Well, you don't have to do everything on your own any longer if you want," Sam said with a huge smile.

"What?" Matthew asked, unsure what Sam meant.

Dante sat forward, resting his arms on the desk, and steepled his fingers. "We want to make you an offer."

"Offer of what?" Matthew was beyond confused by now.

"A permanent position here as a Sentinel," Dante answered.

"A Sentinel? I can't fight myself out of a wet paper bag." Matthew knew what he was capable of, and working out in the field wasn't it.

"You wouldn't be in harm's way. You would work at a distance away from hot zones. We need your computer expertise and your hacking abilities."

"What about Shannon?" Matthew knew she took care of all their computer needs. "I won't take her position."

"No, we would never get rid of Shannon, but she wants more time out in the field, not behind a computer screen," Spider added before standing to retrieve an envelope from the desk and handing it to Matthew.

"Don't make any decisions now. We know this is a bit of a shock. Your contract is in the envelope along with what we're offering. We've worked together in the past; we know what you can do."

Matthew really doubted that. No one knew what he was capable of doing, of building. "If I decide to sign it, and that's not saying that I will, I need a private workshop." Matthew knew that when it came to ordinary day-to-day living, he was clumsy and awkward, but computers, electronics, and weaponry were his passion and he was a pro.

"Done," Dante said.

"You're not going to ask what I want it for?" Matthew asked.

"I would hope you'd tell us eventually," Spider answered.

"I would."

"Then take your time, read over the contract, and if you have any questions, please ask any one of us. We think you'll make a great addition to our team," Sam said, his eyes clear. He was telling the truth; they did want him to join their team.

Matthew had worked alone his entire life, just him and his computers. Would he be able to work as part of a group? Did he want to, and what about Coop? He was looking forward to Matthew leaving.

"There may be another person you need to speak to prior to me making my decision. Coop wants me to leave as soon as I'm healed. If I stay, there might be a problem," Matthew explained.

"Coop won't be a problem. He'll be okay with you staying if you choose to," Dante assured.

"I wouldn't be too sure about that," Matthew advised.

"Don't worry about Coop. Make your decision based on whether you feel you could work as part of this team," Spider explained.

They'd certainly given Matthew a lot to think about. Could he be part of this team? Would Coop be fine with him staying? Or would he cause a rift in the group? He just didn't know. He needed time, and that was exactly what they'd given him.

"If you don't have any questions now, we better go get Coop before he comes down here looking for you," Spider said with a laugh. Matthew wasn't sure what was funny, but that was nothing new.

As Spider reached down and lifted Matthew again, he swore once they were gone on their mission, he was practicing on his crutches until he was able to get around without falling. Matthew held the envelope to his chest, planning to read it when he was alone. If Coop asked, he would be honest and explain that they had made him an offer but he was undecided if he'd take it.

They walked out into the main living area where they found Coop pacing in front of the television. When he saw them, he immediately walked over and took Matthew out of Spider's arms. His face brightened instantly, confusing Matthew even further.

"Done with your meeting?" Coop asked while looking down at the envelope in Matthew's hands.

"Yes, all finished. Can we go up to my room before we go? I have to change," Matthew asked and realized what he'd said. "I mean, I'll change in my room and you can wait outside."

"I know what you mean, Mouthy." Coop smiled and headed toward the staircase as if Dante, Spider, and Sam weren't even there. Matthew would never admit this to anyone, but he kind of liked it.

***

Coop had no idea why he was acting this possessively. He'd never behaved this way before, not with anyone. But here he was acting like a fool and unable to stop himself. He didn't like seeing Matthew in someone else's arms, even though it was only Spider. Coop hadn't been himself since he woke up this morning. The first person he thought of was Matthew, which had been happening with more frequency lately. Then, when he was dressing, he wondered if

Matthew would like the way he looked. Finally, he resorted to pacing in his room until 7:00 a.m. when he could cross the hallway and retrieve Matthew for breakfast.

What's wrong with me? Whatever it was, Coop was powerless to stop it, and honestly, when it came to Matthew, he didn't really want to. Though he was acting crazy, his mind was clear, maybe clearer than it had been in many years. As he carried Matthew to his room, he held him gently but tightly. He wasn't ready to admit how happy he was that Matthew couldn't navigate his crutches.

They walked into Matthew's room, and Coop placed him on the window seat because that was Matthew's favorite spot. He was truly catering to the man; he'd never done that with anyone. Maybe it was a good thing he was leaving on a mission for a few days.

"So what do you need?"

"Coop, I'm capable of dressing myself." Matthew huffed, still holding tight to the envelope Coop had noticed earlier.

"I know you are. I was just going to get what you wanted from your closet before I left."

"Oh, yes, I guess that would help, thank you," Matthew said, his voice soft.

Coop turned to look at Matthew; he seemed dejected. "What's the matter, beautiful?" Coop let the pet name slip out as if he said it all the time.

"Why do you call me beautiful?" Matthew asked.

"Because you are. You're breathtaking."

Matthew's expression changed to confused. "You're either being mean or you're insane because I'm not even good-looking. I might be sort of cute, but breathtaking, not ever. So which is it, mean or insane?"

"Neither. I'm truthful," Coop stated firmly. He wouldn't let Matthew think he was less than he really was. He moved forward until he stood directly in front of Matthew. "You are beautiful. Your hair shines, your eyes are unique and gorgeous, your freckles highlight your milky, soft skin, and your soft lips beg to be kissed."

He was now leaning down only inches from Matthew. Matthew's pupils were dilated, his face flushed, and Coop couldn't resist crossing the distance and taking Matthew's lips in a forceful kiss. A kiss that promised long nights of passion as Matthew responded in kind, at one moment needy and the next demanding. They didn't part until forced to breathe, both panting as they separated.

This kiss left Coop lightheaded for a moment. Once he got himself together, he slowly pulled away to see the beautiful man in front of him. Matthew's eyes were still closed, his swollen lips slightly open, and his face flushed, absolutely gorgeous.

Coop caressed the side of Matthew's face with his big hand, and he rubbed his nose softly against Matthew's. "Beautiful."

Chapter Two

Coop drove one of the Hummers as Matthew sat in the passenger's seat, still reeling from the kiss this morning. He had no idea what to think. That had been the second time Coop kissed him and acted like it was completely natural. *Well, I didn't exactly beat him off me, now did I?*

"Coop, why do you keep kissing me?"

"Do you want me to stop?" Coop asked back, never taking his eyes off the road.

Did he want Coop to stop? Hell no, but he doubted the kisses meant as much to Coop as they did to him. "I didn't say that, but I'd like to know why."

Coop looked out the side window before answering. "Because I like kissing you, is that so hard to believe? If you're okay with it, we're two consenting adults and I see no reason to stop."

Matthew felt like there was something more not being said but left it alone. "Okay, but I'm not easy. You'll have to buy me lunch before you get another one," Matthew teased. Coop gave him that megawatt smile of his, and a few bricks around Matthew's heart fell away.

They reached the men's department store, and Coop parked right out front before coming around to the passenger side to pick up Matthew. He had brought his crutches, thinking Coop wouldn't want to carry him in front of the townspeople, but he'd obviously been mistaken. As they stepped up onto the sidewalk, people strolling by said hello to both of them without even a second look, despite the fact that he was being carried. Brighton was definitely a town like no other.

Coop carefully navigated the door to the men's store and easily carried Matthew to a plush chair by the dressing rooms. "Now, what did you need to pick up?"

"I was hoping to get another pair of jeans, a few shorts, and button-down shirts. T-shirts and, um…underwear." Matthew could feel his cheeks getting warm, but he had only packed for a few weeks not months, and he needed just about everything.

Coop asked his size and then went hunting for Matthew's new clothing. He was surprised Coop was taking such an active role in his shopping. It all felt so normal for a couple, but he was under no illusion. They weren't a couple and never would be.

A couple minutes later, Coop came out of the racks of clothing with his arms full and a goofy smile on his face. "You should see all the stuff I've found. Let's get you in the changing room." He was acting like a kid in a toy store. He was adorable.

Hours later, Matthew was finally done trying on clothing and Coop had gone to take all his bags to the Hummer. He was sitting in the same plush chair when he noticed a man standing at one of the side windows staring directly into the store and at Matthew. He'd never seen the stranger before now, but the man was still looking at him with eyes full of venom and hate. Matthew looked around the shop, hoping for another customer or salesperson, but he was alone and the man just kept staring at him. Matthew's skin crawled. When he heard the bell over the door tinkle and turned to see Coop walking in, relief like nothing he'd felt before washed through him.

Coop immediately went on alert, as if sensing something was wrong, and scanned the area. Matthew looked back at the window, but the man was gone just as quickly as he'd arrived.

Coop kneeled in front of Matthew and reached for his hand. "What's wrong, Matthew?"

"There was a man standing by the side window staring at me. He looked at me with such hatred, but I don't know him," Matthew explained quickly, still shaking from fear. He was the first to admit he wasn't a hero.

Coop stood and walked over to the window, looking both ways down the street. Matthew was beginning to feel like he may have overreacted. But the man had been staring straight at him. Matthew thought of all the work he'd done behind the scenes on missions. Could his name have been leaked?

"Whoever it was is gone. Did you recognize anything about him?" Coop asked.

"No, I've never met him before, but that doesn't mean a thing. With all the work I've done for law enforcement and our government, if my identity has been compromised then it could be anyone. Or I could be overreacting. I'm probably just imagining things. Let's go to lunch." The last thing Matthew wanted to do was ruin their time with his own fears. It wasn't exactly a secret that he preferred to be well behind the scenes, doing his share through long-distance surveillance, hacking, taking over systems weaponry, and so on.

"We should go back to the house," Coop suggested.

"Not a chance. You have to buy me lunch." Matthew laughed, trying to diffuse the situation. His own fear responses had gotten away from him. Some random stranger did not have the power to ruin his day. "Now let's go. I'm hungry, big guy."

"Big guy, eh? I can accept that," Coop said. Matthew hadn't realized he'd used a pet name for Coop, but it did fit him; he was huge.

Coop reached down, picked Matthew up, and carried him to the truck, his eyes scanning their surroundings as they went. Matthew could see no sign of the man and decided it had to be a one-off... He hoped. Soon they were back in the truck and heading toward the diner. Fried chicken Fridays were definitely his favorite time to visit Jesse, his best friend and the manager of the diner.

Matthew only received a few curious looks as Coop carried him into the diner and sat him in a booth. He swore he'd get the crutches under control before Coop came back from his assignment.

"So how long will you be out of town?" Matthew asked.

"Not long, probably only a few days."

"Oh, okay."

"Going to miss me?" Coop asked.

"Hell no, why would I miss your bossy, overbearing ass?" Matthew laughed.

"Oh, I grow on ya." Coop gave his patented, melt-your-pants smile.

"Yeah, like mold." Matthew laughed at Coop's disgruntled look.

Coop gave Matthew a curious look but didn't say a word. He simply smiled and went back to reading the menu. Travis was cooking today, which meant Jesse would be at the construction site of the new youth center. This reminded Matthew that he had a meeting with Jesse tomorrow, to go over the new security system for the center.

"I have a meeting with Jesse tomorrow at the work site," he told Coop. "I guess I'll ask Sam to give me a ride." It frustrated Matthew that he couldn't drive until his right ankle was healed.

"I don't want you trying to go somewhere on your own. Jesse needs to be with you on the site in case anything happens," Coop said.

"Look, Coop, I'm an adult who can and will go where he wants when he wants…at least I will when I'm healed and can drive. But nothing is going to happen. I'll be with Sam and Jesse. If I need help navigating the area, they can help."

"Trust me, I know you're an adult. I'm just concerned about your broken ankle and the stranger from this morning."

"I'll be fine, and the man left. He might have thought I was someone else."

Coop simply shook his head. They ordered lunch and talked about benign topics, nothing too personal. The few times Matthew tried to delve any deeper, he was shut down by Coop. The man refused to speak about personal topics, and if anything, that alone told Matthew where he stood. Matthew wasn't a friend or really considered anything other than an assignment to Coop, the man he happened to have kissed a couple times. The knowledge shouldn't have bothered Matthew, but it did.

The rest of the day was spent working on the blueprints for the security system for the youth center while the team got ready to leave on their mission first thing in the morning. It was well past midnight before Matthew crawled into his king-size bed. He hadn't seen Coop since they returned to the house. He always seemed to be somewhere else in the compound. Vincent had helped him up the stairs to bed.

Matthew lay staring at the ceiling when he heard a soft knock on his bedroom door.

"Come in." He spoke softly, not wanting to wake anyone else up.

The door opened and it took him a few seconds to realize it was Coop standing in his doorway. "May I come in?"

"Yes," Matthew replied. "Is something wrong?"

Coop stepped in and shut the door. He was fully dressed, but his hair was wet, as if he'd just gotten out of the shower. "There's nothing wrong. I just...."

Matthew sat up in bed. Thank goodness he had sleeping pants on, but he was still shirtless and knew he was blushing. "What is it?"

"I just... Can I sleep with you tonight?" Coop asked.

"Whoa, that's a little too fast for me, Coop." Matthew may be attracted to the guy and he may have kissed him, but this was too big of a jump.

"No, I don't mean sex, just sleep...maybe cuddle, but that's all."

"Is this some sort of strange pick-up line or something? Because I don't understand."

Coop came closer and sat on the edge of Matthew's bed. "I want to spend the night sleeping beside you, please."

Matthew was stunned. He'd expected Coop to try to have sex with him, but he never saw this coming. But what harm could it cause if he let him stay? At least Matthew wouldn't spend another night alone. Oh, who was he kidding? Coop was built like a Greek god and wanted to cuddle with him. Hell yeah!

Matthew lifted the covers up and slid over, leaving enough room for Coop to join him. Coop stood and took off his shirt, revealing each and every hard muscle as he went. Next came his pants, leaving Coop standing only in his boxers and Matthew with a hard-on. The bed dipped with Coop's body weight as he got in, stretched out his large arm, and gathered Matthew to him.

There was no way he couldn't feel Matthew's hard cock, but Coop didn't draw any attention to it and simply snuggled Matthew closer to his side. Slowly, Matthew relaxed and let his arm drape across Coop's broad chest. Absently he ran his fingers through Coop's short, blond chest hair, and Coop hummed softly.

The room was dark and quiet. Matthew was warm, snuggled up beside Coop, and almost asleep when Coop spoke. "Make sure you stay safe while I'm gone, beautiful."

"I'll be fine. It's you that I'm worried about. Can you tell me anything about the assignment you're going on?"

"We're going in to take a group of aid workers out of the hands of the local rebels."

"Will Shannon be sending in the drones that I saw today to get a lay of the land? Is she using the new silent XRT drones with armaments?" Matthew asked.

"Yes, we're planning on getting in and out before the entire compound knows we're there."

"I'll help Shannon with the drones," Matthew said.

"It'll be nice knowing you're watching over us." Coop's voice was soft.

"Coop, what are we doing?"

"The only thing I know is that I need to be near you. Is that so bad?"

"No, it's not bad, not bad at all."

"Good." Coop wrapped his arms around Matthew. "Now we need to get some sleep. Tomorrow's going to be a long day of travel."

"How long will you actually be away?" Matthew asked again, now unsure if he liked the idea of Coop leaving. He knew he'd already asked earlier, but he needed confirmation.

"Four days at most. Back before you know it," Coop reassured him, but for some reason Matthew wasn't looking forward to the next four days like he'd thought he would.

When did all this happen? He couldn't stand Coop…right? *Yeah right, that's why I'm in bed with him, because I dislike him so much.* Matthew didn't know when, but Coop had managed to make it past his defenses.

"Please be careful," Matthew said.

"I've never had anyone to worry about me or wait for me to come home," Coop admitted.

"Is that a bad thing?" Matthew asked.

"No."

***

Coop had no idea what he was doing. All he knew was the driving need to be near Matthew. Coop had been truthful; he'd joined the army when he was eighteen, and on deployment, he didn't have anyone to see him off or write him letters. Since becoming a Sentinel, he had the backup of his team and their friendship, but he didn't have that missing piece. The strange thing was, Coop had never cared before now. *Why now? I've never needed this type of comfort before, never been offered it either.*

Life had turned Coop into a cynic of love and relationships. With examples like his parents, who could blame him? Mr. and Mrs. Stenson didn't believe in divorce, though they'd threatened it enough. No matter how dysfunctional their relationship had become, they remained together, sharing their anger and frustration with their son. Once he had a chance to join the army, he left and never looked back. He sought his acceptance among his peers. He knew love wasn't in the cards for him. Love equaled pain; Coop had realized that long ago.

Now here he was lying in bed holding Matthew to him, seeking comfort from the first man to come close to actually making it through Coop's defenses. He couldn't let that happen; he couldn't risk it. Coop looked down at the sleeping man in his arms and brushed a soft kiss on Matthew's forehead. He looked so innocent in his sleep, not the spitfire he was used to. *What makes him so different than anyone else I've met? What makes him so special?*

Coop was too tired to think long on this new turn in his life, and his eyes began to close. He pulled Matthew closer; he'd never been more at peace than he was at that moment.

***

The team had been gone for over a day and a half. They'd been in contact, and the assault on the rebel camp was scheduled for tonight. They had the drones set up and ready for both Shannon and Matthew to operate. Each one had four cameras and modified armaments to protect itself and members of the team.

Matthew had distracted himself by practicing on his crutches, wanting to have mastered them before Coop got home. He'd fallen several times and had various bruises decorating his body, but he could finally make it around the house without tripping over them. He was so proud of himself and couldn't wait to show Coop when he got back.

Matthew had replayed the morning he woke up in Coop's strong arms over and over again since he'd left. The sun had yet to rise, and Matthew lay still, watching Coop sleep. He looked so peaceful. Coop was truly a handsome man with his blond hair, blue eyes, and muscled body, but Coop meant more than that to Matthew. He had no idea when all this had happened or when he'd started viewing Coop as more than his babysitter. *Now what?*

"Matthew... Matthew, are you listening to me?" Sam asked from the other side of the kitchen island.

Matthew looked up at Sam, who was holding a jug of orange juice. "I'm sorry, Sam, what did you say?"

"I asked if you wanted a glass of orange juice."

"Oh, yes, thank you," Matthew replied. "I'm sorry, I zoned out there."

Sam poured two glasses of juice and sat down across from Matthew. "What's got you so distracted?"

Matthew wasn't sure how much to reveal, but he desperately wanted to talk to somebody about this, and his best friend, Jesse, was busy putting the youth center together. "It's about Coop."

"Is everything okay?"

"Yeah, I'm just confused." Matthew ran his fingers through his hair. "Sam, this needs to stay between us."

"Absolutely."

"Coop and I have kissed a couple of times, and I think I have feelings for him."

"I knew it! I could tell something was going on between the two of you."

"You could?"

"Oh yeah. The way you two watch each other, it's like an awareness. And I've never seen Coop like this before."

"Like what?"

"Attentive, gentle, smiling so much more than usual," Sam said. "He just seems a lot happier than before you came here."

"Really, but what about his tendency to love 'em and leave 'em?" Matthew asked. "I can't do a one-night stand. Heck, with my track record, I don't do relationships well either."

"Do you think that's what he's after?" Sam asked.

"I did before he slept with me," Matthew replied.

Sam spilt his juice onto the island. "Slept with you!"

"No. No, not like that. He came to my room and literally just wanted to sleep beside me. No sex, just cuddling. He didn't try to take advantage of me at all. Oh God, maybe he's not interested in me that way."

"Hold on, hold on… He came to your bed and just wanted to cuddle with you?" Sam asked.

"Yes. It was the night before they left," Matthew explained.

Sam stood with his mouth hanging open, staring at Matthew. "I don't think he's ever slept with any of his previous endeavors. From what I heard, he's always back before the team turns in for the night."

"So you're saying he has sex with them but doesn't sleep with them; he sleeps with me but doesn't have sex with me. This is not making me feel better, Sam. Oh my God, what if he goes out after this mission and finds himself another one-night stand?"

"He wouldn't do that, not with you here," Sam assured.

Matthew wanted to believe that, he desperately did, but he was far too realistic to assume Coop would change his ways simply because he'd kissed him. "You can't say that with 100 percent certainty."

"No, but nothing is ever certain in this world. They could be injured on this mission. They could not make it back." Sam's eyes filled with tears, and Matthew realized just how much stress Sam was under, and here he was worried about his own selfish concerns. Christ, Coop could be injured and he was more concerned about any possible hookups. He had to get his head on straight.

"I'm sorry, Sam. I'm not normally this self-involved. They'll be okay. They are very well trained. I would know; I've worked with them before. They're the best. If I were ever in trouble, I'd want them coming for me," Matthew reassured Sam.

"I know you're not a selfish person. Hell, you came all this way to help Jesse, and you hadn't even seen him in fifteen years. And I know Dante and Spider will be safe, but there's always that chance." Sam wiped his eyes. "I just have a hard time when they're gone on missions. I imagine, over the years, it'll get easier."

Matthew stood, grabbed his crutches, and rounded the kitchen island to Sam's side. He carefully wrapped his arm around Sam, lending him any strength he could. "They'll be safe. They have you to come home to. You're a great incentive."

"Thank you, Matthew. It's nice having you around the house. It'd be even better if you decide to stay…. Hint, hint." Sam smiled.

"I haven't decided yet, but as soon as I do, you'll be one of the first to know." With one final squeeze, Matthew released Sam. "I should go check in with Shannon, makes sure the drone communications are all up and running. You'll be joining us to watch the mission as it unfolds later tonight?"

"Yes, I try to watch as many as I can," Sam replied.

"Good, we're all in this together."

Four hours later, Spider announced, "Team one in place."

A few seconds passed before Dante added, "Team two in place."

The team had divided into two groups. Spider, Coop, and Shadow would be going after the hostages while Dante and Vincent stood guard and would provide cover fire if needed.

"Receiving loud and clear. Teams one and two, release your drones," Matthew said through his headset. Shannon was doing final checks. They had already sent in the recon drones to get a lay of the land. Now Matthew and Shannon would each man a combat drone to lend a little extra firepower. They were each fully armed and outfitted with proximity sensors for any uninvited guest.

Shannon took her seat beside him. Both had a set of controls in front of them to operate the drones. Sam sat toward the back watching the screens. Each drone was outfitted with four cameras giving them a three-hundred-and-sixty-degree view of the area. It was nighttime, with only the full moon illuminating the area. Matthew would be following team one to release the hostages. Shannon would stay with team two.

Dante's voice came across the comm system. "We're a go on three. One...two...three." Matthew's drone hovered just above their heads, quietly surveying the area around the three team-members. The team moved out, staying to the shadows as they snuck from one small building to the next. There were two guards standing in front of a tiny hut at the far end of the compound. That was their destination.

Each step was precise. Not a sound was made as they moved like shadows through the night until they reached the back of the hut. Matthew kept his drone hovering several feet off the ground in the darkness, always watching for any rebel who might wander by. Coop, Shadow, and Spider crept around the side of the hut and quickly incapacitated the two guards.

The three went inside while Matthew's drone kept watch. A few moments later, Shadow reappeared carrying a young man who had been severely beaten and was unconscious. Then two ladies appeared, followed by Coop and Spider. *Three survivors out of a group that was supposed to be six, damn.*

The group made their way to the edge of the forest, Matthew ever watchful for any sign they'd been seen, but so far the mission was running smoothly.

They were over one hundred yards away from the rebels and about to meet up with team two when shouting erupted from the rebel base. They'd been discovered. The team ran through the trees with the freed hostages in their arms, trying to reach the rendezvous site. There were two trucks waiting for them to make their getaway to a nearby helipad and the safety that was waiting for them.

Matthew turned his drone around and headed toward the rebels; he had to buy the team some time to get away. Suddenly, Shannon's drone was by his side as they headed back toward the rebel base.

"Nice to see you, girlfriend." Matthew smiled at Shannon, who was sitting right beside him in the control room.

"You think you can have all the fun?" Shannon replied.

"Team one and two, Shannon and I will hold them off as long as we can," Matthew said into his microphone.

"We're almost to the helipad. We only need a couple minutes to get off the ground," Dante reported.

"Got it," Shannon answered for both of them. "You ready, Matthew?" The noise of breaking branches and the approaching voices were getting closer.

"Ready."

The first few men came into the clearing they had chosen where the drones had more maneuvering capability without the risk of flying into a tree. Bullets started to fly, and they found themselves in a firefight. More men came out of the trees as Matthew fired the two modified automatic weapons on the bottom of his military drone.

"We've lifted off," Dante announced.

"Setting self-destruct. We can't leave any technology for the rebels to find," Matthew stated.

"Setting self-destruct," Shannon echoed.

The last thing Matthew saw on his drone monitors were more rebels, some with guns, others with machetes, pouring into the clearing before static took over the screen. Matthew dropped his controller and pushed back from the table. He'd never done anything that intense before; he'd never fired a gun at a real person and not just a target. He may not have been there in person, but he certainly had control over who the drone shot and undoubtedly caused the death of a few rebels.

Matthew knew going into this that he might have to fire on the enemy, but the reality was so much different. His hands began to shake, but he buried them under his legs so Shannon or Sam wouldn't see them.

"Thank you," Sam said as he approached the control screens. "Thank you for keeping them safe."

"Any time, little boss," Shannon said. The team had decided to call Sam "little boss" because he was Dante and Spider's partner in everything.

"Yeah, thanks, Shannon, you did a great job." Matthew voice shook as he spoke.

"What about you, Matthew? You helped save their asses as well." Shannon smiled as she tapped on the screen.

Matthew was happy that he was able to keep the rebels back, knowing they would try to kill the team and the hostages. Three of the hostages had already been killed by the rebels, so why did he feel so much guilt?

"Home base, this is Dante. We've crossed the border and are headed toward the drop-off point."

Shannon had taken off her headset, so Matthew answered. "Ten-four, home base out." They were safe; Coop was safe. That's what was important.

***

Coop sat in the hotel room he shared with Shadow and Vincent. They'd flipped a coin, and he was stuck with the roll-away bed instead of one of the two queen beds in the room. By now, he'd typically be at the nearest bar picking up the first man who caught his eye, but not tonight.

"So, do you want to explain what you're still doing here, Coop?" Shadow asked as he reached for the remote and began flicking through the channels.

"Just not feeling it this time," Coop answered.

"This have anything to do with that cutie back at the house?" Vincent asked. "Or is he free to accept dates from other team members?"

"Yeah, I was thinking of asking him out for dinner when we got back home," Shadow said.

Coop stood to his full height and growled. "Neither one of you are going anywhere near him, do you understand?"

"But if you're not interested—" Vincent was cut off by an even more irate Coop.

"Who said I wasn't interested?" Coop yelled. "And keep your hands to yourself."

"I knew it! Does Matthew know you've fallen for him?" Vincent asked.

"I haven't fallen for him," Coop stated.

"Sure, that's why you're not out looking for your latest conquest." Shadow laughed.

"Leave it alone. He's a good man, and I would never do anything to hurt him," Coop said.

"Finally, Coop's met his match. Never thought the day would happen, but I'm glad I was wrong," Shadow admitted.

"Well, don't go ordering the wedding invitations just yet," Coop grumbled.

Shadow came over and slapped Coop on the back. "It's good to see you happy with him. You think we haven't noticed how you've been around him? The two of you can't take your eyes off each other."

Coop hadn't realized that Matthew was watching him as well, but the news gave him hope that maybe he wasn't the only one doing the staring. But first he had to get Matthew past his reputation so he'd give him a chance. Hell, what did Coop know about relationships? He'd never had one, and the only long-term example he'd had were his parents, and they hated each other.

Chapter Three

Matthew could barely contain his excitement. The team was due back today, and like it or not, he'd really missed Coop. He navigated the stairs now with his crutches as well as the rest of the house. It had taken all four days to do it, but he'd managed with only a few extra bruises for his troubles. As the Hummers pulled up, Sam bounced by Matthew's side.

"Do you want to go outside?" Matthew asked.

"Yes, definitely. I'll get the door."

Matthew hobbled behind Sam. He liked his newfound freedom to get around. At least now Coop wouldn't have to worry about carrying him everywhere. Matthew and Sam walked outside—well, Sam walked and Matthew hopped with his crutches. The team was just unloading their gear, but it appeared Sam couldn't wait any longer and ran for his men, Dante and Spider. They gathered him up and sandwiched him between their two larger bodies.

Matthew had yet to see Coop, so he hopped forward a few steps until he finally found him unloading the back of the vehicle. When their eyes met, Matthew felt it like a caress, warm and soothing. When Coop saw the crutches, his expression changed; it went blank, expressionless, as if the crutches had somehow offended him.

Matthew was suddenly unsure. Maybe he'd read everything wrong. *Maybe he hooked up with someone and got me out of his system.* Now Matthew was having second thoughts and began to turn around to go back inside the house. But, of course, for the first time in days, his crutches got tied up and twisted around his cast, causing Matthew to lose his balance and head for the ground.

Inches before tasting gravel, Matthew was saved by someone behind him. He turned his head to see Coop hunched looming over him, holding Matthew in the safety of his arms.

"Easy, I've got you, beautiful," Coop whispered into Matthew's ear.

Matthew melted into his touch, unable to stop himself from seeking the comfort Coop provided. "I thought you were mad at me."

Coop lifted him gently into his arms and headed for the house. "Mad at you, why would I be mad?"

"You saw me on my crutches, your expression changed."

"Yeah, well, I was just thinking about all the times you must have fallen over the last four days while I wasn't here to catch you, causing yourself pain."

Matthew was touched, but he needed to be back on his own two feet. "It wasn't all bad. I got the hang of it."

"Yeah, I can see that."

"That was a one-off. I was distracted and not concentrating on my crutches," Matthew defended his actions.

"Exactly how many bruises do you have over and above what I can see?"

"Well, um…just a few."

"How many?"

"Maybe five or six." Matthew was getting ticked off. He was an adult, able to make his own decisions.

"Why didn't you wait till I got back to practice?"

"Oh, I don't know, maybe because Shannon can't carry me around and perhaps because I'm an *adult*!" Matthew growled out. "I was so proud to show you everything I accomplished, and all you can do is criticize me. Put me down and hand me my crutches. I can do this on my own."

Coop's face was red as he turned around, brought Matthew back to his crutches and he gently set Matthew down. As soon as Matthew was set, he hopped back into the house, leaving Coop and his hopes behind. He would not be treated like glass by anyone. He was a man, albeit a clumsy one, but still a man able to make his own decisions, and the master of his own actions.

***

Coop stood on the driveway stunned. He'd been so happy to be home, only to have it ruined.

"Way to go, you big oaf. He's been practicing for days trying to get coordinated enough to use those crutches, and the first thing you do is put him down for falling," Shannon said from the back of the truck, where she was helping the team unload. "He was proud that he got the hang of it…well, mostly got the hang of it."

"He's covered in bruises."

"Yes, and those are his badges of honor for not giving up," Sam added, still being hugged between Dante and Spider.

"See, this is why I don't do relationships. I haven't got a clue what's right and someone is always mad."

The swift intake of breath clued him in to someone standing behind him. Slowly, Coop turned around to find Matthew. His face was unreadable.

"I came back to apologize for yelling at you. I'm sorry I took my frustrations out on you, Coop," Matthew said softly and then turned again and hopped back to the house. This time he didn't turn back.

"Oh man, go after him," Shadow said.

Instead, Coop went into the equipment room and began cleaning and returning items to their proper places. He'd hurt Matthew, which was the last thing he ever intended. Maybe it was best to back away. Lord knew he could make things worse.

He was strong enough to admit he had deep feelings for Matthew, but all he could think about was his parents and their horrific marriage. The yelling and screaming, and things breaking. Threats and violence were commonplace. They had stayed together for over forty years—forty years of anger, resentment, and hate. That was why he didn't do relationships. He would just end up angry all the time. He didn't want to be angry with Matthew. He wanted to love Matthew.

Coop froze to the spot. *Love? When did love ever enter the picture? It hasn't, right? I can't be in love. It's only been a few months since we met. And I don't do love, right?*

"You okay, man?" Vincent asked as he brought in another bag to be unloaded.

"Yeah, why wouldn't I be?"

"Because you just crushed the man you're interested in."

"What? Crushed him how?" Coop knew he'd hurt Matthew, but crushed?

"Saying you don't do relationships to the man who's pretty much gaga over you," Vincent explained.

"Gaga, is that a word?" Coop asked.

"Not the most important aspect of the sentence, Coop," Vincent said with a sigh.

"I didn't mean for him to hear that. I didn't know he was behind me. Christ, I'm screwing this all up, aren't I? I've just never—"

"You want a little bit of advice?" Vincent asked.

"You're going to give it to me anyway, so why bother asking?"

"Good, as long as you listen. Go inside and fix this before it's too late. You don't let something like this fester."

Coop stopped cleaning his AK-47 and set it down. Could he have really crushed Matthew with his words? He didn't mean to. Hell, he never wanted to hurt the beautiful man.

"Can you finish up here without me?" Coop asked.

"Not a problem," Vincent replied.

Coop turned and ran toward the house. He didn't know what he was going to say, but the urgency he felt to make things right again between himself and Matthew made him run faster. This wasn't the homecoming he'd expected. Well, he really didn't know what to expect, but it involved Matthew somehow. He checked the entire first floor and no Matthew. Coop took the stairs two at a time, racing upward until he was outside Matthew's room.

He knocked softly, and it didn't take long for Matthew to answer. "Who is it?"

"Coop," he replied and then waited for Matthew's decision to either let him in or turn him away.

***

Matthew sat on his bed absolutely still. What did Coop want? *Hasn't he already said enough outside?* Should he let him in? Did he want to lecture him some more about his crutches? He wouldn't have the answers if he didn't let the man in.

"Come in." His voice shook slightly with the various emotions running through him. Matthew knew this wasn't Coop's fault. He'd been aware that Coop didn't have relationships. But still he managed to fall for the man anyway.

Coop stepped in and shut the door behind him. "Hi."

"Hi," Matthew replied, not knowing what else to say.

"May I sit down?" Coop asked.

Matthew wasn't sure what he would do if Coop came closer—either kiss him or hit him. But he wasn't a rude person. "Yes."

Coop lifted a chair from the corner and brought it over and placed it directly in front of Matthew, who was still sitting on his bed. Coop sat leaning his arms on his legs, head bowed. "I'm sorry."

Of all things Matthew expected, that wasn't it.

"It's okay, Coop. I assumed a lot of things, and I never should have." In truth, Matthew was at fault. Coop never promised anything.

Coop raised his head, his blue eyes troubled. "No, it's not. You're the last person on Earth I'd ever want to hurt. You gotta believe that."

"You're not at fault. Like I said, I assumed a lot," Matthew said as he lowered his eyes.

"Please don't take my comments as gospel. I just meant that I don't know how to have a relationship, and from observation, it always ends up with someone mad."

"I wasn't mad at you, but I was confused. You were so upset at seeing my crutches."

"It wasn't your crutches I was looking at." Coop raised his hand and gently brushed Matthew's right arm, which sported two sizeable bruises. "I don't like seeing bruises on your beautiful skin."

"Beautiful? I'm covered in freckles."

"And each one is beautiful."

"You're insane."

"I might be, but I'm crazy about you."

Matthew stopped and stared straight in Coop's eyes. There was no sign that he was joking; in fact, he looked dead serious.

"What... What does that mean?"

"It means that, if you're willing to take on a beat-up old army vet who has a penchant for running around in dangerous situations on a regular basis, I'm all yours."

"You mean you want to have a monogamous relationship?"

"Definitely monogamous. I don't share."

"Well, neither do I. Ever."

"Easy, beautiful, I'm officially a one-man guy," Coop said, and Matthew's heart beat faster. Coop wanted to be with him, and more importantly, he wanted Coop, even with all his own self-doubt.

Matthew was on board to see where this led. Coop was gentle and kind to Matthew, and the attraction was off the charts, if there was such a thing. Coop leaned forward and wrapped his hand around Matthew's neck, bringing him closer. His blue eyes sparkled as their lips met, insistent and demanding, both desperate to get closer.

Coop leaned away from the kiss, causing Matthew to pull back, unsure what had happened.

"Oh no, sweetheart, I wasn't pulling away from you. But I do need to take a shower before we get any closer."

Matthew let out a breath he didn't realize he was holding. "Okay, I'll wait here."

Coop stood and began walking, but stopped and turned around. He bent and gathered Matthew into his arms before heading to the door. "You can wait in my room. I don't want you that far away from me."

Coop crossed the hall and walked into his own room. Matthew had never been in there before. Coop placed him on his huge bed and kissed him again, making Matthew lightheaded.

"I won't be long. Then we can talk some more, and I'll go down and get us some food and drinks, unless you want to go down for dinner?"

"No, no I'd rather stay up here together." Matthew wasn't leaving this room willingly.

Coop smiled wide and walked into his ensuite bathroom, not bothering to shut the door. Matthew watched as, inch by inch, Coop's gorgeous body was revealed, first his shirt followed by his pants. Then, just as quickly, he slid out of his boxers.

Coop stood still as if on inspection, hands at his sides, a slight blush to his cheeks. Matthew couldn't wipe the smile off his face if he tried. Coop was gorgeous, every last inch of him, and there were a lot of inches to count. "You're the one who's beautiful, Coop."

Coop blushed even harder and stepped into the shower stall. Soon steam covered the glass enclosure and blocked his view. This gave Matthew a chance to look around Coop's room, at least as far as his current location would allow. The massive bed stood dead center in the room, covered in soft blankets and plush pillows. The large wooden wardrobe and dresser sat regally against the far wall and there was a seating area beside an unlit fireplace. It felt like the room was hugging you, it was so lush and comfortable.

This was where Coop found his solace, and he was sharing this with him. Matthew prayed he hadn't fallen asleep in his own bed and this was all a dream, because he was going to be really pissed off.

***

Coop lathered his body as he thought about Matthew in his private domain. Instead of it seeming odd, as he'd expected, it felt good to have someone he could finally share it with. He'd never shared anything this personal with anyone before, except for that one time when he was drunk off his ass and shared his fucked-up childhood with the teammates. He never repeated that again. He didn't need anyone's pity or concern; a lot of people had messed-up childhoods.

He went back to more enjoyable thoughts, like the beautiful man in his bed at that very moment. If he had to put his perfect man together, it would be Matthew. He was smart, kind, caring, and no matter what Matthew thought of himself, he was gorgeous to Coop in every way.

Coop suddenly realized another part of his body was taking interest in the man on his bed, but this was not the right time. He couldn't just maul Matthew, could he? No—no, he couldn't act like a horny teenager. He had to take things at whatever pace Matthew chose. This wasn't a one-night stand. With a few well-placed thumps, he got himself back under control—and though it was painful, it was effective.

Coop finished up in the shower as quickly as possible and walked back into his room in only a towel; he'd put on one of his track pants from his dresser. Matthew was still sitting in the same spot surveying the room until his eyes stopped on Coop. The heat in that one look brought Coop's hard-on back with a vengeance. There was nothing he could do, his towel was tenting.

Coop's face heated up. "I'm sorry, but you're lying in my bed and I—"

"It's okay, Coop. I'm in a similar situation." Matthew moved his arm, exposing a sizeable bulge in his track pants. He remembered feeling that hard cock against his thigh the night they slept in each other's arms. He'd barely held back then; now was ten times worse.

"Oh, babe, you're killing me. I'm trying to be good here," Coop said, his voice deeper than before.

"I think it would be good of you to come over here and help me with this. I'm sure I could find a way to make you feel better too," Matthew said with a big smile on his face, and Coop was doomed. He would give anything to see that smile every day.

***

Matthew had no idea where this brazen behavior was coming from, but it was new. He'd never been forceful with a lover, but something about Coop brought a whole new side out in him, and he liked it. Matthew slid back on the bed, laying his head down on the plush pillows; he began unbuttoning his own shirt.

"Stop," Coop ordered. "Slowly undress for me, baby."

Matthew couldn't help but smile. This was perhaps one of the sexiest things he'd ever done. He wasn't typically this adventurous. Matthew ran his fingers up and down his torso, stopping to play with his own nipples before removing his shirt, slowly moving from one button to the other. His pants were another matter; with his cast, they weren't easy to remove. Thankfully, Coop came to his rescue and gently slid the pants over his cast. Now Matthew lay only in his boxers, and Coop was still in his towel. Matthew desperately wanted them both gone.

"I want you naked, big guy," Matthew said, his voice was much stronger than he felt.

Coop smiled that roguish grin of his and let the towel drop. Matthew's cock throbbed to be set free of its confines.

"Let me help you with this." Coop reached for Matthew's boxers and brought them down and over his cast.

Coop crawled on the bed and began to stalk him—there was no better way to describe it. He covered Matthew with his own body and began kissing Matthew's neck and shoulder. Coop's touch sent electricity straight to Matthew's sensitive balls. Matthew knew he wouldn't last long. Coop's hard cock rubbed against his leg as Coop's lips traveled downward and latched on to one of Matthew's nipples, flicking his tongue as he sucked.

"Coop... Baby, I'm not going to last long if you keep that up."

Instead of answering, Coop reared up and brought their cocks together in one of his large hands. He began to pump while he held his weight off Matthew with his other arm. His intense blue eyes never left Matthew's. It was so intimate, like Coop could see straight into his soul.

"Come for me, Matthew."

He was powerless to stop himself. Fire raced down his spine and straight for his swollen balls, and out his throbbing shaft as he muffled his scream in his hand. A few seconds later, Coop's body convulsed and come splashed onto Matthew's stomach. He melted back into the soft mattress, completely relaxed.

Coop leaned his head down and kissed Matthew with such tenderness that his heart beat faster. He lowered his body down beside Matthew and gathered him into his arms. They lay quietly, neither talking but both content to lie in silence, until Matthew's wet belly began to cool.

Before Matthew could say a word, Coop kissed him and said, "I'll whip us up a warm cloth and get you cleaned, beautiful."

Matthew was touched by Coop's care and wondered if this was a one-off or going to be a regular occurrence. He preferred the latter.

A few moments later, Coop returned with a warm washcloth and proceeded to tenderly clean Matthew. With everything they had done up to this point, this seemed even more intimate, which was strange considering what they'd just shared.

"I'll get dressed and go downstairs and get us something to eat, Matthew. And then we can eat picnic style on the floor in front of the fire. How does that sound?"

"Sounds great, be better if you didn't have to leave," Matthew joked, but now that his hormones had been satisfied, old fears came back.

Coop left with promises of a speedy return as Matthew's self-doubts crept in. He looked down at himself, numbering off his flaws as he went. Freckles covered his body, his skin was too pale, not one defined muscle to be seen, and then there was always his screwed-up multicolored eyes to cap it all off.

He wasn't muscled and tanned like Coop, didn't have his blond hair and deep blue eyes—now *he* was gorgeous. But Coop kept calling Matthew beautiful, so he was either crazy or really did like what he saw—whatever that was. Matthew quickly slid under the covers. It was silly because Coop had already seen him in his naked glory, but he felt too exposed without it.

"Are you cold, beautiful?" Coop asked as he walked in with two plates of food, a bottle of wine, and two glasses. It was a good thing he had big hands. He held up the bottle and smiled. "Thought this might be nice."

Matthew couldn't help but smile back at him. Coop was trying to make everything special; it was a sweet gesture and he appreciated it. Coop set dinner down on the dresser and went over and turned on the gas fireplace, bathing the room in a yellow-orange glow. Matthew sat up, allowing the blanket to fall to his waist. Coop turned and just stared at Matthew with an odd expression on his face.

"What's wrong?" Matthew asked as he pulled the blanket back up to cover himself.

"Nothing, you're just so beautiful," Coop answered. "I'm just kind of surprised you're giving this old army private a chance. Please don't cover up. I'd prefer you to be naked in this room whenever you're in here."

"Fair's fair. You need to be naked as well."

Coop immediately began to strip down, and Matthew let the blanket slip off. Maybe he could live with the fact that he was beautiful to Coop—even if he was the only one who thought so.

Coop gathered a crocheted blanket from a chair and laid it on the floor in front of the fireplace. Then he spread the food and drinks down on the blanket and held his hand out to Matthew. Slowly, he let go of his safety blanket and crawled to the foot of the bed, Coop's eyes tracking his every move.

Matthew slid off the bed and joined Coop in front of the fire. Coop reached out and cupped Matthew's cheek, gently rubbing his fingers across his cheekbones before kissing him breathless. When they parted, Coop's eyes were bright and happy, making Matthew's confidence rise. He could make Coop happy.

He'd missed having someone care for him, considering the last of his family members were killed in a car accident that nearly took Matthew's life as well. It had been years since he'd felt this wanted. Even from previous relationships, the connection hadn't seemed right. This was right. This was the feeling he'd been needing for so long. Now if he could just manage to keep it.

Chapter Four

Matthew took his time climbing into the truck. Sam sat behind the wheel and Coop stood behind Matthew in case he fell. Coop was doing his best to give him some freedom from his hovering and hadn't said a word when Matthew stumbled or got tangled up in his crutches. Coop simply caught him and stood him back up. It took some negotiating for Matthew and Sam to go grocery shopping alone. Dante and Spider were just as protective as Coop. But their men would never hold them back and quickly acquiesced.

Matthew knew Coop was concerned that he might not be able to negotiate the aisles in the store, but they were only picking up a few things, and Matthew felt confident he could do it without incident. He'd been an independent man before the accident, and he was going to damn well be one after.

"So you're sure about this? I can come along you know," Coop asked, that killer smile of his in place.

"Put that away. It's not going to work." Matthew laughed, causing Coop to laugh right along with him. Dante and Spider smiled and watched Coop with interest. Had no one ever seen him laugh in joy before?

"You never let me get away with my completely irresistible, patented smile."

"I guess you shouldn't have gone through the time or trouble of patenting it," Matthew said and then laughed again at Coop's disgruntled look.

Coop leaned in and gave Matthew their first kiss in front of the other team members. Matthew waited for the comments or questions, but they didn't come, not a word. Matthew let out the breath he was holding.

"Beautiful, we're together now, and I'm not about to hide it from anyone. Understand?" Coop whispered.

Matthew couldn't help but smile and nod his head in agreement. He never wanted to hide how much Coop meant to him.

Moments later, they were on their way to town, and Matthew knew Sam wouldn't be able to hold back, so he waited. They reached the main road and turned toward downtown Brighton before the first question was lobbed.

"Soooo, um, anything new?" Sam asked with a grin.

"Nope. Same old, same old," Matthew answered.

"Oh, I'm sure there was definitely something very new… Oh come on, throw a guy a bone here," Sam begged.

Matthew laughed before giving in. "Okay, okay… Yes, Coop and I are together."

"Yes! I knew you two would work it all out. That's great, Matthew."

"Yeah, just as long as I don't mess it up," Matthew replied.

"Mess it up, how?" Sam asked.

"Clumsy may be cute in the beginning, but it wears thin after a while, and my kinda clumsy isn't going to change. I've tried."

"Coop already knows you're a bit accident prone, and why would that make him not want you? He can't take his eyes off you, and he's smiling and laughing. Christ, you breathed a whole new life into him," Sam explained. "I think he loves you."

"Love? That's a little too fast. We've only known each other for a few months. But Coop does seem happy to me." *Love couldn't be on the radar yet, could it?*

"Before, he always seemed to have the weight of the world on him, but now he's got you and he's happy. You have nothing to worry about, Matthew," Sam assured.

Matthew thought about it for a few moments and decided that maybe Sam was right. "Thank you, Sam."

"Anytime. You don't give yourself enough credit. You're wicked smart, you have a generous heart, and you're super cute. What more could he ask for?"

"Super cute, are you kidding? Mildly cute maybe, but super, no way."

"You are. Why do you think so little of yourself?" Sam asked.

"Truthfully, when you're told by your last boyfriend that he stayed with you out of pity, you tend to hold on to those words. He said I was such a freak, from my mismatched eyes to my clumsiness, that in the end he could barely stand being around me," Matthew admitted softly, the memory still painful.

"What an asshole! Obviously, there was something wrong with him because you are no freak, Matthew. I promise you," Sam growled, which was pretty impressive for the gentle man.

"Again, thank you, Sam."

The two sat in amicable silence for the rest of their drive, Matthew caught between believing Sam, and a reality he'd lived with for years. It was hard for Matthew to leave behind his whole perception of himself. It would take time to forget the cruel words, if he could, but he would try.

People waved as they drove down Main Street. This kind of community you couldn't find in big cities, and made Brighton special to Matthew. They pulled up to the grocery store, and he gingerly navigated his injured leg out of the vehicle. The last thing he wanted to do was trip or fall and force Sam to help him up.

Matthew looked across the parking lot and locked eyes with the man who had given him the same hate-filled stare when he and Coop went to the clothing store. He had shoulder-length blond hair, and Matthew guessed he was about twice his size. He was getting a bit freaked out by this guy, and he wondered who the hell he was.

"Matthew, what's wrong?" Sam asked.

He turned to look at Sam. "The other day, when Coop brought me to town to get more clothes, there was this guy who stood outside the window and gave me a death glare. Now he's in the parking lot doing the same thing," Matthew explained.

Both Matthew and Sam turned toward the far side of the parking lot, but the man was gone. "He was just there, I swear."

"I believe you, Matthew. We'll keep an eye out for him. I wonder who he is," Sam said. "Should we go back to the house?"

"No, we can at least get groceries by ourselves." Matthew was trying to regain control and didn't want to run back to the house with his tail between his legs.

"Are you sure you don't recognize him?" Sam asked.

"No, I've never seen him before, but it's starting to creep me out."

"Okay, let's get our groceries and go home. You sure you don't want to go home now?" Sam asked again.

The last thing Matthew wanted to do was overreact. "No, I'm good. Let's go."

He got his crutches underneath him and began heading toward the store. It took a bit, but he hopped on his one good leg and crutches through the front door. To Matthew it was a victory. Sam grabbed a cart and they began moving down the aisles, filling it in no time at all. They were only supposed to do a light shop, but they had a lot of mouths to feed.

Matthew wasn't much help, but he was enjoying their outing all the same. They cashed out and loaded the truck. Matthew was in the process of getting in, and Sam was already behind the wheel, when a car raced across the parking lot headed straight for Matthew. Everything seemed to move in slow motion. Matthew dropped his crutches and pulled himself into the truck by the door handle and grab bar, just as the car sideswiped the truck. The sound of metal screaming as it bent and twisted made Matthew nauseous. He crouched close to Sam on the driver's side, away from his crumpled door as the truck shook. Matthew was covered in glass, and something wet was dripping down from his forehead. He reached up and his hand came away bloody. *Shit!*

The car squealed out of the parking lot, leaving the passenger side door crushed on the ground right where Matthew had been standing. Sam and Matthew sat in shock until several townspeople ran over to help.

"Matthew, he was aiming for you," Sam said, his voice shaking.

"I... I think so," Matthew answered, before the truck was surrounded by people yelling to call the police and an ambulance.

Out of the corner of his eye, he saw his best friend, Jesse, running toward them. By now the blood from his head was almost dripping in his eye. Matthew knew head wounds bled a lot, but this was beginning to freak him out a bit.

"Matthew, Sam, are you okay?" Jesse asked as he leaned in from the now doorless side of the truck. "Matthew, you're bleeding. An ambulance is on the way."

He could hear sirens in the background and knew help was on the way, but he was frozen to the spot. Sam spoke around him and examined his wound, but none of it reached him. Someone was trying to kill him… Matthew felt himself moved out of the truck, but he was still numb to everything around him as they laid him on a stretcher and someone began working on his head wound. In some part of his mind, he recognized the person as being Royce, Jesse's boyfriend and a Brighton paramedic.

There was another squeal of tires, and Matthew couldn't help but curl into a ball. Logically, he knew whoever tried to run him down was gone, but he couldn't help his reaction to the noise.

"Easy, beautiful. I'm here." Coop's voice penetrated the fog surrounding him.

"Coop… Someone tried to kill me," was all Matthew could get out before he began to shake. He thought he could hear his heart beating way too quickly.

"It'll be okay, Matthew. We'll figure this out. I won't let anything happen to you."

"I saw him again," Matthew whispered.

"Who?" Coop asked.

"The man from outside the clothing store," Matthew explained as he slowly sat up on the gurney. Royce had finished bandaging his head, and his tremors were settling down. Matthew was a touch dizzy, but his earlier numbness was slowly slipping away.

"You're going to need stitches, Matthew," Royce said.

"Can I get Coop to take me to the hospital? I don't need to tie up an ambulance for this," Matthew asked.

"You're not tying us up. You're as important as everyone else we help," Royce assured.

"Thank you, but if it's all the same, I'd like to go with Coop."

Royce smiled knowingly. "Of course, Matthew. Just as long as you go."

"He'll be going, I can guarantee that," Coop said. His hand gently rubbed Matthew's leg, calming him further.

"Okay then, you're good to go," Royce said.

"We'll get you right over to the hospital," Coop assured again and lifted Matthew off the gurney.

Matthew's crutches lay on the ground, crushed by the weight of the car, so he had no other choice but to be carried. Oh, who was he kidding? Matthew needed the support and strength he found in Coop's touch more than anything at the moment. Someone tried to kill him, but who and why?

"Do you think someone's discovered my identity and is coming for a little payback? I have hacked multiple criminal organizations during my time working for the government," Matthew wondered.

"We can't rule that out. It could be related to your work, or it could be something completely different. But I swear I won't let anything happen to you, beautiful."

***

As Coop carried Matthew back to his truck, Dante and Spider were still holding Sam between them. They had the same furious look as his own. Their anger wasn't directed at them but at the man responsible for the attack on both Matthew and Sam.

"We have to stop by the hospital. Matthew needs stitches," Coop said. He, Dante, and Spider drove together to get there after Jesse had called them. Coop would be reliving the moment Dante ran into the living room, yelling that Sam and Matthew were in an accident, over and over again in his mind. His heart had finally stopped racing, and he could breathe again now that he had Matthew in his arms.

"Let's get everyone loaded up. A wrecker will come pick up the other truck," Dante ordered. You could always tell when he was furious; he fell back on his military training.

"What about our groceries? They'll be ruined," Matthew said.

"We'll drop you and Coop at the hospital and then take the groceries home before coming back to pick you two up," Dante explained.

"Perfect," Sam agreed.

With that decided, the five of them were on their way, Coop continually scanning the area for anything out of place. Matthew had already described the stranger as having long blond hair and being larger than himself, but that was all he had.

Coop would do whatever it took to protect his beauty. Whatever it took.

***

Matthew's head was pounding from scanning the files on the screen of his laptop all day. He was reviewing each and every case he'd ever worked on, which so far had taken days. Over that time, Coop had taken hovering to a whole new level, but with someone actually out to hurt him, Matthew was okay with that. So far, he'd found nothing in his files, and not one mug shot revealed the man stalking him. Matthew hadn't actually seen the same man behind the wheel of the car, but he couldn't have two separate people after him, could he? *Damn.*

Jesse and Royce had visited and stayed for dinner, allowing Matthew and Jesse to finalize a few options in Matthew's security plan for the youth center and group home. The walls were starting to go up, and soon Matthew would have to do another site visit with the team. He planned to make sure everything had been framed properly. There was a lot of wiring for all the cameras and sensors, as well as the master security office, so there wasn't much room for errors.

Jessie and Royce didn't even bat an eye when Coop sat down beside Matthew on the couch and kissed his neck tenderly. Although Jesse seemed overjoyed, he didn't say a word. He knew Matthew wouldn't feel comfortable being the center of attention. Matthew had gotten another pair of crutches and was now back to navigating the house on his own. So far, he'd only fallen twice.

He and Coop were now sharing Coop's bedroom, but they hadn't done more than rub each other off and cuddle. Matthew was so horny, he was ready to jump Coop in the middle of the night, which was funny considering he was half Coop's size. But he'd give it his best shot.

He had put his laptop aside and was getting ready for bed. Coop was helping him remove his pants over his cast, and Matthew began to harden in his boxers. He wanted to feel his lover deep inside him and had no idea how to ask for what he needed. Should he be forward and just tell Coop what he desired or wait?

"What has you so deep in thought, beautiful?" Coop asked as he dropped their clothing into the laundry hamper.

Well, here goes everything. "I want you to make love to me."

That stopped Coop in his tracks, and he stared at Matthew. His eyes were half closed and his grin gave him an almost wild look. "Are you ready for that, Matthew? I wanted to take things slow. You mean a lot to me, and I don't want to risk what we have by pushing too fast."

Matthew was touched by Coop's thoughtfulness. Coop didn't want to treat him like one of his previous flings. This was special, or at least that's what Matthew hoped he felt. Sometimes he still had self-doubt. Either way, he was too horny to care. He'd been rubbing up against the big guy for days, and he needed some relief.

"Oh, I'm sure I'm ready."

Coop walked toward the bed, his cock already hard, his gaze smoldering. He brushed his unsteady fingers down the side of Matthew's face.

"You're so beautiful inside and out. How did I get this lucky?" Coop said before crawling into bed beside Matthew.

"I'm the lucky one," Matthew countered.

Lips and tongues tangled as Coop kissed him passionately. Matthew snaked his arms up and around Coop's neck and pulled him even closer; he couldn't get enough.

Strong arms held him securely as they rolled across the bed, wrapped around each other, until Matthew lay flat on his back with Coop sucking up marks on his neck. He arched his body to get closer to the sensations while Coop explored lower, torturing one nipple then the other. Soft moans escaped from Matthew's lips as he lost himself to the feeling.

Coop looked up and their eyes locked. "You have no idea what it does to me to hear you moan."

Everywhere Coop touched left him aching with need, his cock begging for attention. Coop kissed and nibbled his way down Matthew's body until he came to his hard cock and, without preamble, sucked him down to the back of his throat. Matthew cried out, not caring who heard him, as pure pleasure flooded him. His hips jerked, pushing him even farther down Coop's throat. His entire body lit up. Coop used his tongue like a finely tuned instrument to bring Matthew to the edge repeatedly.

Matthew had a hard time holding back. His mind reeled with sensations that brought him closer to orgasm until he finally fell over, coming down Coop's throat. Coop let out a satisfied moan before he released Matthew's still-hard cock and flipped him over. A warm, wet tongue pressed against his hole and it sent Matthew soaring. He'd never had anyone lavish this much attention on his body; he felt cherished and loved. Though they hadn't said the words to each other, Coop's actions said it all. Coop's mouth disappeared and was replaced by a slick finger. Matthew had no idea where Coop had gotten the lube but didn't care just as long as he didn't stop.

Soon he sank his finger deep and drew it out slowly before slamming back in. Matthew's mind was reeling as he was assaulted by sensation after sensation. His cock was rock-hard again and ready to shoot. A second and third finger joined the first, and Matthew spread his legs wide, wanton and needy for more. Coop's thrusts increased in strength just before he removed his fingers, leaving Matthew feeling empty.

Coop quickly flipped Matthew to his back. He loved that Coop could move him so easily. His lover reached for a condom and slipped it on before he lifted Matthew's legs to his shoulders, cast and all, and pressed the thick head of his cock to Matthew's hole. In one thrust, he sank deep, and Matthew was thankful Coop prepared him so well, because he was a large man. He began with a slow, leisurely glide that soon sped up until he was slamming into Matthew, pegging his prostate mercilessly. The ecstasy he felt left him speechless, only able to moan his pleasure to Coop. Their bodies moved together in complete unison, grinding and pumping until Matthew's legs shook.

Matthew felt his balls pulling up and knew he'd come again at any moment. "Going to come, baby."

"Yes, come, beautiful. Let me feel your pleasure," Coop said before taking Matthew's mouth in deep, drugged kisses.

That was all it took. Fire raced down his spine, through his balls, and out of his pulsing cock and all over his and Coop's bellies. Coop managed to hold on and keep pumping until his strokes faltered and he groaned long and deep, and heat filled the end of his condom.

Coop rolled them until Matthew lay on top, both gasping for air. In that moment, Matthew knew he wouldn't be able to go on without Coop. His heart was no longer his own; it belonged to Coop.

***

Coop lay awake holding the man he was quickly falling in love with, excited and scared all at the same time. What they'd shared just solidified the fact in his mind and his heart. But love always meant sadness and pain to him. He didn't want to be his parents. The fighting, the screaming, and the hate spewed all over his childhood should have taught him not to go anywhere near love. But this could be different—it would have to be different.

On top of his own fears, he had to keep Matthew safe from some mystery man stalking him around Brighton. When they'd received the call from Jesse telling them that Matthew and Sam had been involved in an accident at the grocery store, his heart had stopped. Then to find out the same man that had been glaring at Matthew could have been the driver spiked his anger to levels he'd never shown anyone.

Matthew began to twitch in his sleep, and Coop knew what came next. The nightmares had been increasing in frequency to the point that now Matthew would wake several times a night. Coop understood that knowing someone was trying to kill him would have an effect on Matthew.

"I've got you, beautiful. You're safe," Coop whispered, helping Matthew to calm.

The fact that he had that effect on Matthew meant more to Coop than he would ever admit. His heart was softening and reaching out to Matthew, and he was helpless to stop it. For someone who didn't believe in love and who had a fear of commitment, he certainly was jumping into the deep end.

He took a good long look at the beautiful man in his arms. Matthew's shaggy brown hair framed his freckled face. Breathtaking inside and out. Something about Matthew drew Coop like some sort of magnetic pull that he was helpless to fight.

But now their future was at risk, and times would only get tougher as they searched for the person responsible for trying to run Matthew down. For any reason, his parents would start screaming at each other; stress only made that worse. Would the stress of what was to come be enough for them to snap at each other? Unfortunately, they would find out all too soon.

The next morning found them at the construction site for the new youth center and group home. Matthew was busy checking and rechecking that everything he'd requested in the plans had come to fruition. Of course, everything wasn't 100 percent complete, but the bones were there and that's exactly what Matthew said he was looking for. Soon they'd run the wiring and then close the walls up before setting the sensors.

Coop watched as Matthew navigated the construction site with his crutches. He really was getting the hang of it, although Coop had had to right him a few times. The building was three stories tall and would house up to forty youths. The architect had done a phenomenal job with his design: there were bold curves and lines throughout that kept the building unique and welcoming all at the same time. Coop had brought along Vincent to keep an eye on everything as he escorted Matthew from floor to floor. He'd never been more thankful for his teammates as he was right then. They'd rallied around them to keep Matthew safe, and for that he'd be eternally grateful.

Coop noticed several members of the community of Brighton working alongside the construction crew, volunteering their time to help out. The White Hair Crew were busy setting up for lunch, the smell of chili filling the air. The second building, which would be the recreation/learning center, was further along than the housing units. There were classrooms and a gymnasium as well as a pool.

They found Travis, the man who worked with Jesse, covered in paint with a smile on his face as he worked away in the gymnasium. The smaller man was being shadowed by a mountain of an off-duty police officer, Bo Mason. Though he was painting as well, it was easy to see that Travis was what really held his attention. Coop knew that feeling; he could barely pull his eyes away from Matthew.

The rec center was set up for the youths staying in the housing units, but also for the youths of Brighton to come and enjoy. Jesse had told them over dinner that he'd had several people wishing to volunteer their time teaching classes and running programs for the center. Brighton was certainly a different town than Coop was used to. The community was tight-knit and always ready to jump in and help out.

"So, what do you think?" Jesse asked as he joined Coop and Matthew. Vincent was nowhere to be seen, but Coop knew better. He wouldn't be far away.

"It's going to be amazing," Matthew gushed, and Coop could see the happiness written all over his face. That was the look Coop wanted to see more often, not the terrified one he'd woken to last night.

"Thank you. I'm proud of it." Jesse blushed.

"You should be. This place will make such a big difference to so many lives," Matthew said.

"I hope so. We'll know in a couple months. We've already sent out word to other LGBTQ+ and youth organizations that we'll be opening in a few months, and we've already had inquiries for rooms and teaching positions."

"That's great. This place will be full in no time, and I'll run the security check on each new hire for you," Matthew said as he leaned into Coop. He could tell Matthew was getting tired, probably from lugging his cast around a construction site.

"What if we fill up and can't help someone in need?" Jesse asked, tension showing on his face.

"Don't be worrying about things that haven't happened yet. If you need more space, we'll make space. You have a lot of people behind you, Jesse, that want to help you succeed," Coop said.

"I know. I've been blown away by the people of this town. By the way, any more incidents of that stranger coming around?" Jesse asked.

"Nothing so far. I hope it stays that way," Matthew said.

"Do you think it will?" Jesse asked.

"No."

Chapter Five

The doctor's office was packed for a Wednesday morning as Matthew waited with Coop. He was sure there were other members of the team hanging around town just in case his mystery man showed up. Matthew had been looking forward to today's appointment. If everything was healing correctly, he might be given a walking cast to make it easier for him to get around. It would continue to immobilize his ankle and foot without adding pressure to his injuries. Matthew couldn't wait to get this plaster cast off. It was hot, itchy, and hard to move around in.

"Mr. Whitton," the nurse called out.

Matthew stood up and, with the help of his crutches, hopped into an examining room. Coop was right behind him.

His orthopedist came in and took one look at Coop. "Mister…"

"Mr. Stenson," Coop answered.

"Yes, Mr. Stenson. Please wait outside."

"No."

"No?"

"Yes, no."

The doctor was taken aback for a moment before Matthew jumped in to defuse the situation. "This is my partner, Coop. I would like him to stay in here with me, please."

"Fine, but stand by the door out of the way."

Matthew had no idea why the doctor was so upset by having both of them in the room, but Coop wasn't going anywhere—Matthew could tell by the set of his jaw. The nurse came in and assisted the doctor in removing the plaster cast, and he examined Matthew's ankle and foot. The skin looked white and wrinkly, but the swelling and bruising were gone. They did a quick X-ray and waited for word from the doctor.

"Well, looks like you're healing nicely, Mr. Whitton. I think we can put you in a walking cast as long as you don't overdo it," the doctor said as he returned to the room.

"I'll make sure he takes it easy," Coop said from his spot at the door.

"Good, now let's get you fitted," the doctor said, finally thawing a bit toward Coop.

Thirty minutes later, Matthew walked out of the doctor's office without his crutches. Though he may have been walking a bit slower and had a cane, he was free of the clumsy crutches. Holding hands with Coop, Matthew was so happy that he almost missed the man following him across the street. His blond hair shone in the sunlight, but his glare made his face look cruel and menacing.

"That's him," Matthew whispered.

But Coop didn't look surprised or concerned at all. He just kept walking hand in hand with him through the parking lot. Why wasn't he doing something? What was going on?

"Easy, baby, Shadow and Shannon are almost on him," Coop said softly, still acting as if everything was normal.

Matthew didn't feel as confident as Coop but carried on all the same. He chanced a glance over just in time to see Shadow grab the stranger's arm, causing the man to pull his other hand back in a fist, readying to strike Shadow. He didn't get a chance. Shannon had him on the ground before he had a chance to throw a punch. Police cars rolled up on the scene, and yet Coop continued to walk away as if nothing was happening.

"I'm going to take you home and come back into town to have a word with the mystery man," Coop said.

"Wait a minute, he's following me. I should be there." Matthew stopped walking and pulled on Coop's hand.

"Do you really want to face him up close?" Coop asked.

"No, but this is something I need to do." Matthew wasn't going to run away and hide. He deserved answers.

Coop stopped them at the truck and looked deeply into Matthew's eyes. "If this is something you need, then I will make sure it happens."

Matthew smiled, knowing his lover wanted to protect him but understood that he couldn't hold him back. That would never work in their relationship.

"Thank you, Coop."

The next thing he knew, he was in Coop's arms being held close to his muscled chest. "You're brave, Matthew."

Now that was one word he'd never use to describe himself, but if Coop wanted to believe he was brave, who was he to stop him? He climbed into the truck with Coop's help and they were off, to come face-to-face with someone who scared the hell out of him. Brave indeed… hardly.

***

Coop wracked his brain as he drove toward the police station. For some unknown reason, he recognized the face of the man who had been harassing his lover, but from where? Could this be about him and not Matthew? Was Matthew a target now just to get to him?

"It'll be okay…right?" Matthew asked, his uninjured leg bouncing up and down.

"Everything will be okay, no matter what we find out."

Matthew looked at him strangely but didn't ask him to explain. They pulled up outside the station right beside Dante and Spider's Hummer. How they beat them there was a mystery, but it probably involved breaking a few traffic laws. He helped Matthew from the truck, and they walked into the building in silence. Coop still searched his memories; he was even more convinced he knew the man. But how?

Once inside, they found Dante in Police Chief Graham's office. They were having a heated discussion, and neither bothered to acknowledge them when they walked in.

"No, and that's final," Chief Graham growled.

"They should be given the choice," Dante said, his voice low.

Coop waited until Matthew sat and then went to break up whatever this was. "Hey, guys, what's got your panties in a wad?"

Both men turned to look at Coop. *Okay, maybe interrupting wasn't such a bright idea.*

"Let them choose," Dante said as he looked at both Coop and Matthew.

"Choose what?" Coop asked.

"The prisoner wants to talk to the both of you," Dante answered.

"Why?" Matthew asked.

"That's the part we don't know. He wouldn't answer any of our questions and stated only his first name. We'll send off his fingerprints to get him identified," Chief Graham said.

"Do the two of you want to talk to him? His name is Robert," Dante asked.

He looked at Matthew to gauge his reaction to the request. "It's up to you, Matthew. We go in only if you want to."

Matthew sat there silent for a moment before he nodded his head. "I want to know why."

"He may not tell you anything you want to know. Maybe he just wants to mess with you," Chief Graham said.

"But I won't know for sure unless I try. I'm going in," Matthew stated.

"We're going in," Coop said.

"Okay, but we'll be watching and listening from the security cameras installed in the cells," Chief Graham said.

"Let's get this over with." Matthew stood and took Coop's hand.

They walked through the maze of desks until they came to the locked doors of the holding cells.

"Ready?" Coop asked.

"As much as I'm ever going to be."

The chief unlocked the door and held it open for them. He and Matthew walked into a three-cell room. Only one cell was occupied. Robert sat on the floor, leaning his back against the bars.

"Ah, you decided to face me with your new plaything," Robert spat venomously.

Coop had no idea why he knew this man, but somehow he did. "Who are you?"

Robert stood so quickly that Matthew took a step back. Coop angled his body in front of Matthew.

"You don't remember me!" Robert screamed.

Obviously the wrong thing to say by the way the man was acting. Matthew took a step forward.

"Why are you following me?" Matthew asked.

The man turned his savage look on Matthew, but Coop wouldn't allow that. The poor guy already had nightmares. "Let's go, Matthew. He only wants to try to intimidate you."

"Really, don't you want to hear how I know your man, Matthew?" Each word was laced with innuendo, and suddenly Coop had an even worse feeling in his stomach.

"Let me guess," Matthew said, his voice calm. "You slept with him."

Both Robert's and Coop's mouths hung open as they stared at Matthew. Coop was floored by the nonchalant way Matthew just said that. Coop couldn't think of anything to say.

"I know about your past, Coop. There isn't anything this man can say that would change how I feel about you. What I don't understand"—he addressed Robert—"is why you're following me if it's Coop you want."

"It's because of you that he doesn't come out to the bars in Rockport anymore."

"I haven't been to Rockport in months," Coop responded with a growl. He didn't like this all thrown in Matthew's face. Sure, he had a past, but Matthew didn't need to be confronted by it.

"So I came looking for you, and I found the reason why you never came back. I must say, I'm very disappointed," Robert said.

"That's it, we're out of here, and you can rot in here for stalking and attempted murder," Coop growled.

"Attempted murder of who?" The viciousness in his voice was gone, replaced by confusion and a touch of fear.

"When you ran your car into Matthew's truck. If anything, assault with a deadly weapon."

"What car? I don't own a car. I take the bus here," Robert replied. "Hey, I may have stalked him a little, but I didn't try to hurt him. I just wanted to know what he had that I didn't."

"I tell everyone I'm intimate with that I don't want a relationship with them. I was straight up about that only being a one-time thing. You would have known that up front," Coop explained.

"But knowing you'd never be back, that I wouldn't get another round with you. It was too much!" Robert yelled.

Coop feared that someday this would happen, that someone would become attached during a one-night stand. Now the results were being played out in front of the man he loved.

The door opened behind them and Dante and Chief Graham walked in. *Great, now it's a party.* Coop couldn't possibly be more ashamed of his past if he tried at the moment.

"You said you don't own a car. Give us your full name and address, and we'll check that out."

"I don't even have a driver's license," Robert said. He was all too willing to give the chief his personal information now.

"As for everything else, you will be charged with stalking and a protection order will be issued against you. If you come anywhere near Matthew or Coop again, I will arrest you on the spot," Chief Graham explained. "Do you understand?"

For the first time, Robert looked dejected; he deflated on the spot as he slid down to the floor and leaned against the bars again. "Yes, I understand."

Coop looked at Matthew; his face was blank. He got this same sick feeling in his stomach just before his parents fought. Would this be their first fight? This was the thing he feared most: he didn't want to be his parents. Coop led a quiet Matthew out of the police station and back to his truck.

As they drove away from downtown, the silence in the truck was deafening. It seemed that Matthew was in his own world. All Coop could think of doing was apologizing profusely.

"I'm so sorry, beautiful. I didn't mean for this to happen."

Matthew looked at Coop with his eyes squinted, like he was trying to figure something out. "Sorry...about Robert? While I'll admit it was a little uncomfortable to be faced with one of your past conquests, it wasn't your fault he followed you here, and that was all before me. I'm not upset with you. I'm upset because I obviously have someone else after me. This isn't over."

Coop pulled the truck off to the side of the road and sat there stunned for a moment. Matthew wasn't mad. He wasn't going to scream or call him names and hit him like his parents used to do to each other. He turned to Matthew, undid his seat belt, and leaned over and wrapped him in his arms.

"Thank you for not being like them."

"Being like who?" Matthew asked.

Coop hadn't meant to say that; this was one area he hadn't divulged to Matthew. "Can we finish this conversation at home? This needs to be explained in bed with you in my arms."

"Sure, Coop, I can wait." Matthew's smile was genuine. How did he get so lucky to have a partner this understanding?

Coop put his seat belt on and pulled the truck back onto the road. Coop's mind was racing. Would Matthew understand his fears or would he think it was an excuse? If history were anything to go by, he'd understand, but unfortunately it would be like ripping a bandage off an old wound for Coop.

It only took another five minutes to get back home, and instead of stopping to talk to anyone, they both headed straight up to their room. Coop was sure everyone was wondering what was going on, but at the moment he didn't care. He was going to reveal the most painful memories of his childhood, and he felt like he was about to throw up.

Once the door to their room was closed, Matthew said, "Coop, it's okay. You don't have to tell me."

"No, I do. I want you to know everything about me. I… I love you," Coop said, laying everything on the line.

Matthew stood motionless, his eyes wide, his mouth hanging open. Coop was about to back away when Matthew hobbled over and stumbled into his arms. "I love you too. I love you, Coop."

He held Matthew close, thankful he wasn't alone in his feelings. He buried his face in Matthew's hair and breathed deeply. The smell of Matthew's shampoo and his natural scent filled his senses. He was in love. He'd never felt this way before, and someone loved him back. He couldn't be happier.

"Why don't we lie in bed and I'll explain about how I was raised in a screwed-up home," Coop suggested, his voice grim.

"Clothed or naked?" Matthew asked, his eyes shining with unshed tears.

"Your choice, beautiful."

Matthew immediately started to strip out of his clothes, and Coop quickly followed his lead. Within moments, they were both naked and holding each other tight. Coop didn't want to let go, but if he didn't, he'd carry Matthew to bed and forget all about talking. So he broke his hold and took Matthew's hand.

"We need to talk before I lose track of what we're supposed to be doing."

Matthew nodded in agreement and followed him to the bed. After they climbed in, Coop gathered Matthew to his chest and lay back. Matthew remained quiet, giving Coop the opportunity to gather his troubled thoughts.

"When I was young, I thought the way you expressed love was by yelling. If not, why would my parents be continually screaming at each other? I learned that love meant pain, arguing, humiliation, and hate. As I got older, I realized that other families didn't fight all the time. I never wanted to fall in love. I always feared it would be the same. My father had a heart attack in the middle of one particularly ugly fight. My mother didn't leave him in peace in the afterlife for long. She passed away less than a year later. I know it's crazy, but I always believed that love meant pain—until I met you, Matthew."

Matthew raised his head and squeezed Coop harder. "That's why you always had one-night stands, so you could walk away afterward without risking having feelings for someone. Coop, I'm so sorry that your parents did that to you, that they taught you to fear love."

"Then you snuck into my life and messed up everything I've ever known about love, and now I'm fighting to keep up with my feelings for you."

"It feels like everything is moving so fast, and it's a little scary," Matthew said.

"Exactly. You feel it too?" Coop asked, hoping he wasn't the only one.

"Yes, but I don't want to slow down," Matthew said with conviction. Coop agreed wholeheartedly.

"I remember one time my parents decided to take me to a theme park. The closest one was a day's drive away, so we jumped into the van and drove there. I was so excited—well, until the fighting started up worse than ever. I was stuck in a car with two people who hated one another. Eventually my father turned the car around when we were mere miles from the park. He said his family didn't deserve a vacation and drove us all the way back home in silence. I don't know which was worse, the yelling or the silence."

"I'm so sorry. No one should have to go through their childhood like that," Matthew said, voice cracking as he spoke. Coop didn't know how he felt about his lost childhood, but his life now was pretty great. He had Matthew and his friends, who were more like family to him than his own had ever been.

"My life is so much better now, but I keep reliving the fears of those days. It's like at any moment, I'm waiting for our relationship to blow up."

"It will take time for those wounds to heal. I believe the longer we're together the less those fears will be, until eventually they're gone. I love you, Coop, and I intend to keep you."

"You do?"

"Yes, I do," Matthew agreed. "You know there will be times when we won't agree and could fight over something, but it doesn't mean I don't love you. What matters is how we work it out together."

Coop pulled Matthew closer, needing to feel his body against his own. He'd explained his childhood to Matthew and his lover understood where his fear stemmed from. He'd consoled Coop instead of running away from him. That meant the world to him. He had Matthew's support, and he had someone in his corner.

Now that his mind was a bit clearer, Coop noticed the warm body glued to his side. He could feel Matthew's hard cock brushing against his hip, matching his own. He lifted Matthew and laid him on top of his chest, while he snaked his hand down to grab hold of his lover's hard-on. Matthew's moan was like music to his ears.

They'd both gotten tested a few days earlier so that they could do away with the condoms. They were in a committed relationship, and this would be the first time he'd ever made love without a condom. He couldn't wait to feel Matthew without a barrier between them. Coop grabbed the lube from under the pillow, released Matthew's cock, and placed a liberal amount of lube on his fingers. He then reached around Matthew's body, as he lay on top of Coop, and found his little hole. He slid one finger in and listened to Matthew moan out his pleasure.

"I love it when you moan, beautiful."

Matthew was pushing into his touch, so Coop added another finger. It wasn't long before he had three fingers inside his lover and Matthew was ready for him. Coop lifted him up into a sitting position over top of his hard cock.

"Put me inside you, beautiful."

Matthew, his eyes glazed over with passion, reached down and lined up Coop's cock with his hole. Coop pushed his thick member in deep and felt the heat and tightness for the first time completely bare. It was wonderful. His entire body lit up as pure pleasure skated through him. Matthew raised and lowered himself as Coop increased the pace of his thrusts. Coop took hold of Matthew's slim cock again and pumped with every thrust until Matthew was begging him to go faster and faster, both of them groaning together.

"Big guy, I'm going to come," Matthew whimpered just before he exploded across Coop's abdomen. Seconds later, Coop came deep inside his lover and partner. He jerked his hips a few more times before he stilled, arms wrapped around Matthew. They lay quietly until Coop heard Matthew's soft snores. He carefully rolled Matthew to his back and pulled free of his body. He went to the bathroom and cleaned up before bringing a cloth back to wash Matthew, who didn't wake. Coop crawled back into bed beside the one man who loved him no matter what his hang-ups were, his beautiful Matthew. Now he just needed to figure out who the second person was that was after his partner and remove that threat. He doubted sleep would be coming to him tonight.

Chapter Six

"So we have another person involved in whatever this is?" Shadow asked from across the table.

Matthew knew this meeting was important, and he felt guilty for involving everyone in his troubles, but it was necessary to keep him safe and he knew it.

"Yes, the stalker has been cleared of having anything to do with the attack," Dante replied.

"I'm so sorry about all this. I honestly don't know who is after me," Matthew said.

"None of this is your fault, but we'll figure this out," Coop said.

"Yeah, this is what we do," Vincent said with a friendly smile. "Just consider us your bodyguards."

"I wish I didn't need bodyguards. Who would want to hurt me?" Matthew asked in frustration.

"We have a few feelers out right now. We should have word back within a couple days," Spider explained as he filled his coffee cup for the third time.

The sun was just beginning to rise, and Mrs. Walker was busy in the kitchen. The team sat around the dining room table, but since the meeting was called so early, their breakfast wasn't ready yet.

"What if it still has something to do with Coop?" Shannon asked.

"Then we'll deal with it the same way as any other threat to one of ours—we eliminate it," Spider growled.

Matthew had wracked his brain and came up empty on possible matches to the person who'd tried to run him down. He'd always led a relatively quiet life, other than being behind the scenes on missions. That's where the excitement ended. Matthew thought back to the contract he had in his dresser. He could be part of the team, a part of this family. He already knew what his answer was, but he wanted to speak to Coop first. After all, this would be affecting him as well.

"Coop, could I have a word with you for a moment?"

Coop looked confused but nodded his head in agreement. Matthew stood with the help of his cane, and he and Coop walked toward the couches. He felt a little unsure. What if Coop didn't want him as part of the team? They sat on the couch side by side as breakfast was served to everyone at the table.

"Coop, I need your opinion on something that will probably affect both of us."

"Is something wrong?"

"No, but do you remember that day I had a meeting with Dante, Spider, and Sam?"

"Yes."

"Well, they offered me a position on the team, working behind the scenes, doing what I do best with computers and armaments. I was thinking of accepting their offer."

"We'd be working together like on the last mission?" Coop asked.

"Yes, if it's okay with you."

"Why wouldn't it be okay with me?"

"Well, we're just beginning this relationship, and then we'll be working together on top of that." Matthew lowered his head. "You might get tired of having me around so much." The cruel words of his last ex still bouncing around in his head: *I could barely stand being near you.*

Coop reached over and cupped Matthew's cheek. "I could never get tired of you. I've spent most of my life alone and too afraid to get close to anyone. Now that I have you, I don't want you anywhere else. If you want the job, take it, beautiful. I'll support any decision you make."

Matthew wanted to cry. Coop wanted him around; he wanted him near. Matthew hugged Coop tightly. "Thank you."

Coop kissed him gently before leading him back to the dining room table. Once he was seated, he turned in Dante, Spider, and Sam's direction. "I would like to accept your offer."

The three of them smiled back at him, and Dante said, "Perfect, you can consider yourself hired as of the day of the mission when you flew that drone."

"Can we start with my shop?" Matthew asked. His workshop was very important to him.

"Wait, is Matthew joining the team?" Shadow asked.

"Yes, we get Matthew's expertise, and this will give Shannon more time out in the field. Matthew will be dealing with our computers, munitions, and various other amazing things he develops," Dante said.

"Other things?" Coop asked.

Matthew looked at Dante, wondering how he knew what he would need the shop for. "We did some digging before we made you that offer. Apparently, there's a general who can't sing your praises enough, said your technology saved his team."

Matthew knew who that general was. It had been over five years earlier when he was perfecting his heat signature glasses, specially designed with the ability to tell friend from foe. They were indispensable when working at night. The glasses allowed the wearer to pick out different heat signatures in the dark. Combined with all the members of the team wearing special uniforms that lit up blue when looked at through the glasses, it became necessary in this instance. As it turned out, that mission had been a trap and the glasses had helped save a lot of lives.

"I believe in using technology to protect. It's a hobby of mine."

"Sounds like a calling to me, and we get to benefit from it," Dante said.

Matthew looked up at Coop and saw the pride shining from his eyes, making Matthew feel ten feet tall. His lover was proud of him. He'd never had that happen before.

"Okay, so let's get your shop up and running as soon as possible," Shannon agreed.

"I have to go back to San Diego."

Coop growled at that and pulled Matthew closer.

"I only have to go back to make arrangements to sell my condo and to bring my equipment down here from my garage, as well as a few prototypes and the rest of my belongings."

That seemed to settle Coop, and he said, "We can make plans to take a couple trucks over and move everything. Will that be enough room or should we bring three?"

"Two should be enough. I plan on selling the condo furnished, considering I'll be living here in this house with you," Matthew said, and Coop smiled even wider.

"Eventually, we're planning on sectioning off land so that everyone can build their own homes," Sam explained.

"We'll get started on your shop and make plans to head to San Diego," Coop agreed.

"The team doesn't have to come with us to San Diego," Matthew said.

"As long as there's a threat to you, we all go," Coop explained.

"Okay, now that that has been settled, let's eat up and then go outside to decide where your shop is going to be," Sam suggested, and everyone dug back into their food as if they hadn't eaten in days, instead of less than twelve hours ago at supper.

Coop stood and went to get two plates for himself and Matthew. He filled them with eggs, bacon, hash browns, and pancakes. There was no way Matthew would be able to eat all that, but he knew Coop would be able to help him finish. The rest of breakfast was spent making plans for the future, something Matthew had never allowed himself the pleasure of doing. Now that he had something to look forward to, the future didn't feel so bleak.

***

Coop was overjoyed with this turn of events. Matthew was preparing to move all his belongings from San Diego to Brighton; they would be teammates as well as partners. For someone who couldn't have anything other than a one-night stand, this was a big leap into the unknown for him, but for Matthew he would give this his all.

Within a couple days, the frame was up on Matthew's workshop, which would be a forty-foot-by-forty-foot building that would house all his experiments and creations. There would be a new firing range created for him out back beside the existing one. Just in case he blew his up, he wouldn't ruin the other range. There would also be a four-post lift added to help Matthew work on the vehicles. Coop was proud of his partner; he was truly an amazing man, and he was all Coop's.

"It looks great, doesn't it?" Matthew asked from the other side of the workshop. They'd hired a few of the construction personnel from

Jesse's job site to work weekends here when they weren't working on the youth center.

"It looks wonderful, Matthew," Coop replied.

"I've never had this much space to work in before. God, the things I'm going to be able to do," Matthew gushed with happiness.

A few of the construction workers had stopped to watch Matthew, and Coop knew interest when he saw it. He had to admit, Matthew looked so happy he was glowing in the sunlight, but that still didn't mean they should stare. Coop walked over and gave Matthew a fierce kiss in front of all the onlookers.

"That ought to have done it," Matthew said with a laugh.

"What do you mean?"

"You were marking your territory. You should know there's no one for me but you."

"I'm not worried about you. It's the rest of these guys that I have to watch."

"You're sweet, but they're not interested in me. You, yes; me, never." Coop was confused. How could Matthew not see it? He was gorgeous, and the men were staring at him. In fact, one of the workers was still staring, which bothered Coop enough to keep an eye on the man.

***

Matthew went on to check out the various hookups and wiring, moving away from Coop and his compliments and the staring men. They couldn't have been staring at him. How could Coop be so blind to the obvious? Matthew went on to check the installation of another security sensor. So far, he'd been impressed with the work that had been done.

By the time he realized he wasn't alone, it was too late. Matthew turned around in the corner to find one of the workers standing close. He had both of his arms pressed against opposite walls, effectively trapping Matthew into the corner.

"Can I help you?" Matthew asked, feeling uncomfortable with the man so close.

"Oh, you can help me with lots of things, sweetheart," the man said with a lecherous smile. Matthew didn't like the sound of that.

"I'll have to ask you to back up. You're too close to me," Matthew said as he tried to back up into the corner.

"But I like being close to you," the stranger said. "I want to get closer."

"He asked you to back away from him. I suggest you move." Coop's voice came from somewhere behind the man, but Matthew's view was blocked.

Matthew had never felt as relieved as he did at that moment. Coop was here. But the mean smirk the man had on his face changed his relief to fear all over again. "I'll be seeing you again," he said before he backed away from Matthew and turned to leave.

Dante came around the corner and must have sensed the tension in the air. "Coop, what's going on?"

The man was still standing between Matthew and Coop, blocking Matthew's path. He didn't know if it was intentional or not, but he needed the man to move.

"Someone has decided to get up close and personal with Matthew. I'm just going to help him find the door. He won't be working on this property any longer."

"Hey, I was just talking to the guy," the stranger grumbled.

"You had him pinned into the corner," Coop growled.

Dante stepped forward. "I'll show him the way out." There were no other words needed; Dante would make sure the man left.

The stranger didn't say another word. He simply smiled at Matthew and followed Dante out of the building. Matthew made a straight line to Coop's open arms. Whatever it was that just happened left him shaken.

"It's okay, Matthew. He's gone."

"Why would he behave that way?" Matthew asked.

"I have no idea. I was just giving you some alone time to look at your new building when I noticed the man missing. It took everything inside me not to rip the guy away from you. His only saving grace was that he hadn't touched you."

"Do we know who he is?" Matthew asked.

"No, but he's not from Brighton. Some of the construction workers from the youth center are from out of town. I'm sure Dante and Spider know who he is."

"Maybe it'll be worth a look into his background," Matthew suggested.

"Bet you a massage Dante is already on it. Let's go check. I could use a back rub," Coop said, and Matthew knew he was simply trying to calm him further.

"Well, my neck needs some attention, so you're on," Matthew played along.

Coop took Matthew's hand and headed for the house where they found Dante and Spider talking. "I didn't like the look in his eyes when he drove off."

"Then we'll have Matthew check him out," Spider agreed. "What do you think, Matthew?"

He looked from Coop to Dante and Spider and knew his opinion really mattered. He belonged to a team that would value his opinion. "Well, the guy gave me the creeps and wouldn't back off, so I think it's worth a look-see."

Dante handed him a file and said, "Here you go. This is his information from his employment record with Jesse. We had the information for all the men working on the property sent over to us."

"I'll get right on this," Matthew said as he opened the file.

"Thank you. It'll make me feel better knowing if there's anything to worry about," Coop said as he followed Matthew from the room.

Matthew led the way to his laptop sitting on the dining room table. They sat down and Matthew went to work.

"So, do we call it even?" Coop asked.

"Even?" Matthew asked.

"Well, I did say they'd be looking into him already, but they were only talking about it, so I can't claim the complete win," Coop explained.

"Then doesn't that mean I won if you can't claim a victory?" Matthew teased as he turned his computer on.

"Oh, come on, beautiful," Coop whined. "Fine, I'll rub your neck."

"And I'll rub your back, because I just love having my hands on you." Matthew laughed and then opened his favorite search program, one of his own creation.

He still felt a little off about the whole situation, but maybe he was overreacting. This may have been a way the strange man picked up men in the past. Maybe this had nothing to do with whoever was after him…right?

***

Coop was still furious hours later. He left Matthew in their room searching for any information on their new "friend" and went to the weight room to work off the extra energy. He decided to work on his upper body strength and headed to the bench press. Twenty minutes later, he was busy working his pectoral and triceps muscles when he heard the door open. Instinctively, he knew it was Matthew. Matthew liked to watch Coop work out, so he gave him a few more reps before returning the weights to the bar.

"Don't let me stop you. I can wait," Matthew said with heavy-lidded eyes. He placed his laptop down on a nearby desk and walked over to where Coop was sitting on the bench. Matthew's tight jeans were doing all kinds of wonderful things to Coop, and all he wanted to do was lay his lover down and ravish him.

Matthew threw his leg over the bench and sat facing Coop. Though they were only inches apart, Coop wanted him closer. He reached around Matthew and lifted him until he was sitting on Coop's open thighs, their cocks rubbing together, causing Coop to moan softly.

"Beautiful, did you lock the door?" he asked while rocking his hips back and forth, heightening his own need as well as Matthew's.

"Yes, the door is locked and the curtains are drawn. We're all alone. What do you want to do about it?" Matthew asked while undoing the buttons on his shirt.

"Oh, I think we can come up with something." Since Coop already had his shirt off, he helped Matthew remove his, his lips and tongue tasting Matthew's skin as he went.

Once Matthew was shirtless, Coop wrapped his arms around his partner and held him close. It no longer felt strange referring to Matthew as his partner, even though he never thought he'd have one. But now he knew he couldn't carry on without Matthew. He was the light to Coop's dark past, the man he loved, his future.

"I love you, Matthew."

Matthew's eyes softened and his fingers brushed along Coop's jaw. "I love you too."

Coop lowered his head and took Matthew's lips in a passionate kiss. He needed to feel his lover's cock against his own. After all, they didn't have any lube with them, and he would never hurt

Matthew, so rubbing each other off was the next best thing at the moment. He reached down and carefully unzipped Matthew's jeans and pulled the hard length free of its barrier. Then he lowered the front of his workout shorts and brought their two hard shafts together.

Heavy breathing and soft moans filled the gym as Coop wrapped his large hand around both of them and pumped slowly while sucking up dark marks on Matthew's neck and shoulders. Matthew's legs wrapped around Coop's hips and he ground himself against Coop.

Fire raced through his veins as each of them sped toward orgasm. Matthew's moans were getting louder, his gaze smoldering. With one final cry, Matthew came all over Coop's hand. Pure pleasure flooded Coop as his balls pulled up tight and he came a few seconds later.

Almost as if someone had been waiting, the sound of a knock came from the door. Coop gathered Matthew closer with no intention of opening the door.

"How are you, beautiful?" Coop asked.

"So much better now," Matthew teased as he cuddled into Coop's embrace.

The knocking on the door started up again and began to irritate him. *Don't they know it's locked for a reason?* He guessed not, considering they were getting louder.

"Go away!" Coop hollered at the closed door.

"Coop, Matthew, there's been an accident. We need the two of you," Dante said.

Well, if anything was going to throw cold water on this moment, that was it. They cleaned up quickly and unlocked the door to find Dante still standing there.

"What's happened?" Coop asked.

"There's been an incident at the youth center site. I can't say accident because Chief Graham isn't convinced it was an accident."

"Was anyone hurt?" Matthew asked.

"Yes, Travis fell about ten feet to the ground. He's at Brighton General as we speak. I need you two to go over to the hospital and see if Travis can remember anything out of the ordinary. The rest of the team will be split into groups. One will remain here with the construction workers, the other will go to the site to begin investigating."

"I hope it was an accident. Jesse's been through enough," Matthew said before collecting his computer from the desk. He always kept it within arm's reach.

"Did you find anything out about the worker we fired?" Dante asked.

"So far nothing, but I haven't gone far enough back to make any conclusions," Matthew explained.

"Okay, let me know if you find anything odd. I expect to have a few answers within the next couple days myself. We have friends looking into this," Dante said.

"I still can't understand why someone would come after me. Maybe it was an accident and they got scared and drove away."

"Do you believe that?" Coop asked.

Matthew thought about where they were parked and the way the car hit the truck and answered, "No."

The three walked out into the living room where Shadow and Shannon were waiting. After a few last orders, Dante left with half the team and Coop and Matthew went to get cleaned up before going to the hospital. Within thirty minutes, they were walking into the emergency room of Brighton General. Thank goodness Sam was working. He took them right into Travis's room.

The lights were dimmed, so they entered the room quietly. Travis was lying in the bed asleep with Bo, in his police uniform, pacing the room. When he saw them walk in, he immediately put his finger to his mouth in the universal sign to stay quiet. Bo took one final look at Travis before joining them in the hallway.

"How's he doing?" Matthew asked.

Bo ran his hand over his face before he spoke. "Doctor Green said he was lucky, just a few bumps and bruises."

"Good, I'm glad he'll be okay. Do you know what happened or where he was working when he fell?" Coop asked.

"Witnesses said he was on the scaffolding. But he told me he was supposed to be cleaning windows all day, removing their labels, not up painting a wall," Bo explained.

"Did he say what happened, or did one of the witnesses say anything?" Coop asked.

"Nothing yet and the witnesses were being interviewed as I jumped in the back of the ambulance. I only heard them say he was on the scaffolding," Bo answered.

Before Bo could continue, a terrified scream broke through the silent hallway. It was coming from Travis's room.

They rushed into the room, Bo in the lead, to find Travis sitting straight up in the bed clutching his blanket in his hands, his frightened screams filling the room. Bo immediately wrapped Travis in the safety of his body, murmuring comforting words. The screaming ended as Dr. Green entered with a syringe in his hand.

"This is the third time he's woken screaming. This can't all be from falling, could it?" Bo asked the doctor.

"This will help calm him. I brought it considering the second time he woke up it took over an hour for him to calm down and he needs his rest to recuperate" he said. "As for the cause of his screaming, I don't know for sure."

"Thank you, Doc," Bo replied as he held the trembling man. "He needs to sleep."

Dr. Green went over to Travis's IV line and added the medication. "I'll give him a few minutes to calm down. Then I'll come back and check his vitals over again."

Coop wondered if they should leave as well, but Travis's own words stopped him. "I knew something wasn't right, but I thought I was overreacting."

Bo laid Travis down on the hospital bed and reached for the tissues to dry Travis's tear-stained face. The medicine Doc gave him must have started working because he was calming a lot faster than Coop would have thought possible.

Matthew approached the bed and spoke softly. "What did you know wasn't right, Travis?"

Travis flinched and Matthew took a step back. He knew fear when he saw it. "I'm sorry, Matthew. I just can't seem to stop myself. I'm afraid of everything at the moment."

"After the accident it would be normal for anyone to be shaken up," Matthew said. "Could you tell me what you meant by you 'knew something wasn't right'?"

"When he asked me to climb up the scaffolding for him, to get his tool belt, he told me his knee was too sore. The boards and poles seemed loose, but I trusted it was safe."

"When who asked you to climb up?" Bo asked.

"One of the construction workers. I don't know his name, but I had a run-in with him once before."

"What kind of run-in, baby?" Bo had taken over the interview.

Travis's cheeks turned red, but he answered. "He hit on me while I was painting the back wall of the gym."

"Hit on you how?"

"Well, it wasn't the nice way. He got up in my space, and I had to do some quick maneuvering to get away from him."

"Why didn't you tell me this?" Bo asked, his face now red.

"Because I didn't want you to get into a fight over me. I was fine, and I can take care of myself," Travis answered a little groggily.

"Would you know this guy again if we show you a picture?" Coop asked. He knew Matthew still had the file and his laptop in his messenger bag over his shoulder.

"Yes, why?" Travis asked.

"We had a similar incident at the site for Matthew's new workshop. The guy had Matthew pinned into a corner."

Matthew's eyes lit up as he caught on. "I have a picture of him from his file. Here, let me show you."

Matthew riffled through his bag and pulled out the file, opening the picture toward Travis. The medicine must have really been kicking in because he didn't flinch this time when Matthew moved closer. Travis looked at the picture and the fear in his eyes said it all. He simply nodded.

"His name is Tony Fentario," Matthew said. "Or at least that's what his employment file states."

Coop pulled out his cellphone to tell Dante about the new discovery so they could keep an eye out for him, since they were at the building site. Coop walked out of the room and his call was answered on the first ring. Coop filled Dante in and sent the picture of the guy to each team member just in case he showed up again. This had to have something to do with this whole mess, and Coop was determined to uncover the reason before anyone else got hurt.

When he got back to the room, Matthew was already on his computer and Travis was asleep with Doctor Green checking him over. Bo was only a few feet away. It was easy to tell Bo was head over heels for Travis, but according to Matthew, they weren't a couple.

"Physically, he should be fine, but mentally he may need therapy if his terrors continue or worsen. I don't want him alone for the next little while until he's healed and the night terrors clear up," Doctor Green stated as he tucked the blanket around Travis. "I'm not a psychiatrist, but it seems there might be more going on here than simply the fall alone."

Bo looked down at Travis with sad eyes. "Whatever he needs, I'll see he gets it."

"We need to go back to the house. I need to do some more research into who this man is before anything else happens," Matthew said. "Could you tell Travis that I'll be by his apartment to check on him tomorrow?"

"He won't be there. He'll be staying with me until Doc says he's okay," Bo responded.

"Is it okay for me to come by your house to see him?" Matthew asked.

"Yes, of course. Here's my card. It has my cell phone number on it. Give me a call first to make sure we're not at a doctor's appointment or something."

"Thank you, Bo," Coop said and took the card.

Coop followed Matthew out, his eyes scanning the area as they went. Once they got back to their truck, Matthew let out a deep breath.

"Are you okay, Matthew?" Coop asked. He knew he wasn't saying something.

"I didn't want to frighten Travis more than he already was, but while you were on the phone with Dante, I researched further back in Tony's life and found nothing."

"So he's clean?" Coop couldn't believe the man wasn't dirty.

"No, I mean I found nothing. Up until four years ago, this 'Tony' didn't exist. He's a ghost."

Chapter Seven

Matthew knew of a few ghosts—men and women who changed their identities every few years. Their main occupation was gun for hire. Get a mission, complete it, and get out without ever being seen. But this guy had been seen by several people already so either he was very bad at his job or someone wanted them to know they were being messed with.

"I need to check out the rest of the construction crew that aren't from Brighton. Can we get the remainder of the files from Jesse?" Matthew asked.

"I'll text Dante and ask him to pick up any remaining files while they are at the site."

They pulled into their laneway and typed in the security code to open the gates. The house was still a ways back from the road, and the whole compound was surrounded by tall fencing. Each building was outfitted with sensors and security cameras, all connected to a security system that could tell the difference between a deer and a person. When he'd first come here, he'd been shocked by all the security measures. Now they made him feel safe.

They pulled into Coop's spot, but he held on to Matthew's hand, preventing him from getting out of the truck. "Matthew, I need you to not leave the house without one of us with you. I need to know you're safe until we have those responsible for this behind bars."

"I'm safe here at home," Matthew said. Surely he was safe on the compound.

"We just had a possible 'ghost' pin you to a wall on this property. Lord knows what else he's done or if he's working alone."

Coop had a point. Matthew knew this and was left with no reason not to agree to have a chaperone outside the house. "Okay,

I'll always take someone with me, but I think we should do the same with Sam. We're not 100 percent sure I'm the only target."

"Do you think he's in danger?" Coop asked.

"It's better to be safe until we know for sure."

"I'll contact Dante to send someone over to the hospital until Sam's off shift."

Coop leaned over and captured Matthew's lips in a gentle kiss before releasing his hand. Matthew decided to retire to the computer room to continue his investigation of Tony or whoever he was. He explained to Coop it was time to crack out the "big guns" as he liked to call them—his personal hacking programs to dig deeper into the background of other programs and follow the trail to where it led. That was an oversimplification of a very specialized talent, but Coop seemed fine with it.

Hours passed like minutes as he worked through system after system, Buddy sleeping at his feet. He'd thought he'd heard Coop come in once, but wasn't sure. He wasn't even sure what time it was. He looked up from his screen and saw a full plate of untouched food. *When did that get here? It must have been a while ago considering it's stone cold.*

Matthew was just thinking of going to find a sandwich, leaving his program running without him for a while on its own, when the computer room door opened and Coop stepped in.

He walked across the room and asked, "Can the system work on its own or do you have to watch over it?"

"It's okay to be left on its own." With that said, Coop picked him up from his chair, careful of his walking cast, and headed toward the staircase. Matthew thought to mention that he hadn't eaten but decided against it. He just wanted to stay in Coop's arms. It was dark outside and the house was silent as they walked down the hallway to their room. Other than his original question, Coop hadn't said a word, which was fine with Matthew. The two of them could sit for hours without speaking, not feeling the need to fill the silence. They were comfortable with each other, and that's all that mattered to Matthew.

Coop opened the door to their bedroom, and the first thing Matthew noticed were all the lit candles scattered around the room, adding a soft glow to everything. As they entered farther, Matthew spotted the picnic set up in front of the fireplace, containing plates and glasses and hot food. His stomach waited until that exact moment to start grumbling in hunger. Coop simply smiled and placed Matthew on the blanket set out on the floor.

"Thought you'd be hungry by now and need to rest," Coop said, and Matthew was so touched by Coop's actions that his eyes misted over with tears. "What's wrong, beautiful?"

"Nothing's wrong, it's just this was so thoughtful. I love you so much."

Coop reached over and wiped away a tear that had escaped. "You're worth it. You're worth everything to me. Now you need to eat. You didn't eat any of your dinner, and it's almost one in the morning."

Matthew hadn't realized how late it was; that often happened when he worked. He could stay up for days on end if needed for a mission. Dinner looked wonderful: roast beef and mashed potatoes, along with corn and fresh-made bread; it was a feast. Coop had a way of making him feel special every day—it may just be a word, or it could be a picnic for a late dinner. It didn't matter what it was, Matthew held each gesture close to his heart.

Matthew finished his meal quickly; he was hungrier than he thought. The last thing he remembered was being picked up off the blanket and carried to bed. It had been a long day filled with revelations and more questions that needed answers before someone else was hurt.

***

Coop was starting to think these incidents were all tied together. That this was a personal attack on their partners. Sam and Matthew in the truck and Travis at the construction site. Even though Bo wasn't part of the Sentinels, he was law enforcement for Brighton. Maybe this was an attack on Sentinel and not on Matthew personally. That would be a way of severely hurting Sentinel without taking them on directly.

If he was right, they had a bigger problem than they originally thought. There was more than one target, and what about Chief Graham's wife, Kate Mason-Graham? She could be a target as well. This was getting out of hand. It was almost six in the morning, and

Coop knew either Dante or Spider would be up by now. One always stayed in bed with Sam until he woke up at seven.

Coop slipped out of bed quietly. Matthew needed more sleep, and he didn't want to wake him. He threw on his sleeping pants and quietly snuck out of the room. He smelled coffee brewing when he was halfway down the stairs, and knew he'd been right. He walked into the kitchen and found Spider hulking over a cup of that dark heavenly liquid, papers in his hand.

"Good morning, Spider."

"Good morning, Coop. How's Matthew?"

"Still sleeping. He was up late last night working on trying to find the true identity of the 'ghost' that's following him. That's what I needed to talk to you about. I've been thinking about all the incidents, and I'm beginning to wonder if it's not all of our partners that are being targeted. Sam and Matthew were both in the truck when it was hit, and then Travis was tricked into climbing unsafe scaffolding by a 'ghost.' The same 'ghost' that was on this property trying to get Matthew alone. I think we need to consider that they all were targets."

Spider sat up a bit straighter in his chair as he thought over what Coop had suggested. Coop knew he was on the right track when Spider's eyes hardened.

"They're going after the people we love the most in our lives."

"I think we need to call Police Chief Graham and Bo Mason to warn them."

"I'm going to wake Dante and Sam. Why don't you get Matthew and the rest of the team; we need to have a meeting."

"You better make more coffee," was all Coop said before he turned around and headed for the staircase. He woke up Shannon, Shadow, and Vincent before he went to wake Matthew, who was still asleep when Coop walked into their room. Matthew was snuggling Coop's pillow, his face buried in the soft cushion. He'd waited his entire life to trust someone enough to let them in. Thank God he'd waited for Matthew. He was everything Coop thought he hadn't wanted but would now never give up.

Coop pulled the blanket down a little and rubbed Matthew's back. Matthew stretched out his beautiful, lithe body, pulling the blanket farther down and revealing soft, milky white, freckled skin. Coop would give just about anything to crawl back into bed with him, but he knew this meeting was important and they needed to be there.

"Come on, wake up, sleepyhead." Coop spoke softly as he continued to rub him. Matthew's gorgeous, mismatched eyes opened and stared straight at Coop with so much love it humbled him. "Morning, beautiful. How did you sleep?"

"I slept well. Is something wrong, or am I late for breakfast?" Matthew asked.

"No, Dante's having a meeting and we need to be there." Coop went on to explain what he'd told Spider, and Matthew quickly dressed.

"Let's go get you some coffee. It'll help wake you up. If you want to get more sleep afterward, that's okay."

"No, I need to keep working on the identity of our mysterious Tony fellow to hopefully find out who sent him, or even if he's working alone or not."

They walked downstairs hand in hand and into the kitchen to find everyone waiting. They each fixed themselves a coffee and then sat as Dante began the meeting.

"I've called this meeting to discuss something Coop's brought to our attention. There's a possibility that whoever it is stalking Matthew may actually be after all the partners instead. Sam and Matthew were in that truck that day, and Travis is special to Bo."

"But Bo's not a Sentinel," Shannon mentioned.

"It's possible they're going after partners of both the Sentinels and Brighton law enforcement."

"Have you contacted Police Chief Graham?" Shadow asked.

"Yes, I just got off the phone with him. I have opened our home to Mrs. Graham, their baby, and Bo and Travis for protection. There are no other partners at the moment to worry about. I'll be giving the Grahams the first-floor suite so they can have some privacy and so their baby has a bit of quiet. We'll put Bo and Travis in a guest room on the second floor."

Mrs. Walker strolled in with two more pots of coffee. "I'll make sure to stock more food this week when I go shopping and add more portions to our meals, as well as baby food. I'll freshen the guest rooms before they arrive."

"Thank you, Mrs. Walker. I'm sorry to add more work," Spider said.

"Don't you be silly. It's a good thing you're doing protecting others like that. Besides, with the amount of food I make to feed you guys alone, I can easily add more," Mrs. Walker explained in her typical no-nonsense way. She was a mother hen to the group of ex-military specialists, and they wouldn't have it any other way.

"Now, until we know for sure, I don't want either Sam or Matthew going anywhere without a bodyguard," Dante ordered.

"But I have to work at the hospital," Sam said.

"We'll get it cleared to have a Sentinel there in the ER."

"But it will be hard to hide someone following me around."

"We'll send Shadow. He'll stay out of sight."

Sam didn't look impressed by the thought of having a babysitter, but it was for the best.

"Does that mean whoever this is, is after revenge against Sentinel and not actually someone after Matthew personally?" Vincent asked.

"We're not 100 percent sure, but it's looking that way," Dante answered.

"And who would be after us?" Shadow asked.

"How the hell do we narrow that down? What drug cartel, terrorist, or mobster wants us dead? Too many to count." Shannon groaned into her coffee.

"It could be anyone," Vincent said.

"Until we have more information, I want everyone to stay on the compound unless necessary," Dante ordered.

Coop thought that was the best idea; that way Matthew would stay safe. But, of course, his love had other plans.

"I have to go back to the worksite tomorrow. I'm not risking the work being done wrong and putting the project behind," Matthew said.

"But it might not be safe," Coop replied. He knew he was overreacting, but this could mean Matthew's life. "I… I forbid it."

Matthew's mouth dropped open and the room was eerily silent. Sam looked as shocked as Matthew. One by one, the team began to rise from their chairs and head out of the room, but Matthew stopped them.

"No, you guys stay. Breakfast will be soon. I'll go," Matthew said as he stood and knocked over his chair in the process. Coop was pretty confident he'd screwed up, and the effect it was having on

Matthew was evident. His hands shook as he reached down to pick up the chair, and Coop quickly picked it up for him. "I'm going to work on my search for the identity of Tony."

"I'll bring you breakfast," Coop offered.

"No, no, I need some time alone right now, or I'm going to say something I'll regret."

Now he knew for sure he'd said the wrong thing, but it had just come out due to his fear for Matthew's life. "Matthew—"

"No, not now, just give me some time, Cooper." With that said, Matthew left the kitchen. He heard the door to the computer room close, and only moments passed before Sam was on him.

"You forbid him? What the hell is wrong with you?" Sam said in a hushed whisper.

"Easy, tiger, let Dante have a talk with him," Spider said as he lifted Sam from his chair.

Coop surrendered and buried his head in his hands. He'd really screwed up this time. Spider carried Sam out of the room, and Dante refilled his and Coop's coffee mugs.

"So, do you want to try to explain to me what that was all about?" Dante asked.

Coop raised his head and sighed deeply. "I really messed up this time."

"I'd say you royally fucked up and you better give that man time to calm down before you go in there."

"If he even talks to me again."

"This isn't your parents' relationship. What you and Matthew have is different. He may be mad at you, but I don't think he's the type of man to shut you out."

"I was just so scared. What if they try something while he's out at the site?"

"That's why you'll take a few Sentinels with you. You just can't forbid a grown man from doing something, especially something he's so passionate about."

Coop knew Dante was right. The moment the words left his mouth, he knew they were wrong. Matthew was a grown man capable of making his own decisions; he didn't need Coop telling him what to do.

"It's just I've never been in this position before. I've never loved somebody this much. I want to protect him all the time."

"Spider and I felt the same way about Sam, but that spitfire set us straight right from the start." Dante grinned as if reliving the memory.

"Thanks, boss. I'm going for a long jog before I go in and beg for forgiveness," Coop said.

"Just be honest with him and there won't be a whole lot of begging."

Coop hoped Dante was right because he needed a miracle to get him out of this one.

***

How dare he even think to forbid me. Matthew was still furious hours later. He'd barely made it out of the kitchen before he blew. He was a grown man after all, able to make his own decisions. Of course he wasn't going to go out without a bodyguard coming with him. He wasn't insane and didn't have a death wish. But the youth center and the attached housing were important to Matthew. His best friend's dream was on the line, and he wouldn't hold up any of the construction.

Matthew was getting closer to the identity of the mystery man, who, according to Jesse, seemed to have vanished from the construction site. As he calmed down, he remembered a few important things. Coop had never been in any relationship before, and he only had his dysfunctional parents as an example, which was not his fault. Matthew knew Coop loved him, and he loved Coop, but he wouldn't be coddled and treated like a child.

He understood that Coop was worried. Heck, he was worried too, but he had to continue with his life, and that meant leaving the compound on occasion. Sam had to leave every day to go to work, and the same with Travis. Why should it be different for him?

They needed to talk, but Matthew had been too shocked and pissed at the time to speak without yelling, so he chose to walk away. He was about to get up and go find his partner to have that talk when there was a knock on the door.

"Come in," Matthew said as he sat back down.

The door opened and Coop walked in slowly. Matthew could see the uncertainty in his eyes, and all he wanted to do was go over and hug him, but they had to talk first. If this was the way their relationship was going to be, there would be no end to the fighting, and Matthew couldn't live like that.

"Can I come in, or are you busy?" Coop asked.

"I've been working all morning. I need a break," Matthew answered.

"And something to eat," Coop threw in but didn't push. "Travis is here. Bo's on shift."

Matthew noticed Coop's hair was wet and assumed he'd been working out or in the shop and had taken a shower. He looked unsettled and leery, but Coop came closer to him and Matthew could no longer stay seated. He knew his love was hurting and had to hold him—even though this was his own fault.

Matthew stood and walked up to Coop, his eyes full of worry, and hugged him tight. Coop wrapped his large arms around Matthew and held him gently while kissing the top of Matthew's head.

"This doesn't mean you're not in trouble, mister," Matthew said.

"I'm so sorry. I don't know why I said it, but I was scared you'd be hurt if you went out."

"You can't forbid me from doing whatever I want, Coop. I don't even know why you thought you could," Matthew said as he backed away from Coop, giving himself space to think.

"I know this is no excuse, but my father would always say that to me. It was a knee-jerk reaction. When you said you were going no matter what, I reacted out of fear. I shouldn't have said what I did. I know I had no right to tell you what to do, but you have to take a few Sentinels with you, right?"

"Of course, I wouldn't go out without protection until this is cleared up. I'm not stupid."

"No, you're not and, again, I'm sorry for how I behaved earlier." Coop honestly looked contrite and ashamed of his behavior.

"You're forgiven. There's going to be a few bumps along the way in this relationship, but know that I always love you."

"I was so worried I'd blown it," Coop admitted.

"One disagreement could never make me leave you. We're going to have them, but we need to talk them out like we just did. But I've gotta admit, there might have been some yelling if you'd have followed me in here a few hours ago."

"I'll remember that: needs calm-down time when boyfriend says something wildly inappropriate."

The computer dinged three times to indicate it had something waiting for Matthew on the screen. He quickly brought up the information, and Matthew couldn't believe he'd finally found the link between the Sentinels and whoever might be causing this, thanks to Dante allowing him into their mission records.

"Coop, do you remember a case involving the Denefusi family out of Chicago?" Matthew asked.

"Damn!" was all Coop said before he turned out of the door and headed back toward the main living quarters. Matthew was having a hard time keeping up with him in his walking cast, but he soon found himself back in Coop's arms and being carried the rest of the way.

"Sorry, beautiful. I shouldn't have left you behind like that."

"That's okay. So you know the Denefusis?"

"Yes, and it's not good."

They arrived in the living room to find the rest of the team and a bruised Travis. "Where is Police Chief Graham's wife?" Matthew asked.

"Chief Graham sent her out of town with family, far away from Brighton," Coop answered before he stood in front of the television, blocking the team's view.

"Hey, we're watching that," Shannon yelled.

"It will have to wait. Matthew thinks he's found a connection between our guy and the Denefusi crime family."

That got the room to quiet down in a hurry. Dante stood slowly and asked, "What did you find, Matthew?"

He had a feeling this was bad. Denefusi was a mobster. They were all in trouble, but why was he coming after the team? "Our mysterious 'Tony' turned out to be Bobby Denefusi, the nephew of Anthony Denefusi. Why would he be trying to hurt us?"

Coop set Matthew down on the couch and sat beside him. Dante remained standing. "You know Jesse's and Travis's boss, the owner of the diner, Clem Mitchell and his partner Rick?"

"Yes, and their adorable nephew, Josh. I've met them a few times since coming to Brighton, good people," Matthew answered.

"Well, a few months before you came to town, Clem and Rick took over the care of Josh after Clem's sister died, and there was a situation. Josh's gambling-addicted father showed up to take Josh and the insurance money. Of course, Clem and Rick wouldn't let Josh go to the unfit man, but little did we know he owed money to

Anthony Denefusi, the head of the Denefusi family. He'd promised the insurance money and his own son to Denefusi to clear his debt."

"Promised him his son, why? What were they going to do with him?" Matthew asked, afraid of the answer

"Human trafficking."

"Oh my God!" Travis yelled.

"Yes, they intended to keep the insurance money and sell the boy to the highest bidder. The father and his colleague were stopped, and we paid Anthony Denefusi a little visit," Dante explained.

"Yeah, a little visit to his private offices after we incapacitated his guards," Vincent added.

"We gave him all the money that was owed to him plus interest; it should have been enough," Spider said.

"Now it seems he's decided to go after what's important to us. Shannon, contact Chief Graham and Bo. We need to discuss this with them."

"Why are they going after me? Bo wasn't involved in the mission, was he?" Travis asked.

"No, but he and the other officers helped protect them from one of Denefusi's henchmen, Luther," Shadow said.

Shannon got up, her cell phone to her ear as she walked out of the room. Only Chief Graham and Bo had significant others on the Brighton police force at the moment, according to Dante.

"But Bo and I aren't even a couple. Why would they come after me?" Travis asked.

"I believe it's because Bo cares about you so much that they put you on the list with the rest of us," Matthew answered.

Travis's cheeks turned red and he looked away. To Matthew, Travis seemed almost innocent, even though he was in his mid-twenties.

"Don't be embarrassed. He's a great guy," Sam said.

"I'm just not used to anyone giving me a second look, let alone pursuing me," Travis said, and his face turned even redder.

"Well, get used to it 'cause Bo has his sights set on you," Matthew said with a big smile, causing Travis to smile as well.

"We should call Clem and Rick just in case they might try for Josh again," Sam suggested, and Spider picked up his phone and stepped out of the room.

Matthew's stomach decided to growl, reminding him that he had yet to eat today and it was past noon. Without saying a word, Coop stood, took Matthew's hand, and led him toward the kitchen. Coop's warm, calloused palm felt good against his own smaller one. Mrs. Walker was working away on dinner when they walked in. She took one look at Matthew and produced a plate of food within minutes.

Coop was deep in thought as Matthew ate his homemade chicken pot pie. He knew this was a bad situation, and the look on Coop's face only confirmed it. He wasn't personally aware of the Denefusi crime family—he'd never come across them in his work—but they must have some serious power if the Sentinels were concerned.

"I need you to stay safe," Coop said.

"I will. I'll always have you with me."

Coop's face was ashen. "I can't lose you, Matthew. I love you."

"I love you too, and I'm not going anywhere." Matthew reached out and held Coop's hand. "I'll be careful of my surroundings, and I'll have bodyguards with me."

"Damn right you will. You need to understand that if anything happened to you, no one would be able to stop me from seeking revenge until I was taken out."

"Don't talk like that."

"You mean the world to me, and I will do whatever it takes to protect you. Whatever it takes."

Chapter Eight

Coop was Matthew's shadow as they walked around the construction site for the youth center. Vincent was close by, his eyes darting between workers and Matthew, making sure no one stared too long or had any reaction at all. They still didn't know how many men Denefusi had sent, but Dante's leads confirmed there was more than one. Coop was happy the tour was almost over. Matthew had just one more room to check and they were out of there.

Matthew was oblivious to the world around him, caught up in the blueprints and his inspection. He'd never see the danger before it was on him. Matthew stumbled and Coop reached out quickly to right him. The glowing smile he gave Coop was breathtaking and filled with love. Coop couldn't help but smile back; he was a lucky man and he knew it.

Matthew quickly finished up the last of the sensors, and the three of them headed back to the truck after their good-byes to the White Hair Crew, who were unpacking lunch for the men and women working and volunteering their time to help build the youth center. Coop noticed something off as they approached their truck. When they got closer, he realized the tires had been slashed and the paint on the body had been keyed. Coop immediately stopped Matthew and checked the area; there was nothing else out of place.

"Vincent, can you call Dante to have someone bring us another truck? Matthew, call the station and let the chief know what's happened," Coop said before he rescanned the area. Coop knew Matthew hadn't had the time to go through all the personal files of the workers from out of town, but obviously there was more than Bobby Denefusi involved. Dante's intel was spot on.

"Dante's on his way," Vincent said.

"Chief Graham is as well," Matthew said as he turned the screen off on his cell phone.

Coop and Vincent positioned Matthew between them and waited for backup. Matthew was quiet. Other than calling Chief Graham, he hadn't said a word since they'd discovered the truck.

"There are security cameras posted across the site, we'll need access to those," Coop said.

"As soon as we get Matthew out of here, I'll get the tapes," Vincent said.

"I'm sorry, this is all my fault," Matthew whispered.

That caught Coop by surprise. "None of this is your fault."

"I'm the one who was determined to come out here today. I put us all in danger." Matthew's voice was small and filled with regret. "Now one of the trucks is damaged."

"This is still not your fault. That lies with the Denefusi family alone," Coop assured him.

Matthew didn't look like he believed Coop, but he remained quiet. Moments later, Dante pulled in, followed by Chief Graham. Coop ushered Matthew toward the other truck, opened one of the back doors, and placed him safely inside its bulletproof exterior.

Coop was in a hyper-alert state; he refused to allow anything to happen to the man he loved. It was obvious whoever did this wanted to scare Matthew and put them on notice of how close they could get to their target, which just pissed Coop off further. They'd gotten too close to Matthew. And why hadn't the car alarm sounded?

As Dante took a look at the damaged truck, his demeanor was calm but his eyes spoke volumes of just how angry he was. Coop was sure his own eyes were doing the same. They needed to go on the offensive and bring the fight back to Denefusi's door.

"I'll write up the report. Did anyone see anything?" Chief Graham asked.

"Vincent's gone to get the security tapes now. They should show who did this," Coop answered.

"It'll probably be another out-of-town worker," Dante added. "We know there's more than one person sent to Brighton by Denefusi. When we get back, I want Matthew to concentrate on identifying each member of the out-of-town portion of the construction crew."

"As soon as we get back to the compound, we'll get right on it," Coop said.

By now, they were starting to draw attention, and he could see Matthew trying to slump lower in his seat. Vincent returned with the tapes in hand and went to stand beside the truck containing Matthew. Coop was grateful for his friends and teammates. They would protect Matthew as if he were their own family. After all, they were a strange family of sorts.

"Take Matthew back to the house to begin working on the names and have a look at those tapes. I'll catch a ride back with Graham."

Chief Graham nodded in agreement. "I need to have a look at those tapes as well, and any information you dig up. So far we only have Bobby Denefusi. We need the rest of them."

Coop didn't wait. He immediately walked up to the truck and opened Matthew's door. "I'm going to take you home now, beautiful. Are you okay?"

Matthew nodded but remained quiet; Coop didn't like it. His Matthew was mouthy, opinionated, vibrant, and full of life, not the subdued man who sat in the truck in silence. But now wasn't the time to talk. He gently raised Matthew's head and kissed him, trying to convey how much he loved him. By the dreamy look in Matthew's eyes when they parted, he must have done a good job.

"Love you," Coop said softly.

"I love you too, Coop."

"Let's go home."

"I'd like that."

Without another word, Coop closed the rear passenger door and called Vincent over. "I want you to come with me just in case something happens. I don't know where it'll come from next."

"Of course I'll protect Matthew. We're family." Vincent gave Coop a slap on the back. "I just hope someday I meet someone who loves me as much as he loves you, my friend."

"You will. Let's just hope he doesn't have a crazy mob boss after him," Coop teased as he rounded the front of the SUV, and he and Vincent got in and drove away.

The road appeared clear, allowing Coop to breathe easy once again. They were halfway to the compound when Coop noticed another SUV coming up behind them fast. The windows of the other vehicle were heavily tinted, so he couldn't make out who was behind the wheel. Coop sped up, and so did the strange SUV. Yep, whoever it was, they were here for them.

"We've got company," Coop said. "Call for backup." Vincent got on the phone.

Coop looked at Matthew in the rearview mirror and hated seeing the terror on his face. The strange SUV sped up and rammed them in the rear end of their vehicle, jarring everyone inside and causing the tires to break free from the pavement for a second. Once he got the truck back under control, he floored the gas pedal and raced down the roadway. Coop didn't know what the other vehicle had under the hood, but whatever it was, it was overpowering his 6.2-liter V8 with 420 horsepower.

The other vehicle came up alongside Coop's and Vincent pulled out his gun, but it seemed their attacker didn't want a gunfight. They wanted to run them off the road. The first hit from the other vehicle sent them onto the shoulder of the road, the tires spinning for purchase on the gravel. The squeal of metal made his skin crawl. Coop slowed and got behind their attacker, rear-ending him this time. The other SUV lost control and headed straight for the guardrails protecting drivers from a thirty-foot drop into a small ravine. The vehicle was moving too fast to be stopped by the railing and plunged over the edge. He could see flashing lights in his rearview mirror and knew help had arrived. He doubted anyone had survived the fall, but he parked his vehicle and turned to Matthew. "I need you to stay in the truck, baby." Matthew was as white as a ghost but nodded his head anyway.

Coop got out of the SUV as Chief Graham's police car pulled up alongside. "Are you three okay?" Dante asked as he stepped out of the car.

"Yeah, but the truck has seen better days."

"I think that's a new record for you, Coop, two vehicles destroyed in less than four hours," Dante said.

"Let's go down. I've already called in the fire department and paramedics. They're on their way," Chief Graham said.

"I'll just be a minute," Coop needed to check on Matthew. He needed to hold him.

Coop went around the damaged truck and opened Matthew's door. Before he could say a word, his arms were filled with a shaking Matthew. "I've got you, baby. You're safe."

"Can we go back to the compound now?"

"We will in just a few minutes. We have to go down and check the other vehicle, beautiful. But just as soon as we can, I'll take you home. I want you to stay right beside Vincent, and I'll be back as soon as possible." Coop nodded toward Vincent who was close by, his gun still in his hand.

Coop placed his love back inside the truck and shut the door. Then the three began the hike down to the bottom of the ravine. The small trail was only big enough to walk one after the other, and the rocks were slippery with moss. When they reached the bottom, Coop was surprised the vehicle hadn't exploded on impact with the ground. It stood in a mangled heap, the front end crumpled in and almost unrecognizable. No one could have survived that fall.

Chief Graham went to what used to be the driver's side of the vehicle and reached in, checking the driver's pulse. "He's dead."

"Is he alone?" Dante asked.

"Yes, as far as I can tell," Chief Graham said.

"Is it someone new or Bobby Denefusi?" Coop asked.

"It's not Bobby. We'll have to go through the workers' files and see if it's one of them," Dante said.

The sirens from the fire truck sounded above them, and all Coop wanted to do was get his partner home and away from all this. Coop went over to the wreck to see if he recognized the guy from the building site; he didn't. Firefighters and paramedics came down the path from the road.

"Dante, I'm going to take Matthew home. We'll get started with the worker's files and see if we can identify this one," Coop said.

"Do you need them to stick around, Graham?" Dante asked.

"No, I'll get statements and pictures of the truck when I drop you off," Chief Graham said.

"Okay, so you three head home and we'll be there as soon as possible," Dante said.

Coop turned away just as the jaws of life began opening the crumpled doors to retrieve the body. He felt no guilt for protecting his family the only way he could. He did what he had to do. It could have just as easily been them down in this ravine instead. Coop made it to the road and got into the driver's seat. The sooner he got Matthew back to the safety of the compound the better.

"We're going home, beautiful," Coop said as he pulled back onto the road.

Matthew nodded but remained quiet. That emotionless response worried Coop more than anything.

***

Matthew was struggling with what happened and his own guilt. Because of him, they could have been killed. One man did lose his life. Even though he was trying to run them off the road, his death was on Matthew. He'd decided to go to the building site; in fact, he'd had a disagreement with Coop about whether to go. He should have listened.

The truck slowed down and parked right in front of the house. Before he knew it, his door was open and Coop had him in his arms again. The second they were inside the house, Matthew calmed a bit further, though his guilt was firmly in place. He knew how dangerous it was, and he'd insisted on going out anyway. *Stupid!*

"Matthew, I need you to look at me," Coop said. "Are you hurt anywhere?"

He was sitting on the kitchen counter… When did he make it to the kitchen? "I'm fine, just a little bruised from the impact with the other truck."

"Did you hit your head at any time?"

"I don't think so."

"Okay, drink this," Coop said as he lifted a cup to Matthew's lips. Herbal tea filled his senses, and he finally noticed Sam standing nearby with a stethoscope around his neck.

"His heart rate is slowing down. He'll be fine," Sam said.

"What's wrong with my heart?"

"Nothing, it was just running a bit fast. But after what you've been through, I can understand," Sam explained.

Shock, have I been in shock?

"Yes, you have," Coop answered.

"Did I say that out loud?" Matthew asked.

"Sam, are you sure he's going to be okay?" Coop asked, concern lacing his every word.

"We'll keep an eye on him tonight," Sam said.

"I need to work on those files. We need to know how many are already here in Brighton," Matthew said as he slid off the countertop and stood. "We need to know."

"Your health comes first," Coop argued.

"I think he can work on the files and he'll be okay," Sam chimed in.

"See? Now if you'll excuse me, I'll be in the computer room." Matthew needed to get away from everyone's concerned eyes. This was all his fault. He didn't say good-bye to Coop, and he didn't even kiss him. His guilt was choking him. He'd almost gotten Coop and Vincent killed. How did he make up for that?

Matthew left the kitchen and walked down the hall to the computer room, where he shut the door behind him, blocking out the rest of the house. How could they be concerned for him when none of this would have happened if it weren't for him?

Matthew pulled out the personnel files of all the construction workers from outside of town and laid them on the desk. He turned on his computer system and waited for his programs to load. He thought back over the time he'd been in Brighton; it certainly had been anything other than dull. First the problems with Jesse and his family, and now this. He couldn't wait until everything was normal again. *Maybe this is my new normal?*

***

Coop stood staring out of the kitchen window for a long time before he finally turned around and exited the house through the kitchen doorway. His mind was reeling from everything that had happened today. He'd brought this down on Matthew. Anthony Denefusi was only after him because of what Coop had done to protect Clem, Rick, and Josh.

He'd put the man he loved in the sights of one of the cruelest mob bosses in Chicago. This was his fault. His partner was suffering because of him. Coop walked over to the building site for Matthew's new shop. Only workers from Brighton were working in the compound now; they weren't taking any chances. The building was coming along nicely and should be all roughed in by the end of the week.

A time when both he and Matthew should be planning their future and moving Matthew's belongings to his new home was now filled with danger. The fault belonged solely to him. Matthew wouldn't be in danger if it weren't for him. He had to figure out a way to end this before anything else happened, but how?

"You want some company?" Shadow asked.

"I'm not in a very good mood, Shadow. I might not be the best company," Coop answered.

"No worries," Shadow said. "Just wanted to check and see if you're okay, man."

"I'll be fine, just have a lot to think about."

"Well, if it's finding a way to make Anthony Denefusi's attacks end, then count me in."

"The only way I can see this ending is if we made another visit to that scumbag. And even then, it's going to only infuriate him more."

"True," Shadow said. "How's Matthew taking all this?"

"Not well. He didn't even want to talk to me. He just went to the computer room. I wouldn't blame him for thinking I brought this all on him."

"I'm sure Matthew doesn't blame you for all of this," Shadow said.

"He wouldn't be under attack if it weren't for me, and that's the truth. There no way to sugarcoat this," Coop said as he rounded one of the interior walls of Matthew's shop.

"So you're just going to assume that's what Matthew thinks as well, without talking to him?"

"Yes," Coop said like a petulant child.

"You need to talk to him."

Coop knew Shadow was right, but what if it was worse than he thought? Anything stressful and his parents would be at each other's throats. By now the threats of divorce would be flying. *Oh God, what if Matthew wants out? What if he's having second thoughts?*

Blood ran cold in his veins at the thought. He loved Matthew. He couldn't lose him.

Coop turned toward the house. "I need to talk to him."

"Yes, you do," Shadow replied.

Coop walked back to the house with purpose. He would find out what his partner was thinking before he twisted himself into a knot with worry. He entered through the kitchen and headed straight for the computer room where he found Matthew leaning over a pile of papers. His beautiful multicolored eyes scanned each page carefully before he went on to the other.

He eventually looked up and acknowledged Coop before looking away. It wasn't a good sign.

"Matthew, I'm sorry for all of this," Coop got out quickly before Matthew had a chance to speak.

His love sat there in silence, looking at Coop strangely as if lost for words, so Coop continued. "I know you signed up for none of this, and I wish I could make it stop, but I promise you I'll protect you."

"Coop, I...." Matthew choked up as he tried to speak. "Today was all my fault, not yours."

Coop rushed forward, took Matthew in his arms, and held him tight. "It's okay, Matthew. None of this is your fault."

Matthew wiped his eyes and looked up at Coop. "But I'm the one who insisted we go today. You tried to stop me, and I didn't listen. Now there's a life lost and two trucks destroyed. I should have listened. We could have died."

"You shouldn't have to worry about going out in the first place. And that life lost would have killed us if he had a chance, so don't feel guilt for that."

"I know, but I still feel like I've messed up everything just because I wanted to go to the work site."

"Is that why you left the kitchen without saying a word to me?" Coop asked.

"Yes, I'm sorry. Everyone was looking at me with such concern when it's all my fault," Matthew explained.

"Again, no it's not. We have no idea when or where they're going to strike. Today could have gone off without a hitch, but the men working for Denefusi chose to attack. We were simply defending ourselves," Coop stated adamantly.

"Then, by the same logic, what's happening isn't your fault. Anthony Denefusi decided to go after an innocent little boy, and you did the right thing by stopping him. He chose to send people to Brighton even though he was paid off. You don't have control of him, so it can't possibly be your fault either," Matthew explained.

"But I brought you into this mess," Coop argued.

"Would you rather we weren't together?" Matthew asked softly, his eyes stormy.

"Never! You're my partner, and there is no way I'm letting you go," Coop almost yelled.

"Good, 'cause I don't intend on going anywhere," Matthew said, before cuddling closer to Coop.

"Do you want to help me with these files?" Matthew asked.

"I'm at your disposal, beautiful."

Chapter Nine

It was well past two in the morning, and both he and Coop were still working on the files. They'd discovered the identity of the man driving the other SUV. He was indeed an out-of-town construction worker and another Denefusi family member. Didn't Anthony have cronies to do his dirty work? Matthew finished the last file, and it was clean, so there had only been two men among the construction workers, and the only one missing was Bobby Denefusi.

Matthew stretched his aching back. Some of the banging around in the truck earlier caused sore muscles and, he was sure, bruises. His head and body ached, and he was seeing things double; it was time to stop.

"I've had enough for one day. I think it's time for bed," he said.

Coop looked up from the papers. "Okay, beautiful, let's go get ready for bed."

Matthew tried to move his walking cast, but Buddy was asleep on it. "Come on, Buddy, up you get."

He immediately stood, and Matthew tried to stand, but his aching muscles had frozen him to the spot. He tried a second time and got partway up before he was wrapped in Coop's muscled arms and lifted off the ground.

"You sore, Matthew?" Coop asked.

"Yeah, seized up a little."

"We'll have a hot bath before bed, beautiful. That should loosen you up."

"Sounds like heaven," Matthew agreed.

Coop carried him up the stairs, to their room, and into the en suite bath. He set Matthew on the closed toilet and put the plug into the bath and started the water. Matthew watched as Coop added some lavender oil in the tub; he'd learned that Coop had a bit of a hedonistic side, and he liked it. Coop came back to Matthew and began removing his clothes. Matthew tried to help, but at the first stretch and hiss of pain, Coop took over. His gentle hands flowed over his skin, ever conscious of the bruising that covered his right arm and hip from slamming into the door when they were hit.

Once Coop was done, he quickly stripped, revealing his tanned, muscled body one piece of clothing at a time. He was magnificent, and he was all Matthew's. He looked his fill and soon found himself back in Coop's arms and stepping into the bathtub. The hot, lavender-scented water felt like silk caressing his skin. Coop hummed softly as he ran hot water over Matthew's body.

His body wanted to respond, but he was so tired his cock didn't even stir. Matthew laid his head down on Coop's chest and relaxed his sore muscles. Coop reached over and grabbed the body wash and the sponge. He lathered up the sponge and gently washed Matthew's body. The tender touches only solidified their bond as they lay together in the steam.

"Feeling better, beautiful?" Coop asked.

"Yes, you're so good to me."

"I'm sure if I was the one hurting, you'd do the same thing."

"Of course, I love you. Hey, you were in the same accident I was; aren't you sore as well?"

"A little bit, but I didn't tense up for the hit, which helped with the muscle strain, and I didn't slam into the door either. I got off easier than you did."

Coop gently sponged away the grime of the day then washed Matthew's hair. Matthew was in heaven, but the warmth and care were starting to put him to sleep. His eyes got heavier and heavier, and that was the last thing he remembered.

The next morning, Matthew woke alone. When he looked at the clock, it was past ten in the morning. He'd slept in. He hadn't done that since moving into the team house. He must have been really tired. Matthew stretched his lithe body and all too late remembered his sore muscles. The pain almost made him cry. This time a little more slowly, Matthew got out of bed and went to use the facilities and take a shower. Once he'd finished, he dressed and walked downstairs to check on the team.

The house was quiet except for Mrs. Walker in the kitchen. Where could everyone have gone? Matthew walked into the kitchen in search of coffee, which Mrs. Walker was all too happy to provide.

"Where is everybody, Mrs. Walker?" Matthew asked.

"Outside working. As a matter of fact, Coop said for you to eat breakfast and then go outside," she said. "So you sit down there, and I'll get your breakfast started."

An hour later and packed full of pancakes, Matthew walked outside the kitchen door in search of Coop. They weren't in their shop, so Matthew decided to wander toward his new shop, which was still under construction. He didn't know how long it would take them to finish, considering a few of the workers had to go back to the youth center site to make up for the two Denefusis, both of whom wouldn't be returning to work.

The first thing he saw was Spider at a table cutting lumber while Dante was carrying lumber to the interior of his workshop and Sam was busy framing walls with some of the workers, Vincent, Shadow, and Shannon. Coop came out of the building and saw Matthew almost immediately. That drop-your-pants look of his was firmly in place. He walked over and gathered Matthew in his arms.

"Morning, Matthew, did you sleep well?" Coop asked.

"Yes, thank you for not waking me. I think I needed that," Matthew said. "What are you guys doing?"

"Helping with the construction of your workshop, so it can be done sooner for you," Coop said in a proud voice.

Matthew's eyes got blurry as he watched his new team and family working hard for him.

"Don't cry, baby," Coop said, holding Matthew a bit closer.

"I'm just so touched that everyone would do this for me," Matthew said.

By now the rest of the team had noticed Matthew and were smiling. "Thank you so much for this, guys. I'm humbled by your generosity, thank you."

"Anytime, Matthew. We'll have the roof on before the end of the day," Sam said before taking a long swig from his water bottle.

"How can I help?" Matthew asked.

"You can help by going to the computer room and finding anything I can use against Denefusi. We need some leverage here, and we need you to find it," Dante said.

"I'll find it." Matthew was honored to be given such an important project.

"That's what we're counting on," Coop said.

After a deep kiss with his lover, Matthew walked back to the computer room and began working on what he hoped would lead to the end to all of this.

***

Coop felt the deep ache of hard work as he hauled more lumber into the shop. It wouldn't be long now and Matthew would be able to use it. He liked seeing the evidence of Matthew settling his life here in Brighton. He loved the man, and Coop wanted his future to include one multicolored-eyed beauty with the penchant for falling over things.

Dante had mentioned going back to Chicago to have a face-to-face with Denefusi, but that would be the last resort. They needed a way of attacking where they weren't the ones saddled with deciding his ending, a way of getting to him without leaving Brighton. He hoped his partner found something that could help, or they would be heading back to Chicago to end this.

All the interior walls were up. They just needed to frame out the last of the huge workbenches Matthew had incorporated into the blueprints. Matthew needed space for special machines that he would use, even though Coop had no idea what they did. This would be Matthew's space, where he could work and experiment with anything he wanted. The building was slated to have frosted security windows for privacy and two security doors, one in the front and the other along the far side. The building was going to be one of the most secure on the property.

Matthew built and created new types of armaments when he wasn't working on his computer programs. He was an asset to the team, which they all knew, except Matthew, who didn't seem to have the same outlook on his abilities. If anything, Matthew thought of himself as commonplace instead of the skilled and intelligent man he was. Coop was going to change that.

For a man who ran from any and all emotional entanglements, Coop had definitely jumped in head first. He was so deep into this relationship with Matthew that he couldn't imagine moving forward without the amazing man in his life.

"It's really coming along," Shannon said. "Should be done in a couple days. Then we'll take a trip to San Diego to pick up his belongings."

"It will be good when he's settled into his new life," Coop agreed.

They were about to call it a day, and Coop was cleaning up his tools when Matthew came hobbling out of the house with his laptop in his hand. He had a big smile on his face, but of course he wasn't watching where he was walking and tripped over a pile of lumber. Thankfully, he landed on his butt with his computer safely held to his chest.

Coop ran up to Matthew and helped him stand up and dusted off his pants. "What are you doing moving that fast without watching where you're going, beautiful? You could be really hurt."

"I know, but I was so excited to show you guys what I've found. I think if we play it right, this might be Denefusi's downfall," Matthew said.

"What did you find?" Spider asked as he joined them along with the rest of the team.

"Well, he had it hidden so well it took me three tries to get into his personal banking accounts and the accounts for the Denefusi family."

"How's that going to help? We have to get him to leave Brighton alone," Dante asked, making Coop want to growl at anyone questioning his partner's ability.

"He'll be too busy explaining where the missing money went to his fellow crime family members," Matthew explained. "He's been skimming off the top of every business dealing the Denefusis had from their legitimate business. I can't imagine what he's done with their not-so-legal businesses."

"He's been stealing from his own family?"

"Yes. As far as I can tell, it's been going on for years. I still have to research more, but I was so excited, I had to tell you guys."

"Good work, Matthew," Dante said, and Matthew smiled brightly. "Now we need to find a way to use the information to get Anthony Denefusi to back off."

"We could blackmail him: either he calls off his men or we share the information with his family," Shadow suggested.

"I say, after everything that man has done, we should share it and he'll have to deal with his family, who won't be too pleased the man they chose to lead them is actually stealing from them," Vincent added.

"Once Matthew has had a chance to investigate further, we'll decide on a course of action," Dante said.

Everyone nodded in agreement and went back to collecting their tools. The work crew was getting ready to leave for the day. Coop held Matthew close. He was so proud of his lover.

"You did great, beautiful. We should be able to use this information to get Denefusi to back off or have him stopped by his own family once they find out what he's been doing."

"I should get back to work," Matthew said. "I have quite a few years to go through, and I have a feeling there's a lot in there he doesn't want seeing the light of day,"

Coop caressed his soft, freckled cheek and gently kissed the brilliant man he loved. "I love you, beautiful."

"I love you too, big guy."

***

Matthew returned to the house but decided to work in the sunroom instead of the computer room. It had taken a lot of digging to get this information. Matthew had been shocked when he finally got into the original accounts and the doctored accounts that were buried even deeper. He worked for another couple hours, while the team were out back having target practice. Even when they weren't on a mission, they practiced continually to stay sharp.

The house phone rang, and considering it was only him and Mrs. Walker in the house, he decided to pick it up—he did live here after all.

"Hello."

"Hello, Matthew."

Matthew didn't recognize the voice. "I'm sorry, who's calling?"

"Ah, you've forgotten me already, and here I thought we had a moment together the other day."

Matthew immediately went on alert. It couldn't be…could it?

"What, nothing to say? You weren't afraid of me that day on the construction site but now you are. That only means you must know who I truly am, Bobby Denefusi. You know I'm coming after you and anyone else who gets in my way."

"You'll never get close enough to me."

"Then how do I know you're alone in the house with that old lady and everyone else is at the shooting range over one hundred yards away from you?"

Matthew froze. How could he have known that? Was he in the compound somewhere waiting to attack someone? Bobby began laughing on the other end of the line and finally hung up. The team was too far away to go to them, so he pulled out his cell phone and called Coop.

His call was answered on the second ring. "Hey, beautiful, how goes the research?"

Matthew's voice was shaky. "I need all of you to come back to the house right now and protect Sam and Travis on your way back."

"What's wrong?" Coop asked after calling for everyone's attention.

"Bobby Denefusi just called me."

"He called you? Our number is unlisted. Bastard."

"And he knew I was in the house alone with Mrs. Walker and that everyone else was at the shooting range. He said he was coming for me."

"I need you to go get Mrs. Walker and get down into the safe room in the basement."

"Okay," Matthew said and hung up his cell phone.

He went and quickly explained to Mrs. Walker and led her down to the safe room. Matthew locked them in and waited. Several minutes later, the door was opened with the secret code and Coop walked in with Travis and Sam.

Matthew limped over and buried his face in Coop's chest. "I was so worried."

"It's going to be okay, beautiful. I need you four to stay in here until we have a chance to look around. Can you access the security camera footage from the day Bobby Denefusi was working in the compound, see where he went while he was here? Use the walkie-talkie to contact us if you see anything."

"Be careful," Matthew said, and Coop smiled, turned, and relocked the room.

The safe room had all the comfort of a living room. There were couches, chairs, a computer system, and even a fridge. Matthew sat down in front of the computer as everyone settled in. He brought up the files from that day and began running through Bobby Denefusi's every move.

Travis came over and sat down beside Matthew. "What did he say to you?"

"That he was coming for me and anyone who gets in his way."

"Shit," Travis said before he started to shake slightly.

"He won't get a chance with our men around." Matthew put his hand on Travis's shoulder to help calm him. "We'll be okay."

He could see the fear in Travis's eyes. He'd also heard Travis wake up screaming in the night. Matthew hoped he would be okay when this was over.

Matthew began to review the security camera footage and zeroed in on Bobby Denefusi. He watched as the man worked on framing a wall. Not even five minutes later, Bobby Denefusi slipped away and went over by the storage units, placing something in the right rear of the building. Matthew stopped the tape and picked up his walkie-talkie, reaching Dante. He told him about what he'd seen and then went back to the tape. Bobby moved closer to the house, near the greenhouse, where he placed something else. He then came back to the work site, where he found Matthew by himself and trapped him in a corner. Matthew remembered that last bit all too well.

He radioed the position of the second thing Bobby had left on the greenhouse to the team. He then turned on the real-time cameras and watched as the team cleared each and every building on the grounds. Matthew zeroed in on Coop, seeing his face etched with concentration, his gun in his hand. One by one, he entered each building, his powerful body pressed against the exterior walls as he carried on. He was magnificent when completely focused on protecting his family.

"Can you find Bo for me?" Travis asked.

"He's here?"

"Yeah, he arrived when we were down at the firing range. He still has his uniform on," Travis explained.

Matthew checked the grounds until he found Officer Bo Mason, who was much in the same position as Coop had been in, clearing buildings.

He got up, gave Travis the seat, and explained how to move the camera to follow Bo. Then he went over to the kitchen area and grabbed a bottle of water, drinking half in one big gulp.

"He called to mess with us again," Sam said.

"Looks like it," Matthew answered.

"He must get some sick joy out of scaring us. I can't wait until this is over," Travis said.

"You and me both," Matthew agreed.

"They'll be done soon, once they clear the property," Sam said.

Matthew pulled out his laptop and, with renewed vigor, went back to searching for Anthony Denefusi's Trojan horse, a way to bring him down. Denefusi had done a good job trying to bury the truth, but it would take a whole lot more to keep Matthew out. The trail went on and on until he found an offshore bank account where all the money had been squirreled away. Now for the communication system. It took less than half an hour to break into their master e-mail account. *They really should have better security.*

The tones coming from the exterior security keypad could be heard from inside the safe room, causing all four of them to stand. They couldn't see who was at the other side of the door—that would have to be rectified, he thought. The heavy steel door opened with a squeal and Coop, Dante, Spider, and Bo came walking in. Air rushed from his lungs as he let out a breath he hadn't known he'd been holding and walked into Coop's open arms. Sam and Travis did the same with their men.

Half an hour later found the entire group sitting in the living room drinking tea and coffee and discussing the tiny cameras found on the property and their next move.

"I think we should go back to Chicago and show Denefusi what happens when he messes with our family," Shadow said.

"That would probably be a setup. We'll walk right into a trap," Coop answered.

"We need to hunt down Bobby Denefusi before he has a chance of hurting someone," Spider said.

"I… I was thinking of another way to get to him without leaving Brighton," Matthew suggested.

"How, Matthew?" Dante asked.

"We use the banking information I found to draw the heat from his family to Anthony Denefusi. I found doctored paperwork and an offshore bank account."

"How would we get it to all the members of the Denefusi crime family?" Coop asked.

"While I was having a look around their inner workings, I found the e-mail addresses to every boss in their organization. We send a mass e-mail, bounce it around a bunch of servers across the world so it can't be traced back, and let the chips fall where they may," Matthew explained.

Everyone sat quietly, considering Matthew's idea and making him nervous. *Should I have said anything?*

"I like it, simple and bound to leave the greatest impact," Dante agreed. "Good thinking, Matthew."

"How long will the mass e-mailing take to set up?" Spider asked.

"To set it up and run it around the world a few times before delivery...honestly, not long, couple hours at most," Matthew explained.

"Go ahead and send the information as soon as you have it ready. It's time for Denefusi to feel the heat of being a marked man," Dante said.

"You think the family will turn on him?" Bo asked.

"There's a reason you never steal from the mob—you don't live long once the information is out there," Dante explained.

"Why do I get the feeling he'll slink his way out of what he has coming?" Vincent asked.

"Because you're a cautious man. We'll have to keep an eye on the fallout," Coop said.

"Okay, let's finish securing the exterior fencing. I want the rest of you to stay indoors for now, and, Matthew, let me know when it's done," Dante ordered as he lifted Sam and kissed him before heading to the front door.

Coop bent over and kissed Matthew softly before following Dante out the door. Matthew grabbed his laptop and headed for the computer room, his second home these days. He didn't mind; he lived for this kind of stuff.

Matthew brought everything up on his screens and began the process of bringing down a crime boss.

Chapter Ten

One week later

Oh, what a difference a week could make. There'd been no sign of Bobby Denefusi since his phone call, and Anthony Denefusi was off the radar. Apparently, once the truth about his embezzling millions of dollars from the family came out, he went into hiding, according to Dante's sources. Matthew knew no one would be able to trace it back to them, but he wondered if Denefusi knew. Matthew hoped so. The man was evil. He'd intended on selling a child and sent men after them, even though he'd received his money to leave the child alone.

The lack of anything happening didn't take away the stress of waiting for it to happen. Would Bobby head back to Chicago to his uncle? Would his uncle, Anthony Denefusi, even still be in Chicago? No one knew just where he was. If his family caught up with him, they wouldn't hold back. Stealing from the Denefusi family had broken trust with the wrong people.

Matthew and Coop had spent the week slipping back into their honeymoon stage and spent a lot of time locked in their bedroom. It had been quiet enough for them to make plans to pack all his belongings and bring them home from San Diego. This peaceful time together only intensified their bond and love. Matthew had never felt this much at home since before his family passed away.

"I'm going out to my shop to have a look around," Matthew said as he put on his shirt. They were both finally getting dressed after two attempts.

"Do you want me to come with you?" Coop asked, still naked and lying in bed like a model.

"Not a chance, big guy. If you came along, we'll be christening my workshop, not working on the layout."

"Yes, but we have yet to do that."

"Oh, we will," Matthew teased. "Just not today."

Matthew laughed and crawled on the bed to give Coop a kiss. He hadn't felt this happy in so long. Matthew left his lover in bed and headed out to his completed workshop. The crew had finished it only days ago with the help of the team. He walked through the living room, waving to the team—his new family—as he went. The sky was clear and the sun was shining. The beautiful day matched his mood.

The building was a lot bigger than he had dreamt of when he asked for a workshop. Two large security doors were open because they had to have their final installation and setup, but other than that, the place was ready to go. Just picturing all his machines in there and all the things he could create made him smile.

He didn't sense the danger until it was too late. The barrel of a gun was pressed up to the back of his skull, sending a cold chill through his body.

"Hello again. Told you I was coming for you," Bobby Denefusi said. "Now we're going to go for a little drive."

"I'm not going anywhere with you," Matthew growled back.

"Oh, I think you will, or when your lover comes out to find you, he will be the first to die, and then I'll go from there."

"They'll kill you."

"Not before I kill some of them, and all because you wouldn't sacrifice yourself. How very selfish of you."

Matthew knew Bobby was playing mind games with him, but he couldn't risk one person. "You won't hurt anyone else if I come with you?" Matthew knew he couldn't trust the word of this psycho, but what choice did he have?

"Nope, just you. Then we leave. You don't give me any trouble, and we'll be just fine," Bobby said as he pushed Matthew toward the side door facing the garage. "Now start walking, and not a sound."

Matthew was stuck between wishing someone would see them and hoping no one got in the way. A truck sat in front of one of the six garage doors, and Bobby nudged Matthew toward it. Matthew knew everyone left their keys in their vehicles when on the compound, so it would stand to reason that there'd be a set in there. This all seemed way too easy to Matthew, but again, he didn't want to run into anyone because he knew Denefusi would shoot them on sight.

"Get in and drive," Bobby ordered.

"I can't drive. I have a walking cast on my right leg."

"Shit." He looked down at the walking cast with a sneer. "Get in and slide over to the passenger seat. If you try anything, you'll regret it."

The only image that kept running through Matthew's mind was Coop coming out of the house unarmed and being shot. He got into the truck and slid over to the passenger seat. Bobby followed, still holding the gun. Matthew knew he couldn't fight the gun away from Bobby; he wasn't trained in combat and would likely get himself shot.

Bobby started the truck and drove past the house on his way to the long lane leading off the compound. When they made it to the gates, Matthew looked back at the house, sorrow filling his soul. Would he ever see Coop again? He prayed it wasn't the last time he saw the compound. Bobby pushed the gate opener clipped to the truck's visor, and Matthew watched in horror as the gates opened wide. The team would know the gates were being opened, which made Matthew wonder how Bobby had gotten on the property in the first place.

The speaker box on the gate came to life. "Matthew, is that you? Where are you going?" Vincent asked.

This was his only chance to tell them what was going on, and he took it. "It's Bobby! He's taking me!"

Bobby smashed the butt of his gun against the side of Matthew's head. The last thing he saw before falling unconscious was Bobby breaking through the half-opened gate.

***

Coop was losing his mind. His love had been taken by Bobby Denefusi. He'd failed the only man he'd ever loved. He'd sworn to protect him; now he was gone. Shannon was working furiously to get the GPS on the truck to work, but it was only working intermittently. They were all suiting up in their gear while they waited.

"Why is the GPS not working properly?" Coop asked.

"It's been damaged somehow; that can be the only viable explanation," Shannon answered.

Police Chief Graham and his men were out looking for the truck, but the team knew the best chance of finding Matthew was with the truck's GPS signal. Every second that they waited, the worse Coop's anxiety became.

"We have to go. We have to go out and find him," Coop growled, his patience growing thin and his fear rising with every minute they waited.

"We have to find them with the GPS first, Coop," Dante explained. "Or we won't even know where to look."

Coop knew the boss man was right, but logic had left long ago. He turned from the table and started for the door. Spider stepped in front of him before he had a chance to reach it.

"Where are you going?" Spider asked.

"To find Matthew. I can't sit here all day and wait. Matthew could be hurt."

"And where do you propose to go looking? We have to wait for the coordinates."

"I know what you're saying is only logical, but I can't wait any longer. He could be hurt."

Coop went to walk around Spider when the phone rang. Dante picked it up and, after a few words, put the call on speakerphone.

"You're on speaker now, Anthony," Dante said.

"Ah, good, 'cause we wouldn't want any of you getting any ideas. If you try to find us, we'll kill him and cut our losses until we strike again. You'll never know when we're coming or when we'll simply take another one of you."

"What do you want?" Dante asked.

"Twenty-two million, the amount that was in my offshore bank account before your team decided to share that information. I know it was you; there's no use in denying it."

"It will take a few days to raise that much in cash," Dante explained.

"You have one or he dies. I've got nothing to lose anymore, so don't try me," Denefusi snapped.

"Where do we meet for the trade?" Spider asked.

Coop was thankful for his team members, because he couldn't think clearly enough to ask any questions.

"We'll call again with the location," Denefusi said. "Don't get any ideas either, or the pretty man won't be so pretty when we get done with him."

Coop growled but held back what he really wanted to say to the bastard. He wouldn't say anything that might get his love hurt. He'd never risk something worse happening to Matthew.

"Twenty-two million and not a scratch on Matthew," Dante said.

"Twenty-two million and there'll be no further damage done to him."

"What did you do to him?" Coop blew. He couldn't have stopped it if he tried. Matthew was already hurt.

"Struck a chord there, didn't I? Well, if you want him back in one piece, get my money," Denefusi ordered before disconnecting the call.

Coop stepped away from the table and began pacing. He had money, but not even close to that much. "I've got only part of the twenty-two million. We have to find him before the time runs out."

"We've got this, Coop. We'll call our accountant and get this settled," Dante said. "He's part of the team."

Now Coop knew the bosses were rich, but to be able to raise that kind of money quickly was mind-boggling. "Are you sure?"

"Of course. It's worth any amount of money to get our teammate back, but we hope not to have to use it. We'll find him before the trade even happens," Spider assured him.

"I've got it!" Shannon yelled. "GPS is up and running."

Coop said the one thing no one wanted to say. "What if they've ditched the truck?"

"Then we go through with the trade," Dante confirmed. "Now let's load up and get our teammate back."

***

Matthew woke lying on a mattress with both his wrists and ankles bound with rope that was digging into his skin. He wondered how far they thought he could go in a cast. The side of his head ached, and he felt a little nauseous, but what really bothered him was the fact that he couldn't open his right eye. It was swollen shut.

With his one eye, he looked around the room and wondered where the hell he was. He remembered Bobby and the gun, but the rest was fuzzy. Matthew struggled against his bonds, but the ropes weren't budging an inch. As he looked around the room, he realized it wasn't a half-bad room. He wasn't in a run-down house. This could be any room in any house. How was the team going to be able to find him?

Voices came from another room; one was Bobby's, the other he didn't know. Something about money, they were arguing about money. Matthew laid his sore head back down on the bed and tried to think of a way out of this. Physically, he was useless. With his cast, banged-up head, and swollen eye, he couldn't fight a flea. Who was he kidding? Even if there wasn't anything wrong with him, he couldn't win a physical fight.

When the voices quieted, he heard footsteps headed his way. He closed his eye and quickly decided to play unconscious for as long as he could. He heard the door open and footsteps walking up to the side of the bed.

"How hard did you hit him? He needs to be in one piece to get our money," the unknown voice said, and Matthew was beginning to think it could be Anthony Denefusi. Who else would be involved in his kidnapping?

"I didn't think I hit him too hard," Bobby said.

"Look at the side of his face. You hit him hard enough. You better just hope he wakes up at all."

"But, Uncle Anthony, he was yelling a warning to the Sentinels. What was I supposed to do?"

Okay, now Matthew knew for sure Anthony Denefusi was in the room. He tried to calm his breathing as his heart pounded.

"Let's go. He ain't going nowhere," Anthony said, before their footsteps retreated and the door shut.

Matthew waited a few more minutes before opening his eye. The room was empty. He wracked his brain, but there was nothing he could do. He'd have to wait until they decided what to do with him.

What felt like hours passed, but in truth, it was probably closer to thirty minutes. The fact that his hands were numb was just adding to the list of things wrong with him. Suddenly, he heard a door being forced open and smashing against something. There was shouting and gunfire. *Oh God, is it the team? Let them stay safe.*

Then there was silence in the other room, and for a few terrifying seconds, Matthew thought whoever it was had forgotten he was there. Heavy footsteps came closer and closer to his door. *It had to be the team.* Only, when the door opened, it was a strange man the size of Coop, with a long scar running down the left side of his face, and not a team member.

Oh shit!

"Well, what do we have here?" the man said to another, skinnier man who came walking into the room. "Seems Anthony was planning on getting rid of someone."

"And if that's what Anthony wanted, you know we have no other choice," the skinny man said.

Matthew pulled frantically at the ropes as the two men stalked closer, the big one pulling out a knife. *Is this how I die?*

When the knife was only inches away, Matthew closed his eyes, not wanting to see it coming. Then there was tugging at his wrists and ankles, a little jostling, and he was free of the ropes.

"What?" Matthew asked in shock.

The larger of the two men came up to him and said, "If Anthony wanted you dead, then you must live, little man."

"You're free to go. If you're heading to Brighton, it's right at the end of the driveway. It's the only town for miles."

"Thank you," Matthew said as he slid to the edge of the bed and stood on shaky legs. He limped to the open bedroom door and walked down the hallway. Once he made it to the kitchen, what he found there turned his stomach: both Anthony and Bobby lay in pools of their own blood. He put his back against the wall and shuffled around their lifeless bodies. Anthony's dead eyes stared unseeing at the ceiling.

He made it out the kitchen door before puking in the flowerbed. Once he got himself back together, he noticed the short driveway to the road and nothing else. The house was in the middle of nowhere. He'd have to limp to the road and hope a car drove by that could take him home or to the police station. A car containing the two men from the house drove past him and sped off into the distance. Matthew continued limping his way toward Brighton. By now his head felt like it was about to fall off from the pain, and the heat of the day wasn't helping.

His head spun and the world tilted, threatened to overtake him. Just when he thought he couldn't handle any more, he spotted two trucks speeding down the road. With the last of his energy, he waved his hands in the air, hoping they would stop for him. Tires squealed, but Matthew couldn't seem to focus anymore. He fell to his knees, the gravel on the side of the road cutting into his skin.

"Matthew, baby, can you hear me?" Coop's voice broke through the fog in his mind. Coop was there.

"Coop, you found me." Matthew felt himself being lifted, but his eye wouldn't clear. "My head hurts."

"We're taking you to the hospital, beautiful. You'll be all right," Coop said, and Matthew heard the truck doors closing. As Coop held him tight, all he wanted to do was fall asleep in Coop's arms, even though his love was telling him to stay awake. Somewhere in the background of his thoughts, he knew sleeping wasn't a good idea, but it pulled at him so hard he was powerless to stop it.

***

It had been nearly a week since the kidnapping, and Matthew was getting ticked off at being confined to bed. Although he was feeling much better, he was still trapped in his room. Oh, it wasn't like it was a great hardship; Coop had gotten him all kinds of things to fill his time. He even bought Matthew an e-reader with a one-hundred-dollar book credit on it. The doctor said it was only for a couple more days, but the room was driving him crazy.

On the day of the kidnapping, part of the team went on to the house while the other took Matthew to the hospital. They reported finding only drying pools of blood in the house. No one was left. The Denefusi family had meted out its own type of justice on their former Don and, in turn, saved Matthew's life.

The door opened and Coop walked in with a tray of food. "I see you're awake, beautiful. How was your nap?"

Okay, so maybe he was still suffering a few effects of the concussion. "My nap was good. Why don't you come crawl in here with me and I'll show you how good."

"No, it's too soon."

Matthew's old fears were kicking in and all his self-doubt flooded back into him like a wave. It'd been a week; maybe Coop had changed his mind? Maybe it was too much trouble having a partner. Maybe he wasn't beautiful to him anymore. When Matthew had arrived at the hospital, they took X-rays of his face and found he had a broken cheekbone and had to have surgery to repair it. He would forever have a scar on his face as a reminder of the kidnapping—as if he could ever forget it.

"Is... is it because I'm not beautiful to you anymore?" Matthew asked, his voice cracking a bit.

Coop stopped so suddenly the water in the glasses on the tray he was carrying spilt over the top of the edges.

"What?" Coop asked as he set the tray down on the dresser. "Why would you say that?"

Matthew turned away from Coop. He couldn't face him, embarrassed at letting one of his new insecurities sneak out.

Coop sat on the bed and gently cupped Matthew's uninjured cheek. "Please look at me, Matthew."

Matthew slowly turned his head to face Coop, and the love he found shining in Coop's eyes was breathtaking. Then, if he loved Matthew, why wouldn't he want to make love to him?

"You are beautiful; you will always be to me. Please don't ever believe I don't think that."

"Then why won't you touch me?" Matthew asked.

Coop looked down, and in a low voice said, "I'm at fault. You're hurt, and I promised to protect you. You have to go through all this pain because of me. I'm so sorry, Matthew. Please forgive me."

Well, that wasn't anything near what he'd expected to hear. Coop felt guilty for Matthew's injuries, but why not touch him? "You have nothing to be forgiven for. But I still don't understand why you refuse to make love to me."

"Because I might hurt you more, and it would kill me to hurt you. I've caused you enough pain."

"There's nothing to forgive. This wasn't your fault. This was Denefusi's fault alone."

"But I should have been able to protect you." Coop wouldn't let it go easily.

"I was on the compound, I should have been safe. Have they found out how Bobby got on the property in the first place?"

"Dante thinks it's likely he snuck back on the property with the construction crew and then hid in the compound until he had his opportunity. There's a new protocol to follow for workers on the compound."

"Good, but you're still not guilty of anything, Coop. You found me when I could no longer go on. You got me to the hospital and stayed with me for the two days they had me, and you have been nursing me better ever since. I love you."

"I love you too." Coop's eyes still looked troubled, but they were a little less sad. Matthew would have to work on this. He'd have his lover back to himself in no time.

"So how about you crawl in here with me and cuddle for a bit?"

"Only if I can bring the food with me. You need to eat," Coop said with a genuine smile on his face. That was a start.

"Okay, as long as you come with it."

Coop grabbed the tray and crawled onto the bed and settled next to Matthew. Matthew cuddled in close to Coop and sighed in happiness. He had the man he loved, who loved him back, in his arms. What else could he ask for?

They each picked up a sandwich and dug in, comfortable and happy together, both wondering how they'd gotten so lucky. Both knowing they'd be naked before lunch was over.

ABOUT THE AUTHOR

M. Tasia is a M/M romance author who lives in Ontario, Canada. She's is a dedicated people watcher, lover of romance novels, 80's rock, and happily-ever-afters (once the MCs are put through their paces, of course), who grew up with a love of reading.

She's a firm believer that everyone deserves to have love, excitement, and crazy hot romance in their lives. Love should be celebrated and shared.

Connect with M.:
mtasiabooks.com
FB: mtasiabooks
twitter: @mtasiaauthor
IG: @m.tasia.author
TikTok: @mtasiauthor

www.BOROUGHSPUBLISHINGGROUP.com

If you enjoyed this book, please write a review. Our authors appreciate the feedback, and it helps future readers find books they love. We welcome your comments and invite you to send them to info@boroughspublishinggroup.com.

Follow us on TikTok and Instagram, and be sure to sign up for our newsletter for surprises and new releases from your favorite authors.

Are you an aspiring writer? Check out www.boroughspublishinggroup.com/submit and see if we can help you make your dreams come true.

Love podcasts? Enjoy ours at www.boroughspublishinggroup.com/podcast

www.ingramcontent.com/pod-product-compliance
Lightning Source LLC
Chambersburg PA
CBHW020822030726
47496CB00001B/40